THE CITY OF MAN

A Trilogy:
Inferno – Purgatorio – Paradiso

Based on a True Story of the Renaissance

by

MICHAEL HARRINGTON

Historical Fiction:

Saving Mona Lisa

Saving Mona Lisa is a story of the complications of creativity and love. It is the story of Leonardo da Vinci and two of his apprentices clashing over the ultimate fate of a painting that had achieved great renown soon after everyone thought it was finished...everyone, that is, except Leonardo.

"Art is never finished, only abandoned."
– Leonardo da Vinci

In God We Trust

A modern interpretation of *The City of Man* and a chronicle of our times, *In God We Trust* is the story of Dante Jefferson Washington, a smart, young, black, religious conservative seeking to make his mark on the Washington D.C. political stage. His lofty ambitions for public service soon become entangled in the web of partisan tribal conflict, religion, and money that defines our national political dysfunction. Dante's journey echoes that of his Italian namesake in The Divine Comedy.

Dante, a social misfit because of his race and political ideals, pursues his Beatrice in a former college classmate, a beautiful immigrant medical student caught between her British Christian and Pakistani Muslim heritage. Their lives and those of their two closest friends are torn apart by the disaster of 9/11 and the war that follows.

Non-Fiction:

Political Economy Simplified: A Citizen's SURVIVAL Guide

An economic policy primer, Political Economy Simplified offers a rich overview of the most pressing policy issues of the day and how to think about them. It skillfully weaves together economics, finance, and politics to present a three-dimensional view of our public policy world for the non-professional.

Trade and Social Insurance: The Development of National Unemployment Insurance in Advanced Industrial Democracies

A national award-winning study of the political and economic foundations of the modern welfare state. Cross-national statistical and four historical case studies of the UK, Belgium, Switzerland, and the USA show how international trade dependence helped shaped national universal unemployment insurance systems in developed democracies. This challenges the conventional wisdom that these programs were mostly determined by labor organization and Left-Labor governments in power

The study won the American Political Science Association's Harold D. Lasswell Award for Best Doctoral Research in the Field of Policy Studies completed in 1998-1999 and was first runner-up to the National Academy of Social Insurance's John Heinz Dissertation Award in 2000.

In the beginning there was only Chaos, an empty void...
        - Hesiod, *Theogony*

Of the two first parents of the human race, Cain was the first born,
And he belonged to the city of men;
after him was born Abel, who belonged to the city of God.
And this founder of an earthly city was a fratricide.
Overcome with envy, he slew his own brother,
A citizen of the eternal city.
        - Augustine of Hippo, *City of God*, XV, 1,5

ACKNOWLEDGMENTS

THIS BOOK HAS BEEN A labor of love over more than four years. It was in gestation for much longer than that. Thus, over the years many people lent their support and assistance.

For readers comments I would like to thank Debbie La Franchi, Ken Mayne, Ansel Hall, Todd Mittleman, Steve Sherwood, Dave Simon, Frank Strakosch and hopefully no one else I may have missed. It's a long book and requires a significant time commitment to read and I appreciate all the comments along the way.

I would also like to thank the Bridwell Library at Southern Methodist University, the UCLA Research Library, the Getty Research Library at the Getty Center, and the servers and friends at Seattle's Best Coffee on Montana Avenue in Santa Monica, where much of this book was written. I would also like to thank Don Weinstein for his help and advice.

For generous financial support I owe heartfelt gratitude and appreciation to Joe Del Signore and Modhi Gude.

My wife, Tushara Bindu Gude, has displayed the patience of Job with this project. Her editing has been brilliant and her dedication through more reads than I would wish on anyone has been a godsend. And I find her constant encouragement indispensible. I would like to dedicate this opus to her and also to my late mother, Nancy Corcoran Harrington, who wished I had written a shorter book.

Contents

FRA GIROLAMO SAVONAROLA, 1452-1498
SCULPTURE IN CHURCH OF SAN MARCO, FLORENCE

PREFACE

IN TODAY'S FLORENCE, CROWDS OF tourists mill about the famed Piazza della Signoria, strolling under the imposing shadow of the government palace, now called the Palazzo Vecchio. Surrounded by art and medieval grandeur, they gaze up in wonder at the statues adorning the Loggia dei Lanzi and the copy of Michelangelo's magnificent David standing by the Palazzo's entrance. Then they stop to sit and rest on the edge of Ammannati's massive fountain of Neptune, perhaps to enjoy an icy gelato under the hot Tuscan sun. By chance, if they look down, they may notice a large brass plaque, roughly three feet across, embedded in the stone pavement towards the center of the piazza. It's inscription, in Italian and Roman numerals, eludes all but the most curious.

As the sun sinks and shadows lengthen, the tourists slowly recede, back to their buses or toward the river, taking with them their most enduring memories of Michelangelo's Giant and the refreshing tang of lemon, mango and coconut gelati. But every spring, on an early morning in late May, wreaths of flowers mysteriously appear around the forgotten plaque—offerings left by some pious modern-day Florentines who still seek to atone for what happened in their city at this exact spot more than half a millennium ago. Translated, the plaque's inscription reads:

After four centuries
this memoriam was placed here
where Fra Girolamo Savonarola and his brothers
Fra Domenico Buonvicini and Fra Silvestro Maruffi
were hung and burned by an unjust sentence
on the 23rd of May, 1498.

COMMEMORATIVE PLAQUE IN PIAZZA DELLA SIGNORIA

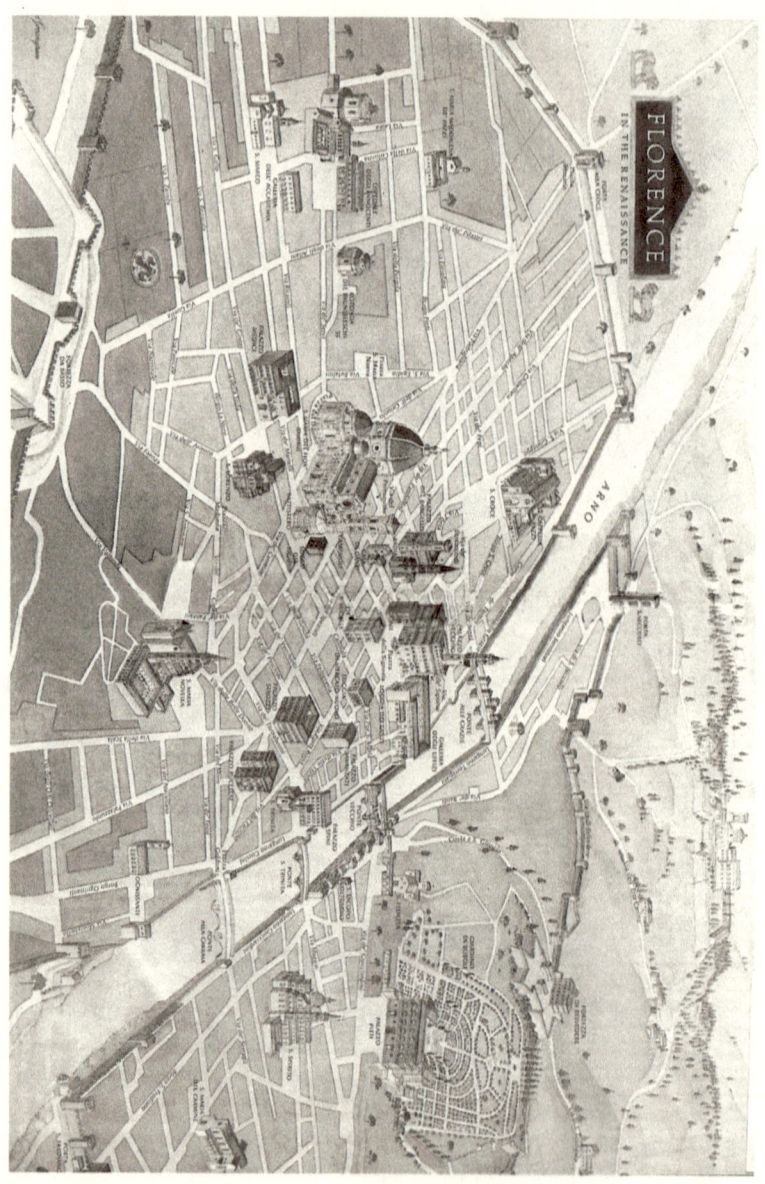

PROLOGUE

MAY, 1498

MISERERE MEI DEUS, HAVE MERCY on me, O Lord!

The prisoner's thoughts screamed *No!* as he saw the floor recede, the rope cutting into his wrists and wrenching his shoulders as the *strappado* hauled him toward the ceiling. He felt his body convulse with the slow, steady squeal of the pulley. Then time ceased to squeal and his body fell from its height like a stone, rushing at the floor until the rope snapped and his shoulders jerked back with a ripping sound echoing up the back of his neck. A white pain flashed before his eyes as his disembodied cry pierced the night.

His cry woke him with a start and his eyes snapped opened. Everything was black. He was still crouched on the floor of his small holding cell, days later, his body shattered, his will broken.

Outside, the shroud of darkness wound itself around the city as the citizens slept fitfully, confined to their homes under the night curfew. Their commune had suffered a fever of discontent for several years and many feared it was now on the brink of open warfare. Guards of the Eight paced out the long hours, cursing their extra duties as they cast their torch lights down hidden alleys and byways. But their startled shadows only danced the macabre before vanishing again into the night. No living soul dared to be caught out before daybreak.

A ripple of church bells announced the hour of Lauds, their solemn tones splashing like holy water over the watchtowers and spires, waking the citizens and sprinkling benediction over saints and sinners alike. But the bells were an absolution for sins not yet confessed.

Nor forgiven.

Roused by the heavenly sound, the prisoner responded with a cry: *Miserere mei Deus…secundum magnam misericordiam tuam Deus qui lucem habitas inaccessibilem…*

The Latin verse streamed forth—a psalm memorized and recited every day since taking his vows as a begging friar of the Order of Preachers, the Order of St. Domenico. Only now the words took on their true meaning. *God, my God, by Your great mercy, behold the misery before You. Take away my misery and blot out my iniquities… Sweet Lord I have sinned… against You, against heaven, against earth…*

His missive caught in the throat of the watchtower jutting out of the

Palazzo della Signoria—the government palace—where he was imprisoned. Silhouetted against the night sky, the tower stood like a sentinel over the city center and the friar's cell was the special one at the top reserved for the Republic's most serious offenders.

The poor mendicant huddled there with his tortured limbs poking through the threadbare tunic, his left arm hanging limp where the *strappado* had dislocated shoulder and elbow. The rough floor timbers cut into his knees and blocks of cold, rough-hewn stone rose up, closing him in with the stench of an unemptied chamber pot. But he fought to deny his suffering. Falling in and out of consciousness, he moved his lips in muted despair:

Miserere mei Deus… miserere mei Deus… miserere mei Deus…

But his petition went unanswered…

The bells fell silent as a thin ray of light slipped through a small lunette, painting a circle high up on the facing wall. The circle of light inched down and across, mirroring the arc of its source across the heavens. But the friar forced his eyes shut, exorcising the light in shame. Shaking from a lingering chill, he wrestled with his soul while his mind sought its escape.

In a moment he was safe again behind the sheltering walls of his convent, gazing at the faces of his brethren, his brothers in Christ as they sang in unison: "*Alleluia! Alleluia!* All praises to *Gesú Cristo!*"

They were as devoted as sheepdogs to the shepherd, following everywhere he led. He marched them out into the city's fray where they stood against the chaos, unified in brotherhood, an army of avenging angels. Advancing upon the enemy, a white light bathed them as they fought grandly for Christ the King. And because God loved them, He favored them with His heavenly glory and they vanquished their foes. With His blessing, they defeated Babylon and built the New Jerusalem.

Alleluia!

The prisoner felt a rush of hope, but his thoughts quickly became jumbled as his vision went black. Somehow, he had failed. How? Where had he gone astray? *Why have You forsaken me, Lord?*

But God was silent. The friar had sinned and now his brothers suffered with him somewhere in this cold fortress at the hands of his enemies. He pleaded in desperation: *Who will take pity on me, Lord? Where shall I go? Everyone has deserted me and cast me off; I am stranger in a strange land…*

Looking down from the pulpit, he saw his flock pack the Cathedral. God had given him Grace and the Word and made him a great preacher—it was God's miracle—and they came from all Christendom to hear him speak. *All hail the prophet!*

Looking out at their faces, his heart rejoiced. Their devotion filled him with purpose and he showed them the way. But they worried him; their faith is like wax, he thought, just a little heat... So he had prayed for their salvation. And prayed until his knees were raw.

But now he saw only their frightened faces amid the commotion—eyes aflame, fists raised, the flash of steel. He felt their fear as the wolves approached. He heard shouts, bleating cries, and the gnashing of teeth. "Save us!" they implored, their faces twisted with love and hate. He was helpless and he covered his face in shame. *Lord, they brand me a heretic. I am abandoned to my enemies. I am the lamb...*

In the darkness he saw Death enter and steeled his will. My trial has begun, he thought. But some animal spirit within scraped for survival. Tucking his legs into a fetal position, he rocked slowly back and forth as he tried to picture his mother. But it was an elderly man's voice he heard: "Did I not warn you, my son, of the evils that dwell in the hearts of men?"

He was a child again, scolded but safe, gazing into the sympathetic eyes of his father's father, renowned court physician to the Duke. He recalled those days when Nonno tutored him in the arcane science of the *medico*, mixing his lessons with a strong dose of piety. Nonno Michele was the font of all wisdom, God-fearing, not like the others. "Open your eyes to life's great mysteries," Nonno said. "Follow me and you will feel how the power of the spirit conquers the flesh. Turn your soul inward and upward to the heavens. Beware the snares laid by Satan."

Though the prisoner knew it was a dream he pleaded, "Please, Nonno, ...help me."

But the old man shook his head with disapproval. It was too late. The prisoner stumbled, tried to rise, stumbled again. He tasted dust mixed with fear and cried in despair, but no sound came forth. *Have I failed you too, Nonno?*

As he struggled he felt an excruciating pain shoot through his left arm. He shuddered from the memory, hearing the rip of the delicate cartilage as the *strappado* tore him. *How they tortured me, Lord, for days and weeks, like butchers ripping apart the legs and wings of fowl...*

Each morning the macebearers had come to take him to face his examiners. The worst moment came when the hooded ones put their hands on him and applied the ropes, before he could steel himself against the pain to come. In these moments, he raced for any sanctuary and would confess to any sin. Then, when the rope released, the agony was past him as he hurtled toward the floor.

They tormented him mercilessly, sometimes six or seven times in succession, until he was sufficiently plied to speak their 'truth.' But after they had wrung all fear from him, he was ready again to defy them with God's Truth.

Forgive them Lord, for they know not what they do.

For days now, maybe a week, maybe two, they had left him in his cell, with a crust of bread and bowl of watery minestra each morning. Some days the Good Men of San Martino—the lay brothers who comforted the condemned and misfortunate—came to visit. But they knew and he knew the macebearers would come again soon. He must prepare himself; he girded his body, but his mind still refused:

No, Lord, no, it was not them, it was not THEM, it was You! O merciful God, from You all things come... these creatures are only the instruments of Your divine will. Why have You forsaken me? Why are You so angry with me?

God's betrayal was only one of many and he knew the Devil mocked him. Then out of the darkness a girl appeared, one he knew long ago. Her flaxen hair was pulled back, its tiny ringlets falling about her face and caressing her fair complexion. The small mouth flushed like a budding rose as she bit her lower lip and her alabaster gown billowed as she held her head erect.

He spoke, reaching out to her, "Mary, ...Virgin Mother, ...Magdalena, save me! Take me from this Godless place!"

The young woman smiled seductively and her beauty beckoned. "Take me," he pleaded as he dared hope she was his salvation. But in an instant her expression changed. Her mouth became hard and cruel as her unfeeling eyes belittled his pride and the vanity. She scorned him: "You are a poor and ugly wretch. Love me if you will, I can't help that."

She haunted him still and her words cut deep. But then he saw the she-Devil and he snarled like a cornered dog: "Harlot! Bastard daughter of Satan! *You* have been cast out without refuge, not I! You strut as if your beauty knows no end, but it too will wither and turn to dust."

His voice broke as fury gave way to self-pity. In an instant the vision transformed before his eyes into a hideous fiend, shocking him into humility. He crossed himself to banish it from his eyes and the Tempter released his hold.

Rising to his knees, he forced his eyes open to behold his pathos. He saw the stains and tears in his tunic and was shamed. *I am lost.* He fought to strengthen his will, then surrendered and plunged headlong into the abyss:

Take me then, Lord! If they shall burn my flesh accept me as You accept Your saints, it is the red hat of blood that I want! Give me strength... Miserere mei Deus... miserere mei Deus... miserere mei Deus...

Delirious, the prisoner collapsed as the circle of light reversed and began its slow trajectory back up the wall.

***

If the friar had remained conscious, he would have heard the sounds of insistent buzzing outside. It was springtime in the great city and the citizens hustled to and fro down the narrow-spoked streets connecting the hubs of crowded piazzas. On market days they gathered in shops and stalls, collecting all kinds of honeyed treasures to tempt the senses: sheer silks, damasks, and velvet tapestries; dazzling gold, silver, and precious gemstones; and fragrances of ginger, cloves, nutmeg and pepper. All these goods traveled along the trade routes between the East and the North; passing through the city, they combined with local manufactures to produce a civic wealth the whole world envied. And this was not even the half of it.

From a window high up in the government palace, just below where the begging friar was imprisoned, a young man spied the scurrying citizens below. There was no dallying today; for today they tasted blood and smelled only fear. As assistant to the Secretary of the Ten of War the young man worried that his fellow citizens had gone *pazzi*, half-mad. The women hid under drab shawls, hairdressers were bankrupt and beauty shops closed, the curfew had silenced the taverns and the gambling dens had gone to ground. Meanwhile, the ruling council of the Signoria dithered. All because of this damned, blessed Dominican.

"How has my glorious city come to this?" he asked himself.

He looked out over the terracotta rooftops and marble spires sprouting toward the heavens. Before him blossomed the fabled city of flowers: *Florentia*—named for the colorful sprays dressing the surrounding hillsides and meadows. For all his life he had lived here, growing up in the shadow of magnificence. The city's symbol was the delicate *giglio*, the lily, and everywhere its simple motif was repeated inside the city's walls: In the great domed Cathedral they named Santa Maria del Fiore, Our Lady of the Flowers; in the stylized lily that adorned the Palazzo walls with marshal pride and graced its soldiers' shields and standards they carried into battle; in the carved capitals atop the columns holding up the churches, palaces and arched loggias of stone and marble; in the golden lilies splayed like a million stars on the azure ceiling of the *Sala dei Signori*; most important, in the lily impressed upon the face of the gold florin—a coin valued and traded the world over.

Everywhere these flowers inspired the city's artisans: her painters and stone carvers, architects, and poets, her goldsmiths, weavers, and jewelers. And, of course, their well-heeled patrons: bishops and cardinals, merchants, traders, and bankers.

Here, amidst the splendor of God and man, rich patricians strolled by, puffed with pride: "Was our fine city not founded by Julius Caesar, as first daughter to Rome?" they crowed. "Did the legendary Charlemagne not rebuild it centuries later? Is ours not the city of the Divine Poet, who wrote heavenly and timeless verse? And of Leonardo, *l'uomo universale*? Is it not the birthplace of Donatello, Masaccio, Ghiberti, and Brunelleschi— a pantheon of artisans unsurpassed? Have we not led the philosophers into a new Age of Man, raising him up to the glory of his Creator?

"Tell us," the Florentines boasted to visitors, "Did Pope Bonifacio not pronounce us as the 'fifth-essence,' beyond earth, air, fire and water as a living force? Are we not the most enduring Republic after Rome (the pride of Virgil and Cicero), a place where liberty and justice reign supreme; on which neither tyrant nor king can fix shackles and chains? Do we not rule over all cities in our realm as their benevolent protector? Is this not our Golden Age, pronounced as such by our greatest philosophers, a glory even Pericles could not envision? Are we not destined by divine favor?"

The peacocks puffed and spouted their dead poets as they went about their daily business of living. Every Florentine was a poet; some better than others, but all borrowed and stole with impunity when reciting their birthright:

> *Since Fortuna smiles at you,*
> *to you, Florence, clear light, I speak;*
> *...that Lord of Heaven who makes all things,*
> *seeing so much virtue reigns in you,*
> *Will want your well-being to increase, to triumph so fully*
> *It makes one rejoice merely to imagine it.*

So in springtime the peasant flower girls, the *contadine*, came into the city carrying boughs of woven cornflowers and lilies to entice buyers on the streets. They sang gaily, indiscreetly promoting the pagan cult of Isis. At such times it was difficult not to breathe in and succumb to the magic in the city's air.

But, the young official lamented, not this year. His might be the City of Flowers, but it was also the City of Towers. Recalling the prisoner locked above, he remembered it was Mars who had been the city's patron before the Christians came. And after this Roman god of war was driven out, his curse remained. The Divine Poet foretold all:

> *I was born in the city where the Baptist*

Replaced the former master, who in his scorn
will always torment it with his art.

So, while the flowers seduced the hearts of his fellow Florentines, the militant towers filled their hungry bellies. The towers shot up like menacing spears of war, where their owners could rain down arrows, stones, and scalding oils on the heads of enemies. The towers once numbered more than one hundred and fifty, creating a picket line of defense behind the city walls. But they were not arrayed against enemies beyond the walls—barbarian hordes or covetous kings from France or Spain, avaricious popes, or the fierce dragon Turk. Instead, the sideways glance of the Florentine caught upon his neighbor, his neighbor's house, his neighbor's wife, and his neighbor's livelihood. His spears were aimed at fellow citizens in an endless vendetta of revenge: faction against faction; family against family; Guelph against Ghibelline; Papist against Imperialist; Black against White; Pazzi against Medici.

Family, Honor, Victory: these were the mantles of the immortals.

Though most of these ancient towers had fallen in blazes of civic strife over the years and a sensible law had restricted the heights of newly built structures, their ghosts lingered on in the bellies of these Florentines, who were forever angling to gain an advantage over neighbor and rival. Long dead Cosimo, *pater patria,* father of his city, revealed the truth when he had said, "There is in the garden a plant which one ought to leave dry, although most people water it. It is the weed called Envy." In this Eden the weed flourished. And Envy never smiles, except at the sight of someone else's misfortune.

The official paced his small office as he weighed the situation: The Golden Age of the Medici was dead; the new pope threatens us with an interdict; and, should we obey the Holy Father, the French king threatens worse. Meanwhile our most evil enemies hide among us. All because of this damned Friar—the one the people foolishly proclaim their prophet. It exasperated him: foolish and cowardly citizens made for a foolish and cowardly republic, a republic that could not defend itself against more determined enemies.

But amidst chaos lay opportunity and the young official's ambition burned. His superior, the Secretary of the Ten, had been removed from office only days ago and the vacancy presented a fleeting chance. He must plan his next move wisely.

As the sun dipped behind the red-flamed hills, the busy bees below wound down after another agitated day. They had become a horde, ready to swarm and attack any who threatened the gathering of nectar, and the name of the friar stuck on the tip of each of their tongues like a fly in honey.

"Perhaps we should sacrifice him to the gods," his enemies spat. "Appeased, they'll permit us to prosper and grow fat again in peace."

"Or possibly," snapped his supporters, "the Almighty will reach down and pluck His humble servant from the jaws of the wolf, raising him up to the heavens in a fiery flame of glory. Then Our Lord shall loose thunderbolts on all you faithless sinners. Yes, perhaps one more miracle will suffice."

Up in the tower the circle of light completed its arc across the cell as the prisoner, lying prostrate on the hard, cold floor, was once more consumed by darkness.

BOOK I

THE INFERNO

See this beast driving me backward,
        help me resist, famous sage,
        For she makes my veins pulse and shudder.
…
Many are the beasts she mates,
        there will be more, until the Hound comes
        Who will give this creature a painful death.
Not nourished by earthly fare,
        But by wisdom, goodness, and love,
        born between Feltro and Feltro,
He shall restore Low Italy…

    - Dante Alighieri
    [*Inferno:* I:88-90; 100-06]

"O God, the heathens are come into Thy inheritance,
they have defiled Thy holy temple."
        -Psalm 78/79:1

CHAPTER 1

CARNEVALE, 1491

CHAOS

THIS DAY WAS LIKE NO other day of the year. It began a week early, slowly building momentum until it erupted in the middle of gray winter with a volcano of color and laughter, an orgy of pagan delights driven by pungent smells and irrepressible urges. Willing participants cavorted in their elaborate costumes, dancing along the parade route as it snaked through the old center of the city.

A youth in a Fool's mask slipped evasively through the revelers, his heart beating rapidly. Over his shoulder he had seen the flash of red and yellow scarves—the colors of the Vipers—and knew what would happen if they discovered him. He would seek a safer route to make his rendezvous in the piazza.

Cleaving his way through the painted faces and odd carnival masks he felt exhilarated by the jesters and harlequins, plague doctors and Death masks, radiant Suns and melancholy Moons, cavaliers, courtiers and kings all flowing by. *Carnevale* was a favorite festival—a perpetual motion of color with echoes of gaiety and laughter as revelers sang and danced and hoisted their jugs of wine—so many pregnant pleasures for a young man with guile and wit. He absorbed all, knowing the masks concealed their wearers' identities, but also revealed their most secret desires and conceits. Anonymity, he suspected, was perhaps, the best disguise of all.

The Fool fell in behind a *trionfo*, a parade vehicle drawn by six lumbering oxen flanked by warhorses. Darting past, he saw a hooded figure whirling about like a dervish on its stage. As two drummers set a thundering tempo, the figure reared back and forth, to and fro, in a corybantic dance. He strained to peer up under the dancer's hood to see if it was man or woman, but found a faceless void. As the spirit twirled, the black cape furled out, blocking the light and chilling the stage. The effect was that of a threatening storm and the audience grasped their cloaks and shrunk back as the fearsome spectacle bore down on them in the narrow street.

The Fool climbed up a torch lamp, anxious to get a better view while keeping a sharp lookout for red and yellow Vipers. The *trionfo* was a pagan Creation allegory. Seated around the stage were several splendid gods and goddesses reclined in luxury, the center presided over by the Mother goddess—her rich brown robes flowing under a cape of verdant green that set off her pale skin and red-hair. To her left the god of Love and attraction lounged in velvety shades of crimson and rose, beckoning to the crowd with his eyes. On the right sat the vainglorious god of the Heavens, his hood of midnight sprayed with stars and a Milky Way of lace. It was a magical ensemble.

The hooded figure dashed in and around these three, fanning his cape and gyrating about, as small star-like figures danced across the stage. Then the wagon halted and a solemn figure in the back stood up and steadied himself at a lectern. Draped in a white toga and crowned with a garland of vines, his voice boomed out as a fanfare of trumpets hushed the crowd:

And in the beginning there was a Void,
and out of the Void sprang Chaos,
and next broad-bosomed Gaea, earth goddess,
the solid and eternal home of all,
and Eros, most beautiful of the immortal gods,
who in every man and every god softens the sinews
and overpowers the prudent purpose of the mind.
Out of the Void came Darkness and black Night,
and out of Night came Light and Day,
her children conceived after union
     in love with Darkness.
Gaea first produced starry Uranus, equal in size
     with herself, to cover her on all sides.
Thereafter she lay with Uranus and gave birth
     to Ocean with its deep current...
Great Father Sky called his children the Titans,
And because of his feud with them he said
     they blindly tightened the noose and
     had done a savage thing
For which they would have to pay
     in time to come...[1]

A raucous laugh alerted the Fool to a blaze of color to his right—the Vipers were approaching. As he climbed down a voice suddenly cackled above the din, freezing him.

"Stop! Signore, take heed!"

The Fool's eyes darted to a small figure sitting on the ground dressed in black under the beaked mask of a raven. In front of this creature, splayed on a coarse linen cloth, was a hand of tarocchi face cards arranged in the shape of a Celtic cross.

"Por favore, Signore," cackled the Raven. "I see an important event in your *futuro*, let us take the Fool's journey together and see if the sixth card turns up in your favore."

A foreign accent with a lisp, maybe Spanish, perhaps a Catalan gypsy. Thinking quickly, the Fool crouched out of the line of sight of those walking by. "*Va bene*, Messer Raven, what have you got?"

He watched the Raven scrutinize him as a commercial prospect: young, fashionable, dressed in black with tight silk doublet and hose—the telltale signs of a young *grandi*. But then the seer's practiced eye dulled as it caught the aged cloak and worn-out soles. As the Raven slowly turned the next card, the Fool held his breath, keeping his ear closely tuned to the sound of the Vipers passing by.

The Raven spoke. "If I may say, Signore, you wear the *máscara* of the Fool today. Perhaps you are at the start of your journey. The cards will guide you through the labyrinth of—"

The Fool held up his hand to interrupt: "*Basta!*" His words cut quick as he pointed to each card in turn: "The Hanged Man? And the Fool, the Tower, the Devil, the Moon, the World... Surely an ill-fated hand!"

The Raven offered a rotted-toothed smile under his curved beak as he opened his arms, his palms facing up. "The cards speak, Signore, not I." Fearing to overplay his hand, he paused. "But, I dealt these *tarjetas* before you chanced by. Perhaps we should begin again? The reading *depende* always on your *domande*..."

Over his shoulder the Fool spied the red and yellow scarves moving off. "I'm too late already, Messer Raven," he said as he plucked a small coin from his doublet and tossed it on the linen cloth. "Perhaps next time you can tell me how to win at *triche-tach*. *That* would better help my fortunes."

The Raven nodded as he pocketed the coin. "Mille gracias, Signore. Hasta luego."

Turning around, the Fool looked both ways then doubled back to enter the piazza from the far side. Dodging a horde of children harrying a gaily-dressed juggler, he passed under two giants on stilts high-stepping above the crowd, then ducked down a small side alley hoping to avoid further trouble before meeting up with his companions.

FORTUNA

Moments later he reached the Piazza della Signoria where the expansive square undulated with rolling waves of bodies. Buffeted by the swell, he searched the crowd for the blue and white banners of his neighborhood gonfalon. As his eyes surveyed the crowd he noticed the inordinate number of Guards of the Eight lined up outside the Palazzo and dispersed through the Piazza. Finally he located his group over near the Pisan canopy and made his way through the crush of bodies. When he arrived he lifted his mask to reveal himself.

A horned red devil swung a wine flask in his face. "*Ciao*, Nico. Where've you been?"

Recognizing Tommaso's slurred voice, he shrugged. "Just a diversion or two."

"Anyone I know?" Tommaso asked, offering his flask.

All around a raucous crowd of masked revelers gathered—friends, neighbors, relations, and servants—all from the gonfalon of the Shell in the Oltrarno quarter across the river. They were dancing and waving their banners, waiting for their *trionfo*—the one he, Niccolò, had helped design—to arrive. Tommaso was his closest childhood acquaintance and sometimes rival, the eldest son of the distinguished Soderini family. Everyone knew Tommaso hadn't a care in the world, his future assured: he was betrothed to Fiammetta Strozzi, the first daughter of *the* richest family in Florence.

Just then a beautiful young sylph caught Niccolò's eye. She was veiled behind an exquisite Carnival mask—her cat's eyes framed in dove-white trimmed with glass-beaded jewels and gold lace. Her long blond hair, covered in fine white lace, swept up toward the top of her head in the French style, and then cascaded down her back over a gown of gold and white damask. If she had not been precariously perched on platformed boots her gown would have grazed the ground.

"Is that Chiara?" he whispered in disbelief.

"Forget it, *Machia*."

It was. Tommaso's young cousin, a daughter of the Corbinelli and another neighbor. Niccolò could not remember the last time he had seen her, surely she had been just a child. Now, with her full-length wool surcoat pulled close against the February chill she resembled a pale yellow lily gripped in a gloved fist, poised at that delicate and dangerous age when feminine allure suddenly blossoms with the discovery of its wondrous power. She must be almost sixteen years and Niccolò doubted he would forget her again. He dropped his Fool's mask down over his face and strode over. Acting the gallant, he bowed low.

"Mademoiselle Corbinelli?" he inquired, mimicking the manners of French courtly fashion. "*Enchanté*."

Playing along, she proffered her hand. "Monsieur Machiavelli, I presume."

Tommaso rolled his eyes and wandered off.

"Did you see the Creation?" she asked.

Immediately he was charmed, but before he could reply a sudden trumpet blast announced the arrival of the next parade float. It was his—their—neighborhood *trionfo*.

Captivated by the sight, Chiara pulled him toward the center of the Piazza.

"Che fantastico!"

"*Il Trionfo del Uomo*, The Triumph of Man," Niccolò said with pride, hoping she would notice where he had slipped in his family standard—the silver field emblazoned with the azure cross and nails in the corners. These nails were the *mal clavellus* that had given his family its name. He presumed she would be impressed.

The stage, filled with masked allegorical figures, was dominated by a large wooden wheel painted with human figures along its rim. They rose and fell as the wheel was turned by three smaller figures adorned with ribbons to mimic the wind. It was the Wheel of Fortune spun by the Three Fates. Next to the wheel stood a masked woman in white holding a horn of plenty, with a ship's rudder propped up at her side. Opposite stood a second masked woman, this one in black, holding a pair of dice and juggling balls.

Chiara pointed to the figures. "Look, Caterina is Fortuna and Isabella, Nemesis."

Niccolò admired his handiwork: Fortuna—the bitch goddess of Chance, who he chased both day and night. Considering his gambling debts, she was fast eluding him. He glanced at Chiara and tried to imagine how easy life must be, born with Fortuna at one's side. Young, beautiful, rich: she was all three and the treasure of the Corbinelli, a respected old family connected through marriage to the most powerful clans in the city. And he, a Machiavelli, a noble name with threadbare hose and holes in his shoes.

As Chiara's cloak fell open, Niccolò noticed the budding breasts and curve of her narrow waist and put his envy aside. What did the noisome priests say? *Thou shalt not covet...* Besides, he thought, the gods always provided mortals with one consolation: One turn of the Wheel and those favored by Fortuna were soon brought down by Nemesis. Perhaps, he thought, it's better the bitch Fortuna keeps me hungry.

Chiara pointed to the figures at the back of the stage. "Who are they?"

"Justice, Liberty, Truth. And behind them: Necessity, Virtù, and Reason."

"I like the Roman centurion, is that Marco?" Chiara waved but failed to get the centurion's attention. Then she pointed to the fantastic creature in the middle with feathered angel wings and a beaked mask with a sprouting crown of feathers. "This looks more like a chicken or cock, no?"

"A chicken?" Niccolò was scandalized. "It's an eagle."

"Don't blame me, Monsieur. I envision Liberty as a lady, not a beaked bird. Just maybe you're a secret Ghibelline—ah, I see the Machiavelli standard there."

"*Basta, basta!* Enough," he admonished, pleased. She's clever for her age, he thought, maybe too clever in exercising her newly discovered feminine skills. Perhaps she secretly admired him. A bet he was willing to gamble.

"So tell me their story," she said.

"*Senti.* Necessity is the mother of action, creating opportunities for man. Then Virtù, together with Reason, battle Evil's dark forces to determine man's actions, for good or for bad—for the ideals of Truth, Justice, and Liberty, or their opposing forces. But man's efforts always suffer the vagaries of the Fates, who serve the whims of both Fortuna and Nemesis. Capricious Fortuna herself may lift men up but, without Virtù, Nemesis brings down the proud and greedy. At other times even the most virtuous are brought low."

Chiara feigned confusion. "And so?"

Niccolò summed up his thesis: "We mortals have only one recourse—Virtù."

Then she challenged him. "If Virtù is all that holds our world together, tell me—how virtuous are you?"

He laughed evasively, knowing she had confounded Christian virtue with Roman Virtù, perhaps deliberately. But as a gambler he knew to hold his cards close, so he hedged: "Only the truly depraved would claim to be wholly virtuous."

Just then Tommaso meandered back their way, swinging his flask and forcing all to imbibe. "Come on, *il Machia*, drink up!" Tommaso was drunk, disconcerting his younger cousin.

"Where's Fiammetta?" she demanded.

"There, with her sisters. I must constantly separate the cow from the herd." Tommaso laughed, taking no pains to be delicate in front of his cousin. He nudged Niccolò. "Hey Machia, seen any ripe fruit?"

Niccolò winced. Tommaso's coarseness was deliberate, if not malicious. Friendship aside, Niccolò was not a serious suitor for a Soderini family treasure like Chiara. But the best-laid plans in the business of marriage were subject to the whims of fate and love; hence Tommaso's wariness. His barbs were a reminder that a Machiavelli's attentions should be focused elsewhere. Niccolò was relieved to see Chiara ignored the remark as well.

Distracted, she exclaimed, "Look, Nemesis dropped one of her balls."

The painted wooden ball rolled off the stage and dropped to the pavement, where a swift-footed street urchin snatched it. As Niccolò shouted after him, the boy darted away and quickly disappeared into the crowd with his prize.

Niccolò cursed as he picked up his fallen mask.

Tommaso needled him: "You see how Chance plays loose with the designs of men?"

"We could use more Virtù in this city," Niccolò muttered.

"As the devil, I must disagree. But maybe you should send your Roman with sword in hand after the scamp." Tommaso quoted the Latin text on the banner draped across the centurion: "*Duce virtute comite Fortuna.*"

"*Sí,* but *Virtù vince Fortuna,*" Niccolò retorted. Yes, Virtù conquers Fortune.

"*Basta,* listen," Chiara hushed them, holding her head still.

As the Triumph of Man retreated along the parade route, the drone of hymnal chants wafted toward them through the air. Waves of bodies washed back across the open space, jostling them as they tried to see. Then a crucifix bobbed into view above the crowd, announcing the approach of the religious orders.

"*Madonna,*" said Tommaso, "it's the black crows. *Andiamo,* let's go."

But Chiara's eyes were transfixed on the approaching monks. "I want to hear the hymns," she said. "Then Bacchus and Ariadne will be coming after." Tommaso shrugged and disappeared across the Piazza as the crowd pushed to make way.

THE FRIARS

As plainchant filled the Piazza, Niccolò felt a tinge of disdain. God's holy army, he thought, dressed in hooded frocks with their tonsured heads bared, their eyes and voices uplifted in blissful ignorance.

Marked by their mode of dress, the various orders were a ubiquitous sight within the city walls. First in line came the white-frocked Benedictines, a small order followed by the much larger contingent of gray-frocked Franciscans. The disciples of the pious and gentle Francis, the *Frati Minori,* made up the most numerous order in Florence and the surrounding region. Like their founder, they wore simple, rough frocks cinched at the waist, sandaled or barefoot. Unlike their founder, many were corpulent. The Gray frocks, as they were commonly called, had many zealous members who closely guarded their holy primacy in the city.

"*Che bellissima!*" Chiara said, closing her eyes. "Mother drags me to the Duomo regularly; the choir is the only thing that makes it tolerable."

Well, he thought as he rolled his eyes, hopefully she wasn't one of *those*. His mother was—a psalm-singer—but these noisome chants soured his ears. The meddling of monks, priests, and friars was a plague on the Christian world, and particularly virulent here in Florence. He remembered as a boy how a certain Fra Barto, an Augustinian at Santo Spirito, had paid frequent visits to a young widow in his neighborhood. The older boys had joked how Fra Barto was comforting Mona Lucrezia with brief glimpses of heaven. And on Sundays, when his mother dragged him to Church, he heard Fra Barto scold the congregation, demanding the last *quattrino* from a poor man's purse. No, most clerics were nothing but charlatans, lechers, and philanderers hiding behind the cloth and making a dirty business of their vocation. Watching them wield the cross like a sword was particularly odious. The ironic truth was that Niccolò's mother had wanted him to join the priesthood, but luckily his father's wishes had prevailed. Fortunately for the Church as well.

"Have I told you the tale of Fra Timoteo?" Niccolò needled, referring to the ribald stories of Boccaccio that captured the irreverent attitude of the Machiavelli household. Chiara, her eyes still closed listening to the plainchant, ignored the remark.

The Franciscans were followed by the smaller order of black-clad Augustinians; these were the black crows to which Tommaso had referred. Behind them came the second largest order in the region and principal rival to the Franciscans: the black and white-clad Dominicans, called the Black friars. These were the learned Order of Preachers—that of St. Dominic, St. Augustine of Hippo and St. Thomas of Aquino—all masters of canon law and staunch defenders of Christian doctrine. The Dominicans were the grand Inquisitors of heretics across Christendom, cursed by their detractors as the *Domini cani*—the baying 'Hounds of the Lord.'

The Dominicans raised their voices in a clear, measured unison as they entered the Piazza, silencing the crowd with the sweetness and enthusiasm of their song. A high-pitched solo, an octave doubling in pure falsetto, cut like a lark through the crisp air:

Ecce quam bonum...
Behold how good and pleasant it is for brethren
to dwell together in unity...

Yes, brotherhood, Niccolò thought—a brotherhood of thieves.

As the procession of chanting monks passed under the shadow of the large government palazzo, their harmony was shattered by a gang of young boys in cheap carnival masks racing in and out of the crowd, snipping at the monks' heels like rabid dogs. The little devils were yelling out profanities while tossing various projectiles.

"Barking dogs!" "Filthy hounds!"

"Prayer-mumblers! Ha-ha! Save your own souls, you bald-headed crows!" the boys shouted, full of bravado.

One young ruffian let fly with a piece of rotten fruit, "Hey Friar Onion! Can you tell who hit you with that one?"

"*Porco Dio!* Up yours! *Sodomiti!*' shrieked another.

These profanities offended the more dignified citizens, who shouted the boys down and briefly gave chase. But the raucous youths were too slick and fast in the crowds, running off down the small alleys to reappear in another part of the vast Piazza.

Niccolò chuckled at the antics of the orphaned street boys, the *fanciulli*. To him, their harassment was divine justice for the moral lapses of God's self-righteous little servants. Ten years ago he might have joined in. Chiara shot him a sharp look. "My mother would not be amused. She goes to all the sermons of the new preacher at San Marco."

Niccolò scoffed, "Priests, preachers and monks…they're all the same." But he silently wondered about this new preacher. Niccolò always kept a sharp ear cocked to local gossip and lately he heard more and more chattering among the street wags about this *Frate* from Ferrara. They said he had visions, that he was a prophet. Niccolò laughed to himself. *Yes, and I'm the king of France.*

"So, Signorina, you have an interest in mystics?"

"I was just saying—"

The crowd buzzed and their attention was suddenly drawn to the approaching sound of full-throated singing. Shouts arose from the crowd: "*Guarda*, look! The chariots of Bacchus and Ariadne are coming! Quickly, get a better view!"

BACCHUS AND ARIADNE

A chorus of male singers marched into view, twelve in all, flanked by flag-bearers on waving their banners in a choreographed routine. With their voices full of merriment and laughter, the singers glanced upwards to the second-story windows and balconies where they caught furtive glances filled with feminine mystique and promise. Inspired, the young men sang out with passion:

> *How sweet is youth, but oh so fleeting!*
> *Let he who will, be merry, for tomorrow, who knows?*
> *Here is Bacchus and here Ariadne,*

Fair and Passionate to each other;
For time flies and is deceptive...
Maids and young men who love,
Long live Bacchus! Long live Love!
Let everyone sport, dance and sing!
Let your hearts be ablaze with joy!
Let there be no pain, no sorrow! What will be, will be:
For tomorrow, who knows?

Their enthusiasm was infectious, causing the audience to join in. Following close behind was a magnificent parade wagon drawn by enormous white oxen. This was the Medici family *trionfo*. It was richly draped with marine-blue tapestry adorned with white lilies and yellow cornflowers. Seated at a center throne were two figures depicting the lovers Bacchus and Ariadne—he in a Roman toga and she in a flowing white robe gathered at the waist. A four-cornered canopy interlaced with vines sheltered the throne while many fauns, satyrs and nymphs languished or danced around the stage. It was the pagan allegory of love and pleasure. Off the back of the wagon masqueraders and spectators merrily filled their cups with wine from the spigot of a huge wooden cask. Niccolò spied Tommaso gamely refilling his flask.

"*Che bellissimo!*" exclaimed Chiara. "Look, there's Lorenzino, ...and Beatrice and Francesca... They told me they would be with Piero. Let's join them." She waved to get the dancers' attention.

Niccolò allowed his eyes to wander lustily over the nubile Ariadne, a face he didn't recognize. These youth were all from the San Giovanni quarter, denoted by the standards of the Golden Lion and St. John's Dragon—the neighborhoods of Medicean clients and supporters. The city's social stratum was defined by this patchwork of little fiefdoms accorded by family names and gonfalon loyalties and the Mediceans were currently at the top of Fortune's wheel. Theirs had been the wealthiest family in the city for the past three generations and though some fortunes, such as the Strozzi, had recently exceeded theirs, they were still the most celebrated and powerful. At the clan's head was the revered Lorenzo—*Il Magnifico*, as his partisans had taken to calling him—who controlled the city by a tight network of family and client connections supporting the family trading and banking empire.

"Wait." Niccolò restrained Chiara as a knight on a large black siege horse suddenly came trotting into the Piazza. It was Piero, son of Lorenzo, grandson of Piero the Gouty, great grandson of Cosimo. His dressage was decorated with gold shields containing the five red balls surrounding a single blue ball with the French fleur-de-lis in the center—

the Medici coat-of-arms. His troop of flagbearers waved an identical standard. As Piero spurred his horse roughly, standing tall and waving his jousting lance, one sensed the bravura of a crusader off to save the Holy Land.

The rest of the troupe followed close behind: two small chariots filled with Piero's younger siblings and his diffident Roman wife, Alfonsina. As the grandiose float came to a halt in the middle of the Piazza, the knight, chariots and flagbearers all gathered round. The entire ensemble was a calculated extravagance to impress and Chiara's body strained to take in the spectacle.

Suddenly red-deviled Tommaso reappeared, his costume blending well with fresh stains of Chianti. He waved his flask toward Piero, who had leveled his lance in the pose of the conqueror. "Here's to the birthday boy!" he sneered. "Look at him, thinks he's one of King Arthur's knights. *Buffone*."

"Tommaso!" Chiara scolded.

"Relax, *cugina*, he's our cousin but he's still an ass. And his Roman wife is insufferable. To think the reins of the Republic may eventually fall into their hands. Anyway, we'll have our fill of them both tonight."

Niccolò knew the wine had loosened Tommaso's tongue, but his antipathy for these younger Mediceans was widely shared. Many aristocratic clans had tried to displace the Medici and failed. Many of these were now banished or dead. Though Lorenzo's power and benevolence were respected throughout Italia, his first son Piero pressed his birthright. Putting on the airs of a prince, he and his friends looked down upon residents of the other quarters, especially those from across the river. This year Shrove Tuesday fell on Piero's birthday, so the Medici would host a celebration at their palazzo tonight even bigger and more impressive than usual. A sad irony, thought Niccolò: a city famed for its republican posturing so beset by petty infighting over power and status.

"My father refuses me permission to go," Chiara said.

Suddenly Niccolò felt two strong hands grip him from behind and saw the ominous flash of yellow and red colors in his peripheral vision.

"What have we here?" said a threatening voice he recognized too well.

Tommaso, sensing trouble with a rival gonfalon, quickly became alert. "Hey Doffo, what are you doing?"

"Eh, Soderini. Your gambling Fool here owes me. Don't you, Machiavelli?"

Niccolò felt the grip on his arms tighten. He saw Chiara's alarm and tried to hide the anxiety in his voice. "I'm well aware, Spini."

"So where's my money?"

Niccolò had no money to pay the bastard and he had been avoiding this gang of gambling cronies for weeks. As he felt the hot breath on his neck, his mind raced for an escape when Tommaso intervened with a hearty slap on Spini's back.

"Hold on, Doffo."

"What?"

"*Senti*, I owe Machia money and Machia owes you money, so I'll pay you and everything is settled. How much does he owe?"

Spini laughed and the hands relaxed their grip on Niccolò. "Four florins plus an extra for my trouble and interest."

Tommaso let out a low whistle. "That's more than I owe, but now my friend can owe me." Playing up the ruse, he winked at Niccolò with a devilish grin. "Anyway, I always wanted to be a moneylender. Come by tomorrow, Doffo, and I'll have it for you."

When Spini grunted his consent, Tommaso wagged his head suggestively toward the Medici trionfo. "Tell me, Doffo, I thought you had dealings with bigger fish."

Without a word the Vipers moved off as Tommaso snickered. "Those roughnecks should keep Sir Lancelot busy. They hate Piero even more than you, Machia. So, I guess you owe *me* your life now."

Niccolò covered his anger by sighing ruefully. "*Con piacere,* if you think you may profit by it." Regaining his poise, he gave Chiara a feeble shrug, but felt exposed as he straightened his doublet. He thought he noticed a change in her mood. Grateful as he was to Tommaso for saving his skin, he knew the aid came at a price—like many in Florence, he was now a client to his rich friend and Tommaso wouldn't let him forget it.

Across the Piazza they watched the ensuing fracas as yellow and red invaded the sea of Medicean blue. The Vipers were from the Santa Maria Novella quarter, where the oldest aristocratic clans lived. The parvenu bankers and merchants had dislodged these families in the social hierarchy, fomenting a fierce and sometimes deadly rivalry. But the Medici controlled the government ministries and within moments the numerous Guards of the Eight Niccolò had noted earlier had converged in force and dispersed the troublemakers. Niccolò wondered if there would be more trouble later that evening and swore revenge against that *bastardo* Spini for embarrassing him.

Suddenly the Piazza was engulfed by a buzz that mingled with a rising thunder of drums. "*Dio mio!* It must be the *Trionfo di Morto,*" said Tommaso. "*Merda*, I should find Fiammetta..." But he hesitated and shrugged. "I can't miss this."

THE TRIUMPH OF DEATH

As the laughter of the Bacchanale receded a masked gang of street urchins propelled themselves headlong into the Piazza screaming: "Here comes Messer Piero di Cosimo's Triumph of Death! Aaaiieeeeyaaaa! *Repente! Repente!* The End is near!"

A somber dirge rose up as a lump of anticipation caught in the crowd's throat. Then a repeating refrain snaked its way through the heavy air propelled by the steady pulse of the drums:

Dead we are, as you can see.

So, one day, we shall see you.

Niccolò stretched to see a large wagon pulled by four black oxen enter the Piazza. It was draped entirely in black contrasted by ghostly white accents. A Grim Reaper sliced his scythe through the air while stalking around a stage littered with coffins. Flagbearers waved banners of skull-and-crossbones while a troupe of flagellants, stripped to their waists, flayed themselves with knotted cords. Many others sang and danced the Dance of the Dead as they alternated their chant with the *Misericordia*: "Have mercy on me, O Lord! O merciful God, save my soul!"

The apparition lumbered into the Piazza as the Grim Reaper bellowed over the crowd: "Behold *Italia*, a prey to war and great famine. God has sent the plague as a judgment on thee! Such are the fruits of thy blindness. O thee of little faith. Alas! Alas!"

"Yes indeed! Alas! Alas!" replied the chorus.

Several old peasant women in the crowd moaned, quickly crossing themselves while crying: "Ai, *Madonna, Il Morto!*"

Chiara shuddered as she grasped Niccolò's arm and retreated behind him. Tommaso was wide-eyed while Niccolò could only laugh, gazing up at the ghoulish portrayal of Master Death.

Up on the stage a spotted leopard, a lion and a hungry she-wolf prowled with the Grim Reaper. Tommaso was delighted to see the sides of the wagon painted with red devils with pointed tails and horns. Their sharp talons clawed the backs of their victims, who cried with their mouths frozen open while red-hot flames licked their scorching feet.

"*Che cazzo!* Look."

Tommaso pointed to the large painted panel standing like a wall almost six *braccie* high over the back of the vehicle, casting the shadow over its stage. It was a fantastic vision composed of strange and horrible images arranged in concentric circles. "The nine circles of the Inferno," said Niccolò. "The gluttons and the lustful, the simonists and the heretics…"

"Seducers and sodomites…" added Tommaso gleefully.

In the center was a three-faced monster fixed in ice. It was Satan himself. The beast flapped its two enormous batwings and in each mouth chomped on a squirming body dangling from its jaws. Across the top of the panel was the inscription:

LASCIATE OGNE SPERANZA, VOI CH'INTRATE
(ABANDON ALL HOPE, YE WHO ENTER)

As the three beasts prowled, the Reaper swung his scythe and the flagbearers and flagellants gathered round. The dancers and singers could hardly repress their mirth as the muffled instruments and trumpets reached a crescendo, their clamor filling the space. The crowd grew silent with anticipation when all of a sudden the coffins popped open and dancing skeletons emerged, chanting:

Dead we are, as you can see.
So, one day, we shall see you.

The crowd buzzed and the old women stifled their screams. The little masked street urchins whipped up a frenzy by running through the crowd and shouting hideously: "Sinners! Fornicators! Whores and Sodomizers! *Repente! Repente! Eeeeyaaaiii!* The End is coming! Save your souls from the everlasting fire!"

"*Fantastico!*" exclaimed Niccolò.

Tommaso chuckled. "*Dio mio!* The Divine Poet would be tickled to see the fright he's put into them."

Chiara closed her cloak against the afternoon chill. "I think it's dreadful. Many mothers have had a child or a loved one die horribly from the pestilence. Isn't it enough to hear about the approaching scourge almost everyday in Church."

Niccolò said, "Oh, Messer Piero and his friends are just having bit of fun. These prayer-mumblers are so excitable, living in fear of the future… reading their fates in goat entrails."

Tommaso grinned and pranced like his fellow devils, mimicking them with a menacing voice: "The *scourge* is coming! It will consume all the evildoers. Unless we repent we shall all be *condemned* to *eternal Damnation!*"

Chiara shrunk from his antics. "Are you going to find Fiammetta?"

Tommaso grimaced with discomfort. "*Merda*, first I need a place to piss. *Andiamo?*"

Chiara shook her head no and turned to Niccolò. With a hard edge to her voice she said, "It's getting dark, I must go." She called to her serving girl to follow.

Tommaso, under the pressure of his bladder, turned to Niccolò. "Machia, escort her home, eh? Make sure she gets there safely too. See you at Via Larga."

Niccolò nodded and turned back to Chiara, who had abruptly walked off in the direction of the Via Calimala. With three quick steps he caught her as her maid followed discretely.

"Life is all very amusing for you two," she snapped, "but my room is like a dungeon. I feel like some precious brooch locked away in the family jewel case, waiting to be bartered away to secure some 'suitable' business alliance—to be a bearer of heirs. I wish I had been born a man!"

A shame that would have been, thought Niccolò, as he wondered at her outburst. Was it because she was missing a party, or something more? She was clever and headstrong, a potent combination for a young woman. Perhaps her family was already making arrangements for her betrothal. He felt a fleeting pang of regret over his 'unsuitability,' but quickly shook it off—she was worth a gamble and he already had too much of the day invested. Taking her arm, he escorted her toward the Ponte Santa Trinità.

Navigating through the crowds on narrow streets, it was almost dusk when they emerged on the quiet street parallel to the river. All the shops had closed for the holiday and in the stillness they heard their footfalls on the paving stones intermingle with the fading echoes of Carnival. Turning a corner, they were suddenly accosted by a gang of youths in carnival masks blocking their way with a long pole. A bonfire crackled in the opposite corner of the intersection. A grimacing devil jumped out and confronted Niccolò: "*Prego, Signore*, a few quattrini for safe passage."

It was a demand more than a request and the devil's voice was menacing. During Carnival it was common practice for gangs to block the streets and demand tribute to prolong their nighttime revelries. Niccolò felt his anger rise, but wisely reappraised the situation—a confrontation might quickly escalate if not handled prudently. He reached into his doublet and brought forth several of the small coins, then gave the devil a cold stare as he handed them over. "*Ragazzi*, take care of the citizens and we shall all enjoy *Carnevale* together."

"*Grazie, Signore*, but of course, we mean no harm to fine citizens such as yourself," the devil mocked with false demeanor. "We must protect you from rival gangs." The boys raised the barrier and Niccolò continued escorting Chiara and her maid down the street toward the bridge.

After a few steps Chiara recovered and started to speak when wild cries erupted behind them and a shower of stones ricocheted off the street and buildings. Behind them the corner exploded in a firefight between two rival gangs. Niccolò hustled the two women across the river.

Safe on the other side, Chiara's anger boiled over. "These *fanciulli* are a plague!"

Concerned with delivering her safely home and seeing his hopes for a romantic tryst fade, Niccolò tried to calm her with typical insouciance. "They only fight among themselves. Perhaps the Eight will increase the watch."

But as he looked back over his shoulder, he thought, yes, a plague on all Italia are these, her children.

CHAPTER 2

A Terrifying Sermon

A NIGHT DRAFT SLIPPED INTO the dormitory cell, flicking the candle flame and sending shadows dancing across the walls and ceiling. A lone crucifix stared down on the Dominican friar hunched over his desk, his head nestled in his hands as long, veined fingers massaged his forehead and temples. A quill rested on the Hebrew Bible over which he had labored nonstop since the hour of Compline. His minute scratches filled the margins, burning the words of tomorrow's sermon into his mind. Thankfully, the intrusion of Carnival had died down to an occasional shout and wine-soaked lyric.

Bracing himself against the desk, the friar rose wearily and crossed over to the open window to gaze down on the shadowed cloister. Hearing the gentle cooing of Brother Domenico's birds caged in the dovecote below, he felt a yearning for a more tranquil past. It was eight years since his first brief assignment to this Convent of San Marco as Lector to the novices, and less than a year since he had returned. In the intervening years much had changed and the cooing doves evoked the distance he had come since those peaceful times of reading, writing, and contemplation—a time when his only concerns had been instructing novices and tending to his own devotions. He yearned for those rhythms of cloistered life that were regular and well ordered.

Those few peaceful years of contemplation were the only ones he had really known in his whole life, except for the early years with his grandfather. As the male child with the most promise from a large celebrated family, he had been predestined to follow in Nonno's footsteps as court physician to the Duke of Ferrara. Under Nonno's tutelage he had witnessed first-hand the magical world of the Court of d'Este, the oldest royal House in all *Italia*. Eager to please with his studies, he had excelled and surpassed all expectations. But Nonno warned him, he had witnessed the malice of court life: it was an ungodly world, filled with debauchery and evil. He could still hear Nonno's stern voice and remembered well this first taste of contempt.

Such memories pained him and the friar turned back toward the crucifix to cross himself, seeking reassurance that the Lord keeps safe the souls of the good and the righteous.

Unlike with his grandfather, he had hardly known his own father. He remembered nights at home with his mother and younger siblings, sadly waiting for his father to return from his trips abroad or from his meetings with colleagues late into the night. It seemed his father avoided his family. After Nonno's passing the boy had tried to fill the void with music and verse, but to no avail. After a few months, his father had begun to berate him anew for his melancholy.

Then there was the promise of the Strozzi girl—*No!*

His mind snapped shut and his body went rigid. He knew temptation was the Devil's ploy. He stared at the crucifix, steeling his will by riveting his eyes on the face of the Savior. *Am I so repugnant?* He knew the answer: *in the eyes of this world, yes.*

He had been right to turn away from pain and seek solace in prayer—unfavored by nature, he would find favor with God. But his father insisted he continue his studies in medicine at the university. He rebelled and his mother wept when he and his father fought. Finally he capitulated, but at the university—that sinkhole of vice and sophistry—his despair only deepened. He turned to prayer and scripture, pouring over *The Confessions* and *Summa Theologica*. Only then did God finally come to him.

He remembered his glorious revelation. At night he had fallen into a feverish sleep and tossed and turned to free himself from his bonds. Then a freezing drizzle spilled down over his head, dousing his fever as he awoke in a cold sweat. From that moment he knew, just like St. Thomas, that he could never find peace in this world. Soon after, without a word, he had stolen away to the Dominicans in Bologna. In letters his father reproached him, telling him how he disgraced the memory of his grandfather and how his mother wept. But this time there would be no surrender. He wrote back: "As you honor my older brother who serves as a soldier of the Duke, so should you grant me the greater honor as a soldier of the Lord."

These had been his last words to his family and he still tasted their bile. The world was ungodly and cruel—all he saw in his young life had proved it—but only great prophets could see clearly. All he needed, all he wanted, was to be left alone to pursue God's truth in quiet contemplation.

By all that was written, on the Last Day, God Almighty would separate the sinners from the righteous. My Lord, my God, I shall serve Your will and only Yours.

The Order of Dominicans suited him perfectly. When he donned the white habit, raised the hood of the black cappa, and tucked the sword of the Bible and crucifix under his arm, he was a true soldier of the Lord. As a novice he honed his mind on Christian doctrine, relishing those puzzles of theology, and in a short time surpassed even his teachers.

Ordained and appointed novice-master, he finally found an oasis where he could breathe freely and devote his life to the Word of God.

But, by God's will, his peace was not to last.

Outside, the shout of a reveler broke the silence and the friar felt a sharp pain in his bowels, a recurring reminder of his body's weaknesses. He drank a cup of water and wondered if he should rush to the privy. But it passed. He picked up the sputtering candle and returned to the window to breath the night air. The struggling flicker made the night seem even blacker.

His was the Order of Preachers. Perhaps he should have joined one of the hermetic orders—the Benedictines or the Augustinians—as he was often wistful for the solitude of contemplation. But the Black Friars were meant to be *in* the world—their mission was to bring the hope of salvation to the needy in the towns and villages. As St. Thomas argued, the mendicant orders blended the active life of the commune with the contemplative life of the convent and were thus superior to both in isolation. But walking the terrain between the provinces of God and Satan was perilous duty.

After his ordination, his superiors prodded him to go forth and preach, to spread the Word, assigning him here to San Marco eight years ago. But, like an awkward fledgling stumbling from the nest, his first attempts were an ignominious failure. His oratory was miserable; his words had the sonority of lead rather than the clear, pure ring of spiritual timbre. He had watched his congregation slowly dwindle to an indefinite few, finally causing his superiors to reconsider. Facing an empty church and resigned to obscurity, he was re-assigned as an itinerant to wander the forgotten towns and villages throughout the Romagna and Veneto.

For several years he plied his ministry and occupied himself with the interpretation of scripture and exposition of Church doctrine. But his travels opened his eyes to the stains on men's souls. He saw the faithful come to parish churches to seek protection from a fast-spinning world, only to be fleeced by clever priests with clever twists of words. Then he spied the charade played by bishops and their bankers as they made their illicit trade in benefices and indulgences. It was rottenness within the House of the Lord that spread outward from the chair of St. Peter. The saints' names these popes took could not disguise their blood ties and true loyalties: Borgia, Delle Rovere, Cibo. It pained him and he felt the spasm in his gut return. *Lord, how is it that Your chosen servants, Your most holy shepherds here on earth, are the most depraved of all?*

For solace he had turned to scripture and prayed for guidance. Then God spoke to him. It was two years ago in Brescia, near Verona, when the words of the prophets jumped out and shook him like a windstorm: *Behold, this people will rise up, and go a whoring after the gods of strangers and break My covenant, which I have made with them. Then My anger shall be kindled against them...*

The Almighty filled his nights with visions and he saw the heavens open wide and all the future calamities of the Church pour forth. The Voice came, demanding to be heard, commanding him to announce it to the people: *The way of life has been shown to you and yet none follows it... Christ is incensed by you and declares by the mouth of the prophet: 'We are weary with calling; for all day do I cry with the voices of the preachers, and no one hearkens unto me.'*

It was the voice of the Revelation of John and he feared the sound of it.

But it was the Almighty's command. He soon found his own voice and when the congregations heard his thunder, they cowed and trembled under his *terribilità*. His voice resonated as he rebuked them from the pulpit and watered their seeds of self-doubt. He shamed them as when Jesus departed from the temple:

See ye not all these things? I say to you, there shall not be left here one stone upon another that shall not be thrown down. And they shall fall by the edge of the sword...and I will lay waste to your cities, and bring your sanctuaries and the land into desolation...

As his fame spread, the churches were soon bursting with penitents. With his new-found fame, he was recalled here to San Marco and thrust once more into the center of this satanic carnival of a city. It was a glorious city—magnificent—but as Rome and Babylon, it had fallen away from the true path. All homage was now paid to wealth, power, and lust; God's temple was overrun. *O Moses, like the stiff-necked Jews, these people dance and worship the Golden Calf and their faith falls away like so much dried-up fruit...*

These days he ministered to the growing hordes of poor, offering them only bread, broth, hope, and faith. The rich *grandi* had built the city's great international wool and silk *fondacci* on the backs of these *poverini* while robbing them of everything, including their faith. With ill-gotten gains these *grandi* then stocked their palaces with the profane, filling every space with family coats-of-arms. All Italia knew their names: Medici, Strozzi, Albizzi, Rucellai. Led by the one they called Lorenzo the Magnificent, they controlled this city for their own amusements. So he had also rebuked them from the pulpit: "*Blessed are the poor in spirit, for THEIRS is the kingdom of heaven. Blessed are the meek, for THEY shall inherit the earth...*"

But this Lorenzo was clever; he distracted them with base and vile amusements. The carnival parades were an orgy of drunken appetites, where painted harlots—men and women both—paraded their perversions and no one turned away in shame. Sodomizers purveyed their unspeakable vices, while courtesans in finery and wigs, lacking all sense of modesty or chasteness, appealed to every other sort. Even the children were wicked, whipped into a frenzy against all that was holy and revered. Every day, every thing was for trade in the market: wealth for power, power for lust, and lust for wealth. It was as written in the words of Paul the Apostle:

> In the last days dangerous times will come, and men will be lovers of themselves, covetous, puffed up, proud, blasphemers, disobedient to parents, ungrateful, wicked, without either affection or peace, incontinent, unmerciful, without kindness, traitors, shameless, arrogant, lovers of pleasure more than God, making a pretense of piety, but rejecting its power. Stay clear of them.

It was the Devil's work. But the preacher was not fooled and he would not bow to a tyrant's pride. He would bring this prince Lorenzo down with God's sword.

That evening in the refectory, before he silenced them with a piercing look, he heard the novices whisper about the riotous displays of today's Carnival: debauched pagan rituals and satanic creatures; even a pagan Creation myth. *But the Creation was revealed to all by the word of God in the Book of Genesis. How dare they redress faith with these pagan legends!* This was the subtlest blasphemy—the glorification of ancient superstitions in the name of some new 'rediscovery of man.' But man was not *lost*—man was found through the teachings of Christ.

So today, the day before the Lenten season, he refused to participate in the procession in both anger and shame at the defilement of the religious orders and their lax morals. Instead, the words of the Book burned through his anger, inflaming his belly. Tomorrow they would rain down from the pulpit: *I hate and scorn your festivals; I take no pleasure in your solemn assemblies. Spare me the din of your chanting, let me hear none of your strumming on lyres, but let justice flow like water, and uprightness like a never-failing stream...*

Justice? He scoffed. The pagan Carnevale made a mockery of the Lenten fast and tomorrow the city would put on its other mask of false piety. But when the congregation crowded into the Cathedral to hear him preach he, like the prophet Moses, would spread the ashes and obliterate them with their hypocrisies:

"Florence, O Florence, for your sins, for your cruelty, for your greed, for your lasciviousness, for your ambition, you have yet to suffer many adversaries! The Lord shall bring a nation against you from afar, from the end of the earth, as swift as the eagle flies; a nation whose tongue you shall not understand…and he shall besiege you throughout all the land, which the Lord thy God has given you…"

He would put the fear of God in them and he would not let them forget because deep down he knew these things would come to pass.

The friar filled his lungs with the night air and tried to calm the turmoil in his belly. *Give me strength, Lord.* For spiritual renewal he turned to the one wall of his cell radiating with light and color. It was frescoed with the Crucifixion—the divine representation of beauty, faith, and sacrifice—painted as an inspiration and constant reminder of Christian virtue. It was the divine work of Blessed Fra Angelico, who for years labored with his talents to lift up the souls of the forgotten friars who inhabited these solitary cells. Here, the crucified Christ spread His arms to embrace His sacrifice for all sinners. With His head bowed in peaceful resignation, an infinite acceptance radiated from the Savior's face as a stream of red spurted from the wound below His ribs. *Lord, You sacrificed Your only Son to redeem us.*

At the foot of the cross a helpless sorrow suffused the expressions of the three figures keeping vigil: the Virgin Mother, Mary Magdalena, and St. Dominic. The friar's eyes lingered on the haloed Dominic. He saw through the saint's eyes, which gazed up at the Savior in solemn devotion. Without thinking, he clasped his hands together in prayer and made a silent promise to spread the Savior's word and fulfill His mission on earth.

Ecce quam bonum…

When the friar looked to the representation of the Virgin, he saw the beauty of her visage and felt his bowels relax. Her face was turned away with the pain of a mother's love and sorrow. Here was the perfect symbol of womanhood: the simplicity of dress, the harmony of form and color, and the softness of tone that created a sense of peace and comfort in the face of great sacrifice. Such was the inspirational gift Beato Angelico had bestowed through God on the spare life of the devotee. It was said he prayed to God before taking up his brush and the Almighty guided his hand across the wall and here was the proof: How beautiful and simple, yet profound, was this representation of the painter's craft. It was a glorification of the pure and holy; it was a glorification of the Holy Mother of God.

Next the friar's eyes fell to the Magdalena, the fallen women. With her hidden face raised up, she knelt at her savior's feet in eternal debt for her redemption, paid for with the lifeblood of her Lord. The friar reached out with his hands to caress the fallen Mary, as the Lord had done to touch her with the warmth of His love and cleanse her of her sins. Then he leaned the side of his face against the wall and embraced the image with his heart.

But the wall's rough chill against his cheek broke the spell, bringing to mind the contrast of this holy representation with the craven images adorning Florentine churches and family chapels. Those private commissions had the likenesses of their patrons' mistresses and courtesans richly depicted in bejeweled finery to represent the Virgin or other saints. Do they imagine the Virgin went about dressed as she is now painted? Do they think they can pull sheep's wool over the Almighty's eyes?

No, the sinners will be scourged, the faithful will be restored, and it will happen soon!

The Lord had revealed these things to him and tomorrow he would tell it to the people.

CHAPTER 3

The Palazzo Medici

NICCOLÒ WAS IRRITATED AS HE made his way back to the center. Chiara was safely deposited in her family home, but in the street outside her door she had rebuffed him with her coyness. He had only himself to blame for playing the stupid game of flirtation, but now the whole afternoon of the city's annual day of debauchery had been wasted. Perhaps he was being too hard—she was only doing what came naturally—but the episode only put him more on edge. He needed a diversion and to save time he cut through the back alleyways.

He was faintly aware of his restlessness these days. He wasn't sure why, whether it was a change around him or from within. He was now just past his second decade, yet could not foresee what the future held in store. Passing the days in taverns, playing cards and dice, drinking with simpletons and enjoying paid women had suddenly become a mindless distraction; unlike Tommaso, his fate was still in play. His immediate fear was that his father would somehow learn of his gambling debts.

Wandering down a dark alley, he was startled out of his thoughts by a low whistle sounding somewhere in the shadows ahead. He felt the hair rise on the back of his neck as he poised for flight—thieves and brigands always prowled the streets after dark looking for drunken Carnival celebrants to fleece. As darkness encircled the small alley, he saw a motion in the shadows ahead—a flash of white—then heard scuffling and running footsteps retreating down another alley. Advancing cautiously, he saw a small figure hunched over in the shadows. The figure appeared to be pulling up his hose when he spied Niccolò. He grabbed his mask off the ground and scampered off like a frightened rabbit. No more than a boy, probably one of the *fanciulli*.

"Filthy buggers," Niccolò said, laughing in relief. Then he saw the red and yellow scarf and reproached himself. He should know better than to pass through the notorious Street of the Furriers on Carnival night. Most likely they thought he was an Officer of the Night, one of those guards who patrolled the streets looking for sodomizers. The unspeakable vice was the favorite sport for young Florentines: horny *giovani* without women buggering the poor *fanciulli*. It was a comic sport at best. Maybe if the magistrates were more permissive of the ladies' arts there would be less of these perversions. He dismissed the incident without further thought.

Back among the crowds of masked revelers, Niccolò detoured through the Piazza della Signoria, where they were torching the traditional pyre of King Carnevale. Fueled by tinder and pitch, this conflagration would burn through the night, inflaming the pent-up depravity of his fellow Florentines, causing most of them to question their sanity tomorrow under the wagging finger of Lent.

The Piazza was a riot of drunks and fools, gamblers and harlots—a place Niccolò felt perfectly at home. He purchased some roasted chestnuts and wandered toward a shadowed corner where several small groups crowded around gamblers playing dice and cards. Looking over the shoulders of one group, he saw a dark-skinned gypsy demonstrating the three-shell game. Many in the crowd were past drunk as they attempted to guess under which shell the pea was hidden. One sodden jester threw down a *grosso* and pointed to the shell on the left. The gypsy turned it over. The crowd groaned and the jester cursed as the gypsy swept the coin up with a deft movement.

"Again, again." The onlookers chanted.

Niccolò shouldered his way to the front and studied the gypsy's nimble movements from behind his mask. He concentrated on the light-fingered hands and caught a glimpse of the pea. The jester again threw down his coin and picked the center shell.

The crowd let out another groan and the drunken jester mumbled in a sinister way, "San Giovanni does not like a cheat."

The gypsy ignored the drunk and swiftly pocketed the coin, once again blurring his hands over the shells. Just as quickly he stopped and Niccolò tossed a *grosso* and pointed to the right shell. The gypsy slowly revealed the pea and the crowd gasped with admiration. The gypsy fixed Niccolò with a stare as he handed him back two coins. Several hands pounded Niccolò on the back with congratulations while the gypsy dropped his eyes and began the game again, his pitch deliberately directed to the crowd. "Who will try now? As you see, even a Fool can win."

Niccolò turned and drifted slowly back into the crowd with a glint in his eye, his thin lips curled into an enigmatic smile. It was the smile of a cat, slow to reveal and difficult to decipher. Fingering the two coins, he let the undertow of bodies pull him back and turn him into the current of revelers flowing toward the Piazza San Giovanni. His small gamble had paid double: reaffirming his gaming skills—but how could he be so unlucky at *triche-tach*?—and delivering to the gypsy a handful of new victims to make up his small loss many times over. Yes, he mused, the game of life required the illusion of hope to continue running its course.

Carried along by his fellow citizens, he wondered why so many held views as narrow as the streets they plodded each day. Driven like pack mules to market, their blinders on, they saw nothing behind or to the sides or above, only to where they were directed by a bag of oats in front and a stick behind. But Niccolò did not focus on the obvious; his mind's eye wandered to the sides and back, overhead and especially down below. Yes, he enjoyed playing the clever mule that outsmarted his master. Someday he would write a tribute to his fellow Florentines, a satire in *terza rima*, and he had already decided on his title: *The Golden Ass.*

Arriving moments later in the Piazza San Giovanni, the religious center of the city, he circled the Baptistery. This was that heavenly-perfect octagon where all newborn Florentines were cleansed of original sin, so as to begin fresh accumulating ones of their own. The oldest edifice of the city, it was said to be built on the former temple to Mars within Julius Caesar's fortifications. Now it housed the city's Christian soul, locked behind Ghiberti's magnificent cast bronze doors.

Standing in juxtaposition was the Cathedral, *il Duomo*, wherein lodged the city's heart with its consuming love for the Virgin. Passing under Giotto's bell tower Niccolò looked up to see a band of angels tossing confetti out over the riotous hordes of masqueraders. He let himself be caught up in the celebration of his city's marriage of convenience between the spiritual and the material. (Normally, he passed his time around the Palazzo della Signoria, where the city's head was found or, more often than not, lost.)

After once circling the Piazza, Niccolò followed the stream of revelers draining down the narrow side streets toward the Palazzo Medici. He stopped to gaze at the imposing fortress rising up like a mountain of stone—its façade of rough-hewn blocks bigger than a man at street level, graduating to smaller, even-spaced rows of carved blocks on the first floor, topped with smooth mason work on the third level. It was a fortress built to exacting, but aesthetic specifications. Radiating power and wealth, these new *palazzi* were built to withstand a battering of siege cannons, if necessary.

To his left a troupe of street singers exposed their wine-besotted condition with leers and off-tune melodies. The object of the singers' attentions were several peasant girls giggling and hiding behind each other with embarrassment. Gaily dressed in tight-fitting multi-colored hose with short doublets fitted above the waist, leaving little to the imagination, the singers were accompanied by a band of ragamuffins playing various instruments, including the lute, tambour, flute, and that bellowing beast from the north, the bagpipe. They sang a common Carnival song, full of obscene innuendos and gestures:

Visin, Visin, Visin, …Come, Come, Come,
If you want your chimneys swept,
To the chimneys, Ladies!
We'll sweep everywhere,
In every nook and cranny,
For chimney sweeping
Is such sweet pleasure.

Is was a popular song, but especially amusing were the antics of the bass singer. At the end of each refrain the bass melody dropped low and slid up in a smooth glissando as the lecher made a sweeping gesture downward and upward, as if plunging a broom up a chimney. Drunken revelers and street urchins mimicked the suggestive motion, leading to more guffaws. Ladies of the night strolled past, adding color and Niccolò let his eyes linger as other *giovani* solicited the harlots' attentions. These women were the common sorts that normally entertained in the taverns but on festival days dressed up in their best finery to parade their wares.

Niccolò felt someone bump his elbow. "*Prego, Signore.* A *quattrino?*"

He instantly recoiled from the dark-stained palm and black fingernails reaching out toward him. Just past the shadow of the beggar he spied a mass of dark forms huddled up against the outside foundation of the Palazzo. Their stained clothing and skin showed these were the dyers, tanners, and carders—the *poverini*—poorest of the poor workers who looked forward to feast days in anticipation of some errant generosity on the part of a well-heeled patron. It was well known that leftovers from a Medici banquet would be distributed after the evening's celebrations. In stark contrast to their condition, Niccolò perceived how their eyes brightened with a shared eagerness to laugh and enjoy the antics of Carnival and its brief respite before Ash Wednesday.

He rubbed the coin he had won from the gypsy, a piece larger than the beggar dared hope for. On a whim, and without looking into the man's eyes, he dropped it into the outstretched hand and turned away, crossing over to the Palazzo.

At the entrance the guards inspected his person, spied his worn shoes and hesitated. He hissed "Machiavelli" and they shrugged and let him pass. Inside the portico, Niccolò looked around the loggia for a familiar face, but all were likewise disguised. Two young women dressed as courtesans eyed him and whispered behind their facial screens. Pleased, he nodded gallantly and made a mental note of them.

In the center of the courtyard a troupe of musicians played a lively Carnival song—Niccolò recognized it as one of Lorenzo's celebrated compositions—while several pairs of dancers performed a formal step choreographed to the music. From across the courtyard, he heard the loud and exaggerated voice of Piero de' Medici, seated at a banquet table with his Roman wife, Alfonsina. Next to them were Bacchus and Ariadne from the parade float and Niccolò felt that pang of desire as he plotted how to maneuver closer to this nubile goddess.

Beyond them, at the far end of the courtyard stood Donatello's fabulous *Judith* with the severed head of Holofernes held aloft. A stern warning of the fate of tyrants, Judith only looked embarrassed by the frivolity of the party banners draping her.

Surveying the room, Niccolò did not see *Il Magnifico* and his ever-present entourage. Then Tommaso, standing in a small circle of Santo Spirito friends, caught his eye and waved him over to the group that included Fiammetta and her sisters. Niccolò acknowledged him with a nod, but turned away, choosing first to wander the perimeter of the courtyard, snapping up bits of conversations and gossip from the masked guests. A good disguise always seemed to loosen tongues, he thought, as he sidled up to a couple of richly dressed merchants.

"…yes, daughters are a poor man's nightmare… the dowry price has gotten out of control…"

"The *catasto* tax is ruining me!"

"Well, its the falling price of woolen textiles what's killing me. Piss on those damn Lowlanders." These two looked like a couple of German burghers.

"…who else would dress up as the king of France?…" Niccolò turned to catch this phrase from a French cavalier, but kept moving through the crowd.

"Oh, yes, then skeletons jumped out of the coffins, singing this dreadful verse. I thought I was being cast into the Inferno myself! *Incredibile!*"

"So I asked, 'Where are you going?' and she says, 'to mass' and I threw up my hands and said, 'and this is Carnevale. Think what you'll be doing when Lent comes around!'" The last phrase, spoken by a portly, well-dressed cad, was drowned in laughter.

Niccolò felt a heavy hand on his shoulder and turned. It was Tommaso, still dressed as the devil. "Whoa, there, Machia. Where you off to? Come on, I've managed to escape for a moment. Let's go find my father and uncles."

He caught Niccolò by the sleeve, pulling him along as he wove a path through the guests. "So, did you get my little cousin safely *a casa?*" he asked. Then he wagged a finger in Niccolò's face. "*Basta, amico*—my uncles have her future planned out, and not with the likes of you."

Niccolò ignored the remark. Personally, he found Chiara's father,

Signor Corbinelli insufferable and hoped he wasn't here. Then Tommaso laughed, reading his mind. "Don't worry, that one's not here."

"Do you know who this Ariadne is?" Niccolò asked.

"A nice piece, eh? She's a cousin of the Ridolfi, visiting from Prato. I know what you're thinking, Machia, and I'm thinking it too."

Turning into the next alcove, Tommaso pointed to a group of older men, looking dignified in their Carnival costumes. "Look, there. Dressed up as the Magi."

As they approached Tommaso's father opened his arms to embrace his son. "Ah, I think I recognize this devil of a son of mine," he said. Paolantonio was the eldest of the Soderini brothers, a devout family man with an ever-expanding brood. "And who is this Fool you have in tow?"

Niccolò raised his mask just perceptively and Tommaso's uncle Piero exclaimed, "Ah, Niccolò di Bernardo. Paolo, a man who wears the mask of the Fool is surely no Fool at all. *Come va*, Nico?"

"Watch out, Uncle Piero," teased Tommaso, "he's a true *beffatore*. He once told me, and I quote: 'I never say what I believe, nor believe what I say... even if sometimes the truth is told me, I hide it among so many lies it's too difficult to find again.'"

The older men laughed, calling him a rascal, and Niccolò's ears reddened though he secretly took pride in his wily reputation. Through the years he had become familiar with all his neighbors, especially the Soderini. Tommaso's family was known for generations of civil service and Tommaso counted more than a dozen *Gonfalonieri* as well as dozens more *Priori* among his ancestors. Tommaso's late grandfather, also named Tommaso, had been a brother-in-law to Piero de' Medici "the Gouty" and was considered the second citizen of Florence in his time. The Soderini business interests, for which Tommaso was being groomed, consisted of various textile and trading enterprises under a single holding company. It was a diversified structure reflecting the conservative approach that was key to survival in the Florentine business world. But what most interested Niccolò were the Soderini's political connections.

"Nothing is ever what it seems," Niccolò parried, bowing graciously. "*Saluti, signori.* You look most magnificent as the kings."

"Careful," joked Piero. "There's only one Magnificent in Florence, and certainly no kings." This brought more amused looks and chuckles from around the small circle. Niccolò noted the sarcasm.

"How goes it with the Strozzi?" Tommaso's father asked.

"Papa, women are women," said Tommaso. "The Orsini and the Medici on one side and the Strozzi on the other—agh! They're all jealous of the Roman Orsini, and she plays it up. Everyone wants to sit on the top step, but there's only so much room. Sometimes I feel the need for less heavy air."

"Patience, nephew," said Piero. "Florence is a small pond with too many big fish, but between Medici and Strozzi, you're in a position of envy."

Yes, thought Niccolò. With the bigger fish always eating the smaller ones.

"Where's Lorenzo, Papa? I expected to see him here," asked Tommaso.

"He's retired to the Chapel with Poliziano, Pico and a few others. These celebrations tire him. They're leaving for the baths at *Bagno a Morba* the day after tomorrow."

Niccolò waited impatiently for the arrow to hit the target of conversation that was always politely avoided, though on everyone's mind: Lorenzo, the leading citizen who held the city together, frequently absented himself from civic affairs due to illness. And no one really knew how serious it was. Meanwhile, rumors spread about public finances since the financial reversals of the Medici banks. Despite their financial setbacks, the family's lavish spending had only increased. With the unofficial appointment of Lorenzo's second son Giovanni as Cardinal at the tender age of fourteen, the celebrations had become more frequent and extravagant, with first son Piero as the primary, though reluctant, host. Niccolò looked around at the banquet tables, the musicians and entertainers and wondered how many florins all this had cost.

The more serious charge, which no one spoke aloud within earshot, was that Lorenzo had unofficially borrowed from the *Monte Comune* to pay the pope for Giovanni's Cardinalate, as well as to maintain the 'official' entertainments in the wake of the appointment. The *Monte Comune* was the public debt financed by the richest families, with interest paid from the tax collected from all. If the fund became insolvent, only the *grandi* would be directly affected. But the public dowry fund, the *Monte di Doti*, where fathers deposited funds for their daughters' dowries, depended on the *Monte Comune* for its solvency. A collapse of the dowry fund, however temporary, would imperil the family fortunes of all the *popolani*—those artisans and local tradesmen on which the Medici depended for support. These rumors caused the grumbling among street gossips, making the ruling class anxious in turn.

Although the Soderini were first cousins to Lorenzo and they had supported the Medici since the time of Cosimo, everyone knew a fierce rivalry persisted between the two families. In years past Lorenzo had often been at odds with his uncle, Tommaso's grandfather, while in more recent years Tommaso's father and uncles had served often as ambassadors on missions that took them far from the city. Many suspected this was Lorenzo's deliberate strategy to keep the ambitious Soderini at bay.

Tommaso continued the banter, addressing no one in particular. "Did you see the Carnevale parade today?"

His youngest uncle, Giovanvettorio, quickly replied, "*Sì*, the Triumph of Death was incredible… and frightening. Piero di Cosimo has such a bizarre imagination."

A feline-masked woman beside him exclaimed, "Ha! Wait until you hear the Lenten sermons of the *Frate* at San Marco. He'll give you nightmares. We've heard him several times now and he is possessed when he ascends the pulpit."

Niccolò was curious. This was the new friar Chiara had referred to earlier in the day and he noticed the Dominican seemed to be popping up in many of the citizens' conversations of late.

"Isn't he the Ferrarese who failed at San Marco so miserably years ago?" asked Piero.

"Yes, but he seems to have had some kind of revelation and now speaks of the coming Apocalypse," Paolo said.

"Well, he better lay off the moneylenders or he'll suffer Fra Bernardino's fate."

"This one's different," insisted the cat-woman.

Confronted by the brothers' skepticism, she fumbled to support her declaration. "I don't know, he just seems to be able to reach out and grab your throat with his words, like he's…".

"Possessed by the devil himself, no doubt!" interrupted a reveler in a black cape, sporting the beaked mask of a plague doctor. Tommaso's father frowned at this unidentified passerby, one who had obviously overindulged. Miffed, the plague *medico* raised his hideous nose and sniffed like a rat, "I'm not contagious, you know."

Signor Paolantonio jerked his head, sending the intruder on his way, and abruptly changed the subject. "I've heard more news from our agents in Naples… Ferrante is threatening the Duke of Milan with war over the succession of Giangaleazzo. His granddaughter is raising a stink over il Moro's wife usurping *her* position as the next Duchess."

Finally, rejoiced Niccolò, a subject he could sink his teeth into. Intrigue these days was centered on the Duchy of Milan where the powerful Sforza clan was engaged in a battle for succession to the Ducal throne. Swarthy Lodovico Sforza, nicknamed *Il Moro*, ruled Milan as regent to his young nephew Giangaleazzo, who had been only seven years old when his father was assassinated. But now Giangaleazzo was of age and married to Isabella, the granddaughter of King Ferrante of Naples, and their brokered marriage assumed the Ducal crown of Milan.

However, Lodovico and his new young wife, Beatrice d'Este, had no intention of relinquishing their hold on the Duchy. And it was said Beatrice took extra pains to show up her younger Spanish rival. Florence had long-term alliances with both adversaries, so now they were caught between the two.

Piero interjected, "Well, if Ferrante attacks Milan, I expect it'll be by a sea route, perhaps in league with the Spanish. I can't imagine he'd try to march across the Papal States and our territory, though I'm sure he'll request our support and the Venetians. Francesco informs me the Doge has no love for the Moor, but would prefer to see him restrained at someone else's expense. Apparently Venice has enough worry with the Turks."

Niccolò knew Francesco, Tommaso's middle uncle and a bishop, was presently in Venice, conducting one of many diplomatic missions for the Signoria.

"Any conflict will be ruinous to our interests," Piero continued. "Even if we manage to stay out of the fighting, the northern land routes will be cut off by marauding *condottieri*. Lorenzo will be hard pressed to manage alliance commitments and talk sense into these foolish princes. Will we never learn?"

It was unclear to Niccolò whether, by 'our interests,' Piero meant the city's or those of his own family. But this was the moment he was waiting for.

"*Scusi, signori*, I'm sure *Il Moro* is aware of the game he's playing with Naples. Perhaps he has some card up his sleeve—say, allying with the French king and inviting him to attack Naples to assert their ancestral claim?"

Piero nodded. "Not unlikely. In fact, I suggested to the Signoria we take a more active interest in French ambitions—we should send an embassy. Charles has consolidated his army, he's young and seems anxious to make his mark."

At that moment two young women, elaborately dressed in the style of the French court, a fashion much imitated in the smaller courts of Italia, sauntered by, silencing the men's conversation in mid-thought. These were the same two who had caught Niccolò's eye earlier. They batted their eyes and Tommaso took the bait, "Speaking of the *Francese* ..." His eyes followed their sensuous movement that was like two swans gliding by and his feet quickly followed. He dragged Niccolò along by the puffed sleeve of his doublet as his father's fading voice exclaimed, "*Basta!* Enough politics, this is a party."

Yes, there was change in the air, and Niccolò could sense it. Distracted, he followed willingly after the gliding swans, watching the tops of their exposed breasts swell as they giggled breathlessly in French, though he was convinced these Venuses were Venetian. This evening may yet offer promising *divertimenti* and one must thank Jupiter for such pleasantries.

CHAPTER 4

LENT

IT WAS THE SECOND WEEK of Lent and Messer Luca Landucci swept at the dirt gathering at the entranceway to his apothecary. It was a task that exercised him several times a day as the swirling wind mocked his efforts by tossing dust back into his eyes. Annoyed, he looked across the piazza at the gaping hole, the heaps of gravel, and those pestering dirt piles, all surrounded by the large blocks of rough-hewn stone. Already this new palazzo had disrupted the area for more than a year and they were still only laying the ground floor. *Madonna*, he thought, the construction will never end.

The building's foundations were colossal, covering a whole city block, and the plans showed a medieval-type fortress towering three stories high, a massiveness that would dominate the quarter. Luca shook his head—probably still too small to house the swollen self-image of Filippo Strozzi and his clan.

Luca remembered when he was a boy the face of the city hardly ever seemed to change, but over the years these grand *palazzi* had sprouted like whiskers on an old woman's chin, each one bigger than the next. This Strozzi monstrosity had required the demolition of many smaller houses and shrunk the piazza by ten *braccie*, permission granted by the Signoria. There was no limit to the ambitions of these *grandi* and the fascination their doings held for the crowds that gathered to watch.

After careful consideration Luca had opened his new apothecary here last summer; it was a good location in the neighborhood of Santa Maria Novella, temporary inconveniences notwithstanding. His shop was on the corner of Via Tornabuoni, one of the most desirable streets in the city, halfway between the church of Santa Maria Novella and the Old Market. All traffic passed through the Old Market and Luca felt he was well placed. Unfortunately, with the construction and the Lenten season, trade was slow.

He had also noticed a subtle change in the daily migratory patterns of his fellow citizens this Lent. They appeared to be flocking less in the direction of the churches of Santa Maria Novella and Santo Spirito, and more toward the Duomo. He supposed this was due to the preaching of the new friar from Ferrara, who had the entire city chattering like birds. Good preachers were town favorites, appreciated for their ability to make compulsory Masses more bearable. Of course, the dismayed apothecary knew High Mass was not compulsory for reasons of faith but because the Cathedral was the place where the citizens gathered together and his fellow Florentines hated to miss any communal event pregnant with potential.

But the gossips said this new Dominican was neither poetic nor entertaining nor jovial, as, for instance, the popular Augustinian, Fra Mariano. He seemed to have a different, though not singular, appeal to his congregation. Even Luca found curiosity drawing him to the sermons of Fra Girolamo.

Luca looked up to see a dusty figure traipsing across the piazza. It was the architect and head builder for the Strozzi, Simone Pollaiuolo, nicknamed Cronaca for his avid story telling. Luca put aside his broom and waved a greeting. Cronaca was the nephew of his old friends the celebrated goldsmiths and painters, Antonio and Piero Pollaiuolo. They all belonged to the Guild of Doctors and Apothecaries; a connection owing to the arcane science of mixing potions for paint colors and medicinal pills, creating odd bedfellows between practitioners of painting and the healing arts. The association had found another, more morbid, avenue of collaboration in the recent artisan penchant for dissecting cadavers.

"*Ciao*, Messer Luca, *come va?*" Cronaca greeted him.

"*Buona sera*. Finished stirring things up for today? My shop is a dustbin!"

"*Sì, basta,* enough. We're off to the tavern for a spell before supper. Come along? I'm meeting the Filipepi brothers there."

Luca shook his head. "To a tavern? It's Lent. Are you artisans all so depraved?"

Cronaca replied to the jibe with a dismissive wave. "We only drink holy wine. It's watered down to taste like the Arno. Besides, Simone these days only wants to talk about the 'terrifying' sermons of Fra Girolamo, so it's almost the same as being in church."

This piqued Luca's curiosity. "Not the Frascato?"

Cronaca's eyes lit up. "That den of gamblers, whores, and thieves? Unfortunately not. We're going to Del Corno's. *Andiamo?*"

Luca permitted a guarded smile. "Well, perhaps one glass of holy wine."

The two men headed down a narrow street toward the Arno, no more than a stone's throw from the Piazza della Signoria and the New Market. The location made the dark and unobtrusive tavern a favorite among low-level city officials, as well as the moneychangers. Poor artisans appreciated the cheap prices.

When they ducked inside they saw the room was not crowded—Lent again—but several patrons greeted Cronaca as he made his way toward the tables in the back. Several young men were loudly gambling over *triche-tach* at a table off to one side as loud exclamations and immodest giggles of women punctuated the rolling of the dice. The two headed for a table in the far corner.

"Cronaca, *amico mio,* how about a story?" an affable fellow exclaimed, clamping his arm around the dusty builder.

"*Basta,* all in good time. First, I want a long draught of that watery wine you're guarding so closely."

Another man rose to welcome them to the table. "Messer Luca! It must be months, *piacere.*"

It was Sandro Filipepi, a celebrated painter close in age to Luca, whose works were scattered everywhere throughout the city and from Rome to Bologna. He was the most popular painter in Florence, a city that boasted the incomparable Leonardo as well as the famed Ghirlandaio. They said when Sandro painted grapes, the birds would peck at them.

Sandro was also one of Luca's best customers for pigments. His most renowned works, such as the *Primavera* and the *Birth of Venus,* hung in the private Medici villas, as the two prominent branches of the family jealously competed for his allegorical representations. In their magnificence and facial resemblances, Sandro's paintings were celebrated as glorious homages to his patrons. Sitting next to Sandro was his brother Simone, who, though not a painter, lived together with Sandro at his workshop. Simone was older, more somber, and Luca remembered he had taken lay orders with the Dominicans at San Marco. The Filipepi brothers were popularly known as the Botticelli, after an older brother's nickname meaning 'the little barrel.'

Sandro called out to one of his assistants, "Filippino, get us another flagon of Trebbiano."

Messer Luca smiled a bit stiffly, ill at ease in a tavern during Lent. "Sandro, a pleasure, though I fear it must be short one." His eyes met Simone's as he nodded a greeting.

"Well, we're here only a moment. I have so much unfinished work and Simone tells me we must attend Mass in the Duomo tomorrow," said Sandro, feigning a look of helplessness. "So, we must drink. Quickly."

Luca noticed Simone was not drinking.

Sandro turned to Cronaca, "Tell me, have you word from your uncles?"

"*Sì,* they're having a devil of a time in Rome with the new commission from Innocente while still trying to complete the tomb of Sixtus. These popes have come to realize they must get their sepulchers finished before they're needed, or their successors will just as soon toss their bodies in paupers' graves."

Cronaca and Lorenzo laughed heartily at this irreverence, but Simone's dark scowl barely lifted. "Rome is a sinkhole," he said flatly.

"*Sì*, Simone," said Sandro, exasperated, "but this is not exactly news. Besides, popes with too much money create good business for us poor artisans, no? If only we could get a Florentine pope, we'd all be swimming in commissions." He raised his glass to a row of cheers.

"To Papa Giovanni!"

Luca knew Sandro's toast revealed the hopes of most Florentines, especially those whose services were in much less demand. For most painters life was a constant struggle, so when Francesco Cibo, otherwise known as Pope Innocent VIII, had bestowed a Cardinalate on Giovanni de' Medici at the tender age of fourteen, all of Florence twittered with the eventual possibility of a Medici pope. (As part of the bargain, Lorenzo had given his daughter Maddalena in marriage to the pope's natural son Franceschetto.) But a Medici pope was at least another generation away. In the meantime, closeness to Rome was a mixed blessing for renowned Florentine artisans.

"Our city would do well to stay clear of the business of Rome," declared Simone, pronouncing the word 'business' with disdain. "The friar has come to warn us of the bitter harvest that will be reaped by these merchants of Rome." Again the sniping tone on 'merchants.' Simone was warming to his subject.

Cronaca interjected, "Have you heard what that Dominican said? Can you believe it?"

"Have you been in the Duomo?" snapped Simone. When Cronaca shook his head the older man continued, "Then you cannot know. Pay no attention to the nonsense of street gossips, they're like chickens scratching for grain. You must go to the Cathedral and feel the words as they resonate off the walls, with the light streaming in from above. Only then will you know."

Another asked, "And why is this one any different from the others? From Fra Mariano? Or Fra Bernardino?" This was Lorenzo di Credi, a painter, goldsmith, and sculptor also in the productive middle of his career. He often entertained them by relating the bizarre tales of Leonardo from when they worked together in Verrocchio's workshop years ago. (Maestro Leonardo, famous throughout all Italia, had now forsaken his native Florence for a favored position at the court of the Sforza in Milan.)

Simone almost jumped from his seat. "Fra Girolamo has the gift of visions. Like Joachim of Fiore he interprets his visions from the Book of the Apocalypse... The most suffering will occur just before the end and will be preceded by the appearance of the Anti-Christ, who shall corrupt the true mission of the Church and the Chair of St. Peter—"

"Of course," Sandro cut in, "Simone expects one of our 'Holy' Bishops of Rome to be the Anti-Christ."

The others laughed but Simone glared at his brother's sarcasm. He spat back, "Eh? Have you seen a more depraved vicar than Cibo? How many little bastards does he have now? And he doesn't even deign to call them 'nephews.'"

"Simone, you're beginning to sound like a *fraticello*," warned Lorenzo. "You and your Friar should remember how eagerly the Church uses the *fraticelli* as tinder for their autos-da-fé. And the writings of Joachim are not exactly favorite reading material at the Holy See. I'd be more careful about public attacks against Roman prelates." Then he broke into a devilish grin as he refilled his cup. "Besides, there's no reason to worry: The Lord ensures we only elect decrepit old popes who die quickly, before they can do much damage."

But Simone was not appeased. "Joachim predicted two religious orders would be born to reform the Church and confront the Anti-Christ. These we have seen with the Franciscans and Dominicans. The Church Militant cannot deny the fulfillment of these prophecies. The Roman Church only fears for its own perdition."

A young, well-dressed man looked up from the *triche-tach* game several tables away and abruptly shouted: "Hey, *Fra* Botticelli, mumbling again about that barking dog of a friar? Think your *Domini cane* has come to bite the Anti-Christ?" The man's voice was thick with sarcasm, addressing Simone as 'Fra' and mimicking a portly 'barrel' with his arms—the common deprecation for a well-fed friar. His drinking companions hooted.

Simone looked darkly across the room. The interloper was Doffo Spini, the rough mannered son of an aristocratic family that had awarded several small commissions to Sandro. Simone did not dignify the insult with a reply, so Spini continued: "You know the best thing your Friar can do is bite the ass of the Medici. But my guess is *Il Magnifico* will soon toss his pesky guest from the city gates, and we'll be back to life as usual."

Spini turned to his companions. "Personally, before I die I'd like to see the world free of these foolish nattering priests."

Sandro tried to diffuse the tension. "*Basta*, Doffo. You should be careful of whom you speak ill within range of the ear of Dionysus." He touched his ear, alluding to the ever-present ears of Medicean loyalists.

Then Luca leaned closer to Simone and whispered, "Is it true the friar says the Church will be scourged and then undergo reform and it will happen soon?"

"Yes," Simone's face brightened. "Fra Girolamo has spoken of these things for two years now, since Brescia. He calls attention to what must be obvious to anyone willing to just open his eyes. Look at the contempt the clergy has for their religious obligations, from the pope and cardinals right on down to the bishops and parasitic priests—everything and anything for a gold florin. Where in the Bible does it say the rich man can *buy* his way into heaven? And it's obscene the way these bishops and *grandi* live! Their skin touches only the finest silks and their bodies are laid heavy with jewels. And their gluttony! While no more than a stone's throw away some poor child is dying from hunger or the pestilence. And then they want us to use pagan allegories to titillate their lust and depravity. Tell me it's not true."

"And what's wrong with a little lust?" retorted one of Spini's companions. It was the acerbic poet Francesco Cei and Simone fixed him with a stony stare.

Spini waved off Simone with a look of disgust. "Has it ever *not* been true? Why do you think I despise these priggish priests?"

But Simone snapped back, "Fra Girolamo is different. He is not one of those hypocrites who scold and then retreat to their comforts and pleasures. He lives by the Lord's example. Never will you see him take the easy way, or recline in worldly comforts. He truly adheres to the example of San Augustino."

The tavern grew quiet, silenced by the conviction in Simone's voice. Then Cei spat in disgust, "Ah, yes, Augustino, Bishop of Hippo—the one with the stiff prick who said, 'Lord! Give me chastity; give me continence.'" Then he paused for effect, grabbing his privates in alarm, "'but not just yet!'"

The tavern exploded in laughter as Cei shouted over the ensuing din, "*Incredibile!* Can you believe it? What does this sniveling 'preacher of the despairing' hope to gain? All these priests are after something in the end—money, power, nuns, sometimes just to be worshipped by half-witted peasants. As sure as the sun revolves round the earth, you'll see this Friar show his true skin."

Spini and his friends nodded in agreement.

Luca ignored the rabble and prodded Simone for more. "What about his sermon last Sunday? Did you hear it? I've heard it described as 'terrifying.'"

Simone's voice expanded and his eyes widened. "Truly it was. He said we would suffer war, famine, and pestilence. He said these scourges and calamities were founded on the Word of God, in the Book of Revelation. And the Church will be afflicted with great sorrows and humiliation and the tyrants punished for all their injustices. The effect was astounding. Many of the women began to wail and some fainted, even though it was not hot at all."

"*Sì*, the Big Weepers," laughed Lorenzo.

Landucci could not imagine words evoking such a reaction.

Disgusted, Spini rose up noisily and delivered his parting shot. "*Merda*, if we Florentines don't have enough problems, God help us if we should have to manage with crazed preachers and hysterical women." Then he departed with his companions.

"*Barlacci*," Simone cursed under his breath.

Cronaca hurried to change the subject, "Don't worry Messer Luca, there'll be many more sermons to hear; at least until the Signoria tosses our new preacher from the city gates. Now, did you see the Triumph of Death Piero di Cosimo and Sandro painted for the Carnival parade? Even I could feel Judas's pain wiggling around in the jaws of Satan. Lorenzo, pass me that jug of holy water."

Cronaca filled his glass and raised a toast. "They say there are two principal things men do in this life: procreate and build. Well, I've had enough of the second and not enough of the first. Here's to redressing the balance!"

Luca flushed as he raised his glass, but did not sip the wine.

CHAPTER 5

A CHESS MATCH

NICCOLÒ CROSSED OVER THE OLD Bridge, the *Ponte Vecchio,* as church bells rang out the midday hour of Sext. It was the first of May, the festival of *Calendimaggio,* when the city celebrated spring and its liberation from Lent. The May festival also coincided with the bimonthly investiture of the Signoria, making it a day reserved for idle pleasures. And today was two days before Niccolò's twenty-second birthday. With a spring in his step he reached down to pick up a stick to clean his nails as he hurried along.

On his way to the Piazza della Signoria to meet Tommaso, Niccolò slowed his pace along the busy Via Por Santa Maria. Though retail shops were closed to business for the investiture, merchants were encouraged to honor their respective guilds and trumpet Florentine prosperity by displaying their finest wares before the ceremonies. The Via Por Santa Maria was the street where the silk merchants located their shops, setting out their bolts of intricately woven damasks and brocades, sheer taffetas and satins, and luxurious velvets. The silks were splayed out in a springtime riot of color: white gold and saffron yellows; deep lapis blues; vibrant and verdant greens; rich purples and opulent violets; all dominated by the luminous cardinal and blood reds for which the city was famous. Accenting the treasured silks were displays of the goldsmiths, with their fine-worked gold and silver set with precious stones.

Niccolò dallied for a moment, playing his eyes over the many well-appointed women enticed here to fuss over fabrics and jewels and plan future purchases. They were queen bees mesmerized by a dazzling flora.

Moving farther along he entered the Via Calimala, or Street of the Wool Guild, where the crowds of the less wealthy congregated around woolen textiles. The city center was well laid out in this fashion, with the various workshops and merchants clustered along streets that bore the names of their respective crafts. One block over was Via Calzaioli, the Street of the Hosemakers. In the workers' neighborhood were the Road of the Dyers and the Street of the Tanners. Continuing along the Via Calimala, Niccolò passed the open loggia of the New Market where the moneychangers congregated, through whom all the gold florins of Florentine wealth flowed. On the next block were the kilns of bakers all bunched in close proximity to the commune's store of grain in the Piazza del Grano. Niccolò fondly recalled the many dawns he was drawn by the sweet fragrance of oven-fresh bread on his way home from the taverns, the time when the bakers were most generous with a spare loaf.

Just ahead was the *Mercato Vecchio*, the Old Market, closed today but filled twice weekly with the abundant harvests of the surrounding countryside complimented, by an endless supply of herbs and spices from the East. The city's trade was ordered in this way so even a foreigner arriving for the first time had no trouble locating exactly who or what he required. In this bustling labyrinth, everything the buyer might wish for could be found within a few short blocks: raw wool from the English, cotton and linen from Africa, leather goods from Spain; and precious gems, stones, gold, and silver from the East refined and reworked with Florentine artistry.

The various manufactures were guarded by their respective guilds to insure the city's reputation for quality. In all, seven major and fourteen minor guilds regulated every aspect of economic life in the city and its surrounding territory. Inspections were frequent, with inferior merchandise summarily destroyed and guilty merchants expelled. More common cheats, such as bakers who shorted their loaves, were locked into the public stocks to be vilified and abused by passers-by. It was a perfectly ordered and jealously guarded world that enriched its citizens beyond their wildest imaginings.

After traversing several more streets Niccolò stopped at a spice vendor and bought a honeyed cinnamon stick, then doubled back toward the Piazza. Not seeing Tommaso at their rendezvous, he watched the square slowly fill for the investiture ceremony. Weaving through the food hawkers, he made his way to the front of the Loggia dei Priori where the standards of the Gonfaloniere waved overhead.

Every two months, on the first day of odd-numbered months, a new nine-member Signoria was installed to govern the Republic. During their tenure the eight Priors of Liberty and their titular head, the Gonfaloniere of Justice, lived together in the Palazzo. There they slept, took their meals, conducted official business, were entertained by musicians and *buffoni*, attended Masses, and confessed—all without leaving the confines of the fortress. They were isolated from their families and business affairs so as not to be influenced during their brief period of civil service. As if such men could or would change their nature for sixty days.

Niccolò felt the burn of envy. He was a born Florentine, citizen of the greatest city on earth, trained since his early years by the best tutors in the seven liberal arts of the *studia humanitatis*. He read Latin like a scholar, devoured the classics of Thucydides, Livy, and Cicero like mother's milk.

But the flower of Florence was for those born into wealth and power and he had inherited neither. It should not have been so. The Machiavelli were an ancient family that had served many times in the highest offices of the Republic—thirteen times as Gonfaloniere. And Niccolò's father Bernardo was a lawyer, a member of the prestigious Guild of Lawyers and Notaries, and closely acquainted with some of most esteemed Florentine humanists. But Niccolò's grandfather, for whom he was named, had not been married to his father's mother and the resulting stigma would forever taint his father's lineage.

Yes, forever Niccolò di Bernardo Machiavelli would be the son of a bastard. Not an insurmountable obstacle if one was rich, but a curse for those of modest means. Worse, he had no head for business, the favored path these days for those who must make their own prospects. Instead, he was consumed by the affairs of men—Aristotle's *Politics*—but had almost no chance of entering the pool of wealthy candidates for the ruling councils.

His envy turned to disdain as he watched the electors fussing with their heavy crimson-robed garments in the shade of the Loggia. Most of these pretenders were only interested in the opportunity to fatten their bellies. Justice was furthest from their minds. They were the true *bastardi*.

"*Saluti*, Messer Niccolò."

Niccolò turned to face two middle-aged men dressed in the wool lucco and fitted cap of the older generation. It was the printer and bookseller, Messer Filippo Giunta, and Niccolò's former university lecturer, Maestro Marcello Adriani—both close acquaintances of his father.

"Enjoying the festivities?" asked Filippo. "I see you've got several of my books with you today. You should come by my shop; I've some new printed copies of Ovid and Petrarca, with woodcut engravings. Perhaps you can interest Messer Bernardo in a new purchase?"

"More printed words for the masses?" Niccolò teased. "I thought you were a connoisseur of illuminated manuscripts, Messer Filippo."

"There's nothing so beautiful to behold—but you usually have to wrestle them away from some avaricious old abbot. But printing—*this* is the future of the written word. The printing press will revolutionize the world."

Maestro Adriani wagged his head to temper Filippo's enthusiasm. "Perhaps. But it's still the same few people who can read, no?" Adriani had written a well-used text for tutoring titled, *On the Education of the Florentine Nobility*.

"In time, in time," conceded Filippo. "But perhaps it would help things if we brought your book to print."

"I'm not sure it would help with this rabble," Adriani replied, inclining his head toward the Loggia. "Well, Messer Niccolò, I'm glad to see you're keeping up with your studies. Please give our regards to your father."

Niccolò bowed his head as the men wandered off. Perhaps Messer Filippo was right about the printing press—news pamphlets and the ability to read were already catching on among the *popolo*, and the fashion would probably someday spread even to the workers and peasants, God preserve us. Even so, the most popular printing was still the Bible, followed by the Psalms, and the Book of Hours.

On the *ringhiera* edging the Palazzo the gowned ministers were gathering for the ceremonies. Niccolò saw Tommaso walking toward their meeting place, clutching his chessboard and case.

"Ciao," Tommaso called to him, sweating as he frowned at the crowds. "*Merda*, it's impossible already." Tommaso spied the books under Niccolò's arm. "Planning some reading?"

"We'll find a place in the shade of the *Tetto de Pisani*."

They made their way across the Piazza and found an open space affording a good view of the Loggia. Niccolò watched Tommaso order the pieces on the chessboard. First he placed the king and the queen, then the two bishops, knights and rooks, finally setting out the front line of eight pawns. As always he assigned himself white and Niccolò black.

A sudden blast of trumpets signaled the start of the ceremony and Niccolò looked up to watch the new Signoria lining up on the public stage. An avid student of *civitas*, Niccolò could appreciate the political symmetry and balance of the Republic—in theory at least, if not in practice. It was an elaborate design dividing offices across the four quarters of the city as well as the major and minor guilds. Of the eight Priors of Liberty who made up the Signoria, two came from each quarter, with the Gonfaloniere selected from each quarter on a revolving basis. Of the eight Priors, six were members of the major guilds and two were from the minor guilds. The Gonfaloniere must also be a member of one of the major guilds.

Below the Signoria were the various ministries that managed the functions of government. The most important of these were the advisory councils of the Twelve Good Men and the *gonfalonieri* of the sixteen neighborhood gonfalons. Defense of the Republic fell under the charge of the Ten of War, while the Eight of the Guard managed local security and policing. Budgeting and financial matters were assumed by the officials of the public debt fund—the Monte del Comune—together with leading representatives of the seven major guilds. Final governing oversight was achieved by subjecting all executive decisions to ratification by the two larger representative councils of the Seventy and the Hundred. In theory, then, the government of the Republic was conducted under an elected, representative structure of balanced and competing communal interests.

In practice, though, one easily saw through the façade: The reins of power were in the firm grasp of Lorenzo de' Medici. He cleverly followed the ploys of his grandfather Cosimo by circumventing the selection of offices and narrowing the powers of the oversight bodies of the Seventy and the Hundred. Because the Signoria's term of office was so brief, officeholders could not acquire the necessary competence and foresight to govern the Republic over the longer term, nor could they amass any power to challenge the status quo. Just last year Lorenzo had engineered the latest constitutional change transferring the selection of office holders from the Seventy to a smaller group of citizens, called the *accoppiatori*. Naturally, the *accoppiatori* was composed almost entirely of Medicean clients and supporters.

With this last change the process was simple. The names of all eligible candidates were selected from the Seventy by the process of the *scrutino*, and put into the *borsa*, a small leather pouch. The *scrutino*, or scrutiny, was the method by which citizens were judged eligible for election to government offices by lot. To be eligible, one must be a member in good standing of one of the guilds and not be delinquent in the payment of taxes. (Thus, for many years, a proven Medicean strategy had been the arbitrary assessment of taxes in order to deny opponents political office.) From the *borsa* the names were drawn at random by the *accoppiatori*. Since the final selection was done in secret, it was no shock when the random selection of offices always fell to a select group of candidates. Of course, this was not the hand of Fortuna at work at all, merely that of Lorenzo and his cronies.

Niccolò fingered his chess pieces, lining them up exactly, centered in their small squares, while straining to hear the official pronouncements.

"Come on," said Tommaso as he moved his pawn forward. "I'll have your king in my hands before they finish their nonsense." But making Tommaso wait was part of Niccolò's strategy.

"Is this Livy's *Histories*?" asked Tommaso, grabbing one of Niccolò's books. He leafed through the pages, then grabbed the other and read the title: "*The History of the Florentine People* by Leonardo Bruni."

Niccolò studied the board and moved his pieces deliberately, utilizing his knights, bishops and queen to control the middle four squares as the game progressed. His strategy established a hidden position of strength from which to attack when an opening appeared. Tommaso was oblivious to defensive strategies; he preferred to race out recklessly with his side pawns to free up his rooks. It seemed to be his favorite piece.

"So, what has studying the Roman Republic taught you?" asked Tommaso.

"For one," he answered, not looking up, "how to win."

Around them the crowd politely applauded as each new member of the Signoria was announced to take the oath of office and receive the crimson mantle and hood. Tommaso looked up and snickered when he heard the alliteration of the last announced name. "Signorino di Signorino Signorini," he repeated, pronouncing the name with exaggerated dignity. "Now there's a name for someone born to the Signoria!"

Niccolò captured another pawn. Tommaso seemed to enjoy sacrificing his pawns to no advantage. Niccolò guessed it was to reduce the number of pieces on the board and unclutter his mind. Tommaso countered and then, distracted, read from Bruni's *History*.

"I see here where you've marked Bruni's words," he said, tracing the line with his finger as he read: 'Wherever men are given the hope of attaining honor in the state, their minds aspire and rise to a higher plane; wherever they are deprived of this hope, they grow idle and their strength fails.' So this where you find your ideas, eh?"

"How does your father feel about the new Gonfaloniere?" Niccolò asked.

"Morelli? Baaaah, another sheep. It hardly matters, eh? The Seventy controls everything." Tommaso advanced one of his knights unprotected.

Yes, thought Niccolò, and Bruni was right. The offices of the Republic constantly rotated among a small select group of weak-willed clients and stronger allies of the Medici. Only occasionally did one of the competing *grandi* slip into office, mostly as a deliberate exception to disguise the artfulness of the game. Recent Priors were dominated by the names of Medici allies such as Ridolfi, Tornabuoni, Martelli, and Rucellai.

Niccolò moved his bishop forward and captured Tommaso's knight. In turn, Tommaso quickly took the bishop. "Sacrifice a bishop?" Tommaso snickered, overconfident.

"A bishop is worth a knight, no?" replied Niccolò, feigning indifference. Tommaso shrugged, distracted by the crowd.

What glory, what justice was there, Niccolò asked himself, if the Florentine Republic continued this way—run by incompetents? He looked up at the Loggia where the officials were preening. That was where he belonged, like so many Machiavelli before him, serving the Republic. But Fortuna had cursed him with his grandfather's sins and a poor inheritance. At best he could hope to serve in one of the ministries, where ability and talent might be recognized and rewarded. If not, he would be forced to live off the meager returns from the family's small land holdings outside the city. *Up yours, Fortuna!*

On the chessboard it was time to strike. "Where's Fiammetta?" Niccolò asked innocently, as he advanced his queen.

"Taking the sun while it's high and strong. Bleaching her hair while covering her face and skin with those stupid hats." Tommaso shook his head. "Women's vanities. She'll be at San Giovanni later, with her sisters and Chiara too. I'd rather go to the Frascato or the Purgatorio. I've had my eye on a little wench at the Purgatorio. *Una bella fica.* Have you seen her, named Francesca?"

"Already had her, *amico. In culo.*" It was the devil in him.

"*Sei stronzo*—you shit—I don't believe a word!" Tommaso took a swipe at Niccolò, who nimbly ducked.

Niccolò shrugged, then, in a series of deft moves employing a combination of queen, knight and rook, he closed in on Tommaso's position. Too late Tommaso realized his predicament and struggled to escape.

"*Porco Dio!* Why don't I see this coming?"

A drum roll signified the completion of the official ceremony and the start of the procession of the new Signoria through the streets. By tradition the new inductees were expected to distribute alms in gratitude for the great honor bestowed upon them and their families. The crowds pressed forward in anticipation.

Without warning a confetti of sugarcoated almonds rained down from the windows overlooking the Piazza and Tommaso knocked his king over in disgust, conceding the match.

"*Cazzone!* I've no patience for this damn game. Soon I'll be owing you money."

Niccolò smiled. He enjoyed these little victories over his friend, and it was a good way to work off his debts. "Don't worry, Tommaso. Every two months you have another chance for revenge."

CHAPTER 6

CALENDIMAGGIO AT THE PALAZZO MEDICI

THE MEDICI GARDENS WERE BATHED in an afternoon light that warmed with the life-giving force of the sun on the earth after the barren chill of winter. With springtime, all living things celebrated their awakening in accord with their nature: young women bloomed like flowers while youths romped like barnyard animals in an open pasture and the older generation turned their backs to the sun to feast at the overflowing banquet table. In the courtyard a choral brigade sang the May Song, *Ben Venga Maggio*—a favorite penned by Lorenzo's closest companion, the luminous poet Angelo Poliziano.

"Agnolo! Over here," exclaimed a young man absurdly cross-dressed as a young nymph.

The youth he addressed, a boy of fifteen garbed as a shepherd, shuffled sheepishly across the courtyard in front of Donatello's magnificent *Judith*. He watched the gaily-colored singers, all handsome *giovani* dressed like forest elves. Their costumes alternated in rows of peach blossom and damask green, giving the intended effect of a colorful spray of spring flowers. The young shepherd felt lost in the middle of this bouquet, even more awkward as his friend cavorted shamelessly in wig and diaphanous gown.

"Francesco!" he whispered, "you look ridiculous."

Actually, his handsome friend looked comely in feminine attire and was doing well attracting the genuine article. Several young girls, including Lorenzo's youngest daughter Contessina, were being entertained by his antics. The shepherd looked away shyly as he became painfully aware of the unfavorable figure he cut in comparison to his friend. Almost six years separated them and Francesco was a head taller and fine-featured, while he was short with a face disfigured by a flattened nose. As his friend's clowning became exaggerated, the girls grew more titillated. Suddenly Francesco broke into song while focusing his attentions on a raven-haired young beauty masquerading as Proserpine:

> *At the dance there is a girl*
> *With lovely eyes, who so beguiles me,*
> *But as for the rest, she will give me nothing*
> *And ever she replies: 'No, no,*
> *Nothing, nothing, nothing doing!'*

The lyric set them giggling as Francesco played up the part of a young girl resisting a man's advances. Feeling ignored, the shepherd boy wanted to slink away to search for lost lambs or something. Just then a page came up and addressed him in a whisper: "Messer Michelangelo, Signor Lorenzo requests you and Messer Francesco to join him in the chapel."

With a sigh of relief, he pulled Francesco away by the sleeve of his gown.

The small, beautiful chapel was designed and frescoed by Benozzo Gozzoli. It was the only private chapel in Florence and one of Michelangelo's favorite rooms in the Palazzo. On entering he saw a small group of men standing around Lorenzo. Behind him, wrapping the walls in the background, was Gozzoli's *Procession of the Three Magi*. There was little resemblance between Gozzoli's idealized portrait of *Magnifico* as the young magus astride the beautiful white horse—the focal point of the large painting—and the man standing before it in the flesh.

The boy magus possessed a fair, delicate beauty while Lorenzo was big-boned and athletic, marked by a swarthy complexion with black hair. The magus was fine-featured, whereas Lorenzo's facial features were oversized. His lantern jaw, crooked smile, and flattened, irregular nose reminded Michelangelo of his own deficiencies. *Il Magnifico* frequently made light of the irony that his burdensome nose did not even enjoy a sense of smell. Lastly, his voice was high-pitched with a nasal tone that grated on the ear when he sang, a favorite diversion.

Taken together it was not a pleasing countenance to the eye or ear. But a careful observer could perceive beyond the unyielding façade a keen intelligence in Lorenzo's penetrating eyes, lofty forehead, and charming wit. In one sense, Gozzoli's rendering was perfectly accurate: Il Magnifico was most definitely the Magi King as the leading citizen of Florence.

Across the chapel Michelangelo saw Lorenzo's intimate entourage of scholars—Count Pico, Maestro Ficino and Maestro Poliziano—standing among several aristocratic members of the Seventy. Lorenzo was preoccupied with a middle-aged man Michelangelo guessed to be a banking associate from the bits of conversation carrying across the room. Lorenzo's son Piero stood next to him, fidgeting and affecting a bored look as the associate addressed his father.

"...we have uncovered serious problems at the Lyon branch, with losses in the thousands of florins. Ser Leonetto does not seem competent in managing affairs. This is our last surviving branch in France as we've lost all our other branches in the north. And in Rome we are beholden to the profligate pope and the spend-thrift cardinals." The man's pitch rose as he exclaimed in frustration: *"Madonna!"*

Lorenzo cut him short with the curt tone of a teacher lecturing a dull student. *"Basta,* I'm well aware of the history. The remaining Lyon and Rome branches are critical to us for reasons beyond money. Giovanni must ingratiate himself with the papal curate, so our fortunes in Rome must have the appearance of ever increasing prosperity. Lyon is less important, but we still need eyes and ears close to the French king. His army is the most singularly powerful in Europe and inevitably he'll want to flex his strength."

During his short stay as a guest at the Palazzo Medici Michelangelo had gotten the impression that matters of business and talk of money frustrated his generous host. Lorenzo treated Michelangelo with a tenderness that gave the impression Lorenzo actually envied the poor young artisan able to devote himself so fully to his art. The grandson of the richest and most successful banker in the history of Florence, Lorenzo had been trained and tutored since youth by the finest scholars—Gentile Becchi, Cristoforo Landino, Marsilio Ficino—and his was a world of contemplation, philosophy, poetry, and romance. Adored by his fellow citizens and anointed *Il Magnifico* by his peers—how could he be dissatisfied? All Florence celebrated the legend of Lorenzo: How he had assumed leadership at the age of twenty after his father died suddenly. How he became the leading member of the three most powerful guilds—the bankers, wool, and silk merchants—and managed the family's position while securing the peace and prosperity of his native city.

Nevertheless, Michelangelo knew his patron was denied the simple freedom to pursue his muse. Once, when they were alone in his study, Lorenzo had confessed the truth of what his grandfather Cosimo had said: Wealth without power was never secure. But the responsibilities of power extracted a high price. Now, at an age when he should be at the height of vigor, he was tired and ill, longing only to secure the family's position and pass these duties on to his sons.

Lorenzo continued instructing his bank manager: "The most pressing problem we have now is to prepare for the celebrations of Giovanni's official coronation after his birthday early next year. We must begin now. Please consult with my secretary to secure the necessary funds."

"Sì, Signor Lorenzo, *capito."*

Lorenzo put his arms around the man together with his son Piero and spoke with an air of finality. *"Bene,* then please, go back and enjoy the party—the food, the women, the dancing. It's springtime. Lent is over.

Let's enjoy!"

Shifting his attention, Lorenzo hailed Michelangelo and Francesco from across the room. "Agnolo, Francesco, join us," he said as he approached them with a roguish look in his eye.

"Francesco, you're looking quite comely today. Perhaps now you'll realize how difficult it is for young maidens to safeguard their chastity. And watch out for the *sodomiti!*"

Francesco visibly reddened, but gamely curtsied as the rest of the company laughed. Lorenzo continued in a more serious tone: "Actually, we were about to discuss the procession vehicles for the Festa di San Giovanni. It's less than two months away and I thought you should participate so we might plan the effort together."

The circle around Lorenzo widened to admit the two young artisans. Francesco was Lorenzo's principal *trionfo* painter, commissioned to design and build the elaborate Medici parade floats for the numerous city festivals during the year. The upcoming Festa di San Giovanni was the most civic-minded of the major festivals, focused as it was on the patron saint of the city.

Lorenzo explained: "Angelo has suggested an allegory from Roman history: the Triumph of the Roman consul Aemilius Paulus..."

Michelangelo listened intently as Lorenzo and Poliziano explained their conception for the procession. It was grandiose, even by Florentine standards, and Michelangelo saw Francesco's eyes widen in fearful anticipation of the task.

"Fifteen *trionfi, Signori!?!*"

"Yes, Francesco," reassured Poliziano, "but most will be minor affairs. You'll need focus only on the three principal vehicles, which will carry the consul and his generals."

"But this will require many additional hands—painters, carpenters... and weavers..."

"Of course, whatever's necessary."

The others seemed detached from the discussion, probably equally dismayed at the scale of the proposal. Two members of the Seventy, Bernardo Rucellai and Paolantonio Soderini, appeared anxious for the subject to change course and finally Rucellai coughed audibly.

Lorenzo looked over. "Bernardo, is there something you wish to add? Something else?"

Rucellai was Lorenzo's brother-in-law and hesitated before he spoke. "Only, Lorenzo, as you know, the friar at San Marco is attacking the extravagant displays and pageantries of private citizens and he will surely take this opportunity to further his attacks. Already the cathedral is teeming with citizens when he preaches."

Despite spending most of his days studying in the sculpture garden out at San Marco, Michelangelo had not yet seen this *frate* who commanded so much interest.

Signor Soderini added: "Frankly, I say the man is a dangerous rabble-rouser who wishes to incite the people against the ruling order of the city. I think we're all in agreement that order and stability are of paramount importance to our continued good fortune."

Lorenzo frowned, visibly displeased by this distraction from his creative endeavors.

"My friends," he said, "do you think it's as serious as all that? My impression of this friar is of an overzealous but sincere reformer. I've heard of his attacks on the wealthy and the ruling citizens—by allusion I know he's principally addressing his comments to me—but do you think he's really a threat? I've been called worse than a tyrant, by worse men than this friar." He smiled again.

Rucellai replied, "But this preacher grows more powerful and his words more provocative each week. I sense a real antagonism toward us. Perhaps it's a sign of the times, but the mood of the city seems to be falling under his spell. He uses the clever technique of prophecy and you know how ignorant fools believe every little superstition. It's better to crush these movements before they get out of control."

"Perhaps the Signoria should issue a decree exiling the friar from the city, at least for a period of time," suggested Soderini.

Lorenzo shook his head. "This seems extreme. Religious matters require a delicate hand. What do you think, Giovanni? Marsilio?"

Giovanni Pico, the Count of Mirandola and Concordia, was the most popular and respected philosopher of his generation. Still in his late twenties, from a noble family, wealthy, handsome, charming and erudite, Michelangelo imagined Count Giovanni as the model of the Florentine ideal. The Count had met the friar almost ten years ago at a Dominican Chapter Council in Reggio d'Emilio and, taken with his intellect and dedication to theology, had pressed Lorenzo to request the Dominican be assigned to San Marco. Pico also claimed he owed his life and freedom to Fra Girolamo, who had intervened when the Church had threatened to try him for heresy.

"I must disagree with our esteemed colleagues," Pico said. "I've attended many of Fra Girolamo's sermons and spoken with him often enough at the San Marco library. He is learned and doing just what we had hoped in raising the reputation and status of the convent. He is a celebrated preacher outside of Florence, as well as within."

Lorenzo looked to Ficino. "And you, Marsilio? Do feel the same?"

The older philosopher thoughtfully weighed his reply as his

habitually twisted the chain of the amulet hanging from his neck. Ficino was a renowned scholar, trained in Greek, and educated under the patronage of Cosimo. He could be aloof, but was the most accomplished of the Florentine philosophers, having translated all the works of Plato into Latin from the original Greek. He had also been Lorenzo's principal tutor through most of *Il Magnifico's* youth.

"*Sì*, Lorenzino, I've had discussions with Fra Girolamo, mostly on theological issues. I find nothing objectionable and much to commend in his teachings. The convent seems astir with new energy and I expect he will attract a greater following among the lay brethren and the novitiates."

"Of course," Ficino added, "on a personal level, he's coarse and lacks the social graces that would endear him to his social betters. This may be a source of discomfort to some, but I believe to banish him would be a grave error. Especially given his popularity with the *popolo*."

Lorenzo shook his head. "I haven't even met the man, which I find a bit strange since I've invited him here. And our House rebuilt San Marco and made it the center of the Dominican Order it has become. It strikes me as ill-mannered."

As usual, Lorenzo suppressed his annoyance with grace. "It's hard to teach a priest manners. Anyway, a man who ventures to see into the future will surely stumble over his own devices; in the meantime perhaps we can temper his message. Shall we ask Fra Mariano to preach a competing sermon? What do you say? A competition between preachers is always entertaining."

"Perhaps if you give them swords," said the acerbic Poliziano. Michelangelo smirked at the poet's bluntness. Maestro Angelo always said exactly what was on his mind.

Lorenzo waved in a way a father might reprove his child. "You're wicked, Angelo. Anyway, my experience with most men is that they are mules: They go their own way, resist the bit, but lay down under indulgence. Priests are no exception. Given the people seem to genuinely follow this preacher and he sticks to Christian virtue, I think we can find ways to make use of his talents. We need only discover what he wants, then show him how to obtain it. If not, it's a small matter to show him out the gates." Lorenzo paused and smiled. "Perhaps we should invite him to a party?"

"I don't think he would attend," said Pico, laughing lightly. "Unless, of course he was invited to preach."

At this, Poliziano groaned. "No, *prego!* If one wishes depressing sermons, one can go with the women to the Duomo. It's the month of May. A time for love, and laughter, youth and rebirth!" He broke into one of his popular spring verses as he focused his ardor on Francesco the nymph: "*I went a-roaming, maidens, one bright day, in a green garden in mid-month of May…*"

As the group convulsed with laughter, Lorenzo commanded loudly: "*Basta* friends, back to the party. *Andiamo.*" As he herded them out of the chapel he added, "Perhaps we can invite the friar to preach to the *Signoria*, eh, Bernardo? We'll weave our net about him before he knows it."

Rucellai nodded sullenly, but Lorenzo had already turned his attention to the commotion in the courtyard below. Michelangelo saw the celebrations were still in full swing with masked guests dancing and singing in the late afternoon light.

***

Walking with Soderini, Rucellai followed Lorenzo, then veered toward the picked-over banquet table and reached for a wine flask. He steered Soderini toward several well-dressed men off to the side.

"*Buona sera, Signori,*" said one of the men expectantly as they approached. "Any news?"

This was Francesco Valori, an ambitious "new man," a member of that class of men without great means or status who aspired to wealth and reputation either as clients to the *grandi* or as competent civil servants. Many changes were sweeping through the Italian peninsula, providing opportunities for those clever enough to take advantage and "new men" invariably held their finger to the prevailing wind, with their personal status and the security of their families as their first loyalty. Under Lorenzo, Valori had served admirably in various official capacities and was viewed as a competent and well-respected citizen. But now, late in life, all knew his ambition still burned.

Rucellai gave a dismissive wave of his hand. "We warned him, but my brother-in-law refuses to recognize the seriousness of the situation. Actually, he probably *does* recognize the insignificance of the threat to his own position, but fails to appreciate the threat to *our* positions. It's all the *grandi* the friar is attacking, but with Lorenzo's patronage and his connections abroad, the Medici can probably weather the firestorm. We, however, will be the ones roasted."

"I won't wait that long," said the conservative lawyer, Guido Vespucci—a threatening tone in his voice.

They were all too aware of the potential consequences of worker and peasant uprisings, like the Ciompi rebellion when many aristocrats were murdered. That was over a hundred years ago, but in Florence time was short and memories long.

"Lorenzo suggested we invite the friar to preach in the *Signoria*," said

Soderini. "Probably not a bad idea: co-opting the friar's message and making it an issue of republicanism versus tyranny."

"Perhaps," said Rucellai, "but we must take action while we can. As official members of the Seventy, I say we must eliminate this problem ourselves."

"*D'accordo*," said Valori, while the others nodded knowingly.

CHAPTER 7

SAN MARCO

A WEEK LATER MICHELANGELO WAS working in the San Marco sculpture garden. With his eyes closed, he read the figure of the satyr with the tips of his fingers as they danced over the rough marble. He 'saw' the obscenely grinning mouth, the wide-open eyes, and the pointed ears. He caressed the raised arm and the rough stump of the other arm that was broken off—perhaps they had held a flute. He ran his hands down the torso and gripped the middle firmly, feeling the solid marble around the seated buttocks and the upper thighs that tapered off in sharp angles to the hoofed legs. These were opposed in two triangles, one up, one down, to create the seated foundation of the figure. The marble was not smooth, but grazed and stained by centuries of wear, the offspring of some ancient Roman carver who copied his art from a more ancient Greek. Dug up somewhere south of Rome, it had found its way here to a strange place in a strange time.

In his hands the satyr came to life, laughing, whispering lascivious tales, and seducing young maidens with his smooth, sweet song. Michelangelo could hear the melody playing, like the mating call of the lark in springtime, and imagined the soft-bellied maidens languidly reclining in the soft grass, their white silken robes open to the warm breeze, as they succumbed willingly to—

"My son, what is it you feel in this stone?"

His vision shattered, the young sculptor opened his eyes to look up at the figure hovering over him. The voice was clear and strong, obviously not that of his aged master. He blinked to adjust to the sudden light, saw the priest's frock and stammered a reply: "Excuse me, Father. I was using the sense of touch in my fingers to feel the art of the ancient stone carver living in this marble."

Using his trained eye Michelangelo instinctively scrutinized the visage gazing down on him. The features were large with a creased brow shadowing a dominating, hooked nose and full lips. The cheekbones were broad and sharply molded and the complexion dark olive, with a touch of sallowness in the cheeks. The face was not handsome or well proportioned, but arresting. It was a face worth sculpting. As his eyes slowly adjusted, Michelangelo caught the burning gaze of two black orbs. He immediately realized this must be the *Frate,* the fiery Dominican from Ferrara. He struggled to rise but the friar put his hand on his shoulder.

"No, please, continue with your lessons. By the look crossing your face though, I would have guessed you were dreaming of something else. Tell me, what do you feel from the cold stone?"

Michelangelo let his gaze fall as his face reddened. He looked up again, hoping the friar could not read his mind, but under those eyes he felt completely exposed. He felt foolish, unable to organize his thoughts.

"Are you the boy from Settignano? What's your name?"

"Michelangelo di Lodovico Buonarroti, Father. But I'm a Florentine."

"I am Fra Girolamo of Ferrara. May I?" The priest knelt down, placing his hands on the satyr. He closed his eyes and ran his long, narrow fingers over the marble. Michelangelo eyes fixed upon the hands. The hands were the color of old parchment, weathered but supple, and the veins stood out prominently on the tops. The fingers were twined roots. They looked capable of a strong grip and reminded him of an ancient, gnarled olive tree clinging tenaciously to a rocky hillside. Michelangelo was astonished because these were a sculptor's hands. He watched as the friar ran his fingers over the marble, noticing they strayed only over the head and shoulders. When the hands halted, the friar spoke with his eyes still closed.

"The stone is cold and unyielding."

Before he could stop himself, Michelangelo replied, "In the right hands the stone yields. It becomes warm, soft, full with the breath of life."

The boy realized his impertinence as the friar opened his eyes and forced a smile. He looked down at his hands ruefully, turning them over, inspecting them for deficiencies. "Then I'm afraid these are the wrong hands for this kind of work."

The friar stood up again. "Do you like these pagan figures you study?" he asked.

Michelangelo was unsure how to answer, afraid of erring. "I wish to learn all of the art of carving marble and these are the only objects I have to study. I don't think much about particular themes as I love all marble, especially when it's still hidden in the mountain."

He must have answered wrong because the priest shook his head. "That, my son, is where danger lies. We must take care to use our talents for a cause greater than our own pleasure. When we create pagan symbols of beauty we risk doing the Devil's work by leading men's souls astray.

"Your teachers may tell you this great art created today is for the glory of man. They feed the humble artisan's hunger to spread his fame and reputation, filling him with pride, as if a single man can be like the Creator. But his pride soon becomes a reflection in a still pool in which he gazes at himself all day. As John tells us: 'Do not love the world or the things in the world. If anyone loves the world, the love of the Father is not in him. For all that is in the world—the lust of the flesh, the lust of the eyes, and the pride of life—is not of God the Father but of the world.'"

Michelangelo felt ashamed, as he often felt under the gaze of his own disproving father. He nodded submissively to show his familiarity with scripture.

The friar continued. "Tell me: Who built the great cathedrals of Christendom?"

Before Michelangelo could respond, Fra Girolamo answered his own question. "We have no names because men built these magnificent houses for the glory of God, so we might worship Him in a place that raises us above our squalor here on earth. When we walk into the Duomo we are transported away from the filthy, sin-filled streets into the anteroom of Heaven, where tired souls find peace and refuge. The paintings and figures adorning God's house should aid us in prayer and not distract us from His Divine presence.

"Ask the painters which pleases more, a figure affected and unnatural or one without such affectation. They will reply the natural figure is better and more pleasing. Beauty is that which is simple, without superficial adornments, and which reminds us only of the Great Creator."

Michelangelo was confused, not sure what to say. He stammered.

"Be calm, my son, you commit no sin. But take care what you learn from the philosophers and poets. They may willingly or unwittingly preach and encourage false doctrines, which confuse and lead us to error. You live at the Palazzo Medici, yes?"

"Yes, *Il Magnifico* is generous and I'm treated well under his roof. I practice my craft and receive instruction here in the garden. In the evenings I'm permitted to attend his discussions with the grand *maestri* Ficino, Poliziano, and Count Pico; I'm sure there are no finer teachers in the world. Sometimes I don't understand, but Lorenzo allows me to read books from the library. There are so many—"

The friar raised his hand to cool the boy's enthusiasm. "I'm sure Signor Lorenzo has a fine library, comparable to the one we have here, granted to our care by his grandfather. But all these books—and I have read many—can confuse the mind, especially the young mind. Remember the most important Book—which is written by the hand of God, available to us everyday."

Michelangelo nodded again; sure he could not help erring, yet hoping to impress the friar. "The Bible is my principal text, it's the source of much of my inspiration. Maestro Ficino says the pagan Greek and

Roman legends are just metaphors for the true lessons of scripture." He recalled the Battle of the Centaurs Poliziano was encouraging him to carve; he was sure the friar would not approve.

At that moment a portly friar came scurrying across the garden from the convent, calling out to Fra Girolamo the entire way. He arrived flustered and panting heavily from the run. Though the friar was not much younger than Fra Girolamo, Michelangelo saw how he regarded him with a great deal of awe and deference.

"Several citizens have come from the Palazzo to speak with you, Fra Girolamo."

"*Sì*, Domenico." Turning back to Michelangelo he said, "We shall speak again, my son. Don't forget your talent is a gift from God. Honor Him with its use."

The young stone carver held his gaze as the two monks retreated back toward the convent, their white frocks and black mantles rolling with the rhythm of their strides. The priest was a strange one. He was causing quite a stir among the people, like an overeager shepherd dog nipping at the flock. But Michelangelo was humbled by the burning presence that overshadowed the friar's vast knowledge and stern manner. He felt something in the brief moment their eyes met. Nevertheless, he was puzzled by the strong reactions he had witnessed during others' discussions of the friar. The mere melody of his name seemed to stoke all the hopes and fears hidden deep in men's souls.

Perhaps the friar spoke God's truth, shining light on good and evil. Michelangelo knew that truth whispered softly deep inside the soul, a whisper so often ignored or shouted down when it became too insistent or in conflict with earthly desire. It was the truth that gnawed at men's consciences because they were inveterate sinners. He thought of another verse from the Book of John:

And this is the condemnation, that the light has come into the world, and men loved darkness rather than light, because their deeds were evil. For everyone practicing evil hates the light and does not come to the light, lest his deeds should be exposed. But he who does the truth comes to the light, that his deeds may be clearly seen, that they have been done in God...

Michelangelo knew his art depended on the light of truth. False hearts lead to false art. He must be open, with all his senses keenly aware; his eyes, his ears, his fingers taking in everything, to be chewed slowly and digested, to blossom renewed in his creations. He must not shrink from his own fear, but embrace it and turn it to strength. Was not he, humble artisan, also one of God's creations? Did God not breathe life through him into a hunk of marble and create beauty in the human form? The friar was not wrong to remind him of his debt to the Almighty. He slowly closed his eyes as he breathed in the fresh spring air and placed his fingers again on the laughing satyr.

***

Back at the convent the two friars crossed the cloister, heading toward a circle of well-dressed laymen engaged in conversation. As they approached, the talking ceased and the circle opened to face them.

The men glanced warily at Fra Domenico, so Fra Girolamo dismissed him and turned to his guests. Feeling his back stiffen, he addressed them formally: "*Signori*, may I offer you something? To what do I owe the honor of this visit?"

A physically imposing man stepped forward and the friar recognized the powerful and wealthy aristocrat, Bernardo Rucellai.

"Father, we shall be brief and not inconvenience you more than necessary. Though you may know some of us from our association with San Marco, may I present myself and the others: I am Bernardo Rucellai, this is Paolantonio Soderini, Francesco Valori, Domenico Bonsi and Guido Vespucci."

Fra Girolamo knew the names and faces, all belonging to Florentine families of high social rank, all Mediceans. These *grandi* knew who filled their bellies. "*Signori*," he said, bowing his head politely in deference, "I am humbled in the presence of some of the most esteemed leaders of our city."

Rucellai continued with a condescending air. "Father, we have longed served the city in various offices and thus we are most concerned with the affairs of the commune. You are not of this city and we must tell you we Florentines have learned how to govern with a delicate hand, as any disorder can lead to serious consequences."

Fra Girolamo noticed two of the men, Bonsi and Valori, begin to fidget, as if their sumptuous clothes were ill fitted. Their forced smiles made plain the meaning behind the deliberate allusion to his outsider status.

Rucellai continued, "We have become aware of the temper of some of your sermons. We feel we must caution you that the tone and substance of your preaching threatens this delicate order."

Three swallows darted through the open air of the cloister as Fra Girolamo's deep-set eyes penetrated those of each of his visitors in turn. Both Bonsi and Valori averted his gaze, watching the swallows. He answered evenly.

"Please, *Signori*, perhaps you will explain the specific references which trouble you as I am only aware I've expanded upon passages from scripture."

Vespucci spoke with a honeyed tone. "Please Father, don't misunderstand. Perhaps we can illustrate our concern with a story of which you are familiar—that of Fra Bernardino of Feltro. In his travels Fra Bernardino often had occasion to visit our city, but several years ago his sermons ignited a riot against the moneylenders and it poisoned the air for all the Jews and disrupted much trade on which the city depends. As a result, the Signoria was forced to banish Fra Bernardino from our territory."

The crudeness of the comparison was not lost on Fra Girolamo, and he found it offensive. He knew of Fra Bernardino, a fiery Franciscan, who was a wandering street preacher with a style designed to frighten and goad his ignorant listeners into a frenzy. His attacks on the usurers hit the purses of the city's merchants, so Lorenzo had ordered the Signoria to send the little rabble-rouser packing. His exile had sent a clear message that disrupting the comfortable order of things would not be tolerated.

But Fra Girolamo felt no compulsion to be cautious. This was the moment he had anticipated and he was emboldened. These Florentine *grandi* dared reproach him as a foreigner—a stranger in this city—but in matters of the faith they were the transgressors, and they hid behind their tyrant Lorenzo. These are the ones Nonno had warned him about, the gluttonous courtiers who grew fat on the poor and defenseless. The ones who had looked down upon his family at the Court d'Este. He was sure when they took the sacraments, they made false confessions in their hearts and paid tribute to wash away unrepentant sins. They were the ones who disgraced themselves in the eyes of God and he sensed their bluster and apprehension. He knew their fear—it was the premonition of the power of God's truth to destroy their earthly designs. His hooded brow cast his eyes in shadow as he drew in his breath to reply, gripping the crucifix of the rosary under his frock. "And the lesson of this story is?"

The question echoed in an embarrassed silence and the friar filled the void. "I believe I understand you perfectly, *Signori*. Let me be direct and brief as well, for I know for whom you speak as you so plainly wear the mask of your patron."

The dignitaries were taken back by this direct affront and Rucellai's expression hardened as the friar continued.

"My intentions are plain—my appointed mission is to bring the word of God to the faithful, to bring them back into the fold of Holy Mother Church by any and all means. If this causes certain *grandi* discomfort or inconveniences them in their worldly affairs, it is not my concern. I'm not here to entertain or condone the depraved practices into which your city has fallen. For that you have your lukewarm preachers."

He saw how his bluntness unsettled them so he pressed his advantage. "I care nothing for your threats of exile—your city is but a tiny patch on the surface of this earth. But I know this new fashion of exposing the truth will triumph and the old lies will collapse."

Rucellai was taken back. "It is the city that concerns us, Father, and this is for the greater good of *all* the people." As Rucellai raised his hand for emphasis, Fra Girolamo noticed the heavy, jewel-encrusted rings on his fingers. The friar's eyes narrowed and his smile became a smirk.

"Yes, I know what you mean by the 'city.' More than forty thousand souls call themselves Florentines, but you only favor some two hundred families as citizens. You Florentines boast of a republic, but it's a mere shadow word used to conceal the true design. I've passed through all these northern cities—from Ferrara to Milano to Bologna and Rimini and here to Florence. We all know it's tyranny that rules these places, with an iron fist."

Rucellai reddened with rage and the others were visibly shocked by the preacher's uncouthness. Fra Girolamo knew this was not what they had expected and his voice assumed the force of the pulpit: "Tyrants are incorrigible, *Signori*, because they're proud, because they love flattery. They corrupt votes and inflict taxes and increase the burdens on the poorest. Then they promote shows and festivals, so the people, distracted, may leave the reins of government in their hands."

Fra Girolamo looked at each of them accusingly, his words challenging their own vaunted sense of dignity. He had struck them dumb. Unexpectedly, he softened his expression and opened his arms in a gesture of supplication. *"Prego, Signori,* I've spent these past few months walking the streets of your city. Not in the Palazzo or the Duomo—those places of magnificence, light and beauty—but in the Streets of the Shearers and the Tanners, the Street of the Cauldrons, the Road of the Dyers; all those dark places of filth and disease. There, workers and their families try to eke out a decent life in God's eyes but have too little food, or clothing, or adequate shelter. So their children die in great numbers. Now, who of you could stand by to watch a child die of want? Can you see your own child there, the pain and suffering in her eyes?

"Tell me, *Signori*, how will you help God's children with your laws and taxes and your *Pratica* councils?"

The men were visibly flustered and Paolo Soderini stepped forward. "Father, you place the Signoria in a difficult position. Be assured our city holds your divine mission in highest regard, but governing the city's affairs is not a matter for priests and preachers. The government would be forced to take action against any who interfere and none of us could prevent it."

Fra Girolamo was unmoved. "But I have no intention of interfering in the business of the Palazzo. My place is in the House of God. You may fear exile, for you have wives and children, but I have no such concerns. My 'wife and children' find refuge in the Church and I take them wherever I go. It is this earthly city of which you speak, but I am concerned with a greater city, a heavenly city—the *City of God*—where all who accept His grace are welcome, whether poor or sick, tired or alone.

"And, if you mean by the 'government,' Signor Lorenzo de' Medici, well, let Signor Lorenzo do what he will. But let him know this: Though I am a stranger and he the first citizen of the city; I am here to stay and it is he who must leave."

Stupefied, the men gazed at him, their eyes widening, wondering if they had heard correctly. He read their thoughts from their expressions: Surely this humble preacher did not believe *he* could drive the powerful *Magnifico* from the city, where popes and assassins had repeatedly failed?

He repeated: "*I* am here to stay, not he."

They glanced at each other in confusion, shuffling their feet in discomfort. Sensing his triumph, the friar let them wallow in their state of confusion, then spread his arms again in a Christ-like gesture of supplication.

"*Signori*, let me put your minds at ease. As you can see, I am but a frail and simple priest. I have no gold. I have no armies. What has Lorenzo to fear from me? I cannot possibly threaten him or do him harm."

The previously silent Bonsi stammered, "Then how will you prevail here in Florence over *Magnifico*? What can you do?"

"What can *I* do? *I?*" Fra Girolamo shook his head and smiled. "Of course, I can do nothing, *Signori*. This is what I've been trying to tell you." His smile concealed his dark secret as he surveyed the peaceful cloister. Now he would throw down the gauntlet and dare them to take it up. He froze them with his black stare.

He slowly pointed the index finger of his right hand toward the sky and said, "It is *GOD*, grand *Signori*. We are all in God's hands and it is *He* who has plans for your city."

The dignitaries were speechless as Fra Girolamo paused to let his words find their mark. He was sure he would clash again with these *grandi*, but he was confident he had struck the first blow.

Glancing purposefully toward the Chapter House, he said, "*Signori*, please, excuse me, I must attend to my duties. But as our guests please enjoy the peaceful surroundings of the convent as long as you wish."

He left them dumbfounded, sensing their eyes on him as the three swallows darted again through the open air in his wake. Then Bonsi, in an involuntary reflex, quickly crossed himself before the five men, their circle irreparably fractured, closed ranks and hurried from the convent.

CHAPTER 8

THE PRIOR OF SAN MARCO

"THE PRINCIPAL OF THE GOOD Christian life is faith—*faith in Jesus Christ crucified.*"

Fra Girolamo felt the weight of the hot summer sun as his words carried out over the radiating heat and descended like a benediction over the bared heads of the novices gathered around him in the cloister. They were boys mostly, with their smooth brows knitted in concentration. He was unaffected by the sun but watched them fidget uncomfortably in their scratchy tunics. In comparing them with his own youthful zeal—when no bodily sensation could have distracted him from his devotions—he found them wanting.

He remembered how his grandfather had tutored him, the hours reading scripture without respite until he would almost collapse from exhaustion. He remembered the one and only time he had deceived Nonno, when he was nine or ten years old. He had told his grandfather he'd memorized his lessons on the earth's four elements and the corresponding humors in the body, when actually he had spent the afternoon in the kitchen playing with the cook and eating sweets. Nonno tested him and he failed miserably, then made another excuse, compounding his lie. He remembered hanging his head in shame, fully expected to receive just punishment for his sins. But then Nonno insisted as teacher he would take punishment in penalty for the failings of his student. He had cried out in protest, but Nonno was firm, insisting his grandson administer the lash himself. He had been horrified as his grandfather ordered him to flay his feet again and again, raising welts upon the old man's leathery skin. His confession welled up with tears, but Nonno had known a far deeper truth about sin.

Fra Girolamo knew how to cure these novices of their bad habits and temptations. When they failed in their devotions, he did not punish them, but suffered for them. He deprived himself of bodily comforts and his anguish shamed them deeply. Bodily pain was but a temporary inconvenience compared to the fierce struggles of the spirit and, like Christ in the desert, the truly pious must learn to endure pain and suffering without complaint. How else was one to resist the temptations of the Devil?

"Without faith and sacrifice it is impossible to please God. The earthly life you abandon lacks unity, but the pleasures of the heavenly life may be infinitely enjoyed in the vision of God, which is of itself supreme felicity."

He watched them lose their struggle to resist the heat as each one puzzled alone with the words, drawing upon his own short catalogue of experience and wondering what this new relationship with God might mean. He knew their thoughts and remembered his own confusion at their age. What would change? Would anything change? Which worldly pleasures led them astray? Which ones branded them hopeless sinners? Surely God must recognize those unworthy of His holy offices. Would He forgive one weakness? *No, He would not.*

During the pause one boy raised his hand. "Father, forgive me. But if God is all-powerful and all-knowing, does man have free will?"

Fra Girolamo tried to hide his amusement; such innocence made his task easier.

"This same question has puzzled all the great philosophers and theologians, but the answer is not so difficult to imagine. San Augustino offers us his guidance: All events depend upon the Will of God and because God is supremely powerful, His Will is never frustrated. He knows prior to the event the exact nature of the action. But there is no contradiction between the foreknowledge of God and the freedom of man's action. Man does not sin because God knew he would sin—he sins because he freely chooses to sin and he is good when he willfully chooses not to sin. Thus, the foreknowledge of God does not make God a partner to man's decisions. God willed man to be free so that he may come to love Him freely. Even though He knows some men will choose sin and thereby earn eternal damnation."

The boy persisted. "But then why aren't all men good? If they have free will and God shows the way to all things, why do they choose sin? From whence comes evil?"

Fra Girolamo continued deliberately, as if reading from a text. "San Augustino has written much on this question of evil. He explains how the angels were created from the beginning, before the world. Through the sin of the fallen angel, the angels were divided into two communities or two cities: one of the light, the good, with God; and the other of the darkness, the bad, with Satan.

"In Book Four of the *Civita Deus* he explains how the first is a community of devout men, the other a company of the irreligious, and each has its own angels attached to it. In the one city the love of God has been given first place, in the other, love of self. So, then, what is sin?"

Several novices looked at each other as they held their breaths, but others already familiar with the friar's rhetorical methods knew he would provide the answers to his own questions.

"Sin," he said, "is the perversity of man's will, twisted away from God, toward lower things, casting away its own bowels, and swelling beyond itself."

Despite the vivid imagery the novices dared not snicker, flinch, or change expression; not if they hoped to escape the friar's scrutiny.

"Remember this: God did not create evil; evil results from man's perversion of God's will. Like the frock you wear—the cloth is woven well and strong but then a hole is rent in the garment and it becomes a defect of the cloth. The weaver did not create the hole. Evil is a defect of men. As the good use the world to rejoice in God, the wicked use God to enjoy the world."

Several of the novices self-consciously fingered the holes in their frocks, praying for a reprieve.

"My sons, earthly goods are not evil—only the *love* of earthly goods is evil because it detracts from true salvation in the love of God. Satan fell because he wished to be God. He puts these same ambitions into the heads of men—that they can be gods and invent some sort of happiness outside of God, apart from God. So men pursue ambition, power, and glory in the things of the world. In so doing they fall from grace."

The boys fidgeted under the hot sun, but, sensing their impatience, Fra Girolamo prolonged their ordeal. "And so, why do we look to Christ? Why do I say the Good Christian life is faith in Jesus Christ crucified? Why did God become man and suffer so?"

He paused, letting his words descend over them before answering.

"To provide the means of salvation through divine grace, to show men and women how to live." His voice rose: "The life of Christ is the role model for mankind."

He paused, then repeated: "The life of Christ is the role model for mankind."

The large bell in the convent tower began to peal and Fra Girolamo waited for its final toll. "We shall gather together in the chapel this evening after Vespers for my address to the chapter. I encourage you to contemplate these questions and read scripture as part of your studies. Our Dominican Order is devoted to study to find the true path to God. As Preachers it is our duty to give others the fruits of our contemplation."

He ended with his favorite motto of the Dominican Order— *Contemplata aliis tradere*—then raised his hand in a final benediction. It was the eagerly anticipated signal that sent the novices scurrying into the coolness of the dormitory for a moment's respite before the next offices.

As he watched them fly away like uncaged birds he was struck by the difficult task before him. Just the day before his fellow brethren had elected him Prior, giving him authority over the governing rules and daily organization of the convent. As Prior of San Marco he was now directly responsible for the souls of all his novices and brothers, as well as his congregation. But he knew his brethren succumbed too easily to the temptations of the world. A true servant of God must learn obedience in order to submit to a higher will; he must be celibate and mortify the flesh; and he must embrace poverty and renounce earthly comforts. This was the first stage of his mission. This evening he would address the chapter for the first time and he was anxious to initiate the necessary reforms as soon as possible. He prayed for guidance:

Lord, give me strength and I will lead my brothers by example. And then San Marco will set the example for the Dominican convents across the region and in so doing we shall pave the way for reform of Your Holy Mother Church.

As the prior headed toward his room to prepare he found two brothers waiting for him at the top of the stairs: Fra Domenico Buonvicini, his main assistant, and Fra Silvestro Maruffi. Fra Domenico was the younger, originally from the small Adriatic city of Pescia. He was a good-natured priest, keeper of the pet doves, a loyal and devout follower. The older one, Fra Silvestro, was a native Florentine prone to bizarre conduct and possessed by an uncontrollable left eye. He grew excitable at times, when his eye would wander independently. At other times he appeared listless and dull-witted. The brothers declared he would often walk the halls in his sleep at night and cry out like a child from nightmares. In the morning he would relate fantastic dreams and visions to anyone who would listen.

"Fra Girolamo," cried Silvestro, breathless, "we heard you intend to make changes at the convent, that precious crucifixes and jeweled rosaries will be confiscated and given to the poor. The older *frati*—"

Fra Girolamo held up his hand to cut him off. The outburst was attracting attention and Silvestro's eye had begun to drift.

"*Prego*, Brother Silvestro, where have you heard these tales? Before you say more, let us retire and not disturb the others."

After the prior closed the door to the outer chamber of his new three-roomed cell, Silvestro was ready to burst again, but Fra Girolamo silenced him with a look.

"Silvestro, where have you been hearing such things?"

"Fra Roberto and Fra Malatesta were outside the library speaking with some of the younger brothers who come from families here in Florence. But I—"

"*Senti*, Silvestro. Do not partake in idle gossip. I plan many reforms for our convent, but no one knows yet what plans I have made. I'm guided by the words of our founder: 'Have charity, preserve humility, observe voluntary poverty; may my malediction and that of God fall upon him who shall bring possessions to this Order.'

"In this sense, is it right for those of our brethren from noble families to possess and hoard gold and silver crucifixes, finely illuminated Bibles and other such vanities? What example does this set for our poorer brothers and our humble parishioners?"

"But Fra Roberto says these things are necessary to holy offices, and to preach against the wealth and necessary possessions of the Church is heretical, and—"

"Fra Roberto is not wrong, Silvestro. But he fails to fully appreciate the consequences on the moral fiber of the convent and the Order and the entire Roman Church. When we permit material vanities from the outside world to enter our cloister we create envy among our brothers and priests, who then feed this envy by making a business of the offices and sacraments of the Church. You see how priests in the smaller parishes hawk tapers and candles and say Masses for money? This is a pestilence spreading through our house."

To reassure Silvestro he added, "But we will not confiscate possessions from our brothers, that is no more than robbery. Go speak with the others and reassure them. Tell them I will present a reform program when we meet this evening. Go now."

Silvestro hesitated. "There is one other thing, Prior. Some of the brothers have been asking if you will now visit the Medici and pay homage to Lorenzo as is the tradition of San Marco?"

Fra Girolamo frowned; this hammer of the tyrant, with its demand for submission under threat of exile, was still raised against him. But months had passed and he was still here. He would not lose this battle against this profligate 'prince' of Florence. His tone hardened. "So tell me then, is it God or Signor Lorenzo who has made me Prior?"

Silvestro's eyes, still unable to focus, flitted to Domenico. He was confused. "God?" he ventured.

Fra Girolamo gestured toward the crucifix on the wall. "Then let me render thanks to Him, not to man."

Fra Domenico stood patiently as the prior dealt with Silvestro. After Silvestro gracelessly snuck out the door, the prior turned to him with a look of exasperation and concern.

"Brother, please watch over him. He is possessed of a simple mind."

"Yes, Prior," said Fra Domenico. "He's excitable and too curious at times, but he's a Florentine and very well known among our congregation. He confesses many of our leading citizens."

Fra Girolamo nodded. He knew how the Florentines treated

stranieri—foreigners—in their city. It was a tightly knit commune and they kept strangers at a distance. But as one of their own, Fra Silvestro could prove useful.

"Forgive me, Prior, do you think it wise to shun Lorenzo?"

"Don't worry, Domenico. God will guide us and it serves us to stay out of the clutches of these *grandi*. We will not be banished from the city, and if we are, we shall return in a short while. You may be assured."

"But the Augustinian from Santa Spirito, Fra Mariano, has been preaching against your—I mean, the prophecies. Surely he is doing so at the request of the Medici."

"Yes, I've heard his theme, '*It is not for us to know the time or moment.*' This is directed toward me, I know. But the Augustinian is no more than a braying ass who does the bidding of his patrons and adapts scripture to their purpose. This manner of preaching for entertainments and amusements is past. The new manner of preaching the truth will prevail. You see how the crowds pack my sermons. Fear not, Domenico, I shall wax as he shall wane."

Domenico nodded and left the prior to prepare his address to the chapter.

***

Later that evening the brethren gathered together inside the chapel. They had just finished singing the hours of Vespers, but the spirit of goodwill evoked by their hymns failed to calm the tension in the air.

The prior stood before them, looking over their faces as they gathered together and sorted themselves into natural alliances: There were groups of the loyal and good; other groups of the jealous and envious; groups of young native Florentines; and other groups of older brethren from foreign cities and distant lands. It was the same disorder as outside the convent walls—each jockeying for position, measuring himself against his neighbor, coveting the position of his neighbor. He must start here, in his own house, to create a new sense of order where one is measured only by his love of God and his fellow man. He must bring order to this chaos.

"My Brethren, you have seen, by the grace of God Almighty, to elect me, your most humble servant, as Prior of the Convent of San Marco..."

To lay out his agenda he began by explaining the reasons for the moral decline of the monastic community: first, how the Church of Rome had suppressed and then embraced the mendicant Orders; then, how the secularization of the Roman leadership had led to benign neglect of the satellite chapters while the clergy—the popes, cardinals and bishops—turned their attention from spiritual to worldly affairs. So the Roman prelates left it to the humble mendicants to care for souls while they took care of themselves. However, with greater independence and interests diverging from the official Church, many chapters and parishes soon began to withhold taxes and tithes from higher authorities. This contributed to the financial crisis of the Church, the main cause of which was the profligate spending of the Roman curate. The result was a scramble at both the top and bottom levels of the Church hierarchy to pursue riches through the sale of indulgences and benefices.

"Just look how we have made a business of the Church," he cried, punctuating his first cadence.

He then explained how reform could only occur by returning to the basic precepts of the religious Orders—to the vows of poverty, charity, and faith of both St. Dominic and St. Francis. These changes must first be implemented at the chapter level, in places such as San Marco, to stop the spread of the disease. Reforms would help the Roman Church return to its pastoral mission.

Then, less they confuse his meaning, he rebuked the Franciscan Spirituals and Dominican Observants. Commonly known as the *fraticelli*, these were radical offshoots of the Orders who took direct opposition to Rome, separating themselves from the true Church because they advocated a militant split and return to pure Christian doctrine. But to renounce accepted doctrine was heresy. The *fraticelli* had been targets of Church pogroms since the time of Pope John XXII, when he had fomented a crusade in 1317 against the French Cathars and Albigensians in an attempt to wipe them out. Many had been burned alive during the recurring pogroms over the past two centuries.

Then he stated how he, as prior, was particularly opposed to the efforts of the Dominican Observants of the Lombard Congregation to enlist the houses in Florentine territory against Rome. Thus, an important element of reform would be to encourage the pope to grant complete independence to the Tuscan Congregation, with San Marco as its lead chapter. But this would be a matter of more delicate politics. Finally, he brought his oration around to the sensitive and divisive issues of immediate changes at the convent.

He reiterated how money was at the center of the Church and where money reigns supreme, sloth, lechery, and pride inevitably follow. To combat this he listed the reforms the chapter must implement: First, they must reestablish the rule of poverty and he fixed his stern gaze on them as he spoke: "The Church has been ruined by wealth. Shall we say then the Church should have no temporal wealth? No, it would be heresy to say this—we submit ourselves to the Church of Rome. But the Church would be better without riches, since she could thus be drawn nearer to God. Wherefore I say to you, my brothers: Seek to adhere to poverty, for when riches enter among you, death too comes in."

The Order's vow of poverty would be enforced by selling those possessions jointly held by the convent, with the proceeds to be distributed to the poor. The brothers and novices would be encouraged to give away or return to their benefactors their prized personal possessions, but these would not be confiscated. Nevertheless—his eyes searched out the rumormonger Fra Malatesta as he spoke—under the new rules members of the convent should be prepared to forgo their vanities and comforts; old coarse robes should signify the *frati* of San Marco. This way their humility will be demonstrated every day to the people of Florence.

At last he explained a reorganization of the work routine of the chapter according to the skills of the brothers and the needs of the convent. These tasks would include administration, teaching, preaching, confessing, alms giving, begging, food growing and preparation, and other necessary tasks. He also spoke of his vision of organizing the study of the manual arts of painting, sculpture, and textiles, so there would be a school within the Order for the creation of religious art and icons.

He ended his address by expounding his grand goal of recreating the Dominican Order of Preachers to take the message of the Christian Church to the East, to the Turks, in order to convert the heathen and reclaim the Holy Land. It was a message of hope and ambition delivered in a voice full of conviction.

As the brothers filed out for the evening procession around the cloister to sing the *Salve Regina,* they found themselves, reluctantly or willingly, caught up in a promise that calmed their natural fears.

CHAPTER 9

THE PASSEGIATA

NICCOLÒ CROSSED THE PONTE VECCHIO, heading for the New Market several blocks away. It was late afternoon and the butchers on the bridge were cleaning up, throwing stinking offal into the water where scavengers would feed on it as it traveled downriver. Niccolò hurried so he could get back to meet Tommaso under the setting sun, to watch and join all the young Florentines in the nightly *passegiata* along the river before nightfall. Weather permitting, it was the favored time to partake in the daily ritual to see and be seen.

Under his doublet he carried a small purse containing the first payment on a loan that had financed the Machiavelli crop plantings from their small land holdings in Percussina. His family lived off the produce and rents from tenant farmers on their land holdings and often needed to borrow funds from the Jewish moneylenders until the fall harvest. The open loggia of the *Mercato Nuovo*, where the lenders and changers set up their booths and counted out their profits, was bustling when Niccolò arrived.

Niccolò felt like a fish out of water among these traders, many of them speaking strange guttural tongues and strongly accented Tuscan. Nevertheless, he knew the lifeblood of Florence flowed through the ink-stained fingers of these moneylenders who, as Jews, were permitted by the Church and the civic authorities to conduct their nefarious art—advancing and collecting funds to grease the wheels of Christian commerce. Of course, interest on loans was usury and usury was condemned in the Bible, so the Church was forever attacking these moneylenders, and these attacks periodically erupted in violence. But as far as Niccolò could see, aside from their dissimilarity in speech and peculiar dress, there was scant difference between the avarice of the Jewish moneylenders and that of the Christian merchants they financed. Did it matter if they believed not in Christ but in Yahweh? It seemed to Niccolò all gods were pretty much the same, whether called Zeus, Yahweh, Jupiter, or Christ. Since the popes and cardinals were some of the most rapacious borrowers, Niccolò saw it as just another convenient hypocrisy of Holy Mother Church.

He arrived at the table of the Jew called Joshua and plunked his purse down.

"Ciao, Messer Niccolò. I hear a sound that gladdens my heart. Sit, while I write receipt," commanded the Jew.

Niccolò watched the old Jew open his account book with its meticulous notes and scribblings—double-entry accounting was one of the mysteries clever Florentines had discovered and taught the world. He wondered how the old man could breathe in this heat while draped in his heavy, black woolen clothing.

"So," Niccolò idly asked, "how does one become a banker?"

The Jew looked up and smiled wryly. "Why, only when one can do nothing else, of course. Sitting here, in heat, every day but Sabbath... all night in bed worrying for everything that can upset one's planning. So many things can go wrong. It's no life, eh?"

"Seems awfully dull to me, but there are compensating advantages, no?"

"Perhaps. I have a riddle for you: What flies all around world, yet never leaves home? Eh? It's the measure of all things. Gives pleasure when you send it away, and greater pleasure when it comes back, and the worst sorrow when it's lost."

Niccolò gave the Jew a satisfied smile and answered by adding to the riddle, "And gives meaning to a man's days?"

The Jew raised his hands up in a self-mocking manner, "Bah! Can it be only money? A man counts his money...and all his days disappear...Aha! But we have an old saying that may interest you, Messer Niccolò: 'With gold in your pocket, you are wise and you are handsome and you sing well too.'"

"Now, that's something I can use, but first I need the gold," said Niccolò, as the Jew handed him the receipt.

Back at the Ponte Vecchio, Niccolò saw Tommaso sitting at the center of the bridge, precariously perched on the wall above the river. He was brazenly observing the young girls and women passing by in small, secure groups.

"Hey, Machia, I've been waiting for you..."

Another pair of girls distracted his leering eyes and he called after them: "*Bellissima*," elongating his vowels and torturing his consonants into a lecherous melody.

Niccolò sat up on the wall next to him. The evening air was warm and there were dozens of young girls out this evening—they made a young man feel wise and handsome, and perhaps able to sing well too. He appreciated how their style of dress wisely emphasized their choicest assets—full breasts and narrow waists—and cleverly hid their faults with creams, rouge, and lipstick; elaborate hair-dos, wigs, and bleached hair to frame plain faces; and long flowing dresses with high heels to disguise short, heavy legs. Occasionally there passed a ravishing beauty who required no aids and hid behind no disguise. Their efforts made him more conscious of his own frayed and threadbare attire.

"Keep an eye out for Fiammetta, eh? Look, Machia, so much beauty and so elusive. Do you know the answer to this riddle: What is beauty?"

"Perhaps you should ask Fiammetta."

"Forget it. Women only want to talk of love. They only want to be *told* they're beautiful."

"Love is the purest desire to enjoy beauty."

Tommaso grabbed his crotch. "Yes, I have *that*," he snorted, "but still: What is beauty?"

Niccolò looked upriver toward the red-pink sky. "Beauty, my friend, is purity of the soul in union with the divine. Like a pure burning fire. Like Dante and Beatrice, Petrarca and Laura, eh? Pure beauty contemplated in a love never consummated…"

Tommaso scoffed, "Buggered poets, you really believe that shit?"

Niccolò raised his eyebrows as if to say, "Who, me?"

"What else have you been doing?"

Niccolò rolled his eyes. "*Niente*, nothing…helping my father with the farm and spending afternoons with the country bumpkins in the tavern in Sant'Andrea playing dice and cards. My father wants me to manage the tenants. Can you imagine? I despise the peasant life."

"How's your luck?"

Niccolò knew Tommaso was alluding to his outstanding debt. But he also sensed Tommaso enjoyed needling him about the obligation more than wanting the money. "Not good. The bumpkins are easily bluffed, but they have no money."

"Eh?" asked Tommaso, a leer in his eye.

"I did manage to deflower a young milkmaid, daughter of one of our tenants."

"Details, details," Tommaso insisted.

"The usual, a bit of rutting in the back of the barn with the other beasts." Niccolò flashed his thin-lipped smile. "There's a bit of the beast in the most innocent *contadina*."

"*Merda,* chained to the damn counting house for most of the day. I think I almost miss Maestro Marcello's lectures. You know, the maestro likes you, even told my father and uncle. Said you have a good head for logic and rhetoric."

Niccolò's mind wandered, Marcello Adriani's university lectures seemed ages ago. Distracted, he looked down at the muddy Arno slowly passing under the bridge. *Fortuna,* he thought, she's like a flooded river meandering to and fro only to be tamed by dams and dikes. A clever little bitch, always looking to thwart man's designs with floods and droughts. *Fortuna*—the goddess who eluded him.

Abruptly he laughed and said, "The Arno is a river that laughs, the only river in Italia that laughs in people's faces."

"*Che?*" asked Tommaso, confused.

Suddenly Tommaso straightened up. "Hey, I almost forgot—about the *Frate* of San Marco. *Incredibile.* My father went to the convent—with Rucellai and some others—to warn him the Signoria would banish him as it did Fra Bernardino if he didn't shut up. They hoped to frighten him but the friar told them *Magnifico* would soon be gone anyway, dead within the year! Later my father heard he added both the pope and King Ferrante of Naples to his list of who would die soon. I said this Friar's crazy in the head, but my father sensed a strange certainty in him. Something dark and forbidding."

Tommaso laughed with incredulity. "The friar said it was God and I think my father believes it."

Niccolò snickered at life's absurdities. He, a young man of keen intellect, well-studied, who couldn't even secure a lowly position in the ministries, while the whole city crowded into the Duomo to hear the ranting and ravings of a deranged, fortune-telling priest.

"The city's in a strange mood," Niccolò said.

"You think there's something to this preacher and his Apocalypse?"

Niccolò tapped his finger against his temple. "No—think. First, Lorenzo is ill and his father died of a similar affliction. Both the pope and Ferrante are old, so it seems a fairly safe bet, no? Anyway, from what I've heard, the friar's ideas sound as much like Dante as Aquinas and Augustine. It's well past time for serious Church reform."

"Dante?"

"*Sì.* It's not just demons gnawing on entrails you know."

Tommaso shrugged as Niccolò continued. "Dante was concerned with the petty rivalries in our city and the degeneration of political life. You should read *De Monarchia.* One of the main causes was the meddling of the pope and clergy in political affairs. He says the Church must confine itself to spiritual leadership while affairs of state remain the province and duty of the Emperor. Neither should interfere with the other."

Tommaso's attention was momentarily diverted by a passing female distraction. "I thought Dante was all about Beatrice and unrequited *love*..." He turned back to face Niccolò and continued, "Okay, okay, I remember some lessons on the *Comedia* and Bruni's critique for putting Brutus in the jaws of Satan. I love that image—"

"Defender of Roman liberty and republicanism, Brutus was a hero for murdering Caesar the tyrant, but I think the poet was influenced more by the treachery of the traitor. In my view, Bruni was right and Dante wrong. Brutus was loyal to the people of Rome and justified. On the other hand, a multitude without a head is useless. A strong leader is needed to temper the spirit of the people..."

"Like the Medici?"

"No, the Medici have created the illusion by fixing the *scrutino*, thereby guaranteeing their position as 'first among equals.' Someday the illusion will crumble. The Roman Republic lasted for hundreds of years, mainly due to strong leadership accountable to the Senate."

"Our noble Signoria?"

"An independent, freely-elected Signoria, not a gaggle of puppets. One must design a government that steers a middle course between the stench of the plebs and the arrogance of the *grandi*. The Greeks knew this, and so did the Romans. Above all, the *polis* must guard against the abuse of power, where the main conflict is between those who have power and those who want to get it. Nobody surrenders power willingly and the Medici are no exception."

"Now I know why my uncle sings your praises, Machia. You sound just like him. But *basta*, enough, you're giving me a headache." Tommaso threw him a sharp elbow and motioned with his eyes. "*Guarda*. Look."

Niccolò saw a tall, dark-haired beauty with a breath-taking figure come ambling toward them, swaying her hips in a delicious rhythm. Her breasts were straining to escape from her tight bodice. "Tell me, Machia," whispered Tommaso, "have you a theory for that?"

The young woman, well known in the neighborhood as *La Bella*, avoided eye contact. She passed slowly, deliberately, before descending down the far side of the bridge.

"Of course," Niccolò asserted. "There, *amico mio*, goes the Theory of Everything."

Moments later the two were joined by Chiara, Fiammetta and her younger sister, Alessandra. The girls were enticing in their summer outfits, simple yet elegant.

"Ciao Nico," Chiara said with surprise.

Niccolò secretly smiled. Though he had been away for a month in the country, he had seen Chiara quite frequently in the spring and their friendship had blossomed with feigned innocence—he toyed with her and she toyed with him. It was a game, like the evening *passegiata*, teasing their emotions while walking in the company of others. But when he wasn't in the mood it exasperated him. He knew the most desirable prize was the one just beyond reach and he chided himself whenever he let his emotions triumph over reason.

"*Ciao, belle,*" Niccolò greeted them. "Tommaso was just asking me what is beauty. I told him to be patient, the answer would soon arrive."

Tommaso rolled his eyes as they all kissed cheeks in greeting.

"But of course, woman is beauty," said Chiara with a coy look.

"*Certo,* of course," the two young men cheerily agreed.

Linking arms, the group descended the north side of the bridge to stroll along the Arno, passing groups of other *giovani* on their evening stroll. Niccolò took Chiara on one arm and Alessandra on the other. They turned away from the stench of the fishmongers, downriver toward the Ponte Santa Trinità. As they passed the fabled spot where the ancient statue of Mars once stood, Chiara held them back.

"Nico, tell again the story of the Buondelmonti. I'm sure Alessandra wants to hear it – it's a beautiful, tragic story—and you tell it so well."

Seeing Tommaso occupied with Fiammetta, it fell to Niccolò to entertain the two girls. He began his tale, employing the pantomimes of a street performer:

"Truly it's a Greek tragedy, the beginning of all of our fine city's troubles. *C'era una volta…*once upon a time Buondelmonte Buondelmonti, a handsome, splendid knight, was betrothed to the young Signorina Reparata degli Amedei. They were both from ancient noble and wealthy families and their marriage would make peace between two powerful, rival clans. Unfortunately, as is usually the case in such arrangements, Reparata was neither so beautiful nor clever and poor Buondelmonte was not smitten."

Niccolò made a sad face as he gauged the attentiveness of his audience. Chiara smiled coquettishly while Alessandra appeared gracious; surely she had heard the famous tale many times before.

He continued: "One day, riding on his beautiful white horse, a certain Madonna Donati called out to Buondelmonte and enticed him into her house to gaze upon her daughter. The signorina was a rare, ravishing beauty with magic in her eyes and Buondelmonte was stricken—he fell in love immediately and not long afterwards they married.

"But the Amidei and their kinsmen, the Uberti, were scandalized by this disgrace upon their family honor. They swore revenge and on Easter Day in the year of Our Lord 1215 waited for the gallant Buondelmonte to ride across the Ponte Vecchio dressed all in white on his white palfrey on his way to the Cathedral. Right there," he pointed to the spot, "at the foot of the statue of Mars is where they dragged him from his horse and stabbed him repeatedly."

He pantomimed the horror that registered on the girls' faces.

"The people of Florence were shocked, indignant over this dreadful crime and soon the whole city was in an uproar, divided between the Buondelmonti and the Uberti. The opposing factions then allied with the Guelph and Ghibelline factions that divided all Italia between those who favor the pope and those who favor the Emperor. And we Florentines have been so divided ever since."

"What ever happened to the young widow?" Alessandra asked.

Niccolò suddenly felt irritated. Though he had absolutely no idea, he said, "Why, she mourned her gallant young husband until the day of her death."

"*Bravo! Che romantica!*" cheered Chiara as she gripped Niccolò closer. Alessandra smiled simply.

"*Bravo?*" Tommaso retorted. "I guess any butchery is okay as long as there's a little romance behind it, eh?"

"Women are children, *amico*, only more foolish," said Niccolò. He just blurted it out without thinking, too late to take back. The girls looked confused and he covered himself with a smile, pretending it was just another jest. But he saw the cool reproach in Chiara's eyes.

CHAPTER 10

DREAM VISIONS

IN HIS DORMITORY CELL FRA Girolamo bent over his desk, poring over the Bible and feverishly taking notes as the shape of his sermon took form in his mind. It was several hours past Compline after all the brothers had retired for the evening. He had not eaten at all today and had only slept in short fits for the past several nights. There was never enough time. A knock on the outer door interrupted his thoughts and he went to open the door.

There stood Domenico and Silvestro, barefoot in their night tunics. "Come in," he said, "I am preparing my sermon."

Domenico shook his head with regret. "Father, we're sorry to disturb you—"

"No, come in, come in. Perhaps it's time for a short respite from my labors."

Domenico said, "I was sleeping when Brother Silvestro came to me. He was disturbed in his sleep and told me of a dream. I don't know, I thought perhaps you would want to hear of it."

"Yes, please." Fra Girolamo motioned for them to sit on his slatted bed, the only other piece of furniture other than his desk. The two monks sat down, looking like children in the presence of their father. "Tell me, Brother Silvestro."

Silvestro began hesitantly, glancing back and forth between Domenico and the prior.

"Fra Girolamo, I was sleeping peacefully when I was possessed by a strong vision. It was full of light ... and there were angels. I was still dreaming but ...I'm not sure. The angels were floating in the air and then they came down to earth. And you Prior were there with me, and Brother Domenico too. The three of us were kneeling in prayer when the angels came."

Silvestro's eyes glanced between Fra Girolamo and Domenico and then stared down at the floor to hide the twitching of his left eye.

"Prior, they were carrying a long chain of gold they bound around us. They wrapped it so we would be bound together, the three of us together. And they were singing. I can hear them still, clearly, singing *ecce quam bonum et quam iocundum habitare fraters in unum.*[2] When they finished singing they told us we should remain united together and make one heart and one spirit of our three. They said God wanted it thus, and we should remain united, because revelations themselves do not provide salvation, but instead are given for the good of the Church."

Silvestro looked up expectedly, but the prior had closed his eyes in a state of prayer. When he opened his eyes, he looked at the two and said, "Brothers, let us kneel together and pray."

They knelt together on the hard floor and recited the Lord's Prayer. When they finished the prior spoke: "Brothers, the ultimate happiness is seeing God fully and completely. Since I was a boy I have been visited with visions at night. I told no one but I heeded the voice of God as He spoke to me through these visions. So it seems you too, Silvestro, are blessed with visions."

When Silvestro beamed the prior warned, "But the world will not accept these signs from heaven. If you tell people of your visions they will say you are *pazzo*. Or worse, you're possessed by evil."

Silvestro's eyes jerked independently as he cried: "Fra Malatesta says it's a blasphemy, those who have visions are possessed by the devil. Their bodies must burn to save their souls. I'm not possessed by the devil, am I, Father?"

"*Calme, calme*, Silvestro. No, I am sure you are not possessed. Pay no mind to Malatesta. God bestows divine revelation by flashing things on the mind, through visions; and also through the intermediation of angels. I'm sure this is why you have been delivered this message by a band of angels. We know Bernard of Clairvaux had visions and also Hildegard of Bingen and the Church has recognized both as saints. We can know a thing by signs or visions. I have never revealed my visions, the ones I have had for many years, because I feared men were not ready. But some months ago the voice came again, scolding me for not following God's will to announce these things."

"But I'm afraid," moaned Silvestro, putting his hands over his eyes. "If people discover I have visions I'll be renounced as a *fraticello* and a heretic."

"Yes," added Domenico, "the Church has condemned those prophecies of Joachim of Flora and many of the *fraticelli* secretly adhere to his prophecies."

Fra Girolamo noticed Domenico's words only increased Silvestro's anxiety. "What is it?" he asked.

Silvestro looked again at Domenico and hesitated, then spoke in a whisper. "Many of our own brethren read the forbidden prophecies of Joachim. There is talk the time has come. They are indiscreet."

Concerned, Fra Girolamo sought to calm them. "My brothers, we should be careful, but we must also heed and obey the word God sends in His own way. Remember the shame of the apostles when they succumbed to their fears. We must not succumb and ignore God's commands. Do not speak of these things. Discourage idle talk in the convent. We must not risk an attack from our enemies. We will reveal the prophecies when the time is right. Now, let us pray together before we retire."

The two priests bowed their heads again as the prior led them with the *Ave Maria.*

After they left Fra Girolamo returned to his desk and wondered if Silvestro's dreams were another sign sent by the Almighty. Surely it must be so. Perhaps the three of them were meant to fulfill their mission together. The friar needed trustworthy companions and God had provided his disciples. But he also had many enemies, even here in the convent. He must be careful and watch for betrayal and also watch after Domenico and Silvestro—they were not clever in the ways of the Devil.

He looked up at the crucifix, closed his eyes and bowed his head as he prayed for guidance.

CHAPTER 11

ALMS FOR SAN MARCO

THE NEXT DAY IN THE Chapter House Fra Girolamo studied Fra Malatesta to take his measure of the man. Malatesta was older, a longstanding member of the convent from an old Florentine family. Though he shared his Prior's antipathy for the ruling families of Florence, Malatesta's hatred was rabid and his disdain more overt. He strongly expressed his disapproval of Fra Girolamo's tolerance of the comforts and earthly attitudes of the younger, richer friars and novices and had come once again to complain about the lax enforcement of the new rules. But Fra Girolamo was unwilling to create unnecessary conflict among his brethren and counseled Malatesta to be patient; the others will come around by example. In truth, Fra Girolamo suspected Malatesta resented that a younger man—a non-Florentine—had been elevated to Prior of San Marco.

Malatesta, visibly irritated, stared back at his superior when they were interrupted by a knock on the door. It was Silvestro and Domenico, whispering in the forced habit within the convent. Silvestro was flushed while Domenico struggled with a heavy purse as they entered.

"Prior, it's a miracle!" whispered Silvestro.

Fra Girolamo looked at Silvestro and then to Domenico in momentary confusion, before Domenico cut Silvestro off with a sharp look.

"Prior, forgive us for interrupting you, but Brother Silvestro and I were just clearing the collection boxes and we discovered many gold florins deposited there. It must have been after this morning's Mass. We have brought them here."

Fra Girolamo looked into the purse and then hauled it over to the secretary's desk. He poured out its contents. Among the many *quattrini* and *scudi* flowed a glittering wave of gold florins. There must have been several hundred there, an enormous treasure that could easily feed the convent for more than a year. The brothers stood dumbfounded before this mountain of gold, looking to the prior to explain such a magnificent and strange occurrence. Fra Girolamo narrowed his eyes in thought.

Silvestro's left eye danced in excitement as he exclaimed, "Perhaps God has seen to make us such a magnificent contribution to ease the burdens of the Fra Girolamo's good works and help pay for the retreat at Monte Cano."

Domenico hushed him "I doubt very much God saw to deposit these gold florins in the alms box—"

Fra Girolamo held up his hand to silence them. "No, I suspect not. Who in Florence could have deposited such a fortune?"

Malatesta was quick to reply. "Only one of the *grandi*: Strozzi or Medici? Or maybe one of the older families, Alberti or Spini—"

Silvestro added eagerly, "But then it could also be a miracle, no?"

"Before we proclaim miracles we should consider more logical explanations. Why would any of the *grandi* make such a contribution anonymously? They rarely commit any small deed of charity without trumpeting it all over the city, and most recently they have responded to our needs with closed fists. This gold must come from a more obvious source and the reason subtler."

Fra Girolamo was beginning to understand. He knew exactly what this game was about as he led them on with his questions: "Who is the most obvious benefactor of the convent?"

"The Medici?" said Domenico.

"Yes. And why would Lorenzo de' Medici make such a contribution anonymously?"

Silvestro was eager to participate in this game. He cried, "But Lorenzo cannot be pleased. The Medici have been frequenting the Church of Santo Spirito for services."

"Yes," said Fra Girolamo, "because they seek to support that buffoon, Fra Mariano, who attacks me, yet fails miserably. So, the tyrant's next strategy is to make a grand contribution to buy favor for his position. I'm sure this is the carrot to tempt the mule who does not respond to the stick."

"But Fra Girolamo, perhaps he made this contribution out of guilt? As an attempt to support our efforts to pay for the new retreat at Monte Cano?" asked Domenico.

Fra Malatesta challenged this. "Then why not come forward in an honest manner and make a contribution for this cause? The Medici have false intentions."

Fra Girolamo felt the power of righteous anger possess him. "Yes, they have resisted my efforts to reorganize the chapter and establish the retreat outside the city. Signor Lorenzo is clever and knows men can be corrupted with bribes and personal comforts. He expects no less in his dealings with priests. In gratitude, he expects us all to do his bidding."

Domenico spoke up. "What shall we do with this gold?"

Fra Girolamo hesitated and felt Fra Malatesta's hot stare. He was being tested and he knew what he must do. He would shine God's light on the tyrant's hidden schemes.

"I will send this worldly prince a message that his money buys no favors in God's eyes. We shall not accept these funds. Instead we shall donate the gold in full to the Good Men of San Martino for distribution to the shameful poor and they shall know from where this fortune comes. And why. Then we shall see what the tyrant will do."

The three friars watched silently as Fra Girolamo swelled with indignation. His black eyes flashed and he no longer seemed to be rooted in their presence but floating in space. He was in the pulpit now, looking down upon the heads of his army of the faithful. He incited their reaction by his righteous fury and waved his arm in a flurry as his voice boomed:

"Yes, you know this is the way of tyrants! But I tell you now: The good watchdog when a thief throws him a bone or piece of meat puts it off to one side and goes on barking."

CHAPTER 12

LORENZO AT SAN MARCO

LORENZO GATHERED HIS FUR-TRIMMED LUCCO close as the afternoon sun retreated below the convent walls, lowering the temperature in the shade of the porticos. Late blooming flowers at summer's end still decorated the center garden while refracted light off the red-tiled roof and faded yellow walls of the cloister offset the chill. Despite the peaceful surroundings, he was irritable.

With his long dark hair and prominent profile, Lorenzo was easily recognized by the friars scurrying in and out of the cloister in noiseless groups of twos and threes, their hoods pulled up to signify their vows of silence. Yet he was ignored. This was the third Sunday he had spent wandering the cloisters and gardens of San Marco and all the monks were surely aware of his presence. In passing, those with heads exposed made sure to bow and reverently murmur *"Buona sera, Signore."*

Lorenzo felt a personal satisfaction as he surveyed the convent; its church and bell tower created an appealing composition of lines and form carefully conceived by his grandfather's favorite architect, Michelozzo. He looked up to see the ubiquitous Medici coat-of-arms, the shield emblazoned with the seven balls or *palle*, displayed at the corners of the bell tower. His grandfather Cosimo had paid out a large fortune almost a half century ago to design and rebuild the convent. Supposedly, Pope Eugenio had ordered Cosimo to the task as penance for his misdeeds, but if so, he had paid more than four times the ten thousand florins stipulated by the pope. This at a time when the Medici Palace on Via Larga had cost a mere five thousand florins. The Church had surely received a generous redressing of the balance of the Medici fortune.

His grandfather had reserved a cell here in his later years to meditate and pray between his frequent clashes with the Bishop of Florence, the first Prior of San Marco, Fra Antonino. As a boy Lorenzo had heard many amusing stories of the feisty little prior who butted heads with his grandfather, but was much loved in Florence. It was ironic he mused: Troublesome priors seem to be a family tradition.

Lorenzo paused to gaze at the large fresco decorating one corner of the cloister. Feeling weary in his legs, he sat on the low wall that ringed the inside of the cloister and regarded the fresco. This was Fra Angelico's *Christ on the Cross Adored by St. Dominic* and Lorenzo felt the mystical aura and artistic tension radiate from the painting. Again it was Cosimo to thank for commissioning these sublime frescoes and paneled paintings by Fra Angelico. The Medici were the grand patrons of San Marco and Lorenzo's contribution was the organized school of sculpture in the nearby gardens. He was anxious to test the capabilities of his protégées, especially the young Michelangelo, who he was sure would far surpass his master Bertoldo.

More important, Lorenzo hoped his support of the convent would insure a revival of religious devotion and creativity at San Marco that would reflect well on the legacy of its benefactor. The Church was the dominant institution in the Christian world and was the only counterweight to the growing strength of France and Spain, so the survival of the small city-states in Italia depended on a strong alliance. Lorenzo's sons Giovanni and Piero were his best hope to solidify the combined strength of Rome and Florence.

Lorenzo smiled at the thought of Giovanni, a clever imp who always outwitted his brothers. Lorenzo's sons were his legacy and he thought how different they were from each other. He often told his friends of the three Piero was foolish, Giovanni clever, and young Giuliano good. But Piero would need to overcome his foolish arrogance and this was the foremost of Lorenzo's worries. On the other hand, Giovanni would need all the careful planning and preparation Lorenzo could muster to insure his ascension through the Church hierarchy. Rome was a sinkhole filled with sly, greedy serpents disguised in robes and miters—to survive one needed to be more than clever, one needed to be blessed by good fortune. The revival of San Marco was an essential element of Lorenzo's master plan.

But he was beginning to have second thoughts about this *frate*. The famed preacher from Ferrara had forged a reputation throughout the northern cities and become a beacon for religious reform in Italia. In this role he could rise high within the estimation of the Church and its followers. So Lorenzo had trusted Pico's recommendation to have the friar reassigned to San Marco. But the purpose was to revive San Marco, not overthrow the existing political order. Now this annoying little priest had decided to preach the Apocalypse and divide society against itself. So easily did power intoxicate men and cause them to overreach.

Even he, Lorenzo, was guilty of such folly when, as a young man, he had invited the hatred that almost killed him and did kill his beloved brother, Giuliano. Giuliano had warned him of the vicious envy that lay in wait for the man who displayed his pride too openly. But Lorenzo had not heeded and now beautiful Giuliano was dead. He fought against the pain of those memories—how the conspirators, in league with the pope, had attacked him with knives and murdered his dear brother during the sacred Mass in the Cathedral. The venom of revenge had turned him into a wild beast. They had hunted down the Pazzi conspirators, every one of them—even that bastard Bandini, who the Sultan had returned from Constantinople. They had all paid dearly with their lives, but retribution had failed to assuage his pain as much as he hoped—especially since the wretched pope had escaped behind his purple robes and then had the audacity to excommunicate *him*.

The ensuing wars against the papal States and its allies had greatly weakened Florence and damaged the reputation of the religious vocation within the city's territories. In those years San Marco had declined terribly. Fortunately, popes are old and soon die and then the next pope is usually the enemy of the previous and all positions are reversed as the wheel of fortune turns. How fleeting were life's fortunes and misfortunes: Now his daughter was married to the new pope's son and Giovanni was a cardinal, the youngest ever. So, slowly, we rebuild our position and focus on the future. *Le temps revient.*

The sun sank lower and Lorenzo knew the hour of Compline was fast approaching when all the friars would retreat to the chapel for final services before retiring. He wondered where the prior was. He had already visited the large refectory and the Pilgrim's Hospice and circled the cloister, admiring the frescoes and trying to calm himself in the peaceful atmosphere. He had occasionally glanced up toward the window of the prior's cell in the second story dormitory and thought he caught a figure standing in the recess of the window but could not be sure. The pigheaded Prior must be sequestered in his cell, even though his patron's presence had surely been announced.

Why, Lorenzo wondered, was this priest so obstinate? Pico and Ficino reassured him Fra Girolamo was a pious man whose sincerity had greatly increased the esteem and popularity of the convent. Soon the convent would attract novitiates from the most powerful and wealthy families and San Marco would become a greater force for Florence within the Church. Lorenzo did not want to clash with the priest, he only wished to associate the success of the convent with Medici patronage to benefit Giovanni among the cardinals in Rome. Did this *frate* not know where his future lay? Didn't he understand he, Lorenzo, was a most benevolent patron? *Instead he chooses to rebuff my every effort at graciousness and refuses to express any gesture of gratitude for my patronage.* They were headed for confrontation, one the friar could not possibly win; but it was a confrontation Lorenzo wished to avoid.

At that moment one of his bodyguards poked his head through the main portico and Lorenzo cursed to himself; it was time to go. Angrily tossing his lucco over his shoulder, he stood up against the chill and swore. Then he heard the soft shuffle of friars as they descended from the dormitory and flocked like so many crows toward the chapel. It was obvious to all why he was here and, as he caught their furtive glances, he sensed their rising discomfort.

LORENZO DE' MEDICI 1452-1494

CHAPTER 13

PICO AND FICINO VISIT SAN MARCO

FRA GIROLAMO ENTERED THE LIBRARY'S scriptorium unnoticed. He moved quietly past the scribes and miniaturists, stopping behind a novice struggling to copy an illuminated manuscript. The boy's shaven tonsure glistened as he worked the small brush on the parchment, glancing back and forth, trying to focus and compare his efforts with the original. The prior marveled at the vibrancy of the colors, satisfied to see those in the copy were close to true. A large red initial "S" flowed with elaborate flower motifs that accentuated the curves and framed the letter in contrasting colors. But the novice appeared to be struggling to duplicate the small faces of the tiny figures contained in the lower portion of the "S." One needed a brush no thicker than a dog's hair to make such a perfect rendering. The painter halted, his concentration broken as he sensed a presence hovering over his shoulder.

"*Bravo*, my son, the flow of the letter and the brilliance of your colors are true to the original."

Startled by the voice, the novice turned to find himself staring into the dark eyes of the prior. He flustered and lowered his gaze. "Prior, you are too gracious. As you see, I cannot manage the delicate expressions on the small figures of the innocents like the original master executed so perfectly."

Fra Girolamo rested his hand on the boy's shoulder. "You must have patience. They say Rome was not built in a day. The master who painted this original *Massacre of the Innocents* was a Camaldoli from the famous *Scuola degli Angeli*. He spent many years on his craft, so you must have the perseverance of Job. Keep faith and you shall surpass your highest hopes."

The old librarian came up and whispered something close to the prior's ear. He nodded and then smiled at the young apprentice. "Faith and patience, my son. Do not lose faith."

Fra Girolamo traversed the long library colonnade and approached two well-dressed men standing at the wooden lecterns, where they were engrossed in several opened manuscripts. He welcomed these guests who came often to make use of the library's vast collection. Count Giovanni Pico and Maestro Marsilio Ficino were the most esteemed of the city's scholars and together they had formed a formidable intellectual partnership to investigate a new synthesis of theology and philosophy.

Fra Girolamo relished the opportunity to sharpen his spiritual message on their philosopher's stone. Looking up as he approached, the two men readily assented to his invitation to join him in the closed room at the end of the library, the one called the Greek Room.

Pico respectfully gestured for Fra Girolamo to sit before taking his own seat. He said, "Father, today we have been investigating the texts of Augustine and Aquinas on the question of the supremacy of will versus intellect. As a man of intellect and reason, *I* take the side of Aquinas and Aristotle while the learned maestro prefers the position of Augustine and Plato."

Ficino grunted, causing Fra Girolamo to smile at their verbal jousting. As the most learned philosopher in Florence, translator of Plato, and leader of the Platonic Academy, Maestro Ficino could hardly be painted in opposition to intellect and reason. But this was just Pico's precocious way of baiting his older colleague. Ficino was a small man, nearing sixty years but still lively, with an unruly mop of curled blond hair atop his head. He had originally been trained in medicine as the son of Cosimo de' Medici's court physician, but his intellectual promise had caused Cosimo to provide for his subsequent training in philosophy and Greek. Fra Girolamo thought it more laudable that Maestro Ficino had chosen to take his vows as an ordained priest almost twenty years ago.

"I fear my position would not likely satisfy either of you, as I would caution that both will and intellect are subject to faith. And I would imagine I am on the side of *both* Aquinas and Augustine, which is sure to confuse the question."

Ficino, fingering the polished amulet hanging from his necklace, replied, "Yes, all things are known through God. And God is the perfect ideal for which men must strive. The wise man is one who seeks union with God. This is the Platonic ideal that Augustine also praises. Thus, the will of man, as conceived in the will of God, supersedes the intellect."

"But the concept of the ideal can only be available to man through the senses," Pico rejoined. "And Aristotle rightly argues man's knowledge is always limited because of the limits of his experience—"

"And thus man must submit to faith," Fra Girolamo interrupted. "We cannot know all things, so we must follow doctrinal teachings and practices based on faith in God and His word. The Angelic Doctor extended the thinking of Saint Augustine on this and shows us reason is employed as an aid to faith."

Ficino protested, "But *all* knowledge is based first on the *idea*. For example, first is the idea of love and charity and then there is the experience of these ideas through giving. All intellect thus derives from the will—the will of God in man."

"I don't disagree," said Pico, quick to respond. "The *idea* of the *ideal* in the abstract is irrefutable, but it remains that we interpret all of the natural world through our senses and our experience. This experience enables our ability to reason and form our concepts of the ideal. Haven't we expanded our knowledge of this world through study and experiment, as has been demonstrated by Maestro Leonardo in both arts and sciences?"

Fra Girolamo sighed. This argument truly was a battle between will and intellect. Such were the follies of men. He challenged them again. "And what *is* knowledge of this world, my friends? For what purpose, if not for union with the divine? Your Aristotle does not even succeed in proving the immortality of the soul; he's uncertain upon so many points, that I truly fail to comprehend why you should waste so much labor on his writings.

"And Thomas, like your Aristotle, writes we can bear witness only to what we have experienced. All our knowledge proceeds from sensations and it is our understanding of ideals that helps us to translate sensations into ideas via intellect. Thus I would agree with Thomas that intellect is primary over will, as we can control our will by intellect. But placing ideas in proper relation to sensations is the difficulty we face. You hope to achieve this with philosophy and reason, but I tell you Love of God and the pure vision of the Deity is attained through faith alone."

Fra Girolamo's tone took on a condescending air as he continued. "It's these philosophers and Sophists who tickle men's ears with Aristotle and Plato, Virgil and Petrarca, but take no concern for the salvation of souls. Why, instead of expounding so many books, do they not expound the *one* Book which contains the law and the spirit of life?"

Ficino looked pained. "Truly, Father, as Thomas has written, reason is an aid to faith. So we may study the ancients in order to find the one true path to God."

"Yes, but I see many who stumble after reason, falling down a false path to become lost in the labyrinth of sophistry. For many years I've been a teacher like you Father Marsilio, but my students are not so gifted and remarkable as the Count here." He gestured toward the smiling Pico and continued.

"My novices ask about good and evil and the unseen presence of God. They struggle against the seeds of doubt planted by challenges to their faith. You, my friends, have the gift of intelligence and vast learning. And you employ astrology and pagan mythology and the mysteries of the Hebrew and infidel texts in your search for knowledge. I cannot know why. Perhaps your faith holds you true, but the poor and the ignorant are easily misled. Pagan philosophies and the worship of pagan deities only confuse the simple-minded."

Looking directly at Ficino, he added, "You know this to be so. Walk through the streets and hear the fortune-tellers and soothsayers, who, with their cards and dice and other devices pretend to foresee the future, feeding upon the fears and superstitions of the simple-minded. Thus, true Christian faith is corrupted by witchery and the devilish arts. In the manual arts, the preoccupation with pagan allegories has allowed the profane to displace the sacred in painting and sculpture."

Fra Girolamo paused. Excusing himself, he went to the door and gestured to the librarian. He whispered something in the old man's ear and the librarian quickly disappeared.

When he returned he saw in his guests' eyes that his words had found their mark. His admonitions were meant as a direct criticism of them both: of Ficino for his practices of divining the movements of the stars and planets and the use of potions and amulets to investigate the mysteries of the unknown; and of Pico for his synthesis of Hebrew, Muslim, and Eastern mystical writings toward an understanding of the one God. He knew the two were silent because as an ordained priest, Ficino was unable to defend his fascination with the occult; and because Pico knew his initial flirtation with the Cabbala and the Church's reaction to the publication of his nine hundred propositions on matters of Christian faith had almost branded him a heretic. Only his own support and Lorenzo's influence had stopped the pope's proceedings.

Fra Girolamo remained standing as he continued his rebuke. "Augustine praised your Plato, but only because the philosopher was opposed to drama and poetry and the cult of pagan gods. But in Florence you have embraced these even though the Saint has argued such practices brought down the great empire of the Caesars."

He watched Ficino shift uncomfortably and cough deep in his throat. The old philosopher was not used to being lectured to, but Fra Girolamo would not be deterred.

"Augustine argued that earthly life is filled with frustration, fear and restlessness—it is an earthly prison. Demonstrations of power and the desire for earthly goods are manifestations of the will to overcome the frustrations of this life. But the pagan gods were powerless to help men overcome deprivation or to find peace and happiness. Reason and the desire to know things cannot fill the emptiness. More dangerous are those who would use power and desire to keep men in that state of fear and restlessness, merely for their own purposes—"

There was a knock on the door as the librarian returned with a large bound volume. Fra Girolamo took the book, bringing it to the reader's lectern in the room to search for a passage. With an air of satisfaction he looked up.

"Yes, here is the reading brought to mind by this discussion. I will read it to you. It is from *Civitas Deus:*

> But the worshippers and admirers of pagan gods delight in imitating their scandalous iniquities, and are nowise concerned that the Republic be less depraved and licentious. Only let it remain undefeated, they say, only let it flourish and abound in resources; let it be glorious by its victories, or still better, secure in peace. What does it matter to us? This is our only concern: that every man be able to increase his wealth so as to supply his daily prodigalities, so that the powerful may subject the weak for their own purposes. Let the poor court the rich for a living, so that under their protection they may enjoy a sluggish tranquility; and let the rich abuse the poor as their dependents, to minister to their pride. Let the people applaud not those who protect their interests, but those who provide them with pleasure.

The prior looked up from the book into their eyes. "It could not be more clear. Has Rome changed yet? And this final sentence I read to you speaks directly to my own experience:

> If such happiness is distasteful to any, let him be branded as a public enemy; and if any attempt to modify or put an end to it, let him be silenced, banished, to put an end to it.[3]

He closed the book with a gesture of finality. "My friends, love of God is the guiding principle that leads man to his goal, and without need for comprehension. We cannot know God by studying Cicero and Aristotle. We can only know God by following the teachings of Jesus Christ. You, Father Marsilio, know this to be true."

Fra Girolamo picked the book up to return it to the librarian, but he was not yet finished. "I know the new ideas, I see and hear them on the streets: how man celebrates the glory of God through his own perfection and that God is in man. And I see how this gives license to interpret God each in his own way. But man is always and everywhere imperfect and it is only through God's grace and love we can find salvation. We must embrace the humility of our own failings because I tell you, *God is not in man, but rather man is in God.*"

***

After Fra Girolamo politely excused himself and exited the library, the two philosophers became preoccupied in their separate thoughts. The impressionable young Count was overcome with mixed feelings. Fra Girolamo was surely correct and Pico felt a deepening reverence for the heart and soul of the priest. But how was one to deny the Hebrew doctrine on which Christianity was based? And the ancient Greeks? And even the teachings of the prophet, Mohammed, or the teachings of the eastern mystics? Are we not all sons of Abraham? From his most careful study, Pico had recognized the commonalities in all of these different faiths and teachings. If all this came from a common impulse within man to fathom his relationship to the Almighty, then why not use the power of reason and intellect to reveal the synthesis?

And other questions still confounded him, questions that addressed the main differences between the faiths of the one God and those of many deities of the East. Was there a personal God who watched over him, to which he prayed directly? Or was God embodied in the world around him in an impersonal fashion shared by all men? Is nature the art of God? Does nature work by reason or chance, or by the will of God? These were questions he dared not ask aloud, remembering the defense he had written against the Church's charges of heresy:

> *I've never philosophized for any reason other than cultivation of the soul and knowledge of the truth. I've given my whole self over to contemplation and this has taught me to weigh things by my conscience rather than by the judgment of others. I've wished to bring into view the things taught not merely according to one doctrine, but things taught according to every sort of doctrine, that by this comparison of many sects and by the discussion of manifold philosophy, that radiance of truth that Plato mentions in his Letters might shine more clearly upon our minds.*
>
> *But certainly God has given man the power of intellect to be used to greatest advantage in understanding the Creator? Man's power of reason is a cherished gift from God to be celebrated. To rise up to heaven, not to crawl upon our bellies like a brute. A philosopher in pursuit of right reason is a heavenly animal. And the pure contemplator, banished to the innermost places of the mind, is not an earthly or even a heavenly animal; but rather a divinity clothed with human flesh.[4]*

His arguments had not been well received then, nor would they be now. The young Count was jerked back into the moment as Ficino grumbled on their way out of the convent. "*Prego?*" Pico said.

"I said, this man is blinded by the strength of one light. He looks straight into the sun and then can see nothing more than the bright light burning his eyes."

"But would you disagree with the substance of his arguments?"

asked Pico.

Ficino was even gruffer in his reply, "The friar is a scholar of impressive depth and breadth. I also believe he speaks from the heart, with great faith. But the man is unyielding and blinded by his holy mission. You know, the older I get the more I learn to temper the certainty of what I know. It was Thomas himself who said 'I fear the man of one book.' Fra Girolamo speaks of humility, but practices it less with the rigidity of his ideas."

"But how can he, if, as he claims, his words come from God?"

Ficino huffed. "He who would know God must first know himself."

CHAPTER 14

PLATO'S BIRTHDAY AT CAREGGI

THE PEREGRINE CLIMBED HIGH UP the gray November sky, folded its wings and plunged like an arrow toward its prey. There was an explosion of feathers as it collided with the small quail and the two birds fell to the ground in a death embrace. When the hunter whistled and waved the lure, the trained bird quickly abandoned its prey and returned to the gloved hand of its master. The falcon screeched and flapped its wings, causing the horses to shy nervously, while one of the beaters ran to retrieve the quail.

"*Calme, carissima,*" said Lorenzo, rewarding the bird with a piece of raw meat. He caressed its wings as the bird steadied, then slipped the leather hood over its head.

"*Bravo,*" said his hunting companion, "there will be no shortage of game tonight. We shall feast like true Greeks."

Lorenzo took in a quick breath of the brisk air. "I'm in love out here, Braccio. I feel truly alive with freedom, like one of these magnificent birds soaring through the sky. I can almost forget the pain."

Braccio regarded the hooded and tethered bird and said, "*Sì,* the vigor of the hunt, the power of the kill helps a man feel in control. The city only stagnates the blood and stifles the spirit. How are your legs holding up?"

"I think it's time to head back to the house before it gets dark." Lorenzo whistled and waved to the hunt master who blew a long blast on his horn to alert the beaters and the dog handlers the hunt was over.

The two men turned their horses as several others in the hunting party road up to join them for the ride back to the villa. Lorenzo winced as he passed the bird off to its handler.

"*Amici,*" sighed Lorenzo, "it's terrible when the body fails just when the mind is ready to soar."

Braccio watched the enthusiastic mood of the hunt visibly fade from Lorenzo's face and offered encouragement: "We'll have a fine evening tonight—good food, fine wine, enjoyable company—all the ingredients of *la dolce vita,* eh?"

Lorenzo was wistful. "I wish I were young again, without a care, a beautiful *amor* to keep me company and the poetry of springtime in my heart. Instead, I'm like one of these wizened old trees, with the passing days falling like dead leaves at my feet. And yet, why should I complain;

what could be more desirable than the enjoyment of leisure with friends? It's what all good men hope to obtain, but which great men alone accomplish."

He sighed again. "But how will Plato help me with the trying affairs of state? I worry." He let the reins slip from his grasp.

Braccio saw Lorenzo's mood shift from shade to sunlight to shade again, like the clouds drifting by in front of the sun. He understood his friend well. They had spent many years together and were just now in the prime of life, but Lorenzo, several years younger, appeared visibly weakened and melancholic. As his banking partner, Braccio guessed at some of Lorenzo's worries. The wars in the north had resulted in enormous losses; those branches had all been closed and most of the bank's business had shifted back to Florence and Rome. But now the city's wool trade was in a noticeable decline, driving down trade receipts.

This had ramifications for all Florentines, but for Lorenzo most of all. It was his fate to manage relations with other royal heads-of-state on the Italian peninsula, while partitioning up a shrinking pie among various Florentine clients. It was becoming increasingly difficult, if not impossible, to keep all discontented parties in line. Whispers on the street had become audible and the major families were anxious, as many of the poor were hungry and restless.

"*Basta*, Lorenzo, as always, we'll survive and prosper."

Lorenzo did not reply but rode on as if he had not heard. After a few moments he said, "Braccio, anyone who envies me is a fool. My life is a daily trial—in the city I am rarely left a moment's peace to myself with a daily line of clients and supplicants trailing out and down the Via Larga. My secretaries spend all their time just managing the constant flow of men at my door who need this or want that, wish to be recommended for this post or that, or have business proposals for this venture or that. On top of this I must focus on issues most men do not even comprehend—writing letters to the pope, managing this rift between Sforza and Ferrante, and sending gifts to the Venetian cardinal who opposes the ordination of Giovanni. And then worrying over the best marriage alliances for my children. And Piero... *Madonna*, it will be the death of me..."

Braccio pitied his friend. Despite the lessons against financing the ambitions of kings and popes, who were notorious for defaulting on their loans, Lorenzo had been trapped into this business by virtue of being the most prominent banker and political leader of one of the most powerful cities in Italia. He needed them and they needed him and it was sucking the life out of him. And his son Piero was off with a hunting party in the Mugello, leaving his wife Alfonsina heavy with child at the family villa in

Cafaggiuolo. Unfortunately, the boy added to rather than relieved his father's worries. Perhaps a child, a grandson for Lorenzo, would finally push Piero into manhood and force him to accept his responsibilities.

***

As day turned to night in the large drawing room of the expansive villa, the party of men settled into cushioned lounges. Candles flicked shadows around the room and a bright glass lamp burned before a large bust of Plato placed next to the lectern. The party was well-fed from the day's hunt and had idled away the evening drinking wine, reciting poetry, telling ribald jokes and stories, and discussing light philosophical fare. This retreat was for their Platonic Academy, begun years ago under the sponsorship of Cosimo and tutelage of Maestro Ficino. The Academy celebrated the rebirth of the neo-Platonic ideal, a new movement away from the hair-splitting logic of Aristotle. It was meant to be the expression of the best to which men could aspire.

The Academy met often here at the Villa Careggi, a short ride north of the city. Nearby was Ficino's small retreat at Montevecchio Cosimo had bestowed on him for his studies. Tonight, the annual celebration of Plato's birthday was limited to a congenial group of nine scholars chosen from among Lorenzo's closest friends.

The festivities had begun with Lorenzo offering a new poem, a verse filled with melancholy. This caused the revelers to groan before Poliziano cheered them with light, witty verses about nature and the Tuscan countryside. Then Cristoforo Landino, the eldest member, guided the discussion into the opposing merits of the contemplative versus the active life. The philosophers naturally extolled pure contemplation over the baneful necessities of social intercourse. But Lorenzo, though he too longed for the peace of quiet contemplation, argued for men in the prime of life to be active in civic affairs. If the most highly trained thinkers did not lead the Republic, he said, they would all suffer as those less talented and high-minded filled the void.

As the midnight hour approached the scholars prepared for their traditional reading of Plato's *Symposium*. As the wine took effect, Ficino stood at the lectern dressed in a Greek toga with a crown of vines playfully set upon his unruly curls. He projected an air of solemnity as he started to read the opening lines to celebrate the birth of Plato, the Academy's patron 'saint.' This was the famous dialogue led by Socrates on the question of love and by tradition each member would rise to take turns reading the different passages. Lorenzo leaned back, easing his swollen legs and closing his eyes to relax and reflect.

He never tired of this annual ritual; the dialogue evoked the true measure of man. It was a contemplation of beauty, love, justice and the divine soul. Socrates argued that the essence of love is uncertainty and process, a constant change on life's journey to divine immortality.

Lorenzo could trace this ascending journey through his own life as it had passed through its various stages. It had begun with youthful lust. He, Braccio, Bernardo, his handsome younger brother Giuliano, had all been rascals, spending their youthful nights in pursuit of earthly desire. Lorenzo had been particularly insatiable. But lust soon gave way to a more sublime expression of love through poetry and grace. With a seriousness more befitting their dignity and sense of honor, they soon turned to composing odes, stanzas, and *canzoni* to the praise of natural and heavenly beauty. Their object was still the same, but by means more delicate and romantic. This was the time when Angelo Poliziano had joined their circle and Lorenzo heard his voice as he took over the verse.

Angelo had arrived in Florence as a youth with an ear for the finest melody and word cadence, combined with a sensuality of emotion. Young Angelo had soon developed a possessive devotion to Lorenzo that had even angered his wife Clarice, God rest her soul. Though Angelo's bark displayed a biting wit and caustic temper, his sublime poetry was renowned all through Italia and his reputation unsurpassed. The two often matched verse to verse, spurring each other on as their poetic counterpoints achieved a measure of notoriety.

But then the Pazzi had attacked, ending that beautiful, carefree life of youth.

Angelo finished his section and Pico rose to read the continuation. He recited the speech of Agathon describing the qualities of beauty possessed by Eros, the most beautiful of the gods, immediately bringing to mind how Pico was the most beautiful of them all.

Lorenzo envied Pico, not for his beauty and youth, but because as a mere boy he had already discovered beauty in the pursuit of true wisdom. He was a shooting star in the heavens of philosophy. As a youth himself, Lorenzo had failed to appreciate the wisdom of his teachers. He had not been ready then, but later, in his thirties after his youthful innocence had died with his brother, Lorenzo discovered a new love: one of justice, courage, temperance, and wisdom itself.

This Roman love served him well in executing his duties as first citizen in the city. After his ruthless revenge on the Pazzi, the ensuing war with Pope Sixtus had exacted a high price on all of Italia and the fierce anger Lorenzo had felt toward his enemies had clouded his vision. Temperance and wisdom had been required to return the city to peace and prosperity; a strong and just philosopher-king was needed to govern the city and prevent the weed of envy from strangling them all.

Now in middle age, Lorenzo was regenerated by a new vigor of the mind. The discovery of love through contemplation had opened a new purpose and gave him inner peace, despite his growing infirmities. This fourth and final stage of the journey was Socrates' ascent to the limits of the mystic vision and Plato, through 'Father' Ficino, would be his guide.

Lorenzo focused his thoughts on this ultimate truth: To know love is to know *God*.

It was Plato's theory of divine love in a universe created according to its rightful order, with the Creator at its pinnacle. The soul ascends on the wings of contemplation in pursuit of truth, to attain the perfect knowledge of God. God is a part of true love and friendship, and true love and friendship is always mutual. Thus, love is the glue that binds all living things together, with the immortal soul at its center. This was the true purpose of the Academy—to facilitate the ascent to a perfect knowledge of God through love, within a community of true friends.

In his darkness moments, Lorenzo knew that to know God was still a fearful prospect, full of uncertainty.

The last reader, the poet Domenico Benivieni, was concluding the *Symposium* when Lorenzo opened his eyes and they all applauded in appreciation. The clapping was also a signal to the housekeeper to enter and refill the wine flasks, as the gathering was sure to linger into the early morning hours.

"*Bravo, bravo!* Brothers, let us toast this evening of pure felicity among friends," Lorenzo exclaimed, raising his goblet. "I never cease to be moved by the recitation of the Dialogues." He nodded toward Ficino. "We are truly blessed by our 'Father' Marsilio for his life's work translating these writings of the great philosopher for the benefit of all in the modern world."

Ficino shook his head in denial. "Only the good graces of Cosimo, you, and your entire family have afforded me the opportunity of such single-minded devotion, without which nothing would have been possible."

"Here, here! To *Il Magnifico*! Long live the Medici and the Republic of Florence!" cheered Braccio and the others joined in.

By force of habit Lorenzo feigned humility. "You embarrass me. I'm just another humble citizen, born of fortunate circumstance. Our city's fortunes are more a reflection of all those who devote themselves everyday to managing its affairs."

"Without your subtle and wise guidance, it would quickly descend into anarchy," said his brother-in-law, Bernardo Rucellai.

Poliziano added: "Yes, and as in *The Republic*, the city functions with justice when all fulfill their appointed duties under the wise guidance of the philosopher-kings, which, of course, are…" He opened his arms in a gesture to embrace all and then smiled conspiratorially toward Lorenzo, who gave a look of disapproval softened by indulgence.

"Enough of your wit," he said. "If the *popolo* get wind of such nonsense, we'll all be chased into exile, or worse!"

Rucellai was quick to respond. "It's that sniveling prior at San Marco. More and more flock to the Cathedral to hear him preach. I think the large crowds and his growing popularity encourage him. He grows bolder and shows no respect for the established order."

Lorenzo got a wicked gleam in his eye that was the hallmark of his youth. "It seems we lesser mortals are unable to protect ourselves from these priests," he said seriously. "And no wonder, considering the long cassocks they wear."

He grinned as the others leaned in for the punch line. "You know, when you're not facing them they can kick you in the ass without your seeing them. And when you're turned toward them they kick you in the balls before you can see their leg move!"

As the laughter receded, Lorenzo grew serious again. "I don't really understand this Ferrarese, a clever fox who seems determined to force my hand. From the pulpit he's made a laughingstock of Fra Mariano, who as a result seems to have lost his pleasing disposition. And just last week I learned the prior contributed the three hundred gold florins I had deposited in his alms box to the Good Men of San Martino, to be distributed to the shameful poor. Then the snake announced this from the pulpit, giving the impression I was trying to buy his silence. I've deliberately visited the convent so he might graciously acknowledge my patronage. Instead I'm ignored like an unwanted relative!"

Poliziano added his own venom: "He's truly *Genus irritabile vatum*."

Lorenzo slammed his hand down on the arm of his chair in a rare outburst. "You see! A stranger has come into *my house,* yet he'll not stoop to pay me a visit or even receive me! I'm losing patience with this damn priest!"

Pico approached Lorenzo and put a hand on his arm. "Lorenzo, I'm filled with regret. I'm responsible for burdening you with these worries. But do not become vexed with Fra Girolamo. I don't feel his intentions are against you. His message is foremost a religious one and he is most concerned with the saving of souls. Marsilio can attest to our conversations, and both Domenico and Giovanni have also frequented San Marco."

The two poets Domenico Benivieni and Giovanni Nesi nodded their heads in agreement. Ficino looked at Rucellai and said, "The religious element is an important ingredient in maintaining social order. Naturally, our Greek philosophers are pre-Christian, but both Plato and Aristotle voiced a clear concept of the divine and recognized the importance of religious belief to the stability of the Republic."

Lorenzo regained his calm. He knew how the corruption of the Church was causing a breakdown in the traditional institutions of order. To the poor, many of the priests and monks were suspect and the rich *popolani* displayed a complete disregard for the substance of Christian teaching. Religious faith had been reduced to the cynical notion of purchasing indulgences toward the end of one's debauched life. He knew that without the moral guidelines of the Church it would be impossible to control the natural passions of men, but the Church had become a business and a dirty business at that. This friar was right in that respect.

On the other hand, reform of such a powerful and essential institution required a delicate touch. There was a crucial difference between gradual change and outright revolution and Lorenzo had witnessed complete breakdown in the social order often enough to fear its consequences. He wasn't sure Savonarola appreciated these distinctions and the reports he had of the prior's methods suggested not. If only he could measure the man in person and dispel his false impressions, but the stubborn mule seemed to resist every overture—as if convinced his moral message will only hold weight through his defiance of the reigning symbol of power. *Fine, then, but why not make contact out of the public eye?*

He must resolve this matter of the prior soon, as civic disorder and instability would be disastrous for the city and likewise for his House.

"Brothers, excuse me while I retire for a moment," Lorenzo said, rising with effort. The older but spry Ficino jumped to assist him.

Lorenzo chuckled, as Ficino supported him on his way to the privy. "Marsilio, who would guess you had doctored me since I was a young child and still you surpass me in good health. I must take time to read your *Three Books of Life* before it's too late."

With Lorenzo gone, the others fell into silence. The discussion of Savonarola raised tensions between the aristocrats and the poet-philosophers. Rucellai was first to broach the subject.

"You tempt fate with this preacher. We've had enough experience in Florence with these *fraticelli*. Perhaps Savonarola is no *fraticello*, but the people react to his message the same way. Soon there'll be mass riots with the *popolo* screaming 'Death to the tyrants!' And who do you think are these 'tyrants?'" He spread his arms to take in the plush surroundings.

"Yes, all who enjoy such splendid living as this."

"Bernardo," said Benivieni, "you overreact to street gossip. Fra Girolamo is a man of most refined learning and piety."

Rucellai retorted, "You think it's just a matter of one religious-minded friar. Who do you think wants to see the present order overthrown, the Weepers in the Duomo? No, it's the *magnati*, the magnate families like the Acciaiuoli, Spini, Davanzati, who will whip up the people by using this unwitting preacher and his apocalyptic message. Fear is power, my friends, for those who know how to use it. You forget they've been kept out of power for more than a hundred years, but they haven't forgotten; they know who runs the city and keeps their taxes high. They lie in wait."

It was difficult for poets and philosophers to comprehend or empathize with the interests of wealthy merchants and bankers. Giovanni Nesi dismissed Rucellai's concerns: "I have no doubt the Signoria can resist any threats from the *magnati*, ...or from elsewhere as well. And it might be time for all in Florence to think again about the salvation of their immortal souls."

Rucellai was contemptuous. "Yes, and how do you feel about the *frate's* predictions of the death of Lorenzo? And of the pope and Ferrante, all to come soon? Do you dismiss these as the ravings of a madman or what? Do you fear the wrath of God?"

The group cowered in the awkward silence of questioned loyalty, confirming Rucellai's suspicions. "Well, my friends, *I* fear the wrath of men."

CHAPTER 15

CARDINAL GIOVANNI'S PROCESSION

WINTER PASSED, ANOTHER CARNIVAL CAME and went. Trapped n the Lenten doldrums, Niccolò was happy for any reprieve and today had promise. The city streets were gloriously decked out with tapestries, silks, and banners all draping from the balconies and windows along the Via Maggio. A brisk day in March, the weather was sunny and the city seemed to glow with the promise of an early spring after a bitter and barren winter. The Medici *palle* was flaunted everywhere and citizens in all their finery packed the parade route. Women glittered with jewels and children were clothed as miniature replicas of their parents. Niccolò, cutting his sharpest profile, particularly appreciated how the young girls dressed to distraction. On such an occasion it was easy to forget his boredom with the dictates of Lent.

The celebrants were anxiously awaiting the triumphal entrance of the boy cardinal, Florence's own Giovanni de' Medici. Many of the leading citizens had ridden out this morning to welcome the Cardinal in Fiesole where he had spent the night and received the red cap. Later, the ambassadorial corps and Church prelates had waited at the city gate to meet him as he approached the city mounted on a donkey. A symbol of Christian simplicity and humility, the charade was unconvincing, for Niccolò had never witnessed such a magnificent display of wealth for a personage not born of noble descent. Certainly never for a native Florentine. It was later said congratulatory gifts had arrived from cities and towns throughout the territory as well as from representatives of all Italian city-states and foreign governments.

Yes, the city had now ascended to the level of pride and dignity accorded to kings, dukes, and popes. Florentines would now bet their last florin that the young Giovanni would someday be pope as they cheered him along the procession route: "Blessed is he who comes in the name of the Lord!"

Niccolò navigated through the jostling crowds migrating in the direction of the Piazza della Signoria where the priors would greet the cardinal at the Palazzo entrance. As usual, he kept an ear tuned to snippets of street gossips. They were filled with bravado.

"Fortuna favors us now, my friends. To hell with those Roman bastards."

"And the Milanese!"

"The Venetians!"

"The Genovese!"

"Screw them all! *Viva Firenze! Viva i Medici!*"

"Blessed is he who comes in the name of the Lord!"

To avoid the sea of bodies heading down the Por Santa Maria, Niccolò dodged right along the Street of the Fishmongers to enter the Piazza from behind the Loggia dei Priori. Looking for a good vantage point, he wedged up against a large outside column of the Loggia to wait for the procession to arrive from the far end of the Piazza. He heard a noisy gang of young men standing inside the Loggia just to the other side of his column. Unseen, the Loggia echoed their conversation clearly.

"Well, the *palle* are moving on to bigger things now, eh? Florence, now Rome, what's next?"

"My father says Lorenzo paid 10,000 florins and granted an additional 100,000 in loans to the pope, and then even had to buy off the opposition of Cardinal Barbo of Venice with another 95,000 ducats in loans. Our money, and they'll never pay any of it back."

"You forget he threw his daughter into the bargain: a virgin child to a forty year-old gambling, bastard son of a pope. *Merda!* In the College of Cardinals the little sniveler will be rolling in benefices, and if he ever becomes pope the Medici will reap ten-fold. With little piss Piero running things here and his Orsini in-laws helping his brother down in Rome, the Medici think they have it all planned out."

Niccolò recognized the voice of Doffo Spini. *Merda*, he thought, the gang from the Unicorn, as he shrank back into the column.

Another voice said, "My uncle Alamanno says we *Fiorentini* have paid through the nose for their benefit—*Il Magnifico* can never say no to any foreigner who speaks well of him. Foreign princes come to Florence with their trunks empty, knowing they'll leave with them packed with our riches."

A Rinuccini, guessed Niccolò. Alamanno Rinuccini was a vocal critic of the Medici and strong advocate of the Republic. Quoting Cicero and Aristotle, Rinuccini had published a political tract titled *Liberty* and his arguments were persuasive, if not a bit rash. The basic criticism was that Lorenzo violated the first principle of liberty—citizen equality—and he used his privileged position of power to freely use the wealth of others as his own. Even Niccolò allowed that Lorenzo was too wrapped up in the things of Venus, delighting in facetious men and playing childish games to an extent unseemly for so great a man. His actions only invited the scorn of his enemies.

"*Ragazzi*, we have been drained to serve one man's pleasures and ambitions for his House. Look, here comes his over-fed pup now, riding on an ass and looking like one himself. *Porco Dio*, we must do something to regain what is rightly ours."

It was Spini's threatening voice again and Niccolò wondered if Lorenzo knew how overgrown with weeds his garden had become.

***

After the procession Lorenzo waited for his sons to join him in the family chapel. It had been a long, cold and, for Lorenzo, suffering winter. But today, though fighting chronic fatigue and constant pain in his limbs, Lorenzo was filled with fatherly pride. He looked up at Gozzoli's *Procession of the Magi* and thought how this was truly the appropriate theme for his family legacy: from humble peasants five generations ago to their present heights of power in Florence and all Europe; three generations with three 'kings' in the line of succession. And now he had accomplished the next most important step in his grand design—promoting the ecclesiastical career of Giovanni. No power was secure without the support of the Church of Rome. With Giovanni within the college of the cardinals, Piero would be more secure as the head of the family in Florence, especially given their financial setbacks. Lorenzo suspected Piero had no more of a head for business than himself, but the benefices flowing through Giovanni would insure the status and wealth of the family for the next generation. And if Giovanni should become pope? Yes, but of course he will.

Lorenzo heard the approach of his sons, who sounded as if they were squabbling again. They fell silent as they entered the chapel.

"*Figli*, come here," said Lorenzo affectionately, but as they approached he felt his irritation. "You are boys no longer, and I expect you to act like men and assume the dignity of your personages."

He smiled at Giovanni, round-faced and fleshy at seventeen years old, regal in a cardinal's purple robes. His naturally large head seemed even more so—it was obvious all the fawning and flattery had its effect. But Lorenzo granted him this moment and said, "In your person we see the greatest dignity our House has ever had."

Giovanni smiled and Piero rolled his eyes noticeably.

"Father—" Piero started.

But Lorenzo cut him off with a wave of his hand. There could be no rift between these two, as the family would require the strong alliance of Florence with Rome to survive and prosper. Noble airs were a heady poison that could infect both his sons and he was particularly vexed with Piero, who at the age of twenty displayed none of the maturity required for leadership of an unruly city.

"Piero," he scolded, "I've had to tell you many times to remember who you are and restrain your pride, but I see you fail in this respect again and again. Despite what you may have heard from the flatterers today, don't be deceived. We Medici are not a noble family, we're not hereditary kings or dukes, and we're not even the richest family in the city. But our position has been strengthened today by your brother's fortune. Together you are the two pillars of the House of Medici and we all rely on you to support each other and the hard-earned position of the family. *Capito bene?*"

Piero started to protest, but his father cut him off impatiently.

"*Basta*, leave us while I have a word with Giovanni."

As Piero stormed off, Lorenzo studied Giovanni, who looked pleased standing before him, knowing he had fulfilled his father's grandest ambition.

"Sit down, *figlio mio*, we have much to discuss before you leave for Rome. I'm not well and the responsibilities of our family fall to you and Piero at an early age, much as they fell upon me when I was just twenty." He watched Giovanni's bluster visibly deflate.

Drawing out a sealed scroll from inside his silk robe, he said, "I have written a letter to take with you to Rome. It's a list of reminders to take with you, as I will not be there in Rome to assist you and give you counsel." He handed the scroll to Giovanni.

"Open it when you get to Rome. Keep it close and read it when you fell the need to speak with me. It's my hope to advise you as best I can. While in Rome remember you have attained the Cardinalate by God's grace alone. Don't forget it. You have shown good judgment in your youth which gives me hope, but in that Roman sinkhole things will be different."

"Yes, Father, I—"

"Let me finish, then we can discuss any questions you may have. In Rome you'll be the youngest Cardinal. You'll be viewed with great envy and many will hope to see you fail. Therefore give no reason or offense to your enemies through your own behavior; lead a saintly, exemplary, and honest life. Don't be ostentatious; favor a few antiques and fine books over jewels and silks. Persevere in the studies suitable to your profession and follow the model of exemplary men in the College. Use your ears more than your tongue and defer to the judgment of His Holiness with humility and modesty. Popes are most grateful to those who don't break their ears."

He was reassured by Giovanni's quick, clever mind. With prudence his son would be secure in an ecclesiastical career and would likely exceed expectations. He only feared his own weaknesses might be passed on to his son.

"Less magnificence and pomp, more moderation. Eat plain food and take much exercise, for many who wear the habit neglect these rules and suffer maladies. Think carefully about the honor of the Holy Mother Church and it should not be difficult to aid the city and our house. For our house is part of the city and the city is united to the Church. *You* are the link. *Capito?*"

Giovanni nodded and Lorenzo saw the young man behind the masquerading boy. "I know you're the cleverest. You must help Piero by helping him temper his pride. With Piero in Florence and you in Rome, our House will be secure. *Figlio mio*, take these words of advice with you and stay well."

With the sounds of drums and trumpets invading his ears, Lorenzo reached out to embrace his young son, feeling the bittersweet mixture of a father's pride and loss.

CHAPTER 16

LORENZO FALLS ILL AT CAREGGI

"O my heart of stone…
Because sweet Jesus is dead,
The world trembles, and the sun dims,
The dead come out of their tombs
And the temple veil is rent,
And the earth, the sky, cry alas,
But you don't hear, O heart of stone."

"WELL, WHAT DO YOU THINK?" Lorenzo's voice was tinged with sarcasm as Poliziano groaned.

"I prefer *Quant'e bella giovanezza,* if you must know," he answered, referring to Lorenzo's famous Carnival song.

Lorenzo convulsed with a hacking cough. It was only a month since Giovanni's celebration when his health dealt him another blow. Bedridden, wrapped in linens and a heavy velvet blanket against the chill, he was sweating, with his long black hair matted against his forehead. "Yes, well, youth is fleeting, that's for sure," he replied with wry amusement. Looking imploringly toward the shuttered window, he begged, "Perhaps just a bit of fresh air?"

Poliziano shook his head. "The *tramontana* has been blowing for three days and the doctors fear the chill."

"*Merda, i Medici,*" Lorenzo said, joking on his name. "If they don't kill me with these pulverized jewels and precious stones, they'll suffocate me with this bad air. Didn't Maestro Leonardo denounce these primitive practices in one of his treatises?"

"I don't know," replied Poliziano, exasperated. He worried for the health of his only true and faithful friend and the strain crept into his voice. "They must know what they're doing, otherwise what would be the point of their profession and all their secret concoctions?"

"Exactly, my friend."

"Well, Ficino is coming to consult with the doctor and oversee your care."

"Maestro Marsilio? Good. We can discuss some ideas of interest while I lie here dying of boredom. But I don't think the Maestro or the good *medico* has yet discovered a way to cure the dying…"

"Don't joke, Lorenzo, please. I can't bear the morbidity..."

"Poor dear Angelo," Lorenzo whispered in compassion to his friend. He wondered if Angelo's delicate nature could survive his absence. "Fear not, we're all dying, but I'm not ready to go just yet. Where's my son? Send him to me and take some rest yourself, you truly look terrible you know."

As Poliziano went to find Piero, Lorenzo felt a sharp pain in his stomach and tried to steady his hand but couldn't stop its shaking. *Perhaps only a miracle can save me now, Lord, but if it should be so I will devote all my time to study and poetry, as this is my one regret.*

The door opened and he covered his shaking hand as his son entered. Lorenzo tried to sound cheerful: "Ah, Piero, please, sit by me. I'm afraid I'm too weak to rise."

Piero strode across the room, moving gracefully in his leather riding boots. "*Sì*, Father, excuse me, I was just riding. Are you feeling better?"

Lorenzo saw the worried look that contrasted against his son's normal bravado and tried to downplay his condition. "I'm tired, but I want to speak with you because when I regain my strength you'll need to take over most of my affairs, as I did for my father. I need the country air, perhaps here at Careggi."

"I understand," said Piero, relieved.

"*Senti, figlio.* Angelo and Lucrezina have been reading Virgil to me and it's brought many things to mind. You know Aeneas was possessed of the cardinal virtues of courage, patience, steadfastness, obedience to the gods, and reverence for his ancestors and with these virtues founded the great Roman state that lasted almost a thousand years. It's this we Florentines aspire to and it struck me again that the foundation of a virtuous society is and always has been *la famiglia*."

His son nodded. "*Sì*, Father."

"You know our family relies on solidarity and a large network of alliances. I've tried to lay foundations for the future with Giovanni and the marriages of your sisters. But the future will certainly be very different from my time. You'll become the *capo* of our house and inherit the burden of too many responsibilities."

Piero was eager. "Yes, Father, I'm ready. What would you have me do?"

Lorenzo prayed it was so. He had been reassured with the birth of his grandson, his namesake Lorenzino, as fatherhood seemed to have had the proper affect on Piero. "In time, in time. My purpose now is to pass on to you some things I've learned and warn you of my own mistakes since I assumed these responsibilities when I was even younger than you are now."

"Sì, papa."

114

"Permit me a small indulgence then," said Lorenzo as he slowly recited the speech he had rehearsed while lying incapacitated. "The path I've traveled has been arduous, full of dangers and beset with treachery; but I console myself in having contributed to the welfare of my country—her prosperity rivals that of any other state. Nor have I ignored the interests of our family. I've always tried to emulate my grandfather Cosimo, who watched over his public and private affairs with equal vigilance. So, at this stage of my life I trust I may be allowed to enjoy the pleasures of leisure and share in the reputation of my fellow citizens."

"Truly, Father, and I'll see to city affairs in the manner in which you have instructed me."

Lorenzo felt his confidence flag; Piero was too sure and quick. "It's important to understand the gravity of these matters—I won't always be here to advise you. The citizens will recognize you as my successor and I don't doubt you'll obtain the same authority. But the commune is a body with many heads and it's impossible to please them all. Remember always to follow the course that appears most honorable according to the good of all rather than individual interests.

"You'll be surrounded by sycophants, but I want you to understand this: The benefits of great wealth must be spent judiciously to affirm the family's status and generosity. To our benefit we have established many friendships inside and outside Florence; something other *grandi* have failed to grasp. We are foremost in Florence because of our alliances in Milan, Naples, France, Rome, Ferrara, Venice; even the Sultan in Constantinople. These alliances are cemented by gifts and elaborate ceremony and this is why we have always spent lavishly on entertaining foreign guests while we live simply ourselves. More importantly, simplicity in everyday affairs serves to reduce the envy of fellow citizens."

Piero responded freely, "I understand these things, Father, and I'll uphold this honor."

But Lorenzo wondered if Piero grasped the depth of his meaning—that others would not forgive his pride in wanting to shine in the shadow of his father.

Then Piero asked, "Tell me though, how should one deal with those persons and parties opposed to us?"

"With many allies among the other powerful families and most importantly by staying in the good graces of the *popolani* and the *popolo minuto*. This requires a generous nature toward clients—like between *padrone* and *amico*. But remember we are all equal citizens in the Republic and you must take care not to offend. Humility will serve you well."

"But what of the current disturbances by the religious? How does one appease these annoying preachers who attack our policies and our persons?"

Lorenzo smiled sardonically, reminded of the persistent thorn of Fra Girolamo. With the rapid onset of his illness over the winter months and more pressing matters at hand, he had tried to forget this minor annoyance. "Ignore them. The elevation of Giovanni will provide us with a line of communication and appeasement to the reform movement. I'm sure Giovanni will follow well my instructions to steer clear of the evil elements in the Church and thereby earn the respect of the religious. As head of state, there's no reason for you to provoke them."

"But this Dominican has predicted your death... I think we should banish him immediately from the city so the opposition will be silenced." Piero rose abruptly to pace the room.

"*Calme,* my son. I've no fear of the friar's pronouncements. Perhaps banishment would make matters simpler, but if his popularity is genuine then it would be better to work to achieve his and our aims together. Remember, faith and fear of God is another way to control the evils in men. It was easier to banish Fra Bernardino, as he did not have the support of so many of the citizens."

"Father, Savonarola incites the people against us."

"Have you heard his sermons?"

"No, I won't listen to deceitful prophecies. We go to mass at Santo Spirito to hear Fra Mariano preach. But I've heard it from my friends, who say the friar's lies are repeated on every street corner."

"This is what I suspected. Savonarola has defeated poor Fra Mariano and left his heart full of snake's venom. Don't believe all you hear. Control your anger and don't make hasty judgments. Be careful with who you keep council. There are many who lie in wait to attack us. Our enemies may try to use the friar and spread many falsehoods concerning his religious reforms. A lie in Florence soon catches the wind." Lorenzo looked away as he was caught in a coughing fit. He motioned for the water from the bedside table and Piero quickly filled the goblet.

Lorenzo struggled to clear his throat. "The friar has no ambitions to take over the city. It's the rival families you must watch. Our fellow *grandi* are like a menagerie of exotic animals that must be tamed and trained to live together in peace. I warn you, it's not an easy task."

Lorenzo saw the bravado return to Piero's eyes, where only moments ago the uncertainty of his own health had shaken him. It saddened him. He was aware Piero shared the Orsini pride and arrogance of his mother and wife, but it would take more than overconfidence to survive the intrigues of Florentine politics. Lorenzo tried to remember if he was as headstrong when he was young. Probably, but now he was humbled by how his extraordinary luck had enabled him to survive all the trials he'd faced. He wondered how his son would fare. Was he too blessed by Fortuna? Lorenzo quietly murmured his favorite motto in lyrical French:

"Le temps revient, mon fils, le temps revient…"

CHAPTER 17

The Marketplace and Portents of Disaster

THE *TRAMONTANA* BLEW IN OFF the Apennines and swirled through the Mercato Vecchio as hordes of buyers rushed about making their purchases before the weather turned again for the worse. It was Friday before Palm Sunday and the weather had been erratic—just the night before a sudden thunderbolt had knocked down parts of the large marble lantern atop the cupola of the Cathedral, scattering blocks of marble several tons in weight as if they were pebbles.

Today the old market was a riot of motion and noise. The largest open square in the center of the city, midway between Piazza San Giovanni and the Piazza della Signoria, it was packed with makeshift stalls filled with fresh produce, dairy, livestock and every imaginable item of use. Carts and mules choked the entrance streets, their drivers competing with hawkers who screamed an unceasing refrain describing their wares for sale. The ring of pots and pans clashed with a cacophony of caged animals and birds, and a colorful splay of woven textiles and linens dressed out the gusts of wind that carried the scent of herbs, spices and smoked meats across the piazza. Women freshened their utensils and others slaked their thirst at a fountain in the center where perched above on a granite pillar was Donatello's statue of Abundance, holding her overflowing cornucopia. Gilded in the gold currency of trade, she stood there in perpetuity, overseeing all.

Just off one corner of the market, along the *Via Calimala*, a barber had set up his red and white striped pole over a chair and small table holding the tools of his trade. But the wind was playing havoc with his client's hair and he cursed as the wisps of the man's thinning hair flew around in the breeze.

"Don't break my balls! *Madonna mia*, this wind is impossible!"

The men seated around the open stall were laughing to the consternation of the barber's poor client squirming in the chair.

"Eh, Jacopo," one teased, "have you come to have your hair cut or to be bled?" It was the young painter, Francesco Granacci.

"*Basta*, Francesco," barked the barber. He changed the subject to distract his nervous client. "Have any of you seen the fallen lantern of the cupola? I passed it this morning. A large piece was buried in the paving stones of the Via dei Servi and another piece struck the roof of Ranieri's house, crashing all the way through and burying itself in the cellar.

Brunelleschi must be turning in his grave."

"*Sì*," replied his customer. "Everybody's talking about it. Luca Ranieri is saying it's a miracle no one in his family was hurt. So strange the lightning struck without warning, not a cloud in the sky."

"Hah!" said Francesco, "Can you believe that? That a lightning bolt would strike from nowhere? Who told you, did they see it?"

"I don't know, but I heard it from a gypsy over on Via dei Cimatori."

"A gypsy? A *gypsy*? *Incredibile!*" retorted Francesco.

Two old peasant women selling their eggs, milk, and cheeses in the next stall overheard the conversation and eagerly joined in.

"It's true, Nello," said one, addressing the barber. "It is most definitely another bad sign. There's a shooting star burning in the sky at night too. You can see it from the hill atop San Miniato when it's clear."

The other woman nodded vigorously. "*Sì*, a lightning bolt is a sure sign straight from Heaven. And there was a madwoman on Sunday screaming in Santa Maria Novella about a vision of a bull with horns of fire. She said she saw it burning the whole city. She was possessed." The woman quickly crossed herself.

"Ha!" Francesco laughed again. "And were you there? Did you see it too?"

"I heard it from Monna Clara, my neighbor, and she—"

He quickly cut her off. "*Sì, sì*, I understand perfectly: We live in a city of *chiachiaroni*, ceaseless chatterboxes. You arrive at one gate and tell a tale and by the time it reaches the center of the city it's transformed into a fantasy."

The first woman became irate. "Bah, *giovane*...what do you know? The cupola *was* struck by lightning last night, there *is* a shooting star in the sky and the good friar has taken his predictions straight out of the Old Testament, the very *Word* of God. These must be signs from God. Are you a non-believer?"

The older men nodded as if weighing grave matters. "*Sì, sì*, one cannot ignore the facts."

Nello paused his clipping to add, "There *is* a strange humor in the city. Perhaps the friar's prediction is upon us."

The first milk woman nodded rigorously. "For a month Lorenzo has stayed outside the city, an invalid at Careggi. There are vigils at Santo Spirito and San Lorenzo where many faithful pray to the Virgin to save his soul... and save us all..."

"There are dark days ahead," warned the second. "My husband has put aside stores for the winter and every day for the past week I light a votive to St. Zanobi."

Francesco threw up his hands, exclaiming contemptuously, "*Va bene, va bene,* let me speak with the gypsy, so then *I too* will know how to plan for the coming disaster."

As the women turned back to their stall, one whispered to the other, "Bah, he's a painter... I've also heard the gypsies say Lorenzo is doomed because he let the genie he possesses in his magic ring loose to save himself and the spirit has turned against the city."

"*Madonna mia,*" the other woman muttered, crossing herself again.

Giving up, Francesco spied a small company of actors across the Via Calimala. He thought he saw a familiar figure and then recognized Michelangelo, engrossed in the entertainment. The troupe was performing a rough recitation of Dante's *Comedia* with the lead actor dressed in the long lucco and outmoded cap often used to depict the poet. He also wore a mask to obscure his identity or perhaps to suggest that of the Poet as he recited his verses. He gestured toward another actor whose shirt and hose so were stuffed with sackcloth he looked as rotund as a stuffed pig.

> *Your city, so full of envy that the sack spills over...*
> *The name I took,*
> > *Among you citizens is Ciacco;*
> > *The sin of gluttony brought me here...*

The rotund actor danced as if on hot coals as the crowd laughed.

> *Tell if you can the divided city's fate,*
> > *And of the citizens: is any one just?*
> > *And tell me why such schism threatens it.*

Then the corpulent actor stopped dancing and stretched tall to mouth the words of the orator:

> *After long argument they must*
> > *Descend to bloodshed, and the rustic bloc*
> > *With much offense will expel the other first.*
> *Then through the power of one who while we speak*
> > *Is temporizing, that party too will fall*
> > *Within three years, the ousted coming back*
> *With head held high; and long will they prevail*
> > *Despite the others' cries of shame and despair*
> > *Under their burdens. Only two men of all*
> *Are truly just—whose words the rest ignore,*
> > *For the triple sparks of envy, greed, and pride*
> > *Ignite their hearts.*[5]

At the end of the canto the orator paused and the crowd clapped in appreciation while one of the actors passed the hat.

"*Ciao*, Angelo, what are you doing here?" said Francesco.

Startled, Michelangelo turned. "Francesco. I was just coming from my father's house. He never ceases to nag about every little thing—I know it's because he's worried for his own position as Lorenzo's client. With my eldest brother joining the Dominicans, my father frets over who'll now make the money needed to care for him and my sisters. It seems the Buonarroti lack the Midas touch."

"Nonsense, my friend, your father's blind; everything you touch turns to gold."

Michelangelo laughed in self-deprecation. "Maybe you should talk to him."

"Messer Lodovico? Not on your life, he hates me. Listen, all this verse puts me in a mood for a bit of wine at La Casa Dante. Care to join me? "

With a wistful look at the antics of the actors, Michelangelo reluctantly trudged off behind the blithe Granacci and then stopped. Francesco turned. "Well?"

Michelangelo suddenly looked ill, as if something he ate strongly disagreed with him. "I'll make you a bargain, Francesco. First we go to Santa Maria Novella …to drink in Masaccio, and then I'll be ready to drink your wine. *Va bene?*"

The frescoes of Masaccio were also Francesco's favorite inspiration; his eyes lit up as he broke into a wide grin. "*Sì, va bene così.*"

Reaching the church, they entered through the main door and walked the length of the nave toward the fresco, their eyes adjusting to the darkness. The large fresco reached almost ten *braccia* high and five across and they stopped before it at a distance about equal to its height. It was an awe-inspiring representation of the Trinity and Crucifixion. From where Michelangelo stood the flat surface of the wall appeared to recede deep into a barrel-vaulted chapel. Inside this illusory chapel there was an altar, in front of which stood the cross with the martyred Christ who had just expired. Filling the chapel behind the cross and up upon the altar stood the imposing figure of God the Father, holding up with apparent ease the heavy cross that bore His son. On either side of the cross knelt the Virgin Mother and John the Evangelist. Outside the chapel, one step down were the profiled portraits of the patron and his wife, kneeling in prayer. Another step down a large recessed stone tomb was set underneath the altar and revealed inside the sarcophagus was a skeleton with a Latin inscription carved in the hard cold marble. It said: *I was once what you are and am what you are yet to be.*

The total composition of the fresco was perfectly balanced and the entire image seemed real enough to touch. Yet, in reality there was no vault; it was only paint on a flat-walled surface.

Francesco's whispered voice echoed in the empty church. "Masaccio's art remains an enigma to me, Angelo, no matter how long at stare at it. I feel I could climb up over this tomb and walk into that chapel."

"*Capito,*" agreed Michelangelo. "It's a remarkable effect. The more I sculpt the more I appreciate the transformation of the three dimensions of my hands into the two of my eyes. In Lorenzo's library I found a copy of Alberti's treatise on painting, where he explains the problems of perspective."

Michelangelo walked closer to the fresco. "I think Masaccio learned the geometric structure of perspective from Brunelleschi."

Francesco shook his head. "I can't understand mathematical treatises, I only paint what I see."

"Yes, but what you see is not always what is, no?"

Francesco appeared confused.

"Here, look." Michelangelo stepped back to the original spot where he stood. "Imagine just above the tomb, below the base of the cross, and before the step. Right there." He pointed. "There you place a nail. Then run a string from that nail to the tops of the columns, and also down to the base. Can you imagine the lines now forming the balance of the composition?" Francesco nodded and Michelangelo continued. "Now, also imagine you run a string from your eye where we stand to the front of the altar, to the back of the chapel, to the top of the chapel. Do you see?"

Francesco grunted. "*Che?*"

"This is the perfect spot, *a posto,* to view the fresco and see the illusion of three dimensions. If you move too close," Michelangelo took a stride closer, and then to one side, "or to this side or that, the effect is different. *Davero?* What you perceive is different depending on where you stand. It helps to have a good knowledge of geometry, and some understanding of the theories of the Greek mathematician, Euclid."

Francesco was skeptical. "Is the point of using perspective only to play tricks on the eye, deceiving us into believing we're seeing something different than we are?"

"Exactly! Because from different angles, different perceptions are apparent. What you perceive depends on where you stand. I have found this to be especially true of sculpture, which treats the subject in the round."

"What is true about that?"

"That's the point, Francesco, our eyes are not always true. Imagine it like the song of a bird that is actually an imitation by skilled bird caller. Or the shimmer of water off the burning hot summer hills. What we *see* is not always what *is*. Leonardo writes that perspective aids us when judgment fails and our senses give us a false impression. As painters and sculptors we must overcome such limitations."

"A trade secret, eh?"

"*Sì*. Maestro Pico told me there's a painting in Urbino by Piero della Francesca. It's a *Flagellation* that's incredible in its use of perspective. It appears almost like three paintings in one, yet all lies in spatial balance. There's another one, a *Madonna and Child*, painted for the Duke of Montefeltro. Maestro Pico told me Piero della Francesca has written a treatise on the use of perspective in painting. Unfortunately, Lorenzo doesn't yet have a copy."

Francesco became animated. "I'd like to see these paintings. Lorenzo di Credi told me Maestro Leonardo is painting a fabulous fresco of the Last Supper, in Milano in the refectory of Santa Maria delle Grazie. He is using an entire end wall to make it appear like an extension of the dining hall. It would be great to visit Milano to see it. *Allora*, so much possibility, now I'm thirsty for that wine."

Just as quickly, Michelangelo felt the expanding world begin to shrink again. For both of them these were important years to make their mark, and to do so it was necessary to win competitions for commissions. But with Master Bertoldo's passing last winter and Lorenzo's debilitation, the sculpture garden at San Marco had closed, its future in jeopardy. And without a patron and paid commissions there would be no possibilities to go to Milan or Urbino or Rome. The young sculptor's life seemed suspended, hinged on Lorenzo's health. Perhaps indulging his spirits with Francesco while he was still able was not such a bad idea.

CHAPTER 18

Lorenzo's Deathbed

THE AIR IN THE BEDCHAMBER was fetid and the men struggled to control their emotions. Pico and Poliziano had spent most of the late afternoon with Lorenzo as he fell in and out of a fitful sleep. Periodically, his daughter Lucrezina or sister Bianca would enter to change the linen wrapped around his chest and throat when it became damp with sweat. Pico fingered the copy of Virgil's *Aeneid* from which he had been reading verses to comfort Lorenzo. None of them had eaten anything for several hours and Pico felt his belly complain. Poliziano was visibly distressed, sitting forlornly on a chest close to the bedside when Lorenzo stirred and opened his eyes.

"Ah, my friends, you are too faithful," he whispered in a hoarse voice. "But it gladdens me to see you. The company of true friends and family is the only real comfort a man can hope for."

Lorenzo motioned with a half wave. "Pico, please read to me again that passage of Jupiter, the part about every man's last day…"

Pico leafed through the book, looked down and read in a mellifluous cadence:

Every man's last day is fixed.
Lifetimes are brief, and not to be regained,
For all mankind. But by their deeds to make
Their fame last: that is labor for the brave.

Lorenzo struggled to concentrate as he repeated the verse, "…but by their deeds to make…their fame last… that is labor for the brave…"

He looked up and smiled. "I only hope I haven't failed in my efforts. I wish I'd been able to complete our library. It's my one true regret, *car'amici.* Have you any news from Lascaris?"

"Not in almost a month," said Poliziano, "But we believe he's still in Greece. Our last communication was from Athens and from there he's traveling to Salonica before he returns to Florence by way of Venice. He writes that he's purchased many fine manuscripts and sellers are eager from fear of the Turks."

"Well, you both must take charge of the effort for me. It's the legacy of my grandfather and my father and, as members of the Academy, this task falls to you …a task of the utmost importance. I only wish I could be here to read them with you."

"Save your energy, rest," said Pico. "I'm sure you'll be with us for a long time to come."

"No, my friends, I'm too tired to struggle. Did you hear the thunder again in the night? It's as if the Almighty is calling me to account."

"Another storm," said Angelo. "Two nights ago the lantern on the cupola was struck by a thunderbolt and parts of the structure tumbled to the ground. It's amazing no one was killed, it'll take a long time to repair the damage."

A dark look came over Lorenzo and he became agitated. "A thunderbolt? The lantern fell? And toward which side did it fall?"

"On the north side, near the Via dei Servi," Pico said.

Lorenzo deflated, "*Dio mio*! It fell toward my house. It's surely a bad sign…it's God's will…" His voice trailed off as he stared vacantly at the shuttered window. "It's only a short time… "

He raised his hand to silence their protests. "No, I wish only to satisfy one last request. One wish…" Lorenzo paused, the guilt like a heavy weight on his chest, stifling. He turned to look at them, as if summoning the strength to continue.

"I want to speak with the prior of San Marco and receive his blessing before I die."

Poliziano registered his shock and then exploded in protest. "That priggish friar? Gloating in his self-righteousness? No, you must not give him the satisfaction. Please, Lorenzo, I can't bear the sight of the sniveling priest."

Lorenzo grew short tempered. "Angelo, don't be disagreeable toward a man's dying wish. Perhaps the friar has been in touch with the Almighty all along and it is *we* who are blinded by pride. I know no honest friar save this one, please send for him immediately."

It was an order and Pico rose up and bowed in deference. "I shall send a messenger to San Marco, immediately."

Annoyed with Poliziano, Lorenzo feigned a desire to sleep while the friar was collected from San Marco. *Surely he would not refuse?*

For a year now Lorenzo had felt his body failing fast, forcing his thoughts toward his mortality. He spent most of his time in quiet reflection, disguising his preoccupation by attending to only the most necessary functions of his position. These had pertained to the succession of his sons—to secure the Medici legacy. But his satisfaction with these activities did not quell his regret. Despite the envy he knew his position invited, his life had never fulfilled its promise. He was most fortunate, yes, born to many opportunities life had to offer, but his time had been stolen from him. It had been offered up for his family and his city. It was ironic that all one's free time gained by wealth should be spent in managing and defending that same wealth. Surely one would be better off with a simple, secure life.

He opened his eyes again and smiled as he heard Poliziano snoring through his bedside vigil. Gazing around his shrinking domain, Lorenzo's eyes wandered over the fine objects adorning his bedchamber. In the corner stood an exquisite double-handled Venetian vase made of red-dappled jasper filigreed with finely worked gold, a gift of the Doge. On his night table there was a black ewer of onyx gilded with silver and enamel to hold his water and a goblet of rock crystal encrusted with sapphires and rubies from which to drink. He picked up the crystal goblet, drank down the last drop of the water and turned it over in his hands. Such a wealth of earthly splendor gathered, possessed, and savored with a jealous hold on life. These things that lift us up and then weigh us down. He thought of all his precious objects located elsewhere in other residences he would never see again and felt a sudden distress. It mattered little, but he knew to be denied one last thing in this life was to suffer. But to suffer needlessly. He put the goblet down and forced himself to think of other matters.

This morning he had confessed his sins and received absolution, but he was sure it could not possibly be enough to absolve a man from a lifetime of small regrets. He was mindful of the Lord's judgment and the past weighed upon him with the guilt of one who knows he cannot make full restitution. What would he say when the innocents at Volterra greeted him in the afterlife?

How had it happened? Twenty years ago the rebellious Volterrans had sought to reclaim the alum and alabaster mines on which Florence depended and he had felt pressured to make a strong example. So, he instructed the *condottiere* Federico Montefeltro to besiege the town and exact tribute, but the mercenaries sacked the town after it surrendered and slaughtered many citizens for pure lust sport. The news had devastated him and the Volterrans blamed him, and justly so, for the impasse could have been negotiated. Twenty years had not dulled his regret.

Several years later the Pazzi conspirators put him to the test again and he failed to control his rage. After they murdered his brother, his revenge knew no bounds. For weeks the bodies of the murderers hung from the walls of the Signoria and the Bargello and even poor Sandro had become distressed when commissioned to paint their effigies on the walls as a warning to traitors. Later, the feral little street urchins had exhumed old Jacopo Pazzi several times from his grave and dragged his putrid corpse through the streets, desecrating the dead with their games, and no one had interfered. What malice lies in the heart of the human beast! *Homo homini lupus...*

Afterwards his position among the citizens inspired their silent fear and wary respect, no more was he greeted with collegial warmth. He was forced to travel with an escort of guards and his life became more like a prison than the life of a free man. But he supposed his worst sin came last.

Due to the misfortunes of the Medici bank and the financial pressures upon his House, he committed a sin less forgivable because it was done willingly. He had used his position of power to misappropriate funds from the *Monte* and divert them to his own purpose of promoting Giovanni to the Cardinalate. He had hoped to replace the funds but the bank's fortunes had not reversed and now his enemies whispered their suspicions louder each day. He rationalized that the glory of the Medici was one with the glory of Florence, so the success of Giovanni would shower riches on them all; they must only be patient. But meanwhile the dowry would be insolvent for those young women who came of marriageable age.

Poliziano stirred and Lorenzo felt the full weariness of life weigh upon his chest. Strange, how life becomes an inconvenient wait for death. He dreaded the darkness to come but willed himself into a fitful sleep.

Sometime later the incessant barking of his hunting hounds woke him. He felt a sudden wave of trepidation. The prior must have arrived— had he come now to claim a soul? There was a knock on the door and Pico stepped into the room to announce his guest's arrival.

When the black-cowled figure entered gripping the Bible in one hand and the crucifix in the other, Lorenzo had another fleeting premonition of death. But he forced a smile and radiated a fading spark of life.

"Fra Girolamo, please. Welcome to my home. I thank you for granting my request and venturing out on this forbidding night."

The friar threw back his cowl and smiled enigmatically. "There is no need to express gratitude. It is our duty and great joy to comfort those in need of God's grace."

Lorenzo relaxed; the man wasn't the Devil after all. "Would you care to eat something, Padre? Or perhaps rest after your journey?"

"No, in God's service there is no time for comforts of the body. I understand you requested my presence and I have come to offer what assistance I may."

"I desire to speak with you on many things, Father. Perhaps the others will permit us a few moments alone in peace." As his family and friends shuffled out of the bedchamber, Lorenzo beckoned. "*Prego*, Padre, sit here beside me."

As Savonarola approached, Lorenzo smiled graciously, projecting the warmth of his personality. "It seems we have had our small differences, Father, but I wish you to know these are of little consequence now. I've asked you here because I'm curious and apprehensive about what is to come, as all men must be when they face the inevitable consequence of life."

Lorenzo paused, but the priest did not soften his grim countenance. Lorenzo looked into his eyes, but could not decipher any meaning there. The eyes were black and deep, the skin sallow, and the friar's large features strongly dominated his face: the large hooked nose, prominent brow, strong bones, and full lips. Lorenzo felt empathy for another face unblessed by beauty. He continued, "I've confessed my sins and received absolution, but it gives me little comfort. Surely the Lord God cannot be satisfied by small routines and rituals performed by witless souls?"

The friar maintained his stony gaze, so Lorenzo continued. "I wonder if you're different, Father. I think in some ways we're more alike than you know. We are both learned men. We both see the truth, though you speak it plainly while I use it to my advantage. I admit I'm a practical man, but I imagine such talents will be of less use to me in the afterlife. Father, I wish you to tell me what you know. Do you believe I can be saved?"

Savonarola slowly lifted his Bible, cradling it as if it contained the secrets to which Lorenzo inquired. "I don't know, Signore. Only God knows the fate of men, but faith in God is the only true path for men to follow."

"But how do we know when we have true faith? How did you prophesize my illness? What did you hear or see that made it clear, so you knew?"

"But I did not know. Man cannot divine the unknown and I'm a mere man. It's by God's grace alone we're given signs. God flashes visions on our minds, but we must still interpret his meaning. God has granted me signs, but possibly I err in interpretation.

"I don't know if you will be saved. But death awaits all mortal men, so we must prepare for the time we're called by the Lord. If God chooses to call you now, you must face death with true faith, and, if He should spare you, you must live a virtuous life. Christ teaches the path to salvation is through faith. We can strengthen our faith by doing penance for our weaknesses, which are our sins."

"But how do I find true faith?"

"By confessing your sins and doing penance. There are four steps to penance that give true meaning to the sacramental ritual you belittle: First, the acceptance of sin; second, the expression of regret and contrition; third, confession and acknowledgment of error; and finally, the actual performance of the penance itself. One must complete these four stages to give true meaning to the sacrament of penance and receive the grace of God. Have you performed these necessary steps?"

The friar's manner was pedantic and reminded Lorenzo why he had difficulty accepting the simple prescriptions of the religious. He wished to probe deeper into the mysteries of life and death. "The guilt I have carried in my heart for many years confirms the acceptance of my wrongs. I've deeply regretted these sins and confessed them. I've been granted forgiveness and absolution—"

"But," the friar interrupted, finishing the thought, "perhaps your penance is insufficient." Then he laid his wooden crucifix on Lorenzo's chest. "Tell me of your sins and together we will determine the nature of your penance."

"There are three crucial sins to which I have confessed, Father. First, I was responsible for the murder of many innocents at Volterra by the mercenaries. Next, I took God's own retribution in hand with an evil vengeance on the Pazzi traitors. Last, I'm guilty of deceiving and robbing my fellow citizens by appropriating funds from the *Monte* for the purpose of satisfying the pope and cardinals. I meant to return it, but…"

"These are serious sins. You have violated God's own commandments and also contributed to the corruption of the state and the Church, which is God's house. What were the terms of your absolution?"

"Only that I pray to God for forgiveness and trust in His mercy."

"And this seems insufficient to you?"

Lorenzo did not reply. He felt like a child in confession, forced to catalogue his sins for the sake of the ritual. He gazed into the friar's staring eyes.

"Yes, and so it is," said the priest. "You must meet three conditions to fulfill the act of contrition and receive true absolution. First, you must acknowledge your faith in God and responsibility for your sins. Have you done so?"

"I cannot deny these things and I pray to God for his mercy and forgiveness."

"Second, you must grant restitution to those you have stolen from. Have you done so?"

"No."

"Are you willing to submit to an accounting of restitution and grant it to those you have injured."

"Yes, where possible."

"Third, you have violated the sacred trust of those poor citizens who depend on the just behavior of their leaders. This is a most serious offense because it eats at the heart of the community and hinders all in their personal search for God: unjust rulers prevent all in their charge from finding salvation. The third condition therefore must rectify this situation."

Lorenzo was silent. He felt the silence engulf him as he searched the black orbs of his accuser. He waited for the consequence to fall.

"Liberty must be restored to the people."

The words fell like those marble blocks that had tumbled off the Dome of the Cathedral. Lorenzo was unable to summon the breath to reply. His feelings of empathy with the prior were shattered in that moment and he felt his anger well up. He knew men might accuse him of a tenacious will to power but to relinquish power was to surrender one's fate and the fate of all to an unknown outcome. So many times Florence had suffered the anarchy of true liberty. But true liberty was an abstract fantasy—one is always subject to some higher power. Men of books could not understand this and religious like the prior could not see the almighty power of God was sometimes insufficient here on earth.

He stared back into Savonarola's cold, black eyes. They were unyielding and Lorenzo felt naked and weak under their piercing gaze. The friar's righteous condemnation burned into his breast, but he refused to take blame for the way things were. A strong leader must bend the good of all to fit a higher purpose, and sometimes he must go against Christian teachings to accomplish his ends. Resolutely, Lorenzo turned away from the friar's gaze.

The two men remained there in the room, speechless, facing off in a stalemate of wills as the night temperature dropped precipitously. Sometime later, only Pico remained awake outside the door when the friar left the room. He quickly rousted the sleeping escort to accompany the prior back to San Marco.

***

On his long walk back to San Marco in the dark, Fra Girolamo felt the chill in his bones. Now he knew the rightness of his mission. Here was this man—for all his intentions a learned, cultured, benevolent man—yet such a man could not resist the temptation to bend the good of all to fit his purpose. This was even truer of men less wise and just than Lorenzo de' Medici. The tyrants of Italy were too numerous to count and struggled to outdo one another in ruthlessness. Most serious was how this poison had infected the Church and given rise to a College of Cardinals and a succession of popes to shame the Devil. The only solution was to rid the earth of these rapacious wolves—cut off the head and the body will die.

CHAPTER 19

LORENZO'S FUNERAL

LUCA LANDUCCI WALKED PAST HIS shuttered shop on his way to the Piazza della Signoria. The bells of Santa Maria Novella were droning, as they had off and on for the past two days. *Il Magnifico* was dead.

The whole city seemed to be a chamber of ringing bells; not only the many churches but also *La Vaca*—the Cow—lowing from the tower of the government palace and heard as far as an hour's ride into the countryside. It was a mournful sound and it hung on the faces of the people moving toward the procession route from the Palazzo della Signoria to San Giovanni, continuing on to the Church of San Lorenzo. This was the route Lorenzo would travel on his last pass through the city from the Church of San Marco to his final resting place in San Lorenzo. The funereal route was lined with thousands of citizens, foreign visitors, ambassadors and emissaries, even workers and peasants. All commercial activity had ceased and the markets closed in mourning for the city's favorite son.

Luca occasionally caught a glimpse and feeble wave from someone he knew but, finding it too difficult to navigate through the pushing bodies, let himself be sucked up in the flow. There was sense of timelessness as people crowded up against each other at the street entrances to the Piazza. Many chattered away as if they were attending one of Lorenzo's public parade spectacles, while others stared in eerie silence.

Luca found himself wedged against a wall along the Street of the Hosemakers, just next to the miracle shrine of Orsanmichele. He looked up at the imposing figure of St. George the Dragon Slayer, beautifully carved by Donatello, staring down on him. In the next niche was St. Matthew, carved by the famed Ghiberti of the Baptist doors to honor the patron saint of the bankers.

The humble apothecary was dismayed by the vainglory of men. Last year it was Filippo Strozzi, the richest man in Florence, who met his final judgment and this year it was the Magnificent Lorenzo. These men were the most illustrious, the richest, the most dignified, and the most renowned among mortals. Signor Filippo envisioned his overblown palace as a monument to himself, but now he was dead and his palace will last eternally: has not his pile of stones mastered him then?

And Lorenzo: Everyone declared he ruled Italia and possessed great wisdom. He even succeeded in getting his son appointed cardinal, a great honor for his House and the city. Yet, in spite of all this, he could not live one hour longer when the end came.

Luca shook his head at the commotion around him. *Man, O man, what have you to be so proud of?* True humility is the only fit human attribute. Each time we grow proud and esteem ourselves above others, we exceed the limits of humanity; and everything that exceeds its limits is evil. We are not masters, only dispensers and man is nothing, if not what God has made him. All lies in God's hands and all praises are His due...*may He pardon our sins.*[6]

Two old peasant farmers chattering next to him interrupted his thoughts.

"*Dio mio*, did you hear what happened to Signor Lorenzo's *dottore*, Pier Leoni? Found at the bottom of a well. Fallen, or perhaps murdered!"

"With such a name it's inevitable he would meet a bad end. It's another sign. First, the lantern atop the Duomo and then, during the same storm, the city's lions fought and killed the finest of the pride."

"*Merda*, it's no time to be a lion or even have the name of one."

His friend's reply was thick with sarcasm. "No, you ass. We're just more likely to be eaten by one."

How true, how true, thought Luca, admiring the country wit.

***

Niccolò and Tommaso traversed the Ponte Vecchio on their way across the river to the Signoria. They were dressed in funereal black, as were most of their fellow citizens crowding the streets. The two young men were on their way to meet Tommaso's uncles, who would be in the Loggia dei Priori with other government officials. Tommaso's father was one of the bearers of Lorenzo's casket and would accompany the funeral wagon on its trip to the church. As they reached the end of the bridge Niccolò's attention was arrested by a figure dressed in the garb of a soothsayer, like those from the East beyond the Holy Land. The seer was dressed in colorful flowing rags and his head was wrapped in a moth-eaten silk scarf partially covering his face. He waved his arms about as he moaned a verse Niccolò did not recognize. The passing citizens ignored the vagrant, but something caused Niccolò to stop as he caught Tommaso by the sleeve of his doublet.

"*Momento*," he said as he drew closer to hear the seer's words.

Nobody sees Death,
Nobody sees the face of Death,

Nobody hears the voice of Death.
Savage Death just cuts man down.
Sometimes we build a house, sometimes we make a nest,
But then brothers divide it upon inheritance.
Sometimes there is hostility in the land,
But then the river rises and brings floodwater.
Dragonflies drift on the river,
Their faces look upon the face of the Sun
But then suddenly there is nothing.
The sleeping and the dead are just like each other,
Death's picture cannot be drawn,
When the great gods assembled,
They appointed death and life.
They did not mark out the days for death,
But they did so for life.

Tommaso pulled Niccolò by the arm in exasperation. "*Andiamo, dai!*" he importuned. "We must meet my uncles before the Piazza gets too crowded to pass."

As Tommaso pulled him away, Niccolò continued to stare at the seer, who returned his gaze. The man appeared to smile, then lowered his turbaned head and raised his clasped hands in the universal symbol of divine worship. The image of the man, his odd accent and the strange magic of his words stayed with Niccolò as he caught up with Tommaso. He had a recurring sense of a portent. He knew it had something to do with Lorenzo's death.

He was still preoccupied as they elbowed their way through a roiling sea of bodies to finally arrive at the Loggia. All three of Tommaso's uncles were there and Niccolò noticed Piero Soderini conversing privately with two of Lorenzo's supporters from the Council of Seventy, Piero Capponi and Francesco Valori. As Tommaso's uncle Giovanvettorio greeted them, Niccolò thought he heard the name "Piero" mentioned several times.

"A colorless day for the city," said Giovanvettorio, looking up at the cheerless sky.

Niccolò nodded as he strained to hear the hushed conversation behind him. But then the men parted and Piero Soderini returned to the family group. "Francesco," he said, addressing his brother the bishop, "both Capponi and Valori agree we must give Piero de' Medici support against any *ottimati* plots to wrest control of the government."

The maneuvering had begun before Lorenzo was cold in the ground, thought Niccolò. Every succession of the Medici invited treachery from their enemies: first with Cosimo, then with Piero the Gouty. But in previous times the Medici were much more secure and he recalled the words of resentment he had heard whispered during Cardinal Giovanni's procession. With Piero, the Medici looked weaker than ever.

Francesco whispered back. "Yes, of course, but what of the prior of San Marco? He prevailed against Lorenzo and his reputation swells. Paolo feels strongly about the friar and thinks the government should find a way to work with him for the good of the city—for both its soul and its lifeblood."

Piero sighed in frustration. "It's true, he's gaining followers by the day. The young Medici seems unwilling or unable to deal with him, but our own camp is dividing between those for and against the religious reform: you, Paolo and Valori in support and Rucellai, Del Nero, Capponi and Vespucci strongly opposed. Me? I'm a man stretched between—on the rack." Piero smiled with self-deprecation.

"But Uncles," interjected Tommaso, "don't we confuse religion with the politics of the city. Surely a priest will not wield power over the Signoria?"

"The division is never as clean as we suppose, nephew," said Francesco. "When we become divided by mixing religion with politics, we make ourselves vulnerable to those who would banish us in their own lust for power. This is what inflicts the Roman Curate now."

Piero added: "This is what we must guard against—as the Medicean party splits, we weaken, and the *ottimati* can pounce like our own hungry lions. The Republic must hold or we'll suffer by it."

Listening intently, with a secret joy, Niccolò itched with anticipation: Everything that seemed so set was now in flux, just as he was discovering politics was his true mistress and strategy his sword. There would be a power grab and he recited in his head one of those verses by the Divine Poet (perhaps a better poet than politician):

> *My deeds were not those of the lion but those of the fox*
> *the wiles and secret ways—I knew them all*
> *and so employed their arts that my renown*
> *had reached the very boundaries of earth.*[7]

Piero continued: "We agree Paolo must rise to the top of those who blindly follow the friar. Valori also is leaning in this direction. If a new faction forms behind Savonarola it may gain influence with or without Medici support."

Francesco added, "My position may help. Though I credit Fra Girolamo, I suspect the Church will resist many of his proposals. His ardor may carry him too far against those in power."

"*Va bene*," said Piero, nodding his assent. "I will provide tacit support for both the Mediceans and the Frate until it becomes clear which will prevail. But we must watch the *magnati* too—they still make cause with the *ottimati*."

These old *magnati* families were those who clung to the last threads of their noble status—aristocrats who had been deemed ineligible for office in the Republic to prevent them from exploiting their power of wealth and land ownership. But the new merchant and banking families—the *ottimati*—were now competing for control, and many of these were tied to old *magnati* clans through marriage. To marry land and title to new wealth was a proven formula.

Niccolò interjected, "*Signori*, perhaps Tommaso and I can help keep an eye on these. Many of the sons are the same age and we come in frequent contact with them." He nodded across the Loggia toward the front door of the Palazzo where several of the aristocratic families gathered. "In true Florentine tradition, they whisper their secrets loudly and incessantly."

Tommaso looked askance at Niccolò, knowing his antipathy for these rival gangs. "*Sì*, Uncle, I…we see them often—Spini, Gianfigliazzi, Acciaiuoli, Albizzi…"

Niccolò caught Piero Soderini's eye as he carefully weighed their proposal. Tommaso's uncle Piero was the most ambitious of the Soderini brothers and, though blessed with nephews, had no children of his own. Since Tommaso was expected to enter the family trading business, Niccolò calculated perhaps Piero would find him a useful protégé. He was determined to prove his value, as the Soderini represented the best opportunity for his own advancement.

At that moment a fanfare of trumpets announcing the funeral wagon had entered the Piazza. Many of Lorenzo's friends and supporters walked alongside and Niccolò recognized Braccio Martelli, Bernardo Rucellai, and at the end, Tommaso's father, Paolantonio. In the small entourage he also saw the famous poets and philosophers, who, along with the Medici family members, walked with bowed heads. Behind them was Lorenzo's son Piero, mounted on his horse leading a troop of flag bearers showing the Medici coat-of-arms and several of Lorenzo's devices, including the embroidered banner from his celebrated joust displaying the words '*Le Temps Revient*.'

***

Michelangelo and Francesco marched in the funeral train alongside the older painters, Sandro Botticelli and Benozzo Gozzoli, all following close behind the three *maestri*: Ficino, Pico and a forlorn Poliziano. The train halted in front of the Loggia where several eulogies were read, the most long-winded delivered by long-time Medicean client Chancellor Bartolomeo della Scala. Then the funeral wagon exited the Piazza and traveled along the Street of the Hosemakers. They were heading north toward the Piazza San Giovanni with the Signoria and the rest of the civic leaders in tow to join the religious community at the Cathedral.

As they walked, Michelangelo heard Sandro comment on Scala's oration, "A fitting eulogy for *Magnifico*, eh?"

Michelangelo saw Poliziano stiffen and Pico turn toward him. Without warning Poliziano let loose his vitriol: "*Figlio de putana!* Messer Bartolomeo ...it makes me ill just to listen to his drivel... that such a pompous ass should be the one to honor Lorenzo. Fortunately," he sniffed, "his words will be soon forgotten while the tribute *I* write shall shape the lasting legacy of my dear *Laurentia*."

Maestro Sandro did not seem offended—Poliziano's outbursts were frequent and his antipathy for Chancellor Scala well known—but the anxious silence of Michelangelo's fellow artisans hinted at the uncertainty clouding their future patronage. Lorenzo had promised Michelangelo he would be welcome at the Medici household unconditionally, but the young sculptor wondered whether this promise could be fulfilled from beyond the grave. It was obvious to all his son Piero took little interest in the arts and was more consumed by his passions for sport, hunting, and competitive games.

The temperature turned cold and a thick mist descended over the city streets. As he trudged along, Michelangelo witnessed the bizarre counterpoint of blank faces and troubled countenances among the crowds of people: the trepidation registered visibly on their faces. When the procession passed Orsanmichele on the left, Michelangelo saw the gray outlines of the magnificent statue of St. George, carved by the great Donatello. As *La Vaca* throbbed, the brave Protector valiantly held up his powerful shield against the dragon, but he failed to dispel the gloom hanging over the city.

CHAPTER 20

A New Pope – August, 1492

THE OLD MARKET BAKED IN the summer sun and the two busy friars sweated under their woolen frocks. After buying provisions, Domenico sent the laden mule cart back to San Marco, then hurried after Silvestro. The native Florentine relished every opportunity on market day to gossip with his fellow citizens.

Today the market buzzed with rumors of the newly elected pope. Yesterday the bells had pealed all day while chants of *"Viva il Papa!"* announced the news. The death of Pope Innocent VIII, a few months after Lorenzo, had fulfilled the friar's second prophecy and the citizens bowed at the mere mention of his name, referring to him as the "Prophet." Their reverence was extended to all the brothers at San Marco and both friars glowed with self-importance—especially Silvestro, who could hardly contain himself.

On their way back to the convent, they noticed a small group of monks and laymen outside the Baptistery. As they approached Domenico saw several Augustinians, Benedictines and a few Franciscans in animated conversation, no doubt over the election of the infamous Spanish cardinal, Rodrigo Borgia. Legends of the debauched Borgia were colored with concubines and mistresses, bastard children, incest, murder, simony, and deceit. They said he was driven by a wolf's hunger for power.

Domenico hesitated warily, but Silvestro plunged into the center of the conversation.

"I find it strange they elected the Catalan," said a young Augustinian monk. "I thought the first and second votes were split between Sforza and delle Rovere."

Several others shrugged and shook their heads at the mystery of the Vatican enclave.

A gray-frocked Franciscan retorted, "Didn't you read the words of the official announcement of the appointment: 'In the year of the Lord 1492, on the 11th day of August, which was a Saturday in the early morning, Rodrigo Borgia, nephew of Calixtus III, was created Pope and named Alexander VI. Immediately after assuming the Papacy he distributed his goods and gave them to the poor.'

"What he distributed were bribes—Cardinal Sforza received the Vice-Chancellorship and just after the election several mules laden heavy with silver and jewels were seen delivered to his palace. As Supreme

Pontiff, Borgia will replenish his treasure chests tenfold."

The young monk persisted. "But how could they elect the Borgia devil? He's a Spaniard and they hate Spaniards in Rome. And what of all his treacheries? Poisoning his enemies and confiscating their properties? And his fornications? They say his bastard children visit him in his private apartments in the Vatican."

An older blind Franciscan was resigned. "May the Lord save us, brothers, I can smell the stink of Rome from here. Will the reign of black popes never end?"

At this, a layman chastised them all with a laugh, "*Roma*, it's the place where everyday Christ is bought and sold. So what else is new? The closer to Rome, I say, the farther from God."

At this Silvestro jumped in: "*Attenzione*. Listen, brothers and believe. The Fourth Age of the Apocalypse is upon us."

The others gave him a guarded look but he continued, eager to hold their attention.

"As written by Joachim and your Franciscan brethren, this age would be marked by the tepid ones—those who permit the degeneration of the Church and follow the lead of the anti-Christ. Perhaps this black pope is he? Thus he'll be vanquished by a great scourge on the corrupt Christian cities by an invader from the north: the Second Charlemagne!"

Domenico gave Silvestro a sharp look, but Silvestro would not be restrained.

Another Franciscan was skeptical. "Tell us then Maruffi, what does your Prior say about this pope? Is he the Anti-Christ?"

"Fra Girolamo predicted the death of Innocente and now it has happened. That devil met his rightful end, probably on his way straight to the eighth circle of the Inferno. Neither mother's milk nor the blood of three innocents could save his mortal body and only the Lord's mercy can save his soul."

Like a suspicious old woman, Silvestro crossed himself as he continued. "The Borgia is no better, he purchased the tiara with riches stolen from the Church. He worships only power and money. Fra Girolamo says the entire Church requires cleansing of this filth and this pope or that matters little to God's plan, for after the scourge the next age will be heralded by *il Papa Santo,* the Holy Pope who will restore God's House."

Silvestro relished his self-appointed role as the prophet's apostle and Domenico gave him another warning look he ignored.

The first Franciscan challenged him. "So, your Prior is just regurgitating the prophecies of Joachim of Flora and the Spiritual Franciscans? Is he directly opposed to the Roman Church?"

A fearful look crossed Silvestro's face and Domenico saw his left eye betray him. "No, no, I never said that. Fra Girolamo is faithful to the true Church. He only interprets the words of the Lord our God directly from the written Word. His visions come from God and the facts speak for themselves. Did he not predict the death of the pope and the tyrant as well? Do you doubt this?"

In the ensuing silence, Silvestro grew more confident. "Even the clever and wise Lorenzo, whom all the blind Florentines worshipped like sheep, knew the prior spoke the truth."

Then he lowered his voice. "Did you know the Medici requested absolution from Fra Girolamo as he lay on his deathbed? Yes? But you don't know the whole story."

"Enlighten us, Maruffi," said the Franciscan

"When the Medici requested absolution, Fra Girolamo would grant it only if he agreed to three conditions: first, that Signor Lorenzo acknowledge faith in God and admit his sins, to which he readily assented; second, to make restitution to those he had wronged in his life, and to this he also agreed since he had little use for his remaining riches; and third, he must restore liberty to the citizens of Florence."

He paused. "But this final condition the tyrant refused. Why? Because he could not free himself from his lust for power, so he was denied absolution and within moments his soul expired. Now I'm sure it burns in everlasting fire, with many fellow Florentines of similar treacheries, while here we suffer under a new tyrant—his son Piero."

As the others weighed the credibility of the source of this fantastic story, Silvestro puffed up and added, "But not for long, my brothers."

Domenico had had enough. He reacted before the others could elicit more loose gossip from Silvestro's tongue. He said forcefully, "*Basta!* Enough. We must return to the convent. *Now!*"

CHAPTER 21

DREAM OF TWO CROSSES

LATE INTO THE NIGHT FRA Girolamo huddled over his desk, writing quill in hand. He raised his magnifying glass to carefully reread a copy of the letter he had dispatched earlier to Rome in the care of two brothers from the Convent. It was to be delivered into the hands of Cardinal Caraffa of Naples, the Protector of the Dominican Order. The Cardinal favored the separation of the Tuscan chapter from the Lombard Congregation and his influence with the new pope would be critical to the petition. A separation would accomplish two important objectives: first, it would sever San Marco's from the radical, anti-Roman congregation of the Lombard Observants and second, it would make him, as Prior of San Marco, the new Vicar General of an independent Tuscan Congregation. This would promote his independence and empower him to institute the necessary reforms at San Marco without outside interference. One only wondered at the direction the new papal administration might take.

He knew he could count on the support of Caraffa to counter the opposition of the Lombards, especially that from Cardinal Ascanio Sforza, brother of the Duke of Milan. The Sforza did not want to lose control over the Tuscan Congregation and its influence within the Church hierarchy. The Duke had plans for the expansion of his duchy and his brother had his own designs on the papacy. On the other hand, Caraffa's objective was to further weaken Milan and the Sforza in favor of Naples. Fra Girolamo knew this web of Church politics was an intricate one and survival depended on the most delicate maneuvering.

Surprisingly, the petition had received the support of Piero de' Medici. Fra Girolamo remembered from his visit to Lorenzo's deathbed six months ago how the boy had stood apart in diffidence. At the time he had guessed at the boy's resentment toward his father's nemesis and since then Piero had communicated only infrequently by messenger and cut a wide berth around San Marco. But Piero's insecurities made him an unworthy opponent; his attitudes and actions were somewhat predictable. The prior had not expected him to grasp the mutuality of their interests on this issue, but apparently Piero had received good council—perhaps from Count Pico—because he had sent his own representatives to communicate with the pope and give support to the separation.

Of course, the Medici were trying to win favor with the pope and the king of Naples for their own reasons. Nevertheless, Piero would present few obstacles to his plans and, at best, might prove an unwitting foil against other opponents of the reforms.

Fra Girolamo knew many of the *grandi* families were obstructing his efforts to build a monastic retreat in the countryside at Monte Cano by withholding at the collection box. He had wanted to create a place there for his young novices outside the city, sheltered from the temptations and influences of their families. Every ambitious family knew the Church was the most powerful institution in Christian society and all desired their own advocates inside and close at hand. San Marco's novices and brothers were not all devious—most were just unwitting pawns—but Fra Girolamo knew he needed to break this connection in order to root out simony and corruption from within.

He felt his temples tighten and rubbed them with his open hands. He no longer felt hunger pangs, but the cramps in his lower abdomen persisted—a reminder of his body's weaknesses. Perhaps a short rest might invigorate his waning energy and quiet his rebellious gut. Retiring to his sleeping chamber, he lowered himself onto the slatted pallet and closed his eyes to pray. *O Lord... my faith calls upon You, I shall seek You as I call upon You, and call upon You as I believe in You...I would not exist, O God, were You not in me... I would not exist at all...*

The prayer renewed his confidence and strengthened his resolve. It was always this way—prayer rejuvenated the soul. He felt a wave of peace wash over him as the tension in his temples, wrists and fingers slowly released and his breath became more even. With his eyes closed, the blackness of night began to recede with the dawn, lulling him into a restful respite.

As he gave himself up in prayer he felt himself raised up off his pallet, transported as if on the wings of a giant bird. Then a flash of lightning and crack of thunder shattered his repose and darkness blotted out the morning light. He must be dreaming, but could not rouse himself; his arms and legs were frozen, as if under a heavy weight. He felt a helpless panic. Then another flash of lightning lit up the sky and he saw the vision of a giant cross, black against the angry clouds. It's top reached high into the heavens, its arms extending completely over the land below. At its foot he saw a walled city—it was the Vatican beside the winding River Tiber—filled with crowds of frightened people. Above all, written in the clouds, were the words CRUX IRAE DEI.

Immediately the weather became violent. Bolts of lightning and arrows hurtled through the sky as it rained hail, fire, and swords; all blown by a howling wind. These projectiles pierced the people on the ground and he could hear their screams. Among the former crowds, only a few escaped. He tried to cry out but could not as the weight on his chest suffocated him, crushing his breath. The thunder rumbled and lightning flashed, and he panicked, fearing he would be tossed into the conflagration. *It was the vision of damnation – the Cross of God's Wrath!* Time stopped as he poised in midair over the abyss. *Lord, my God, save me!*

Just as he was sure his racing heart would burst, the lightning and thunder ceased. Gradually the sky cleared and the destruction faded from view. He was now floating down on a gentle breeze and he heard the songs of angels. As the light of dawn broke, a feeling of safety flowed over him and he slowly recovered.

After some moments of peaceful calm he saw another cross in the clearing sky, as big and high as the first. He sensed no threat or fear this time, as the cross was golden and radiated like the sun. Below was another walled city and within he saw the Holy Temple of Jerusalem. The cross, so resplendent it lit the entire world, had another transcription written over it: CRUX MISERICORDIAE DEI.

Crowds of people from all parts of the world crowded into the golden city. They were dressed in white and smiled as they came forward to embrace the cross in adoration. He was overwhelmed—truly this was a vision of salvation. Then a strong voice spoke to him, but he became confused as bells tolling in the distance rang louder and closer.

With a start his eyes popped open and he became disoriented. It was the dark. Where was he? How did he get here? Then he realized he was still lying on the slatted pallet in his cell. It was night and the convent bell was tolling the hour of Matins. He must have slipped into sleep for several hours. He closed his eyes and tried to transport himself back to the vision of his dream. Struggling to remember the details, he rose and took up his quill to record what was still fresh in his mind.

It was the two cities—the vision of Babylon and Jerusalem from the Book of Revelation as chronicled by John. 'Fallen, fallen is Babylon the great! The mother of whores and of earth's abominations. And the whore is the great city that sits upon seven hills!

Yes, the great city was Rome! And then the Lord said, 'Come out of her, my people, so that you do not take part in her sins, and so you do not share in her plagues… and with such violence the great city will be thrown down, and will be found no more…'

And then there was the holy city under the Cross of God's Mercy. He wrote feverishly: 'And I saw the holy city, the new Jerusalem, coming down out of heaven from God, prepared as a bride adorned for her husband…after this I heard the loud voice of a great multitude in heaven, singing Hallelujah! Salvation and glory and power to our God…'

The friar saw it all clearly now, the choice God Almighty was offering them: Fall into depravity and sin like Rome and Babylon, condemned forever; or be redeemed by faith in God's everlasting mercy and be rewarded as the New Jerusalem. He went to the window and looked out over the sleeping city. He must wake them from their slumber. All he saw must be torn down in order to be rebuilt. The Lord had spoken and he wanted to shout for all to hear: "Let us become *Civitas Dei*, the City of God."

CHAPTER 22

PIERO DE' MEDICI AND MICHELANGELO

ANOTHER WINTER DESCENDED AND FOR two days and nights blankets of white floated down, draping the streets and making the city look strangely pure and virginal. It was a miraculous occurrence, even in the dead of winter. Despite the bitter cold, the snowfall engendered an adventurous mood among the aristocrats gathered at the Palazzo Medici, where Piero was holding court with his wife Alfonsina. It was now almost a year since his father had died and Piero had grown more confident in his preeminent position in Florence.

Hosts and privileged guests lounged in the main parlor before a roaring fire where at mid-afternoon a large banquet table had already been well picked over. Only the remnants of a sumptuous feast of game and fowl remained, dominated by the half-eaten carcass of a wild boar. Amid many empty carafes and scattered goblets of wine, Piero raised a toast his friends and supporters: the rich young scions of merchant trading and banking families.

"My friends, to our good fortunes and to the good fortunes of our fair city, which looks so appealing to the eye this day."

"And to our host!" shouted one of the guests.

"Bravo! Bravissimo!" rang the chorus.

"Have you spoken with your cousin since you cuffed him?"

"No," said Piero. "My cousins are ungrateful bastards, speaking ill of my father after he treated them so well. They complain to the Ministry of Justice with lies about how we stole their share of our grandfather's trust. But didn't we give them Castello and our farms in the Mugello? They just envy our success." He drained his glass and then shouted to his manservant.

"Is it impossible to keep my guests replenished with fresh food and drink? Vito, tell the kitchen to supply us with some confetti and berlingozzo cakes."

Turning to his guests, he added. "My servants spend most of their time listening to sermons these days—seeking salvation for their souls— but they forget who feeds their bellies. Thank God that noisome preacher is away in Bologna this season. Is he grateful I helped him secure his independence from the Lombards? The man doesn't know the meaning of gratitude. Let the Bolognese have a taste of him for a change."

Piero's future brother-in-law, a Ridolfi betrothed to his young sister

Contessina, said, "It's but a brief respite. This Fra Menico from Ponzo has taken up the slack. Do you think he's the eyes and ears of Milan?"

Piero was dismissive. "The Moor is caught between his fears and ambitions. This stupid Franciscan may be his spy—we'll find out. Sforza knows I favor the pope and the pope is aligned with his fellow Spaniards in Naples, so he encourages these preachers to whip up our citizens against the pope, thinking we'll fall into his lap. He's in for a rude surprise if he thinks Florentines harbor any love for the Milanese. My father humored them in order to keep the peace, but the Moor is only a pretender to the Duchy and soon either the French or the Aragonese will reclaim it. We must swing our weight toward the South—the overwhelming strength of Naples makes it the more important ally."

"But," Ridolfi persisted, "what about the French king? The French have long been friends with us, even the fleur-de-lis is on your arms."

"France is far away, we have no quarrel with them. Here in Italia, King Ferrante and the pope together outweigh all others. Remember," he winked, "we now have an important representative in the College."

Another guest agreed. "*Davero*, I'm sure Cardinal Giovanni will be a quick study in the ways of Rome. On a recent visit with my father, after witnessing all the pomp and lofty magnificence, I experienced a violent desire to become pope myself. I can't imagine any grander ambition. No longer do I marvel at these prelates desiring so ardently to procure this dignity, and I believe every lackey would sooner be made a pope than a prince!"

Piero winced at the sarcasm, not sure whether he was being mocked in comparison to his younger brother. The party was suddenly interrupted by the sound of children racing down the hall toward the room. The door burst open and in tumbled Piero's siblings: brother Giuliano and cousin Giulio, followed by a more composed Contessina.

The excitable Giuliano cried, "Piero, let's go outside and play in the snow. It's almost two *braccie* deep! I've never seen so much before."

In front of the older guests and her future husband, Contessina tried to control her voice, "Yes, let's go outside. It's whiter than Carrera marble and we can make a giant statue. Alfonsina, will you come?"

Alfonsina wrinkled her nose, cringing at the notion while inclining toward the fire. "I would freeze."

Piero stood up. "I've got a better idea. Why should we expose our hands and feet to this bitter cold just to build a poor snow statue when we have one of the finest sculptors right here in our employ. He waits patiently for a commission, so let's commission him! I'll have him carve us a giant Hercules in the courtyard."

Pleased with himself, Piero called to his manservant, "Vito, summon

Michelangelo."

***

The freezing snow numbed Michelangelo's bare hands as he packed it into solid balls of ice. Nevertheless, a burning anger warmed him. Trained as a sculptor of marble, he had languished here at the Medici palace without a commission for almost a year. Now, the foolish ass invites him to execute his first commission in snow! For the amusement of his friends, no less. Michelangelo felt his frustration. Piero had no appreciation for the sublime in art—he only understood the competition of sport and chase of the hunt, always riding his horses and parading around like a prince. Michelangelo knew Piero's desperate attempts to prove himself were necessary to compensate for being a mere pretender to the field of battle. How did this louse issue from his great father and grandfather?

He was convinced Piero had always envied him; resenting the privileged position accorded him by Lorenzo. Now, as *capo*, Piero openly displayed his contempt and Michelangelo knew this was the reason he was out here on a bitter, cold afternoon carving a sculpture from snow—snow that would melt in a day and leave no trace of his skill.

He heard light footfalls behind him. He turned to see Contessina bundled up against the cold in a long, hooded cloak with gloves on her hands. He tried to soften the angry look on his face, but she saw it clearly. Michelangelo could never learn the art of hiding his feelings.

"Agnolo, don't be angry. I'm sorry for the ill manners of my brother, but actually, I'm to blame. I'm the one who wished to make a statue with the snow, trying to please Giuliano."

He looked at her and his countenance brightened. "It doesn't matter. What else I can do in this weather. It's not so unpleasant. I've been imagining for some time a giant Hercules to commemorate your father and so now I'll just work out my ideas with snow. At least, it's more malleable than marble." He tossed a handful in her direction.

"How big will you make it? There's so much snow piled up here."

"As high as this scaffold, I think, perhaps five *braccie*. Look, here, I've already made a small model."

Contessina looked at the knee-high snow carving of a Greek hero and gasped with pleasure. "How exquisite! I'll get Giuliano and Giulio and we'll help you. We'll do it together." She ran back up the stairs.

A reluctant but determined smile returned to his face. Well, he thought, if it's a snowman he must make then he'll make a magnificent one—one to entertain the young and astound those who fail to appreciate the power of his talents. Word of the magnificent Hercules will spread quickly throughout the city and the grandeur of his skill will silence their laughter and cover his humiliation. It will be his best revenge.

The only real difficulty will be when his father hears of it.

CHAPTER 23

THE JEW

AS THE YOUNG WENCH LAY exhausted on the straw pallet Niccolò ran his hand over her bare backside; it was still firm and apple-shaped, not ample. She moaned again under his touch—he smiled, she was the adventurous sort—but he was already late as it was. He stood up to adjust his doublet and left the room.

He passed through the cool cellar of the tavern where he had just whiled away the hottest hours of the day in delightful decadence: playing dice, cards, and drinking copious amounts of wine. He had even won. Outside he squinted in the bright afternoon sun, trying to adjust his eyes from the darkness. The August heat hit him like the Inferno, especially after the dank coolness of the Frascato.

He felt full and satisfied as he headed back to the Oltrarno to meet the Soderini. Tommaso and his family had been in the country, with all sensible Florentines in August, but had returned early to celebrate Tommaso's formal engagement ceremony with the gift of the ring to Fiammetta Strozzi. For the shrewd Soderini, cementing this alliance was cause for celebration.

As Niccolò crossed through the Old Market he was surprised to see it almost deserted. When he turned and headed down the *Via Calimala* toward the Old Bridge, he saw the New Market was also deserted. The merciless heat had driven everyone indoors. As he passed within a block of the Piazza della Signoria this peculiar quiet was broken by the shouts of a crowd echoing down the narrow street. His natural curiosity pulled him toward the noise. Entering he heard a preacher thundering from the causeway recently constructed between the Loggia and the Palazzo. *Madonna mia*, he thought, another street sermon.

Several hundred people gathered around the rabble-rouser. Encouraged by the popular success of the prior of San Marco and wary of the imperialist papist policy of the Borgia pope, and as a check on the Medici, the Signoria had allowed these apocalyptic preachers to proliferate like locusts. In addition to the friar at San Marco, there were at least three others driving the citizens into a frenzy with their daily preaching, directed predominately against the corrupt Church. Though the Signoria thought itself clever to promote an anti-Roman agenda to check the pope, Niccolò knew it was a strategy that could easily spin out of control. Especially when conducted on the streets rather than within the tempering confines of the Church.

As he got closer, Niccolò recognized Fra Bernardino da Feltro, shouting out his diatribes against the 'enemies' of God. This itinerant madman had been banished from Florence five years ago but, due to the change in policy, had received permission to return. A mistake, thought Niccolò, which might have been avoided with a stronger leader than Piero de' Medici to restrain factions within the government.

From the faces of the crowd it appeared Fra Bernardino was eliciting his desired reaction. As Niccolò hovered on the fringe—close enough to hear, but far enough away not to get caught up in the frenzy— he heard the preacher's fiery message above the rabble: *"No one can persuade you that usury is sinful... you defend it at the peril of your souls!"* The crowd jeered and cheered.

Typical, thought Niccolò. The usurer was the favorite whipping boy of the Franciscan Order, vilified even more than that trinity of sexual sinners: sodomizers, prostitutes, and adulterers. It was the cornerstone of a pattern among reformist preachers, who attributed all moral corruption to avarice and the worship of mammon. Of course, it didn't stop there— much blame was also put to pure lust and the raw pursuit of power—but the moneylending Jews were an easy target and provided a ready scapegoat for the moral failings of Christian congregations. Ultimately, Niccolò believed, the condemnation of the Jews was rooted in envy. Everyone knew Jews were forbidden to join the guilds, cutting them off from manufacturing or the professional trades. But they were permitted to lend at interest and thus almost forced to ply their trade. Then, when discovered to be successful, were condemned for it. It was a paradox most Christians thought just punishment for the crime of murdering Christ.

Niccolò looked into their eyes and saw the preacher had driven out all reason. Like the relentless summer heat, his words seared into their raw insecurities. *"The usurers and their protectors hate the man who teaches justice and detest anyone who declares the truth. For their trampling on the poor man and for extorting levies on his wheat..."*

The rabble cheered on cue, for who among them had not felt trampled on by the rich? They lashed out like rabid dogs, the heat fueling their temper. Niccolò started to worry for an escape route when a sudden roar emitted from the far end of the Piazza. Niccolò looked and saw another crowd moving toward them, swarming the prison wagon of the Podestá. In the center of the wagon was a post with a prisoner tethered to it.

As the wagon pulled closer, Niccolò felt his stomach turn. Both the prisoner's hands had been severed at the wrists—leaving two bloody stumps. His severed hands were tied together and draped around his neck. He was shackled with a leather collar and appeared to be in a state of shock, unaware of the commotion around him. Shouts went up:

"It's the Jew who defaced the Virgin!"

"Murderer! Christ-killer!"

"Stone him! Stone the defiler of the Blessed Virgin!"

The two angry crowds merged in a boiling sea as many *fanciulli* raced around the wagon, whipped into a frenzy. As the frightened guards lost control of the situation Niccolò inched toward the alley leading to the river on the far side of the Loggia. The street boys hurled stones at the prisoner and Niccolò heard sickening thuds followed by screams as the stones tore into the man's flesh. He turned away in disgust and found himself running down the alley toward the Ponte Vecchio, his heart pounding in his chest.

Instead of crossing the bridge, he turned toward the quay, past the stench of the fishmongers, and stumbled down the embankment to the river's edge. Sitting down, he closed his eyes but could not erase the images of the Jew with his bloody stumps, nor could he silence the man's screams. Feeling woozy, he lay back on the embankment and tried to rein in the thoughts galloping through his head. All of a sudden he leaned over and convulsed, vomiting. Drawing in gulps of breath, he tried to calm his fear and disgust.

As he slowly recovered, he tried to comprehend what he had just witnessed. The basic tenets of human nature, reason, and logic became all jumbled. What kind of beasts are we? What fear turns God-fearing citizens into crazed animals? We're worse than the beasts... even animals don't kill for bloodlust... only man kills, crucifies, and despoils other men. It was primal—when animal fears dominate their nature, all men are truly cruel and brutish...

He was now convinced that fear must be conquered to restrain the beast. It would take strong laws and a virtuous state. Virtù needs a strong sword wielded in the name of a ruthless leader as Almighty God had with leaders like Moses who cut down disbelievers and blasphemers. This must be an unforgiving God, the Hebrew God *Yahweh,* not the Christian God. The Father, not the Son, the Christ who forgives man his sins and sacrifices himself on the cross. The malice in man must be rooted out, his fear conquered, and, if necessary, the unrepentant soul sacrificed. Otherwise, these malevolent beasts suffer no earthly consequences for the evil they commit—they merely confess to temporary madness and beg forgiveness. Perhaps this Jew was guilty of the sacrilege, but even so, the punishment of death must be administered by the rule of law and order. Madness only begets more madness.

Overwrought and confused, Niccolò tossed until he collapsed in exhaustion on the embankment.

He awoke later, still lying by the river. The sun was low in the sky and its warm red light showed through the porticos of the Ponte Vecchio. Though he was now several hours late, he must keep his appointment with the Soderini. He brushed off his hose and doublet and tried to clear his head as he crossed the river at a brisk pace, stopping at a fountain to wash his face and rinse out his mouth.

When he arrived at the Soderini family compound Tommaso greeted him at the door and chastised him for his tardiness. The family dinner was finished but the family was still relaxing in the afterglow of self-congratulation. Even Chiara was here with some other Soderini cousins, uncles, and aunts. But Niccolò's face betrayed him.

"What's wrong? You look unwell."

"Tommaso, *prego,* listen. I'm truly sorry... But I need to talk alone first."

"Of course, come in, we'll go to the library."

In the large well-appointed library, Niccolò paced back and forth with nervous energy as he relived the gruesome scene in the retelling. When he finished he was still shaken and Tommaso sat there in disbelief.

"It's incredible, barbaric. The Jews are sure to flee. I'm sure my father and uncle Piero will want to hear of this."

Niccolò paced as he waited for Tommaso to return with Messers Piero and Paolantonio. When they came into the room, Niccolò related the story once more. The two older men were disturbed but not surprised—Florentine history was littered with stories of similar atrocities.

Piero spoke first. "The Signoria has gone too far. Now they must banish Fra Bernardino again. Too late, I'm afraid, to comfort our Jews."

"It would be better for them to become good Christians," Paolo said.

"But how would we finance our trade without moneylenders and moneychangers?" Piero asked facetiously. "Besides, it's the pope and cardinals who borrow like Sultans. Look at the foolish Spaniards with their Inquisition—every year more *marranos* seek refuge here and it appears we'll drive them off as well. It disrupts our business and makes no sense."

Paolo countered, "Now you see. Fra Bernardino argued many years for a *Monte di Pietá* to loan to the poor and drive the usurers out of business. Even Fra Girolamo supports this idea, though he won't incite against the Jews."

"Well, perhaps it's not a bad idea, but it's too late for Fra Bernardino now. It's a shame we can't send that other loudmouth, Fra Menico, back to his master in Milan." Piero threw up his hands in frustration. "These damned preachers are just another problem. And these young Medici can't begin to grasp the intricacies of power and diplomacy. They're more concerned with accumulating benefices through the pope and pleasing the Spanish than in maintaining the delicate balance between the Republic's allies. I'm sure Sforza is now confused and suspicious of our intentions; he'll do something rash if he feels threatened."

Niccolò's mind was working fast. Today's events made clear to him the city was in a dangerous position with enemy forces gathering. He was also mindful of the growing split between Paolo and Piero over the friar. Recovering his composure, he interjected: "*Scusi, Signori.* The pope has already married his daughter off to one Sforza and his youngest son is betrothed to Ferrante's granddaughter. I believe he wishes to please both the Milanese and the Napolitani, strengthening his alliances for a strategic move to regain papal lands in the Romagna. They also say he plans to appoint many new cardinals to raise funds and consolidate his allies."

"But we've no direct ties to this Borgia pope, except through the Medici," said Paolo "In a clash between Milan and Naples, the pope will lean toward Naples. Neither threatens us but the pope has little regard for our independence and uses the Medici by promising more benefices to Cardinal Giovanni."

Piero pondered this. "I don't trust this pope. And we should be wary of the Medici, as Piero appears to favor his wife's Orsini connections. In the Seventy many of Lorenzo's supporters are distancing themselves from Piero and some of the younger members of the patrician families have openly defied him."

"Yes," added Tommaso. "There was that violent skirmish in Piazza Santa Croce between Piero's crowd and the Vipers last week."

Now Paolantonio pressed his point. "Fra Girolamo presents the best opportunity to foil any attempt by the *ottimati* to make a grab for power. He's in a much stronger position as Vicar General with of the Tuscan Congregation; he's also more learned than these ignorant Franciscans and sensitive to the city's welfare. Most important, the *popolani*, the poor, and the country peasants follow him in ever greater numbers."

Suddenly Niccolò saw the friar's usefulness in gaining advantage over the unraveling political situation. His preaching could influence the will of the masses that no faction could overcome. Before he could speak Piero clamped his arm around Tommaso and sighed, "*Dio mio*, all these calculations and complications for what should be a simple life. At least we're fortunate to reap this alliance with the lovely Fiammetta. Eh, nephew?"

As Tommaso grinned, his father was more circumspect. "Signor Filippo had a big brood and we're not the only ones—a Ridolfi has already married one of his daughters and the Rucellai and Capponi have their eyes on the others."

But Piero looked satisfied and winked knowingly. "Well, our family tree's got as many branches as any." This was true, the web of the Soderini family was growing every year—Tommaso now had five siblings with another due and a brood of cousins.

Piero addressed both Niccolò and Tommaso. "*Giovani*, it's clear our world is changing fast—it will soon be much different than the one we know. Why, one day maybe we'll even follow that crazy Genovese sea captain to his New World. Vespucci says his nephew Amerigo is now planning a voyage. They say the climate's so warm that fruit trees abound and natives cavort without clothes, like Adam and Eve in Paradiso!"

They all laughed as Piero put his arm around Niccolò. "*Allora, andiamo.* Come see the ring, Nico, and join us for another toast to the happy couple." Niccolò gave him a look of determination that spoke of other things on his mind. It would have to wait.

They exited the library and returned to a large sitting room where the Soderini and Strozzi women were gathered around Fiammetta. Niccolò saw Chiara's eyes brighten when their eyes met, but he was in no mood for gaiety; he was still shaken from the chaos and murder he had witnessed earlier. Anyway, what was the use? She was the next pawn to be played to strengthen the Soderini family alliances, and it wasn't going to be with a poverty-stricken Machiavelli.

CHAPTER 24

ALMS FOR THE POOR

FRA GIROLAMO FELT THE WINTER wind bite as he led his brethren out of the convent into the Piazza San Marco on one of their regular missions to deliver alms to the poor working neighborhoods along the river. Their excursions always took place on the day before the Lord's Day so the faithful would be reminded of the source of their salvation. There were a dozen of them altogether, all novices except for Domenico and Silvestro. Fra Girolamo recruited a different group each week to teach them the practical aspects of their vocation. They needed to experience the gross injustices of a society that left its least fortunate to fend for themselves. And they must learn to fulfill their duty to alleviate the suffering of all God's children.

Seeing them turn away from the bitter cold, he exhorted them: "Come, let our blood flow with the warmth of brotherhood. Let us sing *Ecce quam bonum* as we extend our charity and good will toward all." And so the troop, dressed in their white frocks and laden with food baskets, marched in two columns like a regiment down the Via Ricasoli singing their prior's favorite hymn.

In addition to their baskets of foodstuffs, Fra Domenico hauled the purse of offerings from the Church collection box, as well as monies earned from the sale of printed copies of the prior's sermons. The printer Fra Bartolomeo di Libri, a good Dominican, now devoted his presses full-time to transcriptions and each week Domenico's purse grew heavier. Fra Girolamo's labors for the Lord were now yielding fruit for the bellies as well as the souls of his congregation.

The wool workers and their families lived and worked in the Santa Croce quarter, but first the friars would take a route passing through the center of the city along the Via Calimala, the Street of the Wool Merchant Guild. This was deliberate. The city's textile merchants peddled silk, cotton, and various leather goods on these streets, but it was the wool trade that was preeminent. On the Via Calimala, they passed by a variegated rainbow of luxurious overgarments, woven carpets, bed and table coverings, tapestries and other items. For two hundred years the Florentines had grown fabulously wealthy and famous throughout the world on this trade and the prior wanted to be sure his novices witnessed the contrast of this swollen wealth with the abject poverty and neglect they would soon confront. As usual, their infectious hymn attracted a small crowd of *fanciulli* following close behind, while the merchants and their clients bowed in humble deference as they passed by. Fra Girolamo was sure they lowered their eyes to hide their shame.

From here they passed along the Street of the Hosemakers and turned down the Street of the Cauldrons before they arrived in the neighborhood of Santa Croce. As they entered the Road of the Dyers they encountered an army of grimy-faced children. These were the ones too young to work in the factories, but old enough to watch over their younger siblings while their parents worked. The children were uncommonly silent and expressionless with hunger written on their faces. They clung eagerly to the frocks of the mendicants as old women leaned out of their upstairs windows to shout at the children not to grab at the good friars. The old women then lowered baskets from their perches to collect a few coins from Fra Domenico's purse. Meanwhile, Silvestro directed the novices to fan out and enter the houses to distribute their alms.

As he surveyed their efforts, Fra Girolamo noticed several older children peering out from the shadows and a few shadowy figures duck behind closed doors. These were the ones with no work and he noticed each week their numbers grew. Without work the situation for these families grew worse and he remembered the excuses he had received when he had confronted the Signoria and the Guild leaders. Business was bad they said, competition in woolen textiles from the north was thinning the profits of the wool trade and there was nothing to do. These *grandi* acted the beggars, turning their empty pockets inside out.

But he knew they maintained their profits by paying less to their workers, who were then forced to toil from dawn till dusk for wages barely enough to keep them and their families alive, leaving them exposed to disease. One-third of the workers in Florence worked in the wool trade and they were living in squalor. The weakest suffered most from this decline in trade and this, he told them, would not escape God's notice. In response, the Signori praised his charitable efforts and passed a decree to encourage almsgiving. It was nothing. The charity of the mendicants was the poor's only lifeline.

Fra Girolamo ducked his head to enter one of the small, dark hovels and inside found two young girls watching over a toddler. There was a brazier smoldering in the corner but the room was chilly. The older girl held out her hand and smiled when he smiled back. Then he called out to the novices to bring fresh bread and the flask of goat's milk and offered bread to the two girls and the goat's milk to the toddler. As the girls happily devoured the bread and the toddler sucked ravenously a woman came rushing through the doorway from the street. She was out of breath and when she saw Fra Girolamo, she fell quickly to her knees and bowed her head, mumbling in prayer:

"Grazie a Dio, Padre é gentile frati…"

The woman was meanly dressed in a peasant's frock of torn linen, her hair pulled up and covered in a scarf. She looked too old, but was obviously the mother of these children. She smelled of ammonia and her rough skin and tortured hands told him she worked as a carder or spinner of wool.

"Rise, Signora. Take this bread and water and feed your babies."

The woman grabbed the friar's hand with a desperate plea. "Blessed Father, I must return quickly to the *fondacci*, I said I was ill… I only came to be sure my young ones received a small bit of bread and some milk. We have no food and no wages until next week. Please, Father, give us your blessing," she pleaded as she lowered her head again and let her hands fall upon the folds of his frock.

Fra Girolamo recoiled on impulse. His growing reputation as a "prophet" had caused these frequent confrontations where the poor desired to grab at him and touch him in the hopes of some miracle.

"No, no," he said. "Rise up. I do not bring you salvation, only these meager rations. You must put your faith in the Lord and pray to Him for your children. Your God is merciful. He has said, 'Blessed are the poor in spirit, for theirs is the kingdom of heaven and blessed are the meek, for they shall inherit the earth.' Say your prayers to the Virgin Mother, for she keeps watch over all her children."

Then Domenico came into the room looking for him and the prior took a handful of small coins from the purse and offered them to the mother. "Here, take these few coins and buy your children some bread and soup to tide you through the week. Don't despair. Tomorrow, come with your family to the church of San Marco to celebrate the Lord's Day. Rejoice and be glad, for great is your reward in heaven."

"Grazie Padre, grazie à Dio, grazie à Madonna e Figlio e Spirito Santo…"

Fra Girolamo looked at Domenico. "Come, we must go now and visit the workers. Be with God, my children." He smiled to reassure the young ones and blessed them all.

***

They marched down to one of the factory buildings close against the river and descended into a large room filled with boiling cauldrons surrounded by spools of raw wool. The workroom was stifling hot and the stench of urine used to cure the wool was overwhelming. With their clothes and skin darkly stained by the many dyes—all blended together in a murky, brownish black—the workers resembled those black shadows condemned to the *Inferno*. Ammonia and alum burned the skin and destroyed the lungs while the contaminated workrooms lacked fresh air and clean water. Their hellish life on earth would be brutal and short.

The laborers looked up when the Dominicans entered and interrupted their activities in a show of respect. As work activity ceased, the foreman turned with a scowl, which turned to an effusive smile when he saw Fra Girolamo.

"Welcome, Father," he said as he gave a hasty bow. "We have eagerly awaited your visit," he added, with a noticeable lack of conviction. Then he shouted above the din, "*Ragazzi! Attenzione!* The Prior of San Marco."

Fra Girolamo raised his right hand and projected in a clear, powerful voice, "Please, my brothers, we have come to distribute alms to alleviate the suffering of your families in this harsh season." He turned and instructed the novices to distribute the alms from Domenico's purse as the foreman made a face of pained forbearance.

The workers bowed their heads and whispered their thanks as the friars passed their offerings around the workroom. As Fra Girolamo began his impromptu mini-sermon, one worker whispered to another: "With the death of the King of Naples, three of his prophecies have now come to pass. It's a miracle."

His companion whispered back, "Yes, I would never believe it, but by God it's true. My wife and I attend all his sermons when we're able. I'm waiting for his next prophecies."

As they whispered the friar's words echoed through the room.

"...and we come to join with you in the brotherhood of the faithful, the brotherhood of man who lives together in communion with God. For He who said, 'Let each of you look out not only for his own interests, but also for the interests of others. Let nothing be done through selfish ambition or conceit, but in humility let each esteem others better than himself...'"

Glancing at the stern-faced foreman, the first dyer said gingerly: "No wonder the *grandi* fear him. He speaks not only of justice in the next world, but in this one too."

When the friar paused, a worker across the room called out: "Father, forgive me, I mean no disrespect, but please tell us how can we celebrate this community with God when our work pays so little we cannot feed our families. Where is this brotherhood in the city? Where is God's justice in this world?"

A murmur rose up and then quieted as the foreman hushed them and Fra Girolamo answered: "My son, there's no shame in poverty though there is pain in hunger. You may have little bread to show for your efforts, and when your children cry in hunger, the rich and powerful close their ears. Our city suffers from a lack of charity and this is no fault of the poor. But we must work together and by our efforts correct these injustices. I encourage you to keep faith, do not lose hope and do not despair.

"Don't envy the rich, for they are poor in spirit. God has sent me a message with a vision, a vision by which the rich and powerful will suffer His wrath for the injustices they visit upon the poor. Remember the words of the gospel: on the final day, the last will be first and the first last."

The hum rose again and the foreman looked worried. Their nods and mumbles affirmed the words of the friar as he spread his arms in a symbolic embrace to calm them.

"My brothers, I remind you there is power, goodness, and justice beyond evil. God has destined us not for wrath but for salvation through our Lord Jesus Christ, who died for us so we may share in the kingdom of Heaven. I ask you to follow our example at our convent of San Marco. We have turned away from the luxuries of this world and banished them from our sight. We beg for alms and we toil for the salvation of those in need and for the glory of God. If you have need, please come and take what you need—it will be given. But heed the words of our Lord and do not love the world or the things in the world. If anyone loves the world, the love of the Father is not in him. No one can serve two masters—either he will hate the one and love the other, or else he will be loyal to the one and despise the other."

The room grew silent as Fra Girolamo found his rhythm: "I have told you the scourge will come and those who have defiled the temple of the Lord will be destroyed. Woe to those fornicators, idolaters, adulterers and sodomites. But if you keep faith with the Lord, your God, do not let fear consume you. For I say if you truly amend your ways, if you truly act justly one with the other, then the Lord will dwell with you in this place. Let faith and charity be your watchwords and then mercy, peace, and love will be yours in abundance."

Then one of the whispering workers called out, "Father, when will these things happen, how long must we wait while our little ones go hungry?"

Fra Girolamo's face became stern. "Watch, for we cannot know when the master of the house comes. He revealed to me it would be soon, so watch, I tell you, lest He finds you sleeping." The buzzing grew louder as the prior led his brethren in their hymn of brotherhood before departing.

***

On the way back to the convent one of the novices quickened his step against the cold and drew up alongside the prior.

"Pardon me, Father," he said, "but why does God visit the undeserving poor with tribulations? How can He allow this? What sins have they committed to deserve such a fate?"

Fra Girolamo immediately was reminded of the lessons of his grandfather and replied softly: "My son, remember when we spoke of Job? How God allowed Satan to visit such suffering and tribulations on his faithful servant? Satan the Tempter was sure Job would curse his unmerciful God after he lost his wealth. But Job did not question God. Then he lost his children and again he did not curse God. Job's friends convinced him he must have committed some great sin to deserve such suffering, so he prayed for forgiveness. Finally, Job lost his wife and fell into a deep despair, but still he did not turn away from God. Do you remember the lesson of these trials?"

"That God inflicted such sufferings on Job to test his faith?'

"Yes, as God will often test the faith of his strongest followers. Job did not curse God but affirmed his faith, and as a reward the Lord restored Job's fortunes twofold. This too is our reward. What appears to our eyes as evil must be a part of God's plan. Remember, it is not our place to question the ways of the Lord, if we keep our faith we shall be rewarded."

The novice absorbed the prior's words thoughtfully, then asked, "And the pestilence, Father? Does God test us with the pestilence?"

The friar sensed the boy's fear, but could offer no words of comfort.

CHAPTER 25

SODERINI-STROZZI WEDDING

NICCOLÒ WANDERED THROUGH THE WEDDING party, a select circle of the most esteemed and privileged persons in Florence. There were Medici, Tornabuoni, Rucellai, Vespucci, Soderini, Strozzi and more filing through the courtyards and foyers of the Soderini family complex where the banquet had taken place due to the displacement of the Strozzi awaiting the completion of their new palazzo.

It had been a long day as Tommaso and Fiammetta's wedding celebration had unfolded like a magnificent tapestry of Florentine honor and pride uniting two powerful families. It was perhaps not as ostentatious as a Medici affair, but close. Today was the Festa di San Giovanni, the most important festival in the city's civic tradition and the most auspicious for marriages, so the preparations had started early, before the raucous civic parade began. Niccolò had been one of the gallants who complimented the bride with bouquets of flowers as she was delivered on horseback to the Cathedral. Flowers were strewn along the streets as she passed, accompanied by her many ladies in waiting, Chiara among them.

The wedding mass was said by the Canon of the Cathedral and accompanied by a choir. Later, the wedding party was feted with innumerable courses of food delivered by an endless regimented parade of stewards, all attended by trumpets and singers. Niccolò surveyed the carnage: banquet tables overflowed with the remnants of all sorts of dried fish, chicken, pheasant, veal and wild game; the side tables were piled with fruits, nuts and sweetmeats; and the barrels of various wines included heavy blood-red Trebbiano and Chianti, light white Vernaccia of Crete and too sweet Malvasia of Greece. Not a bad selection given the year had been a sour one for wine. Obviously the sumptuary laws had been overlooked for this occasion. As the banquet wound down the musicians would soon take up the cue and the choreographed dancing would begin.

Niccolò observed the uneasiness many of the guests showed toward Piero de' Medici, who, as usual, overplayed his presence. It was now more than two years since Lorenzo's passing and Piero was day-by-day becoming less popular. The rumors arriving from abroad told of a brewing conflict between France and Naples and many were losing confidence in Piero's leadership. Today the large Strozzi and Soderini clans were overwhelming in numbers and Niccolò suspected Piero felt even more insecure outflanked by his relatives and family rivals.

But this was not a day for the Medici; it was one for the Soderini. Even Tommaso was resplendent in his role as groom, coveting his bejeweled bride. It had been almost a year since the official engagement and Niccolò had the impression Tommaso had finally taken possession of his treasure, the value of which he had just estimated. With the size of the dowry Fiammetta had brought, Tommaso was now a wealthy man in his own right and Niccolò felt an uncharacteristic wave of warmth for him—one must not envy happiness. Could his dispassionate friend have actually fallen in love?

Nearby was Tommaso's brooding father, Paolantonio. Surrounded by his clan of children, brothers, sisters and nephews, he seemed almost burdened by a fragile contentment. Tommaso was his first son of eight children by two wives, but third son Francesco had died suddenly several years ago and the second, Tommaso's brother Alessandro, was now seriously ill with consumption and the toll showed on their devoutly religious father. Then again, the cruel scales of life were balanced by the birth of two new sons in the last three years. God giveth and God taketh away.

"Enjoying yourself, Nico?"

Niccolò turned to face Piero Soderini and his wife. "Signor Piero, Signora Argentina," he said, bowing low to his hosts. "Yes, it is truly a joyous occasion."

"It's a blessing to have children and watch them grow. We are most fortunate in our nieces and nephews," said Piero. "Life passes so quickly," added his wife, wistfully.

Niccolò smiled graciously at Signora Argentina. Piero had made an acclaimed marriage twenty-five years ago to this daughter of the Marchese of Fosdinova. It was a noble match, but they had not been similarly blessed with children.

The dance music began and Signora Argentina excused herself. As the young people gathered in the courtyard, Piero leaned closer as if to confide a secret. He had begun to treat Niccolò as a confidant and Niccolò inclined his ear, expecting some inside political gossip.

"Remember, Nico, there are only two requirements for an ideal marriage."

Just a witty joke, but Niccolò played along. "Two?"

"Yes,' said the older man, suppressing a grin. "First, the husband should be deaf as a stone, and second, the wife should be blind as an oyster. That way the wife can't see her husband's escapades, and he can't hear her constant nagging."

Niccolò smiled broadly as Piero chuckled. Then quietly, Piero added, "I believe our strategy is working to our advantage. The *popolo* flock to the friar and the *popolani* are following along in greater numbers."

"Yes, his star rises as the *palle* falls, at least for the moment."

"I think I can convince Capponi of our policy, and Paolo's in a strong position to help. But perhaps we shouldn't burden him with our plans—better if I manage it."

Niccolò nodded his assent, implicitly understanding the value of discretion, especially among family members.

"Look, here come my lovely nieces. Here's your chance for a dance." Then Piero moved off to follow his wife.

The clique of girls crossed the courtyard, circling together like a flock of doves. Niccolò caught Chiara's eye and she greeted him coyly—the wedding ritual had flushed her with romantic notions.

"Did you see Fiammetta? She's ravishing! And Tommaso looks so elegant."

The musicians struck up the music for a new French dance choreographed for four couples called the *reogarza*. Niccolò held out his arm to Chiara, who smiled as she took it. Hearing the girlish titters behind him, he was about to step into the dance area when they were shunted aside by four couples from the Medicean quarter, led by Piero de' Medici and his wife Alfonsina.

CHAPTER 26

Piero Plays Football

STYLISHLY OUTFITTED IN THEIR RESPECTIVE team colors of red and green blouses and tight breeches, the young men sweated profusely under the hot summer sun as they chased the ball around the large campo in the Piazza Santa Croce, where these games of *calcio* were frequently played. It was a fast-paced, violent game scored by kicking a stitched ball of leather through opposing goal posts. Many spectators had come to watch a hotly contested match between the rival San Giovanni and Santa Maria Novella quarters and to admire the play of Piero de' Medici, the most skillful player on the Greens of San Giovanni. They whistled, waved their banners and screamed encouragement to their favorites.

At the far end of the campo Piero Soderini stood on the steps of the Church of Santa Croce, casually viewing the match with two of his colleagues from the Council of Seventy, Bernardo Rucellai and Piero Capponi. They were well acquainted—each having served at various times as Priors in the Signoria—and were here in their official capacity to survey the damage from a severe flood the previous week when the Arno had inundated this quarter with mud and debris.

Soderini queried Rucellai. "Have you spoken with Piero about the next lottery for the Signoria? Has he made a decision about when we shall send another embassy to Charles?"

Rucellai shook his head in disgust. Signor Bernardo had long been an intimate of the Medici circle, a loyal supporter of his brother-in-law Lorenzo, but the generational gap with Lorenzo's son was wide.

"I've only spoken with Bibbiena, that lackey, who keeps repeating the excuse his *Lord* Piero is busy, which means he's either out in the Mugello hunting, or here, as we see, kicking a ball."

The energetic Capponi was more blunt: "The world hasn't stopped because the Republic languishes without leadership. Charles's army is crossing the Alps and he travels with a hundred siege cannons drawn by horses—I've seen them, you know, and I tell you no walled city can withstand their bombardment. They'll be marching the length of Italia and we're directly in his path. I don't think Naples, or anyone else, can resist an attack by these legions."

Just last month Capponi had led a diplomatic mission to the French court to meet the king and since returning Soderini noticed he had become more brusque and outspoken. His patience with Piero de' Medici was wearing thin.

Soderini agreed. "Piero has aligned with the weak monarchy in Naples while also offending the Sforza in Milan, all of which could spell disaster for us. The French will request our cooperation, but our bargaining position is seriously weakened. This flood ruined the crops and our grain supplies are insufficient for any winter siege campaign." Addressing Capponi, he asked, "What do you think of our negotiating position with Charles?"

"The king has no quarrel with us. I believe he expected we would side with him against the Aragonese in Naples. His father was close with Lorenzo and Piero the Gouty, but the sons have never met and some in the French court are critical of Piero's casual disregard for French interests. We tried to reassure the king and his advisors that, contrary to Piero's actions, the Republic stands fast to our long friendship with the House of Valois."

"And?" Soderini persisted.

"I fear we have enemies as well as friends within the king's court. Charles is indecisive and easily influenced; his only deep desire is to use his army to expand his territories, thereby showing he's got the balls of a king if not the body. This deficiency makes him vulnerable to courtiers, though I believe his ambassador, de Commines, is favorable to us."

"Sforza's the real problem," interjected Rucellai. "The pope rebuffed Milan, forging ties with Naples with his son's marriage to the king's daughter. This leaves Sforza isolated, a usurper to the Duchy of Milan. Tyrants who rule in fear often act rashly."

Capponi disagreed. "The Moor is only afraid of Naples and the consequences of his mistreatment of his nephew. Beyond that, he's what we should expect—a petty despot who wishes to expand his family's territory together with a brother in the College of Cardinals. Sound familiar?" He paused before continuing. "We must do what we can to counteract this foolish policy that is really no policy at all. The Council's grown strongly critical of Piero's actions and the citizens have become anxious. They've enjoyed a certain peace for so long that just the thought of war unnerves them. Panic is our worst enemy."

Soderini nodded in agreement as they descended the steps on their way back to the Palazzo. Capponi spoke with the sureness of an experienced Florentine merchant who knew the risks in managing business affairs. He brought the same serious of purpose to his role in government, which was why it was expected he would soon be selected again as Gonfaloniere. The unspoken implication though, was a direct break with the Medici.

This was the opportunity Piero was waiting for. In an off-hand manner, he said, "My brother Paolo believes the friar of San Marco might help us survive the Medici's bungling—Savonarola's as popular as Piero is despised."

Rucellai bristled at the idea, as Soderini expected, but Capponi contemplated it in silence. It was Nico Machiavelli who had suggested the friar might be the key to managing the city's deteriorating affairs. Savonarola's fearful preaching was just what was needed to keep the people in line. All the former supporters of Lorenzo—men like Capponi, Rucellai, and Vespucci—were jockeying for position in the face of Piero's inadequacy. As Niccolò had pointed out, if there was a free-for-all the *popolo* would be the decisive factor. Soderini was sure with Paolo's help and the friar's influence, he could prevail over the rival factions. Capponi would either be a strong ally or a dangerous foe.

As they exited Piazza Santa Croce, the shouts and screams of the spectators reached a crescendo as the final moments of the match were counted down. With his team well ahead in scoring, Piero taunted the opposing players, controlling the ball to keep it away from them. At the final trumpet blast he ran into the arms of his teammates and collapsed to the cheers of the crowd.

Stripping off his green blouse, he raised his arms in a pose of victory and shouted over the mayhem: "*Car'amici tutti*, in honor of our victory I invite you all to my house for an evening of celebration! Let us eat, drink, and enjoy the moment!" With Piero's pronouncement, the crowd erupted in joy and moved as one out of the piazza.

CHAPTER 27

SCOURGE OF GOD SERMON

MICHELANGELO RAISED HIS EYES UPWARD to behold the rays of the sun shooting through the colored lunettes high within the nave of the Cathedral. He watched the light play across the nave and the transepts, a rainbow of crossed swords carving the three-dimensional space into light and shadow. His eye traced the thrusting stone pillars, which sprang up from the earth to join together at the top in arches and vaults, like fresh lilies reaching for the spring sun. Hearing the choir, he closed his eyes and felt his soul expand. As the clear voices punctuated the Mass with hymns, starting with the Kyrie and ending with the Agnus Dei, he felt the harmonic vibrations carry his soul up into the heavenly dome and fill its vast expanse.

He had positioned himself near the cupola in order to admire Brunelleschi's magnificent handiwork. It was incredible to behold this hollow mountain of stone floating up so high, providing a protective roof over the souls huddled below. Every detail was exquisite and the sum infinite; here was the most beautiful building in all of Italia. He thought if God would only grant him the opportunity to create a work of such strength and beauty in his short lifetime, he would die complete.

At the end of the Mass the packed Cathedral began to buzz and Michelangelo surveyed the sea of bodies hemming him in. Their faces were etched with lines of fear and worry. For two and a half years, since the death of Lorenzo, the people had suffered this creeping anxiety as scant hopes in Piero dissolved into further disappointments and impending threats to their safety. Three weeks earlier the great French army had crossed the Alps, bypassing Milano, and were now heading straight for their throats. Allies or not, a legion of bloodthirsty mercenaries and foreigners couldn't contain their lust for the spoils of war. In the past two months country peasants had crowded into the city with all they could carry and, as these refugees overflowed all available living space, the mood of the townspeople had become increasingly inhospitable. With no place to go and little to do, the homeless and their reluctant hosts crowded together into the Cathedral to seek deliverance under the moral guidance of their famed prophet.

The friar's sermons had become a series of chapters in an unfolding drama where the thread of the last sermon continued into the next and the entire city became caught up in suspense to know the ending.

Michelangelo saw most of Florence crammed within the massive Cathedral, elbowing each other for hard-won vantage. The air was permeated with the scent of incense and the odor of stale sweat, an odd mingling of hope and fear.

Looking down the nave toward the front entrance, he saw the pulpit hover above the heads of the crowd. This was where the friar would preach and Michelangelo was satisfied with his position. Close by he saw Count Pico and Maestro Angelo, with whom he had come but had been separated by the crowd. Beyond them a large curtain hung down the center of the nave dividing the women from the men. There would be no co-mingling of the sexes within the House of God, at least not when the prophet spoke.

The hum of the crowd became more insistent as Fra Girolamo ascended the pulpit. The friar wore his simple white woolen frock with the black cappa with hood pulled up over his head. The crowd hushed when he raised and spread his arms out over them. With his hood up, Michelangelo thought Fra Girolamo resembled a frightening representation of the Grim Reaper. The silent, frozen image heightened the audience's sense of suspense until finally, at the moment of peak tension, the Preacher threw back his hood and his voice cracked like a thunderbolt.

"Florence, O Florence! For your sins, for your cruelty, for your greed, ...for your lasciviousness, for your ambition, ...for all these and more, you have yet to suffer many evils!"

The words echoed off the high walls of the Cathedral and fell like heavy hammer blows. The congregation cowed and Michelangelo heard women wailing from the far side of the curtain. His audience wounded and their attention riveted, the friar then tempered his voice and addressed them with his drafted sermon.

"...Florence, you know for sixty years you have had an armed man in your home...he robbed you of your goods and your women, and you were compelled to bear all with patience. You know of whom I speak..."

The friar went on to condemn the "tyrants" who used power and wealth to achieve their personal ends to the detriment of the community. Lately he had been unleashing his vitriol on the Medici and it played well. Michelangelo reacted with mixed feelings to these indirect attacks on Piero, and by inference on Lorenzo and Cosimo before him. On one hand, he was glad to see Piero receive his comeuppance from the prior and the Florentine public. In over two years Piero had still not approved any new commissions for him and Michelangelo had reached the end of his patience with the posturing princeling. Rejecting his small stipend, Michelangelo had moved out of the Palazzo back into his family home, to the consternation of his father.

But conversely, Michelangelo was concerned for his own welfare because he was known primarily for his association with the Medici. If the Medici were driven from the city, who knows how he would fare and he feared for his own safety. Thoughts of fleeing to Bologna or Venice for work and refuge recently occupied his mind, but he told no one, not even Francesco or his family. The friar's voice cut through the pregnant silence:

"Let me describe for you this city. In these days there is no grace, no gift of the Holy Spirit that may not be bought or sold. The shepherds of the Church now lie with the wolves. The poor are oppressed by grievous burdens; they are hungry and sick. When they are called to pay sums beyond their means the rich cry unto them, 'Give me the rest.' But heed my warnings—you who are rich and powerful—your punishment will come. God will set it right and Florence will no longer be a city of flowers. It will be called a den of thieves, of vice and bloodshed... "

***

Several meters away, Count Pico saw the heads of the well-dressed *grandi* near him bow lower as they pulled in their necks, like geese hoping to escape the farmer's axe. He sighed inwardly. The foolish Piero had no one but himself to blame for the public's loss of confidence and simmering frustration. Piero's rejection of the Duke of Milan in favor of the king of Naples had put them all in harm's way and the friar continued to remind the people of their years of complacency and the price they paid. Pico knew Fra Girolamo had privately criticized Lorenzo's methods of control but those methods had been justified by expediency—Lorenzo had always been a worthy leader of his city and it seemed necessary at the time. But his son's weaknesses have led to stupid mistakes and now the people were calling him the Unfortunate in cruel comparison to the Magnificent. But Pico could do no more as Piero rejected his counsel and even that of Angelo, who had tutored him since he was a child.

Pico looked over at Angelo. His friend was pale and weak, slowly wasting away after the death of his adored Lorenzo. His will to write and create—to live—had vanished. Luckily, Pico was able to convince Angelo to accompany him and Ficino on their regular visits to the Library of San Marco, where they now held discussions of the Academy. In time, Angelo had softened his antagonism to Fra Girolamo and even came to embrace the visits as solace for his melancholy. Pico himself had willfully come to acknowledge the righteous wisdom of the prior and was preparing to join the Order of the Preachers. The intellectual pride he had known for so many years would now be humbly directed to saving souls. Pico looked up as Fra Girolamo expounded on scripture, knowing another deluge of words was coming.

Savonarola waved his arms as he spoke: "…and the Lord said, 'See these great buildings? There will not be left one stone upon another that will not be thrown down. And when you hear of wars and rumors of wars, do not trouble yourself, for such things that signify the end shall not yet be. For nation will rise against nation, and kingdom against kingdom, and there shall be earthquakes and there shall be famines and other troubles. We are in the grip of evil and these are only the beginnings of our sorrows.'"

The congregation started to plead the *Misericordia* as the friar picked up his tempo and began to hammer his fist on the lectern.

"I have told you how Noah was a righteous man and walked with God. But God saw the earth was corrupt, for all flesh had corrupted its ways upon the earth. And the Lord was sorry He had made humankind and it grieved Him to His heart. So God said to Noah, 'I have determined to make an end of all flesh, for the earth is filled with violence because of them; now I am going to *DESTROY* them along with the earth.'"

Savonarola's voice became high-pitched, echoing sharply across the large chamber of the Cathedral. He raised both arms high and cried out:

"Divide, O Lord, divide once again the waters of the Red Sea, and let the impious perish in the flood of Thy wrath! And God said, '*Ecce ego adducam diluvii aquas super terram!* I am going to bring a *flood* of waters on the earth, a *flood* to destroy from under Heaven all flesh in which there is a breath of life…*EVERYTHING ON THE EARTH SHALL DIE.*'"

Pico was startled by the fury in the friar's voice as cries and shrieks of fear loosed from behind the dividing curtain. He was sure the women were fainting as he heard cries of *"Madonna mia!"* He felt the hair rise on the back of his neck as fear snaked through the crowd around him. Then Savonarola disappeared from view and darkness descended over the congregation. He had a sense of foreboding and turned to see Angelo pale and then collapse in slow motion, though the crush of bodies prevented him from falling to the floor. Pico quickly grasped him under the arms and lowered him against the large stone pillar.

***

From his position a few meters away, Michelangelo watched the crowd roil like an angry sea whipped by the wind. He no longer saw Pico or Poliziano where they had stood. The friar had dropped from view but his hands were still grasping the front of the lectern. Michelangelo experienced a brief feeling of dizziness, as if they were all on a ship being tossed by large waves. He leaned up against the pillar to avoid the shoving crowd and waited for the storm to pass.

After a few tense minutes the friar stood up again and raised his arms to calm the multitude. His voice was now soft and calm, a respite from the tempest, and the men in the congregation fell silent as the Preacher took up the thread again.

"But, I tell you, good people of Florence, Noah was a righteous man. Noah found favor in the sight of the Lord ... and Noah and his kind were saved. So you too, must do as the Lord says: Wash yourselves, make yourselves clean, cease to do evil, learn to do good, seek justice, rescue the oppressed, defend the orphan, plead for the widow. Let us build together an ark of the spirit to survive the flood.

"'If you are willing and obedient, you shall eat the good of the land. But if you refuse and rebel, you shall be devoured by the sword, for the Lord has spoken."

Moans of the *Misericordia, "Lord, have mercy,"* commenced in earnest, as the average Florentine knew where he or she stood on the Day of Judgment. Savonarola raised his voice above the din.

"For some months now I have told you the Sword of God will come from the North, as was prophesied. I have seen it in a vision! But the Lord said the day and the hour was known by no man. But take heed, the scourge of God, *flagellum dei*, approaches with his vast and powerful army!" The Preacher thrust his right arm upward. "The Great King, Charles, comes as Cyrus to Jerusalem. To vanquish the evildoers and restore the land to the faithful."

A single shout rose from one of the congregation, "The second Charlemagne!"

A second shout followed, "Save us from the French invaders!"

Savonarola's voice reached a feverish pitch, cutting through the clamor as he thrust both hands into the air, his voice echoing through the vast chambers of the Cathedral.

"Be afraid of the sword, for wrath brings the punishment of the sword, so you may know there is a judgment. Behold, it is the Lord God who is leading these armies... *Behold, I shall unloose waters over the earth*... the prophecies are fulfilled. It is not I, but God who foretold it. Now it is coming. It has come! *Ecce gladius Domini super terram cito et velociter!* The Sword of God is coming to earth, *SOON AND FAST!*"

He crashed his arms and fists down on the lectern and collapsed over the pulpit with a gasp. Michelangelo had never witnessed anything like it: It was as if a burning energy of unworldly power flowed through the friar until it spent in one fiery burst, a shooting star flaming out across the sky. The aftermath accentuated the frailty of the man, who lay in a heap of sackcloth upon the pulpit. For a timeless moment the sound and fury of the friar's voice resounded in Michelangelo's ears, "The Sword of God is coming to earth, soon and fast!" and he saw the imagined fury of an angry God. He closed his eyes and saw flashes of images similar to the illustrations of the *Inferno* by Botticelli—all those burning, tortured souls screaming for mercy in the boiling pitch fires of Hell. He saw the Last Judgment at the throne of the Almighty, with the lifeless souls of sinners damned, descending into Satan's fire. He felt dizzy as he opened his eyes to take in the scene before him.

The reaction of the congregation was equally fantastic. There were screams from the women and shouts among the men, reminding Michelangelo of sheep scattering in a pasture during a lightning storm. The choir sang *Gloria in excelsis Deo* as several laypersons ascended the pulpit to assist Savonarola down. Sensing the sermon was over; the crowd scurried for the doors. They clogged the large doorways as Michelangelo stayed frozen in his place against the pillar, absorbing the surrealness of the moment, the *Gloria* still ringing in his ears. In the thinning crowd he saw Pico helping Poliziano rise from the floor. He hurried over to assist the Count and saw the confusion in his eyes. These two learned titans of Michelangelo's young world now seemed weak and sickly.

"Oh, there you are Agnolo. Yes, please, help me hold him. He's not well and I think the stale air and the heat caused him to faint. Perhaps the friar's words also had some effect. We must get him outside."

The two men easily supported Poliziano out the side door of the Cathedral where he revived a little in the fresh air. The people were still streaming out onto the streets in a rush to return to their homes.

"Will you take him to Via Larga? Can I assist you?" asked Michelangelo.

"Yes, yes, please, thank you, Agnolo. We miss you these days at the palazzo."

Michelangelo did not reply as he pulled the hood of his cloak up over his head and grabbed hold of Poliziano's arm. As they hobbled down the crowded street toward the Palazzo Medici, the citizens darted by, oblivious to the three men—the poet propped up between the philosopher and the sculptor, all formerly the brightest stars in a now fading Medicean constellation.

CHAPTER 28

PIERO DEPARTS FOR CHARLES'S CAMP

PIERO DE' MEDICI PACED BACK and forth, the heels of his riding boots clicking an impatient rhythm on the stone floor of the courtyard. With him were three of his closest companions as they waited the arrival of the fifth, Piero's cousin Lorenzo Tornabuoni.

"Vito!" Piero screamed, his annoyance echoing through the vast palazzo, "do the stable hands have my horses ready?"

Fate had dealt a cruel blow to his plans. Just two months ago he had entreated in Arezzo with Alfonso, the new King of Naples. Though Alfonso was not the bulwark of strength his father Ferrante had been, Piero at least had felt his alliance with Naples secure. When the French army advanced into Italia, Alfonso had sent his navy north to besiege the ports along the coast and Piero's plan was to mobilize around the fortified cities of Sarzana and Pisa. But the French fleet arrived and routed the Neapolitans at Rapallo and just three days ago, Alfonso died suddenly in Naples—probably in terror of his coming fate.

The French army was now on the border of Florentine territory, stronger than ever, and Piero was on the wrong side of the French king's favor. The city was in grave danger of an attack from an overwhelming hostile force and the moment had come for drastic action. Piero imagined what his father would do: *Il Magnifico* would use the force of his reputation and his bravery to rescue the city, as he had done during the Pazzi wars. In his mind Piero relived his father's legend, delivering himself alone into the treacherous arms of the enemy to successfully sue for peace. His father had received a hero's welcome upon his return. Now this moment would be Piero's finest hour.

"Have you notified the Signoria, Piero? Do we have an official writ to negotiate with the French?" Piero's future brother-in-law Ridolfi asked.

"I've sent a letter informing the Signoria of my entreaty with Charles. I don't need an official writ. Don't forget the *fleur-de-lis* blossoms among the Medici *palle*—the House of Medici and the House of Valois are joined by the honor of a royal family alliance. I'll manage the king and those shits in the Signoria will see how I've saved their pricks from the steel of the French sword. Hasn't my family always won the day?"

Worried looks passed between the others as Piero stomped around the courtyard under the eyes of Donatello's Judith. When Lorenzo finally came rushing into the courtyard Piero looked up, exasperated. "Ah, finally, cousin. Come, let's ride."

A moment later, the early morning calm was broken by the clapping hooves of five horses galloping toward the Porta al Prato.

CHAPTER 29

APPROACH OF THE FRENCH

IN HIS APOTHECARY, LUCA LANDUCCI busily prepared powders and molding pills with his assistant, rushing to fulfill the sudden run on medicinals.

Outside, Cronaca was kicking idly at loose stones as he sat facing the Palazzo Strozzi—widespread panic over the impending French invasion had stopped all work on the palazzo and everywhere else in the city and there was little to keep a masterbuilder busy. He yelled to Luca: "The whole city's gone crazy. Maybe all Italia's crazy! Where are all these people going to run? Where can they hide?"

Luca finished the batch of pills and went out onto the dusty street. "They say the Swiss pikers sacked Rapallo and put everyone who resisted to the sword."

"Well, then I guess the lesson is not to resist when the sword is poised over one's neck, eh? Surely the Signoria will strike a bargain with the French king. It's just a matter of how many thousands of florins."

"But the Medici alliances with Rome and Naples complicates things, no?"

Cronaca made an obscene gesture. "What do they expect, putting our fate into the hands of a twenty-year old? It's truly amazing how this city survives."

"They say the king is mindful of our friar and prophet."

"Now there's our saving grace, eh, a man with God on his side. According to the number of pilgrims, the words of our prophet have traveled far and wide across the northern countries, but I wonder will the mercenaries believe it."

"Fra Girolamo assures us Charles is the redeemer and his mission is a divine one."

Cronaca was skeptical. "Yeah? I would guess the boy king mostly has his eyes on the luscious fruits of Naples—God help him, those witches will have his prick."

In a surly mood, the builder stood up and kicked at a pebble. "A crusade only means the French will be expecting tribute and new recruits from good Christian cities. Seen any fighters around here?"

Cronaca spread his arms out across the mostly empty, disarrayed piazza, answering his own question. "No—for us it means we pay and pay. I'm sure our clever magistrates will do their best to convince Charles our purses are light." He let out a laugh like a drunken man. "It's amazing we Florentines expect anything to change just because of a little thing like war."

"No," said Luca, "our average citizen just wants to be sure he isn't the one stuck on the end of a Swiss pike. The people are hoarding."

"Yes, I wonder I'm not there myself, watching them clean out the market and scatter into their holes like squirrels." He cast an angry look at the still half-finished Palazzo Strozzi across the way. "If the damn French disrupt the city for too long this monstrosity will never be finished, at least not in my lifetime."

"What will you do?"

"What can I do? The work can't proceed and there'll be no new commissions while everyone thinks first for the safety of their own necks. Botticelli's *bottega* is deserted; Sandro has virtually ceased painting while Simone has become a devout Weeper. They spend their time up at San Marco. And Lorenzo di Credi told me the young sculptor, Buonarotti of the snowman, departed last week for Bologna or Venice to find work. Probably not a bad idea, the poor boy naturally fears the rising anger against Piero. Maybe Simone is right, that only the friar can pull us from this fire…"

A rider galloping through the piazza from the direction of the Porto al Prato interrupted their conversation. A small crowd was chasing after him on foot as the rider continued through the Old Market in the direction of the government Palazzo. One of the crowd shouted, "It's a messenger from Sarzana. He brings word that the avenging French army has sacked Fivizzano and put all the citizens to the sword!"

"*Merda*," hissed Cronaca.

Another shouted: "The French army is more than sixty thousand! With more than one hundred large cannon!"

Cronaca looked at Landucci with raised eyebrows and Luca replied, "All right, *momento*." After instructing his assistant, he and Cronaca hurried off after the crowds of anxious citizens racing toward the Palazzo.

***

That afternoon, after one of his trysts in the back room of the Frascato, Niccolò was walking back across the Ponte Vecchio on his way home to the Oltrarno. First, he intended to stop by the Palazzo Soderini to visit and speak with Tommaso and his uncles. With the news from Fivizzano today, the city had turned into a scene of chaos and madness with people running around like chickens without their heads. Tavern business seems to be the only one not disrupted.

Farm wagons drawn by nervous mules were coming and going to and from the Old Market as peasants flocked into the city for protection while others hurried out with their provisions. The well-to-do were also running to and from the market, laden with grain, livestock and other winter stores. Certainly some planned to hole up behind the city walls while others headed for their country villas and farms. Everyone had his or her own family survival strategy.

Niccolò heard constant refrains from groups of passers-by. "They've sacked Fivizzano! *Tutti morti!*" "*La Bombarda* is coming!" "Who will protect us from this scourge?" "What will the Signoria do?" Young boys on the bridge brandished sticks like swords, fearlessly playing like soldiers.

Everyone knew the French ambassadors had arrived in the city last week while Charles and his army were encamped near Sarzana, just outside Florentine territory. The French had requested safe-conduct, but the Signoria hoped to encourage Charles to direct his forces south, past Pisa, avoiding the city altogether. Niccolò recognized the French held all the winning cards in this game because the magistrates, with their lack of direction and ceaseless infighting under the weak leadership of Piero de' Medici, had responded too late to the crisis. And Piero, with his ties to the French House of Valois and his machinations with Naples, was still a wildcard in the game. Meanwhile the French ambassadors waited impatiently, confined to their rooms in the Palazzo.

Piero Soderini had already confirmed the Signoria led by Capponi was leaning heavily toward enlisting the friar, who, it was hoped, would have some influence over the negotiations with Charles. Savonarola had been preaching of the divine mission of Charles for weeks now and it was said the French king was intrigued with their prophet. Cardinal delle Rovere was also in the French camp and Niccolò was sure the Cardinal was encouraging the king to march on to Rome to drive out the pope, the Cardinal's hated rival.

Niccolò knocked on the main door to the Soderini palace but no one answered. Tommaso's sickly brother Alessandro had died only a month ago and the heavy solemnity had not yet lifted from the household. He knocked again, louder. After a long moment, the small peephole in the door opened and he saw eyes looking out at him. At last he heard the door being unlocked.

Tommaso greeted him. "Ciao, Nico. Sorry, everyone here is busy with preparations."

"Preparations?"

"Yes, we're sending my sisters and cousins to the Carmelites in

Fiesole for their safety. Fiammetta and her sisters are also going. Chiara is here now. Hopefully, it won't be for long…as none of them have plans of becoming nuns."

Niccolò spoke quickly. "I've just come from the center. It's a *casino*—the sack of Fivizzano and rumors of the invasion have put the fear of death into people. I think panic may be a greater danger to us than the French army."

"*Avanti*. My uncles are in the library."

As they entered the library Tommaso's uncle Piero looked up. "*Buona sera*, Nico. As you can see things are unfolding quickly."

"*Sì*, Fivizzano… but what of the French ambassadors? Any word from the Medici?"

Piero related the latest developments. "The Signoria failed to convince the ambassadors to dissuade the king from entering the city—he's heard such great things of our city he wishes to see with his own eyes. They say he'll either be welcomed or enter by force. So, we must try to prepare for an agreeable visit.

"The council is now negotiating the terms under which the army will be quartered. There are almost forty thousand, so almost every household will need to host soldiers. The quartermasters will be here tomorrow or the next day to chalk houses so the Signoria is presently drafting legislation instructing the citizens how to accommodate the French and not cause trouble."

Tommaso cut in. "Many are stockpiling weapons."

Piero wagged his head in dismay; conflict would be dangerous. "We should not rile the French—in good faith, they've promised to pay for provisions."

Paolo interjected, "Yes, with our own money, no doubt. What of tribute? What do you think the king will demand?"

"I don't know. There's no talk of payments yet, though I'm sure it will come."

Tommaso's youngest uncle, Giovanvettorio, asked Niccolò's question again. "But what of the Medici?"

"We've no word from Piero since we received the letter. We believe he's in Charles's camp at Sarzana now, with several others. The letter is comic in its desire to mimic the tone of Lorenzo's mission to Naples—all these nonsense about 'risking his life for the glory of the Republic.' Capponi has been making much fun of it at the Palazzo. Piero's in a real mess: first, Ferrante dies and then his successor, the Duke of Calabria, dies too. *Merda*, this Medici is truly unfortunate."

After pausing, Piero continued. "Capponi's lost confidence in Piero; he'll invite Charles to spend the night at his villa just before entering the city, to speak to the king clear of his advisors. The negotiations will require a firm hand with a delicate touch."

"Fra Girolamo will be useful," said Paolantonio. "He predicted the coming of Charles as the redeemer of all Italia and is sure the king will listen to his message from God. He believes he can bring the force of his prophecies to bear on the impressionable young king."

"Let's hope so," said Piero, who turned back to the business at hand. "We must prepare. Giovanvettorio and Tommaso should be back tonight after escorting the women to Fiesole. Some of us must remain here to manage any problems with the French and protect our interests. I will likely be selected if we send an embassy to Charles in Sarzana. Niccolò, what of your family?"

"They're in Sant'Andrea in Percussina and my sisters are with their husbands. I'll stay at my house with two of the servants."

"If you need assistance, you must let us know immediately. Unless there are some unforeseen catastrophes or stupidities, I don't think we'll have serious problems with the French. I don't believe Charles is ill-disposed toward us and I hear his army is well disciplined. The French have an appreciation for beauty and women, so hopefully our *belle donne* around the Old Market can soften them up and keep them pleasantly occupied." Piero forced a knowing smile at Tommaso and Niccolò.

When they were finished, Niccolò left the library with Tommaso and saw Chiara with several of her cousins in the courtyard. She saw him and approached. She did not walk with her usual light step and Niccolò saw fine lines etched into her forehead and a tired look in her eyes.

"*Ciao bella,* off to join a convent?"

"*Ciao* Nico. It's no joking matter... Forgive me. I'm glad to see you before we're forced to flee our homes. The Lord must truly be testing us."

"Careful. They'll keep you at that convent if they hear you say such things."

"My family has suffered too much. Seriously, you don't find it strange Fra Girolamo has predicted so many of these things that have befallen our city over the past three years?"

"You've cut your hair."

"Yes, the less to fuss over," she said as she reached into her bag to pull out some pamphlets. "Here, read his sermons. Compare what he preaches to what has happened."

Indulging her, Niccolò took one. It was one of the many rough printings sold by the mendicants on the street corners that had littered the city in the past year, causing Niccolò to question this blessing of the printing press. As he perused it, his eye caught one paragraph referring to the Marzocco—the martial symbol of pagan Florence. He read the passage aloud:

> *O Marzocco, I will tell you of that time and how you will fare. The wrath of God will descend to flay you and cut off your tail and ears, then you will be attacked by lesser beasts and suffer as if dying. And then the Lord will reappear when you have had time to contemplate your ways and the Lord will revive you with a medicine that will send all attackers back to their lairs. The medicine is that of humility to purge the sin of pride. Those who are firm in their faith will not suffer the tribulations.*

This sort of thing was exasperating. The French crisis was invited by their own lack of foresight. It was not so much the sin of pride as the sin of folly—the pettiness of all Italia invited stronger monarchs to invade and reap the spoils and the interference of the religious only exacerbated the problem.

To cover his irritation Niccolò was flip. "Sounds grim. I see our prophet has an admirable gift for metaphor." He heard his tinged sarcasm and tried to soften it. "He does hold out hope for us, no? Perhaps I should read more."

"Take these. My mother has a whole collection. I'm sure where we're going there'll be little else to do but to think and pray on such matters."

"*Grazie a Lei, Signorina,*" Niccolò said, using the formal pronoun with respect and bowing low to kiss her hand. "May you be safe and return to us soon. The city will mourn with its most beautiful flowers hidden away."

As he turned to leave, Niccolò thought about how quickly the carefree vitality had drained from the vibrant, playful girl he had known. He felt a pang of regret, but quickly let it go—these things were inevitable.

CHAPTER 30

THE SIGNORIA REACTS

PIERO SODERINI SAT AT HIS bench in the *Sala dei Signori* and watched the young Medicean squirm before the eight magistrates staring down at him from their throne-like chairs. The youth, a cousin of Piero's, put up a brave front as he waited to be questioned by the Gonfaloniere. He gazed wide-eyed around the imposing room, its magnificent frescoes and panel paintings by Domenico Ghirlandaio framed under a ceiling of midnight blue sprayed by a constellation of gold lilies. This was where the Signoria received testimony and advisories from the various ministries of the government and to testify here on an important issue of state should be a great honor for a *giovane* of a respected family. But the youth's worried expression betrayed him; something was terribly wrong.

As Soderini had calculated, Piero Capponi was the new Gonfaloniere, and he was pleased it was Capponi conducting these proceedings. Like a cat with unsheathed claws, Capponi stalked his witness as he conducted his interrogation:

"Messer Tornabuoni, will you please explain this communication from Piero de' Medici you delivered into my hands? Please speak loudly and clearly so the priors will have no doubts as to the facts and the scribe will be sure to record your testimony accurately."

"*Sì*, Your Excellency. Piero de' Medici together with myself, Gianozzo Pucci, Jacopo Gianfigliazzi, and Piero Ridolfi traveled a fortnight ago to the French camp of Charles VIII, King of France, to negotiate the terms of an agreement between the king and the Republic."

Capponi cut in. "And was this an official embassy commissioned by this body, the Signoria?"

"Not that I know, Excellency. As preeminent citizen, Piero acted on his own initiative to secure the fate of the Republic and prevent a hostile invasion. But I understand he sent a written letter of his intentions before his departure."

"Yes, we received this letter *after* your departure, Messer Tornabuoni. Now, please repeat what transpired between your—what? Your 'excursion party?'—and the king of France."

The young man spoke in measured tones, trying to hide his apprehension. "We were received with great courtesy by the king and his advisors. Piero conveyed his feeling of honor and gratitude for the friendship of the king's family, the Valois, with the Medici, his father and grandfather and—"

Capponi cut him off. "Skip the ceremony, Messer Tornabuoni. What were the terms of the agreement Piero offered the French king?"

The youth hesitated, perhaps thinking on how to word his answer. "Well, Excellencies, Piero did not actually make an offer before the king's Secretary dictated the requested terms of an agreement."

"*And?*" prodded Capponi.

"They wish to receive control of the fortresses and cities of Sarzana, Pietrasanta, Livorno, Librafatta, and Pisa until the end of the war campaign."

The magistrates reacted by mumbling among themselves. To silence them, Capponi raised his voice for his next question.

"Do you mean all five of the cities and fortresses guarding our western and northern borders to the sea?"

"*Sì,* Your Excellency, the five cities."

"And what else did the king request?"

"A payment of two hundred thousand florins…to support his campaign…immediately."

With a start the magistrates expressed their dismay: "*Impossibile!*" "This is an outrage!" We would be ruined!"

With a hard stare, Capponi silenced them again as he asked, "And what was Piero de' Medici's response to these terms?"

"We had just received word they had sacked the city of Fivizzano and we were fearful they would do the same to us—"

"To what terms did he agree?"

"He granted them all, Excellencies."

Now the magistrates jumped from their chairs, erupting all at once: "This is treason! Piero de' Medici has no authority to agree! These terms are outrageous! We must retract this agreement at once!"

The room was thrown into anarchy. Tornabuoni was perfunctorily dismissed with instructions to remain in the city until the Signoria finished debating the matter and decided on a course of action.

The priors of the Signoria were now in a state of crisis and Soderini sat back to observe. Two hundred thousand florins would bankrupt the city, they insisted. And the loss of the fortresses along the western seaboard would expose their territorial defenses to the treacherous Duke of Milan, Genova, or even Venice. Worst of all, the loss of control over Pisa would greatly damage the city's economic interests as almost all imports and exports traveled up and down the Arno River between Pisa and Florence. A Florentine protectorate, Pisa was forever plotting to throw off the yoke; surely the French king must understand this. What was this Medici fool doing? We must recall the young Medici as quickly as possible, said one, and try to undo this damage. But what if the French king supports Piero's position as the rightful leader of the city? The House of Valois has always collaborated with the House of Medici.

After half an hour, Gonfaloniere Capponi was losing patience with the circularity of debate. He galvanized them all with a strong voice and a pounding fist.

"Signori, we *are* a Republic, *not* a monarchy or a principate. We must explain this in forceful terms to the king. Piero de' Medici is not fit to rule and has no authority to speak for the interests of the city without an official commission granted by the government. We must refuse to grant that authority. *The moment has come to shake off this baby government!*"

This last phrase caught the other magistrates by surprise and Soderini knew the glass had finally been broken. It was a direct challenge to the large party of Medicean supporters throughout the government. Yet, the break had been fracturing for some time.

The subsequent silence was broached by Jacopo de' Nerli, known for his loyal support of the Medici. "And what then shall be our course of action?"

Capponi was resolute. "We must send an embassy to Charles at once. It must leave tomorrow. They will explain to the French that the government must ratify the terms of any agreement for it to be valid. The agreement with Piero de' Medici is to be voided."

One of the priors raised the question: "And why should the king agree? He already has Piero's word and if he so chooses he can install Piero as his puppet right here in Florence, backed by a French garrison."

Capponi was not deterred. "The king must understand Florentines will never stand for usurping their liberty and their Republic. These will never be terms for peace. And Florence will not so easily be taken by force." He raised his hand to cut off further debate.

"We also have another card to play with Charles," he added. "We shall send the friar with our delegation to Charles. Fra Girolamo will expound his prophetic powers to remind the king of his divine mission to press on to Rome and Naples to cleanse the Church. Some of us have consulted with the friar and he has told us interpretations of his visions. He assures us God does not wish His sword to strike here in our city and we will be secure by allying with the French. If the king fails to adhere to his mission, then God will punish him and make a catastrophe of his campaign. I've heard confirmation the king is much impressed by our 'Prophet.' We must place our faith in the friar's power of persuasion."

"Who shall we send?"

"The Pratica recommended we send Tanai de' Nerli, Pandolfo Rucellai, Giovanni Cavalcanti, and Piero Soderini. Are we in agreement then?"

The vote quickly affirmed Capponi's motion—his forcefulness had carried the day and the tide had turned against the Medici. Piero Soderini was especially pleased—by allying with both Capponi and the friar, he and his brother had cleverly straddled the gap between the two.

CHAPTER 31

CHARLES'S CAMP

FRA GIROLAMO WALKED NIMBLY PAST the soldiers' encampment along the road outside Sarzana, clutching the Bible and crucifix as he followed close behind his two companions and their haggard mule. The three friars looked commonplace in their simple frocks and drew no notice from the resting soldiers, but Fra Girolamo felt his pulse quicken as he passed over the endless contingents of disciplined infantry, cavalry, and cannon batteries. These, he thought, would be won over to the cause. These would be God's armies now.

An escort met the friars outside the city's walls. The Florentine embassy had arrived the day before and was waiting with the French delegation in town, so Fra Girolamo and his companions were escorted directly to the city palace where Charles was staying. The Florentine ambassadors were there in a room consulting when Fra Girolamo entered alone. Piero Soderini greeted him.

"Ah, Prior, we've awaited your arrival. We hope you had a pleasant journey. *Prego*, sit and rest. Would you care for something to drink or eat?"

Fra Girolamo shook his head and remained standing as Soderini informed him of the initial negotiations with the French. The day they arrived Piero de' Medici had left Sarzana to return to Florence in an air of diffidence and the French ambassadors were now holding hard to the concessions they had won from him.

"We've explained to the king that we, as appointed envoys, represent the citizens of the Florentine Republic—of which Piero de' Medici is but one. And without final ratification by the Signoria, no agreement can be binding. But the king is indecisive and makes no moves without consulting his ministers, from whom he receives conflicting advice. His military captains have intimated they will take the city by force if necessary."

"What is the king's attitude toward the Medici?" Fra Girolamo asked.

Pandolfo Rucellai shrugged impatiently. "This dwarf king has no thought of his own. His minister Beaucaire whispers in one ear while Cardinal delle Rovere whispers in the other. Beaucaire has his eyes on all Italia, but the cardinal is Napolitano and only hates the pope."

Soderini added, "The king's torn between Piero's flirtations with

Naples and the French court's disdain for dealing with a Republic rather than a noble house. He's unsure of where his interests would best be served."

Savonarola contemplated this. These men were all political animals and foremost the French king must be used to reform Florentine politics. It is to be God's Republic and the Medici must go. "We must help the king see the light of God's truth."

Soderini crossed his arms and paced. "We've informed him we require the fortresses and towns on our borders for our own defenses. We've offered to allow him use of these while he passes through, but they must be returned to our control after he leaves. Pisa must be the exception—it must stay in our control. The Pisans will take advantage of any interference to declare their independence and we cannot afford to lose our link to the sea.

"Two hundred thousand florins is far beyond our ability to pay. We've attempted to impress upon him the value of our friendship. He must understand the city is opposed to the policies of Piero de' Medici and that we favor our longstanding alliance with France."

"Yes," said Rucellai, "but his response is to keep mumbling about how 'all should be arranged once in the great city.' Naturally we prefer the terms be agreed on *before* we open the gates."

Fra Girolamo was not distracted by political arguments. He remained resolute to a higher purpose: "God has already decided the terms of Charles's mission and, if he should go against God's will, his grand ambitions will be shattered. I must pray for guidance now before the king receives me."

He retired to the next room, filled with a sense of destiny. He distrusted these political animals and he had no intention of allowing Florence to fall into their hands. But this is how I have foreseen it, he thought: A wrathful God has endured the sins of Italia for too many years and awaited her repentance. But the brazen harlot has only multiplied her crimes, so He will execute a harsh judgment upon her. Now God has brought everything to pass, down to the last detail—details as small as a man's fingernail. *At last you, Charles, the Sword of God, have come as God's minister, the minister of His justice.*

That afternoon Fra Girolamo was presented in the king's chambers. Several ministers hovered near the king and two cardinals conferring together in French. The younger cardinal was French but the other—an imposing prince of the Church—was easily recognized, even though he resembled a *condottiere* more than a Church prelate. Tall and bearded, this was the renegade Cardinal delle Rovere of St. Piero Vincoli in Rome, nephew of the infamous Pope Sixtus IV. Since Sixtus had expired ten years ago his nephew had fiercely coveted the papal throne, but the Spanish Cardinal Borgia had outmaneuvered him in the last election. This ensured the everlasting enmity between the two. Earlier in the year it was reported the Cardinal had fled Rome in fear of his life and lighted in France at the court of Charles VIII. Now delle Rovere was most anxious to encourage Charles to take Rome and depose Alexander VI. So, to that end he was favorably disposed toward the Florentines.

As their eyes met, the friar smiled softy but remained wary of this wolf in sheep's clothing, hoping he would prove useful.

Fra Girolamo slowly approached the king and the room went quiet. As he bowed he noticed a sweet pungent smell mixed with more foul odors and he struggled to suppress an unpleasant grimace. Then, looking up at the king, he was momentarily shocked. He tried to hide his surprise. The great monarch was too small, with spindly legs and a head too large; it seemed an enormous weight for the small body. His nose was wholly out of proportion to the rest of his face, which contorted each time he changed expression. His eyes were large and vacant and his complexion pale and sickly. When his mouth gaped open it gave him the look of an idiot.

Ah, he thought, such were the ways of the Lord. Recovering, Fra Girolamo spoke in a fluid Tuscan dialect to the wide-eyed king, who fidgeted uncomfortably, seemingly void of comprehension.

"O most Christian king, thou art an instrument in the hand of the Lord. He sends thee to relieve the woes of Italia. He sends thee to reform the Church, which lies prostrate in the dust. With joyful heart and cheerful countenance, we welcome you. Your arrival has filled every servant of God with joy."

The king looked impatiently at his translator, who repeated Fra Girolamo's words in French. He appeared restless in replying to the perfunctory greetings.

"Yes, yes. Brother Girolamo, we have received your letters and thank you for your kind solicitations. We should most like to hear more of these prophecies. In our country we've heard much of the great prophet of Florence. My own royal physician has also had visions of our destiny as a reformer and defender of the Cross. Tell us of your visions and how God has chosen us as his divine instrument."

Fra Girolamo related his dream visions of the Sword of God hovering in the sky pointing down over the earth and the two crosses over Rome and Jerusalem. Then he spoke of the corruption of Rome and how the priests and prelates had despoiled the true Christian Church for their own avarice and ambition. He told of the message he had received:

That the Church would be scourged and then reformed and it would all happen soon. Then he drew upon the Biblical analogies of Cyrus and the prophecies of Isaiah, Ezekiel, and Leviticus about the Sword of God that would come down from beyond the mountains and mete out God's justice upon the sinful city. This appeared to spark a glimmer in the vacant eyes of the king. The friar continued his narrative with the rebuilding of the holy temple of Jerusalem and the rejuvenation of God's Heavenly City. After a time the king became distracted and appeared lost within the maze of words and images.

As Fra Girolamo neared the end of his mini-sermon he noticed the royal feet encased in their odd, bulky shoes, also worn by all the king's ministers. They were squared off and cloven, like hooves. He'd heard rumors these special shoes were designed to accommodate the king's six-toed feet, but they gave his court the beastly appearance of pagan centaurs. He quickly finished.

"And so, most holy Christian King, God's mission to cleanse His house has fallen to you. For His Church must be regenerated with the strength of faith to then drive back the infidels with a crusade to recapture the Eastern Empire and finally the most Holy Land of Jesus of Nazareth."

The translation of this final statement set the ministers grumbling among themselves. They quieted as the king spoke after conferring with his advisor Beaucaire.

"Yes, well, you see, such a great undertaking needs a large army, and such a large army costs the royal house mountains of gold. We require the generous support of all Christian communities with fighting men and funds. The government of your city has resisted our requests, which had been graciously granted by Piero de' Medici."

"Be assured, Majesty, the Florentines hold dearly to the alliance with their French brothers. The policies of Piero de' Medici have greatly dismayed his fellow citizens and because of this they gravely oppose any suggestion they submit to the dictates of one man, be he tyrant or prince. The Medici are but private citizens of the Republic and must submit to its laws and the rules of government." Then he added gravely: "And to God."

Beaucaire whispered again into the royal ears before the king spoke. "Yes, yes, with most respect to you, my dear prophet, you can see this army, these infantry and cavalry, these cannon cannot be denied. The resistance we have met was easily and quickly vanquished. Your government ministers must understand we will dictate the terms of our agreement."

Fra Girolamo's voice was firm behind the ingratiating smile.

"Forgive me, Majesty, but I see we speak of different things. You speak of the earthly designs and actions of men whereas I must speak of the will of the Almighty. I bring to you His words as it has been foretold. My people labor under the burden of many sins, yet count among them many servants of God. For their sake, you ought to preserve the city so the faithful may intercede with God for the good success of your expedition. If wickedness should by your means be increased, know that the powers given to you will be withdrawn."

Fra Girolamo's voice took on the scolding, formal tone of the preacher. "If you be not just and merciful; if you should fail to respect the city of Florence, its women, its citizens, and its liberty; if you should forget the task the Lord has sent you to perform, then He will choose another to fulfill it. His hand shall smite you, and chastise you with terrible scourges. *These things say I to you in the name of the Lord.*"

Even before the translator nervously repeated Fra Girolamo's words, the king grimaced in discomfort and his body shuddered involuntarily. The message was clear and the king's feeble mind instinctively grasped the meaning behind the forbidding tone.

CHAPTER 32

OVERTHROW OF THE MEDICI

PIERO DE' MEDICI STOMPED IMPATIENTLY across the stone courtyard of the Palazzo della Signoria, his youthful fury boiling over. He had arrived back in the city yesterday, expecting to be revered by his fellow citizens for averting a terrible siege by the French forces. But he had been greeted only by a veiled contempt as he and his party rode through the streets. He had even thrown out *confetti* and small coins and provided wine to those outside his palazzo as a gesture of goodwill, but to no avail. The people purposely shunned him. Then his cousin Lorenzo told him how the aristocratic families and the Signoria had poisoned the people against him. Now was the time to take decisive action, but the guards here at the Palazzo refused him entrance until after he disarmed and entered without his own guard; an insult to his dignity and status as first among citizens. Now he stewed as the magistrates delayed in receiving him.

He heard the noise increasing on the other side of the large doors as the Piazza outside filled with people. These Florentines smelled trouble, but if they knew the truth he was sure they'd support him against these petty usurpers. Meanwhile the magistrates were playing this game, keeping him under the watchful eye of armed guards.

His nervousness and fear finally undermined his confidence and he demanded to leave. Outside he found his friends and supporters huddled together, standing on the steps. As Piero heard the doors lock behind him, the Palace bell-tower started to peal with a rumbling tone like distant thunder. It was *La Vaca*, and its tone carried far and wide across the valley of the Arno. This bell was an alarm, used only to summon a *parlamento* and rally the citizens to repel a threat to the Palazzo or the city. Under the standards of each of their gonfalons, they would come armed to the teeth with knives, swords, sticks, hoes, and even stones, rallying to the city's defense.

Piero looked at the faces crowding the Piazza and saw their momentary confusion and indecision. He must rally his supporters now, as his father had during the Pazzi conspiracy, or the people would turn on him and tear him apart. His friends looked at the crowd and saw it too. Then they saw panic in his eyes as he cried, "Come, we must rally the *popolo* to support the *Palle!* Quickly!"

Mounting their horses, they waved their swords and shouted their rallying cry: *"Palle! Palle!"* But their exhortations fell on deaf ears as the crowd stood frozen in momentary confusion. Suddenly there was a rebellious answer: *"Abbasso le Palle!"* Then the shout caught fire, spontaneously igniting the multitude: "Down with the Balls!"

The fireball exploded and the mob unleashed its wrath and fury with the Republic's most primal rallying cry: *"Popolo e Libertà!"* *"Popolo e Libertà!"* "Liberty and the People!"

Piero and his party circled furiously near the entrance to the Palazzo, their desperate cries of *"Palle"* drowned out by the firestorm sweeping across the Piazza. Stones rained down on them and Piero screamed to his companions to follow him to the quarter of San Giovanni to regroup at the Palazzo Medici. The riders raced away down the Via del Gondi, still waving their swords and shouting: *"Palle!"*

***

Niccolò buttoned up his doublet as he hurried across the Ponte Vecchio. He had heard *La Vaca* sound a *parlamento* while napping in his house and now wondered what extraordinary circumstances required a vote to suspend the constitution. The *parlamento* was used mostly as a cynical device to manipulate the masses to achieve some specific desired ends for a small group of governing elites, but he wondered if this time it signaled a problem with the French. He passed many scattered groups of advance soldiers from the French army, but they appeared as confused as everyone else.

As he ran toward the Piazza he saw the shopkeepers closing up and heard the republican rallying cry of *"Popolo e Libertà!"* and saw men brandishing sticks and iron tools and other makeshift weapons. Then he heard one man shout *"Abbasso le Palle!"* and he knew—it was a rebellion against Piero de' Medici. The time had come. The people had been seething after hearing of the treaty Piero 'negotiated' on their behalf; impoverishment and subjugation to a foreign monarch was more than Florentines would tolerate. Now something or someone had incited the Signoria and the people.

The Piazza della Signoria was a madhouse, as if there was a fox was loose in the hen house. He demanded of one young tough brandishing a pike, "Tell me, what happened?"

"Piero de' Medici attempted to storm the palazzo but was barred from entering with his party. The Signoria barricaded the doors and rang *La Vaca*. Then Piero and his fellow *grandi* attempted to rally the *Palleschi*, but rode off when we rebelled against the little bastard."

Niccolò's thoughts raced: Nothing in Florentine politics was truly spontaneous. Piero Soderini had not yet returned from Sarzana; so, who had orchestrated this plot against the Medici? Capponi? He fought his way through the crowd to the doors of the palazzo but the guards refused to let anyone pass.

Niccolò turned to look back across the vast piazza. From its western entrance he saw a group of riders enter waving swords and yelling "*Popolo e Liberta!*" Leading the charge was Francesco Valori, who had become the most vocal supporter of the friar and leader of the pro-religious faction. Valori's group bulled its way to the entrance of the Palazzo and turned to form a front line of defense. But there was no military threat now and Niccolò moved away down along the ringhiera. The square was filling fast with a frenzied and dangerously armed crowd, half shouting: "*Popolo e Liberta!*" while the other half screamed: "Down with the Balls!" There were no cries of *Palle!* to be heard.

A sudden hush quieted the crowd and Niccolò saw an official come out of the Palazzo. The official held up a proclamation, trying to shout over the din of the crowd. The proclamation was an order forbidding any and all citizens from aiding or abetting Piero de' Medici on pain of death, and ordering all foreigners to lay down their arms and not interfere with the city's political affairs. It was uncertain how the French forces would react to this sudden civic upheaval.

When the official finished, the crowded Piazza became a deafening roar of rallying cries and shouts for vengeance. There were cries to storm the Bargello and the Stinche prison, and also to attack the house of the officials of the Monte. Across the Piazza, near the north end, Niccolò spied a large group coalescing around anti-Medici cries and raising their weapons into the air. This group suddenly surged, like water over a burst dam, down the Street of the Hosemakers and Niccolò knew they were headed toward the Palazzo Medici. He quickly fought through the crowd to follow.

When he arrived minutes later at the Via Larga, he found a large, mean-spirited crowd agitating outside the Palazzo Medici. Gangs of young street toughs were throwing rocks and stones at the shuttered windows while others rammed the barricaded doors. He shouted to the nearest man, "Where's Piero? Is he inside?"

"No, he was here only half an hour ago with some of the Tornabuoni and Ridolfi but they were driven back. His brother the Cardinal led an armed band of supporters toward the Signoria, but Valori stopped them before they reached Orsanmichele and they retreated as well. Most of the *Palleschi* galloped off with Piero by way of the Porto di San Gallo—they say Giuliano is waiting there with soldiers of the Orsini." The man raised his hoe and exclaimed, "They're finished here now, lucky to escape with their skins! One of their manservants who dared cry *Palle!* was quickly silenced." The man drew his finger sharply across his throat with a fiendish grin.

"Where's Cardinal Giovanni now?"

"Still in the Palazzo—with his sisters and the rest of the women. Hiding behind their skirts no doubt! It won't be long before we break down that door and sack this place. Down with the Balls!"

Niccolò shuddered at the quick reversal. Lady Fortuna had blessed three generations of Medici, from Cosimo to Lorenzo the Magnificent. It had seemed a perpetual reign, which had caused young Piero to assume Fortuna's favor as his birthright. But then, as happens so often, Nemesis sweeps down to punish the proud and the arrogant. Nemesis was now Piero's bride. He'll be destined forever as Piero the Unfortunate.

Niccolò felt no pity—Piero was a fool and now the Republic might find better leadership—but all the Medici would suffer his fate. On his way from the Signoria, Niccolò had seen many people already tearing down the banners of the Medici and defacing the *Palle* from the walls and cornices of buildings. It was too late to restrain them and the rioting would continue until their passions were spent.

The rabble finally rammed through the barricaded doors and rushed into the Palazzo's courtyard. So much would be ruined or lost in the pillage: paintings, sculpture, tapestries, silks and precious decorative arts. Hopefully the looters would respect the inviolable beauty of Donatello, Verrocchio, Gozzolli and others whose works were inside. So much wealth acquired and accumulated over generations, gone in a few hours.

It occurred to Niccolò that tomorrow would bring a new set of threats and opportunities. The Mediceans would be purged from the government ministries and councils and there would be a mad dash to fill the void. And the mob would strike out with vengeance. The Signoria must quickly issue orders to mobilize the guards of the Eight and impose a curfew to restrain the citizens from destroying all in their path. There was nothing more to do now but return home and wait.

CHAPTER 33

CAPPONI, SODERINI, AND VALORI AT SAN MARCO

FRA GIROLAMO BOWED BEFORE THE crucifix and prayed, struggling with so many conflicting emotions. At dawn the message had arrived from Ferrara: His mother had died. He tried to remember her face. She had been strong and willful, unlike his father. Now both were gone from this world and he prayed for the salvation of her soul. He wondered why he felt little and felt guilty for it.

As a child he had been close to her; she had connected with his melancholy and in her own way shared his loneliness. Perhaps she too suffered from an excess of yellow bile or an unhappy life, he never knew. He often imagined her then as his Monica, the faithful and long-suffering mother of Augustine. She encouraged his piety, but in the end could not understand when he left to join the Order. He had never seen her again.

He shifted his thoughts to the Virgin Mother, but unfortunately there was no tender rendition of the Madonna frescoed on the walls of this cell. When he opened his eyes he saw only the crucifix—the nails, the crown of thorns, and the bloodied gash in the Savior's side. This was the Son of God *and* man. He must put personal matters aside—in the confusion after the expulsion of the Medici there was still much to do before the French arrived.

There was a warning rap on his door and Fra Domenico peeked in. "Prior, the officials from the Palazzo have arrived. Silvestro is with them in the Chapter House."

"Then let us join them."

Waiting in the Chapter House were several government officials: Paolantonio Soderini, Francesco Valori, and Piero Capponi. In their desire to share the glow of the friar's popular appeal, these three had come to rely heavily on his advice. Capponi, the present Gonfaloniere, often received Fra Silvestro in the Palazzo for confession. As for the other two, the friar had come to know them well. Since their unpleasant visit to San Marco some years ago, Soderini and Valori had become devout believers in the moral value of his religious teachings and his main allies within the government.

"Fra Girolamo," Valori began, "we are at a dangerous moment. Charles's army is poised to enter the city in two day's time."

Capponi added, "We've heard Piero de' Medici has been in touch with Charles and his wife's family, the Orsini, has petitioned the king to reinstate the Medici in return for an alliance."

"Signori, when I accompanied Charles to Pisa I took many occasions to impress upon him the Florentines' determination to defend their freedom. Some of his ministers would prefer to buy off the Medici tyrants and subjugate the city—like all tyrants, despots find common cause in subjugating the freedom of their citizens.

"More important, I made Charles understand it is God's command to respect the sanctity of Florence. In this I believe Cardinal delle Rovere proved helpful. He convinced the king to emblazon the French standards with *'Voluntas Dei'* and *'Missus a Deo.'* This will serve as a constant reminder of the divine nature of Charles's mission. When I left Pisa I am sure the king accepted the Almighty's terms for his mission to Rome and Naples."

But Soderini warned, "Father, we must not underestimate the treachery of Piero and his henchman. The Signoria has placed a bounty of two thousand florins on the heads of Piero and Cardinal Giovanni, five thousand if they're delivered alive."

Valori added, "The citizens also fear the mercenaries may try to sack the city. Three times in the last few days we've rung *La Vaca* based on rumors of an imminent attack. Each alarm proved false, but the French captains have not failed to notice the fierceness of the people's reaction. They're being asked to sacrifice to quarter the French soldiers with little assurance they're not letting the fox into the henhouse."

Fra Girolamo shook his head. "Signori, we must keep the people wary of the tyrants they know and reassure them against the tyrants they imagine."

"There's also this problem of Pisa rebelling two days ago," said Capponi.

Valori continued, "Father, we've had trouble since the Medici were driven out. The citizens reject all authority. The Signoria instituted a curfew and the Eight patrols all gonfalons, but still some incidents have caused grave regret, as I'm sure you've heard."

Yes, he had. When he returned from his entreaty with Charles, Domenico and Silvestro had informed him how on the day Piero was expulsed the people had stormed the Bargello and the Stinche, freeing all prisoners. Then the mob had taken revenge on several Medicean supporters, hanging the administrator of the *Monte* and threatening the same to an official of the Chancery. To avert more violence, the Signoria had dismissed Bartolomeo Scala, the First Chancellor. But removal of the tyrant was enough, now divine order and peace must be restored.

He replied, "This lust for revenge, the southern mentality for *vendetta*, is opposed to everything I've preached. It promotes an endless cycle of violence and is opposed to the fundamental Christian virtue of forgiveness. I will devote my next sermon to counseling forgiveness, but the state must also contain these passions and support amnesty for former members of the Medici regime."

Capponi protested vigorously. "No, we cannot risk the treachery of the Medici. We must break their support, *here* and *now*." He pounded his fist for emphasis.

But Fra Girolamo was adamant. "There should be no tolerance shown to Piero and his conspirators, but those citizens who found it necessary to become clients of the Medici must be forgiven and accepted back into the fold. To do otherwise will tear the fabric of the city in two. Likewise, we must welcome back those former enemies of the Medici who languish in exile, as they will strengthen our hand."

Fra Girolamo paused, but there was more. "I cannot condone the reward placed on the head of a representative of the Holy Mother Church, though Cardinal de' Medici should remain banished from the city. In truth, my brothers have told me how they assisted the cardinal, who escaped the murderous crowd in the guise of a poor friar."

He motioned toward Domenico and Silvestro and then permitted himself a smile as he added, "They were also able to dissuade the rabble from pillaging the ancient statues in the sculpture garden."

Domenico lowered his eyes while Silvestro beamed with pride.

Soderini added his support to Fra Girolamo's view. "Yes, our city should not suffer the loss of so much just because of the foolish actions of one man. Let us suggest the Medicean art treasures and library be put under the care of the convent of San Marco."

Capponi was still reticent. "I counsel a watchful eye on these *Palleschi*. Piero's cousins—Lorenzo and Giuliano—have already returned, but I, for one, am not ready to embrace them with brotherly love. I'm sure they plot, waiting for the chance to regain their position."

Fra Girolamo smiled. "Signor Capponi, you are too guarded. I am sure Fra Silvestro has instructed you on the wisdom of forgiveness. Remember, Christ conquered by turning the other cheek."

The Gonfaloniere gave the friar an incredulous look, but held his tongue.

Fra Girolamo returned his gaze. These men of the world, he thought, committed the same errors again and again. They were trapped in an endless cycle of good and evil, blind to their own follies.

The discussion over, the men excused themselves to return to the Palazzo to prepare for the arrival of Charles and his vast army. As they reached the door, Fra Silvestro whispered to Capponi, who halted with a look of surprise and regret. He turned back to Fra Girolamo.

"Father, Fra Silvestro informs us you received word today of the death of your mother. Please accept our deepest sympathies and our sincerest apologies for disturbing you on such a grave occasion." Nothing could command more deference in Italia than a son's loving devotion to his mother.

Fra Girolamo smiled painfully to acknowledge Capponi's condolences and cast a disapproving glance at Silvestro. Without emotion, he replied: "My mother shed tears for many years. I let her do so. It is enough she must now know she was wrong to do this."

CHAPTER 34

THE FRENCH ENTER FLORENCE – PICO DIES

TWO DAYS LATER THE AFTERNOON sky hung like a gray mantle over the city as crowds massed along the streets Charles and his vast army would pass. Many preparations had been made for the king's arrival: the streets were draped with banners and tapestries; standards graced with the *fleur-de-lis* hung from windows and the sides of buildings; and the coat-of-arms of the royal House of Valois was draped over the main entrance of the Palazzo della Signoria. The ransacked Palazzo Medici on the Via Larga was cleaned out and decorated to house the king during his stay and two large columns were erected on either side of the doors at the entrance portico, both emblazoned with the king's coat-of-arms.

As peeling church bells announced the city's hopeful anticipation of this Most Christian King, the Florentines crowded the streets to behold his troops. Their heads sprouted from the windows and balconies along the route and many others packed the rooftops and turrets to enjoy the grand vista of the army winding its way like a serpent from the far horizon in through the gated walls.

Down the *Via di Santo Spirito* came the tramp of marching boots and the clip-clop of horses on the paved street. Then the gaily-colored infantry troops passed, arranged in ranks with pikes, crossbows and small arms. The short, rat-like quickness of the Gascon infantry contrasted with the tall, Swiss pikers in their multicolored hose and the hairy Scotch archers with their long wooden bows. To the refined Florentines these fierce northerners looked almost ape-like and were regarded with a combination of awe and apprehension.

Following close behind was the magnificent horse cavalry consisting of French knights in full regalia. These gallants were the flower of French aristocracy—decorated with gold mail and other precious ornaments and draped in mantles of rich brocade. They wielded finely wrought weapons and waved their bright-colored standards. As they passed, their regal bearing made an indelible impression on the aesthetically minded Florentines, who showered them with confetti and cheers of *Viva Francia!*

The parade continued for many hours as the king wove slowly through the streets, waving diffidently to the people and acknowledging their cries. He sat astride his powerful white charger, clad in black velvet with a mantle of gold brocade draped over his shoulders. For the Florentines there was only one blight upon his noble visage: The king carried his war lance leveled at his knee, a martial symbol of the conqueror which gave great offense to the free citizens and increased their anxiety.

By the king's side rode the ambitious and confident Cardinal delle Rovere and several French marshals. The cardinal, dressed in full battle regalia, seemed to enjoy the spectacle more than the king. The procession passed over the river and then into the Piazza della Signoria, where the king admired the imposing government palace and leaned over to comment to the cardinal. It was almost twilight when the royal party turned in the direction of the Cathedral.

The crowds were milling around the Piazza San Giovanni, anxiously awaiting the arrival of the king. Outside the doors of the Baptistery, Sandro Botticelli pulled his lucco close against the chill weather and stamped his feet to keep warm. Cronaca and Luca Landucci were with him, hoping to get a glimpse of the king. Sandro looked up at the magnificent bronze doors of the Baptistery, but Ghiberti's Gates of Paradise cast an unwelcoming bluish-gray.

"*Merda*, where is this most celebrated King of France?" said Cronaca. "I'm cold and hungry. And this endless parade of soldiers on their *Missus a Deo*, I wonder where *they're* going to eat."

"From your soup bowl no doubt, Masterbuilder."

Cronaca turned, surprised to see one of his idle stonemasons.

"Well, Maso, there's scant soup left. There'll be no work while these soldiers fill up every available space."

The mason nodded. "My cupboard's already emptied, but my scabbard's full. They say the king promised his soldiers the treasures of the city, so all the gonfalons have prepared for battle. Every man with a French soldier in his house will have a sharpened knife under his bed. And half the street stones have been pulled up and stockpiled. Lucky for us the artillery was diverted along another route and the infantry is scattered. We'll have no problem picking them off when the time comes."

Sandro leaned over to say, "I pray it doesn't come to that. Simone says Fra Girolamo warned the king of God's wrath if he should violate the Florentine maiden. Simone is confident God will prevail over king."

"Perhaps, perhaps," said the mason, "but there's still the Medici to worry us. The king's sure to favor noble privilege over republican liberty. Piero can still hope to gain his favor."

Cronaca said, "Well, nothing will surprise me this year. First terrible weather, then a hot, dry summer with no rain, next the French army marches through Italia, and now we have a bounty on the Medici and the possibility for a new government. I even heard the *other* Medici have already returned to Florence. Have you spoken with them yet, Sandro?"

"No, but it's true, Piero's cousins have been welcomed back into the city. They actually changed their family name to Popolano."

Cronaca laughed heartily at the irony. "That's rich—like a leopard changes its spots! We need only change a name from 'tyrants' to 'men of the people' and all will be forgotten. Not bad. Anyway, maybe you'll regain a patron or two."

Sandro shrugged. "I don't know. Perhaps when things settle down."

Sandro fell back into his dark mood. In truth, he desperately needed new commissions though he resented the idea of painting merely to satisfy the needs of some avaricious patron. His household had fallen into complete disarray. His niece, who was his ward, had become uncontrollable and Simone was consumed with the teachings of the friar, spending most of his days attending sermons and serving at San Marco. Perhaps Simone was right about Fra Girolamo. Messer Luca believed it and even Cronaca was being persuaded. Here, before their eyes, was a new Florence, a city liberated by a foreign monarch and a people swayed by moral reform—all fruit borne through Fra Girolamo's efforts. Was Charles the Sword of God? The new Cyrus? The Second Charlemagne? The ground was being cleared for the rebuilding of the Temple, but would it really be a New Jerusalem? And what would be the need for the old pagan representations and depictions? What would be the need for paintings like his? Or painters like him? Suddenly, approaching the age of fifty, he felt old.

A blast of trumpets announced the arrival of the royal guard.

"Finally," said Cronaca, "our savior has arrived. Looks impressive with his retinue. Take note, Sandro, you may have to paint this."

The king and the cardinal rode into the space cleared in front of the Cathedral, only a few paces from where they stood near the Baptistery. The crowd was loud, screaming "*Viva Francia!*" over the din of the trumpets and the drums. Then the king put up his lance, dismounted, and stood next to the tall Cardinal delle Rovere. His large sword scraped the ground.

A hush fell over the crowd. The Florentines were aghast. "My God," exclaimed Cronaca, "he's a dwarf! An awfully ugly one too. His face is put together all wrong. This is our Cyrus? Our Second Charlemagne?!"

Messer Luca leaned over to whisper, "His reputation is based more on the thunder of his artillery."

The stonemason was indignant. "Did you see him riding with his lance leveled? Like a conqueror."

A hushed whisper coursed through the crowd: "There, look at his feet."

The spindly legs of the king ended in the odd hoof-shaped shoes that were the malicious talk of Europe. Only a devil could have such a deformity as six toes. Suddenly the overall impression the king made was comic and everyone knew tomorrow the street gossips would be merciless; their tongues only held in check now by the awesome might of his army. The people roused again their shouts of *Viva Francia!* but the words only aroused fear and contempt in their hearts.

***

Count Pico strained to raise his head. All day he had heard the ringing bells and the trumpet blasts heralding the arrival of the French king. But here, in a small cell in San Marco, bare except for a crucifix on the wall facing one of Fra Angelico's radiant frescoes, Pico clung to life. Across the room sat his nephew, a precocious lad only a few years younger than himself, keeping the vigil.

Pico acknowledged the truth quietly: "All the prophecies have come to pass, the words of Fra Girolamo have proven true."

By speaking it, he accepted what Lorenzo and the others had suspected, as foretold in the Testament of Our Lord. The Golden Age of the Medici was dead, the Sword of God had arrived to cleanse them of their sins. Charles heralded a new age of spiritual reform, in which the glorious city would shine brighter than ever before. It was as foretold— Florence would become a beacon for the humble and faithful, the 'New Jerusalem.'

He fell back, exhausted. His strength was fading and his will to live seemed a losing battle with time. Only two months before, right after the terrible sermon, dearest Angelo had passed, his spirit slowly withering in the two years since Lorenzo's death. Soon after, Pico had moved to San Marco with his last companion, Domenico Benivieni, to prepare to take the habit of the Dominican Order. For almost two years now he had been preparing himself under the tutelage of Fra Girolamo and finally he saw clearly the heavenly light that glowed brighter as earthly darkness engulfed him. His life had flamed too bright too early and now was fading too soon.

His thoughts wandered to his early years studying canon law, learning Greek, and reading Plato. And the glorious year at the University in Paris where at the age of twenty-two he was already renowned as a scholar versed in the Cabbala and the Qur'an. The world was his and never once had he denied himself the hedonistic pleasures available to him under the title of Count of Mirandola and Prince of Concordia.

At a precocious twenty-three, he had returned to Rome to publish his Nine Hundred Conclusions reconciling the world's great religions and philosophies. This was his masterwork showing how all the practices of prophets and sages, oracles and mystics, philosophers, astrologists and cultists concurred only in proving the one true divinity of the Christ.

Incredibly, the Church prelates misinterpreted his Conclusions and, in disputation of his theses, accused him of seven counts of heresy and six more possible counts. The narrow-minded theologians and the ill-informed pope were incapable of entertaining the slightest departure from Christian orthodoxy, so they attacked him, forcing him to flee. When he finally found refuge in Florence, under the protection of Lorenzo, he entered the company of those learned men who welcomed new ideas. Or rather, old ones of the pre-Christian world they reconciled with the teachings of Christ.

This was when he had encouraged Lorenzo to request Fra Girolamo's appointment to San Marco. In time the friar had opened his eyes to the ultimate futility of reasoning one's way to God or of divining the truth through the occult. As Benivieni and Poliziano had conceded: it was not the place of the poet or the prophet to ask "Why?" for they could never explain.

Then he had written a celebrated oration '*On the dignity of man,*' which explained how two natures were planted in our souls. By the one we turn inward to find oneness and love in the Holy Trinity, and by Faith, Hope and Charity we are lifted upward to the heavens. By our other nature we fight like fearful beasts in a deadly competition for status and survival, thereby slipping downward into the lower world. The battle between these two natures was the measure of our souls and our times.

His last work, encouraged by Fra Girolamo, was a refutation of astrology that had caused the break with Maestro Ficino. But even Ficino, despite his truculence, was a member of the priestly brotherhood to which Pico was wedded this very morning when he had taken his final vows. As Pico looked over at his frock and mantle folded neatly by his nephew, his soul was at peace. His only regret was he would not have the privilege of spreading God's word as a poor mendicant in the village squares throughout Italia.

We have entered a new age, he thought, but I am destined for a different mission. As his breath grew short he recalled the opening words of the poet's journey:

Nel mezzo del cammin di nostra vita
mi ritrovai per una selva oscura,

che la diritta via era smarrita.

The thought that he had, after some time, finally found the right road—the path to Paradise and the way of the true faith—expired peacefully with his last breath.

BOOK II

PURGATORIO

We have given to thee, Adam, no fixed seat, no form of thy very own, no gift particularly thine... In conformity with thy free judgment, in whose hands I have placed thee, thou art confined by no bounds; and thou wilt fix limits of nature for thyself... Thou canst grow downward into the lower natures, which are brutes. Thou canst again grow upward from thy soul's reason into the higher natures, which are divine.
- Pico della Mirandola
  On the Dignity of Man

May you be damned, O ancient wolf, whose power
*   can claim more prey than all the other beasts—*
*   Your hungering is deep and never-ending!*
O heavens, through whose revolutions many
*   think things on earth are changed, when will he come—*
*   The one whose works will drive that wolf away?*

Dante Alighieri
[*Purgatorio*, XX, 10-15]

CHAPTER 1

MACHIAVELLI AND THE FRENCH CAPTAIN

NICCOLÒ WASHED DOWN THE LAST of the *minestra* with a full-bodied Sangiovese from the vineyards at Fiesole. Then he broke a crust of stale bread to swab the remainder as he watched the French captain across the table search the bottom of his bowl for the last few beans. The captain, a cavalry officer and *bon vivant* of the French aristocracy from Orleans, had been quartered as Niccolò's "guest" for more than a week along with some lancers who were staying in the servants quarters. While most Florentines complained of their occupiers, Niccolò calculated his inconveniences—a bed already empty, a few bowls of *minestra*, some bread, and more wine—a small price to pay to satisfy his curiosity of the French military. Exciting things were happening and Niccolò could not suppress his inquisitiveness; fortunately the captain spoke passable Italian as Niccolò plied him with questions.

"*Mon ami*," said the captain, a sour look on his face, "I don't mean to appear ungrateful, but it's been weeks since I've eaten meat. *Fagioli, pasta*, and more *fagioli*—is this all you have in this city?"

"*Au contraire, mon Capitaine*," said Niccolò wryly, showing off his rudimentary French, "before you came we had capons and chickens, pheasants, veal, and wild boar and venison. There were figs and artichokes and pears—some so fat and juicy we called them Nun's Thighs. Alas, since your mercenaries have stripped the countryside bare, we must ration even our beans. And this," he added, raising his cup, "is the last of the drinkable wine."

The captain rocked with laughter, he had come to relish Niccolò's wit. "I don't believe you, you Florentines are too clever. I'm sure you hide it all from us, for the banquet after we depart."

Niccolò gave the captain his razor smile. "So, you *do* plan to leave?"

"I hope soon. I don't want to be *en Italie;* I want to be *en France*. It's not good for soldiers to stay in one place too long, but we must defend the House of Valois and its rights to the kingdom of Naples." The captain shrugged. "So far we've seen very little fighting—our Swiss *burbars* do most of the dirty work and our cannons do the rest. But fighting men grow restless."

Niccolò shared the captain's unease over his soldiers' idleness—he had witnessed their gambling, whoring, and drinking in the city's taverns. Recalling how Rapallo and Fivizzano were sacked, he was afraid it would happen here and he had already observed a few nasty fights. Then there was the dwarf king. Charles was a weak, indecisive ruler, too easily swayed by more clever advisors, and yet here he was, the conqueror. He asked the captain, "You believe in your king?"

The captain became alert. "You don't like kings—you and your Republic—but the nobility is a great force for the unity of our nation. Under the monarchy we have become strong. And we have a *Parlement*, you know. In Paris."

The more Niccolò ate, drank and played cards with the captain, the more he admired the French *esprit de corps*. Here was a clear case of the power of *patria* and duty the modern Florentine found completely incomprehensible. These soldiers even took pride in their uniforms and appearance, spending half their days polishing their swords and light armor (before heading off again to nighttime debauchery). This noble attitude trickled down to the infantry as well; it must have been how it was in past centuries with the Florentine *magnati*. But the city-states now are defenseless; Italia desperately needed her own patriot sons.

The captain was well mannered and did not condescend, but couldn't help wondering aloud how these Italian cities managed anything. Niccolò discoursed eloquently and at length on classical theories of government, of Rome and the glory of the Republic, but his *discorsi* rang hollow. With the French he had witnessed first-hand the power of new weaponry under a centralized authority. A national army was now imperative to a people's survival. It was Dante's *Monarchia* in action.

CHAPTER 2

THE SIGNORIA CONFRONTS CHARLES

AS THE DAYS PASSED AND the French lingered, the air thickened with apprehension. Most shops were closed and the Old Market deserted, leaving idle citizens and soldiers free to rove the city streets and loiter in the squares. There was a tension that reminded the Florentines of an arranged marriage between rival family clans. The soldiers' presence humiliated and oppressed the Florentines, grating on their pride while their grumbling irritated the imperial ears of the French and their mercenaries, who showed their disdain for a foe conquered "with chalk," without a fight. The citizens soon became reckless and defiant, fomenting small confrontations with the soldiers that threatened to explode into random violence. Suddenly, from nowhere, a hail of stones would rain down on the soldiers, as hasty blockades hemmed them into narrow streets. And when they angrily brandished their swords the enemy quickly vanished into a maze of alleys and hidden passageways. In this atmosphere the Signoria and the French captains did their best to diffuse tensions with strict curfews, but the matter of the king's purpose dragged on.

After the Signoria explicitly rejected the terms negotiated by Piero and renounced all proposals including the return of the Medici, the king demanded an immediate payment of one hundred twenty thousand gold florins and an additional twelve thousand florins per month during his campaign. This was in addition to indefinite control of the border fortresses to garrison his troops until he passed again on his return to France. The Signoria refused, reacting with dismay to such exorbitant terms and pleading the dire state of the city's finances. This was where the negotiations had stalemated, with patience on both sides wearing thin.

With little recourse, the Signoria, under the leadership of Piero Capponi, turned to the friar to reprimand the king with his divine authority. So Savonarola met with Charles and Cardinal delle Rovere at the Palazzo Medici and the Cardinal joined with the friar exhorting Charles to resume his divine mission to cleanse the Holy Roman Church. Delle Rovere was most anxious to return to Rome at the head of the French army to face his Borgia rival.

Afterwards, Fra Silvestro dutifully spread the word and the street corners buzzed with accounts of the meeting: "Most Christian Prince," the prophet had said, "your stay here is causing great injury both to our city and your own enterprise. You lose time, forgetful of the duty imposed on you by Providence, and to the serious hurt of your spiritual welfare and worldly fame. Listen now to the voice of God's servant: Pursue your journey without delay! Seek not to bring ruin on this city and thereby rouse the anger of the Lord."

Such words had their effect on the irresolute king, while his soldiers fidgeted under the watchful eyes of the Florentines. The citizens gathered in the piazzas and under the loggias playing dice and cards, waiting, determined, concealing knives and scabbards under their jackets and luccos. They watched the king attend mass at San Lorenzo and again when he visited the menagerie of lions at the Signoria, snickering when the diminutive king alluded to these fierce "fellow monarchs" of the animal kingdom. Finally, they looked up from their gambling with apprehension when they spied an official delegation leaving the palace to meet again with the French at the Palazzo Medici.

The four delegates marched through the streets with resolve, escorted by a troop of green-liveried servants. At the head of the delegation was Gonfaloniere Capponi, regal in his cloak embroidered with gold stars and lined with ermine collar and cuffs. Capponi, a veteran of many campaigns as both soldier and commander in defense of the Republic, had become the people's hero. His several diplomatic missions to France made him sure of his ability to measure the French national character, especially that of the dwarf king. He was accompanied by the familiar figures of Francesco Valori, Guidantonio Vespucci, and Domenico Bonsi.

When the delegation entered the vast sitting room on the second floor of the Palazzo Medici—where the former residents had once entertained under different circumstances—the room was filled with French barons, captains, and ministers, all hovering around the seated king. The Signori stood waiting as the king deliberately took time to confer with his ministers. Minister Beaucaire had advised him of the strength of his position against the Florentines and the need to extract as much tribute as possible to support his financially strapped campaign. The Italians were clever cheats, said Beaucaire; they would lie shamelessly to hide their treasures. The Medici had promised more, so the city must be able to pay. The king must stand firm in his demands.

But Charles's captains were shaken by the possibility of conflict and the logistical problems of fighting in close quarters on narrow and unfamiliar streets. Ensconced in their houses and towers, the Florentines were a tenacious foe and subduing the city would be a deadly enterprise. The captains were anxious to depart for the open air of the southern campaign.

The king was hesitant when he finally looked into the eyes of his petulant host, Piero Capponi. He did not possess a decisive temperament, preferring to vacillate and allow events to unfold while delegating tactical decisions to his diplomatic ministers and military captains. But he sensed these quarrelsome Florentines were testing him.

"Signor Capponi," said Charles through his translator, "we have presented our terms for the treaty between the Royal House of Valois and your Republic of Florence, but your Signoria has refused to sign. Our patience is wearing thin. What news have you brought us today."

"Your Majesty, Most Christian King," said Capponi, bowing low, "I regret to say the terms of the treaty presented to us by your ministers have been deemed unacceptable. This, after careful deliberation by the rightful representatives of the people of Florence. Perhaps it's difficult for an all-powerful monarch to understand, but we cannot circumvent the wishes and interests of our citizens. To do so would invite their wrath, as was demonstrated most recently against the previous rulers."

Charles gave a dismissive wave of his hand and replied contemptuously. "So, who is it who will make a decision here? Does your city have no reigning authority? Where does it hide? No wonder your cities lay down like lambs before my army!"

These insults from the mouth of the uncouth French provoked the Florentine and Capponi's reply was equally haughty: "Majesty, the legacy of a freely governed republic based on a constitution of laws long predates the existence of the Spanish, English *or French* monarchies. The peoples of Europe were Roman citizens long before they were English, Spanish, …or French."

The court grumbled at Capponi's audacity and even the other three Florentine delegates shifted nervously.

"*Capon, mon capon,*" said Charles, emphasizing his words with a threatening smile, "this is not the Roman Empire and it is *our* army that occupies *your* city. Our terms are final and these negotiations will be concluded thus."

He motioned to his secretary to read the terms of the treaty ultimatum as he feigned a look of royal ennui. When the secretary had finished, Capponi turned to his fellow delegates and spoke rapidly and softly in Florentine dialect. They nodded their heads in agreement as Capponi turned to the king again.

"Majesty, I regret to say we, as duly elected representatives of the citizens of the Republic of Florence, are unable to agree to the terms. I assure you the citizens would refuse to recognize our actions if we chose to sign this treaty, with grave consequences to our persons and to the state of peace."

The king was incredulous and his dwarfish body convulsed. Jumping to his feet, he turned on them in a white fury: "So be it!" He waved to his military captains, as if commanding them. "Then we will sound our trumpets!"

Now Capponi turned red, fuming as he strode forward. He tore the treaty from the hands of the secretary and approached the king. His voice exploded without trace of fear or hesitation. "And we shall ring our bells!"

He proceeded to tear the treaty into many pieces before the astonished eyes of the French, then he turned and marched out of the room followed by his fellow delegates. This was as close to a declaration of war as one could come.

Charles was struck momentarily speechless and pandemonium broke out among his ministers and captains. This would mean blood in the streets—both Florentine and French. Charles looked at his ministers and saw Beaucaire's fixed smile while his captains nervously avoided his direct gaze. This was not what a king had come to expect—Charles had no experience with those who would refuse his commands. Acting impulsively, he quickly told one of his military attachés to retrieve the Florentine delegation. He then sunk into his chair and forced a smile.

As the delegation was led back into the room the king called out in a joking manner, "*Capon, capon*, you are a naughty capon, *mon ami*. You have the hot southern temper. Please, sit, we shall find a compromise and complete these tiresome negotiations."

Less than two hours later Capponi led the Florentine delegation back to the Signoria, after having secured a compromise treaty with the French that greatly reduced Florentine obligations. The terms stipulated that Charles would receive the title of Restorer and Protector of the liberty of Florence; for which the king would receive one hundred twenty-thousand gold florins in three installments, the first one being fifty thousand; the French would retain the fortresses for not more than two years; and the Pisans would receive a pardon as soon as they resumed their allegiance to Florence. The bounty on the Medici was revoked as a concession to the friendship between the Medici women and the king, but Piero and his brothers remained banished from Florentine territory and their estates confiscated. The Signoria quickly ratified the treaty.

That evening the people were in a delirious mood. The curfew was lifted and the streets spilled over as candles, lanterns, and torches lit up the night. While the Signoria and the French met in the Duomo for an official swearing ceremony, the citizens and soldiers celebrated outside together in cautious relief. The city's new champions were Gonfaloniere

Capponi and the friar of San Marco. The two were hailed continuously over the din of the celebrations as the young street toughs returned to their mischievous ways, running through the city shouting out their new battle cry: "And we shall ring our bells!"

CHAPTER 3

POLITICAL REFORMS

AFTER THE FRENCH EXITED THE city, less grandly than when they entered, they left a sobering void. His guests gone, Niccolò put his own house in order and wondered who would fill the void and how the city would recover from the previous month's turmoil. Shops had been closed for weeks and all trade in and out of the city had collapsed. Construction projects and crafts work had ground to a halt and workers stood idle. In the countryside roving mercenaries and French soldiers had pillaged everything, leaving food and produce scarce and forcing many peasants into the city seeking refuge. The townspeople hoarded the few possessions and food still available, leaving little for sale in the market. Absent the civilizing rituals of daily life, gangs of young men clashed and vented their aggression in the streets.

With the expulsion of the Medici there was no clearly accepted authority to manage the crisis. Four days after the French departed, in the euphoria of the moment, the Signoria had convened a *parlamento* in the Piazza della Signoria and all articles and laws since 1434—the first year of Cosimo's reign—were annulled by popular vote. The institutions swept aside included the Council of the Hundred and the Seventy, both established by Lorenzo. In their place, twenty able citizens were appointed to a new *accoppiatori* to oversee the Signoria and other offices until an election could be held. What form the new government would take was still to be decided and there were hopeful rumors of a new constitution designed to widen citizen participation in the governing councils. But for now, control of the Signoria and the new constitution was the main prize coveted by numerous competing factions.

The political situation was fluid and Niccolò did not yet have a feel for it. The Soderini were well positioned, with Piero consulting Capponi and Paolo close to the friar. But no single faction controlled the *accoppiatori*, so the battle for supremacy would be hard-pressed. The danger was that the *ottimati* and *magnati* opponents of the republican regime would strike while the city and the government were unsettled.

Though the politics was muddled, the mantle of spiritual leadership was firmly affixed to the famed Fra Girolamo, acclaimed now by poets as the "True Prophet of Florence" as well as the "Socrates of Ferrara." Niccolò and the Soderini had recognized the power of the people's adulation and were hoping to harness it for republicanism. Ambitious officials wore a path between the Palazzo and San Marco to consult with the friar and today Niccolò knew Paolantonio Soderini would be there with Francesco Valori and Domenico Bonsi, attempting to forge a coalition for the popular regime.

***

"Please, *Signori*," Fra Girolamo said, gesturing toward the chairs before his desk in the Chapter House. He knew his three guests well—they formed the core of a new party of his supporters in the Palazzo, called the *Frateschi*.

As they settled into the chairs, Valori leaned forward to address the friar. "Thank you, Father. We've come to discuss the accoppiatori. There are many intrigues regarding the new form of government and your advice and support is invaluable to our cause for a just and moral community."

Fra Girolamo nodded perfunctorily. He was tired. In these days he had toiled endlessly, taking to the pulpit each day to provide spiritual guidance for the salvation of the city. He had counseled charity, organized a procession to collect alms from the four principal Churches, and distributed the funds to the deserving poor. He had counseled forgiveness and amnesty for the former Medicean partisans while denouncing the sinful hanging of the official of the *Monte*. And he encouraged merchants to open their shops to employ their workers and exhorted all to fasting and prayer. At the start of the Advent season he had begun preaching from the Book of the prophet Haggai and the Duomo overflowed with thousands each day to hear his sermons. But he knew it was not enough—he must also combat those in the Palazzo who would undo his efforts for their own ambitions. Fighting his fatigue, he forced himself to focus on Valori's words.

"Our Popular Party controls the group's proceedings, but some members are scheming for a return to the old regime before Cosimo. These hypocrites pretend to speak for the Republic by denouncing the Medici, but we know they represent the Medici cousins—the Popolani, Alberti and other *ottimati* families."

The friar had heard much of this new gang of opposition. They were called *Arrabbiati*, the Angry or Rabid Ones. It was an appropriate label for this pack of feral dogs. He dismissed Valori's concerns: "We can easily counter such lies."

"*Sì*, Father, but they fashion their arguments against a popular government. They attribute the our political troubles to popular revolt, which degenerates into chaos—like the Ciompi rebellion. The ignorant merchants and townsfolk are easily agitated by such nonsense."

Fra Girolamo contemplated Valori's point. Ambitious men, with their ready lies, never cease their efforts to hide the truth with the opposite. He must shine God's light upon their falsehoods because the defense of order was critical to the administration of God's justice.

Then Paolo Soderini added, "It's not only the *Arrabbiati,* but also the argument put forth by the Whites and Grays. They want strict control over offices and elections in order to serve their narrow interests. It is a *governo stretto,* a narrow government they seek. My brother Piero says even Capponi is a strong advocate of a narrow election process overseen by a few well-chosen leading citizens, subject to the approval of a larger council. Rucellai is even more adamant—"

Bonsi anxiously interrupted, "The people have not fought for liberty just to preserve power for the same men who were ruling before. They will rebel."

"I agree it's impossible," Soderini said. "Republican ideals have been twisted to serve the interests of a small group. The result is degeneration of civic participation, disaffection with arbitrary laws, and the collapse of moral and spiritual authority."

Valori then stood to drive his point. "We agree on this then: we must install a *governo largo,* of wide participation, that cannot be co-opted by a small group. And we must resist the suggestion to choose offices by election, which are easily rigged by insiders. Better to choose by lot from a *borso* of eligible candidates so all have an equal chance."

"But this is what we had with the *scrutino,*" complained Bonsi, "where the *borselino* was stuffed with Lorenzo's favored candidates. And anyone who was deemed unacceptable or out of favor was disqualified by a hastily assessed tax."

"But we can prevent this abuse with clear laws and procedures," Valori countered, "subject to oversight of a larger council. A council like the *Consiglio Maggiore* in Venice, approximating a true representation of the citizens. This could not be controlled by one group."

Soderini sighed. "We're back then to the issue of a large unruly body vulnerable to manipulation through its own ignorance. Squabbling among factions is the bane of our history."

Fra Girolamo stood to pace, he knew he must guide these men to a higher order of reasoning. "*Signori,* you are our most esteemed civic leaders and I am but a religious teacher and a foreigner. But it strikes me a new order should include careful consideration of all the possibilities the best minds can offer. The ideal procedure would have all sixteen *gonfalonieri* bring forth proposals after consultation with their people. Also the existing ministries—the Ten of Liberty and Peace and the Twelve

Buonomini—should also present their ideas. Then the city can debate the merits of the plans in an open manner and reach the just plan acceptable to all."

They nodded, but Bonsi asked: "Yes, but what end or purpose should guide the final design? Many will see the best solution from where they stand."

"This is a question to which I've given deep and careful thought," said the friar. "As Thomas of Aquino writes, 'Man is by nature a social and political animal.' It is by this very nature that men must live in society. But how should this state be formed? How to avoid the chaos of each man seeking his own advancement? A state is only good if ruled for the benefit of the whole, but who shall take charge of ensuring the common good?"

Valori stated flatly, "The philosophers profess that rule by one man, a benevolent king, is the best model, but I don't believe it."

"True—a king too easily becomes a tyrant. While an aristocracy, as favored by Signor Capponi, often becomes the rule of a few rich to exploit the many."

Soderini completed the circular logic. "Yes, but a polity ruled by the masses soon becomes a rabble."

Fra Girolamo had struggled to reconcile this paradox of governing men. He was convinced the monarchy functions best among northern peoples, who possess a more complacent temperament. Florentines were too spirited and greatly valued liberty—like stubborn mules they chafed under the bridle and threw the bit.

"Broad participation in the electoral and law-making processes is necessary in such a community to insure *both* freedom and peace. The Venetian Constitution appears to be a blend of the three classical ideals of government."

"*Sì,*" concurred Valori, "*La Serenissima* enjoys the benefits of a monarch in the Doge, an aristocratic Senate and democratic participation in the Great Council."

"But in the end it's a government of the aristocracy. How would we ever be able to accept a Doge?" asked Soderini.

Fra Girolamo shook his head; no, no earthly king was possible. "The Florentine character has a weakness for ambition and your city has suffered too often the evils of tyranny to ever trust one man. But we must have a Great Council that includes all those various elements in order to counter the ambitions of any small group. Only Christian virtues ensure the stability and peace of a broad-based government. This is why our program of spiritual reform is so necessary. Men must be restrained not by fear of the king or tyrant but by fear of God and everlasting damnation. The corrupt clergy has undermined this foundation with its deceitful trade in indulgences. And the Roman curates..." He waved his hand in disgust as his voice trailed off.

But the others were inspired. Valori exclaimed, "With a true sense of justice and piety, we may be able to defeat those who oppose us. We'll vanquish them once and for all."

Fra Girolamo quickly tempered their enthusiasm. "*Signori*, forgiveness is a fundamental Christian virtue. We must root out the vicious cycle of vendetta and revenge. We must advocate a blanket amnesty for the previous regime and embrace all in the new community."

He watched their faces fall as one, their expressions suggesting a mix of incredulity and shock. The cycle of revenge was a poison—but it was the only way they knew. They believed the words of tyrants who warned that states couldn't be ruled with paternosters, convinced their enemies must be vanquished once and for all. But thankfully they held their tongues.

To persuade them he began to sermonize: "I've begun a new cycle of sermons for this Advent and the Epiphany. My emphasis will be on the Christian virtues and a reaffirmation of Christian faith. The Lord has delivered us from tyrants and shown us His mercy. Now we must show ourselves worthy of His favor. I will lead the community in prayer and I will declaim the sinful practices of the past, inciting the faithful against gamblers, profaners, and sodomizers. I will advocate charity for the poor and a reform of the tax system to lighten their burdens. I will advocate an amnesty for the Mediceans and persuade the people to place the good of the community ahead of their own and to enforce God's justice as we are taught through the Holy Bible and the example of Jesus Christ, His son."

Fra Girolamo ended this willful statement by looking closely at each of the three men. "And now, *Signori*, you must each do your part in the councils."

Glancing among them, Soderini spoke first. "Perhaps you should also preach support for a new constitution based upon the Great Council of Venice and advise against the designs of those who would subject the people to new tyrannies."

Fra Girolamo fixed his eyes into that penetrating stare with which he froze his listeners. "You can be sure there will be no rest for tyrants as long as I live and breathe. For too long injustice has reigned in Florence, it is time for us to reinstate God's justice in the name of the Heavenly Father."

CHAPTER 4

POLITICAL SERMON

NICCOLÒ AND TOMMASO SLOWED TO keep pace with Tommaso's father and uncle Piero. As they crossed over the Ponte Vecchio, the older men stopped momentarily in the middle of the bridge to gaze at the view downriver. It was late Sunday afternoon and the four were headed for the Duomo, where the citizens were gathering to hear the announced sermon by Savonarola. It was to be about a new political order and a new constitution and only men were permitted to attend.

As Niccolò gazed west toward Pisa, with the sun reflecting off the liquid gold of the Arno, his mind spun from the strategic complexities of trying to keep one step ahead of the changes that had overtaken his city in just the past two months. The political landscape had been completely plowed under and with the insight of Piero and Paolo, he was just beginning to see how the battleground was reforming.

The main line of opposition was drawn between the Popular Party at one end and the anti-republican *ottimati* families at the other. The masses were strongly for the Republic, so it was unlikely the *ottimati* could prevail except by force. To this end, the Popular Party leaders agitated constantly against the specter of military coups, inciting the citizens to frequent mobilizations against a phantom enemy, usually in the person of Piero de' Medici and his small band of fellow exiles. The real purpose was to keep the masses actively engaged and mobilized against internal enemies of the popular regime.

A more subtle approach was employed by the *ottimati* party, the *Arrabbiati* or Angry Ones. Under the conservative Guidantonio Vespucci they used anti-Medicean vitriol against the former Mediceans in the Popular Party while also attacking the religious fervor stoked by the friar. The younger generation of these Angry Ones had organized themselves into a gang united in their hate for the pious and self-righteous Friar. They were commonly referred to as the Bad Companions, or *Compagnacci*. Many of Niccolò and Tommaso's peers were associated with this group of privileged roustabouts and Niccolò knew their leader was Doffo Spini.

The *Bigi*, or Grays, were an offshoot faction of former Mediceans led by Bernardo Rucellai and Bernardo del Nero. These Grays were wary of popular government and religious fervor, like the Arrabbiati, but were also suspect of harboring Medicean sympathies.

Though one might expect the Popular Party to be in firm control after the Medici exile, Niccolò understood the party's unity was illusory. The leadership—Capponi, Valori, and the Soderini—all had competing perceptions of how the Republic should be governed, and these differences lay just below the surface of their uneasy alliance. Tommaso's father and Valori were firmly in the friar's camp. It was impossible to deny the power of the friar's hold over the hearts and souls of the people and these *Frateschi,* seduced by the friar's moral arguments, were adamant to combine religious and political reform.

As head of the Whites, Capponi was more in favor of a narrowly based Republic with a governing elite firmly in control. Similar to the Grays, Capponi believed in the rule of the Roman Senate, of which he would be the leading member.

Piero Soderini envisioned a more pragmatic governing structure that would adapt to changing circumstances. In his view, which Niccolò shared, the problem of the last sixty years was the matter of succession and the city's good fortune had finally run out with the incompetent Piero de' Medici. Unfortunately, the hereditary rule of one family had also undermined the spirit of republicanism. As regards the friar, Niccolò himself agreed with Dante: Religious belief and virtue was essential to good government, but religion and politics were separate realms. Two hundred years ago, the poet attributed Italia's political troubles to the mixing of politics and religion and the subsequent corruption of both. One could observe the same today.

"Giovane," Piero addressed them as he gazed down the Arno, "you've heard often how we Florentines sing the praises of *Libertà* but I tell you our fidelity is as fickle as a woman's. Like romantic love, love of liberty is but a convenient myth; we discard it in an instant in the face of fear. We've done so time and again, no?"

"I agree," said Paolo, "but isn't faith the antidote to fear? Isn't this why true faith in God is required to insure both liberty and peace?"

"True," said Piero, "but faith only in God? Faith in God's mercy is one faith with which to conquer fear but not the only one. Did the Romans not have faith in their Senate and in their armies, which allowed them to overcome the dark abyss? Or the Greeks' faith in their gods, their philosophers and their democracy? What do you think, Nico?"

Niccolò thought for a moment. His convictions had hardened after the occupation of the French king and the ease with which Charles's army marched through Italia. Even a weak, indecisive monarch prevailed over a divided city-state. The ruin of Italia owed to petty rivalries, dissolute rulers, and mercenary armies under corrupt, self-interested condottieri. This all went against the wisdom of the ancient Romans. It was obvious to him that security and prosperity could only come through unity and *patria,* like the French. The citizens must unify behind a sense of loyalty and sacrifice for the common good—if not them, then who else? And for this ultimate sacrifice they needed wise and resolute leadership.

He answered carefully. "I believe the greatest good one can do, and the most gratifying to God, is that which one does for one's country."

Piero smiled broadly. "Well said—a true patriot! You'd think he was applying for a position!" The three Soderini smiled and Niccolò suspected some family ruse.

"But," Piero continued, "I think Paolo would argue God's country, the heavenly domain, takes precedence over our earthly domains."

"It may well be, but until I am delivered unto heaven I must act upon what I know from what I see here on earth."

Now Paolo challenged him. "But what can you see, *giovane?* What do you know here on earth compared with all you don't know about the heavens? God is more to do with what you don't know, than with what you do. Will you base your decisions on your own ignorance compared with the infinite wisdom of God's universe, or will you follow His word as He has given it to you?"

"Certainly God's word is absolute, but interpretations of His word by those who would use it for their own purpose are more suspect. To distinguish between the two I must often defer to the guidance of *maestri* more experienced than I."

Niccolò gave a small bow in deference to his older mentors.

Piero laughed. "Well said. Leave off, Paolo. Our boy Nico knows well how to deflect a challenge with either a sharp wit or a honeyed tongue. Come on, let's go hear our humble prophet speak with the 'words of God.'"

As they walked Piero continued to talk of the current goings-on behind the Signoria's doors. "We're in a good position, Paolo. I've convinced Capponi of the amnesty. This will guarantee the safety of the Grays and help bring them into the Popular Party fold against the *Arrabbiati.*"

Paolo replied in a cautionary tone. "There are practical as well as charitable reasons for amnesty. But I wonder how long before Rucellai, Del Nero and the others turn against popular republicanism. You know it goes against their nature."

"Perhaps, but they have more to fear from Vespucci, Corbizzi, and the Angry Ones. And the new constitution will greatly restrain the mischief any one faction can do against the government. The Popular Party will have the support of the *popolo minuto* and the citizens will control the Great Council. Capponi is fighting for a Council of Eighty as a Senate to ratify the actions of the Great Council and this will have a tempering effect on popular sovereignty. You and I may well find a comfortable home there."

As they crossed the Piazza della Signoria, Piero stopped and looked up at the Palazzo tower, putting his arm around Niccolò. "You know Nico, there's a famous saying in Italia: 'if you have someone to whom you wish evil, send him to Florence as a city official.' My father often told this to me and I can attest to the truth of it."

The three Soderini chuckled again, hinting again of a conspiracy. Piero pointed toward the Palazzo and said, "Since Scala and Guidi were dismissed from the Chancery, their offices have been vacant, but after the new constitution passes there'll be positions to fill. A good opportunity, eh? One appointment will be scribe and assistant to the Second Chancery and I'm in a strong position to influence the choice."

Niccolò looked into Piero's dark eyes to decipher his meaning and saw his own reflection. Piero smiled. "I can reveal to you now that Capponi has already agreed to your appointment to this position under the new Secretary of the Ten, probably Pandolfini or Braccesi, or even Maestro Adriani." He paused to gauge Niccolò's reaction. "Will you accept?"

Tommaso clapped him on the back and said, "Think carefully, Machia, before you answer. This means you'll work like a slave for the pleasure of the Signoria. No more gambling or idle pleasures!"

Niccolò was taken completely by surprise. He had anticipated riding Signor Piero's coattails, but had almost completely lost hope of ever finding a legitimate position. With no aptitude for business and bored by the philosophers, his father had been pushing him to become a notary. Now, finally, he would get to participate directly in the ultimate game of politics. He would receive an income to cover his debts and show his father and mother some fruit for their labors. With a position in the Palazzo a whole host of opportunities would open to him and the possibilities unfolded before him—perhaps even a profitable marriage arrangement. First, he would replace these beggar's clothes. He could not remember later how he answered. Indeed, he remembered little else before finding himself packed into a crowd of men hearing the penetrating voice of the friar echo throughout the Duomo.

Drawn back to the present, he listened with a deepening curiosity as the sermon veered into politics. The friar seemed to be weaving a political argument derived from the writings of Aristotle and Aquinas mixed with a bizarre twist on climate and human temperament. The audience appeared in a trance as the simplest minds attempted to follow the friar's wandering thread of logic:

"Citizens! Rule by a single person is best when that person is a good man, but when the ruler is evil—a tyrant—there can be no worse sort of rule. In warm climates where people have little blood and in cold ones, where they have plenty of it, but little intelligence, men are apt to submit to a single ruler. But in countries neither too warm nor too cold, as in Italia where plenty of blood and intelligence are to be found, men are not willing to submit to a single ruler. Each person wants to rule others, each one being in command and not under command. This is the cause of all Italia's troubles. Hence, wise teachers recommend the rule of more than one. This is especially true of our city of Florence, where men are unusually full of blood and intelligence."

That's Florence for you, Niccolò thought: plenty of blood and intelligence. He supposed the friar meant to compliment the Florentine character by neglecting to mention the serious lack of common sense. It was a Venetian ambassador who said Florence was a democracy where people did not understand the art of rule due to pride and envy in the Florentine character. The friar forgot to mention this as well, but perhaps its meaning was contained in his reference to 'plenty of blood.' Niccolò looked at the Soderini and noticed Piero's thin smile. He turned back to listen as the Preacher provoked his audience with a reference to the legendary admonition of Cosimo de' Medici:

"And who is to say States are not ruled by paternosters? Who have you heard say this? Eh? ...Remember then, this is the maxim of tyrants, of men hostile to God and the common welfare. Good men flee from such a city, for they see the evil toward which it is heading, while murderers and bad men rush to belong to it.

"I tell you when the love of God is lost, strife enters in, for the community needs moral virtue and the knowledge of God. Note, then, Florence: In your government you ought to raise up good men, those who have the virtue of humility. Proud and wicked men do not deserve to be raised up; it's the humble who fly from power who you ought to elect to govern."

Niccolò sharp eyes looked out over the congregation and saw many of the ambitious and ruthless citizens who lusted for power and personal reward through control of government offices. How many of these, he thought, would fly from power out of humility? Who of these possessed true piety? Where were the humble men of Florence? Surely not in the offices of government. Then he remembered, now he too had his foot in the door.

Suddenly the friar's voice reached a more fevered pitch, crying out: "O Florence, if you desire a good government, you must submit it to *GOD*."

Niccolò noticed the men nodding their heads and shaking their fists to underscore the friar's words. But what does that mean exactly, to 'submit it to God'? Savonarola paused for a long moment and then extolled his program of religious reform. His oratory impressed Niccolò. The preacher was equally interested in educating as in evoking the emotions of his audience. But it was not only the substance of his message that explained his power—his message appealed to the heart, mind, and soul. And his personal charisma mesmerized his audience.

As he continued, the friar elaborated on an allegory Niccolò thought he recognized from St. Augustine. It was of original sin and the life of pleasure in the flesh: how the earthly city was overrun by animalistic, flesh-loving, carnal man. This was in contrast to those who lived according to the dictates of the Holy Spirit. These latter were the inhabitants of the heavenly city, the City of God. One city was marked by pride and avarice while the other by humility and charity; one by wickedness and the worship of false idols, the other by love and faith in the true God. And these two cities were divided against each other like Cain and Abel. The earthly city was both Babylon *and* Rome, cities of the devil, while the heavenly city was Jerusalem.

He then spoke of the seven-day scheme of the Apocalypse and how the world was currently between the Fourth day of the pale horse and the Fifth day of the Antichrist and the conversion. But soon, after the conversion, after the reform, Florence would become the City of God with the rebuilding of the fallen Temple.

Niccolò found it difficult to decipher this cascade of metaphor and allegory. But it dawned on him that the Preacher was relating the allegory of St. Augustine to the recent events in Florence: how the French king was God's scourge who was sent to punish the corrupt Roman Church and the religiously indifferent; and Florence would be spared God's wrath through a reconfirmation of spiritual faith and religious piety.

Niccolò was not yet sure who was the Antichrist.

Then his thoughts suddenly wandered to Chiara. Tommaso had told him earlier Fiammetta and Chiara were still at the convent and how Chiara had declared her intention to become a novice in the Carmelite Order. He had been shocked by this news and confused by the change in Chiara over the past year. He wondered if it was a reaction to the trauma of the city's upheaval and fear caused by the French invasion. Or perhaps she was fleeing from familial duty and the prospect of a loveless arranged marriage.

Suddenly the men around him were pumping their arms and crying: "*Gloria Firenze!*" It was as if he was in the midst of a political rally. The friar incited his congregation with a loud, commanding voice that cut through the rising commotion.

"I announce this good news to the city: Florence will grow richer and more powerful than any State, her empire spreading into many places. First, glorious in the sight of God as well as of men. And you, O Florence, will be the reformation of all Italia, and from here the renewal will begin and spread all over, because this city is the navel of Italia. Your councils will reform all by the light and the grace that God will give you. Second, oh Florence, you will have innumerable riches, and God will multiply all things for you. Third, you will spread your empire, and thus you will have power temporal and spiritual."

At this point Savonarola returned to the particulars of the constitution and recommended the model of the Republic of Venice. He proposed a *Consiglio Maggiore* composed of all eligible citizens be established in Florence and this Great Council would choose the Signoria from among them by lot. The Council would then ratify or reject all laws and directives submitted by the other functionaries of government. But the audience became subdued and Niccolò guessed this was caused by the reference to Venice where a single ruler, the Doge, was elected for life; it was a highly contradictory suggestion for a city that had just banished the Medici.

"But, O Florence, remember how I said the climate and temperament of our city makes it unfit to submit to the rule of one man, like the Doge in Venice. The best rule is by a good king but there is only one king worthy of our fair city."

The audience went mute in anticipation and Niccolò came to attention.

Suddenly the friar raised his crucifix, waved it in front of the multitude, and exclaimed: "That king is *Jesus Christ!* The Son of God ...and of man! O Florence, behold! This is the Lord of the universe! Will you have Him for your king?"

He paused, waved the crucifix and repeated: "Will you have Him for your king?"

The congregation erupted: "Vivo Cristo! Vivo Cristo!" "Long Live Christ Our King!"

There was a great commotion as the friar exhorted them in their chant. Then, as he turned and descended the pulpit, the men pumped their fists into the air and moved as one mass toward the exits of the Duomo, carrying the rally out into the Piazza San Giovanni. In disbelief, Niccolò and Tommaso were carried along on a wave of emotion that spilled out the Cathedral doors. There they gathered themselves and found Tommaso's father and uncle pushed off to one side.

Adjusting his lucco, Piero Soderini exclaimed in amusement, teasing his elder brother, "Well, Paolo, that was exhilarating. Your prophet will prove interesting to work with. I'm relieved though—last month we were all going to Hell, but now, with a few well-placed prayers, it seems we'll be richer than Midas!"

Watching the crowd pass by Niccolò also wondered how many of the stains on these men's souls had been purified in the past two months. There's a certain power gained from mouthing well the words men want to hear.

Tommaso's father scowled at his brother's levity. "The pope would do well to heed the friar's warnings."

Piero laughed again, "Better His Holiness than us!"

Darkness was falling as the four hurried away from the fevered crowds back toward the Piazza della Signoria. There they parted, with the elder Soderini returning across the river while Niccolò and Tommaso headed toward the Santa Croce quarter to toast Niccolò's pending appointment. As the two young men passed through the large Piazza Santa Croce, Niccolò still heard "*Vivo Cristo!!!*" ringing in his ears. He found it unsettling.

"When will Fiammetta return from the convent?" he asked.

"*Merda*, I'm not sure. Chiara's going to stay and I think she wishes Fiammetta to stay and keep her company. Perhaps after winter passes and things have settled down again, I hope. Not much of a marriage so far, eh?"

Tommaso hesitated and cleared his throat, signaling a change of subject. "I should tell you now. My father instructed me to join the *Compagnacci*."

Niccolò started. "*Davero*? Really?"

"Yes," he replied with sarcasm, "I suppose it's part of our political strategy—just in case, you know. Now I can renew my old friendships with Doffo Spini and his debauched gang, while you slave away transcribing letters for the Second Chancery."

"Won't they suspect?"

Tommaso was guarded and avoided Niccolò's eyes. "I don't think so. I've known most of these wastrels all my life and the life-style of a hedonist fits my character, don't you think?"

"Yes, well, try not to act the complete jackass."

CHAPTER 5

THE NEW CONSTITUTION

NICCOLÒ CURSED THE BLUSTERY MARCH wind as he hurried across the Piazza della Signoria, heading for the main entrance to the Palazzo. Today an important Pratica was scheduled to debate a controversial amendment to the new constitution and he had little time to prepare. He pulled his new wool lucco close as he passed under the shadow of the impressive edifice and menacing tower that, together with the Duomo and Giotto's Bell Tower, defined the city's profile seen from afar. The Palazzo was built almost two hundred years ago to protect the government from all conceivable attack, but principally from the noble *magnati* families that ruled before being deposed by the modern Republic. Inside one discovered a self-contained, well-ordered world, devoted entirely to the single task of managing the city's many affairs.

Niccolò gave a familiar nod to the guard as he passed through the main portal and traversed the courtyard to ascend the stairs to his small office on the mezzanine. The monstrous fortress was organized by civic function: militia on the ground floor; large halls for deliberating laws and Pratica councils on the first; the Ministries and Signoria on the mezzanine and second floors; and household staff on the attic level. Halfway up the tower was a holding cell for important political prisoners (called the "Alberghetto," where Cosimo de' Medici had once been detained) and finally, the tower itself topped by *La Vaca* and the lookout parapet.

Niccolò had acquainted himself with the Palazzo in the three months since his appointment, but still he could not help being overwhelmed daily by the quantity and quality of beauty that decorated the seat of Florentine power. The walls and rooms overflowed with frescoes, paintings, and sculptures by the city's most famous artists, many depicting religious and civic icons evoking the Republic's glorious history. At the first landing he passed a homage to the Medici, a large panel painting of the Adoration of the Magi. Next to this was a large St. Christopher, the Protector. The most magnificent room he had seen was the second-floor *Sala dei Signori*, where the Signoria would convene privately and dine. Its gold-guilded ceilings were adorned with rosettes and *fleur-de-lis,* girdled by a frieze of lions holding wreaths, with wall frescoed by Domenico Ghirlandaio. These depicted St. Zenobius, a patron saint who, it was believed, had saved Florence from conquest by the Goths a thousand years ago. There was also a freestanding statue of

David in marble by Donatello and another of John the Baptist over the doorway by Benedetto da Maiano. Over the entranceway was the Wheel of Fortune with a sonnet that had become Niccolò's favorite touchstone with its opening lines: *"Se la Fortuna t'ha fatto signore."* It is Fortune who has made you Lords.

His favorite allegory was a cycle of Ghirlandaio paintings in a second floor saletta sealed off from public access. These depicted the Famous Men of the Roman Republic, including Brutus, Cato and Cicero— symbols of republicanism from which the magistrates drew analogies and examples for their long-winded oratories. Often, Niccolò fancifully imagined himself conversing among these Roman Senators as he conducted his secretarial tasks each day in the Palazzo.

Reaching his office on the mezzanine next to the *Sala dei Dieci*, where the Ten of Liberty and Peace decided foreign policy, Niccolò removed the wool lucco and brushed off his silk doublet—one of his first purchases after his appointment. Then he eagerly sat down at his desk to prepare and organize his work for the day. As the new government struggled to be born, every moment was filled transcribing proceedings of various advisory councils, debates, and votes on executive orders. As scribe and assistant to the Secretary of the Ten—a plodding, overfed notary named Ser Alessandro Braccesi—Niccolò was granted access to almost every Pratica and meeting of the Signoria and the other ministries. His task was to compile and summarize these proceedings into concise reports for Braccesi and First Chancellor Scala, who had been reappointed a month after his forced resignation. Niccolò was also required to read and summarize the various dispatches from the city's wide-flung ambassadors. His daily routine made him privy to almost all of the confidential information passing through the Florentine political world and he knew Piero Soderini had recommended him to this job exactly for this reason.

On his desk were the most recent reports from the ambassadors in Rome and several dispatches from Pisa. Digesting these was the task Niccolò prized most. From Rome was a report on Charles and his army. After leaving Florence, the king and his forces had descended on Rome, forcing Pope Alexander VI and his Spanish entourage to flee the Vatican and take refuge in the Castel Sant'Angelo. Eventually the Borgia haggled a temporary peace and Charles turned his attention to Naples. Then just two weeks ago the most recent king of Naples, the boy Ferrantino, had fled just before the French overran his kingdom.

Pisa was more troublesome, with disappointing reports on Florentine efforts to regain control of this vital port. Recently Capponi and Valori had been dispatched to negotiate a peace but the Pisans refused to yield, alleging Charles had assured their independence. What followed had been a seesaw of battles and skirmishes between Florentine and Pisan forces, which threatened a long and costly campaign at a time when Charles's envoy was demanding the second installment of seventy thousand florins. Paolantonio Soderini was now on his way to Naples to entreaty with the king and press the city's claim to Pisa.

Niccolò was anxious to address these diplomatic issues, but today there was more urgent business. In true Florentine fashion, factional infighting over the constitution had reared its Hydra heads, but the friar's sermons had swayed the final outcome. This handed an important victory to the Popular Party, especially the *Frateschi* championed by Paolo Soderini and Francesco Valori. The hallmark of the new constitution was the Council of the People and of the Commune, called the Great Council. Eligibility to this legislative body was limited to all male citizens at least twenty-nine years of age who had paid up their taxes and previously served as a magistrate or could claim at least one ancestor who had served. These *beneficiati* numbered almost three thousand and was considerably more inclusive than the Hundred who had controlled things under the Medici.

The Council would elect all officials to executive and legislative offices in the government, with candidates drawn by lot. The Signoria would continue in its previous form with the Eight Priors of Liberty and the Gonfaloniere as it leader. To appease more conservative supporters, such as the Whites, the authority of the Great Council was balanced by a Council of Eighty, made up of citizens over the age of forty. All legislation would be ratified by the Eighty before being submitted to the Great Council, providing a double check on new laws. Capponi, Piero and Paolo Soderini were already among those elected to these offices.

With ultimate authority residing in the Great Council, it was expected the government would be secure from narrow private interests and party factions. The overall constitutional design was in accordance with the ancient customs of the state, whereby participation was open to the citizenry but held in check and balanced by various functionary bodies. Like the Venetian model, it sought to combine the benefits of monarchy, aristocracy, and democracy. And since no mortal man was fit to rule as monarch, the symbol of Christ the King was the innovation added by the friar.

Though Niccolò considered the reforms a vast improvement over the previous regime, he had raised doubts about its ability to tame the Florentines' fractious political nature. Paolo was confident of the Popular Party's triumph, citing their recent successes. Most notably, the tax system had been overhauled with Cosimo's unjust *catasto* replaced by a new tax on real property called the *decima*. This was based on the friar's recommendations to ensure basic fairness among the rich and poor. But planned reforms were continually sprouting new branches and opening up new areas of contention and Piero shared Niccolò's reservations.

Their most immediate concerns were the anti-republican elements in the new government. Though the opposition's attacks against the friar's political meddling had failed, the Angry Ones would bide their time and surely strike again. Niccolò expected a skirmish in today's Pratica concerning the amnesty for former Mediceans and the right of appeal, and with the Soderini away it fell to Niccolò to measure the temper of the opposition.

Niccolò recalled their discussion before Paolo had left for Naples.

"The law of the six beans must be changed, everyone knows this," Paolo said.

This was certainly true, thought Niccolò. According to existing law, all political and criminal offenses were tried by secret ballot by the Eight of the Guard and on special occasions by the Signoria. A 'yea' vote was denoted by a black bean and a 'nay' denoted by a white bean. Six black beans out of eight were enough to pass final judgment and sentences ranged from imprisonment and confiscation to exile and even death. With offices of the Eight changing so frequently amid an atmosphere of party hatred and revenge, this law had resulted in many outrageous and unjust sentences merely for political vengeance. The reform called to submit all judgments for political offenses to a court of appeal to curb any excessive and potentially abusive authority of the Eight or even the Signoria.

"Yes, but what of all these amendments to the proposed law? And the amnesty? Who knows what final form it will take," cautioned Piero.

"It doesn't matter," said Paolo, "the Angry Ones cannot go against Fra Girolamo or the popular will. Bonsi knows this."

Niccolò knew there were several opposing viewpoints on the right of appeal, with one strongly advocated by the friar in his frequent sermons and pamphlets. Niccolò had read several pamphlets and been impressed by the logic of justice promoted by the friar. And it had gained widespread popular support. But the *ottimati* had frequently controlled the Eight and used the law to punish their enemies. Niccolò knew they would not yield without a fight, especially the wily jurist Vespucci.

As he gathered up his papers and journal to go down to the Hall of Two Hundred, he was eager to appraise the strategies and tactics of the opponents. Taking his seat near the front, Niccolò inked his quill and drew lines in his journal, as if graphing out battle lines.

When the members finally settled into their seats—there must be at least sixty, thought Niccolò—the Notary called the Pratica to order, and then droned out the proposed amnesty:

> Considering the need for union and concord in a well-constituted republic, and in order to follow in the footsteps of our Lord, who, in all He did, whether journeying, preaching, or resting, always enjoined peace; and considering the same is to be seen in all natural things, which ever seek for unity, according to their kind, wherefore the strongest virtue is united virtue; and finally, being admonished by the supernatural events we have witnessed this year, in the establishment of our new government, and the mercy vouchsafed us by the Lord, the magnificent Signoria and Gonfalonieri hereby ordain a general peace be made, that all offenses be pardoned and all penalties remitted unto the supporters of the late government.

Niccolò looked up from his journal as the secretary paused, waiting for the murmurs of approval to quiet. An amnesty for Medicean partisans was surely an overly generous gesture—it was part of the friar's promotion of Christian charity and forgiveness intended to end the cycle of revenge plaguing the Republic. But Niccolò questioned its wisdom, given the unrepentant and grasping nature of the Florentine character. Cicero and Livy had taught him how the stability and longevity of a republic or principate frequently depended on the swift and ruthless elimination of its enemies, for its own immediate safety and as a warning to others with similar designs. He suspected this proposal was tacked onto the law of appeal for tactical reasons and jotted a quick note in his journal as the notary continued:

> That every citizen eligible to public office who, for any political offense, should be sentenced by the Signoria or the Eight either to death, to corporal punishment, to reprimand, imprisonment, or to any fine above the sum of three hundred florins, should have the right of appeal, for the term of eight days, to the Great Council. That, in case of such appeal the Signoria should be bound to allow anyone to speak in defense of the accused; and within the term of fifteen days to bring the case before the said Council as many as six times in the space of two days, and furthermore, to acquit the accused if two-thirds of the assembly should vote in his favor.

Niccolò immediately noted the reform's opponents had craftily amended the proposed law. The original motion advocated by the friar had stipulated a special judicial council of eighty to a hundred members to consider appeals. Such a limited council would be made up of wise and experienced judicial experts to evaluate the merits of a case. But submitting appeals to the entire three thousand member Great Council would invite deviousness rather than insure justice. The foolish ignorance of the many would prevail over the wisdom of the few and the resulting disorder would play into the hands of those who wished to subvert the Council's authority. Now Niccolò wondered how the *Frateschi* would defeat this distortion of the law's intent.

When members of the Pratica were requested to give their opinions and recommendations regarding the amended proposal, Messer Domenico Bonsi was the first to address the magistrates:

"Excellencies, on the issue of the amnesty, in the spirit of Christian charity as espoused in the teachings of Our Lord, Jesus Christ, as well as by those learned statesmen of the Roman Republic, I am reminded of the words of that esteemed orator, Marcus Cicero, who warned of the most grievous mistakes men are prone to make. Two of these are: refusing to set aside trivial preferences and differences; and second, harboring the delusion that individual advancement is made by crushing others.

"We Florentines have made these mistakes often. I exhort you to take to heart the words of both Cicero as well as the good Prior of San Marco that 'justice is founded on good faith.'"

Yes, thought Niccolò, but Cicero also said 'every evil in the bud is easily crushed: as it grows older, it becomes stronger.'

Niccolò heard a muted whisper cut through Bonsi's oration: "This wretched monk will bring us ill-luck." It came from the direction of the *Arrabbiati* partisans.

Bonsi prattled on about communal peace and harmony in rhetorical style, quoting from the Gospel of Paul, then Demosthenes, then Aristotle, causing Niccolò to wonder how impossible these deliberations would be under the new constitution. Fortunately, only up and down votes were permitted in the Great Council.

Finally Bonsi reached the point: "...on the law of the right to appeal, it is my opinion such a measure is needed but the form it has taken has divided us. Personally, I fear the law may be excessive in its application." Then he became tentative and abruptly sat down.

The man next to him jumped up to second the opinion: "How many good servants and highly respected citizens of the Republic have suffered at the hands of the Eight? Families scattered from Naples to Padova, wives separated from husbands, brothers from sisters, and sons from fathers—for no other reason than the pettiness of politics! What riches were squandered when Palla Strozzi and his family were banished? Or even Dante, our favorite son, sentenced to exile or death? We must end this abuse of justice. But this law of appeal to the Great Council will invite new abuses. Perhaps it should be considered only as a temporary measure."

Niccolò coolly noted how the *Frateschi* were struggling to make a positive case for amnesty while cautioning against appeal to the Great Council. But this proved difficult when they had previously argued for the justice of the Great Council and how it prevented the co-option of the government by small factions. Now they were being forced to admit that under certain circumstances, such a large body might be vulnerable to abuse.

Then Luca Corsini, a leading member of the Popular Party, rose and the crowd grew still. After extolling at length on the principal of unity and reconciliation to counter external threats, he turned to the question of appeal:

"The Republic consists of one body alone, and this body is the whole people. When doubts, disorders, or dissensions arise, there is no injustice in recurring to the Great Council, which represents the people; nor can the authority of the Signoria be diminished by an appeal to the people to whom the whole of the Republic belongs."

Niccolò counted many nodding heads in the large room. The seductive appeal of the Great Council as the representative of the *popolo* and ultimate authority was too much for the republicans to resist. He was busily writing and shaking his head in dismay when a loud throat clearing silenced the room again. Eyes turned to the opposing bench as Messer Guidantonio Vespucci rose to address the Signoria. He first praised the preceding speakers, saying Cicero had also warned that democracy often degenerated into the 'despotism of the multitude' before moving on to the proposals at hand.

"For my own part, the only viable plan would seek to establish perfect equality among the citizens; if the old road will lead us to that goal, let us follow it; if not, we must choose another path. I deem the old law to be perilous, just to give so much power to the Signoria without also granting right of appeal against their decisions. In France, appeal can be made to the Council of Paris against the verdict of the king, the pope can reverse imperial decisions, and the sentence of the papal Chair itself can likewise be appealed to a Council of Bishops. If princes, who are bound by no law, are willing to allow the right of appeal, why should it be refused by magistrates whose authority is wholly derived from the people?"

Niccolò noted this argument was delivered by a man who had voiced strenuous opposition to the new constitution only three months before. The major opponent to republican liberty was now extolling its virtues and Niccolò felt a twinge of admiration as Vespucci continued spinning his web.

"By granting this power of appeal we shall only restore to the people its own right, and repress the immoderate pretensions of the over-ambitious. Accordingly, I see not what harm can be caused by destroying the pernicious authority of the 'six beans.'"

The room hushed at this turnabout. Heads nodded in agreement, ignoring the contradictions with Vespucci's previous position. The Great Council had become the magic touchstone of liberty in the new Republic and the reservations of the *Frateschi* could hardly be expressed now, except in opposition to their own Great Council. There was little choice but to ride the wave of public opinion as the common folk would fail to appreciate the distinction between a limited council of legal experts and the entire Great Council.

The tactics of Vespucci and the Angry Ones impressed Niccolò. He was sure they saw the breakdown of the Republic as their saving grace and were most eager to push it to the extreme to hasten its demise. The Popular Party and the *Frateschi* had been outmaneuvered and Paolo would be furious, but Niccolò would not be fooled again. It was sure to be the first of many skirmishes and he had seen the subtle sleight of hand of the shell game and knew where to watch for the pocketing of the pea.

CHAPTER 6

MICHELANGELO RETURNS

THE SPRING SUN WAS JUST beginning to moisten the cold ground as Michelangelo dismounted his mule at the Porto San Gallo. He had ridden several hours after departing before dawn from a small inn on the road from Prato. He was traveling with a small troop of penitents from the Veneto eager to hear the famous Prophet of San Marco. It was more than eight months since Michelangelo had fled to Bologna, shortly before the Medici had barely escaped the wrath of the mob with their lives. He had found work in Bologna, carving several marble statuettes for the Church of San Petronio, but, after moving on to Venice, there were no commissions to be had and he'd been idled for more than three months in the lagooned city that afforded him little serenity. Now, as he arrived outside the gates of his city, he immediately sensed the changed atmosphere.

News and rumors traveled fast along the arteries of trade, to Bologna where he had stayed almost four months, then following him to Ferrara, Padova, and Venice. All Italia was in turmoil and Florence was at the center of it. Charles had spared the city and was now occupying Naples. When Michelangelo was in Venice, the pope's ambassadors had met there to organize a Holy League of States to drive out the French. The pope's legates had convinced the Duke of Milan to renounce his French alliance and join forces with the papal States together with Venice, the Holy Roman Emperor Maximilian, and the King of Spain. The League was now arraying its forces in the north to attack the French army upon its return.

Florence was the wild card in this face-off and the League had demanded the city break its alliance with Charles and join with it. But Charles was still God's champion according to the friar and his army still held the entire south of Italia. He was also Florence's best hope of regaining control of Pisa without a protracted war of attrition. So the Florentine-French alliance had rendered all Florentines *persone-non-grata* in cities allied with the League and Michelangelo imagined this had added to his difficulty in finding commissions in Venice.

On the positive side, heartening news of the Prophet of San Marco had traveled even faster and wider than the doom and gloom of war; all the cities Michelangelo had passed through were abuzz with hope for the salvation of good Christians everywhere. The roads were filled with pilgrims like his companions, making their way to Florence to do penance and hear the friar preach. During their journeying together, the young sculptor had become celebrated among these penitents with his stories of Fra Girolamo in the sculpture garden at San Marco. Michelangelo had also noticed many suspect characters along the way doing a brisk trade in holy relics attributed to the friar.

Though the Republic had regained its liberty and a new constitution had been established, rumors also claimed Piero de' Medici was scheming to retake the city. This is why the guards at the gate were so apprehensive and diligent in their duties. The city was under a strict curfew and the gates locked and guarded from nightfall until dawn.

After he obtained leave to pass, Michelangelo's curiosity regarding his city was instantly confronted by a scene just inside the gate: the monastery of San Gallo had been burned to the ground. Lorenzo had built the monastery for Fra Mariano and the neo-Platonists had gathered when not at one of Lorenzo's villas The charred remains and the hollowness of destruction shocked him and he became uneasy about other Medici landmarks in the city.

He thoughts raced. What of the Palazzo Medici? What of all the art collected by Cosimo, Piero the Elder and Lorenzo? And the books! Were they destroyed? Pilfered by the French? Then he thought of his own work. Thank God he'd been able to keep the two marble carvings he'd completed: the *Madonna of the Stairs* and the *Battle of the Centaurs*; they would still be safe in his father's house. But all his patrons and mentors were gone—Lorenzo, Poliziano, Pico—all departed from this world. Michelangelo could barely hold up his head against this loss. He was twenty and what did he have to show for all his talents and years of work? Where would he find new commissions? In coming home, he had hoped his city had settled into peaceful prosperity and goodwill, a place he would be able to work without worry.

As he led his mule he wondered which direction to go. First, he must go to his father's house where he had sent word of his pending arrival. Then, where? Whom would he find? He wondered if Francesco was working. He was very anxious to show his friend the copy of Piero della Francesca's *On Perspective of Painting* he had received as a gift from his patron in Bologna. Perhaps he should try Ghirlandaio's bottega first, or maybe La Casa Dante? Surely Francesco would know he was expected and would seek him out, but he hadn't heard word from his friend for several months.

He heard his name hailed and looked up to see his traveling companions waving as they veered off toward the Convent of San Marco. He wondered about the large influx of religious into the Dominican order and if his brother Leonardo was there or still in Pisa and what had become of the sculpture garden. They said the neo-Platonists now gathered at San Marco and were known as the *Accademia Marciana* rather than by the former Medicean name of the Platonic Academy. He wondered if his name was still associated with the Medici and how this might affect his prospects for commissions. And he wondered if his former pagan themes would spoil his reputation in this city of Christ the King.

Michelangelo watched the penitents as they smiled with joyful anticipation of meeting their prophet, oblivious to the weight bearing down on the young artisan. He saw a dourness in faces he passed on the street—the gay Florentine spirit had been tempered. Suddenly he had the sense of being a foreigner, a stranger in his own home. He forced a wan smile as he waved back to the penitents, then led his mule in the opposite direction toward Casa Buonarroti.

CHAPTER 7

BOYS OF THE FRIAR

AS FRA GIROLAMO APPROACHED THE chapel, he felt his soul transported by the sound of plainchant spilling out into the hallways and courtyards of the convent. Song gladdened and opened the heart and the friar noticed the effect on the faces of all the devotees in the cloister as he passed. More of these pilgrims had arrived every day until he and his poor brethren had been overwhelmed. The pilgrims' strange faces and foreign tongues filled every available space; San Marco had become a new Tower of Babel. And the city outside was full of them; when he preached in the Duomo, fourteen, fifteen, sometimes sixteen thousand devotees packed the Cathedral. In addition, many *giovani* from the wealthiest and noblest families came with offerings and hopes to be selected as one of the novices to the Dominican Order. It seems Lorenzo's desire to raise the prestige and reputation of the convent by inviting him to San Marco had been more successful than anyone dared imagine.

The friar suspected the *grandi's* revived interest in the ecclesiastical calling was less a devotion to God than a keen understanding that power had shifted from the marketplace back to the Church. So each family was grooming one or two sons for the clergy. He knew many of them were also determined to thwart his reforms and they would infiltrate and infect like the pestilence if given the opportunity. It was his expressed intention to ferret them out and he tested them by renouncing their families' gifts, giving them over to charity for the poor and needy.

The plainchant slowly decayed, concluding the offices of Nones and the brothers silently filed out of the chapel to return to their duties in the interim before Vespers. As they passed, Fra Girolamo motioned for Domenico, Silvestro and the Choirmaster Fra Bonifazio to follow him into the Chapter House. Once inside the prior motioned to Fra Bonifazio to close the door.

"*Sentite, fratelli*, indulge me for a few moments. I wish to discuss with you a proposal I've been contemplating."

The three friars grew attentive and Fra Silvestro spoke eagerly, "Yes, Fra Girolamo, things go well with the civic reforms and we have good relations with the Signori, especially Signori Capponi and Valori." Silvestro was proud to be confessor to some of the leading citizens and spoke openly of his frequent meetings with these men.

"Yes, Silvestro, we've made much progress with the reforms and I'm deeply grateful for the communications you've conducted with our friends in the Palazzo. But our enemies also multiply and our purity of vision is diluted by some of those who join our ranks. I suspect some of our novices' loyalties lie first with their patrimony."

Silvestro's brow clouded. "I have my suspicions. I hear whispers of dissent, but I'm familiar with the family histories of these Florentines, so I can help you on these matters. Some have close relations with our *Arrabbiati* enemies and their nasty offspring, the Bad Companions, who harass us everyday outside the convent walls. In particular, I'm wary of the Rucellai, Amidei, and—,"

"*Sì*, Silvestro," the friar replied wearily, "but the farmer can hardly spend all his time chasing vermin in the grain storage. We must devise a better method to combat these foes and solidify our reforms."

Domenico shot an impatient look at Silvestro, who appeared confused by the peasant analogy.

Fra Girolamo continued: "The capriciousness of city politics is the simple truth of Florentine affairs as they now stand. The magistrates set their sails to the prevailing wind—it will sometimes go with us and sometimes against. We must break this cycle of duplicity, corruption, and fraud. How so?"

They returned only blank, expectant looks, so he continued: "I believe we must direct our efforts away from the elders, they will not change their ways. We must focus on the youth before they learn those bad habits ingrained in men."

Domenico was dismayed. "But the *fanciulli* are ruffians and little devils. They're like feral animals. How can we tame them?"

Fra Girolamo gazed warmly into his brothers' eyes before he answered. They are simple and good, he thought, but they are like sheep to his shepherd. "With the power of the Lord's grace. And some insight into the methods that appeal to the youthful spirit. This is what I wish to discuss."

Seeing their confusion, he continued: "The problem and promise of children is a case on which much has been written. As we know, children are born innocent but with the stain of original sin. After Holy Baptism they enter the corrupt world of men. Many of these children, especially the boys, are often mistreated as infants, with either too much or too little affection, discipline, or nurture. Their fathers are more concerned with making them wealthy than with making them good. The young ones follow the bad examples they see in their fathers' behavior and then adults indulge and encourage young men to debauchery and drunkenness and allow them to sleep off hangovers until the afternoon."

The friar thought of his own upbringing and the example of his father—a model of moral lassitude. Only the grace of God and his pious grandfather had saved him from the debauchery he witnessed all around him in Ferrara. And the many temptations he had experienced.

"Young men are naturally hot of blood and desirous of the flesh. They're tempted and corrupted by the public and private spectacles of dishonest women, who lure them into gaming and the wicked life, with fornication and obscene gestures. I will not even speak of the other vice. It is a life filled with vile verse and poetry and depictions of naked wantonness."

The eyes of the three friars widened as they listened to the friar's graphic descriptions.

"With such an upbringing, is it any surprise these *giovani* grow up to be corrupt and dissolute rabble-rousers? And when they enter the clergy for material gain, is it any wonder the whole world has lost respect for religion?"

They shook their heads with the shame of it all. But these were the ways of men—what could one do? Fra Girolamo gave them his answer.

"Brothers, it's my idea to organize the youth into an army—an army of angels for Christ. We shall give them a purpose where they have had none. We shall give them a home where they have been abandoned. We shall show them how the power of goodness can vanquish evil. And with their aid we shall cleanse the filth from the streets."

Silvestro became visibly excited, but Domenico was reticent. "Prior, already the youth gangs attack us and commit all kinds of terrible deeds just for sport. They pelt us with rotten fruits and vegetables. How can we turn these little devils into angels of the Lord?"

"With care, Domenico, just like with your doves," he answered. "Do you not believe children are led astray? And with proper care they can be brought back into the fold of the good and the faithful?"

"Yes," Domenico said, but sounded unconvinced.

"All we need do is discover the means by which to accomplish this. The Signoria has already assisted us by recognizing the need for spiritual reform, thereby raising the status of the religious vocation. This is one reason we've been deluged with applicants from the *grandi* families. All young persons love the regimentation of discipline and the sense of belonging to something greater, but they no longer receive this from their elders. So they establish small gangs with leaders and strict hierarchies and then they defend these 'families' in deadly skirmishes. We need to provide discipline and self-respect through the power of faith. We will dress them in white surplices and give them little red crosses to carry to mark them apart from other citizens.

"And young people love music and songs, to sing as we do in simple

unison in the spirit of togetherness. I've heard them singing those vile
Carnival songs and they sing for the joy of singing, regardless of the
lyrics. Even Lorenzo knew the power of popular songs to direct the
energies of the young." He turned toward Bonifazio. "And this is where I
need your assistance, Brother Bonifazio."

"*Sì*, Prior?"

"You've heard my sermons denouncing the common, secular
music—those songs that delight the senses but not the spirit. Even
though these songs may be sweet to the ears, nevertheless they do not stir
the soul. For this it's necessary to return to the original simplicity of
sacred music, so God may always be praised."

"But will youth versed in bawdy Carnival songs sing sacred hymns?"
asked the Choirmaster.

"No, that is not my meaning. In Church and in the offices, brothers
and novices shall sing sacred hymns as we have always done. But for the
popular taste I've written verses of sacred *laude* to fit the melodies of the
most common Carnival songs and street madrigals. The poet Girolamo
Benivieni has also composed *laude* for these purposes and set them to the
most popular melodies. Thus, we shall elevate the soul through the power
of music praising the divine. This brotherhood of song will also serve to
hold our army of *giovani* to the right path. Here, listen to an example I
wrote."

The friar sang in a sweet, soft voice a pleading lyric to Jesus the
Savior:

Gesú, Gesú, Gesú,
let everyone cry out Gesú.
Call this name with heart and mind,
and experience how it is sweet and merciful;
Whoever calls it faithfully,
feels Jesus in his heart.

But the brothers' eyes widened in surprise: The melody they heard
was the vile song of the chimneysweeps and their faces registered their
shock and red-faced shame. But Fra Girolamo sought to reassure them.

"Trust me, brothers, with repetition, sincere devotion, and
concentration on the new text, you will soon cease to hear the old.
Bonifazio, I need your help to write and transcribe more *laude* so we will
have a complete hymnal from which we can train our boys choir.
Domenico, you and Silvestro will undertake this important task of
organizing and training the *fanciulli* to do God's work as the army of
Christ the King. I've a list of rules and instructions to guide you in
training the boys that I will discuss with you later. *Va bene?*"

The three friars nodded obediently in acceptance of their appointed missions, but were each struck incredulous by the prior's proposal. Domenico, firm in his faith and devoted to Fra Girolamo, feared those who conspired against them would not be thwarted by children. The prior had recently focused his sermons on the corruption of the Roman Curia, especially the pope and the young cardinals he had recently appointed to serve Borgia interests. And it was also rumored young Cardinal Giovanni de' Medici, now in Rome, was soliciting the pope's support to reclaim Florence for his brother Piero with promises to support the Holy League against the French.

On the other hand, the Signoria had accepted the prior's argument for the French alliance, so perhaps it was God's will they were to be His instruments of reform. Nevertheless, Domenico knew sometimes God was sleeping and that was when Satan ensnared the hearts of men.

Silvestro, his left eye twitching, only heard a discordant blend of obscene street lyrics from his youth mixed with the devoutness of the prior's new text.

CHAPTER 8

A VISIT TO THE CARMELITE CONVENT

"SILENCIO! SILENCIO!"

FRA DOMENICO HAD lost control of his unruly charges. Dozens of them were making a riot of the Piazza outside the convent, shoving each other and shouting as he and several assistants attempted to herd them into some semblance of ordered rows. The white surplices they wore could not obscure the unkempt griminess of these street orphans, and to Domenico they resembled more an unruly flock of wayward sheep than a flock of Angels. He found the task before him demoralizing and longed to be left to peacefully care for his doves.

Suddenly, like magic, the little urchins froze and hushed their chattering into a low murmur. Domenico looked around in the bright sunlight to discover the source of this miracle and saw the prior at the main door of the convent, accompanied by two novices.

"Ah, Fra Girolamo," Domenico said with a desperate cheeriness in his voice before raising it sharply again: *"Silencio! Silencio!* The prior wishes to speak with you."

Fra Girolamo appeared taken back by this mob of unruly youth but quickly regained his composure. Clutching his ever present Bible and crucifix, he raised the cross up in his right hand.

"My children, you are here to become Angels of the Lord, your God. He is the Almighty One. If you serve Him well, with purity of heart, you will know His great kingdom in Heaven."

A small cry of *"Vivo Cristo"* escaped from the center of the crowd and fanned out in repeated ripples.

Fra Girolamo waved the crucifix to silence them. "Yes, *Vivo Cristo.* But listen carefully: Learn and obey the word of God through His Ten Commandments. We must turn away from the temptations of sin and renounce the worldly pleasures afflicting your elders. If you see persons engaged in gambling, believe them to be no Christians, since they are ministers of the evil one, and they celebrate his rites. They are avaricious men, blasphemers, slanderers, thieves and murderers, and they are hateful to God."

This evoked more cheers of "Evil-doers! Burn the devils! *Vivo Cristo!"* and Domenico tried to hush them.

Fra Girolamo continued: "Rather, observe and follow the example of your teachers here at the convent. Dress and behave simply, with great humility, according to the true Christian virtues of Faith, Hope, and Charity. And together we shall all serve Christ and cleanse our city of the sins of the evil-doers and drive out the merchants of Satan."

The boys cheered like an army of infantry for their general. Ranging in age from five to twelve, the true meaning of the friar's charged words flew beyond their young minds, but the emotions of the moment fired their hearts. Their elders may revere or fear the friar, but they had become intoxicated with the power of God's righteousness and clamored to serve their friar's cause. But Domenico found their uncontrolled zeal disconcerting.

Bemused, Fra Girolamo leaned over to whisper to Domenico. "Perhaps you can discover a way to scrub some of the street grime off these poor boys, so cleansed they may present a purer image for their holy mission. Perhaps, well, ... you can take them bathing in the Arno. Be sure to go upriver." Then, with a vanishing smile, he turned and motioned to the novices who were waiting to accompany him on his journey.

Domenico gave his departing prior a horrified look. "Bathing in the Arno?" he muttered to himself. He couldn't swim and envisioned himself being swept all the way to Pisa and drowned in the sea.

***

Fra Girolamo hurried up the dusty road to Fiesole, forcing his two young novices to struggle to keep up. Today was the feast of St. Catherine of Siena and he had consented to visit the Carmelite sisters near Fiesole to preach at the request of the prioress. It was early and the journey to the convent would take more than an hour.

This morning Fra Girolamo was invigorated. The success of his program of reforms had helped him overcome his recent exhaustion and painful digestive disorders and he was pleased his army of little angels was proving so popular. With their overwhelming numbers, he now had the means to turn back his enemies and insure the city's spiritual redemption and salvation. But it would take time. His only concern was whether Domenico could manage all the new recruits.

In the Palazzo the Great Council was passing new laws inspired by the Word of God and he was confident of his influence over a small circle of respected citizens and civic leaders—Valori, Paolo Soderini, Bonsi, and several others—who visited San Marco often to consult with him. But despite his successes, he knew he could not rest. His avowed enemies still lurked in the shadows and he was forever suspicious of the changing winds and the true motives of worldly men; he was sure they only deferred to reform when it suited them. They were practical men and the temptation to reassert their ambitions would resurface. He suspected many were just pagan republicans who found common cause with him against their enemies and would follow him only for as long as they walked the same path together and no farther. Grown men did not shed their true skins.

But providing the people followed him without question, Fra Girolamo was confident of his position. So many came to fill the Cathedral when he preached: citizens, workers, peasants, and foreigners. He could rally them in an instant to his cause and none of the *grandi* could oppose their concerted will. But popular moods were always short-lived. This is why he had decided to form new men from the *fanciulli*—new Christians created in the spirit of Jesus Christ the Redeemer. From these youth he would mold Angels of the Lord, to cleanse the city and enforce the regime of Christ the King. The young were untainted and he would use them to enforce peace and harmony, good will, and adherence to the scriptures. Like Moses he needed his own army of faithful followers. They would collect alms, sweep the streets, and chase gamblers and wanton women from public places. In time their elders would die off and be replaced by this next generation of pious and ardent devotees— worthy citizens of the City of God.

He turned to see his novices struggling to keep up, revealing their eagerness to visit the sisters' convent. He knew the source of their enthusiasm, the tales they heard of the coupling of priests and nuns, with orphans mysteriously appearing at the doorstep of the foundlings hospital. But it was the Devil's work, disguised as woman.

With those of the female sex, his task was the opposite as with the men. His most ardent devotees were the old women—wives, mothers, grandmothers and widows—who dressed simply and reverently. With age they discarded the frivolous vanities of youth and turned to prayer and the inner spirit. They came to his sermons tirelessly and filled the Duomo for each Mass. They came to the convent and crowded the cloister to offer their services distributing alms and other works of charity.

But the younger ones were filled with the promise of life, their nature brimming with fecundity, pride, and vanity. And when they lost their innocence they became Satan's temptresses. Fra Girolamo knew how nature had weakened Adam's resistance to Eve, so his Angels must not be tempted by lust. To protect them he must turn his attention to the impressionable and curious young women. He must enlist the pious nuns and novices to keep these temptresses in line.

Fra Girolamo turned this subject of his sermon in his mind. His theme would be the two Marys: the Virgin Mother and the Magdalena. The Madonna was the true mother of the faithful, the symbol of female purity and model of Faith, Hope and Charity. In Christendom, the icon of the Virgin was ubiquitous: on city streets, in the cathedrals and churches; in corner niches; in country villages and shrines along travelers' waysides. She was mankind's helpmate on earth and the patroness of forgiveness and redemption. The faithful prayed to her to intercede with the Father to forgive the transgressions of mortal men.

The other Mary, the Magdalena, was the fallen woman, the temptress Eve who led man astray. These were the prostitutes and whores who flaunted their flesh to sate the appetites of men. These women used nature to serve the Devil, to bring men down to the level of beasts. These were the women he chastised from the pulpit with the words of Ezekiel:

> O Women! You provoke God by your extravagance, by the excessive length of your trains, your low-cut dresses, the paint you daub on your faces, and your indecent garb in church. You women, who glory in your ornaments, your hair, your hands, I tell you: you are all ugly. Would you see true beauty? Look at the pious man or woman in whom spirit dominates; watch him when he prays, when a ray of the divine beauty glows upon him when his prayer is ended; you will see the beauty of God shining in his face, you will behold it as it were the face of an angel.[8]

The Lord had interceded to save Mary Magdalena. She was turned away from the sins of the flesh and found redemption for her immortal soul. This was the message the Preacher brought to bear in his sermons against vanity and lust.

Later that afternoon in the Carmelite chapel Fra Girolamo delivered his sermon on the two Marys. These sisters chose to follow the path of the first Mary, the Virgin. The Church was the symbolic Bride of Christ and her nuns were His literal Brides. In their chasteness, they were an example to their lay sisters. Yet he admonished them, for all told of the frequent violations of chastity within the convent walls. He knew that among them were "courtesans who opened their doors to fine *signori* who visited them." He warned them against priests, monks, and rich patrons who would take advantage of their weaknesses by appealing to their vanities. They must resist the temptation of the flesh and, like Magdalena, find redemption in their chaste devotion to their Savior. They must renounce their vanities, their rouges and paints, wigs and fine dresses, and adopt the humble examples of the Madonna and the saints. He inspired them with stories of Hildegard of Bingen and Catherine of Siena, two exemplary women who had served God exclusively and through their selfless devotion were canonized as saints.

When he finished he was gratified to see their eyes cast downward and ended the service by leading them in singing the *Ave Maria*.

After his sermon, the prioress received him and his novices in the refectory to express her gratitude for their visit and offer refreshment before their return journey. In a hospitable manner she ventured her views on Church politics:

"Vicar, we've heard word of your sermons against the Roman Curia and the Holy See. Are not such words, though infused with truth, sure to invite strong sanctions from the Vatican and the College of Cardinals?"

Fra Girolamo looked sharply at the prioress through narrowing eyes. She was a good and honest servant of God but, like so many others, perhaps she shrunk from the hazards of her duties. So many of the clergy, the monastic and confraternal orders were lukewarm to the reforms. Change threatened and a body at rest succumbed to some powerful force of nature that made men and women feel safe. This was the tide he was forced to row against. He softened his features into a smile as he begged the question.

"Should we temper God's word to satisfy those hypocrites whose actions disclose their true loyalties?"

"Of course, I would suggest no such thing. But we're a small Order. Many of our sisters come from important and powerful families, but we depend wholly upon the generosity of charity and alms contributions. We serve you as our Vicar General, but if we incite the displeasure of the Roman Curia, our cherished independence may be threatened. Remember, our independence was granted by the Holy Father and can be easily rescinded."

Fra Girolamo felt he was being chastised and his voice grew stronger, baring his irritation. "Prioress, I can only say that in our times prelates and preachers seem more adept at destroying Christian life than building or conserving it. In the early Church it was the chalices that were made of wood and the prelates were men of gold; today it is the prelates who are made of wood and their chalices rich in gold.

"Who will question what everyone knows: that priests, who once had the grace to call their sons nephews, now call them sons sons, pure and simple. When I say these truths I think not of their displeasure— because they are guilty of these sins. I only desire to shame them and drive them from God's Temple. And if they should attack me, I recite the words of Our Lord, 'Blessed are you, when men shall revile and persecute you.'"

The prioress bowed in deference, wisely recognizing such righteous passion would not be swayed by appeals to reason and circumspection.

A sudden knock on the door of the refectory interrupted them. A young novice entered slowly with her head bowed in reverence. The girl was fair with a simple beauty, but appeared thin and fragile. Behind her was a young laywoman slightly older in age, dressed in simply fashioned clothes that failed to hide the elegance of their rich and costly fabric. This woman's hair was also fair but flowed down her back and her dark eyes smoldered with a barely hidden sexuality. This creature flushed with life and Fra Girolamo noticed the eyes of his novices riveted on her vulgar beauty.

Without raising her eyes, the novice spoke: "Excuse us, please, Mother Superior. We beg to take leave as we must depart soon to arrive in the city before dark."

"Come in child." She turned to Fra Girolamo. "May I present one of our recent novitiates from your city, Signorina Chiara di Giovambattista Corbinelli. Perhaps you know her family, it is an old and esteemed name. And her mother is from the Soderini."

Fra Girolamo's brows rose as his eyes brightened. "Yes. I've worked closely with Signor Paolantonio Soderini and his brothers. They come often to San Marco to discuss political matters."

The novice demurely raised her eyes. "They are my uncles, Father."

"I am pleased to see a member of such a distinguished family take vows. I will compliment your uncles when we meet next."

Chiara lowered her eyes again. "If I may be so bold, Father, your teachings inspired me to take the vows of the Order."

Fra Girolamo smiled warmly. "Then God has granted me one additional reward here on earth. One of my natural sisters is named Chiara, but she is in Ferrara and I haven't seen her in many years."

"Chiara has only been with us about six months, since the French came," the prioress said. "May I also present Signorina Corbinelli's companion, Signorina Fiammetta di Filippo Strozzi…"

The prioress continued her introduction, mentioning something about the Strozzi and the girl's connection to the Soderini, but Fra Girolamo failed to comprehend anything after hearing the name. He stared at the young woman as she smiled politely, but his eyes clouded over and he felt a weakness in his belly. He looked at her body beckoning from under the fine silk damask: her tightly cinched waist; her breasts fully formed under the lace shawl. Its power, which he had not felt for so long, filled him with fear. Involuntarily he mumbled the name "Laodamia" as he felt his body revolting, struggling to suppress emotions welling up inside him. His face must have betrayed him, as he saw confusion invade the faces of the prioress and the two women. He fought to control his distress.

"Father, is something wrong?" inquired the prioress. "Are you well?"

"Yes, no..." He labored to reply. "Excuse me, I... I must be tired. We should be heading back to San Marco now."

The prioress was solicitous. "Perhaps you would care to accompany the young ladies, as they have a liveried coach—,"

"No!" he cried, too stridently, then in a more measured tone: "No, I always walk." He forced a smile. "It would be better for us to walk. But...thank you for your graciousness."

Moments later, as the sun slipped below the horizon and darkness swallowed the silent travelers on the dusty road, Fra Girolamo was sufficiently recovered to reflect on the young woman at the convent. He was distressed by the power of Nature, to lie deep within him all these years, only to leap out and enslave him at will. His mind was strong—he had disciplined his will on a daily sacrificial regimen—but his body was weak, its instincts difficult to control. He remembered those strong urges of the flesh when he was just a foolish boy and the dream of the freezing water dousing the carnal fires of his flesh. He thought he had conquered the beast, but now he knew the Devil was never vanquished and he prayed. *Lord, you have favored me as you did your servant Thomas. You cleansed me of these desires, as I have mortified my flesh.*

But Strozzi, Strozzi, Strozzi...what was her given name again...Laodamia? He saw her face again across the alley from the room of his father's house. No, he was only imagining it. The battle raged between heart and soul and he winced as a sharp pain pierced his lower belly. Closing his eyes tightly, he gripped the Bible and crucifix and prayed. The Devil within must be crushed by the force of God's grace. Crushed.

That night, in the privacy of his cell, he scourged his body unmercifully.

CHAPTER 9

A CONSPIRACY

TWO DICE RICOCHETED OFF THE masonry wall of the loggia as the crouching youths leaned in to see the lay. The player who cast, a dwarf, cursed loudly when the dice showed 'snake eyes' and the opposing player pocketed the coins with a chuckle.

"Spini, you're a lucky bastard," exclaimed the dwarf.

"Ah, my dear Mariotto, it's *you* Fortuna frowns upon. The game has nothing to do with luck. Eh, Francesco?"

Francesco Cei was playing his lute and replied without looking up. "Agreed. Winning is a matter of strategy. But the strategy is to woo Fortuna into one's bed and deny the same to her dark sister."

Spini laughed as he pocketed the dice and tossed the winning coin in the air. "Hey, Tommaso, wake up!"

Tommaso was leaning his back against the wall with his eyes closed. Spini prodded him again. "Hey, Soderini, what do you think?"

Tommaso stirred, opening one eye. "Me? I think it's time to go to the Frascato and christen the day with wine and women before it's lost."

"No song?" inquired Francesco.

"You can sing if you want."

Spini looked out over the Piazza della Signoria, which was bustling with workmen hauling materials to the back of the government palace. "Enjoy your freedom, *amico*. How goes it with your new wife? Seen her lately?"

"She's still at the convent at Fiesole with my cousin."

Francesco chimed in, in tune with his lute: "Ah, yes, your cousin, the young Chiara di Corbinelli. I hear we've lost another jewel to the nunnery."

"It's a fashion these days," sneered the dwarf.

Spini's cursed. "*Porca Madonna!* More and more nuns, fewer and fewer women and they wonder why the buggerers multiply. It's the work of this sniveling preacher. He's a curse on us all." He threw the gold florin down ringing and spinning on the masonry floor.

"Look!" he said, as the coin came to rest. "*Senatus Populusque Florentinus* on one side and *Jesus Christus Rex Noster* on the opposite—he's even taken control of the money. Now the bastard *fanciulli* are doing his dirty work. I cornered a couple of them yesterday and they had the balls to denounce dice and cards to my face. I sent them off with a swift kick in the ass."

Tommaso chuckled. "It's comic, no, Doffo? Young boys in white surplices, carrying small red crucifixes, haranguing the older citizens into line? Nothing to get worked up about."

"They're little shits. Call us *Compagnacci,* Bad Companions."

Tommaso laughed. "Angry Ones, Rabid Ones, Bad Companions, Snivelers, Prayer-mumblers, Big Weepers, Little Weepers…our city has a colorful cast of characters, don't you think? Francesco, you're a poet, can't you write some lively verses about our politics? Be our Dante. The friar's little angels are even singing hymns to Jesus using the melody of *"Visin, Visin!"* Tommaso tried to hum the tune through his laughter.

"A comedy, yes," Francesco said, "but because of this fool we may all be sent out to fight the Pisans soon."

Tommaso gave a wave of his hand toward the Palazzo. "If my good neighbor Messer Niccolò Machiavelli ever has his way, we'll all be fighting for our liberty and never again depend on these foreign condottieri and their mercenaries."

Spini said, "Why do you waste your time with that little prick. Wipes the ass of your uncle now, doesn't he?"

Tommaso was nonchalant. "Like you say. Between my father and my uncle, it's hard to get any peace in my house. Anyway, Machia owes me money, so I must keep track of him."

Francesco said, "Well, what about Pisa? The war's a disaster and the Signoria, enslaved to the Popular Party, is helpless to resolve the conflict. Taxes and mercenaries, and more taxes and mercenaries, always accompanied by the sanctimonious refrain of the *Domini cani*…."

Spini's voice rose with indignation. "That's the other reason this situation is intolerable. The Medici are finally off our backs, but now everybody swoons in the Duomo while the city languishes. And this prophet is too convenient with his reasoning: if a good prophecy fails it's because the people have sinned; if a dire prophecy fails it's because the people have become holier; and if any prophecy unfolds, well that just proves he's a true messenger from God!"

Tommaso said, "Well, the part baffling me is now that we've been saved from our moral depravity, the friar promises the city will be richer than ever. But with all this piety, I guess we're not ever to taste it! An interesting paradox, no?"

Spini was not interested in subtle arguing points. "I can tell you this, this damned monk's days are numbered." Then he lowered his voice. "There are agents now here in Florence from Rome and Milan who campaign for the Holy League. The pope and *Il Moro* intend to drive out the French. They need us Florentines and the friar stands in the way."

Tommaso perked up. "Yes? What have you heard?" Tommaso had known Doffo Spini for most of his life and knew he was a proud and arrogant fool, full of envy, but clever at self-preservation. His family was an ancient one and Doffo had resented the Medici for years with a burning passion.

"And…" Spini paused and shrugged, "Nothing. I don't really know. But I can tell you, the friar's days are numbered."

Francesco changed the subject. "Hey Tommaso, now that you're married you need one of those little advice manuals. You know, to tell you how to keep your wife happy and at home, how to have a boy child, or a girl child, or how to prevent having children at all…full of useful information. For example, do you know how to conceive a boy child?"

Tommaso played along. "Besides sending your wife to the baths at Petriolo? I've heard something about tying up the left *coglione*."

"That's part of it. *Senti*, first you put a tourniquet on the left ball and then you turn the woman onto her right side during copulation so the seed from the right ball flows to the right side of the woman. Because the heat of the seed determines whether the baby is a boy and the right side is hotter because it's closer to the liver. And of course, you must wear hats so the warm humors do not escape from the head, and you must look lovingly into one another's eyes. Let me see, have I forgotten anything? Oh, yes, after copulation the woman must curl up with her knees and turn on her right side and stay in that position for one hour."

Francesco now had their undivided attention. "Listen up, Tommaso. Perhaps you want to write this down, it's all very exact. If you make a mistake and your seed from the left ball spills over to the right side of the woman, you will sire a female child in need of a razor. And if the seed from the right gets implanted on the left you get a *femineo,* a boy who wears dresses. Apparently Florentines frequently fall into this error, which explains all you sodomites."

The young men laughed and scoffed. "*Cazzone!* Do you know all this from practice, Cei?"

"Well, only the part about not conceiving at all, the rest I've read from a source that, uh, may surprise you …" Francesco paused in anticipation.

"Come on, spill it!" Spini demanded.

"Actually, it's all in a little book written by an esteemed medico named Dottore Michele Savonarola of Ferrara, who just happens to have been the grandfather of our meddlesome little Prior of San Marco."

"*Davero?* Really?"

Francesco held up his right hand. "I swear it's true."

"And what about the French boils? Does he have any advice on how to treat that?" inquired the dwarf, who suffered from the affliction.

"Yes. Become a monk like his grandson. But a celibate one!"

Spini had heard enough. "*Che cazzo! Basta!* Enough of this priggish monk. Let's go to the Frascato and live a little."

Hours later, as Tommaso and his companions imbibed and flirted with the prostitutes at the tavern, Tommaso spied Spini and Cei seated at a table in a dark corner speaking closely with a third man. Tommaso peered through the dim smoky light, but could not recognize the dark-complexioned face of their companion.

CHAPTER 10

ARTISTS DISCUSS REFORMS

"GRANACCI! OVER HERE. JOIN US."

Michelangelo heard the familiar voice of Cronaca pierce the din of Del Corno's tavern. "Eh, Buonarroti, welcome back!"

Following Francesco, Michelangelo approached the table tentatively as Cronaca looked him over. "You've grown. We heard of the fine statuettes you carved for the Bolognese."

Looking at the faces, Michelangelo recognized some of the most renowned artists of the region. In addition to Cronaca, there were the painters Sandro Botticelli, Filippino Lippi, Lorenzo di Credi, Benedetto Ghirlandaio, Giovanni della Robbia, Baccio della Porta, Piero di Cosimo, and the sculptor Benedetto da Maiano. It was an imposing group and he was surprised they acted so familiar with him.

Cronaca was effusive. "Take a seat. Here, share some wine. Granacci here's been keeping us abreast of your travels. But you've missed a grand *casino* here at home."

"I feel almost a stranger," Michelangelo said sheepishly, nodding to the others at the table.

"We have a new Republic now, much like the one you just visited— but without the Doge," said Cronaca, raising his wine goblet in a toast. "Christ is our king now, and so far he likes us artisans."

Francesco took a draught from his goblet and explained. "Cronaca was awarded the commission to build the new *Sala dei Grand Consiglio* in the Palazzo to house the Great Council according to San Gallo's design. He's *il capomaestro* now, which is why we let him buy the wine."

Cronaca laughed off the teasing and winked. "Yes, keep it in mind— I'm here every evening. Soon we reconstruct the foundations. Then we'll finish in record time, by early next year."

"In eight months? Is it possible?"

"Well, it must be. The friar demanded it and all reparations on the Duomo have ceased, just so we can work solely on the Great Hall. The Council has no place to meet all together so the hall must be ready as soon as possible. Of course, the interior decorations will come later. For this I will have the help of the illustrious da Maiano brothers."

Cronaca slapped Benedetto on the back, then winked at Michelangelo. "But I'll need some competent painters too, I imagine.

What do you say? Can you paint?"

Michelangelo shook his head. "I'm a sculptor, Francesco is the master of buon fresco." Nursing his wine, he looked around the table and inquired delicately, "So, Fra Girolamo is now setting government policy?"

"More or less," said Francesco. "You should hear his sermons—the city's in a fever for our prophet. So far it's all to the good: the Signoria and the guilds have begun to request proposals for new commissions."

"Yes, a little peace is good for business," Cronaca added. "The friar wishes to guide the construction and intends the creation of other good works as well. The Great Hall will be a glorious monument to the Republic—a hallmark of justice. Let me tell you the words he used in pressing the Signoria; I memorized them:

> *Truth is born on earth and Justice stays up in Heaven and looks down to earth. And Truth looks up and says:*
> *Justice, what are you doing? What do you look at? Come down here, Justice.*
> *She replies, 'I want to come, but I look to see what I will receive, and I don't find a place prepared for me.'*
> *People, do you want this Justice? Make a beautiful room. Do this so that she may come and not be impeded.*"

Then he pantomimed the friar in the pulpit. "Thus I say to you, Florentines, it is time to build anew the house of the Lord and renovate your city."

"Cronaca's become a true believer," said Piero di Cosimo disparagingly.

"Yes, and I'll make a beautiful room. I've come to see the good of this new regime that spreads wealth and work for the good of all. The Signoria is of one mind and those who would poison the regime have been silenced. This is good for the heart, soul...*and* belly of the city. Simone has convinced me and...except for you, Piero. "

Piero retorted, "Yes, your good friar is beyond reproach. But what do you think of his Most Holy Army of Infant Inquisitors?"

Cronaca was dismissive. "What—a few children? Look at what good these boys have done for the city," he countered. "The *fanciulli* used to be ruffians who caused no end of trouble. Now they're cleaning the streets, singing laude and erecting little crosses so people don't piss in the corners and alleyways."

Piero was unmoved. "I'll piss wherever I want. It goes too far. The friar makes a grave mistake: he believes children are innocent and innocence is always good. But it's not true. If you give power to children, they'll abuse it because they lack the wisdom and empathy that comes with age. Remember the horrors these innocent scamps committed against the Pazzi?"

Piero continued, "Yes, dragging old Jacopo's corpse around the city, playing with it like a Carnival puppet. This is the dark side of the friar's innocence and we'll see it soon enough."

Piero paused, but a new thought launched him back into his tirade. "And I'll be damned if a little snot-nosed shit will pass judgment on my painting. Last week Simone brought some into Sandro's workshop and instructed them on acceptable and unacceptable images in painting!"

He mimicked a childish voice: "'Only the simple as rendered by light is beautiful. Color, proportion, and form are only distractions from the divine simplicity.' Shall we abandon our artistic style then? Shall we have the chicks teaching the hen? I, for one, will not stomach it."

Sandro held up his hand to intervene. Together with Benedetto da Maiano, he was the oldest and most accomplished of them and commanded deference accordingly. But Michelangelo noticed Sandro looked exhausted, as if suffering from sleeplessness. When he spoke his voice was strained: "Simone can be too zealous, but the friar has made legitimate criticisms of popular images in our painting, especially religious images. I see nothing inappropriate in encouraging artisans to be more mindful of the sacred. Christian faith and the cultivation of the soul must take priority and govern the manual arts. I, myself, am more aware of it now. Children won't have the chance to pass judgment if we first do so ourselves."

Piero di Cosimo was not placated. "The friar condemns the use of pagan mythologies and a naturalistic style, so you can imagine where that leaves me. Am I supposed to paint Madonnas for the rest of my life? And what are you painting, Sandro?"

Botticelli ignored the rebuke, though Michelangelo could see it cut deep. "Condemn is too strong a word," he said. "Fra Girolamo encourages a more Christian style, but only speaks out against the lewd and obscene."

But Piero pressed his point. "And is the natural obscene? Is Boccaccio obscene?"

"In certain cases, Maestro, perhaps," said Baccio. "Quite a few of Boccaccio's stories pander to the base instincts," he said. "Of course, that's what makes them entertaining, and one is not forced to read it. But in the Church and chapel, decorum is called for. Lusty images of concubines in the images of saints and madonnas are justly criticized." A popular young painter with a lusty reputation, Baccio had formerly studied with Piero, but Francesco had said he increasingly spent more time at San Marco these days.

"Fine, Baccio," retorted Piero. "And what do you think of the comportment of our fair women? Do you like the convent style?"

Baccio smiled, taking the bait. "This is another question entirely. The friar will meet his match if he tries to deprive Florentine *donne* of their God-given right to pamper and paint themselves. And it will cause all sorts of havoc for their husbands as well!"

The others laughed at Baccio's remark, but Michelangelo was troubled by Piero's question. If the natural could be deemed obscene, how could one determine natural beauty from vice? He thought he knew the difference but now was confused. When is a naked body beautiful and when is it sinful? Could it be a matter of sensibility or interpretation? Was artistic representation to be censored by religious authority? Was there a law governing such things and was the matter absolute, unchanging? What about Greek sculpture? He tried to remember some of the conversations he had with Fra Girolamo in the sculpture garden. The priest had not shied from pagan images.

As he struggled with these questions he regarded the older and wiser Botticelli. Sandro looked drawn and Michelangelo realized each of them would be tested in his own way according to his art by the uncertainties of this new world. Meanwhile, Cronaca had shifted the conversation to the friar and the pope.

"My uncles have written that the street gossips in Rome are already talking about the friar's strong words against the 'Pharisees' of the Church. Surely it's come to the Borgia's attention."

"The pope has bigger problems with the French breathing down his neck."

But Piero di Cosimo was more cautious: "The Catalans have a reputation for removing obstacles with more subtle tactics, like assassination by poison. Perhaps the friar should take care of what he eats. Anyway, Charles has already departed Naples on his return north. One wonders what fate awaits us when he returns."

Granacci looked to Michelangelo. "What was the word in Venice on the Holy League?"

Michelangelo was evasive. "I don't really follow such things. Except the Venetians are adamant about Florence joining the alliance and the mood was decidedly anti-Florentine in most areas in the north. But mostly I try to keep my head down and out of politics."

As he said this, Michelangelo looked into his empty goblet and wondered if this was truly possible in Italia these days. He desperately hoped he could find work in his native city now, but with the republican revolution there were few private patrons willing to spend lavishly on commissions. Granacci was pestering him to come to Ghirlandaio's workshop to paint fresco, but he was a sculptor, not a painter, and he only wanted to carve stone. And he preferred to work alone, not amidst the confusion of a crowded workshop. If he could not find work here he would have to leave again.

It was always war and politics, war and politics, and more war and politics—always these destructive arts, which laid waste to the creative. Was this the Glory of Man? Michelangelo felt crushed, like one of his figures enslaved in the stone, struggling to break free.

***

The artisans argued back and forth until afternoon passed into evening and the wine gradually subsumed the discussion. As the group thinned, Sandro withdrew and put his head down on his crossed arms. He had been stung by Piero di Cosimo's remark and was conflicted by the views of his peers. But neither wine nor social company relieved him of an unshakable morbidity. For twenty years, since the Pazzi conspiracy, his celebrated allegorical painting had been pagan. And the Pazzi commission...he remembered how sick he had felt with Lorenzo's request to paint the hanging effigies of the dead conspirators on the walls of the Bargello, lifelike reminders of a gruesome death that awaited all traitors. With their necks broken and their black tongues distended, the paintings had given him nightmares for months. Though the effigies were eventually scraped away, they lived forever in the back of his mind. And ever since he had been painting pagan allegories for his Medici patrons. Now his patrons were gone or out of favor and Simone kept admonishing him to paint new religious allegories to redeem himself.

He was sketching and blocking one out now, a Crucifixion with the Virgin Mother and Magdalena, inspired by the friar's sermons and encouraged by Simone. But there were no patrons willing to pay for such paintings and he despaired of receiving civic commissions because of his long association with the Medici. He hoped Simone was right. *God would show the way.* In the twilight of life there was only God, nothing more. Man on earth perished into dust and Sandro needed redemption.

Sensing Botticelli's despair, Cronaca offered to accompany him back to his workshop. When they arrived, they entered his workshop and Sandro lit several torches and candles. Then Sandro watched as Cronaca grabbed a torch and gazed at the large cartoon hanging on the wall. It was a crucifixion scene with Mary Magdalena. It was actually two scenes divided by the crucified Christ in the center. On the right a storm raged with swords, arrows, and fireballs raining down like hail. In the foreground, an angel held up a fox-like beast by its hind leg and whipped it. On the left was a panorama of Florence identified by red crosses on white shields arrayed overhead in a clear sky. In upper left God the Father was seated, holding an open book as a circle of light shone down on the Magdalena grasping at the foot of the cross. She was prostrate as a symbol of repentance and renewal, with a wolf escaping from the folds of her robes.

Sandro knew the mood of the cartoon was dark and austere. Cronaca was silent, fueling Botticelli's apprehension. Then, with a sympathetic tone, he finally spoke. "The Signoria will need to commission frescoes for the walls of the Great Hall. I know the friar is most interested in Christian allegories. He especially likes the Madonna and Child, the saints, and depictions of Heaven and Hell. Perhaps something like this might be considered."

But Botticelli sensed the lack of conviction in Cronaca's voice and tortured himself with his own doubt. "You don't think it too dark?"

The word he meant but could not say was foreboding. Cronaca shrugged, providing the answer he feared. Sandro tried to explain. "I'm not yet sure of this. I've had to rip each detail from the depths of my soul. I fear I've lost the ease with which I used to work. It's inspired, of course, by the Apocalypse from the eleventh chapter of the Book of John, adapted to the present situation."

"Like the friar's sermons."

"Yes, I wanted to depict the spirit of his themes in visual imagery. I'm not sure I succeed with this. I've begun and abandoned the composition so many times in the last weeks. It's discouraging." Or perhaps I've succeeded too well, thought Sandro.

Suddenly a door slammed and a crash came from the adjacent house. As the two looked toward each other, Simone came bursting into the workroom, wild-eyed. He was dressed in his Dominican frock.

Sandro started. "Simone, what—,"

"They tried to assassinate him!" Simone cried, struggling to catch his breath.

"Who? What—?"

"After the sermon... as we were returning to San Marco."

"Where? Is he—?"

"No, they failed. In the Via del Cocomero."

"*Who* failed?" demanded Cronaca.

"It was dark, they wore masks... hiding in the shadows."

"Calm down, Simone. Tell us what happened."

Simone sat down to catch his breath. "I was with several of the brothers, walking ahead when we heard a commotion behind us. The friar was with Fra Domenico when three men jumped out of the shadows. They were dressed in black and Domenico said he saw the glint of their knives. They cornered them in an alcove."

"What happened then?"

"Almost immediately there were shouts and four men came running from the Via Alfani with swords drawn. They ran toward the assassins who were advancing on the prior, surprising them. The assassins cursed and ran and the swordsmen gave chase. By then we were running back to help Fra Girolamo and Fra Domenico. They were unharmed."

"And what of the bandits? And those chasing them?"

"We saw no more of either. We quickly sent word to the Palazzo to summon the Guard of the Eight and they escorted us to the convent. The guards searched the streets in the vicinity but found nothing. I'm sure the assassins escaped—they were a fleeting shadow. They appeared and vanished in an instant—like spirits."

"And the men with swords?"

"I don't know—no one knows. *Grazie a Dio* they came when the assassins attacked."

"No one knows who all these men were?" asked Cronaca incredulously.

Simone's face twisted with malice. "I'm sure it was some of the *Arrabbiati bastardi*. They were young and quick, probably several of the *Compagnacci*. I would question Spini, I'm sure he would know."

Sandro tried to calm his brother. "Simone, do you think those wastrels would really be so bold? If caught they'd surely be executed."

Cronaca added, "And can we be sure they meant to kill the prior? Perhaps they only meant to threaten him."

"Well, if that was their intention, they failed. Almighty God intervened to protect His holy messenger. The *grandi* hate Fra Girolamo. They will not cease their evil designs until they're eradicated—either banished from the city or by the hand of God."

"Others also wish to eliminate the friar, as well as harm the city," said Cronaca. "It's not unreasonable to suspect agents of Il Moro or even the Borgia of such acts."

Simone's voice was filled with contempt. "Let them do what they will. Having failed, surely they'll try again. But now we are ready and we will protect Fra Girolamo, because it is God's will to drive this evil from His city."

CHAPTER 11

THE STRUGGLING REPUBLIC

NICCOLÒ PULLED HIS SHAWL TIGHT against the draft snaking through the closed shutters, feeling the rough wool against his neck. He was still wet. Rain had fallen unceasingly for almost eight months and the rotten weather had become a malevolent beast resisting all attempts to keep it at bay. The townsfolk had become fatalistic: Was it the disfavor of God or Fortuna causing the natural elements to conspire against them?

Feeling his hands cramp, Niccolò rubbed them over the candle, his sole source of warmth and light. The physical discomfort only added to his agitation. The struggle for power within the Palazzo had recently turned nasty and the Whites were under attack. Just last week several anonymous accusations had denounced more than thirty notable citizens for sodomy, Piero Capponi and Piero Soderini among them. This was an obvious political ploy—forcing officials to defend themselves against false accusations to tarnish their reputations and disqualify them from office. But still, it proved an embarrassing and effective distraction.

Piero seemed unconcerned, but Niccolò had learned one thing in his year of service in the Ministry: one could never rest easy in Florentine politics; the tide could change in an instant. He also had a renewed appreciation for the marvelous good fortune and sublime skill of *Il Magnifico*.

Like debris blown in by the inclement weather, the bad news kept piling up. The most serious difficulty was the pope's Holy League. On his way north Charles and his forces had skirted Florence and the city's fears of an alliance between Charles and Piero de' Medici came to naught. But the Holy League routed the French at Fornovo and Florence's principal ally had limped home, leaving the city isolated and surrounded in a sea of enemies. To date, the French alliance had yielded only empty promises, so the war to regain Pisa dragged on. And Florence's enemies in the League—the Genovese and the Venetians—were supporting the Pisans, hoping to stalemate the conflict. Meanwhile, the Florentine ambassadors in France had sent word the English king had also agreed to join the League against the French.

As these diplomatic calamities multiplied, the magistrates became desperate to regain Pisa while defending Florentine liberty against all intruders, including the pope, the Venetians and especially the Medici. To incite the people's ire, the Signoria had auctioned off the last of the

Medici artifacts and confiscated the two main symbols of tyrannicide, the Donatello sculptures of *Judith and Holofernes* and the bronze *David*, installing them at the entrance to the government Palazzo. Then they reinstated a bounty on the heads of Piero and his brother Giuliano. The real fear was the city's foreign enemies would use the Medici to attack and subjugate them to new tyrannies. To these one must now add the ambitious Duke of Milan who, after switching allegiance from the French to the pope, had declared himself sole ruler of Milan after the mysterious death of his nephew, the rightful heir.

If this was not enough, the disfavor of either God or Fortuna caused Nature to combine with these man-made misfortunes to make them suffer even more. The unrelenting rain had destroyed the harvest, driving up the price of corn more than ten times, threatening famine. And the Arno had several times overflowed its banks, wreaking havoc in the city's center.

Ominously, the pestilence hovered unseen but ever-present. It often struck without warning, coming out of the ground with the rats or flying through the air on the wings of crows. So far the outbreaks had been minor and brief, but when it descended it poisoned all, spreading death and fear. It was the closest thing to divine retribution Niccolò could imagine.

Some believed the friar was the city's only saving grace. The Soderini were still conflicted—Paolo always in favor and Piero frequently against—but Niccolò argued the friar provided an important advantage. With his sermons and the support of the Signoria, Savonarola rallied republican support and kept the people vigilant against their enemies, especially the anti-republicans within their midst. This helped the Whites maintain their strong position within the councils. The friar also provided a critical link to the French king, who was expected to return to Italia in the coming year.

The only problem was the preacher had started goading the pope. In turn, Alexander had repeatedly summoned Savonarola to Rome to explain his revelations from God. But Savonarola resisted, holding firm to a long list of excuses—a wise tactic, thought Machiavelli, as many of the Borgia's enemies had been left to languish and die in the dungeons of Castel Sant'Angelo. Also, the friar was in enough danger from assassination attempts here in Florence without risking the dangerous passage to Rome. So the pope and the friar continued their deadly game of chess.

Personally, Machiavelli believed the Borgia and the papal army was the greater threat to the independence of the Republic. But, if handled carefully, with the support of the French, this conflict with the friar could keep the pope's ambitions at bay. The risk was if they provoked his wrath the pope could wreak havoc upon the city's commercial interests. Already, Capponi had spoken out, warning the Signoria and the Council of Eighty of the brewing conflict between Florence and Rome and the papal threats the government had received. But the ambiguity of the conflict played into the republican government's long-standing weakness to sit on the fence and dither. They held fast to their favorite Tuscan maxim: "Wait. Watch. And hope."

To improve his mood and get his blood flowing, Niccolò wandered out to view the work on the Great Hall. It was almost finished and he had come to enjoy his everyday banter with the affable master builder.

As he entered the construction area on the far side of the Palazzo, he was impressed by the rapid progress. The Great Hall was almost ready for use and it hadn't been seven months since the foundation had been laid. Such civic projects usually took years, wandering at a snail's pace through the maze of government councils and advisories.

Spotting him, Cronaca came striding over. *"Buona sera,* Messer Niccolò! What intrigue have you for me today?"

"I've only come to escape my little cave where the sun never shines. You're almost finished," Niccolò said, pointing to the ceilings and walls.

"Yes, we work without pause until the light fails, and then we drink in the tavern for our sustenance until the sun comes up again. It should be ready for the Great Council by the end of the month. I imagine the Works Committee, the Signori and the friar will be satisfied?"

"The friar will declare it another miracle."

Detecting the sarcasm, Cronaca was reproving. "As it will be—and not the first miracle our city has seen this year."

"Davero? What miraculous events have you witnessed, then?"

"Look around you, on the streets: no ruffians, no gambling, all swept clean... did you witness the Procession of the Boys of the Friar on the day before Lent? An amazing sight—a band of little angels filling the air with the pure sounds of sacred *laude."*

Niccolò found this less of a miracle than a curse. "Personally, I reminisce for the days when we called it Carnevale. I don't sing, but I do enjoy my little distractions." He gave a knowing wink.

"Yes, well, flies are only drowned in sweet wine, eh? But you and I both know unrestrained pleasure can only lead to perdition."

"I'm still learning—,"

"You're a student of history, look at the Greeks and Romans."

"The rise and fall of great states is a complex affair. I'm not sure a band of little angels could have saved Rome."

"Like me, you can make a joke of anything, but I don't think these trials we face now can be dismissed as mere coincidence."

"Naturally. We bring many of our miseries down upon our own heads. Man is most often a fool and *Fortuna* plays with him as she wishes."

Cronaca was adamant. "There's more to it. I have a friend who keeps a chronicle of events and news items from abroad. He told me several stories that portend the prophecies of the *Frate*."

"Pray tell," Niccolò teased, "I love a good story."

"Well, they say a woman appeared to a shepherd in the region of Naples and said to him, 'Give me one of those sheep.' When he did she said, 'Cut it in half.' And then there came out of it all sorts of serpents, vipers, and scorpions. Then she said, 'Close it up and join it well and it will come back to life.' And after this was done, she said, 'Go, tell the pope there will be a great plague and everyone must do penance and fast, and not eat meat for three days.'"

Niccolò nodded his head gravely, mocking Cronaca's seriousness. "Hmmm, I've never seen a sheep sewn back together."

"Don't believe it then. Stranger things have happened. There was another report from Milan that the murdered Duke, Giangaleazzo appeared in the street and gave a letter to a man, saying, 'Carry this to Signor Lodovico.' And when it was carried to the court, the Chancellor could not open it. But as soon as the Moor took it in his hand, it opened; and when he read it, he bent his head, lost in wonder. And when the messenger asked for a reply, the Moor said, 'It has been given.' And the messenger immediately disappeared."

"*It has been given*," Niccolò repeated with melodrama. "Well, what does it mean?"

Cronaca gave him a look of forbearance. "These stories are talked about everywhere. They've inspired much fear of a coming catastrophe. A woman in Viterbo became possessed by a spirit and in a trance declared the true prophet was in Florence. Is this all just coincidence?"

"Well, we're most fortunate to have the true prophet with us then, eh? The friar serves a useful purpose and only a fool would ignore a prophecy, no?"

"Fear of God can be a good thing," Cronaca sniffed.

Most definitely, thought Niccolò, flashing his enigmatic smile. He never ceased to learn new things about human nature. There was a strange mood in the air since the French invaded Italia, or perhaps even earlier, when Lorenzo had died. That mood was poisoned, and just like some virulent form of the pestilence, it afflicted the hearts and minds of all.

And what of the pestilence? What was it and where did it come from? Pockets of the disease had broken out, but it was early in the season and so far they had been spared a full-scale attack. Was it a curse of nature or retribution from an angry God? Who knew? It almost seemed to be a war between the pagan gods and the Christian one, with hapless man caught in the middle. Perhaps the friar would save them. But if it struck, there was no cure, it would ravage the city and run its course and those who survived would only wonder why they lived when others more worthy died.

CHAPTER 12

CESARE AND THE CARDINAL'S HAT

THE RIDER FORCEFULLY REINED IN his black Arabian in the shadow of the towering Palazzo. He was young, no more than twenty, of strong bearing, with long, black curled hair, a close-trimmed beard, and a hard look in his eye. His vigorous appearance was somewhat out of character with the mantle of cardinal's purple draped over him. With his escort of Swiss guards, he had entered the city from the south, through the Porta Romana, and marched slowly but deliberately under the hot midday sun toward the center. He was followed along the way by the watchful gaze of the Florentines, who knowingly spied the standard of the Scarlet Bull. The government palace would be his first stop, to be welcomed there by the city magistrates. But this was not a state visit, so his entourage was small and unobtrusive. Later, after he and his train had settled into lodgings, he would tend to the business that brought him.

This was the cardinal's first visit to the fabled city, which was described by all who knew her as the flower of Italia. When crossing the mountain passes and coming upon the valley of the Arno earlier this morning, he'd been struck by the beauty of the city's outline. The vision inspired his imagination and what he saw was a bejeweled goddess reclining among the surrounding hills, resplendent in a gown of flowers with a life-giving spring flowing by, giving respite and refreshment under a hot Tuscan sun. The rounded dome of the cathedral was the goddess's breast, into which, he imagined vividly, the entire populace could enter and suckle on the Virgin Mother's grace. Surrounding the Cathedral, the city's bell towers rose up like sprouting saplings, standing guard behind a stone wall that girded the goddess like a belt with so many gated buckles. But foremost, this goddess's virtue was guarded by the strong masculine presence of the powerful fortress with its piercing tower, which from a distance resembled Poseidon standing guard over Aphrodite with his trident. He now understood what his father had told him: this city was a precious gem. And now he coveted it.

What also struck the young cardinal on his passage through the streets was the subdued atmosphere. Everything was so quiet, staid and colorless—a striking contrast to the riot of Rome. There was little street entertainment, and the few women he spied were dressed in drab colors and modestly covered. The famous Florentine beauties were nowhere to be seen. The cardinal chafed under his ecclesiastical robes, an occupational nuisance, as he wondered if this was all the preacher's doing—a city suffering a terminal case of holiness. Fortunately, the jaded Romans were immune to this sort of thing.

He dismounted in front of the Palazzo and stopped to gaze into the fiery eyes of Judith holding the severed head of the tyrant Holofernes aloft. He would enjoy subduing such a bitch, he mused; then he read the inscription on the statue's base:

> *Kingdoms fall through luxury, cities rise through virtues; behold the neck of pride severed by humility. Piero, son of Cosimo de' Medici, has dedicated this statue of a woman to the union of strength and liberty so that the citizens are led back by an invincible, unswerving courage to the defense of the Republic.*

The young cardinal grunted at the irony: this Piero, son of Cosimo, was long dead and his namesake grandson had already felt the sting of severed pride. This *lauda* was just a noble sentiment to the Republic—Rome was full of such things. But what sort of men ruled inside?

***

Fra Girolamo walked aimlessly through the gardens of San Marco; distracting himself as he picked his way around the ancient statues littering the grassy knolls. It was quiet and he missed the activity of the former school of sculpture run by Master Bertoldo. Brother Lionardo had told him his natural brother, the young sculptor Michelangelo, had also departed for Rome in search of new commissions. Apparently Rome was now the center of artistic expression and ambition intended to glorify the flamboyant egos of popes and cardinals. Here, at San Marco, the creative energies of the convent were redirected to painting and illuminated manuscripts. Many of the young friars exhibited a marvelous talent for such techniques and the workshop was turning out a considerable body of new work. For the glory of God and not man the brothers found a just purpose in art.

Fra Girolamo's disposition varied these days with the changing weather, darkening like the clouds full of rain before brightening again as the sunlight glimpsed through to judge the contrition of the city only to start the random cycle again. Nevertheless, he had much to gladden his mood.

The Republic was thriving, with the Great Council firmly in control of the *Frateschi,* led by the tenacious Valori. Recently the Council had established the *Monte di Pieta,* a loan bank for lending to the poor and needy so the moneylenders could not victimize them. Soon after the

Council passed a law ordering the Jewish moneylenders to leave the city within the year.

The program of moral and spiritual reform proceeded apace with his Army of Angels growing to several thousand strong. The boys policed the streets, promoting a spirit of Christian peace and harmony while encouraging their elders to give up their vanities and vices. And the Word reached the faithful in ever-larger numbers as they crowded into the Duomo to hear him preach.

Over long nights in his cell he had labored for months with his writings, finally completing his *Compendium of Revelations*. It explained the progression of his inspiration through visions and messages from God and how these were to be interpreted in the earthly events. Printed and widely distributed, the truth was now readily accessible to all who could read and wished to enlighten themselves.

But dark clouds still passed over, threatening the city in its inconstancy. After the assassination attempt last year, rumors had circulated continuously about agents of the tyrant of Milan or those of the rapacious Borgia, the *Arrabbiati,* and the Medici partisans. Like Satan's minions, they all were seeking the opportune moment to strike him down. But he felt the invincible shield of God's armor protecting him from these nuisances, as well as the armed escorts provided by *Frateschi* partisans and the Eight. Today there was a more tangible threat looming, he thought. He turned to go back to the Chapter House.

At his desk he leafed through the papal briefs and his own posted replies, anticipating the coming confrontation with his expected visitor. For a year now he had received these briefs filled with directives and subtle supplications from the Supreme Pontiff. His eyes scanned the first brief he received from His Holiness:

> To our well-beloved son, greeting and the apostolic benediction. We have heard that of all the workers in the Lord's vineyard thou art the most zealous; at which we deeply rejoice, and give thanks to Almighty God. We have likewise heard thou dost assert thy predictions proceed not from thee but from God. Therefore we desire, as behooves our pastoral office, to have speech with thee considering these things; so that, being by these means better informed of God's will, we may be better able to fulfill it. Wheretofore, by thy vow of holy obedience, we enjoin thee to wait on us without delay, and shall welcome thee with loving kindness.

He reread the last three words and recoiled, dismayed by the exquisiteness of the spider's deadly web. This pope and his court were accustomed to using honey to entrap unwitting flies, but God had fortified him against flattered words from a false prince of the Church. This pope was not interested in hearing about God's will, but wished only to silence the messenger. He could only wonder why the Almighty raised such men as this to the highest station in His earthly temple. It must truly be the work of Satan, a Satan fortified by the lack of grace and faith among Christian peoples.

In his first reply, Fra Girolamo had submitted to the pope's censure but declined his summons to Rome, pleading illness and the need to tend his flock in Florence. If the pope and his advisors wished to learn more of his revelations, they had only to read the little book he had enclosed, his Compendium. That had caused the wolf to snap in anger, charging him with impertinence and insubordination, and forbidding him to preach. Then His Holiness appointed the Vicar General of the Lombard Order to investigate the matter and for good measure ordered the reunification of the Tuscan congregation with Lombardy.

Beleaguered, he replied again, deliberately defending himself point-by-point. He accused his enemies in Rome of misleading His Holiness with lies and falsehoods. Then he rallied his brethren to reject the reunification with the Lombards, rightly declaring this could only be sanctioned by the entire congregation. He continued to preach, as was his sworn duty by the request of the faithful, and begged the pope's forbearance.

This was followed by a flurry of briefs from Rome—alternately angry and conciliatory—claiming perhaps Fra Girolamo erred not through evil motives, but from simple-minded zealotry. At this he only smiled. With such a lack of principle the pope had bared his true motives and Fra Girolamo became more certain of his convictions. The briefs halted for a number of months and then he received word he was being investigated by a consistory of Dominican theologians on charges of heresy and false prophecy. Now he expected to hear Alexander's reaction to the court's decision from his emissary, who was scheduled to arrive momentarily. He gathered up the papers and put them in his desk.

Just then the door opened and Fra Domenico poked his head in. "Prior, His Eminence, the Cardinal Bishop has arrived."

Fra Girolamo rose as the young cardinal strode into the room. He was tall and comported himself with confidence in his purple robes. He smiled down on his host as Fra Girolamo greeted him: "Your Eminence."

Though the title left a bitter taste on the prior's tongue, he smiled graciously at this bastard son of a pope, Cesare Borgia. He can't be more than twenty years old and it has already been two years since he was appointed to the cardinalate. What a business this Church has become! The names of these new 'boy cardinals' were laden with the wealth necessary to purchase their offices: Medici, Orsini, Farnese, Sforza, d'Este, Borgia. It was a litany of shame. This young pup, a strutting Prince of the Church, acted more like a princely heir than a humble priest. But Fra Girolamo knew, and they knew, and he knew they knew, that wealth and power had no purchase on the Day of Judgment. Let *them* be cautious.

"Prior, I bring you heartfelt greetings and benedictions from His Holiness. He has sent me personally to convey his good wishes."

Fra Girolamo inclined his head graciously but was silent, wishing to cut short these formalities and hypocrisies, their only purpose to sugarcoat the coarseness of these business exchanges. He motioned for the cardinal to sit.

The cardinal's self-assurance only made Fra Girolamo more determined to unseat his easy arrogance. The cardinal's eyes tried to read him but he sat stone-faced as he listened. Disconcerted, the cardinal smiled and said:

""Naturally, Prior, I've come to speak of other matters. As you may know, a consistory of esteemed theologians of your Order was convened to review your writings on matters of the Christian faith. The purpose, of course, is to discern the nature of divine guidance that is the source of your revered reputation as a messenger and servant to the faithful." The cardinal paused, but Fra Girolamo's eyes emitted no flicker of curiosity or emotion, so he continued.

"The Church has always gratefully encouraged the mendicants in their mission of ministering to the community of Christian believers. Both Dominic and Francis were received into the bosom of the Roman Church and raised to its highest station soon after their deaths."

Fra Girolamo knew this was a self-serving revision of history. The Church had battled ruthlessly to eradicate the reformist movements for most of the past three hundred years, usually with the Inquisitor's tools of torture and holy fire. It was little more than sanctified murder. Only the moral force of Dominic and Francis had swayed the Holy See to co-opt their reform movements into the official body of the Church.

The cardinal continued, "We realize now, more than ever, the Church requires the help of its devoted servants in the mendicant orders to achieve its mission. It's in this spirit the Holy Father has asked me to convey to you his sincere appreciation."

It was ironic to hear the bastard son make a double reference to the "Father" of the Church, his natural father. Fra Girolamo wondered perversely if, by choice of words, the cardinal was implying the pope was offering to raise him to sainthood, like Dominic and Francis, after first causing his 'natural' death.

"So, the consistory is satisfied? And His Holiness?"

"More than satisfied," replied the cardinal with a sly cat smile. "Their recommendation is to offer you the Cardinal's hat. It is my pleasure to deliver the Holy Father's exact words: It would please His Holiness greatly to receive you into the College of Cardinals as a spiritual and moral force for the goodness of the Holy Church."

Fra Girolamo felt a surge of strength as he fought to hide the satisfied look on his face. He stood up to look away as the taste of victory caused a smile to form on his lips. The Lord had revealed plainly to him Satan's desperate ploy. Now he would vanquish the Devil and in so doing raise himself higher in the people's esteem. He turned to face the cardinal.

"Your Eminence, I am moved by such an honor bestowed upon me by the Holy Mother Church. But I am merely a simple priest of humble origins. The fine silk and ermine robes of a princely prelate would ill suit me."

"All the more reason to set an example in the College."

"I must consider my mission here and my congregation."

"Your mission can best be served in Rome."

"Perhaps. I will pray on the matter."

Fra Girolamo was pleased to see the look of incredulity cloud the cardinal's face—that a poor monk would reject a cardinal's hat. The cardinal's confusion gave way to the aggression of his true nature.

"I fail to understand your reticence, Prior. It strikes me such an honor would solidify your position within the Church. I trust it would not be indelicate to also mention your position here in the city is tenuous; the city itself is in dire straits. I spoke with the magistrates and they are most concerned by events."

"All the more reason to remain, Your Eminence. Florence is now God's Holy City with Jesus Christ as King. It would be wrong to leave it in the hands of those with lukewarm faith. I believe the Signoria is of the same mind."

"And so you risk His Holiness's displeasure? I spoke directly with your Chief Magistrate Gonfaloniere Capponi and he is most concerned. I believe four separate papal briefs have been issued that have been conveniently ignored by you and your government. Something to do with your frail health?"

"As I explained in my letter, His Holiness has received false council on these matters. Surely you have copies of all my printed sermons and I believe your consistory has confirmed the content to His Holiness's satisfaction, else why would Your Eminence be here?"

He let this point prick the arrogance of his young adversary before continuing: "As Your Eminence well knows, the enemies of true Christian faith are many. And yes, my health and the dangers of travel make it unwise for me to visit Rome at this time."

The cardinal suppressed his frustration as he parried back: "As you say. But I find it strange then God would visit such tribulations on His anointed city. If I may say, it's common knowledge the war with Pisa goes poorly and famine decimates the countryside while the pestilence strikes down the weak. And the French have brought you little more than the pox. Perhaps God is sending you a different message than the one you hear?"

Fra Girolamo was angered by the young Cardinal's insolence. God did not 'speak' to him, as he had made perfectly clear in the Compendium. The brazen little bastard was mocking him. His dark eyes flashed at the Cardinal and his voice strengthened. "Cardinal Bishop Borgia, as God's humble servant, *you* would know *His* work on earth is never done." The subtle insult was deliberate. "Nor is Satan's. The Lord expects His shepherds to be constant and not fly at the first howl of the wolf. We have received word from the French that Charles will return within the year to finish what he started."

He saw the cardinal struggle to control his anger. His words had hit their mark: the French threat was an intolerable weapon used against the papal States and the son knew the "wolf" was an indirect reference to his father, the avaricious pope. The cardinal's smile faded. "Much can happen in a year," he muttered.

Savonarola quickly changed the tone of his voice and became conciliatory. "Excuse our inhospitality, Your Eminence. You must be tired and hungry. I will request some wine to drink. Will you be staying long in our city?"

"Only long enough to receive an answer for His Holiness."

"As I said, Your Eminence. I will pray on the matter. If you are able, attend the mass in the Cathedral tomorrow afternoon and you shall have your answer."

***

The next day Cesare shed his church robes and attended the friar's sermon dressed in a long black cloak with the hood pulled up to hide his face. Only one attendant accompanied him as they stood in the shadows near a side door. The Cathedral was packed with portable wooden stands arranged along the walls to provide additional seating for a large choir of white-robed boys carrying little red crosses. There must be more than a thousand. As they raised their voices as one the Duomo reverberated with their deafening hymns. He watched the women as they filed in, young, old and in-between, all dressed in somber clothes with veils hiding their hair, nary a smile revealed. He laughed to himself and thought: How long did this priest hope to force men and women to go against their nature? It wouldn't be long before this all exploded in his face; it was just a question of whether the preacher was fool enough to stick around and sit on the powder keg. He turned his head to listen with anticipation as the friar launched into his sermon.

This priest was a strange one, no knave or fool, Cesare conceded begrudgingly. But was he really such a stubborn mule, so dim-witted and dull as to reject a Cardinal's hat? Surely not. As his father said: "Men can be moved with either the carrot or the stick, one must just discover the smallest carrot or the biggest stick necessary." This Friar would reveal his price eventually, but it was equally unbelievable to Cesare the priest would play cat and mouse with the pope's offer.

The preacher's sermonizing was the usual haranguing of religious righteousness, causing Cesare to chafe under his father's imposition of a Church career on him. Pope Alexander VI wanted his son to become pope in turn, convinced a papal dynasty was the only way to insure the survival of the Spanish Borgia family's fortunes in Italia. But Cesare had not the temperament or patience for Church affairs. He was a man of action and the thought of negotiating and waiting on the whims of foolish monks was maddening. His solution was simple: Let the monk become a cardinal, get him to Rome in the College, and then do with him what you will. Throw him in the dungeons of Castel Sant'Angelo or have him suffer an untimely attack of the pestilence, either way, be done with it.

Cesare started as he heard Savonarola tell a story about how St. Dominic had refused a bishop's miter three times. Then he told the story of Antonino, the beloved little archbishop and favorite son of Florence, who, in his turn, had denied the offer of a cardinal's hat. *Merda*, thought Cesare, this little worm was going to reject it. His father would be infuriated and blame him. Cesare's ears and face reddened underneath the hooded cloak as he forced himself to listen to what Savonarola was saying. The people in the congregation were beginning to respond to his exhortations, the women crying and moaning, the men shouting.

The friar was now telling them the Roman Church had offered him a cardinal's red hat. But, he said, it was nothing more than a naked attempt to silence him and the truth he spoke. Furthermore, he proclaimed, it was a plot to bring down the glorious Florentine Republic!

Cesare was beside himself with disbelief. The bastard was using the pope's carrot as a stick to whip him.

Suddenly a woman screamed: "Look, a halo of light over the *Frate*! And two angels floating above!"

The preacher's voice echoed through the Duomo, burning into Cesare's ears: "I want no hats, ...no miters great or small. I only want the one You, O Lord, gave to your saints, ...DEATH. A crimson hat, a hat of BLOOD, ... that is what I want!"

Cesare headed for the door, furious and disgusted with how he had been used. His father would be incensed. He wanted to get away quickly, to leave this city of crazed fanatics and hysterics. But he must make one more stop before leaving. This preacher would pay, he swore, they would all pay. A martyr's death? Is that what he wants, a hat of blood? That's not a problem. That, too, can be arranged.

CHAPTER 13

Procession of the Madonna dell'Impruneta

NICCOLÒ CARRIED HIS OFFICIAL PORTFOLIO under his arm as he exited the Palazzo and crossed the short distance to the Loggia dei Priori. He turned the corner and found Tommaso waiting in the shadows. Glancing up at the clouded sky and out over the sparse Piazza, he gave Tommaso a somber nod. The loss still weighed on him: only two weeks ago his mother had passed away. Always slightly embarrassed by her over-mothering, now he felt her absence deeply and worried for his father as well, who was staying in the country with his sister's family. He hoped all his mother's prayers were a saving grace for her now.

"*Ciao'mico,*" Tommaso said, "*Andiamo,* let's go."

On their way to the Oltrarno several beggars accosted them near the fishmongers along the river. As most respectable Florentines, they steered clear of the unwashed hands, but one could hardly avoid them these days. The rains had destroyed the last harvest, driving the price of corn up to more than fifty soldi from its normal price of thirty. The price of bread and other foodstuffs had risen similarly and famine threatened to devastate the population.

As they crossed the Ponte Vecchio, Tommaso said warily, "Spini plans to cause trouble tomorrow."

Niccolò knew this complicated their plans, which is why they were conferring today. Arriving at the Soderini compound minutes later, they went straight to the library where Piero and Paolo greeted them with sympathetic looks. Niccolò hadn't seen them since his mother's funeral, but they had known his mother for many years too and he knew they shared his sorrow. But he wanted to take his mind off it.

"Nico, have you eaten?" asked Piero.

Though it was the midday *pausa* and he was hungry, Niccolò waved off Piero's solicitation as he opened his portfolio and removed his notes. He knew the seriousness of the situation: Capponi, leader of the Whites and Piero Soderini's strongest ally, had recently been killed in a skirmish near Pisa. Though a setback for their cause, it was also opportunity for Piero to rise to the leadership. But such a distinction was also perilous.

"With Capponi gone," said Piero, "the *Arrabbiati* will renounce the French alliance and demand we join the League." As he expected, Niccolò heard Piero's natural cautiousness, or was it lack of courage?

"The more immediate problem," Niccolò said, "is Livorno." Then he reviewed for them the recent reports from the western campaign. In the northern regions the Holy League was pressing its advantage, trying to consolidate its gains against a possible return of the French. Once again, the duplicitous Duke of Milan had precipitated a crisis by inviting the German emperor Maximilian to enter the fray. Now the forces of the League, combined with the small forces of the Emperor, were pressing Florentine forces in the Pisan campaign and the city's isolation was becoming precarious. The death of Capponi had not helped the situation.

In response, the Signoria, under the friar's influence, still maintained hope in the French alliance. Reinforcements and supplies had been sent via the sea route from Marseilles to the port of Livorno, but Livorno was under siege—its port blockaded by the Venetian fleet with land access cut off by the League. Meanwhile the supply ships were being held offshore outside the harbor, lashed by the inclement weather. Only the petty rivalries among League allies delayed disaster, with none wishing to allow the other the spoils of victory.

Paolo supported the pro-French alliance. "In his last sermon Fra Girolamo rallied the people against any and all who would threaten the present government. And tonight the Madonna dell'Impruneta is being transported to arrive at the Porto San Piero Gattolino at dawn. Tomorrow the whole city will be united in the procession."

Niccolò considered the substance of this response. Prodded by Paolo and the *Frateschi*, the Signoria had turned again to its holy prophet, pleading with Savonarola to defy the pope's decree and mount the pulpit. The friar had finally done so yesterday with a rousing call to Christian faith and hope, inciting the people to root out the evildoers in the city, and trust in the grace of God. Then he had called for a Procession of the Madonna dell'Impruneta, appealing to the city's miraculous icon to protect it from famine and drought.

But what kind of strategy was this, Niccolò reasoned, his level of frustration rising. All this talk of sacred images and saints was really beside the point. What good came of all this praying? What good had it done for his mother? He was now beginning to see limits of the friar's usefulness—Florentines would not be united, they would stay divided. And to be associated with a failed policy would be a personal disaster for each of them as well.

"I don't see how this solves the Pisan problem," he said. "Perhaps it brings a certain sense of hope and calms the rabble, but how does it help us resist the League? We need to break the blockade, receive reinforcements and supplies, and pursue the campaign to recapture Pisa. The friar keeps promising God will return Pisa to us, but I don't see how we can win it back with prayers. And without control of Pisa both our commerce and defense are vulnerable."

Tommaso spoke up. "The *Compagnacci* plan to disrupt the procession, blaming Savonarola for the city's misfortunes."

Niccolò was emphatic. "See? If the friar can't produce a miracle, it only strengthens the Angry Ones and complicates the Pisan campaign."

Paolo disagreed. "The *popolo* don't expect miracles every time they glimpse L'Impruneta—it's just a petition, it reinforces faith and instills hope. It can only help our present situation. Despair and fear undermine authority and *that's* what the *Arrabbiati* prey upon."

Piero nodded in agreement. "It's an acceptable risk. We must secure our authority foremost. We must prevail and it's important we rally the people against internal threats. The friar is best for this and the *Arrabbiati* really have nothing positive to counter with. After, we can regroup to address the problems of the Pisan campaign."

"And Fra Girolamo is confident the French king's support will arrive in time," added Paolo.

"So, what do we do about the *Compagnacci* tomorrow?"

"The Signoria is aware. The militia will be dispersed throughout the Piazza."

Then, looking closely at Niccolò and Tommaso, Paolo challenged them with a hard look. "Besides, have either of you considered the possibility it might work?"

What, praying for miracles? Niccolò shrugged, swallowing his retort. The new politics required boldness, the spirit of *animo* to accomplish great things. But old men were conservative—their *animo* dissipated and their politics mostly the art of trickery and tomfoolery—so perhaps hoping for miracles was just another part of the game. He knew Piero only wanted the friar's help to resist new attacks by the *Arrabbiati,* but he still suspected they were courting disaster and the consequence of failure would be chaos. Then again, the gamble of Fortuna might be the most convincing explanation of history and perhaps it only required blind faith. *We shall see.*

***

The city woke the next morning under the same bleak fog. The shops remained closed for the occasion, but crowds gathered along the route, nervous with anticipation. To insure the Madonna would not be offended by a lack of devotion or conviction, every able body was required to march in the procession. As was proper, men and boys marched separate from women.

The image was a sacred icon of the Virgin painted on a panel by an unknown artisan. She was blessed with miraculous powers and housed in the baptismal church of Impruneta, two hours walk outside the city. There she remained throughout the year, veiled to the eyes of pilgrims, until called forth to by the city to plead its case to God in times of crisis. The appeal was usually to influence the weather against drought or flood, but on certain occasions the Madonna was solicited to grant relief from the suffering of war or the recurring pestilence.

The procession started the night before. The veiled Lady was transported in a large tabernacle on a litter strewn with offerings—mostly shawls and overdresses of the finest silks and brocade offered by merchants of the Silk guild. As the procession passed in the night all those who lived outside the city gates joined in. Before trumpeters announced her arrival at the Porta San Piero Gattolino at dawn, the city clergy hurried out to meet her, carrying sacred relics and talismans for the procession.

She would spend the day in the city, visiting several locations from which to survey her domain, before returning to Impruneta by nightfall. Her first stop was always the Piazza San Felice, across the Arno, near the Ponte Vecchio, where the veil was lifted from her face so she might view her penitent subjects as they paraded before her.

Normally, the clergy would lead this procession in their finest vestments, with the archbishop in the lead followed by the canons, parish priests, and mendicant orders. But today the prior of San Marco took the lead and the churchmen's dress was appropriately subdued to conform to the friar's disposition.

Following close behind were the Boys of the Friar, singing sacred *laude* and waving their little red crosses as they led the mendicant Orders. The Signoria and the various officials and council members of the Republic were next, then the main body of the citizens, men and boys first with women at the rear. The citizens dressed simply and soberly, mixing together without regard to status or wealth to emphasize their equality before the Madonna. The women in the rear prayed, moaning and wailing the *misericordia* to heighten the commune's fragile emotional state.

By mid-morning the procession was snaking over the Ponte Vecchio and straddling the river as the marchers filed past the unveiled Madonna. The line on the bridge was moving at a snail's pace and the young painter Francesco Granacci was impatient to glimpse the image. He peppered his older companions with questions.

"Do you know who painted the image? Is it done well? In what style?"

"Nobody knows, Francesco," said Cronaca. "I've only seen it a few times myself. The style's not common, but in this case, artistic technique is of little consequence. More important are its miraculous powers."

"I'm not sure I believe any of it, but I'm curious to see what all the fuss is about," whispered Francesco.

"Watch your blasphemies," Cronaca chastised. "This is our last hope you know. I went to the *paneria* yesterday and there was not even a crust of bread."

Then Messer Luca reprimanded the younger painter sternly. "Young minds find many things difficult to understand, but the legend of Our Lady of Impruneta is beyond coincidence or suggestion. The stories are many and the pattern clear. Just read the chronicles of Matteo Villani, Giordano da Rivalto, Naddo da Montecatini, Pietrobuoni—so many times crops were saved from drought after Impruneta was importuned."

"But we have no drought," Francesco pointed out.

The apothecary dismissed his youthful impertinence. "Or she stops the rain. The Madonna is not deaf to the sufferers of the pestilence or to the threats of murderous barbarians. Fra Girolamo called for this procession to protect us from our enemies. Surely, we'll be delivered from these calamities. God moves in mysterious ways."

"Too late for some, *Signore*."

Francesco turned to look at a haggard ghost of a man. "What do you mean?"

"I'm from the Mugello. I had a neighbor, a widower, and the rains washed out his crop. His family was so famished he was forced to come into the city to beg. But he left his three small children and when he returned they were starved and could not be revived. So he took a rope and hung himself. Mysterious ways God moves." The peasant's tone hardened.

A youth next to him said, "Uncle, don't despair. God so far has spared us, so He must have a purpose for us. May He show us His mercy." With youthful bravado he shouted: "May the Virgin Mother and Her son save us! *Ave Maria! Vivo Cristo!*" His cry was echoed halfheartedly by those around them.

The artisans were moved and Cronaca affirmed the boy's plea. "In His wisdom God cannot possibly deny us redemption. Fra Girolamo has spread the grace of God throughout the city and the people have changed. We must have faith in His mercy and our deliverance."

As they slowly shuffled along, Francesco muttered, "But many still behave in the old ways. The *grandi* and their spoiled offspring haven't changed—surely God has noticed. As Dante wrote, the way to Hell is lined with Florentines. If we lose this battle against the Holy League, the city is doomed. My only salvation will be to join Michelangelo in Rome."

Cronaca silenced him with a cuff on the head, saying, "Then stop whining and say a prayer to the Virgin."

***

Later in the day, when the sun dipped low in the sky, Our Lady of Impruneta sat enthroned on the ringhiera outside the Palazzo della Signoria. The Signoria was seated along the ringhiera as the clergy performed benedictions on the unveiled Madonna, inciting the lamentations of the citizens who were packed close like sheep in a pen. As the smell of incense hung heavy in the humid air, Niccolò watched from his place with other officials and members of the Council of Eighty.

The histrionics of his fellow Florentines never ceased to amaze him. The friar had spoken earlier, whipping them into this trance before retiring to his convent and leaving them drunk on the sour wine of self-pity mixed with a heady brew of miracle visions. What amazed him was his fellow citizens never connected their foolish, shortsighted behavior to its logical consequence. The government councils dithered and dallied, refusing to make a decision until events forced some action upon them. By that time it was rarely to the Republic's advantage. They prosecuted this war with Pisa by bits and pieces, like slowly peeling an onion, blinded by the tears that flowed during the torturous process. After his experience in the Palazzo, Machiavelli had formulated his own iron law for making and executing official decisions: the more parties to the process, the slower to reach a decision and the less favorable the outcome. Aristotle was right, monarchy was the best form of rule, at least for efficiency and effectiveness.

So these various misfortunes were brought down upon their heads. Instead of making corrections to this faulty stratagem, his imprudent compatriots now put their faith in divine providence. He watched as the crowd swayed together, alternating between a solemn silence and the groaning moan of the *Miserere mei deus*—the great rallying cry of the Savonarolan Republic: "*Have Mercy, O Lord! Have Mercy On Me.*"

In this case they intended to evoke the sympathies of Mary, the Virgin Mother. She was their favorite patron because of her maternal, forgiving instinct and her ability to soften the stern judgments of God the Father. But God Almighty would have slammed the door on these pathetic Weepers.

Niccolò willingly conceded religion had its rightful place: in the individual soul and in the Church. One place religion did *not* belong was in the Palazzo. This was his principal objection to the *Frateschi*. Expecting prayer to save one from the penalties of bad government was pure folly. In these sentiments he was in perfect agreement with Dante, poet and politician.

His quick eyes surveyed the crowd, fearing the tension was sure to snap with some incident or other. He spied small groups of troublemakers hovering around the perimeter of the Piazza and recognized some of the *Compagnacci* Tommaso had warned them about. Several groups of militia were also distributed around the Piazza, but the crowd was far too large to control any spontaneous outbreak.

Suddenly the mob surged from the direction of the Street of the Hosemakers across the Piazza. Niccolò's sharp eyes focused, expecting the worse. He spied a horseman struggling to make his way through the tightly packed swarm of bodies and several men shouted, but their words drowned in the commotion. Niccolò moved closer from his position under the Loggia. He could see the horse was covered in lather and had a feral look in its eye—most probably its rider was a courier bringing timely news to the Palazzo. The courier had a scarf tossed cavalierly across his neck affecting the impression of fleet-footed Mercury and was waving an olive branch in his hand. As the crowd parted way they shouted: "*Popolo e Libertà!*" His words finally cut through the noise.

"We are saved! We are saved! A fierce wind broke the blockade. The same tempest propelled the French fleet full sail into port!"

The crowd exclaimed as one. "*Che miracolo!* The Frate's sermons have saved us again!"

The Piazza erupted with joy as people shed their somber cloaks, danced and sang with festive abandon, and shouted their celebratory choruses: "*Grazie a Dio!*" "*Grazie alla Madonna!*" "*Gloria in Excelsis Deo!*" "*Vivo Cristo!*"

Soon the bells of the Palazzo and the churches began to peal. In the pandemonium Niccolò did not receive the full gist of the report until much later. Apparently the capricious goddess, *Fortuna,* had intervened with a wicked wind to drive the Holy League's galleys off to sea, allowing the French galleys to enter the port of Livorno. Encouraged, the Livornese then went out and routed the camp of the Emperor and some of the Pisan forces. All this happened while the Madonna dell'Impruneta was in the city, so the miracle was proclaimed.

In retrospect, it was not a great victory, as the Holy League soon regrouped and pressed the siege. But only two weeks later another storm struck, this time scuttling the League's fleet, with many ships and lives lost. A special galleon carrying the Emperor's personal belongings and treasures was lost, and Maximilian himself narrowly escaped drowning.

Soon after, he abandoned the enterprise and decamped for Germany.

The events were hailed as a true miracle comparable with any of those in the Hebrew Bible. And the friar's esteem rose to new heights.

CHAPTER 14

Vanities Reform

FRA DOMENICO LEFT HIS DOVES cooing in the cloister as he hurried through the portico, passing through the kitchen and into the storage area where he had left the three novices after instructing them to restock the cords of wood used to fire the stoves in the kitchen. As he approached he heard loud talk and laughter that ceased when he pushed open the door. The young novices were sitting on the floor with a Bible lying open on a crate. One of them quickly snapped it shut and put it aside.

"Have I interrupted some pleasant diversion?" Domenico asked, his voice full of authority.

The novices, no more than fresh-faced boys, averted his eyes. One answered in a weak voice, "No, Brother Domenico, we were just finishing... with the wood and..."

"Perhaps you were refreshing your weary souls with some readings from Scripture?" His reproving tone precluded an answer and the novices remained silent. He easily guessed what they had been doing: opening the Bible to a random page and then pointing a finger at a passage to be read aloud. It was a common trick to declare God guided the hand and prophecy could be inferred from the randomly chosen passage.

Domenico sprang upon their incriminating silence. "Do you think the Almighty is amused with these childish games? Do you think He's pleased with the mockery you make of His sacred communication? And what do you think the prior would say about such frivolities?"

His last question raised the necessary specter of fear. Apparently God was too remote to frighten them, but the prior's stony disapproval was more tangible.

One of the boys looked up. "We mean no disrespect, Brother Domenico. The Holy Book is the source for the prior's divine visions, is it not? We only wished to make a trial."

"A trial! What are you then, jurists? What do you think God's judgment will be? Do you think He employs idle tricks to communicate His will? These are the ruses of charlatans and itinerant street preachers. You know the prior doesn't use such methods or do you need to reread the *Compendium Revelationum* where he explains this for weak minds?

"You've seen with your own eyes how tireless he is in prayer, and how he suffers for your sins. And you've witnessed the power of the revelations and visions—how he called for the Impruneta and that same moment the city was saved from its dire fate? Time and again the result is the same, as he foretold. Why must you flaunt your ignorance? Is it not enough just to listen and obey?"

Domenico was exasperated. He forgot they could hardly even read Latin. So many novices pledged to join the monastery there were insufficient teachers to monitor their training. Fra Girolamo was completely occupied with government affairs, assisted primarily by Silvestro, and Domenico himself was exhausted by the weight of his duties organizing the army of 'angels.' Already he had appointed a small staff of younger friars and novices to assist him and these were three of his charges. He sighed to himself, if God had only left him to tend to his peaceful birds, like St. Francis.

"Yes, Brother," they said, their small voices full of contrition.

Domenico saw how they were shamed and worried he had been too harsh. "Come now. You must meditate on God's words to achieve wisdom; it's not a devil's trick. The prior has called us to the chapel to make an announcement of our plans for the coming Lenten season."

The three novices dutifully raised themselves up to follow Fra Domenico, but before they left the room, he turned and asked in a whisper, "So, then, what was the passage?"

"John, Chapter eight, where the Pharisees make to stone the adulteress before the Lord intervenes," said the oldest boy.

Curious, thought Domenico, repeating the verse to himself: "And the Lord said, 'Let he who is without sin be first to cast the stone.'"

***

Fra Girolamo gathered his thoughts before leaving his cell to address his brethren. Months after rejecting the cardinalate, he had felt increasingly burdened by the trials testing the city. It had rained continually, with crop failures and persistent famine; and the roving presence of the Holy League's armies had left the people feeling vulnerable. At the same time the recurring horror of the pestilence incited their worst fears and imaginings. As these calamities closed in, his enemies played upon those fears to turn the people against him.

So he had turned to God. He had fasted and prayed, and God had delivered—pulling them from the fire at the last moment with the miracle of the Impruneta—proof he still enjoyed the Almighty's favor. Still, he knew it was not enough. Such favor must be repaid and sacrifices were required for the Almighty to receive His due.

The famine and the pestilence rages because the citizens are not constant in their faith. They cower, repent, congratulate themselves on their deliverance, and then slip back into sin. Their moral defenses must be built up to withstand the relentless temptations of Satan's devices. He knew this needed more than words and reproaches, no matter how strong and persistent. His words needed reinforcement by actions, by symbols, by rituals. These were the tools employed by clever men like Lorenzo to keep the people in line, to serve his needs and do his bidding to the detriment of their own souls. This is the lesson the friar had learned, so now he would use it for good, because God wished these tools to be put into His service. The army of little angels was thousands strong and they fanned out over the city, keeping the peace, admonishing sinners, and collecting alms. They discouraged displays of vanity, cleaned the streets and alleys, and tended the holy shrines. They served as a constant reminder and example to their elders to strictly observe the commandments of God and Church, to attend to the sacraments, to renounce worldly pleasures, and to conduct themselves with simple manners and simple dress.

But Satan still plied his trade. He tempted the faithful with so many seemingly small vices: gambling, lust for the flesh; food, drink, and luxurious comforts; and displays of vanity and social rank.

He looked out over his brethren as he explained these things to them. The coming season of Carnival was when Satan's provocations were most rampant and unchecked. The most crucial moment was Shrove Tuesday, the last day before Lent, when all the pent-up emotions spilled forth in an orgy of drunken pleasure, when the pagans danced around a fire, like savages—singing pagan songs and engaging in pagan rites. With a shout he proclaimed: "Satan and his minions must be driven from the city once and for all!"

He told them he had a plan, a plan God had revealed to him. All this license would all be cast away—replaced with a holy procession. They would sing sacred hymns and *laude* written especially for the occasion. And they would build a large pyre in the Piazza della Signoria, piled high with the foolish vanities people used to indulge their nefarious arts: the gambler's dice and cards; the prostitute's paints, wigs, and garments; the poet's ribald verse; and the painter's wanton images. Their army of angels would canvas the city and encourage the citizens to submit and cast their vanities into the cleansing fire.

The friar raised his arms high as he envisioned the towering inferno lighting up the night sky—the Burning of the Vanities. He imagined the voices of the faithful rising up with the flames to praise the Glory of God and His Son, Jesus Christ, King of Florence, who would smile down upon His holy city and bless it with His grace.

CHAPTER 15

A Visit to the Gonfaloniere Valori

"Make way for Fra Girolamo! In the name of Jesus Christ, King of our City, and of the Virgin Mary—make way for the Prophet of San Marco," shouted the boys.

Marching resolutely in their white surplices and red crosses, the small band were escorting Fra Girolamo and Fra Silvestro down the Via dei Servi connecting San Marco to the Duomo. Through the Piazza San Giovanni, past the Baptistery, and continuing down the Street of the Hosemakers toward the government palace, they glared at the citizens as they passed. The shopkeepers and their customers stopped and stared, then bowed their heads and made hurried signs of the cross, dutifully paying reverence to the prophet. Of late, the friar's presence had become more remote—his message mostly conveyed from the height of the Cathedral's pulpit or by way of the many printed pamphlets of his writings distributed by the San Marco brothers. The infrequency of his public appearances lent an air of seriousness to the prior's actions and the people were not surprised to see his entourage heading for the Palazzo. The *Frateschi* faction now controlled the Signoria and the friar's most vocal proponent, Francesco Valori, had just been elected Gonfaloniere.

At the entrance to the Palazzo, the friar dismissed the boys and they scampered off on their surveillance missions with renewed enthusiasm. After the guards admitted the two friars a page escorted them up to the second floor to the Gonfalonier's office.

At the landing to the first floor Fra Girolamo paused and motioned to the page to wait, as he wished to view the progress on the Hall of the Great Council. He and Silvestro turned the corner and entered the expansive room, large enough to hold more than five hundred members. This had been the friar's most inspired civil project—to enshrine the new constitution with a physical space, making concrete the abstract notions of justice. He had designed it and it had been executed to his satisfaction. This was a place where earthly justice would reign so the people could rest in confidence, knowing their representatives would insure the various councils governed for the good of the whole community. Though it had been in use for almost a year now, the Hall was still being decorated to match the grand artistic style of the rest of the Palazzo and the unfinished ceiling and the walls waited while the Works Committee organized a competition to award the commission. Nevertheless, the carved portals over the doors had been recently completed and the friar looked up to read the Latin inscription he had inspired. It was a commandment to those who would dare to transgress God's justice in this place:

This council is from God, and ill will befall anyone who tries to go against it.

The Palazzo was now united with God's House and would rule according to God's Laws. With the vanities reforms it would soon be joined by the daily practices of life in the marketplace and on the streets. United as one, the three pillars—Palazzo, Duomo, and Mercato—formed a Holy Trinity that provided the foundation for the transcendence of all worldly trials and final ascendance to the Divine presence in the next world. It would be the City of God on earth.

The friar felt a wave of pride reinforcing his will and rejuvenating his weakened body. He nodded to the page to continue the journey up to the second floor office of the Gonfaloniere. As the page presented them, Francesco Valori rose to welcome them.

"Fra Girolamo, Fra Silvestro, thank you for coming. As you can see, as Gonfaloniere, I'm more prisoner than free man. Fortunately, it's only for two months. Fra Silvestro, I assume you will visit me here for my confession."

"But of course, Excellency," replied Silvestro effusively, "It is our mission to carry God's word to those who desire to hear it wherever they be."

Fra Girolamo smiled graciously but stayed silent as he took in the luxury of the Gonfaloniere's quarters and the ermine-lined crimson cloak embroidered with gold stars that Valori wore to signify his exalted rank. He settled slowly into the chair Valori offered, feeling uncomfortable as he sank into its plush velvet softness. These signori lived like princes, if just for a short time.

He judged his host a vain man, and full of false humility. Fra Girolamo remembered when they first met at San Marco, in the first year of his reappointment to Florence. Valori had come to the convent with the other Mediceans—Rucellai, Vespucci, Bonsi, and Soderini—to rebuke him for offending Lorenzo. Now, Valori and Soderini were his most committed supporters while Vespucci and Rucellai had chosen the hated opposition. Florentine politics was an intricate web spun by the Devil's mischief and the friar guessed Valori's leadership of the *Frateschi* party was for personal ambition more than faith. Though these earthly men might prove useful for God's purpose, he must keep his guard.

Valori addressed him directly. "Fra Girolamo, I've asked you here to consult with you on some important matters. You know the many difficulties we face—the Pisan war, the famine, and now the return of the pestilence. The city is overflowing with unruly peasants from the countryside, which has provided an opportunity for mischief from evil elements within the city."

"The inconstancy of His congregation is surely trying God's patience," he replied in an admonishing tone.

"Yes, of course, and the burning of the vanities will keep the citizens mindful of the new reforms, but our enemies are constantly plotting to undermine our efforts. Since we have taken control of the Signoria, they are constantly agitating in the councils about the Pisan war and, with the death of Capponi, I fear the Grays see their opportunity. Perhaps to annul the new constitution or advocate the return of Piero de' Medici. I'm sure Bernardo Del Nero and Bernardo Rucellai are convinced they can use the Medici to regain control."

Silvestro grew agitated. "It's true, Prior. I know from the pamphlets they distribute that they employ the filthy Franciscans, Fra Menico da Ponzo and Francesco di Puglia, to spread lies from the pulpit about the *Compendium Revelationum* and your sermons. Then they send these lies to Rome to deceive the pope."

Fra Girolamo was rueful as he thought of St. Francis and St. Dominic so often depicted as two brothers joined in a crusade for a renewed Christian faith. Now the angelic cherubim and the ardent seraphim were locked in a death embrace. This enmity depressed him and he replied, "Yes, our founders would be ashamed at the decline of our Orders into petty squabbling, and the abandonment of the cardinal virtues of Lady Poverty and humility." His mind wandered, but Valori's voice called him back.

"We know from our ambassador in Rome that Fra Mariano and Cardinal Giovanni have the ear of the pope and plead aid for Piero. This is why I fear the imminent possibility of a plot by the Grays."

Savonarola was pensive. Piero de' Medici was without favor—the Magnificent has been succeeded by the Unfortunate—but the Grays posed a danger. "Who do you fear most in the councils?"

"Del Nero, Rucellai, Vespucci, Tornabuoni... I'm sure all these still sympathize with the Medici and secretly oppose the Republic," answered Valori. For good measure he added, "As well as the religious reforms."

Fra Girolamo was curious about the faces behind the factions in Florentine politics. He knew Rucellai and Vespucci, his foes since he first arrived at San Marco. He knew another Vespucci, Giorgio Antonio, who was a priest and the Bishop of Santa Maria del Fiore. These brothers were as different as night and day—these Florentine families were often strangely divided against themselves. "What of the Angry Ones?" he inquired.

"The *Arrabbiati* have been silenced by the strength of our party and the people's rancor against the aristocratic families. They have few representatives or supporters in the Great Council."

"What about Soderini? Have you spoken to Signor Paolantonio?" Fra Girolamo counted on the strong support of Paolantonio Soderini, but knew he was Valori's chief rival for leadership of the *Frateschi*.

"No, I don't trust the Soderini. His brother Piero is one of the leaders of the Whites and he's sure to harbor political ambitions. The Soderini family was too long in the service of the Medici."

Fra Girolamo detected the envy in Valori's tone. "Yes," he said, "that seems to have been the case for most families in Florence, no?"

Valori reddened slightly at this reference to his past confrontation with the friar and maintained an embarrassed silence.

"So," asked the friar, "what do you propose to counter the Grays in the councils to insure they do not gain control of the Signoria. I assume this is the objective."

"Yes, this would threaten our position and the pace of reforms. I believe with Cardinal Medici's support in Rome, Piero is a constant threat to the Republic. We must insure he doesn't receive any assistance from within the city. It's been suggested the age of eligibility for the Great Council be lowered from twenty-nine to twenty-four years. This will enlarge the Council and make it more difficult for the Grays to receive a majority or elect its members to the Eighty or the Signoria."

"Do you have the necessary support? What do wish of me?"

"We control the Signoria and I believe we have enough support to sway the Pratica. This should be sufficient to secure the necessary majority in the Great Council. But, of course, I asked you here to explain this change and seek your endorsement. If the Council knows you endorse it, the law will surely pass."

Fra Girolamo contemplated the situation. It seemed every family had its Cain and Abel and the envious Cains, with their incessant plotting, were a plague upon mankind. He was determined to defeat them once and for all. If men in their arrogance thought they could appropriate God's will and purpose, then it was necessary to tip the balance. Enlarging the Council could only make it more representative of the people and the people were his main ally. He saw nothing wrong with this strategy. "Signor Francesco, you can rest assured our words of approval will reach the necessary ears."

"*Grazie*, Father. May God grant us His guidance and mercy."

Then he looked harder at Valori to extract his end of the bargain. "Yes, and in return God expects His servants to do His will. We expect the Signoria will encourage the collection of the vanities and promote a religious spirit for the Carnival season."

Valori smiled too easily. "Of course. The Signoria fully agrees with the spirit of the reforms and the citizens' renewed commitment to faith. The militia of the Eight will be instructed to encourage compliance with the collection of vanities."

CHAPTER 16

THE VANITIES CRUSADE

A WEEK INTO CARNIVAL SEASON Niccolò and Tommaso were crossing the Ponte Santa Trinita on their way to the Frascato to enjoy some pleasant afternoon diversions.

"Look, Machia," said Tommaso, as he surveyed the street traffic. "Not a pretty ankle or lock of hair in sight."

Though it was mid-February the bright sun was uncommonly warm today and both *giovani* were dressed provocatively in tight-fitting hose and doublets. Carnival being the high social season before the downdraft of Lent, they were most intent to enjoy it. Unfortunately, it didn't appear as if many of their fellow citizens were of the same mind.

"You're a married man now, *amico*. Would you risk hellfire with such devilish temptations?"

Tommaso made an obscene gesture. "Up yours. Fiammetta's a good wife and I'm a good husband, but I'm married, not castrated."

He motioned with his head. "Look. Here come the little shits. If they wave those goddamn little crosses in my face I'm going to kick their asses."

As the gang of rambunctious boys came within earshot, Niccolò heard them accosting several women with their familiar refrain: "In the name of Jesus Christ, the King of our city, and of the Virgin Mary, we command you to cast off these vanities; if you do not you will be stricken with disease."

It was a dreadful practice—these reformed delinquents threatening simple people with the pestilence for partaking in life's simple joys. Niccolò found it even more amazing how many of his fellow citizens willingly submitted to these tactics. For him the city already was too holy—it was more and more difficult to find a decent game of tarocchi or triche-tach these days. He thought the friar and the *Frateschi* should be satisfied with their success and not push too far. Were they now only permitted to contemplate their eternal fate in either Heaven or Hell, rather than just enjoy a day of self-conscious beauty?

As the boys came closer, Niccolò sensed Tommaso tensing for a row. He grabbed him by the sleeve and whispered, "No. Deception is always sweeter than confrontation. Don't speak, just follow my lead."

He called out, "*Ragazzi, attenzione.* There are some big fish to catch across the river. We've just come from the Via Maggio where we saw a den of dice players plying their despicable trade. You'll catch them if you hurry."

The boys stopped and eyed them suspiciously. They spied the tight, suggestive clothes, looking for a soft underbelly of loose morals to attack. Niccolò knew what they were thinking: Dressed as they were, these two might be sodomizers. With an imperious air, Niccolò addressed the tallest one, guessing him to be the leader.

"I am Messer Niccolò Machiavelli, secretary for Second Chancellor Braccesi. This is Messer Tommaso Soderini—his father is Signor Paolantonio Soderini, leader of the *Frateschi* and close colleague of *Gonfaloniere* Valori. Now go, quickly."

Impressed by the cascade of reputable titles, the boys scampered off while shouting, "*Vivo Cristo!*"

"*Sì, sì, Vivo Cristo!* Now, get lost," he muttered once they were out of earshot, pressing his lips together in a razor smile. When the boys disappeared from sight Tommaso roared with laughter.

"You're right, Machia. A ruse is far more gratifying than a kick in the pants. But now they know who we are and we played a trick on them, no?"

"Bah, they know nothing. Unfortunately, the dice players disappeared just before they got there." Then he broke into a devilish grin. "Then again, on the Via Maggio they may just stumble across exactly what they're looking for."

Back in a jovial mood the two young men continued toward the Old Market. When they reached the Frascato, they found it shuttered with a sign hanging from the door, reading: Closed by Order of the Eight and the Signoria.

"*Merda!*" Tommaso exclaimed with a scowl. "What now?"

"The Inferno? Purgatorio?" said Niccolò, suggesting other taverns nearby.

"No, they're closed as well," said Tommaso. "But I do know a place. It's not publicized, so I'm sure our lady friends will be there. It's on *Borgo Allegri* in Santa Croce. Unfortunately, it's also where the *Compagnacci* gather. I imagine they'll be there."

Niccolò shook his head. "No, they shouldn't see us together. Besides, they're a bunch of twits—I don't think I could contain my sarcasm. What's new with our fellow Bad Companions anyway?"

"Well, they've taken to calling you my uncle's 'little hand,'" teased Tommaso.

Niccolò felt his face burn, but controlled himself. He knew Tommaso was baiting him with the insult. Besides, Spini and his gang of *ruffiani* were beneath contempt.

Then Tommaso waved off the joke. "Ah, they're just full of piss, thoroughly defeated by the miracle of the Impruneta."

"Shall we meet at the Ponte Vecchio later?" asked Niccolò.

"No, I've got an appointment with Fiammetta at her uncle's."

"Ah yes, the obligations of marriage." Niccolò smoothed his close-cropped hair. "Well, then, I think I need a cut and a shave. Perhaps Nello's chair is free. *Addio.*"

***

When he arrived at Nello's open booth the market was overflowing with peasants, though there was little they could buy—the famine was still afflicting the countryside and many of the rustics came seeking charity. But here, with the price of corn up to four lire a bushel, they would only face slower starvation. Due to the unsanitary conditions there were several more small outbreaks of the pestilence, sending many of the townspeople scurrying behind locked doors, venturing out only to buy necessities and curse the intruders. There had been demands the magistrates close the gates against travelers and non-citizens, but as most of the *grandi* wished to escape to the countryside, no quarantine was yet imposed.

Many of the peasants found refuge and solace in the friar's sermons in the Duomo. Niccolò imagined they were praying for another miracle on the order of the loaves and fishes. Often with no place to go and little to do, these itinerants wandered the marketplace looking for a scrap of discarded food or an offer of charity.

At the barber's concession he was greeted by several acquaintances, including his father's friend the bookseller, Messer Filippo Giunta.

"So, Messer Niccolò," asked Nello, as Niccolò settled back into his chair, "What news do you bring us from the Palazzo."

"Nello, for news these days you should go to San Marco and shave heads," he joked. "With Valori as Gonfaloniere, it's the friar who's guiding the state's affairs. With his own little army to do his bidding too."

Niccolò winked at Filippo and looked over to see if the two peasant women who sold their produce in the next stall would take his bait. "This morning I saw some of the friar's little angels harassing good citizens, so I sent them chasing the wind over in the Oltrarno."

"Yes, well, some good with the bad, some bad with the good," said Nello. As a member of the barbering trade, Nello was also a natural philosopher. As he wrapped a cotton towel around Machiavelli's neck he said, "With all these foreigners and uncouth peasants, perhaps it's a good thing the friar's Boys keep a sense of order and restraint."

Niccolò was indignant, feigning outrage. "Restraint? God help us! It's Carnival, you lout—a time to forget our woes for a moment before the gray mantle of Lent descends again. But look at them," he waved his hands toward the crowded market, "all serious, all solemn, all dressed in drab. Does God really wish us to look all the same? To *be* the same? To *act* the same? To *think* the same?"

This outburst got the attention of the old peasant women and they bustled over to scold him. They were like mother hens and baiting them gave Niccolò endless amusement.

"Messer Niccolò, such outward displays only confess to the sins of earthly pride. The friar counsels us to put aside frivolous vanities that divide the community. Look for yourself at the results." The woman spread her arms wide to take in the somber marketplace.

"I am," said Niccolò with exaggerated disappointment.

"Don't be a *diavolo*. Look at the way people behave now. The Great Council passed laws against usury, blasphemy and the "unspeakable vices" of young and old men alike, *and* those shameless *putane*." This last remark was explicitly directed at his rakish reputation.

"They've instituted the *Monte di Pietá* and outlawed the Jewish moneylenders…" The woman stopped to catch her breath and her sister stepped into the breach:

"Even the greedy bankers and tradesmen have restored ill-gotten gains to customers and clients. No more cheating, by grace of God. There's been an outpouring of charity and more citizens are attending to the salvation of their souls by staying at home and reading the Bible—,"

"And what has all this charity brought us?" Niccolò interrupted, thinking of the fresh young women he missed. "A bunch of unwelcome guests to fill our streets and an outbreak of the pestilence to boot." Both of the old peasant women quickly crossed themselves.

"One cannot spare the body to save the soul," said Nello, moving on to theology. "Besides, I've met many of these pilgrims and they all praise the peace and goodwill in our city and our prophet. It's not a bad thing, no?"

The first woman rejoined, "Yes, and the cleansing fire of the vanities will insure we continue on the path of reform. If it pleases God, perhaps we'll be saved from the famine and pestilence."

Niccolò wanted to knock some sense into these pumpkin-heads. "Another miracle? Well, why not? The cold weather will control the pestilence and the spring harvest will ease the famine—it's miracles galore! But tell me, how many of these *fanciulli* are the same who were playing the stones and barricading the streets and harassing citizens just a few Carnivals ago? Is this any different? Who will reason with them when they set upon your own house? Why, I hear they even snitch on their own parents. Messer Filippo, help me here, it would be nice to pass the afternoon with a game of chess, eh? But who dares tempt their annoying censure?"

Filippo shook his head in acknowledgment of the sad state of affairs but refused to enter the fray. He knew Niccolò's game.

Then Nello said, "They came through our neighborhood yesterday demanding contributions for the pyre. It's not a big thing for my wife to rid herself of a few face paints and baubles." He shrugged. "I also added some printed *novelle* of Boccaccio."

The peasant women both glowed. "It will be a glorious sight to see next Tuesday," they said in unison.

Niccolò was incredulous but amused; it was time to redeem himself with a bit of charm. He addressed the first woman: "Monna Beatrice, like your beloved namesake, you have no need of such beauty aids. But what of the poor women not so blessed?"

The old woman blushed. "Eh, Messer Niccolò—you and your honeyed talk, though I know it doesn't cost you a *grosso*. I'm long past the age of vanity. The friar said in his last sermon a mighty pestilence would come and force the women to rid themselves of their vanities. God's will cannot be denied." She crossed herself again.

Niccolò held his tongue. He asked himself: Did these foolish Florentines really wish God's laws to govern the Republic in all things? Does the Bible really proscribe dress? If so, will there be no more fashion? It was folly. Laws to govern behavior may be based on absolute principles, but man's laws can adapt these principles to the day and age. Should we now apply ancient Hebrew law to our modern age? It was absurd idea and they couldn't see it could only lead to disaster.

After Nello finished with Niccolò's hair he started to lather and shave him. "The friar even put forth the proposal for one or two women to be selected from each quarter to form a committee to recommend religious and moral reforms," he said, whispering close to Niccolò's ear. "I think the Signoria rejected it just to prevent women having a say in the making of laws."

"A wise policy, I would guess," Niccolò whispered back with a wink. Then he said loudly, "Well, ladies, if it's a bonfire you want, then it's a bonfire you shall have. I would caution you though. I expect trouble."

"How so?" asked Nello, "The Angry Ones? They're far outnumbered now. And the Eight doubled the Guard."

"No, they'll be bold, especially the *Compagnacci*.."

Nello gave him another questioning look.

"The *giovani* are also mostly against the friar, which may cost the

Frateschi their majority. Signor Valori has made a tactical error."

After Nello wiped his face, Niccolò gazed into the looking glass the barber supplied and admired his spare, groomed reflection. His eyes twinkled, pleased with what he saw. Not bad, he thought—he cut a good figure today. But where to apply it, with all those unlucky maidens locked away with their prayer books and rosaries? Maybe the final week of Carnival will draw out a few.

CHAPTER 17

BURNING OF THE VANITIES

ON SHROVE TUESDAY SANDRO FOUND himself sitting despondently in his workshop shuffling through a bundle of old drawings. Earlier he and Simone had sorted through the old inventory and selected out all those they had agreed violated moral decency and religious piety. These were mostly nude studies for his celebrated pagan paintings now held in private collections. He had hardly remembered these sketches, which had lain about, forgotten, in his workshop for years. As he fingered his creations, especially the sketches he had made of the beautiful Simonetta Vespucci as *Venus*, he was torn but knew what he must do.

This morning he had woken to the expectant ringing of Church bells calling the citizens to assemble for the day's grand *spettacoli*. At mid-morning he and Simone had joined with the *Piagnoni*, or Big Weepers, who came pouring out of their houses to attend a High Mass in the Cathedral celebrated by the friar. It was a magnificent scene. During the Mass thousands of children's voices had raised up in song to proclaim the triumph and glory of God the Father and Jesus Christ, King of Florence. Sandro could still hear the *Kyrie, Gloria,* and *Agnus Dei* echoing through the nave and resonating in the hearts of the congregation. After the Mass Fra Girolamo had exhorted the congregation to humility and charity in the name of Holy Jesus. Then he had led them in prayer, beseeching the Infant and Virgin Mother to intercede with the Almighty for the salvation of their souls and the safety of their commune. Finally he had instructed them to return to their homes for a mid-day repast marked by contemplation and prayer, to return in late afternoon to the Piazza San Marco for the grand procession.

A slow crescendo had been building for months as the Boys of the Friar, with the tacit consent of the government, had gone from house to house gathering the vanities. From rich and poor alike they collected all sorts of worldly possessions: dice, playing cards, chess pieces, masks, wigs, make-up powders, perfumes, hats, mirrors, dolls, lutes, ribald books and verse pamphlets, lascivious drawings and paintings, carved cupids and nude sculptures. Sandro had watched as they carted all these items to the center of the Piazza della Signoria, where they heaped them upon a large octagonal pyramid packed with brush and tinder. The pyramid was thirty *braccie* high and one hundred twenty around and was crowned by a grotesque figure symbolizing pagan King Carnival. The cask of gunpowder in the center would insure a dramatic climax to the sacrifice.

Sandro started to tie the bundle together with a string. He longed to look at them—the youthful models who were now either dead or withered—but dared not. Instead, he looked back at the two large canvases set upon the easels in his work area. These had occupied him continuously for most of the last two years. The *Crucifixion* with Florence in the background he had started first was almost complete. The second was the more recent work, a *Nativity* scene. Still in progress, it showed the marks of constantly being reworked. His interpretation of the theme was taken from a passage in the friar's *Compendium of Revelations* Simone had copied out for him. It told of a vision the friar had of ascending to Heaven as Florence's ambassador to the Blessed Virgin Mary. There— surrounded by singing angels, saints, Apostles and Old Testament figures—she addressed him directly, urging Florence to maintain its faith, offer up prayers, and remain patient.

But no matter how he tried, Sandro could not capture the *mysterium terribile et fascinans*—the elusive spirit he sought in the facial expressions of the Madonna and child. Perhaps, like Fra Angelico, one needed to be inspired by God to paint such images, and he was not so favored. He looked deep into the rough, indefinite outlines that sketched out Mary's unfinished head and face. Closing his eyes he prayed, silently beseeching the image eluding his eyes: "*Ave Maria, gratia plena, Sancta Maria, Mater Dei, ora pro nobis peccatoribus, nunc, et in hora mortis nostrae. Amen.*"

His eyes teared and he turned away. He must find Simone and prepare to go to San Marco, where the procession would begin. He took the bundle under his arm.

At the appointed time the procession embarked from the Piazza San Marco enroute past the Cathedral through the Piazza San Giovanni. At its head was a large figure of the Infant Jesus, originally carved by Donatello, borne by four boys dressed as angels. Behind them marched the prior of San Marco and his brethren in close ranks, all singing the infectious *ecce quam bonum*. The perimeter was crowded with the white-robed Boys of the Friar carrying their red crosses while intoning the hymns led by the Dominican brothers. Many of the Boys carried alms trays, soliciting contributions as they passed through the crowded streets. The citizens opened their purses and later it was said more alms were collected on that one day than previously received throughout the entire year. The rear of the parade was joined by thousands of Weepers.

The procession wound around the Duomo and the Baptistery and then turned toward the Piazza della Signoria and the pyre of vanities. A rowdy gang of *Compagnacci* stood in a corner of the Piazza and watched as the boys and the friars spilled in from the Street of the Hosemakers. Tommaso Soderini was among them and they had spent much of the day in the Carnival spirit, drinking and carousing in defiance of the public prohibitions. In a foul mood, they taunted the religious with lewd Carnival songs to drown out the sacred laude. One of the friar's Boys angrily waved his cross in the face of Spini, who grabbed it from him and threw it to the ground, splintering it on the stone pavement.

"There, you little shit! You wave a damn crucifix in my face again I'll cut off your balls! If you still have any!"

Several of the friar's Boys boldly interceded to support their comrade. They shouted at Spini and the others: "Filthy buggers! *Compagnacci!*"

Spini and several of his gang pushed toward them. "Come on, you little turds! I'll wring your necks!" he yelled.

Banding together, the boys grew bolder: "May the sword of God strike you sodomites down and send your souls to burn in the deepest Hellhole!"

"Better there than here with you, you pious little bastards! Stay off the streets or you're fair game tonight!"

Several friars hurried over to break up the combatants. Francesco Cei saw a familiar face and called out derisively: "Hey Bettucio! I didn't recognize you in your monk's dress. Nice haircut. Tell us, how do you like your boys? Or maybe you've discovered the secrets of the nuns' habits? What do you think, should we join too?"

Fra Benedetto, known formerly as the pleasure-seeking painter Bettuccio Luschino before taking vows at San Marco only three months before, fixed his former acquaintances with a withering scowl as he stepped between them and the boys. His face was red but his voice stayed calm.

"*Basta, ragazzi.* Show some respect and leave off these boys. Have you no shame? They do you no harm."

"*Scusa, Padre,*" mocked Spini. "We only wish to teach them respect for their elders. It seems at San Marco they've only learned to harass and chastise. Did you think we would just roll over and have you priests dictate our every action here on earth?"

"Doffo, take a moment and think about how you waste your brief time on earth with worthless pastimes. Take off the spectacles of Satan's pride and assume those of Christ's humility. Instead of attacking your fellow man, why not join hands with him as you both follow the same path to eternal salvation."

Spini laughed loudly. "*Merda,* I think I'm going to puke. Bettuccio, you sound like you actually believe that crap coming out of your mouth.

Fortunately, that's not yet the way of the world. Go back to your convent, paint miniatures and pray. Piss off!"

Shaking his head, Fra Benedetto gave Spini a last piercing look, then turned his boys around and began again to sing the *lauda* to Jesus the friar had composed.

Spini loudly sang the same melody but substituted the original obscene lyrics of the Chimneysweep song. Tommaso and the others joined in as the Boys and other *Piagnoni* backed away with scowls of disapproval.

Fra Girolamo and his brethren had set up in front of the Palazzo facing the crowd packing the Piazza. The singing children were arranged on the ringhiera and under the Loggia dei Priori. When all were in place the crowd was hushed by a loud blast of trumpets and wind instruments as the poet and humanist, Girolamo Benivieni stood on the ringhiera and recited a verse he had composed for the occasion:

> *Arise, O New Jerusalem and see*
> *Your Queen and her beloved son.*
> *In you, City of God, who now sit and weep*
> *Such joy and splendor will yet be born*
> *As to decorate both you and all the world.*
> *In those days of bliss*
> *You will see all the world come to you,*
> *Devoted and faithful folk,*
> *Drawn by the scent of your holy lily.*

When he finished the crowd let out a cheer and the Boys sang other verses mixing pleas for God's mercy for the city with retributions against their enemies. Finally, to the staccato of drums, the Boys chanted a long call and response *lauda* mocking pagan King Carnevale. They harried him for his games, his masks and bags of stones, banishing him from the reformed city. They sent him off to chastise the Romans and warn them of the dire prophecies to be visited on that corrupt city. This performance unfolded like a Greek drama, captivating the audience straining to hear the verses, which were punctuated by frequent refrains of *ecce quam bonum*. At the conclusion of this playful comedy the trumpets and winds blared again, silencing the crowd and announcing the lighting of the bonfire. Instantly young men with torches raced around the pyre, igniting the brush and fanning the roaring flames.

This was the moment Sandro had anticipated. He watched the flames leap and the fire grow fiercer. Next to him he saw the faces of his fellow artisans warmed by the sudden red and yellow light. Turning to his other side he saw the consumed face of Simone with the reflections of the flames dancing in his eyes. As Simone stared, Sandro stepped forward and tossed his bundle on the fire and then watched as his fellow artisans followed in turn. They all stared curiously as the flames lashed out, quickly swallowing the fragile paper and canvas.

In this sacrificial act Sandro experienced the surrealism of a dream. His heart felt weighted and unweighted by both an unburdening and sense of loss. Around him many others quickly stepped forward and tossed various articles into the flames, each 'sinner' making a public act of atonement that masked a secret act of true or false confession. It was a declarative act, one of compliance and concordance with the commune, resulting in an overwhelming feeling of release that soon erupted in an immoderate celebration of song and dance.

***

From his perspective under the Loggia, Niccolò watched this orgy with wry amusement in the company of Filippo Giunta and Maestro Adriani. As the crowd sang and danced with zeal, the flames leapt up to tickle and then devour King Carnival.

Niccolò leaned over to whisper, "Doesn't strike me as much different from last year. Some wine has flowed—but even with holy wine, the effect is much the same."

But Messer Filippo was in an ill humor. "The friar accomplishes much of merit, but the burning of printed books strikes too close to the heart. Boccaccio may be a rascal, but his *Decameron* deserves a better fate. If the pestilence descends again it may provide our only comfort."

Adriani consoled him. "Don't fret too much, Filippo. One can't expect monks to have any love for Boccaccio, but I don't think the written word suffers much in this sacrifice. Nor do I believe the friar is hostile to the better writings. His convent has taken to preserve the Medici library intact and the book collection at San Marco is their most precious treasure."

Filippo was not reassured. "I suppose. It's just that one always wonders how far such passions go before they burn out—forgive the expression. I can't condone this program."

"Nor I," said Adriani.

Niccolò noticed the dour solemnity of the women around the Piazza. "I don't think many of the women, especially the young ones, find it easy accommodating the latest monastic fashion either."

"My wife," said Filippo said, "is appropriately somber, but her younger sister and my niece are chafing at the restrictions. One wonders what the rites of spring will bring."

Niccolò retorted, "If it doesn't bring rain and grain, we'll all be praying for our daily bread."

At that moment the gunpowder exploded, collapsing the towering pyre in on itself with a crash of sparks sending the Weepers shouting with glee. Then they sang a chorus to Christ the King:

> *Viva, viva, live in our hearts,*
> *Christ the king, leader and lord.*
> *Let everyone purge his mind, memory, and will*
> *of earthly and vain affections.*
> *Let all burn in charity,*
> *contemplating the goodness*
> *of Jesus, King of Florence.*
> *Through fasting and penitence*
> *let us reform ourselves inside and out.*

Cries of "*Vivo Cristo!*" pierced the night as the trumpets gave one final blast. Niccolò looked across to the front of the Palazzo and saw the friar gazing intently at the flames. Savonarola's eyes were transfixed and Niccolò detected a self-satisfied smile between tightly compressed lips. But he was sure this holy edifice the friar had erected would not last long.

CHAPTER 18

A PAPAL SUMMONS

THE PAPAL PREFECT OF CEREMONIES at the Vatican opened the door to the anteroom and approached the two clerics: one a pale, ample young man in the purple robes of a cardinal and the other, an older monk of the black-clad Augustinian Order. The two looked up from their chairs with hopeful eyes—they had been waiting patiently now for more than four hours.

"Your Eminence, ...Fra Mariano," the Prefect addressed them in turn. "His Holiness will receive you now." Then he turned to lead them into the *Sala dei Santi*, the large reception hall in the private apartments of Pope Alexander VI. They entered the long hall from the side at the far end whereupon the Prefect walked to the center, made a defined right-angle turn to the left to face the pope's throne at the far end, and then advanced toward the reception area.

As they approached, Cardinal Giovanni looked up to see the pope conferring with some members of his court, so he and Fra Mariano were left waiting once more in attendance. Pope Alexander was a large, effusive man, a dark Spaniard, and he looked more imposing in full ceremonial regalia. The underlayers of amice, alb, and stole were enveloped in a red seamless cope that flowed freely across his body and his large head was crowned with the pope's miter. Even when seated, it made him as tall as those standing around him. His physique and manner well suited the symbol of the Borgia Bull.

The delay gave Giovanni time to appreciate the splendid paintings adorning the vault and walls of the reception hall. Pinturicchio of Umbria had recently executed these frescoes displaying a series of famous tribulations in the lives of the saints, as the name of the room implied. But what caught Giovanni's eye was the depiction of the pope's familiar daughter Lucrezia as St. Catherine in the *Disputation*. Lucrezia was a pretty girl of seventeen who had already been married off for political reasons to the Duke of Milan's nephew, Giovanni Sforza. Rumors told the union would be dissolved to facilitate a more favorable alliance with Naples. Giovanni's curious eyes searched without success for a depiction of Giulia Farnese, the lustful pope's beautiful young mistress, known throughout Rome as *Giulia la Bella*.

Looking up at the ceiling vaults, Giovanni saw several large representations of the mythical Egyptian pagan deities of Osiris and his wife Isis. One segment showed Osiris resurrected from his tomb as the bull Apis, the Egyptian god of agriculture, peace and abundance. It was a strange theme for the holy Vicarage of Christ, but not surprising given this pope's predilection for all things great and ancient—after all, he had appropriated the name of Alexander for himself and Caesar for his first son.

These pagan frescoes reminded Giovanni of those in his home in Florence—beautiful creations now lost to him due to the narrow-minded rabble that had usurped his city. Like his father, Giovanni loved the beauty created by skilled Florentine artisans. Many had migrated here to Rome and he did his best to continue the tradition of Medicean patronage—recently he had recommended his childhood friend Michelangelo for a commission from Cardinal Riario. In the meantime, he prayed for God's favor and hoped good fortune would eventually return his family seat. And he prayed his father's last words of advice would not fail him now.

Up on his throne Alexander was fully aware of his guests' presence, but waited until a dignified time had passed, and then some. Finally, he dismissed his coterie of advisors and nodded for the Prefect of Ceremonies to announce his guests: "Holiness, I present His Eminence, Cardinal Giovanni de' Medici of Firenze and Vicar General of the Augustinian Order, Fra Mariano of Genazzano."

As was customary, the two clerics ascended to the throne and knelt to kiss the pope's exposed foot. As they rose up with heads bowed, Alexander quickly bestowed a blessing and motioned for them to sit on the stools provided near his throne.

"Eminence, to what do we owe this pleasantness?" he asked politely, though he already knew the answer.

"Your Holiness, we have come with a petition regarding the predicament of my brother Piero and my family. I beseech Your Holiness, not only in the interest of my family, but also in the interest of resolving the unsettled situation in Florence, which remains an obstacle to the interests of the Vatican and the Holy League of Italian States."

"Yes, it has been a constant thorn in our side." The pope blinked nervously—a nervous habit belying his steely will—then leveled a penetrating gaze at the young cardinal. Personally, he had little sympathy for the Medici. When he had needed votes in the *Collegio* for his election, this newly appointed pup had sided with Caraffa against him. In addition, the Medici were allied with the Orsini by marriage and the Orsini had treacherously betrayed him against the French invaders. Just last month his son Juan had led the papal army into battle against the Orsini and besieged their castle at Bracciano. But Juan had suffered a humiliating defeat and the pope had been forced to make an unfavorable peace and restore the Orsini lands and possessions. To strengthen his hand against these duplicitous Italians, he had felt it necessary to appoint four new Spanish cardinals.

Cardinal Giovanni continued, "Of course, we have many agents still in the city and we know it's a small group of ambitious upstarts who've used the veil of liberty and the mouthpiece of the friar to achieve their aims. But the city suffers intolerably from these selfish pursuits and we expect more political unrest. Citizens hope for a return to the stability and peace they knew under my father."

Alexander sighed, making his indifference plain—the aims of the Medici were quite beside the point. "We have repeatedly expressed to the Florentine government our desire for it to join us in the Holy League against these barbarians, but they have resisted and tried our patience. And the Holy See has also been most tolerant of this Dominican preacher called Fra Girolamo. We have sent many Briefs requesting him to attend to us here in Rome, yet he has defied us and tested our leniency."

Fra Mariano almost jumped to his feet, startling the pope with his vehemence. "Your Holiness, I tell you this friar is an instrument of the devil, the perdition of the Florentine people! I'm well acquainted with his falsehoods and heretical teachings, as I've preached against them. But he's very clever—he disguises his true meaning and deviously twists events to confirm his false prophecies."

Alexander's smile turned into a sneer. "It seems this preacher has many powerful enemies, we've heard the same from the cardinal from Milan. So, why does your government insist on giving him free reign to attack us?"

The young cardinal answered in a more measured tone: "Your Holiness, those in control in Florence find the friar useful to their purposes. They employ him to incite the people against their enemies in the city and outside. They do all this in the false name of republican sentiment. To maintain power they resist the Holy League and trumpet the French alliance. However, the party of the Grays—containing many of our supporters—argues for a new alliance with the League, but the friar attacks them from the pulpit and provokes the people against them."

Alexander blinked, thinking how true it was that fear was the most useful means of control. "Better to be feared than loved," his son Cesare always advised. But the Holy Father had more subtle tools at his disposal. *Why must these Florentines be so obstinate?* The pope grew vexed as he listed their transgressions:

"We have ordered this friar to cease preaching and yet we continue to receive copies of his sermons. We have issued a Bull uniting the Tuscan congregation to the Roman under the control of the Protector of the Dominican Order, Cardinal Caraffa. But this rebellious friar and his brethren defy the Bull, stating it goes against the Constitution of the Dominican Order—as if this supersedes papal authority! He chooses to make legal arguments against those of us who are trained in canon law."

"He's a heretic, Holiness," barked an excited Fra Mariano. "He calls the Church a shameless harlot and compares the Holy See to lustful Babylon, referring to the prelates as lowly beasts and abominable monsters. He—,"

Alexander cut off this diatribe with a wave of his hand. He had no need to be publicly reminded of the insults heaped upon his person. "My sons, as you know, our first duty within the faith is to obey him to whom God has given supreme authority and to whom we are bound in supreme respect. The Church is threatened with more serious tribulations—we are beset not only by the French and the Spanish kings but also the Turks. After having subjugated Asia and a great part of Europe, they have twice already descended on Italia, destroying everything with fire and massacre. The dragon now threatens the very center of our religion, the city of Rome. If he were thus able to crush the head, the rest of the Christian body would quickly perish.

"We are the shepherds of the flock and we are set upon the watchtower precisely so we may keep it safe. It is a duty for others to follow our example. You see how this preacher is forcing our hand and yet your government supports him."

For Alexander the matter was plain: the Church hierarchy had long been wary of mystics within its ranks. These self-proclaimed visionaries constantly popped up all over Christendom and a delicate hand was required for handling them. Some, such as Bernard of Clairvaux, Hildegard of Bingen or Catherine of Siena were tolerated and then canonized after death into the pantheon of saints. Others, like the *fraticelli,* were quietly but firmly hounded by the Church Inquisitors and quickly burned to save their souls, making the *auto-da-fé* a common and highly anticipated public entertainment. Whether it was God or their own dementia speaking through them would never be known, but the answer was immaterial to Church interests. The threat was obvious: if it was possible for the faithful to entreat with the Divine directly through revelation and visions, what need was there for the control and guidance of an established Church? How, then, would order prevail?

"Tell us," the pope said, "What do you propose?"

"Your Holiness, despite the stories of the latest Carnevale

extravaganza we've reason to believe the political situation may grow more favorable to our cause. In the last month there have been two bread riots where the common people ransacked the public granary. Now is the propitious moment to overthrow the existing government by a show of force under my brother Piero, who still enjoys much hidden support inside the city walls. If Piero should be reinstalled in Florence, he can assure Your Holiness a favorable alliance and the elimination of this other problem. To accomplish this he needs additional funds to raise a military force and the support of Holy League allies."

"Your request, Eminence," said Alexander, "will require close council with certain members of the Curia, as well as consultation with diplomatic representatives of the League. We can promise nothing at this point except to assure you we shall consider your proposal. You will receive word when we have come to a decision."

With a simple wave of his hand the pope indicated the interview was concluded and signaled to his Prefect of Ceremonies. After the two Florentines left the room, he commanded: "Summon Cardinal Cesare and also the papal Secretary and deliver them to our private chambers. Then send a request to the Florentine embassy and have the ambassador attend to us at his earliest convenience—tomorrow."

***

Cesare impatiently paced his father's chamber in his black leather riding boots. The papal Secretary was taking notes as the pope, reclined on a velvet settee, dictated a brief addressed to Fra Girolamo Savonarola, Prior of the Dominican convent of San Marco in Florence:

"...We are disturbed at the troubled state of affairs in Florence, the more so in that it owes its origin to your preaching. For you predict the future and publicly declare you do so by the inspiration of the Holy Spirit when you should be reprehending vice and praising virtue. Such prophecies may easily lure the simple-minded away from the path of salvation and obedience due to the Holy Roman Church. Moreover, these are not the times for such teaching, calculated as they are to produce discord even in times of peace, let alone in times of trouble... now, read it back to me."

Cesare was annoyed at having to listen twice to the same dictation. It was a waste of time trying to reason with this monk. Better to have Michelotto garrote him in a dark alley. Michelotto never failed. His father continued dictating the brief:

"...Our duty, however, prescribes that we order you, under holy obedience, to cease from public and private preaching until you are able to come to our presence, not under armed escort as is your present habit, but safely, quietly and modestly as becomes a religious, or until we make different arrangements. If you obey, as we hope you will, we for the time being suspend the operation of our former brief so you may live in peace in accordance with the dictates of your conscience…"

After the entire letter was read back one last time, the pope instructed his secretary to copy it out in final form and then to affix his seal and dispatch it by courier to San Marco in Florence, with copies to be delivered to the Signoria of Florence and Cardinal Caraffa here in Rome.

After the secretary left the room, Cesare approached his father.

"Cesare, my son, Cardinal de' Medici has proposed we provide support to his brother Piero to recapture Florence. They offer a new alliance and promise to rid us of the annoying preacher."

Cesare returned to his pacing. "Piero de' Medici is a pompous fool, with no talent for inspiring or leading men. His brother is harmless enough, preferring to wallow in the lap of luxury while pretending to be abstemious."

"An astute appraisal. We do not favor the Medici. They connive with our enemies here in Rome, especially the Orsini. And this generation displays little talent for governing Florence—they whimper like lambs in the lion's den."

"So you'll reject their proposition?"

"No. We wish to encourage Piero and the cardinal as they can provide us some advantage. We'll give them enough encouragement to attack Florence, but not enough support to be completely successful. Florence is a tenacious adversary; we must weaken it before we can control it. A Medici regime in Florence does not serve our eventual goal of controlling the city and its territory, with you or Juan as ruler."

"What about the friar? Will you still negotiate with him?"

"No, this letter is merely preparing the way for a different strategy. We've summoned him again to Rome but he'll reject it, strengthening our hand against his insubordination."

Cesare continued to pace. "We should act quickly. The priest is clever—he hopes to play the French king against us. The king can be manipulated to move against us with a call for a Reformation Council to depose you—your Holiness. If he should invade again—,"

"It will never come to that, my son. If the French king returns, you can be sure he won't find the friar waiting to greet him. But that is of little concern at the moment: Charles's army is far away and the miscreant is more concerned with siring an heir than pursuing another adventure in Italia. For now we'll deal with the problem through more delicate means.

We've summoned the Florentine ambassador to an audience tomorrow and we'll propose one more solution to this problem."

"Which is?"

"There's only one sure way past the thick skull of a Florentine: through his purse. In return for an alliance with the Holy League against the French we offer the return of Pisa. In addition, if Florence complies we'll even allow them to keep their preacher as long as they instruct him to confine his preaching to matters of faith and desist from attacking the Holy See."

"They're a bunch of peasants. What if they refuse?"

"Then we will give serious thought to issuing a Bull of Excommunication."

Cesare wondered if excommunication was really a sufficient deterrent to apostates. His father was applying in small increments his lesson of the carrot and the stick, whereas Cesare believed one must eliminate one's enemies with a fatal blow. Incremental pain only steeled resistance. At times Cesare found his father's presence stifling. With age and power comes timidity and that was the real reason principalities fell. He, on the other hand, was determined to be decisive and unsentimental in the exercise of power.

Regarding his son, Alexander knew he resisted advice like a horse under the bit. In this he was like all young men, only more so. Only an experienced man grasped how the judicious exercise of power required restraint and circumspection, not rashness. Those who were too reckless and bold exposed themselves to the vagaries of fate and misfortune. As pope, his true power lay in the symbolic, not the instrumental. In this new world of monarchs and nations, symbols of power were more important than rushing headlong into battle— that was for captains and condottieri. No, princes and kings must hold back to manage the responsibilities of the greater enterprise of the state and he was prince of the Church. The great enterprise of the Christian Church had ingrained this lesson in its best leaders for centuries and the rest of the world was just now catching up.

"Trust me, Cesare. In the end we will prevail. The preacher's power rests first on his hold over the people and the Florentine government cannot ignore the masses. But an excommunication will restrain the faithful and weaken his popular support. The magistrates in Florence are practical men, when time is favorable they will sacrifice a monk or two, but we should not make a martyr of this priest. The Augustinian who was here with the Medici may also be useful—he hates the Dominican with a passion that reveals his own weaknesses."

Alexander raised himself up with effort. "Our decision has been made. Extend just enough rope to allow Piero to hang himself and a weakened Florence will fall willingly into our lap. Enough of this talk, we tire of our duties. Tonight we will dine together: you, Juan, Lucrezia, Giuliana and Monna Adriana—a quiet family gathering."

"That brings another issue to mind, Father. What shall we do about the idiot Duke of Pesaro? He and the rest of the Sforza contest the annulment based on nonconsummation. Hiding in Pesaro, he alleges we wish to do him harm."

"Marriages must receive the blessings of the Church and *we* are the Supreme Pontiff. He'll come to his senses and see the futility of this marriage, with a bit of gold to assuage his pride. The Milanese are no longer useful to us and Lucrezia must be free to make an alliance with the progeny of our new King of Naples. Now, let us retire."

Cesare turned away from his father. "I'm sorry, Holiness. I've another...ah, appointment this evening." Then he quickly excused himself.

CHAPTER 19

THE NEW SIGNORIA

PIERO SODERINI WAS BESIDE HIMSELF. "We've lost control of the Council. I warned Paolo to distance himself from Valori, that *idioto*. The man is an ambitious fool."

Yes, and ambition and folly made for a dangerous combination, thought Niccolò. As the older man paced, Niccolò opened the shutters to welcome some fresh air and light into his office. The lively midday chatter of the Piazza floated up, cheering the room.

As Niccolò had anticipated, the new younger members of the Great Council had voted against the friar's party and the fragile coalition of Whites and *Frateschi* had lost their majority. So the Grays captured the most recent Signoria and their leader, Bernardo Del Nero, a Medicean sympathizer, was elected Gonfaloniere. Now the Grays were seeking to strengthen their position by attacking the friar.

"I warned Paolo too," added Piero. "When the friar takes credit for all that goes well, he leaves himself vulnerable when things go wrong, as they invariably do. Who is the man God has not chosen to test? Anyway, the Signoria will need to do more than blame the friar for the current unrest. They must offer a decisive plan to relieve the famine, otherwise the city will descend into chaos and we'll all end up in the Inferno."

Niccolò replied, "They dither, as usual, hoping for additional shipments of grain from France through Livorno. They've also convened a Pratica to discuss a new law against hoarding and the possibility of fixing the price of corn."

Since the burning of the vanities, the Lenten season had been marked by a rapidly deteriorating chain of events. The Signoria had received two briefs from the pope: one demanding the government uphold the papal censure of Savonarola; and the other offering the return of Pisa for a new alliance with the Holy League against the French. The Grays had used the first issue to argue against the friar in the councils but rejected the second outright, recognizing it as a disingenuous offer. The papal forces had been supplying Pisa for more than a year and, in any event, the Pisans would never consent to such an arrangement.

These problems of state were further complicated by another crop failure, with the price of corn reaching unprecedented heights and the weakened population increasingly susceptible to disease. Several food riots had broken out in recent weeks and the streets were simmering in desperation. Compounding the city's gloom were unchecked rumors of an attack by the combined forces of Piero de' Medici, the Orsini and the Holy League.

"I read your minutes of the Pratica," said Piero. "The pope is seeking to divide and conquer by offering us Pisa; the new Signoria was wise to reject his offer. But what concerns me most is Del Nero and the coincidental return of Fra Mariano from Rome. I'm suspicious of the Grays. Have you heard anything?"

"The dispatches from our ambassador confirm the cardinal and Fra Mariano petitioned the pope, most likely for an alliance. Also, rumors reach us from Arezzo that Piero is attempting to enlist the Venetian *condottiere,* Bartolommeo d'Alviano."

"Well, I've no doubt our walls can withstand Piero's forces, but perhaps not if he gets reinforcements from our enemies. And the betrayal of those who would open our gates."

"The Eight have placed the militia on high alert, but the Ten of War have not yet recalled forces from Pisa," said Niccolò.

"Well, Paolo told me the friar has denounced Piero from the pulpit and predicted his utter failure should he attack. I wonder if he'll succeed again with his prophecies."

"If he emboldens the people's resistance, perhaps it's self-fulfilling, eh?"

Niccolò added, "There's also the *Arrabbiati* and the *Compagnacci.* They've grown more violent, especially against the friar's supporters. Their pamphlet war sparks street fights almost every day now."

"If it's not one faction, it's another. May they all burn in Hell." Soderini started to say something more but stopped as the crowd buzz coming up from the Piazza suddenly grew louder. It's steady cadence sounded like a march. The two men quickly stepped to the window to look below and saw a large crowd spilling into the Piazza. The people were chanting something like *"Pane! Pane!"* and all the marchers were women. *Merda*, he thought, it was another food riot and the horde was headed toward the Palazzo.

Soderini said, "Come on, we must alert the Eight to call more guards and summon the Gonfaloniere to calm them down.

As Niccolò hurried from his office he thought he heard an ominous variation of the chant crying: *"Palle! Palle!"*

CHAPTER 20

PIERO MOUNTS AN ATTACK

HEARING THE ALARM OF *LA VACA,* Niccolò raced across the Old Bridge toward the Palazzo and saw the morning rain had swelled the Arno. When he arrived in the armory on the ground floor he found a mass confusion of captains and guards of the Eight mustering the militia for battle. Word had come Piero was leading a large force of Sienese and Orsini troops to attack from the south.

He raced up to the first floor to find the Captain of the People huddled with several members of the Signoria and the Eight. The captain was arguing with several of the Grays. Apparently the Medici were leading a force of six hundred horsemen and four hundred foot soldiers to attack the city at the Porta Romana. The captain had dispatched a hundred foot soldiers to defend the gate but insisted more forces must be mustered to defend the perimeter of the city walls along the southern part of the Oltrarno. With the call to alarm there would soon be thousands of citizens in the streets and the magistrates seemed more worried about which way the mobs would turn.

The captain said he was ordering the Palazzo sealed and guarded with all members of the Signoria and other officials held inside. This was the main source of the disagreement with the Grays. Niccolò did not see the Gonfaloniere, Bernardo del Nero, who must be in his chambers. He thought of what action he could take, but soon realized he could do nothing trapped inside the Palazzo with the Soderini outside. He went to his office to wait, wondering if or when the Palazzo would be attacked. Feeling a mixture of trepidation and excitement, he imagined how he would fare under fire.

***

Piero de' Medici felt the cold rain drip down his back under his armor, as he impatiently sat his horse under a protective canopy of trees not more than a stone's throw from the Porta Romana. His troops were miserable and disorganized, arrayed up and down along the Via Senese. They were cold and drenched by the day's rain after the long march from Siena. Along the top of the wall Piero saw the city's archers and pikers waiting to repel his attack. Trapped by the thunderstorms, he was furious as a wet cat, wondering where the Venetian troops were and the promised reinforcements from Rome. He cursed the weather and his stupid foreign allies. No matter, he would attack and take the city without the Venetian and Romans and to hell with them. He pulled on his horse's reins as waited for his supporters inside to open the doors and welcome him back as the city's savior.

He had heard much of the misery of his fellow Florentines under the ineptitude of the republicans and their crazy friar—famine, riots, pestilence—but he would return his city to its former glory and expel those who caused these calamities. All men falsely believe they are leaders of men, but few are well trained to the task; this, he assured himself, was his birthright and today he would take back what belonged to him. He watched the tower above the gate but nothing had changed.

He called out to one of his captains, demanding to know the status of their invading forces and the execution of the plan of attack. The man gave a weak reply about the archers on the ramparts and then rode off to get a report from the rear guard. The rain turned to a drizzle and still there was no change on the tower. Piero waited.

An hour passed and the captain returned, saying he received a scouting report there was a Florentine force returning from Pisa to defend the city and it would arrive within the half day. They did not have much time. Piero lost patience—*what is happening inside this city of cowards? Where are his allies?* He spurred his horse toward the gate, shouting as he rode back and forth in front of the large wooden doors. Suddenly he was answered by a hail of stones. Along the top of the ramparts gangs of youths appeared, hurling more stones accompanied by jeers and curses:

"*Vaffanculo!*" "*Vai via, bastardino!*" "*Il Sfortunato!*"

Piero quickly returned to a safe distance, red with anger as the laughter of the Florentine youths filled his ears. His saw his troops look away, feeling no less miserable over their predicament.

In the Palazzo, Niccolò had passed an uneventful afternoon. Florentine infantry were being recalled from Pisa, but meanwhile nothing happened while reports kept arriving on the status and movement of Piero's forces. Apparently no allies had risen up in his defense, nor arrived to supplement his private army, so the city was still secure. In the meantime both Valori and the Soderini had gained entrance into the Palazzo. By early evening the final reports came in: Piero and his troops had ignominiously retreated, harassed by the *fanciulli* from the walled ramparts of the city. Niccolò could only marvel how the friar had proved prescient again.

CHAPTER 21

A SECOND CONSPIRACY

THE TWO MEN SPOKE IN hushed tones as they melted into the dark shadows of a deserted street in the Oltrarno. They conversed for almost a half hour before the one with a Spanish accent, his face partially obscured by a hat and a black scarf, untethered his horse and led it through the streets under cover of darkness toward the Porta Romano before the gate was locked for the night. The other man turned in the opposite direction to cross the river for a rendezvous at an unrepentant tavern hidden in the Santa Croce quarter.

When he arrived he saw his friends at a table in the back surrounded by emptied jugs of wine and several familiar courtesans. Coming upon them, he opened his arms wide and exclaimed, "My *Compagnacci*, you're truly a disgrace to the holy sentiments of our city. Don't you know tomorrow is Ascension Day? You'll surely burn in Hell for your sins!"

"We look forward to it, Doffo," said Tommaso. "It has to be better than Florence these days. So what's your pleasure this evening? Wine? Women? Perhaps you'd like to borrow a rosary and do penance?"

"Piss off. I'm in good spirits this evening and I feel lucky. *Fortuna* is about to shine on us, *ragazzi*. Where are the cards?"

After several hands of *tarocchi*, punctuated by insults and money changing hands, the gang of *giovani* settled down with the wine. Tommaso was casually fingering the cards when Spini shooed away the women and dropped the level of his voice.

"Okay, my friends, are we agreed on the time?"

"I don't know, Doffo. What if the Signoria or the Capitano learns of it? We'll be banished ... or maybe worse."

"Don't be stupid, Duccio. The plan is set and we won't be discovered. Besides, the Signoria is sympathetic. They've forbidden him to preach after tomorrow, so we won't get a better chance. The Eight is also against the friar; we need not fear any reprisals from the Palazzo."

"But the friar's followers will turn out in force for the sermon."

"There won't be a sermon after we're through. Besides, the Weepers are like rabbits; they scatter at the first sign of trouble. In the Council the feeling against the friar and the *Frateschi* has grown. The Gonfaloniere hates the friar and the Signoria's more afraid of the pope."

"But look how the people rose up against Piero de' Medici and his troops last week. The common rabble are completely unpredictable," said

Francesco Cei.

Spini scoffed. "Piero's a stooge, used by the Grays, as well as the Sforza and Borgia. And he's completely ignorant of it. Why, even the little shit *fanciulli* pissed on him. *Veni, vidi, fugi*...I came, I saw, ...*I ran.*"

They all laughed at this running joke about Piero.

Spini added, "I've received assurances both Il Moro and the pope are convinced *we're* their best chance to get rid of the friar."

Tommaso looked up from the cards. "What about Rucellai and Del Nero?"

Spini waved his arm in a sign of impatience. "The Grays can do nothing without raising suspicion. The *popolo minuto* and the peasants are already rioting over the price of grain. All we have to do is spark this tinderbox for it to explode. Tonight we set the stage. *Basta.* Are we agreed?"

As the others nodded their assent, Tommaso put down the cards and stood up. "I'm not adverse to the plan, it may work. Unfortunately, I won't be able to participate, as tonight I'll be occupied with my wife. She wouldn't understand my excuse for such festivities, you know."

"Another servant of the Strozzi, eh? What about tomorrow?"

Suppressing his annoyance at the slur, Tommaso forced a smile. "I wouldn't miss it," he said. Spini waved him away with a look of disgust and turned back to the others. "Okay, then, the rest of us shall meet after midnight in Piazza Santa Croce."

***

Later that night a half dozen black-clad figures arrived in the empty piazza where they huddled in the shadows behind two wagons. They sat and waited until the night guards made their last rounds of the sleeping city. There was a disgusting smell coming from the wagons.

"*Porco Dio*, Duccio, that shit stinks," said Spini. "What did you put in there?"

"We found an old rotting mule carcass down by the river and slit it open. We also emptied out the manure and pig shit from several stalls at my uncle's farm. It helps if you tie a scarf over your nose."

"*Merda*, that priest will die if he tries to breath, much less preach. Come on, let's get on with it before I choke."

The men pushed the wagon on a roundabout way toward the Cathedral to avoid the Bargello and the Stinche, where the night guards were housed. They entered the Piazza San Giovanni on the south side of the Duomo and proceeded to the side door closest to the pulpit. They struggled to haul the stinking mule carcass off the wagon and drag it across the deserted Cathedral. With a concerted effort they heaved it up the stairs to the top of the pulpit and draped it over the sides. Then Spini took a mallet and drove some iron spikes, nailing the carcass in place. The spikes protruded where the preacher often pounded his fists. Next, they shoveled the manure into the pulpit and over the stairs. Soon they were covered in filth and the vast Cathedral was filled with an overpowering stench. When they finished they stole outside to collect the wagon and sneak off through the dark narrow streets.

Spini sneered, "That should cramp his style. Pass the word: we meet in the Piazza San Giovanni at Nones and be sure to carry a knife. If the braying jackass tries to preach we'll instigate a riot and in the commotion we'll fall on him and his damn prayer mumblers. We have the advantage of surprise and once it's done there's nothing his supporters can do."

"Do we have enough accomplices to overcome them?"

"Word of the sermon has spread among the *Compagnacci* and the *Arrabbiati,* so there'll be a crowd. They'll be anticipating a disturbance and once it begins they'll come together."

"So, how does it begin," asked Francesco.

Spini shrugged. "You're the poet, you'll think of something. *Madonna,* we smell like shit. Come on, let's wash off in the river."

CHAPTER 22

ASCENSION DAY RIOT

IT WAS SHORTLY AFTER THE hour of Terce and Fra Girolamo was steeped over his desk, glossing the day's sermon by adding notes with his quill, when Fra Domenico came to his door.

"Prior, forgive my intrusion, but Messers Domenico and Girolamo Benivieni and Fra Bartolomeo have just returned from the Duomo and they say the situation there is growing dangerous."

Fra Girolamo motioned impatiently for Domenico to enter. The wicked ones in the city were constantly making threats and bluffs against him, but it only made him more defiant. There was even a rumor they had threatened to blow up the pulpit with a powder keg.

"*Prego*, Domenico, tell me what worries you. I know our enemies seek to frighten me from performing my duties, but I am determined they shall not prevail."

"Fra Girolamo, forgive me for not telling you earlier. At dawn, immediately after Lauds, several of the brothers checked the Duomo to be sure our enemies had not committed some terrible deed as they had sworn to do today. It wasn't true, but Fra Bartolomeo told me of a most despicable act. The villains desecrated God's house with a mule carcass and they heaped the pulpit with offal and dung from the horse stables. All morning our brothers have labored to clean away every scrap of filth and restore the pulpit, but now a large crowd gathers outside. Messer Domenico implores you not to go as he's sure they mean to do you harm."

Fra Girolamo put his hand on Domenico's shoulder to reassure him. "Brother Domenico, the Ascension is the day appointed by the Lord to His disciples for going forth to spread the His word through the world. To fulfill His command many of those same disciples suffered torture and death. Remember Peter was martyred in Rome.

"Our enemies hope to strike fear into our hearts and make us doubt. They hope to scatter us in the wind, so they might regain power. It's what we expect. But no earthly fear shall induce me to deprive the people of their sermon on this day. I know who they are and I know their designs. We are prepared and we shall defy them, Brother Domenico. We must."

Resigned, Domenico said, "*Sì*, Fra Girolamo, I'll tell the others. But perhaps we can organize some protection?"

"If it makes you feel calm, Signor Valori has assured us of his protection."

After Domenico left the friar gripped his quill and made an addendum to his sermon.

***

"You lose heart too easily. You are sad when you should rejoice."

The friar's words resounded over the congregation. As he looked down on the multitude, he could smell the traces of the offal with which they had fouled the pulpit. There were no women in the congregation today and he easily perceived the contrast between his supporters and his enemies in their mode of dress. His enemies flaunted their disdain for the vanities crusade with their rich attire. They smiled crooked smiles and stared with insolence as he spoke, daring him to confront them. In comparison, his supporters dressed simply and soberly and huddled in groups for protection as they listened to his words. It was like seeing wolves among sheep and he, the shepherd, must drive off the wolves to protect his flock. He raised his voice to the challenge:

"The days of trial have come. God grant I be the first to endure them. Already I must bear great ingratitude from the *tiepidi*—those tepid ones who do unto me as Joseph's brothers did unto him when they sold him to the merchants of Egypt. They cry I am no prophet, yet they themselves fulfill my prophecies. I tell you again Italia will be invaded by barbarian hordes and destruction will befall this perverse land. But you who are righteous—offer your prayers and the Lord will show you mercy."

A low murmur arose as some of the Angry Ones stamped their feet and hurled insults toward the pulpit while others shouted down the disrupters. Fra Girolamo raised his voice accusingly over the tumult:

"*YOU* who are wicked! You seek to fight against me, but in so doing you make war upon the Lord. You say I sow discord but Jesus Christ Himself came to raise strife among men so they might be saved from the wrath of the Father. You say, 'O Friar, you should not preach when forbidden by the Signoria.' But I cannot refrain from preaching from fear or by the command of man. I shall continue to preach unless my God wills me to stop."

Murmurs of approval and support rose from the pockets of *Piagnoni*. Encouraged, Fra Girolamo continued to harangue his enemies:

"So do what you will, play with any fantasy you like, imagine what you want. But this I tell to you: this reform, you will never be able to beat it down; it will continue even after I die, for it is Christ's work."

Shouting now to cut through the din, he incited his divided

congregation. "I warned you before and I say it again. To those who would aid tyrants: 'Cut off his head, were he even the chief and head of his house; cut off his head!'"

With this provocation the dissidents flew into a rage, yelling angrily to disrupt the sermon. In the thick of the congregation a group swarmed and the friar glimpsed the flash of steel blades. Suddenly a loud crash rang through the Cathedral and the crowd panicked. He heard the banging of pews and benches and saw a gang of ruffians push their way toward the pulpit. The crowd pushed one way and the next, seeking to escape. Then the Cathedral doors opened and a company of men armed with lances and drawn swords pushed into the Church. Clenching his crucifix, the friar watched his followers panic amid the unfolding chaos. He felt their fear as he raised his arms to cry out above the roar:

"Ah, see! The wicked refuse to hear their fate! But they cannot escape the judgment of the Lord thy God. Wait! Be calm. Have patience. Don't fear them!"

Apparently the armed reinforcements were actually *Frateschi* partisans who fought their way to the front of the congregation to cordon the pulpit and protect him from attack. Below, he saw men pushing and shoving and more threatening flashes of steel, but no bloodshed. Next to him several friars from San Marco were guarding the stairway to the pulpit. Looking out over the confusion he thrust the crucifix over his head and cried out: "Stop! Have no fear! God is on our side! Believe in THIS! Fear nothing!"

With a final burst of energy he trumpeted one last appeal, "*Miserere mei Deus!*" and then collapsed to his knees, still holding the crucifix aloft.

Those in the congregation with their wits still about them shouted: "*Vivo Cristo! Vivo Cristo!*" and the cry was taken up by all his supporters in the Cathedral.

Below the pulpit the *Frateschi* brandished their swords against the surging Angry Ones and their Bad Companions. When one of the magistrates of the Eight pushed to the front of the crowd, a furious Francesco Valori knocked him to the ground. Faced with formidable opposition, the attackers retreated as the brothers of San Marco carried the spent preacher down from the pulpit. The *Frateschi* then cordoned a circle around the friars and pushed back against the crowd. Forming a phalanx, they banded together to escort the friar back to the convent under armed guard. They were followed out by many of the Weepers chanting "*Vivo! Vivo Cristo!*"

As the friar's supporters spilled out the side entrance leading to the Via del Cocomero, Tommaso Soderini emerged quietly from the shadows near the main door and slipped away through the milling crowds unnoticed. He made his way quickly down the side streets, skirted behind the Palazzo, crossed the river, and stopped when he came to Machiavelli's house. Let in by a servant, he waited for Niccolò in the small foyer.

"I was just in the Duomo, Nico..." His words rushed out: "Savonarola preached and they... we... you know, the *Compagnacci*, started a riot. I was near the main entrance when Francesco Cei lifted up the alms box and sent it crashing to the floor. Spini and the others made a deafening noise banging on the pews, then swarmed toward the pulpit. Many Arrabbiati joined them, but the *Frateschi* rallied and protected the friar from attack. Tosinghi and some others, I think... Valori was in the midst of it but, *grazie a Dio,* my father stayed away."

Niccolò nodded. "So, the *ottimati* fail again."

"They were bolder than I expected. Vespucci, Salviati and the other Angry Ones have egged them on."

"In the Signoria and the Eight as well. They attack the friar and his Weepers while they can. The new ordinance forbidding preaching takes effect tomorrow."

Niccolò fixed Tommaso with a barely perceptible smile. "Did you know the Signoria rescinded the order against the *Frascato* and several other taverns and brothels—just so you and your 'naughty companions' can come out of hiding and cool our religious fever."

Tommaso looked embarrassed. "Spini and Cei want to plunge the whole city into panic and chaos just to get rid of Savonarola. And the *Frateschi* are just as eager to vanquish their enemies."

"Of course, one against one and all against all. What else would we expect," Niccolò commented wryly.

"Spini's in contact with foreign agents, but I don't know who or how much they're involved. He keeps his own counsel."

"Perhaps he suspects."

Niccolò was convinced Rome and Milan already had agents conspiring in the city. The Borgia pope had been very busy aggrandizing his family, granting four territories out of the papal States to his sons in the last two months. He was sure the pope had his eye on Florence.

"Stay close to him. I fear *Il Papa* and *Il Moro* will join forces and then fight like dogs over our carcass."

"What did my uncle say?"

"He's anxious for the Whites to regain the Signoria. After Piero's failed attack the Grays have lost all support in the Great Council. The main threat now is Vespucci and the *Arrabbiati*, so he hopes to convince Rucellai and his allies to combine against them. Like you said, the Rabid Ones would just as soon destroy all peace and order in the city in order to regain power."

"But where does the friar fit in? My father still believes the Whites should join forces with the *Frateschi*. Frankly, I'm sick of all this religious nonsense. I always said he was *pazzo*."

Niccolò gazed upward toward divine providence. He almost wanted to beg God to spare them from His foolish servants, for Savonarola surely must have God or *Fortuna* on his side. "The friar has no sense for governing men—it's a dangerous weakness. The vanity campaign goes too far and costs him. Florentines want to live, no? He wants to be Moses, but forgets Moses had an army. And so does the pope."

Tommaso countered, "Today he had a phalanx of lancers and swordsmen ready to rally to his defense."

Niccolò was unconvinced. "The mob is fickle. Valori's his champion for now—an ambitious fool who thinks he's Cosimo de' Medici. But Valori lacks cleverness. I wouldn't bet on him against more skilled and ruthless men, such as the Borgia."

"But for this we have the king of France."

"Yes, I've found kings are always good to have up one's sleeve, …at least in cards."

CHAPTER 23

EXCOMMUNICATION

CRONACA SAT ON A STOOL in the doorway of Landucci's apothecary gazing out upon the half-finished Strozzi palazzo. He was fed up.

"Messer Luca," he shouted into the shop, "can you tell me: will I ever be free of this pig of a palazzo?"

Construction had proceeded at a snail's pace and was becoming a labor of Sisyphus. The foundation and ground floor were completed four years ago, almost a year after the *capo* of the Strozzi clan, Signor Filippo, had died. After, the first floor, with its rows of arched windows, had taken almost two years. But since then, little more had been accomplished. First came the disruption of the French, then the Great Hall. Then the ongoing conflict with Pisa and the Holy League. Now, after legal complaints lodged by the Strozzi heirs, he was back at it, splitting his time with repairs to Brunelleschi's cupola. But with the famine and the pestilence felling his work crews, his difficulties as head builder were growing more acute—today he had only one mason and six laborers on a job requiring five times that number.

"I'm not a seer, you know, but I believe at some point in this life we're all released from life's labors," the apothecary shouted back.

"Yes, but that's at its end. Can't we expect any comforts before then?"

He looked out at the empty, dust-blown piazza and kicked at the pebbles under his foot. The city, like this piazza, was empty as well. After the riot in the Cathedral all public sermons and other large gatherings were suspended, ostensibly to check the spread of the pestilence. But everyone knew it was a disguised effort to prevent the friar's preaching, for it passed soon after his supporters defeated an edict to banish him from Florence.

Landucci came out to the front of the shop. "If you believe the scriptures, our rewards do come in the next life."

"But must we suffer so in this one. You know, I've spoken with Sandro and Simone, and I agree our situation is exactly as the friar warned. We've turned away from the Word of God to write our own words and paint our own images. Maestro Leonardo and Piero di Cosimo, Ficino and poets like Boccaccio and Petrarca have argued for the glory of Nature. Their intentions do not oppose Christian faith—they only wish to incorporate the beauty of Nature into the mystery of God.

But I think those of us with lesser talents misinterpret these sentiments. We reject saintly images and religious virtues to paint what delights us."

Cronaca looked up into Landucci's eyes. "Have you ever noticed the nature of the misfortunes punishing our city? It's not just man's foolishness; it's floods, famine, terrible storms ...crop failures, ... now the curse of the pestilence—rats have already come out of the sewers to show us our own fate. These calamities are not man-made—they're visited upon us by Nature herself, who we propose to worship with our arts. No, God is not opposed to Nature, there's no separation between God and Nature or this world and the next. Nature is God's handmaiden and He uses her to whip us for our incessant pride and ambition."

Messer Luca tried to console him. "You're too hard on yourself. You painters and sculptors are dependent upon the whims of your patrons for your bread."

He pointed toward the half-finished palazzo across the piazza. "It's the *grandi* who, in their desire to accumulate fine things, build these monuments to their pride. This is what angers Our Lord. Like Moses' Jews who worshipped the golden calf, we Florentines have come to worship the golden florin and all it buys. Everyone wishes to be a head taller than his neighbor, but to do so they must climb up on the backs of the weak."

Cronaca shook his head. "No, we're not blameless, Messer Luca. We had it good, we had our Golden Age of more than seven fat years and we grew pleased with ourselves. Now we're faced with seven lean and I doubt we have the stomach for it."

"Well," said Luca, "it's a crime to prevent Fra Girolamo from preaching. His divine guidance is our only hope now."

Cronaca threw up his hands. "The Signoria operates from fear—fear of the mob, fear of chaos, fear for their own necks, ...perhaps even fear of the pope. But what they truly lack is fear of God Himself and His final judgment. So they fulfill their own worst fears by failing to act against the growing divide in the city. We are forever Guelphs and Ghibellines long after these identities have lost their meaning; only the names have changed. Now we're Weepers, *Frateschi* and Prayer-mumblers against Grays, Angry Ones and Bad Companions. Have you read any of those pamphlets fluttering around the city?"

Messer Luca nodded. "Yes, the friar's sermons and his epistles; also some of the laude of Benivieni and Nesi. Bartolomeo di Libri's runners drop off a few almost everyday. Last week they distributed the friar's latest epistle addressed to the *Piagnoni*, 'To all God's chosen and faithful Christians.' I read it. He warns us to expect ever-greater persecutions. The prophecies are being fulfilled and he says our persecutions will increase step-by-step in order to raise faith, virtue, and courage to an ever-higher pitch. This is the way of the Lord: suffer for faith and rejoice, for salvation will be our final reward."

"Yes, I've read some, but at Sandro's bottega the *Compagnacci* drop off mean-spirited insults from the opposition. Some are childish and amusing."

"I wouldn't know. When I see a pack of the Angry Ones or their Companions, I turn the other way."

Suddenly the bell at Santa Maria Novella began tolling, shattering the lazy quiet of the piazza.

Landucci started. Puzzled, he asked, "What's the hour?"

"I'm not sure, but judging by the sun I would guess more than one hour past midday."

The bell towers of the other churches also began to chime in chorus, but there was no reason for them to sound at this hour. It must be a signal.

Messer Luca called to his assistant in the back room, "Jacopo, watch the shop, we're going to Santa Maria Novella. We'll return shortly."

The two men hurried down the street and joined a gathering in the large piazza in front of the church, by the main entrance. They pushed their way toward the front door where the crowd was clustered around an official notice posted there.

"*Porco cane*, what's it say?" someone asked.

"Can anyone read? Tell us what it says," shouted another.

"It's a papal Bull from Rome."

"What's it say?"

"Fra Girolamo is excommunicate!"

"*Impossibile!*"

"*Davero*, it's true."

"Somebody read it aloud," another pleaded, then saw the apothecary. "Messer Luca, please, read it for us."

Landucci elbowed closer to read the notice:

We have heard from many persons worthy of belief, that a certain Fra Girolamo Savonarola, at this present said to be Vicar of San Marco in Florence, has disseminated pernicious doctrines to the scandal and great grief of simple souls. We had already commanded him, by his vows of holy obedience, to suspend his sermons and come to us to seek pardon for his errors; but he refused to obey, and alleged various excuses, which we too graciously accepted hoping to convert him by our clemency. On the contrary, however, he persisted still more in his obstinacy; wherefore, by a second Brief, we commanded him, under pain of excommunication, to unite the Convent of San Marco to the Tuscan-Roman Congregation recently created by us. But even then he persisted in his stubbornness, thus, ipso facto, incurring the Censure. Wherefore we now declare said Fra Girolamo excommunicate, and to be held as such by all men, for his disobedience to our apostolic admonitions and commands; and under pain of the same penalty, all are forbidden to assist him, hold intercourse with him, or abet him either by word or deed, inasmuch as he is an excommunicated hereon, and suspected of heresy.

-Given in Rome, 12 May, 1497.

The crowd became vocal.

"*Madonna!* Excommunicate? Heresy? What?"

"Here." With his finger a man traced the words for the illiterate to stare at. "Basically, the pope wants to kill the friar," said a *Piagnone.*

"No! You blaspheme," cried another. "The friar is an apostate, he's defied the Holy Father so many times. He *must* be held accountable."

Another voice softly asked, "What is this *ipso facto?* What's the meaning?"

"Shut up, you pumpkin head!"

"Pernicious doctrines? What are those?"

A wry voice shouted back, "It's how Rome now describes the Bible."

"No, the friar professes to speak with God. He's full of lies, deceiving the ignorant, a heretic," countered an excited foe.

The crowd divided into two camps facing off against each other and Landucci and Cronaca moved off to the side to avoid the fracas. The friar's enemies taunted his supporters with a verse:

> *O ungrateful people,*
> *Thou art caught by a cry,*
> *And follow a guide*
> *All full of hypocrisy.*

This angered the Weepers and the scene grew ugly. "Shut up, you pups of Satan," one yelled. Then the group chanted back at their adversaries:

> *With laughter and verse you mock the divine word,*
> *But wait till the hard lash straightens your backs.*

Buzz then, you bluebottle flies; crawl, you black beetles;
whirling hornets, use your venomous stings!
But remember that justice and chastisement will never fail …

The opposition countered by yelling curses and insults as they jostled the Weepers. "*Figli di putane!* You sons of whores! Your stupid priest is excommunicated by the pope. He can't preach or administer the sacraments and anyone who holds discourse with him or aids him is excommunicate as well. The Holy Inquisitors will burn him and send him to Hell where he belongs!"

"That's a lie! The Bull says he is only suspected of heresy. The Holy Father is deceived by so many lies from you worms and your Fra Mariano. Fra Girolamo commits no heresy or blasphemy, as you do everyday."

Swords were drawn and the crowd scattered. Landucci and Cronaca withdrew and hurried back to the apothecary. As they quickened their pace, Cronaca grew agitated. "The mob is crazy and the Signoria's playing into the hands of rabble-rousers. Every day it's the same."

Messer Luca was silent, conflicted by the pope's Bull of Excommunication. Often such actions were political and used to defend the Church against attacks on its temporal authority. There had been excommunications in Florence before, most notably Lorenzo de' Medici by Pope Sixtus IV. Often these political conflicts were resolved and the excommunication rescinded. But the friar was excommunicated for his challenge to the pope's spiritual authority, whereas Christian doctrine stipulated the sanctity of St Peter's successor on all such matters. Luca was confused; for laymen who feared for their immortal souls it was impossible to challenge the spiritual authority of the Roman church. This was a serious charge.

Later that evening, while still mulling over the excommunication, the apothecary heard shouting in the street outside his home. He went to his window and saw groups of men carrying torches and yelling out news that the Duke of Gandia, the pope's second and favorite son, had been found murdered in the Tiber outside the Vatican in Rome.

This, the Weepers were shouting, was proof of God's judgment. God had seen to punish the degenerate Alexander for his unholy life and his unjust excommunication of the true prophet. Luca sat back in his chair, more confused than ever. Could it be true? It was incredible.

CHAPTER 24

FRA GIROLAMO WRITES TO HIS HOLINESS

FRA GIROLAMO SAT AT HIS desk in the Chapter House and stared at the documents before him. He was agitated and had not slept for the past two nights. The pope had threatened excommunication, but the friar had never foreseen how it would come to this. He had prayed on the matter, but it was not yet clear to him which path he should take. Surely the sanction was unjust, yet he was troubled. As his dilemma stared back at him he struggled, weighing his conscience against the consequences of his actions and the stark choices contrasted by these two documents. His fate was sure to lie in the balance.

The first was a missive composed for his congregation against the excommunication, titled: "Epistle against the surreptitious Excommunication, addressed to all Christians and friends of God." He had written it to preempt Alexander's threats, which had begun more than a month before. By delivering this epistle to his followers he would be clearly defying the papal authority in Rome. If he did not he was sure the excommunication would undercut his support in Florence and threaten all God's work he had so far accomplished. He was not certain of the pope's purpose, but his was sure this was the aim of those who advised him with their pernicious lies.

The second document was a letter of condolence to the pope over the recent death of his son. Because the pope had wielded his naked power unjustly with the excommunication, God had dealt him a crippling blow by taking away his son. The connection was irrefutable. The friar was sure if he could open His Holiness' eyes to these truths, he must rescind the excommunication.

After the murder, it was said Rome was scoured for clues to capture and punish the perpetrators, but the murder had become an unsolvable mystery. The Borgia had too many enemies: the Orsini; the Sforza; even his other sons Cesare or Jofre acting out of fraternal jealousy. Then, suddenly, the inquiry was quietly terminated, adding to the rumors.

During this time the friar had received a letter from Cardinal Caraffa at the Vatican conveying Alexander's remorse and his intention to make restitution to God for his personal transgressions. Caraffa wrote how Alexander was inconsolable over his son's death. On receiving the news he had barricaded himself in his room in the Castel Sant'Angelo for three days and three nights, denying his body all comforts. All Rome had heard his plaintive wails of pain and grief haunting the hot summer nights. When family members and Church prelates begged him to open the door, he refused. At the end of his penance he emerged exhausted. With renewed conviction he confessed: "Though we would willingly give seven tiaras to bring him back to life, Almighty God has punished us for our sins." He promised a reform, saying, "We have fallen headlong into corruption; we must begin our reform here—here within our Roman Curia." After which he had appointed a commission of six cardinals headed by Cardinal Caraffa to offer recommendations.

In a second letter Caraffa reported the proposed reforms: a prohibition on the sale of indulgences; the practice of simony to be punished by excommunication; church monies to be spent for pastoral purposes only (not on idle entertainments for clerics and churchmen); and bishops required to be resident in their dioceses. Lastly, Alexander had renounced nepotism in Church appointments and sent his three children to live outside Rome so he would not be tempted to indulge them. Caraffa hinted the pope had even considered abdication in order to save his condemned soul. In any event, the cardinal was optimistic the reforms would answer the popular criticisms against the Roman Curia and also grant a victory in principle for the friar's position.

This all seemed according to God's plan, but the friar was not so easily convinced of the Devil's abdication. He long suspected there were few moral or religious principles involved in Alexander's tactics. He was not shocked or surprised by this; the Church required good administrators to run its affairs. Prelates who rose to the top, like Rodrigo Borgia, were trained at the universities in canon law; consequently they were spiritually and morally deficient. Alexander's sporadic attacks against him shifted with the political winds and the man was a proven nepotist— it was obvious his main priorities were his family fortunes pursued through the power of the Church Militant. His actions revealed his strategy to subjugate Florence to support his ambitions and the friar harbored those concerns as he weighed his renunciation of the unjust excommunication:

> *This Excommunication is invalid before God and man, inasmuch as it is based on false reasons and accusations devised by our enemies. I have always submitted, and will always submit, to the authority of the Church, nor will I ever fail in my obedience; but no one is bound to submit to commands opposed to charity and the law of God, since in such a case our Superiors are no longer the representatives of the Lord. Meanwhile, seek by prayer to make ready for that which may befall you. If this matter is pursued further, we will make the truth known to all the world.*

For his rebuttal, the friar had turned to the writings of St. Bernard of Clairvaux, who had castigated the Roman Church more than three hundred years before. Bernard had said then "the plague of the Church is inward, and it is incurable." Bernard argued that the saint blessed by revelation was in all ways superior to the Church hierarchy in authority, so no earthly prince of the Church could condemn a 'messenger of God.' The corruption of the Borgia pope was common knowledge and to submit to the judgments of such an earthly sinner would be a sacrilege against true Christian faith and belief. It was to follow Satan into Hell.

But the pope was the Vicar of Christ on earth, the head of Holy Mother Church, the spiritual leader of the faith. Was he, a lowly friar, willing to force a break with the Holy Father and suffer the pope's damnation? And how would his congregation react to his choice? What if Alexander truly repents and the reforms are enacted? Could he then reconcile with Rome? This was his dilemma: He risked his soul either way.

The friar closed his eyes and clasped his hands in prayer. What was God's will on this matter? Did He punish Alexander to condemn the sinner, or to encourage his redemption? How was the unjust excommunicant expected to interpret these events and act accordingly? Was it possible to steer a stable course until the way became clear? The friar felt the acid of indecision burn in his stomach as sleeplessness clouded his mind. He got up to walk and clear his thoughts.

At the door exiting the Chapter House he looked up to see Fra Angelico's magnificent *Crucifixion* frescoed over the doorway. He looked at the painted figures arrayed before the three crosses on Golgotha: the Holy Family; the saints and founders of the religious orders; and the three Church Fathers: Jerome, Ambrose and Augustine. Underneath, along the lower border, were smaller medallions depicting the most illustrious men of the early Church—seventeen defenders of the faith in all. These were the true heirs of St. Peter and he sadly wondered where such men in the future would be found.

He wandered through the cloister to breathe in the night air. Stopping at Domenico's dovecot to contemplate the peaceful birds, he felt his tension release. How easily the gentle birds slept. The convent life was a rewarding one; it was pure. Measured only by the rhythm of prayer and meditation, one's heart beat slowly and regularly—it only quickened when going forth into the frantic city, where everyone raced to get from here to there. The convent was the last refuge for the oppressed and wearied soul. The thought struck him suddenly: This was the ground in which to plant future shepherds of the Church—in a soil rich with piety, humility and grace, not in those fetid sewers of Rome.

He thought of the past papal briefs, how Alexander attacked his reforms as a "new mode of life," at odds with Church practice. No, he thought, it's a mistake to say we have entered upon a new mode of life— it is only a return to the principles and example of our saintly predecessors. To build poorhouses; to wear a rough, old and patched habit; to eat and drink within the limits of sobriety; to live in a poor cell; to cultivate silence and solitude; to separate oneself from the world; and to give oneself to contemplation—these are not innovations. He had written as much in his letter of condolence to the pope.

The rewards of such a life were many, but most important was the sharing of God's Word with the faithful from the pulpit. Would he be denied this through the false judgment of an unholy pope? *No! Senza predicare, non posso vivere—unless I preach I cannot live.* He *must* bring the word of God to the faithful. The Holy Father had erred by listening to the wicked lies of his enemies.

Reinvigorated, he returned to the Chapter House and picked up his letter to reread it. Toward the end he returned to the power of faith:

> *...Faith, most holy Father, is the one and true source of peace and consolation for the heart of man. Let your Holiness respond to this call and you will see how quickly sadness turns to joy. All other consolation is trivial and deceitful. Faith alone brings consolation from a far-off country. Let your Holiness forward the work of faith for which I labor, and do not give ear to the wicked. ...May God console you in your distress.*

This was the right course and the only course. He must tread lightly but resist firmly until the pope revealed his true self. He would desist from preaching until the pope rescinded the excommunication and granted him permission to resume or when he chose to defy and renounce the unjust excommunication. God was at his shoulder to guide him.

***

Later that night in his dormitory cell his body collapsed into fitful exhaustion and mind finally traveled on another journey. He was a fisherman setting sail to search for the day's catch, but the wind failed and after several hours under the beating sun he was blinded by the white-hot reflections off the water. He felt his parched tongue dry upon the roof of his mouth and the salt caked on his skin. Suddenly he knew he was alone: he looked around and saw his companions had deserted him, and felt a wave of fear well up. He looked to all four points of the horizon but there was no sign of land and his sails flapped aimlessly. He burst out into loud lamentations and cried out, but no one heard him. Delirious, he imagined sea demons rising up from the dark waters to devour him. The sky clouded over and the sea grew angry and fierce. It upended his small boat and he felt the cold, black water engulf him. His body tensed from the shock and he woke with a start in the bewildered blackness of his cell.

CHAPTER 25

PLAGUE

AS HE STEPPED OUT OF the cool Palazzo into the infernal heat, Niccolò wrapped the silk scarf over his mouth and nose. The piazza was empty except for the odd solitary figures scurrying by, swathed like Egyptian mummies. This week the dreaded devil's breath had finally exhaled in full force over the city, bringing with it unbearable heat and poisoned air. Already he had seen more than a half dozen of his neighbors' bodies borne away by the *becchini*.

As he crossed the piazza a sudden gust whipped up a small whirlwind that danced around the perimeter of the piazza and tossed dust into his eyes. He turned away to shelter his face. It was a mystery where the pestilence came from or how it traveled. Some supposed it was the crows circling overhead or the rats skittering from dark corner to dark corner, while others swore it was the gypsies and the Jews. But it was indiscriminant and when it arrived it drove people into fearful isolation. In this way Niccolò recognized it was a more serious calamity for the city than even military attack. Attack united the citizens against their foes; it was a fear that caused them to become stronger. But this plague ate away at them from within and divided them against themselves. Suspicion lurked behind every furtive glance as friends and neighbors abandoned each other to the scavengers. The only saving grace was it struck the same fear into their foreign enemies—no one would attack a plague-ridden city.

When Niccolò turned onto the Ponte Vecchio he noticed a small group of citizens hovering near the center of the bridge. As he drew closer he recognized the foreigner he had seen early one morning this week in the empty Piazza della Signoria. The mystic was sitting cross-legged covered in a black hooded cloak as he recited a strange verse:

"In the East, hard by Greater India, in a certain province, horrors and unheard of tempests overwhelmed the whole province. There was a rain of frogs, serpents, lizards, scorpions, and many venomous beasts. Then thunder was heard, and lightning and sheets of fire fell upon the earth, mingled with hailstones of marvelous size, which slew almost all. Then fire fell from heaven and stinking smoke, which slew the rest and burned up all the cities and towns in those parts. By these tempests the whole province was infected; the foul blast of wind that came from the South and has traveled West on the wind…"

The mystic's small audience kept their distance, their scarves pulled up over their faces.

"*Madonna mia*, it's God's wrath, just as the friar said."

"All the warning signs were there—the scourge of the French, the famine, the Pisan war—each time we were saved by the good friar, but many refused to listen to his warnings. Now we shall all suffer God's retribution."

The mystic raised his head, but his eyes were closed. "When the poison wind arrives the air is inhaled by good and evil ones alike."

"It's true, you know, even the holy priests are struck down."

Another scoffed, "What holy priests? Most of them light out at the first sight of a dead rat."

"But not all," said the first. "Many administer to the victims and even they, with their great faith, are not always spared. At San Marco, Fra Girolamo has created a sanctuary and he treats the afflicted himself. Several of the Sisters' convents do the same." He lowered his voice, "They say he administers the sacraments, even though he is excommunicate."

The mystic ignored the chatter and continued his oration: "Soon the wrath of the heavens will pour forth a deluge, hurling thunderous bolts over the earth, wreaking havoc and chaos upon the land. Fierce lightning will strike fear in the hearts of both man and beast. And the humble beasts will become wild and devour their own. Cattle and sheep will trample fields and meadows as shepherd dogs fight each another and turn on the lambs. Pigs gorging at the trough will explode their entrails in fear, while rivers shall rage and mountains shake and the tallest trees in the forest will tumble. Then the light of the sun will be blotted out from the sky and darkness will engulf all. Meanwhile, man, cowering in his fear, will try to hide himself in the shadows. Only then will the great Marduk come to slay the dragon Tiamet, cleaving her body in two: with one half to become the sky and the other half the earth. And finally the light shall shine down from the sky, chasing away the darkness, and only then will man be healed…"

"*Dio mio*, what's he's babbling about?" an old woman asked.

Before anyone could answer, clinking bells and the hollow call of the *becchini* scattered the gossipers, leaving the mystic without an audience. Niccolò continued on his way to the Oltrarno from where the *becchini* was approaching with his ill-fated cargo. These plague wagons drove through the city streets each day collecting the blackened, rotting bodies of victims abandoned by their fearful families. With victims now numbering more than sixty a day, the government recently had had to authorize the appointment of another contingent of *becchini* just to keep up. The diseased bodies were collected and heaped ingloriously in a pile, blessed by a brave cleric, and then buried in shallow mass graves outside the city walls, as it was the law no victims of the pestilence could be buried on hallowed ground. As he passed, Niccolò held his breath but could not close his ears to the haunting, jingling sound of death. He heard it almost constantly now, echoing down the empty streets at dawn.

They said it was a horrifying, ugly, merciless death. It struck suddenly, first with the appearance of fever and *buboes*—large boils in the groin or armpit areas—that hemorrhaged beneath the skin, creating blotchy black discolorations. After the fever wracked the victim for a day or two a momentary madness struck the mind before welcome death, all in a matter of days. For some the attack was even swifter—an apparently healthy person might cough up blood and fall dead before the day was out.

It was highly contagious, due to poisonous vapors escaping from the center of the earth or by contact with infected or unclean persons. They said even the mere gaze of an afflicted person could strike down a healthy one. The only course of action was quarantine. Those who could packed up their wagons and carriages and fled for their villas in the countryside, while those who remained suffered in isolation, praying for their slim chances of survival until the poison air cleared. The pestilence's most terrifying aspect in a crowded city was forcing one to face fear, and possibly death, forsaken and alone. It was a nightmarish end for a people most devoted to temporal beauty and social station.

***

At the Convent of San Marco a steady stream of victims arrived seeking comfort and last rites. The friars quarantined the sick in the Foresteria, a long corridor of guest rooms under the library. There they were ministered to by a few of the brothers, as well as several nuns who had come from their convents to aid the sick and dying.

The prioress of the Carmelite convent in Fiesole with several of her sisters and novices led the effort to treat those victims with a slight chance of surviving while Fra Girolamo administered *extreme unction* and comfort to those without hope. The dead were wrapped in shrouds and placed in the large cloister of San Domenico, behind the church and away from the dormitories, to await burial at the end of each day.

This evening, just before vespers, the friars gathered in the chapel to attend a funeral mass conducted for Fra Antonio da San Quintino, a middle-aged friar who had been stricken and died a painful death. Fra Girolamo delivered a heart-rending eulogy that brought tears to the eyes of the friars. Afterwards they sang plainchant and sacred hymns, ending with *ecce quam bonum*. After vespers and Compline the brothers gathered in the Great Refectory, as they had every evening for the past two weeks to perform a ritual reinforcing their faith.

In a large circle they sat cross-legged on the floor and followed Fra Bonifazio as he led them in hymns. As they sang, Fra Maurelio, the recently ordained natural brother of Fra Girolamo, entered dressed as Jesus in a flowing white robe and sandals and sat at the center of the circle. At the appointed signal the friars fell silent and those closest to 'Jesus' rose in turn and offered their hearts to the Savior in return for the granting of a favor in the form of a prayer. The first to rise this evening was Fra Benedetto, the miniaturist painter. Fra Benedetto begged for the salvation of the soul of Fra Antonio. This was followed by the other brothers reciting the names of each of those souls freed from their bodies this day. After these testimonials more hymns were sung and an icon of the Virgin Mary was brought in to sit next to 'Jesus.' The brothers prostrated themselves before the Blessed Virgin, calling her "Nostra Mama," and pleading again for the salvation of the souls recently departed. To end the ceremony, the friars stood up, linked hands and sang.

"My Brothers," said Fra Girolamo when they finished, "tonight will be our last night together…"

He raised his hands and hushed their exclamations and protestations to continue, "Only for a short while, until this pestilence has passed. Too many are exposed in the close quarters of the convent. For your safety and the good of the convent, I must ask you to leave and pass the time at our retreat in Monte Cano."

Despite their protestations, there was a thinly veiled collective sigh of relief.

"Prior, who will help with the sick and minister to the dying?"

"I will remain here where I belong. A small group of brothers and sisters will assist me."

"I'll stay, Prior!" shouted 'Jesus,' his younger brother Fra Maurelio.

Fra Girolamo shook his head and smiled at this son of his mother, a brother he hardly knew. He wondered if she were watching over them. "No, Brother Maurelio. There's much work to be done to prepare Monte Cano and I need you there. Almost all of you will pass the rest of the summer there. I'm sure by autumn the pestilence will have passed and you can then return to the convent. It's not far and your families will rest easier knowing you are safe. I, also, will rest easier knowing you're out of harm's way. Fra Roberto will be in charge at Monte Cano. Now let us sing once more together."

And the monks sang *ecce quam bonum* for the third time that hour.

CHAPTER 26

THE BIGI CONSPIRACY

TWO WEEKS PASSED AND SAN MARCO convent was deserted except for the few friars and Carmelite nuns tending to a dwindling number of plague victims. The Boys of the Friar were dispersed, with a few aspiring novices accompanying Silvestro to Monte Cano and the others mostly quarantined with their families. With insufficient staff to care for new victims, the prior directed the majority to various hospitals and plague houses around the city. These were places of scant hope from which few emerged except on the wagons of the *becchini*. But there was nothing more to be done—the convent could now minister only to a small number of clerics, local parishioners, and patrons.

The prioress came out of one of the cells in the Foresteria and saw Fra Girolamo with his Bible and crucifix in the hallway. She shook her head sadly.

"This one is coughing blood," she said, referring to a middle-aged matron of a wealthy family.

Fra Girolamo paused before entering the room. "We must send the last of your sisters back to Fiesole. It's too dangerous to remain here."

The prioress nodded in agreement. "Some of their families have made urgent requests for their daughters' welfare, especially the Corbinelli and Soderini for Sister Chiara. But still she refuses to leave. She inspires the others."

Over the past few weeks the young nun had surprised Fra Girolamo and touched him deeply. The niece of Paolantonio and Piero Soderini, she came from an illustrious Florentine *grandi* family. Yet, instead of retiring to the safe and luxurious existence that was her birthright, she had chosen to join the Order and devote her life to God. Without fear she tended to plague victims and assisted in the daily chores of the convent. She performed the most menial tasks without complaint, even with enthusiasm. Regarding her in her daily routine, he was confounded by the purity that often emerged, like a fresh spring lily, from the foulest of earthly soil. He cherished her presence, but was mindful of Signor Paolantonio's wishes.

"Tell her it is my wish she and the others leave for now."

"What of you and the others, Prior?"

"God would never forgive me if I were to abandon my duties here. Even though the Signoria has forbidden my preaching, there are those who come to the chapel or I can visit in their homes. The Lord's shepherd should never abandon his flock."

The prioress hesitated. "But if you should continue to administer the sacraments, the Roman Curia may make a case of blasphemy against you. And the excommunication extends to all who aid and assist you."

Fra Girolamo's eyes flashed coldly with the thought. "If it is God's will," he stated flatly. Then he warmed. "But then you and your sisters are also at risk here, yet you do not run from the dictates of your faith. Should God expect anything less from me?"

He entered the plague victim's room and saw the bedclothes stained with blood and sputum; the poor woman's face was blotchy, her eyes swimming in delirium. It would not be long. He laid the crucifix beside her and felt the consuming fire as he anointed her forehead. She was the God-fearing wife of a well-to-do merchant and mother, but in final moment it mattered not at all—all souls became as one. Suddenly he felt her grip on his arm, a desperate hold to save herself from falling into the void. It was the fear of loneliness in death, a final reckoning with the loneliness we all feel in life. He wondered: why this woman and not the next? Why now? Is it truly God's wrath? Has He condemned them all, or will He spare some? Fra Girolamo rebuked himself as he administered the sacrament—he must not question God's will, he must just do his duty.

Emerging moments later, he was met by a wild-eyed Silvestro.

"Prior, Messers Francesco Valori and Tommaso Tosinghi are waiting in the small refectory. There has been new treachery in the government—,"

Fra Girolamo did not wait for an explanation, but swept past Silvestro in mid-sentence. Entering the small refectory at the end of the hallway, he saw the two men standing there. Valori quickly stepped forward, agitated.

"Prior, we've come with important news."

Fra Girolamo motioned for them to sit. "Please. Brother Silvestro, go to the kitchen and have something brought to drink."

Valori continued: "As you know, we were commissioned to investigate whether citizens were secretly aiding Piero when he attacked the city in April. Last week we took two citizens into custody when they entered Florentine territory: Lamberto dell'Antella and his brother Alessandro. Upon questioning they told us they were in Siena with Piero and Lamberto had on his person a letter detailing a conspiracy of citizens to aid in overthrowing the Republic. It was a list of citizens Piero was expecting to rally to his cause. The Eight are holding the Antelle at the Bargello and further questioning has exposed several *Bigi* traitors."

The friar sensed the relish with which Valori condemned his *Bigi* enemies, but he needed the unadorned details. He had many questions. "Why do you believe this Lamberto is telling the truth and why have they turned against Piero?"

Valori was sure of himself. "The Antelle are bitter because Piero turned on them when they returned to Siena after their failed attack. Lamberto said Piero 'treated them worse than dogs,' requesting the Sienese throw them into the *Carnaio* dungeon. This should be of little surprise to those of us familiar with the arrogant fool. And four turns on the rack for Lamberto left little doubt of the veracity of his confession."

Fra Girolamo fell silent, imagining the unspeakable means of extracting such confessions from suspected traitors. Just then Silvestro returned with a carafe of water and several drinking cups he filled for the guests.

He continued with his questions: "Who were the conspirators?"

"They revealed several names, five of which have been apprehended by the Eight," said Tosinghi. "These are Gianozzo Pucci, Lorenzo Tornabuoni, Niccolò Ridolfi, Giovanni Cambi, and Bernardo del Nero."

The friar tried to register the names, anxious to learn the extent of the conspiracy. He was familiar with Pucci, Tornabuoni and del Nero, as all three had frequently attended his sermons and openly professed support for the reforms of the past three years. They had all given the impression they had abandoned the Mediceans to support the *Frateschi*. He was not familiar with the name Cambi, but Valori said he was a rich cloth merchant and probable client of the Medici bank. Ridolfi, the head of a large wealthy and extended Florentine family, had always stood aloof, but several of his relatives had joined the Dominican Order at San Marco.

Most astonishing was the elderly Bernardo del Nero, one of the most powerful and respected officials in the city. He had been the Gonfaloniere during the two-month period leading up to Piero's failed attack. The implications of these accusations left a momentary vacuum of silence.

Valori finally broke it with a triumphant tone: "This morning the traitors were arrested and imprisoned in the Bargello. The five will be questioned and put on trial—for treason. More were involved, but these five will serve as a warning. The *Bigi* will not raise their voices for a long time."

Tosinghi was more cautious: "Many problems remain concerning this affair, despite the support of the Signoria. The opposition parties will use confusion and fear to undermine the pursuit of justice."

But Valori jumped to his feet. "We must be vigilant and stamp out this treason!" he exclaimed. "The *Bigi* will use every tactic to save the traitors, only to betray the Republic at a later date."

Fra Girolamo felt a burning sensation behind his eyes and became disoriented. He was shocked and angered by the audacity of the conspirators who were so quick to betray their fellow citizens for personal gain. This brazen treachery was inherent in the Florentine character. But he also had a foreboding sense of the same fanatical lust for power among his own supporters, these *Frateschi*.

Feeling exposed, he became confused. For many months he had been struggling at nights with a weighty new treatise titled *The Triumph of the Cross* and he felt himself being torn in different directions. His thoughts wandered to the words of his treatise: *the chief aim of the Church is Justice and an irreprehensible and unspotted life...* and then to the words of the Christ: *ego veni ut vitam habent et abundantius habeant...*[9] He was surrounded by evil and wished to seek guidance in prayer.

Valori asked, "How many of the friars have remained here? Who's taking care of all the plague victims?"

When he responded his voice sounded drained and distant: "Only a few of us remain, I've instructed the nuns to return to Fiesole. We send the sick and dying to the hospitals of Santa Maria Nuova and Santa Maria degli Innocenti. Also to the plague houses of San Francesco and San Miniato."

As his eyes glassed over he heard Valori say: "Yes, may God grant their souls rest in peace." Then the two excused themselves.

At the door Valori turned and added, "The state, too, is like a hospital—if men were not morally ill we would have no need of it."

CHAPTER 27

CITY TURMOIL

IT WAS LATE AFTERNOON WHEN Cronaca entered Del Corno's tavern. The interior was dark as usual but offered a cool respite from the relentless mid-summer heat. It was mostly empty due to the fear of plague and the builder wearily deposited himself at a table of his fellow artisans. The group had dwindled with the recent death of Benedetto da Maiano and the self-imposed seclusion of Simone and Sandro Botticelli.

"*Madonna,* my bones ache and my head splits under the cursed weight of the House of Strozzi," said Cronaca. "Give me something…a reason to live." He reached out to fill a goblet from the communal wine jug in the center of the table.

Lorenzo di Credi retorted, "You're going to die and assuredly go to heaven for your troubles. But only if you stop whining about your circumstances, for the Lord is testing you."

"*Merda,* why don't you just throw me to the *becchini.* Poor Benedetto, I miss his steady mood and industrious talents. I don't know where I'll find another with as much skill to finish the gables and porticos." He glanced at Granacci. "Except maybe young Buonarotti. When's he returning, Francesco?"

Francesco held up his hands in a gesture of futility. "To what? The only thing here is pestilence, starvation, a barren city, and government officials who fight like dogs for the privilege of taxing us to a slower but surer death. Besides, he's written me about several commissions in Rome. He's been put off by Cardinal Riario but is carving a marble Bacchus for a wealthy banker. And there's talk of a commission for a *Pietà* for a French cardinal's tomb that will surely take a couple of years. I have his letter here. I received it two days ago and he begs me to write him news from Florence." Francesco reached under his tunic to bring out the folded letter.

"A marble Bacchus!" exclaimed Lorenzo, raising his glass in a toast. "And here we only get to commemorate Bacchus by indulging him everyday. Tell us, what does our young friend say of Rome?"

Francesco read out passages of the letter:

> "My dear Francesco, I've not had a letter from you in some months and I'm eager to hear news. We only receive rumors, but foreigners and Romans are exceedingly hostile to

Florentines who live and do business here. The infernal city has been in turmoil since the murder of the pope's son, but nothing has yet come of either the crime or the proposed reform. Meanwhile, the pope grants pardons and plenary indulgences by the wagonload. As the local wags quote him: 'It is not God's wish that a sinner should die, but that he should live—and pay and pay.' We've heard of the excommunication of Fra Girolamo. Here Fra Mariano is preaching against him, declaring that he deliberately violates the Bull of Excommunication. Cardinal Giovanni is more restrained, but rumors have it he lobbies the pope incessantly for his brother and his family's position.

Travelers say the pestilence is ravaging Florence this summer and I worry for my family. Now and again I receive letters from Buonarotto but it would comfort me greatly if you could visit them and send me word."

Francesco scanned down the letter. "Here he describes the Bacchus he's carving for the banker, a large figure with a smaller satyr. There's a small sketch." Francesco passed it around so the others could admire his friend's handiwork.

"Yes," said Cronaca, "this is the man I need to finish the Palazzo Strozzi."

"Unfortunately," said Francesco, "I'll advise him to stay in Rome. With the arrest of the Grays, things will surely get worse. There are better opportunities there—I almost wish I could go myself."

Cronaca shook his head. "A Tornabuoni, Ridolfi and del Nero tried for treason. Blood will boil and spill with *la vendetta*... and the rest of us as frightened as chickens under the axe."

Piero di Cosimo chuckled. "I thought the peasants would die of fright when the moon passed in front of the sun last week—a sign the end of the world was at hand. No wonder my Triumph of Death scares them silly every year."

Lorenzo stood up. "I think we need another bottle of Trebbiano, *amici*."

***

Across the river there was a frantic pounding on the front door of the Machiavelli house. With the family and house servants away in the country to avoid the plague, Niccolò opened the door to find a distraught Tommaso Soderini.

"*Grazie a Dio,* you're here," Tommaso gasped.

"What is it? *Avanti…*"

"It's Fiammetta… I don't know what to do, she's fallen ill. I'm afraid. She's at my family house, quarantined from the others. Chiara has come to care for her, but I fear the worse. *Madonna mia,* now I can find good reason to pray."

Niccolò noticed Tommaso had avoided the word expressing his worst fear—the pestilence. He escorted him into the sitting room where the shutters were all flung open, though there was not a whisper of fresh air to provide relief from the heat. Niccolò felt a deep sense of helplessness for his friend. He also shuddered when he realized how much Chiara was at risk. Somehow, her being locked away in a convent had given him a false sense of satisfaction for his own mixed emotions. His feelings surprised him, as he had not seen or thought of her for months. He was at a loss for words. "I'll get some wine," he said.

"I don't know what to do," said Tommaso. "It's so sudden. She became feverish last night and today the fever's worse. She won't let me see her and I fear the buboes… What can I do, *Dio mio…*" He grasped his head.

Niccolò offered Tommaso the wine. "It's out of our hands now, as our precious life always is. Perhaps it's not the worst if there's no sign of blood in the lungs or buboes. Also, many survive, the young and strong have a better chance. Chiara will give her care and perhaps her devotions will now bear some fruit."

"But she won't let me near… And there's more—my cousin, Lorenzo. My father and uncles fear the conspirators will be tried for treason. It's fairly certain they're guilty, but my uncles don't wish to inflict any lasting pain on the Tornabuoni."

"It's likely they'll only be exiled for a time."

"But Uncle Piero fears tempers in the Signoria will demand the death penalty. First my brothers, now my wife, my cousin…" Tommaso dropped his head in his hands.

"We must do what we can to see that cooler heads prevail," said Niccolò, knowing this was easier said than done. Managing the impulsive behavior of the Great Council and the actions of the Signoria was proving to be a complex and delicate task; one could never be sure when the Fates would cast the best laid plans awry. The *Bigi* were opposed to the Whites, but blood was thicker than politics. "What does Signor Piero suggest?"

"He believes Lorenzo is least culpable and may benefit from an appeal for clemency. Del Nero is the most egregious offender since he was Gonfaloniere and failed to report the conspiracy in order to defend the Republic. But my father says the *Frateschi*, especially Valori and his faction are furious to make an example, particularly of del Nero."

Niccolò was sanguine. He remembered the clever trap Vespucci had laid with the law of appeal. This might now help the conspirators. He explained to Tommaso, hoping to lift his spirits. "Under the right of appeal any judgment imposed by the Eight can be appealed to and overturned by the Great Council. The right of appeal was originally the friar's proposal, so it will be impossible for the *Frateschi* to oppose it. And since the Angry Ones cleverly made the appeal apply to the entire Great Council, it's unlikely the severest penalty will be imposed—more likely, confusion and compromise will result. The five come from powerful families too well-respected to be condemned, though this means any further support for the Medici will be dealt with severely."

Tommaso had drifted into silence and Niccolò knew his thoughts had returned to Fiammetta and the impossibility of waiting for God or Fate to determine his future happiness. If Fiammetta died Tommaso's whole future would change—the Strozzi connection would be lost as well as the enormous dowry. But Niccolò suspected Tommaso was not thinking of this and he felt guilty for his callous calculations and inability to comfort his friend.

As he sat there it struck him how his countrymen's love of family and kin was both a blessing and a curse. In ancient Rome the family was sacrificed for the good of the state, and in return citizens received honor and glory. But now the rulers of Italia were quick to sacrifice the state to the temporary advantage of their families, and there was no honor or glory in it, only love for a fragile life.

He wondered how things had changed—whether a weakened state had caused stronger blood ties or, vice versa, stronger blood ties had weakened the state.

CHAPTER 28

THE SIGNORIA DELIBERATES

NICCOLÒ SENSED THE TENSION FILLING the Hall of Two Hundred as the Signoria waited to hear the Eight pronounce the verdict on the five conspirators. The trial had taken place over the past three days under the aegis of the Eight assisted by two advisory councils of twelve additional citizens. The charge of treason was taken seriously and the evidence presented had been damning. Lamberto dell'Antella testified to a widespread plot in which Piero de' Medici was to have been smuggled into the city while many of the citizens were away in the country to escape the heat and the plague. Piero had planned to arouse a popular revolt against the government by distributing food and money to the poor and then inciting them to ransack the houses of the rich.

There was little doubt some form of a guilty verdict was warranted, but there was still the question of the degree of guilt and the appropriate sentence. The *grandi* families, many of whom were linked by marriage, were up in arms over the prosecution while defenders of the Republic were demanding the severest penalties. As a participant on one of the advisory councils, Piero Soderini had made a strong case arguing for Lorenzo Tornabuoni and Niccolò Ridolfi, who were only guilty of association and not directly involved in treasonous acts.

Hence, there were those who desired to free the five, those who wished to condemn them wholesale, and others who wished to split the difference. It was a judgment worthy of Solomon and despite the pestilence, the city streets swelled with citizens clamoring to defend their interests and peasants flocking in to witness the proceedings. In response, the Signoria was forced to mobilize the guards of the Palazzo as well as the troops of several mercenary captains to insure civic order. Niccolò again noted the conflict between family and state in city politics—this would be a ferocious battle with potentially deadly consequences.

Niccolò tried to decipher the temper of the magistrates. The Eight of the Guard appeared uncomfortable and daunted, trying to hide their apprehension at inciting the hatred of so many powerful families, no matter what the verdict. They avoided direct eye contact and whispered among themselves. Among the nine members of the Signoria, it was apparent the eight priors were evenly split for and against the prisoners, with Gonfaloniere Bartoli tipping the balance against. But according to law, a total of six votes were required to carry any measure.

The meeting was finally called to order and Bartoli requested the Chief Magistrate of the Eight to pronounce their verdict.

"Your Excellencies," said the magistrate, rising amid a pregnant silence. "We, the Eight, regret to say we are unable to pronounce a verdict in this matter—,"

The room buzzed and Bartoli cut in loudly, "*Che*? Unable or unwilling?"

"Excellency, we are unable to comply and we beseech Your Excellencies as Priors of Liberty to assume the responsibilities of our office in this case..."

There was a wave of grumbling among the priors as Bartoli replied, "You know this would be in violation of the constitution. The Ministry of the Eight is charged with the administration of justice in criminal matters and actions against persons of the state. Is there some question about the evidence?"

As the Eight conferred in whispers in lieu of a direct reply, Niccolò knew everyone was acutely aware of the problem: the evidence was plain but any verdict would split the city in two and invite violence of one form or the other. Perhaps splitting the difference would be the best result.

Gonfaloniere Bartoli spoke again to break the impasse: "According to the law giving the right of appeal, the defense may submit the case to the decision of the Great Council, which constitutes the supreme Court of Appeal."

There was a nodding of agreement among the Eight as they sensed a narrow escape. Niccolò surmised such a tactic would bog down the proceedings in the anarchy of the three thousand-member body and would favor the defendants. Then the chattering lawyers for the defense jumped up and the lead counsel requested to speak.

"The defense is strongly opposed to an appeal to the Great Council on the grounds it would be unwise to communicate the secrets of the state to so great a multitude. We also believe it is unnecessary to run the risk of so many different opinions when the verdict of the principal magistrates should suffice."[10]

"All well and good, but we have failed here to reach a satisfactory verdict," said Bartoli with evident sarcasm. He turned and conferred with several of the other priors.

Niccolò was taken back: apparently the defense wished to obfuscate and delay the decision. A new Signoria would be elected in less than two weeks and it was a good bet the balance of opinion, with the crucial six votes, would shift in favor of the defendants. They were gambling on each day as another reprieve for the five.

Finally Bartoli turned to address the assembly. "The lack of a verdict and the inability of the Eight to reach a satisfactory verdict forces the Signoria to convene a new Pratica to be held two days hence."

The members buzzed, forcing Bartoli to raise his voice over the din. "This new Pratica will be a Pratica *larga* and will consist of the sixteen gonfalonieri of the Companies, the Twelve Good Men, the Ten of War, the Eight of the Guard, the officials of the Monte, and the Council of Eighty."

The assembly erupted in pandemonium as everyone rushed for the exits. Niccolò saw Valori was enraged, recognizing the bald tactics of the Grays. The Pratica Bartoli described would be an unwieldy mob of almost two hundred persons and the likelihood of reasoned compromise was non-existent. But there would be adequate cover for individual responsibility. The defendants would live to see another day and share another dance with Fortuna. Why care for principles of justice when one can gamble and find safety in numbers? Such were the ways of Florentine 'democracy.'

CHAPTER 29

SISTER CHIARA VISITS SAN MARCO

FRA GIROLAMO COULD NOT KEEP his wearied mind from wandering in the languid afternoon heat. The convent was quiet, the plague had abated and the friars were not due back from Monte Cano for several more days. Forbidden to preach these past few months by order of the Signoria and under excommunication, he felt alone and isolated. In addition, he was distracted by this trial of traitors.

To refocus his efforts he had poured his energy into this treatise, *The Triumph of the Cross*, with its pages splayed across his desk. It was a detailed explication of the Christian life, a comprehensive clarification of faith and a guide for human action. But the work was a struggle. How was one to proselytize on the Christian life demonstrated by the example of Christ the Crucified, in the face of the relentless nature of man? He felt besieged on all sides—by the pope and the Roman prelates, by the city's enemies, by the tyrants entrenched in the Palazzo, even by his own lukewarm brethren and congregation. What were the lessons gained by Christ's sacrifice? He reviewed his words:

> *I undertake to defend the glorious triumph of the Cross against the impious volubility of the sophists and wise men of the world…*

This enterprise is bold and beyond my strength, he said to himself, and it was true. He had labored to provide the proofs of faith and the knowledge of the one true God. He renounced the efforts of the philosophers but realized, in looking over his own painstaking arguments he had resorted to those same powers of human reason he deemed insufficient. He was attempting the impossible: *to use reason to prove faith and disprove reason.*

Like all men he was a prisoner of his body—feeble and weak. This was why he must have faith, which God bestows on man through grace alone. This was why he must finish this treatise to aid all men in their struggle with the cruel contradictions of earthly life: *that our nature demands that we know what we cannot and that we understand that which cannot be understood.* But he could not help feeling he had failed.

He grasped the crucifix in his hands. Looking into the eyes of the Savior, he prayed: You died to save mortal men from such failures and in this You provided the only hope for all mankind. Christian faith and the example of the crucified Son of God is the cause of the perfect life and

349

the redemption of the helpless sinner's existence...

A knock interrupted his prayers and he laid down the crucifix. It was his new secretary.

"Excuse me Prior, you have a visitor. Sister Chiara, the young nun who administered to the plague victims, has returned and wishes to speak with you."

"*Grazie*. Please instruct her to wait in the cloister. I shall be down shortly." His heart gladdened in anticipation, though he wondered what brought the young nun to San Marco. Stepping out into the cloister he felt the heavy heat of the sun and saw the white-habited nun sheltered in the shade admiring one of the frescoed lunettes of Fra Angelico. It was the *Pietà*.

"My child, it brings me great pleasure to see you again."

Sister Chiara turned and bowed without looking into his eyes. "Father, I wish the circumstances of my visit were more...pleasant," she said, fumbling for words.

Fra Girolamo's joy gave way to concern. "Please, let us retire to the Chapter House where it's cooler. Tell me what troubles you, child."

"Father..." She struggled to speak with restraint but was overcome. "It's my cousin, Lorenzo Tornabuoni, who is on trial for the conspiracy with Piero de' Medici, who I must confess is also my cousin."

Fra Girolamo was taken back. He knew the young woman was a member of the respected Corbinelli family and was the niece of Paolantonio and Piero Soderini. But he had never made the connection to the Medici. Like most of the former Mediceans, the Soderini had renounced their association with Piero after he fled into exile.

"Father, my cousin is a well-respected citizen and the Tornabuoni are a dear relation of my family—my grandmother was Signora Dianora Tornabuoni. My father and uncles say cousin Lorenzo was unwisely associated with the conspiracy of the Grays, but he took no direct part. My uncle Piero argued this in the trial, but to little effect. The virtues of Christian charity and forgiveness are not widely shared in the Palazzo."

Fra Girolamo was pained. Valori had briefed him on the trial and he had become incensed over the Mediceans' attempts to harm the Republic and undo his work.

"I'm aware of these events, but I'm not sure what I can do. I cannot meddle in matters of the state and you know I am under the sanction of the Church."

"Father, I only ask that you speak out for the right of appeal, as you did so eloquently when it passed two years ago."

He felt a distaste rise in his throat and felt himself stiffen. He got up from his chair to pace and avoid the young nun's gaze. His response was dry.

"The affairs of government are more complex than we are led to understand. The enemies of liberty seek only to use the laws to manipulate justice to their own ends. I understand when the Gonfaloniere offered an appeal to the Great Council it was rejected by their defense. After, a large Pratica of almost two hundred of the most respected citizens was convened, and when they determined a guilty verdict the defense quickly changed course. Now they seek the right of appeal they formerly rejected. Can you see how they only seek to disrupt the pursuit of justice?"

The young nun broke down in tears, further perplexing him. Overwhelmed, she spoke through her sobs: "I don't know, I don't understand. I just know my cousin Tommaso and I cannot bear the loss of our cousin Lorenzo. There is so much death, not again, not so soon..."

Fra Girolamo was ashamed of the coldness of his manner. He reached out to touch her but pulled his hand back. "What is it, child? What troubles you?"

"My sister, ...my friend, ...died last week of the pestilence. She was the wife of my cousin, Tommaso. It was...it was...horrible. I cared for her, I watched as the disease ravaged her, her beautiful face and her skin." Chiara raised her watery eyes to look into those of the prior.

"When she was in pain she asked me, 'Why is this happening to me? What did I do?' I told her the Lord had special reasons we cannot understand, and we must pray..."

She closed her eyes and dropped her head, shaking it from side to side. "But I didn't believe it and I don't believe it now. My faith is—,"

"Child!" He cried sharply to stop her from blaspheming. She looked up again.

"They were married only two years, Father. She was only twenty-five years; she was trying to have a child. And I loved her like my sister. Tommaso is in shock, he cannot eat or sleep and now this... this executioner's axe hanging over the head of another close to us."

Fra Girolamo was conflicted. He wanted to reach out to comfort the distraught girl, but could not. His mind reverted to thoughts of his own. He knew this girl she spoke of, she was the one he saw at the convent— that breath of life, so full of temptation. But she wasn't the temptress of his youth. She wasn't the one who had scorned him—the arrogant, bastard daughter of an exiled Strozzi, who had laughed at him and belittled his family name. This one was innocent and he felt shame and compassion. He sat down to try to comfort the young nun.

"I beg you, Father. This is our only hope. Speak out ...for the justice of appeal. Tommaso says if you spread your word of support to the people the Signoria will be compelled to grant it."

He did not reply. Valori had warned him of dangerous plots against the Republic, of Medicean sympathizers who sought to recapture power and reverse the reforms he struggled so hard to enact. Valori was right: The Florentine tyrants were relentless and the people were easily deceived. The agents of Milan and Rome were in league with these traitors, waiting for any weakness or disorder to strike a blow against Florentine liberty. To the *grandi,* liberty was the pestilence that gave hope to the poor. It was a threat to their hold on power, a threat to the established order of things. "We must give no ground," Valori had said and reminded Fra Girolamo of his own words to "cut off the heads" of tyrants and those who would aid them. These men were traitors and they were out to destroy him and the peoples' faith in God. There was unrepentant evil in the world and it must be cast out. He could not yield.

"Sister, I remind you the Holy Father has forbidden me to preach to my congregation. As for an epistle, you've seen the pamphlets fluttering in the streets—for and against the conspirators—mine would be just one more leaf in the wind. And, as a religious, it would compromise my vows to appear so directly involved in the affairs of state."

"But you have spoken out before, in your sermons. And many others have already spoken for the appeal, including Maestro Ficino and Messer Guidantonio Vespucci—,"

The friar held up his hand to silence the girl. Marsilio Ficino had ceased to visit San Marco, preferring so he said, to rest and study at his villa in Montevecchio. But Benivieni reported in recent months Maestro Ficino had become more critical, refusing to support the moral reforms, and attacking him in private councils. As for Vespucci, well…he was truly the devil.

"My child, Messer Vespucci is eloquent with words but his intentions are plain: he would embrace Satan himself if he thought it would serve his purpose. When I refuted the notion that states are not ruled by paternosters, I meant the state requires the moral guidance of faith, not that men of God should become involved in worldly matters…" He stopped suddenly when he heard his own words. Did he truly believe it anymore? Everything was becoming lost in a fog.

"But Tommaso—," she pleaded.

"I think perhaps your cousin overestimates my influence. The *popolani* are determined to defend the liberty of the Republic."

Chiara's voice became bitter. "Father, to me all this talk of *libertà* is false. With my own eyes I've seen how these men are all the same. Vespucci, Valori, Albizzi, Tosinghi, Spini – all men who grasp for more."

"Even your uncles?"

The nun paused, self-conscious of her youthful passion and bias. "Father, I'm young and not wise but I follow your teachings faithfully. I remember most the words of love for Jesus and the Virgin Mary. Since taking my vows to serve Our Lord Jesus Christ I've learned much from the sacrifice of our Savior. If we are unable to forgive our enemies, hatred will consume our hearts and souls. Then what will God make of us?"

Fra Girolamo felt a sharp pain and closed his eyes as he stood up. "My child," he whispered, "God is the breath of life. He is the still, small voice in all of us."

He walked over to a cabinet and took out a handful of printed pamphlets. These were some of his voluminous collections of writings, his short epistles to the faithful. He shuffled through them until he found the one he wanted.

"My daughter, I believe you are wiser than many of the blind old men who lead us. But often prayer is our only recourse. Please take this to help you through these troubled times. I will do what I can to recommend clemency for your cousin, but I fear I've little influence over these matters."

Through eyes red with tears, Sister Chiara read the title of the pamphlet: *Ten Rules For Praying in a Time of Great Distress.* The words on paper pained her like the lash on a flagellant. She thought again of Fiammetta and the tears started to flow. She raised her head, stared into the friar's dark eyes, and whispered, "Why?"

He knew he had no words, no answer for her. But he willed a surge of righteousness, knowing God's will would be done.

CHAPTER 30

TRIAL AND EXECUTION

NICCOLÒ PUSHED HIS WAY BACK through the crowd packing the Hall of Two Hundred to take his seat next to the Second Chancellor. During the brief recess circles of overdressed men had vehemently struggled to pronounce their various opinions, creating little more than a cacophony of semi-ordered mayhem. It seemed every ministry and administrative office was represented in the room. This was the high theater of the absurd and no one in the city wished to miss an act. Even the Piazza outside had been overflowing with crowds all day with more than three hundred foot soldiers called out to keep the peace.

The Practica of two days ago had resulted in a guilty verdict on charges of treason, so the defense had reversed itself and requested an appeal. As expected, the Grays argued the convenient rhetoric of "democracy, liberty and absolute sovereignty of the people," as represented in the Great Council—the body they had previously done their best to eradicate. The prosecutors belittled their obvious hypocrisy. They stated the previous Pratica *larga* had already pronounced a guilty verdict and the defense tactics were only to delay until a new Signoria was elected. This would only give the Republic's enemies more opportunity to organize another assault. To support their case, ambassadorial dispatches and private letters had been read out before the last recess asserting the enemies of Florence were plotting at this moment in Milan and Rome to aid in the overthrow of the Republic.

Across the room Niccolò saw the worried looks of the Soderini seated at the benches of the Eighty—their plea for Lorenzo Tornabuoni was in jeopardy. A death penalty for all the conspirators would be a crushing blow so soon after the death of Fiammetta but neither Piero nor Paolo could press their case for fear of retribution. And Paolo had refused to press the friar to speak out for the appeal, denouncing it for the naked political ploy it was. Niccolò was not sure the *popolo* would grasp this subtlety; on the face of it the *Arrabbiati* were calling the friar the hypocrite.

It was nearing midnight and the decision was stalemated, the priors again split four to four. Niccolò had spent the last two hours drawing circles on his notepad while the crowds outside, resigned to the disappointment no final decision was forthcoming, had quietly faded away.

To call the assembly to order the president, Luca Martini, hammered his gavel for another roll of the various ministries. The spokesman for the neighborhood gonfalonieri rose first to declare the sentencing should proceed without delay. But then he equivocated by saying some in his group were still disposed to concede the right of appeal.

The spokesman for the Ten of Liberty loudly rejected this opinion: "The greater disturbance you make in the city, the better you will assist our enemies' designs. It's clear all the princes of Italia have plotted against us and Rome is the center of every intrigue. The object of the desired appeal is not to learn the will of the people, which has already been expressed, but merely to gain time, and invoke foreign aid."

In quick order each official body expressed the same opinion, but also deferred to any decision decided upon by the Signoria. However, the Signoria remained split. Then Bartoli spoke, advocating caution, which was the time-tested survival tactic of representative government. Niccolò was dismayed—it was like watching turtles stick their necks out and then quickly pull back into their shells. Sure the final verdict and sentencing would be delayed again, Niccolò caught himself beginning to yawn.

In an instant, Francesco Valori sprang forward from behind his bench and rushed the magistrates, throwing official etiquette to the wind. In a fury he seized the ballot box and rapped it violently on the table. The assembly snapped to attention as he shouted: "Let justice be done, or there will be a revolt!"

The resulting uproar supported Valori's boldness and Niccolò looked hastily at Piero and Paolantonio Soderini but their expressions betrayed no emotion. Luca Martini hesitated, but Valori stared him down, forcing him to put the question again to the vote of the nine magistrates. Again the vote was five against the appeal and four in favor. But Valori vehemently stood his ground.

"Why then have your Excellencies summoned all these citizens, who every one of them, as recorded by the notary, has already voted against these plotters?" He waved his hand around the Hall. "Have not all present confirmed their vote? Do you not hear the universal cry of all who care to insure the public safety?"

He paused to gather restraint.

"Your Excellencies should remember you are placed here by the people for the purpose of defending the liberty of Florence. If you betray your duty in order to favor traitorous citizens, you may be sure there will be others to defend so just and holy a cause, to the peril of all who are opposed to it."

It was a bald threat and Niccolò watched the priors squirm. He sensed a change as the room became silent as a tomb. Valori grabbed the ballot box again and forced it on Martini, who solemnly pronounced a new vote and passed the ballot box to each of the priors and the Gonfaloniere.

When he read out the vote this time it was unanimous—all nine votes found against the accused. Martini pronounced the verdict to the stunned audience: "Seeing that the councils and reports of the magistrates, the Senate, and other citizens are all in favor of execution; and seeing that delay would lead to greater peril and disturbance, it is hereby ordained that without delay, this same night, the Council of Eighty shall put to death the five citizens upon whom they have already pronounced sentence in this meeting."

Niccolò was shocked—they had caved in to Valori's intimidation. Again a sacrifice was to be offered to save the majority. Before anyone could recover, the sentence—death by beheading and confiscation of all property of the condemned—was pronounced and the prisoners consigned to the Eight. The prisoners—dazed, barefoot, and chained— were led out of the Hall to be delivered to the Bargello. As they passed, the rage and scorn of the crowd was heaped upon them.

***

After a hasty word with Piero Soderini and a quick stop in his office, Niccolò raced across to the Oltrarno. He must warn Tommaso. It was after midnight and everyone was asleep except for Tommaso, who was waiting for his uncle and father to return from the Palazzo. When Niccolò told him the news he was crushed; on top of his grieving for Fiammetta, it was the final blow. As they raced back across the city to the Bargello, Niccolò heard him venting his anger and pain by cursing Valori and the friar.

When they arrived at the Bargello, the gathering crowd was steaming with passion, both for and against the verdict. Armed guards ringed the courtyard, which teemed with curses and insults like the pit in the ninth circle of the Inferno. Niccolò felt the hair on his skin rise as he remembered past instances of civil chaos—once released, there was no restraining the beast in man. He tried to calm Tommaso as those in the courtyard were armed and tensions against the *grandi* families were running high.

The scene unfolded slowly, like a Greek tragedy. Each of the condemned, accompanied by a criminal judge and a confessor, was led out to take his place at the executioner's block. Del Nero was first, holding his head high with an air of defiance before kneeling and placing it on the block. This unrepentant demonstration incited the crowd to curse his betrayal as the executioner's axe swung.

"This is all the work of Valori," Tommaso hissed. "The bastard hides his ambitions under the frocks of priests." Niccolò put a hand on his arm, but Tommaso would not be restrained.

"And the friar, what did he do to prevent this vengeance? He crows about justice, but only when it serves his purpose."

One of a group of wide-eyed toughs armed with small swords glanced sharply at them, trying to distinguish Tommaso's loyalties. Niccolò guessed they were *Arrabbiati* but nevertheless elbowed Tommaso deliberately as a warning not to attract attention. Valori and his supporters had carried the day and there was little to gain by inciting more vengeful acts. Niccolò tried to assuage his friend: "Tomorrow is another day and the boldness of this act will not be forgotten."

Ridolfi and then Cambi were led out to meet their fate. As Niccolò witnessed the axe fall and each severed head roll off the block, he couldn't silence a silly little couplet running through his head:

Treason doth never prosper, what's the reason?
Why, if it prosper, none dare call it treason.

He had mixed feelings and betrayed no emotion. He was gratified to see the traitors punished severely—even Livy had condemned his own sons to death for conspiring with the enemy and this fate was certainly deserved by the traitor del Nero. But he also sympathized with the Soderini in their desire to save their kinsman, who was not a bad sort. Death was final.

Next on the executioner's block was the youthful Gianozzo Pucci, who elicited some sympathy with his sorrowful expression of regret, but to no avail. Last came Lorenzo. A cultured and respected member of the *grandi,* he split the crowd neatly between pro- and anti-Medicean factions and when he laid his head upon the block, Tommaso turned away.

"What will I tell Chiara?" he said when he heard the axe fall and the thud of the severed head.

With the conclusion of this tragedy, the families of the condemned men were left to collect the bodies as the satiated crowd slowly retreated into the darkness. It was now the middle of the night, close to the hour of Matins. Niccolò was tired. The long day had shaken them all and the repercussions would be felt for weeks, months, even years, to come. A deliberate injustice, committed out of vengeance under the guise of civic duty, was an affront that could never be forgotten in the Florentine collective memory. The executions had deeply cleaved the divide again, and vengeance would be demanded. It was a cycle that played itself out again and again, until all were exhausted. Or dead.

CHAPTER 31

CONFRONTATIONS

AS THE CONGREGATION TRICKLED OUT of the Duomo, the young brother asked, "Fra Silvestro, What will we do with the rest? Almost everyone has left."

They were handing out printed copies of the prior's new treatise, *The Triumph of the Cross,* after the sermon delivered by Fra Domenico. Fra Girolamo was still under sanction of the excommunication and had preached only a few times in the six months since, and then only in San Marco.

"We'll wait for Fra Domenico, Benedetto. Then we'll distribute the rest at San Marco after the evening service. More of the faithful come to the convent these days than here."

They asked only for donations in return for the pamphlet, but Silvestro's purse was light. After the Bigi execution, attendance had declined precipitously. Fra Benedetto did not voice his concerns, but he was troubled nonetheless. The double jolt of the excommunication and the execution had cast a pall over the convent. The prior appeared tired and distracted, sequestering himself in his dormitory cell for days. Exhorted daily by Domenico and Silvestro, the majority of the brothers stood fast, but the wariness and censure of the citizens were difficult to bear. The younger friars had grown uncertain and impressionable, and already Fra Malatesta and Fra Roberto had begun again to question Fra Girolamo's authority.

Fra Silvestro scowled and pointed across the Piazza San Giovanni. "Benedetto," he said, "take care, here come the Mad Dogs." He whispered under his breath, "*Bastardi…*"

"Hey Maruffi! Bettuccio!" It was their nemesis, Doffo Spini, accompanied by several of his hangers-on. Among them Benedetto spied Paolo Soderini's son, Tommaso. "How's business?" said Spini, "Not so good, eh?"

"Doffo, don't make trouble," warned Fra Benedetto.

"Ah, my friend, I could create no more mischief than your hypocrite friar. What convenient lies is he spreading now?"

"You *ruffiani* are Satan's lap dogs," snapped Silvestro. "You'll be damned by your disrespect for all things holy."

"*Basta*, Maruffi, you wild-eyed loon. Are you dreaming again, telling your prior all sorts of nonsense?"

The others jeered, encouraging Spini to bait Silvestro. "Your false prophet's days are numbered. Have you noticed how few of your followers attend the Masses and heed your incessant barking? The pope branded him a heretic and everyone can now see he's just a puppet of Valori and the other *Frateschi*. When Valori goes..."

Spini ominously drew his finger across his throat.

Silvestro became hysterical, his wandering eye making him appear deranged as he cried: "Lies! Have you heard the Carmelite who confirmed the prophecies? God revealed to him Fra Girolamo is a holy man. Whoever has resisted him and spoken ill of his divine work, whether Signori, monks, or great *maestri*, their tongues will be torn out and thrown to the dogs!"

"Another fantasy of a drunken monk. Do you think we're all crazy like you, Maruffi?"

Fra Benedetto stepped forward to shelter the older friar from Spini's abuse. "Doffo, I said don't cause trouble."

Spini smiled and relaxed. "My good Bettuccio, you've lost your sense of humor. This holy fever has addled your brain. You know as well as I your good friar has revealed his hand, and it's neither clean nor pure. Our good friend Soderini here can tell you, since you murdered his cousin. And the excommunication—will you defy your vows to obey the Church and the Holy Father?"

Fra Benedetto extended a copy of the friar's treatise. "Doffo, perhaps you and your companions should read this to save you from your ignorance. You will see there is nothing remotely heretical or hypocritical about Fra Girolamo's teachings. Please take it, no donation is required in the service of truth."

Spini refused the pamphlet. "I don't care to read fables."

He withdrew his hand from underneath his cloak and tossed a small coin on top of the pamphlet. "Here, take this *grosso* instead, since you don't care to profit by my advice."

The troop of young men walked off, laughing among themselves.

Fra Benedetto turned to Silvestro. "Forgive their ignorance, Brother. It's a contagion in our city."

***

In his dormitory cell Fra Girolamo pressed his hands into his face and rubbed his eyes to keep himself awake through the night. His exhausted body refused to respond as he opened his eyes again to look up at the crucifix. His fingers grasped each other in a tight embrace as he prayed:

Lord, show me the way.

But his inner vision was lost. Valori had triumphed and the traitors purged, but the friar still suffered the greater peril of excommunication. He asked himself what more could he do? He had written the Holy Father again to beg forgiveness. He justified his actions in detail—he was falsely accused and the excommunication unjust—and swore allegiance to the Holy Mother Church. After two months he still had received no reply. Nothing had changed.

Then Valori said the Signoria had received dispatches from their ambassador in Rome stating Alexander refused to rescind the excommunication at this time. Instead the pope had issued a new brief with a different offer: the pope would grant Florence the return of Pisa and would also rescind the excommunication if the city would denounce the French alliance and join the Holy League.

It was another blatant political maneuver and was summarily refused, as the pope sought only to weaken both his adversaries by severing their alliance. The *Frateschi* controlled the Signoria these past months and Valori assured him the Signoria and the Ten would continue to reject any treaty offers that depended on trust of the Roman Curia.

Lord, this world is truly a dangerous, sinful place. You give Satan too much sway. How can I obey this pirate in whom you have entrusted the keys of St. Peter?

The friar continued to pray, but he stood poised over a precipice. How could he defy Holy Mother Church? How could the excommunicant be welcomed into Heaven? I am deprived of the Holy Sacraments—why, why does Rome attack me in this way? Have I strayed, Lord, from my mission to bring forth the Word and save souls?

Then he exhorted himself as he did to the multitude from the pulpit and his anger took form: No, his trials had nothing to do with faith and belief—not a bit! The princes in Rome only wish to impose the tyrant over Florence; a fig they care for Christian living. Everyone knows of their courtesans, squires, horses, dogs; their houses filled with carpets, silks, perfumes, and servants. Their pride fills the world and their avarice matches it. All they do, they do for money. They preach nothing but food… money… candles…

So says the Lord, my sword will hang above your sons, upon this brothel which you are, upon your whores and your palaces, and my justice will be made known to all.

Yes, Rome! You have made yourself a brothel for all and this Alexander is the worst. Nothing had come of the proposed reforms, nothing had changed. How can we discipline priests for living with mistresses when the pope does the same and flaunts his bastard offspring before the public? How can we exalt holy poverty when the pope flagrantly sells benefices to the highest bidder? This pope is no more than a lustful earthly prince. *He is NO pope. He is NO Christian.*

The friar stared up at the crucified Christ and spoke.

"Lord, you have chastised the sinner with a sign so plain—the death of his treasured son—and yet still he refuses to repent and change his ways. Lord, show me how to fight. I am a tool in Your hands and I will fight to the death to defend the true faith. But how can I fight? I have only the words you have given to us and yet I languish here in the silence, as in a tomb behind these walls. I must preach, without preaching I cannot breathe, I cannot live."

Then the Lord replied to him and he heard the words form in his ear as he beheld the crucifixion:

> *Leave all to me. It will be with them even as it was with the Jews and Romans, who thought to destroy me by nailing me on the cross, and instead made my name known throughout the earth.*

Fra Girolamo grasped his quill to write. He must—he must return to the pulpit, no matter what the consequence. He must defeat his enemies. He must bring the words of the Lord to the people, to give them hope and comfort their fears. He must enter the fray, if only to save his own soul. He must defeat his enemies. God will show the way.

CHAPTER 32

BROKEN TOOL SERMON

FRA GIROLAMO STOOD IN THE pulpit with eyes closed, listening to the murmuring of the congregation echo off the walls of the Cathedral and carry the breath of life to his lungs. His hands gripped the pulpit as he inhaled and waited for the choir to finish singing the *Gloria*. As the last strains of the children's voices faded, resounding with "*et in terra pax hominibus bonae voluntatis,*" he opened his eyes and saw the close-packed heads of his audience. Thousands had come to defy the excommunication and the curtain divider separated the bare heads of the men from the covered heads of the women. He raised his right hand to make the sign of the benediction:

"Gloria Patri, et Filio, et Spiritui Sancto. Sicut erat in principio, et nunc, et semper, et in saecula saeculorum. Amen."

Without speaking further he focused his eyes on those of his congregation as they lifted their heads up. He measured them, anticipating their reactions to the sermon to come. He knew few had come for devotion, most from curiosity. They were anxious to hear what he would say, but he made them wait. This was his army (though there were traitors in its midst), but they were apprehensive. They behaved as infantry at sea, frightened and sickened by the motion of the waves. With each rising swell they rocked back and forth, from doubt and bewilderment to passion and zeal, then back again to fear and confusion. But, like all armies before the battle, they would only be as confident, strong, and resolute as their captain. It was time to fortify their courage.

He gestured toward the child choir and riveted his audience with his opening words: "O Lord, from the mouths of these little ones shall Your true praises proceed."

He paused, then continued: "Philosophers praise You Lord according to the light of the world, but these little ones according to the light of heaven. Philosophers praise You from self-love, but these children from simplicity. Philosophers praise You with their lips, while these children do so with their works."

He averted his eyes and redirected his gaze to the high vaulted ceilings of the Cathedral.

"But, Lord, their elders turn from You. They are lukewarm in their hearts and indifferent to Your teachings. They show their scorn for religion and true faith and are consumed with worldly politics. They flaunt their wisdom and say the state cannot be ruled with paternosters, but to those I say: you have not done your reading and your memory is short.

"Go, I say, read in the chronicles of the Order of St. Dominic what he did in Lombardy, and likewise what St. Peter Martyr did here. How they intervened to pacify the state. It was Cardinal Messer Latino of our Order who made the peace between Guelphs and Ghibellines. And St. Catherine of Siena who arranged for the peace during the war with Pope Gregory. And our own Archbishop Antonino—how often did he go to the Palazzo to prevent the making of bad laws?"

He stared back into the audience, watching the heads bobbing in affirmation.

"And what does this tell us? …I will tell you: it tells us there can be NO just politics without FAITH. There is NO commune without FAITH. God has given you his honey, Florence; He has chosen you for His own. But if you refuse to do penance and be converted to Him, He will take away your honey and give it to others. This is as true as the fact that I stand here in this pulpit!"

He paused for a reprieve and the congregation started to murmur as he awakened their passion. He sharpened his eyes, penetrating those he met in his audience, to demonstrate how he was speaking directly to each.

"And now we must speak of the dangers we face. You have heard of these briefs that have arrived from Rome. They call me the son of perdition. But this humble friar before you has neither catamites nor concubines. He preaches only the faith of Christ. His spiritual daughters and sons do not pass their time perpetuating wickedness—they live godly lives. This friar would help build up the Church of Christ, which those in Rome would destroy. But I say to you: leave me to answer these letters from Rome. Time will open the casket, one turn of the key and such infection, such filth shall arise from the city of Rome, that it will spread through Christendom, and corrupt the whole atmosphere!"

Fra Girolamo raised his arms and reached out his hands for emphasis. "O Rome, what do I ask of you? Only a Bull to allow people to live decently. That is all I ask of you. But here, on the contrary, we await a Bull that will trample all semblance of a decent way of life."

He paused and lowered his head in repose as he waited for the congregation to absorb his words. When he spoke again he pulled back in tone to allow them to acclimate before ascending to the next level.

"The righteous prince or the good priest is merely an instrument in the Lord's hands, but in our times prelates and preachers seem more adept at destroying Christian life than building or conserving it. When moved by the wrong hand for the wrong purpose, an instrument under

God's agency becomes a *ferro roto*, a broken tool!

"But who is to tell you when the tool is broken? Examine and see whether what he commands is contrary to the principle of all wisdom. If what is ordered is contrary to this, you can be certain that a broken tool is at work and that no obedience is due."

"I cite to you now the case of Jean Gerson, the Christian Doctor in Paris who labored to heal the Great Schism in our Holy Mother Church. He said we must show humility and meekness to the sovereign pontiff, but when humility fails, then we must assume a courageous freedom!"

Cries of "*Vivo Cristo!*" punctuated the friar's words before fading into humbled silence.

"There are those here among us who, by their lying reports, have procured this sentence of excommunication. So tell me, what is their aim?"

He felt their rising fever and braced himself against the pulpit. "You know they seek to drive away virtuous living and righteous government, and open the door to every vice. No sooner was the excommunication pronounced then they returned to drunkenness, profligacy, and every other crime. Thus, I will not acknowledge the Bull, for I cannot act against charity. Anyone who gives commands opposed to charity is excommunicated by God. Were such commands pronounced by an angel, even by the Virgin herself and all the saints: *anathema sit.* If pronounced by any law, or canon, or council: *anathema sit.* And if any pope ever spoke contrary to this: let him be declared excommunicate!"

The murmurs rose higher. He had identified the enemy and now his army bubbled in the uncertain state between passion and bewilderment. A direct confrontation with the pope was not a trifle for those with something to lose—and he knew these thoughts would cloud their minds first. So he unleashed a second tirade.

"It is feared by some that, though this excommunication be powerless in Heaven, it may have power in the Church. For me it is enough not to be interdicted by Christ. Therefore, anyone who obstinately upholds the excommunication and affirms I ought not to preach these doctrines is fighting against the kingdom of Christ and supporting the kingdom of Satan. He is himself a heretic, and deserves to be excluded from the Christian community!"

The congregation became agitated as those inflamed with zeal searched to find those among them who failed to declare for Christ and the friar. There were more shouts of "*Vivo Cristo!*"

Then Fra Girolamo held up some keys and jingled them to gain the attention of his audience. He smiled, playing upon the symbolism of St. Peter's keys signifying papal authority.

"Would you like to know who will absolve you from excommunication?" he teased. "Just do this." The jingling keys sounded like coins jingling in one's pocket, coins used to pay priests and prelates for absolution. It was an unmistakable allusion to Alexander's penchant for selling benefices and indulgences. As the sound echoed through the Cathedral, many in the audience laughed and nodded their heads.

Moments later, as the friar descended from the pulpit and the congregation exercised their emotions, a watchful Machiavelli stole out the back of the Cathedral.

CHAPTER 33

MACHIAVELLI'S LETTER

Most Illustrious Signore Ricciardi Becchi, Ambassador to Rome[11]
9 March 1498, Florence

IN ORDER TO GIVE YOU, in accordance with your wishes, a full account of matters here concerning the friar, you should know he has preached many sermons (several of which you have already received copies). On Septuagesima Sunday, he attacked the Supreme Pontiff, calling him a "broken tool," and continued to preach in the same vein until the Sunday of Carnival. After speaking at length on Carnival day in San Marco (after the Arrabbiati chased his followers away from the second burning of the vanities), he invited his entire audience to take communion and said he would pray to God that if what he had predicted did not come from Him, He might display a very clear sign of it. Some say he did this in order to unite his partisans and to strengthen their defense of him, fearing lest the new Signoria, already chosen but not yet made public, might be against him. Once the membership of the Signoria was made public last Monday, because he believed it was more than two-thirds hostile to him and would not support him, and the pope had sent a brief summoning him under pain of interdiction, he decided—either because of his own choice or because of a warning from others—to leave off preaching in the Duomo and go to San Marco. Therefore, on the Thursday morning the Signoria took office, he said—still in the Duomo—that, in order to avoid strife and to preserve the honor of God, he would withdraw and the men should come and hear him at San Marco and the women should go to Fra Domenico at San Lorenzo.

Now that our Friar was in his own house, if you heard with what boldness he began preaching and with how much he continued, it would be an object of no little admiration. Because, fearing greatly for himself and believing the new Signoria would not be reluctant to injure him—and having decided that quite a few citizens should be brought down with him—he started in with great scenes of horror. His explanations were quite effective to those not examining them closely. He pointed out that his adherents were excellent people while his opponents were most villainous, and he drew on every expression to weaken his opponents' party and fortify his own. Because I was there, I shall briefly relate some of these matters.

The text of his first sermon at San Marco was this passage from Exodus: "But the more they oppressed them, the more they were multiplied, and increased." In explicating this passage, he delineated three types of human beings: namely, the good—they are those who follow him; the wicked and the obstinate—they are the adversaries; and there is another type of person, the intemperate—given to pleasure—neither obstinate about doing evil nor inclined toward doing good, because they cannot distinguish one from the other. But whenever some actual disagreement arises between the good and the wicked, people recognize the malice of the evil and the integrity of the good, because opposites are more evident when placed near one another. Because everyone naturally shuns evil and willingly follows good, therefore, during adversity the evil diminish and the good multiply. (On the contrary, my experience in the affairs of men has shown just the opposite.)

I am telling you about this briefly because the brevity of a letter does not call for a lengthy account. After he had digressed as is his wont, in order to weaken his adversaries further and to provide a bridge to his next sermon, he continued by pointing out that dissension might cause a tyrant to rise up who would bring down our house and lay waste to our land. This did not contradict what he had already said, that Florence should prosper and be dominant in Italia because it would soon come about that the tyrant would be driven out. And with this he finished his sermon.

The next morning, still expounding Exodus and coming to the passage where it says Moses slew an Egyptian, he said the Egyptian represented evildoers and Moses the preacher who slew them by exposing their vices. Then, comparing himself to Moses, he said, "O Egyptian, I want to stab you." (He fashions himself as Moses but he carries no sword, a prophet unarmed!) He then said again that God had told him there was someone in Florence who sought to make himself a tyrant, and he was engaged in schemes and that the desire to drive out the friar, to excommunicate the friar, and to persecute the friar meant nothing else than to seek to create a tyrant. And he made so much of this that later people speculated publicly about someone who is about as close to being a tyrant as you are to Heaven.

Afterward, since the Signoria had written to the pope in his behalf he realized he no longer needed to be afraid of his adversaries in Florence. So, instead of trying, as he once had, solely to unite his party through hatred of his adversaries and through frightening them with the word "tyrant," he has changed coats—now that he understands he no longer needs to act in this way. He no longer mentions either the tyrant or the wickedness of the people. Instead he seeks to set all of them at odds with the Supreme Pontiff and, turning toward him and his attacks, says of the pope what could be said of the wickedest person you might imagine. Thus, in my judgment, he acts in accordance with the times and colors his lies accordingly.

Now, as for what the common people are saying and what men hope or fear, I shall leave to you. You can determine these matters better than I inasmuch as you are fully aware of our temperament, the nature of the times, and, because you are in Rome, of the pontiff's state of mind. Only this I ask of you: if reading my letter has not been too much trouble for you, then do not consider it too much trouble to tell me in your reply what judgment you make concerning our affairs. Farewell,

Yours,
Nicolaus di M. Bernardus Machiavellus

The courier to Rome was scheduled to leave within the hour and Niccolò felt a flush of pride as he read over the dispatch one last time. In the past few weeks political rancor had begun to stew and strategic complexities within the Palazzo multiplied accordingly. Niccolò had been tracking the undercurrent of tension at its source: the parry and thrust between Florence and Rome in the persons of the friar and the pope. With the *Frateschi* in control the friar had grown bold, defying the excommunication and returning to the pulpit at the request of the Signoria. But the Pontiff then upped the ante by threatening additional sanctions if the friar was not silenced. With fear of conflict pervading the government councils, the pendulum had swung the other way, ushering the *Arrabbiati* into office. So the friar had retreated to San Marco, while escalating his attacks on the pope. Now the government councils were of one mind to deflect the pope's wrath, but were at odds over the friar, the choice being whether to muzzle him or repudiate him.

Niccolò and Piero Soderini attempted to straddle this divide with hopes of staying one step ahead of events. With Maestro Marcello Adriani's appointment as First Chancellor to replace the deceased Scala and Paolantonio's election as Gonfaloniere, they were confident. The correspondence between Rome and Palazzo had become the highest priority of the Ten and the Signoria, with couriers racing daily back and forth between the two cities, but this particular dispatch was not transcribed for his superior, Second Chancellor Braccesi, or First Chancellor Adriani. This was Niccolò's own handiwork, with additional suggestions by Piero, and his reports had been compiled confidentially at Becchi's request. Chancellor Braccesi was an ardent *Piagnoni* and *Frateschi* and might protest, but Niccolò was sure Adriani would approve. He wondered though how Signor Paolantonio as Gonfaloniere would react to his brother's machinations.

As he affixed the Chancery seal to the dispatch, Niccolò contemplated his strategy. Would it be shrewd now to sacrifice a bishop, or perhaps a knight, to advance a rook?

CHAPTER 34

PAPAL THREATS

"DAMN ROMAN HOUSES," CURSED THE ambassador as he yelled for his servant. "Beppo, cover the windows with something to keep the wind from howling through."

The three men huddled in the chill room of the ambassador's residence across from the Castel Sant'Angelo. Second Chancellor Alessandro Braccesi and Domenico Bonsi had been sent as special envoys to resolve the crisis between the pope and the friar. They carried with them a special dispatch from the Signoria to be delivered to the pope, a copy of which was open on the table for the ambassador, Riccardo Becchi, to review.

Becchi looked back at the dispatch. "Look, I'm glad it's you who has to deliver this to His Holiness. He's refused to grant me an audience for almost two weeks."

"The Signoria is firm," said Chancellor Braccesi, "at least for now. The Ten also concurred with Soderini, who argued the pope must be made to understand the city will not join the League at any price and the government could never risk the city's security."

"Gonfaloniere Soderini?"

"Si, Signor Paolantonio. He still strongly supports the friar," said Bonsi.

"And you?" Becchi asked, looking at Bonsi.

"I've much respect for Fra Girolamo, but it's becoming impractical to make distinctions based purely on principle. In my opinion a conflict with the pope would do us great harm."

Braccesi disagreed: "The pope is no friend of the republic and uses Venice and Pisa to harass us. The French alliance is our best leverage against the outsized ambitions of the Borgia, especially with his son Cesare. We should not discount the importance of Fra Girolamo to our purpose. He is also a servant of God, while Borgia is a devil."

Becchi sighed, averting his gaze by looking out the window toward the Vatican. "I've been in this God-forsaken city longer than I wished and I don't have the advantage of measuring the friar for myself. So I've asked and received communications from your undersecretary for the purpose of informing myself since Savonarola has become an obsession with the Holy See, occupying the majority of my time."

Braccesi was surprised to learn of this sideline of his subordinate.

"Messer Niccolò di Bernardo?" he asked.

"Yes, Machiavelli, and I find him very useful. Just yesterday I received another letter. Not very flattering to your Friar, but keen on insight. He says Savonarola 'trims with the times and colors his lies to suit them.' Here, read it if you wish."

Bristling at this breach of his authority, Braccesi waved the letter away with his hand and said, "It matters little how my lowly scribe colors this matter or any other. The Ten are convinced the false reports of our enemies have brought this trouble upon us. The Signoria made its decision and now it's our task to convince the pope of the rightness of our position. Naturally, we wish to shift the focus to the other issues addressed in the dispatch. Now, can you advise us of the situation?"

Becchi reviewed protocol: "First, the pope's secretary has sent word Alexander will receive you immediately after you arrive, but I wouldn't be surprised if he makes you wait a long day or two in his antechamber. It seems to be a papal privilege he enjoys exercising."

"But what can you tell us about the pope's state of mind and his disposition toward our case?" Bonsi asked.

Becchi shrugged. "Well, as he refuses me an audience, much of what I know is hearsay. It's common knowledge the Holy Father is incensed with the friar—he received a copy of the 'broken tool' sermon, you know. And Fra Mariano, acting for his Medici patrons, has stepped up his attacks. I suspect Alexander now takes the friar's attacks personally and will refuse to consider any other points, especially Pisa or any tithes on Church properties, until he receives satisfaction. Surely the Signoria understands this."

"Perhaps we can use the tithe as a bargaining chip?" said Bonsi.

"For what? The pope is happy to see Florentine finances weaken—it strengthens his hand—so why would he grant a tithe on Church properties to shift revenues from his pocket to ours? No, I don't see any easy way out of this impasse, unless you can convince His Holiness Fra Girolamo is no threat. I suggest you devise a convincing argument, whether true or not."

Braccesi and Bonsi looked at each other with resignation.

Becchi sat down again. "There is one hope in our favor. Many of the cardinals have attempted to deflect the pope's anger, warning him a conflict with the friar might threaten the well being of the entire Church if the reform movement should cause a schism. But I wouldn't mention this to His Holiness."

Becchi stood up with an air of finality. "*Allora, signori*, there it is. You see the task before you and all I can say is *buona fortuna*."

***

The next day the two envoys stood in front of the Supreme Pontiff. Becchi was right; Alexander had kept them waiting for more than six hours. After the pope's secretary had read aloud the dispatch, Alexander flushed as he addressed the stout Braccesi.

"Your Signoria has written us a wicked letter. We are *not* misinformed. We have read your friar's sermons and spoken with those who have heard them. He dares to say the Supreme Pontiff is a 'broken tool,' that it's heretical to believe in the efficacy of the excommunication, and he would rather go to hell than ask to be absolved."

Braccesi cleared his throat as if to speak but the Supreme Pontiff's glare silenced him.

"Messer Secretary, this is the third time you have come to us. But though we see you grow fatter than Ourself, your missions grow more meager and lean. If you have nothing more to say to me, you may be dismissed from our presence and go back at once to your post."

Braccesi could do nothing but play the supplicant. "Your Holiness, the Signoria has instructed us to explain we are unable to obey your commands because, in obeying them, we would act unworthily toward our Republic, and unjustly toward one who has deserved so well of his country. Even if we had the will, we lack the power to obey without exciting popular dissension and placing many persons in danger, so great is the favor won by the friar's integrity. We are pained these matters have turned the heart of Your Holiness against us but, nevertheless, we shall continue to maintain our allegiance to the Church and the Christian faith."

"Your Holiness," Bonsi added, "in humble submission to your last brief, Fra Girolamo has withdrawn from preaching in the Duomo and retreated to his convent at San Mar—,"

"Enough!" roared the pope, with a swipe of his arm. "Words! You offer us only words. We should never have supposed your audacity would rise to the point of contending with us concerning the affairs of this chatterbox of a friar, almost as though it were a question of carrying on a family quarrel, and forgetful of your duty of rendering to Caesar that which is Caesar's, and to God that which is God's! I should never have believed you could treat us so!"

The pope's large presence dominated the room like an angry thundercloud hovering over the papal throne. He glared, cowing the Florentine envoys into silence.

"We well know all this comes of your faith in the prophecies of that parable-monger of yours. You allow him to lacerate us, insult us, threaten us, and trample upon us, who *licet immeriti,* now occupy the Holy Chair of St. Peter!

"We therefore strictly command you to send this Fra Girolamo to us without delay. We promise if he comes and shows himself penitent, we shall receive him and treat him kindly, both for your sake and because we do not seek the death of the sinner. Until then, we command you to confine this son of iniquity, as a rotten member, in some private place where he can be cut off from communication with others. If these orders are not obeyed and you go on giving your support to this pernicious excommunicant and suspected heretic, we shall lay your city under an interdict and proceed to severer measures."

As his last words thundered through the audience chamber, the Pontiff turned away sharply to signal his displeasure and dismiss his audience.

CHAPTER 35

A PRATICA CONSIDERS THE POPE'S DEMANDS

"BONSI SENT ANOTHER DISPATCH TO the Signoria." Niccolò handed a notebook to Piero Soderini as they settled into his small office on the first floor of the Palazzo. "The original is in cipher but these are my notes."

Soderini glanced over the scribblings while Niccolò recounted the contents of the dispatch. "Bonsi has lost hope. His Holiness refuses to deal with the matters of Pisa or the tithe until he receives satisfaction from the Signoria on the question of the friar. Bonsi fears for his safety and begs to be recalled."

"He's a reed who bends in the slightest breeze," said Piero, dismissing Bonsi as if shooing a fly. "What about Braccesi?"

"Ser Alessandro defers to Bonsi, though I am sure he is steadfast behind the friar."

Piero looked up from the notes. "Paolo tells me the Ten are also in the friar's camp. They've rejected Borgia's naked attempts to break with the French alliance."

"But Bonsi says we can count on an interdict if nothing is done about the friar. The pope also threatens to imprison every Florentine merchant in papal territory unless we suspend all his preaching and send him to Rome. The Cardinal of Perugia informed our envoys that if we do not respond, the pope plans to send a prelate to escort the friar to Rome under guard."

"The people will demand we defend our jurisdiction and repel any such act with force—putting us in direct conflict with Rome. *Porco Dio,*" cursed Soderini. "This will split the city in two, just what Vespucci and the *Arrabbiati* need to disrupt the Council. With an interdict the *popolani* will be the first to jump."

"Where's the King of France when you need him?" Niccolò joked. He well knew the dire fear merchants had of an interdict. The Soderini especially had much to lose. "I would venture the last brief sent to the pope by the Signoria under the influence of Vespucci was exactly intended to provoke Rome in this way."

"*Sì,* Tommaso said Spini had his hand in this too. No offense Nico, but I strongly regret allowing *giovani* into the Great Council."

Niccolò could not see it any plainer. The time was now. The new Signoria was hostile to the friar and he saw the plot unfolding and how they needed a counter strategy. They must abandon Savonarola to his fate or risk war with the pope. Now he must prod his overly cautious mentor to commit to a decision.

"We're at a crossroads, Signor Piero. The friar put himself in this position. He played to the masses but then refused to support the appeal, allowing Valori to execute Messer Lorenzo and the others. He violated the law he himself made and by so doing, he's unwittingly revealed himself to be partisan and ambitious, ruining his reputation. Now his attacks on the pope only increase the threat."

"But this Dominican has more lives than a cat. The Signoria ordered him to stop preaching, but the people still praise him and Paolo believes he'll prevail."

Piero was too comfortable sitting on the fence and Paolo was still swayed by the friar, but Niccolò was bolder. "No, more citizens each day feel oppressed by the friar's policies and their animosities will be purged only by offering up a scapegoat. The sacrifice is a fundamental practice of both pagan and Christian beliefs, no?"

Piero appeared shocked by his cold reasoning and did not reply.

"Besides," Niccolò added, "the pope has an army."

Piero conceded this point. "He won't need to use it if he hits the Florentine merchants where it really hurts." He looked at the angle of the shadows coming through the window. "It's time for the Pratica."

Niccolò, determined to overcome this lack of *animo* in the older man, followed Piero out of the office.

***

Niccolò sat at the bench of the Ten of Peace and Liberty near Paolantonio Soderini, carefully observing the members of the Pratica as they filed into the Hall of Two Hundred. All the government magistrates were arrayed near the front while the backbenches contained the various appointed representatives of the gonfalons and the major guilds. Piero Soderini sat with his neighborhood gonfalon, the Dragons from Santo Spirito.

The audience settled as the Notary of the Signoria read aloud the papal brief. As all were aware of its contents, this was merely a formality to bring the meeting to order. When the representatives from the various benches were called upon to express their opinions the first to rise was a member of the Twelve Good Men.

"Excellencies, granted we have great respect for the good works of the prior of San Marco and praise the excellence of his life and doctrines ..."

The man droned on for several minutes, praising the friar in a vain attempt to paint himself as a reverent and impartial judge. It was largely a cover as the speaker quickly shifted to the injuries an interdict would bring upon the city's commerce:

"...for my own part, I would say we must render to everyone that which is his. In this respect I would even go farther and hand over the friar to the pope, who has a right to punish him. Remember the city of Troy was burnt and destroyed because of its refusal to give up Helen. Shall we deny the pope his own?"

In response, Paolantonio, on the behalf of the Ten, rose to denounce this political dissembling; calling the reply sent to the pope "an apple of discord purposely thrown into the city by enemies of the Republic." He alluded to Venice and Milan and ended by denouncing the pope's attempts to dissolve the French alliance and join Florence to the League.

Encouraged, one of the officials of the *Monte* jumped up to declare: "One should rinse out one's mouth before speaking of Fra Girolamo, instead of proposing to hand him over to this pope. Where would we be without his aid? Why should you fear an interdict? Haven't we weathered others before?"

Then another rose in support: "It's needless to refer to heathen examples! The Old and New Testaments suffice to show Fra Girolamo is a true prophet. How can the pope excommunicate him? I do not dispute the authority of the pope, but I say he is liable to error, and I fear God's wrath more than his."

Many of the *Frateschi* voiced approval of these opinions, forcing the president to hammer the gavel for order. Niccolò was suddenly concerned the tide was flowing the friar's way again. But it was a doomed policy to threaten war with the pope.

Then Guidantonio Vespucci rose to speak. "This is a serious affair," he began in a carefully measured voice, "we should weigh carefully the good or evil that may result to our city..."

These lawyers are slippery serpents, thought Niccolò. They crawl on their bellies and insinuate themselves into the affairs of men until they tighten their grip on every ill-gotten gain. Slithering with dexterity, Vespucci argued legal syllogisms and sophistries, "on this hand, this" and "on that hand, that," etc., etc. Niccolò waited for Vespucci to reach his conclusion and see how the mood of the Pratica responded.

"...all things considered, it is wiser to yield to the pope. We desire the tithe on Church property, the return of Pisa, and the absolution of the friar. It's foolish to ask these favors of the pope while giving him offense. Whether Fra Girolamo is right or wrong, you will gain nothing from the pope without giving him something he desires in return. And if the interdict is imposed, our commerce will be ruined. But..."

Niccolò held his breath—here it comes. He caught the eye of Piero Soderini as Vespucci worked his sleight of hand.

"...as one reflects on the harm of restricting the friar's sermons, we should remember, as the command comes from our lawful superior in all religious matters, *no sin is incurred by ourselves*. We should guard the honor of God, but it is certain the power of the pope is derived from God, whereas it is suspect whether Fra Girolamo is truly a messenger of the Lord."

This angered the *Frateschi* and one rose from the citizen's bench to speak against it: "God came to our aid even when all Italia was against us. Why should we abandon the safe course pointed out to us by the friar, to enter on a doubtful one? The pope is an authority on spiritual, not temporal things. The members of my bench are not afraid of the interdict. We believe our trade would go on as before, and bales of wool will be packed and unpacked as usual."

At this a guild merchant rose to contest: "Are we to put ourselves against the whole world? All of my bench wishes to vote for the suspension of the sermons. The interdict would cause grievous harm, and many of us have already ceased sending merchandise to Naples and elsewhere. If Messer Enea had anything to lose he would speak in a different tone. My wine casks are scattered all over Italia and I shall be unable to meet my obligations. We shall be pillaged on all sides."

Niccolò noted the subtle shift in temper as Vespucci's argument seduced the Florentine character. He had stirred up a tried and true potion concocted from three main ingredients: fear, inaction, plus the prospect of assigning blame elsewhere. Others sensed the change as well. They tried, but were powerless to turn the momentum.

Francesco Valori rose for a final appeal from his bench. "Not one word is said of closing San Marco, for this monastery is a school of virtue, and will be in higher repute fifty years hence. I advise you to honor and venerate the prior and cherish him more dearly than anyone who has ever existed during the last two hundred years. These briefs do not emanate spontaneously from the pope, but are wheedled out of him by our enemies. Our city has never recognized any superior power, and I remind your Excellencies our freedom must not be subject to the will of the Pontiff. This wheel we turn will only raise a larger disturbance."

Ah, but virtue, Niccolò chided, is not one of the three aforementioned ingredients. Neither are justice, freedom, nor moral conscience. As he expected, the magistrates sat waiting with arms crossed, seeking to close the debate.

In the end the Pratica endorsed the status quo, upholding the suspension of preaching and putting off the question of delivering the friar into the pope's clutches. As usual, the minimum and nothing more was done and so the chess match would be extended.

CHAPTER 36

LETTER TO THE PRINCES

IT WAS JUST PAST THE hour of Nones, soon after the friars emerged from their afternoon prayers, when Fra Domenico interrupted the prior in the Chapter House to announce his two visitors. Bishop Francesco Soderini and the prioress of Santa Maria della Grazia of Fiesole were waiting for him in the cloister of San Antonino. Fra Girolamo put away his papers and went out to stroll with them in the last hours of daylight.

"Prioress, Excellency, it gives me great pleasure to receive you both. So much do I feel like a hostage here these days, separated from my congregation and denied communion with my parish."

"Surely it's a difficult situation, Prior," said the prioress. "We at the convent all hope it will soon be resolved. The sisters have missed your visits."

"I'm not so hopeful. The government and the Holy Father seem set against me. Can you tell me any word of Sister Chiara?"

The prioress hesitated and looked at the bishop, Chiara's uncle. "Sister Chiara has returned to the convent after several months resting with her family. Many, you know, have not come back. We're all still recovering from the pestilence and pray to God it won't afflict us again." As she spoke she grasped the cross hanging from her neck.

They continued to speak obliquely of recent events in the city and the impact on their respective parishes, skirting the subject of the visit until the bishop finally came to the point. "We've come to speak with you about the Signoria and His Holiness, Father Girolamo. We worry about the consequence to you, the Church, and the religious orders if the conflict is raised to the level of the Christian kings against Rome. The prospect of a Council is a dangerous one for all involved."

"Yes, Your Excellency, I've struggled with my conscience and I'm aware of the dangers involved." And so he had, though he was reticent to speak plainly with the bishop. Bishop Soderini had supported the reforms and he was the brother of Paolantonio Soderini, who was a champion for the friar's cause in the government. But the Soderini were *grandi*, wealthy and ambitious, and the bishop surely had his sights on a cardinalate.

He continued carefully: "When I saw clearly that my leaving the city would mean the spiritual and temporal ruin of the people, I could not obey any living man ordering me to abandon it. This order would be contrary to God's will. It is the intention of the laws which we are bound to obey, not the mere words."

The bishop was not in the mood to be preached to by a subordinate. He replied, "This is past a matter of principle or intention. It is one of consequence. I need not remind you how the Church has struggled from the time of Constantine to Gregory VII to rise above worldly princes. The Holy Father, as successor to St. Peter as Bishop of Rome and the leader of the Holy Mother Church anoints the Holy Roman Emperor. Subordinating the pope to the judgment of the Christian kings risks the future independence of the Church, and our true mission to spread the Christian faith."

Chastised, Fra Girolamo fumed. He needed the support of the bishop and other prelates, yet despised his predicament. He was alone, always alone. He sensed his time was short, as already word reached him the pope planned to send a prelate to force him back to Rome. Once in Rome, in the devil's embrace, he knew he would never be freed.

"In no way do I wish to disturb the Church in Rome nor to challenge the sacred office of the papacy. Excellency, as all know, I only speak out against the present occupant of the office. His reign is an unspeakable scandal, but it is not the first. I can cite many cases where the papal authority has strayed from its path, merely out of lust for personal ambition and earthly power—Boniface VIII and IX, John XXII, also accused of heresy, and—,"

Bishop Soderini cut him off. "And I can cite as many cases where kings have sought to subject the papacy and the Church to their own political designs. But we need not split hairs like Scholastics, Father. Should we hand more weapons to our foes?"

"In due respect, Excellency, do you truly believe the moral power of the Church will be enhanced with the abuses it suffers under the Spanish Borgia? My only wish is to save the Church from further scandal, but this pope uses the sanction of excommunication unjustly to punish his foes. Just as Lorenzo de' Medici was excommunicated, this excommunication is illegitimate and invalid. I will not be going to Canossa to kiss the feet of this imposter."[12]

His voice had become tinged with contempt, causing the bishop to step back and regard him closely.

"Under his tutelage, Rome has become a sink hole of vice and plunder—,"

Bishop Soderini cut off his tirade: "Granted—His Holiness is found wanting in some qualities defining his holy mission—but it merits little to your cause to inflame the ire of the entire Roman Curia by calling him a 'Pirate' and an 'unbaptized Moor.' You must temper your words in public. Your enemies deliver them directly to Alexander's ears. If he declares an interdict, you know how the Florentine merchants will react, no matter what they think of Borgia or you…"

"And Father," said the prioress, trying to calm him, "the Franciscans show no misgivings in attacking your doctrines. Fra Menico in Santa Maria Novella …and also Fra Francesco di Puglia assailed you viciously in his Lenten sermons at Santa Croce—,"

The bishop was more blunt: "The words he uses are 'heretic, schismatic, and false prophet.' These words are filled with peril."

Fra Girolamo paused, turning away as he thought of these cackling crows. It was true—San Marco was abuzz with the attacks by the Franciscans. He said, "Again… like with Michael of Cesena and William of Occam…"[13]

"This is no time to provoke the *odium theologicum*. They will accuse you of exciting the *fraticelli* against the Church," said the bishop, his voice heavy with finality.

Later, as the friar sat at his desk in the Chapter House, he looked down at the draft of the letter before him and read the words he had written:

> The moment of decision has arrived. The Lord commands me to reveal new secrets, and make known to the world the peril by which the barque of St. Peter is threatened owing to your long neglect. The Church is teeming with abominations from the crown of her head to the soles of her feet. Yet, not only do you apply no remedy, but you do homage to the cause of the woes by which she is defiled.

He weighed these words against those of the bishop and the prioress. In their own eyes they were right. They had much to lose from a conflict within the Church. The letter before him would ignite a fireball and no one knew how much it would consume. And he could not disagree with the ruthless methods of the Church against schismatics and heretics. Peace and order for the salvation of souls required dogmatic adherence to the faith. For more than three hundred years innocent souls had burned in sacrifice to insure the unity and strength of Holy Mother Church. In this long history perhaps his soul was next. If he chose to put the letter back in its drawer, maybe he could escape that fate.

But, his conscience argued, how could the doctrine of St. Francis and St. Dominic be heresy? The Inquisitors who burned the heretics believed. They believed in Holy Fire and its power to cleanse and redeem the soul. But these Cardinal princes have *no beliefs*. They care for nothing beyond the comforts of their own persons and the weight of their purses.

They tolerate all sorts of blasphemies and hunt down only those who threaten their own positions. This Borgia bull is only the worst of many. He is the beast. He orders me to cease preaching by the powers vested in St. Peter, but as Peter and John replied when asked to stop preaching: *non possumus, I cannot.*

He scratched with his quill to finish the letter:

> Now, I testify, God being my witness, *this Alexander is no pope*, nor can he be held as one. Leaving aside the mortal sin of simony by which he obtained the papal chair and daily sells the benefices of the Church to the highest bidder, and also leaving aside his other evident vices, I declare solemnly he is no Christian and believes in no God. Infidelity can go no further.

There must be a Church Council to depose the infidel. What Charles failed to do by the sword, must now be done by true defenders of the faith. Filled with moral indignation, he continued writing and when he finished he called for his secretary.

"Brother, you must copy this letter five times tonight. Then tomorrow we will send each by trusted messengers directly to the various kingdoms."

"Which?"

"The royal houses of France, Spain, Hungary, England and the Holy Roman Emperor."

CHAPTER 37

THE INTERCEPTED LETTER

CARDINAL CESARE BORGIA SMILED INWARDLY as he waited for Vesuvius to erupt in a fiery rage. Burchard, the papal Master of Ceremonies, and Cardinal Ascanio Sforza, also stood silently as the pope rumbled around his private chamber, the letter shaking in his hand. The dispatch had been intercepted on its way through Milanese territory several days ago on its way to France. Duke Sforza had immediately forwarded the intercepted letter to his brother in Rome, where it had been received just this morning. Cardinal Sforza had eagerly delivered it directly to the Holy Father. As his father turned, Cesare saw the expression of raw anger shaded by the shock of disbelief.

"This presumptuous, wretched little worm…he dares to say I am no Christian, that I do not believe in God? That I am *no pope!?* He calls me a thief as well!"

Alexander struggled to hold his temper, but Cesare noticed he had dropped the formal plural pronoun in referring to the papal person.

Cardinal Sforza could not contain his delight. "Holiness, this foolish preacher has lost all sense of propriety with regard to his superiors within the Church. My brother, the Duke, also has several agents in Florence who send him reports on a regular basis."

Cesare saw his father's expression change, as if this undisguised reference to spies had momentarily sidetracked his thoughts about possible repercussions if the letter had reached it destination.

Sforza continued his probing. "This copy was on its way to King Charles VIII, but careful questioning of the courier revealed it is but one of several to be delivered. Our sources in Florence have confirmed this."

It was too much for the pope's disposition. "We have tried our patience with this vile monk, but where has it got us?" He lifted his eyes from the letter to look at Cardinal Sforza. "Well? Are you going to tell us the other recipients?"

"The kings of Spain, Hungary, England, and the Emperor."

"Fa—, Holiness," interjected Cesare, "there is no chance the barking of a foolish Italian monk will sway these other monarchs."

The pope snapped: "The King of France has army enough to cause us trouble. And perhaps enough to encourage other princes with designs on Italia and Church holdings. You know delle Rovere is eager to fan these flames." He cursed softly as he turned to Sforza. "Are you sure only one copy was sent to France?"

"My brother spares no means when questioning his enemies. The courier revealed no others. But, I'm sure this friar will try again... if he's not stopped." There was a pregnant silence as Cardinal Sforza looked from Alexander to Cesare and back, then continued. "Holiness, may I offer additional information received through my brother, directly from Florence? The Franciscans there are incensed with this Dominican rabble-rouser and have begun to attack him. In their sermons they accuse him of heresies. With encouragement, perhaps these religious may be successful in swaying public opinion against him."

Alexander was unconvinced. "What of this despicable government in Florence? They play the Church for a fool with this friar's game. They are the true obstacle."

"Holiness," said Cesare, "the Florentines, especially those who live in the government palace, are faithful to one thing only: their ample bellies. If you impose the Interdict they'll be the first to throw the friar to the wolves. Their principle fear is the *popolo*—it's imperative we break the preacher's hold on these ignorant peasants."

The pope, used to getting his way, would not be mollified. "Must we depend on more preachers? Have you heard this inept Augustinian, Fra Mariano? More and more he sounds like some diseased appendage of the Medici. With enemies like these, our little Dominican has little to worry."

Alexander was beginning to tire of this tactical discussion. "We must think on the correct course to pursue to rid us of this problem. Messer Burchard, would you please escort His Eminence out."

Cardinal Sforza bowed. "Your Holiness."

When the pope was alone with Cesare, he spoke again. His voice was flat and cold. "Cesare, this problem of Florence and her preacher exasperates me. You have met with the priors and also spoken with the friar. Give me your opinion."

"Father, the government is a circus of ineptitude. The vain Florentines prefer a comedy to strong rule and those in control practice the vanity of all vanities. You can be sure they confound *amor patriae* with *amor nummi*,[14] but an interdict will quickly put an end to this confusion."

"We detest this predicament. To have our hand forced this way. What of this pesky fly? What does he want?"

"Father, the Dominican fancies himself as the true successor to the founder of his Order. He's a zealot and not open to reason or compromise. He has dreams and visions and falsely proclaims himself a prophet of the Lord. We should hesitate no longer. Let me call Michelot—,"

The pope cut off Cesare with a quick wave of his hand. "In two weeks time we will send an envoy to escort the friar back to Rome under guard. Perhaps, God willing, it will not be necessary."

Back at his palace Cesare felt a wave of satisfaction warm him. Now it was time to deal with the friar and the Florentines in a decisive manner. His father would not wish to know anything of the details, but with his obliqueness he had given his tacit consent. Cesare was certain men of this world only understood one thing—the power of the sword. It was far more expedient and effective than the endless intrigue of the Roman papal court. Someday he hoped to be free of these cumbersome purple robes to fulfill the role he was born to.

He called for his manservant to summon Don Michele.

CHAPTER 38

ANOTHER CONSPIRACY

THE TWO HOODED RIDERS BLENDED with the black night as they rode out through the Porta Romana toward a small inn on the road outside Arezzo. After an hour's hard ride without a word, they slowed as they approached the lighted inn. Tethering the horses, they entered the inn, requested lodging for the night and some food.

"Are you traveling south, *signori?*" asked the innkeeper.

"No, we've been hunting and it's too late to ride back to the city. Do you have some wine?"

The innkeeper nodded and motioned them toward an adjacent tavern room dim with candlelight. He followed with a carafe of wine and two goblets and set them down on a table. "Any luck with the hunt?" he inquired, but only shrugged when met with silence.

He motioned toward another table in the corner. "There's another traveler here, from Rome. Says he's riding toward your city tomorrow." In an aside he whispered, "A Catalan, by his accent." Again receiving no response, the innkeeper turned to leave. "My wife will bring food shortly."

The two new arrivals carried their wine over to sit at the foreigner's table.

Without raising his eyes from his plate, the man spoke. "So we meet again, Messer Spini. Who's this?" He spied the stranger out of the corner of his eye.

"Messer Paolo, da Milano," said Spini, not revealing the man's family name.

The dark Spaniard nodded without looking up, cutting his meat with his own dagger. "The eyes and ears of the Sforza, eh? Well, I hope with the help of Milan and Rome, we might finally clear up this little problem in your city."

The Spaniard irked Spini. He resented this reference to previous failures. "And what help does Rome have to offer, Don Michele? Besides words."

The Spaniard finally looked up, pointing his dagger. "I'm here, am I not? I will take lodging in Florence and remain, inconspicuous, until this matter is settled. My, uh, patron is most impatient to end this conflict once and for all."

"*Va bene*, our Milanese friends are most eager as well," said Spini as he nodded toward the other man.

"And what do you propose this time?"

"The friar would be dead by now if not for the idiocy of his Weepers. But things are different now."

"How so?" The Spaniard was naturally cautiously.

"In the Great Council we can prevent Savonarola from preaching. Silencing him, we cut off the head of his movement. And the mood has gone against the friar among many families because of the execution of some Mediceans. The pope's excommunication has also helped sow confusion among his followers. Now, when we attack there will be no outcry of support."

"No miracles?" teased Don Michele.

The Milanese interrupted, "This too may be the friar's downfall."

"Don't talk in riddles, friend. I'm not a patient man."

Messer Paolo explained: "We have strong allies among the Franciscans: Fra Menico in Santa Maria Novella and Fra Francesco in Santa Croce. Fra Francesco has challenged the prophet to prove his doctrines with an Ordeal by Fire. A large conflagration will be lit in the Piazza and whoever walks through the flames unscathed is proved right."

The Spaniard laughed. "Of course, catch a monk with a monk! And fry them both."

"This fornicating preacher has been too clever," said Spini, "but we'll force him to accept the challenge or forfeit his right to speak for God. I say it should be no problem for a 'true prophet' to call up a miracle or two. Christ did it, no? Besides, the friar can't resist the pleas of his Weepers, they're true believers."

"But is the Franciscan willing to burn for you as well?"

"All monks are expendable," scoffed Spini, "if not this one, another. But I doubt it will come to that and the Franciscans know it. Think, my friend, there are only two possibilities: the friar enters the fire and he's burned; or he refuses to enter and loses all credit with his followers. I'll bet he doesn't; then we'll have the opportunity to raise a furor, and during the chaos seize him. Either way, the fowl is cooked."

Don Michele swilled wine from his goblet. "Will your Signoria ever approve of such a circus? It goes against Church policy to encourage such spectacles."

"We control the balance of power in the Signoria and the Gonfaloniere is with us. Will the pope interfere?"

"Materially, I think not. But the Roman Curia will probably condemn such foolery. Cardinal Delle Rovere will see through this ploy in an instant."

"Then we must hurry the plan as quickly as possible, before the next election of the Signoria, and before the cardinals can force the pope's hand."

"Spini, if this fails I will resort to my own tried and proven methods."

Spini's tone was indignant. "It would be better if neither the hand of Rome nor Milan was revealed in these events. We Florentines prefer to take care of our own problems."

CHAPTER 39

SAN MARCO AND THE ORDEAL

ALL THE BRETHREN CROWDED TOGETHER, their whispers filling the large refectory with anticipation as they waited for the prior and Fra Domenico. For the past several weeks two Franciscans—Fra Menico in Santa Maria Novella and Fra Francesco in Santa Croce—had attacked Fra Girolamo from the pulpit, slandering his writings and sermons. Fra Menico hurled appalling personal invectives while Fra Francesco was repeatedly issuing a direct challenge for an Ordeal by Fire. But, forbidden by the pope to preach, the prior had been forced to let the challenge go unanswered.

It greatly angered the brothers to absorb these blows and watch their reputation suffer. With their intellectual conceit, the Dominicans looked down on the Franciscans and the unmet challenge incited a competitive desire to vanquish their rivals. Finally the previous Sunday, their own Fra Domenico, preaching in the prior's place, had fervently and impulsively accepted the challenge himself. The prospect of victory now excited them and the friars in black mantles and novices in plain tunics flocked together like cackling magpies and insistent crows.

"The Graysacks disgrace their founder," whispered one young friar.

"These *frati minori* have forgotten Francis's rule: friars must own nothing and serve the Lord in poverty and humility," replied an older brother. "They're all ignoramuses. Why, I don't think half of them can read."

Another said, "Menico's a puppet of the Sforza and Francesco sells his soul to the devil himself."

"Well, he'll burn for it. Just like the *fraticelli*," hissed the first.

These flames of emotion flickered and caught fire, spreading through the small circles.

"We must fight back, in the name of the Lord."

"I, for one, will join Brother Domenico in the fire!"

"*Sì!*" "*Anch'io*, me too!" A chorus of buoyant martyrs rose in unison.

"*Basta!* Shhhhh," admonished an older friar, silencing them as Fra Girolamo entered the room followed by Domenico and Silvestro. "The prior does not wish to encourage this *spettacolo*."

As they settled down, Fra Girolamo looked into their eager faces. How their faith burns with zeal, he thought. They believe, as Domenico believes, as Silvestro believes. But the Devil lays traps and he must do his best to restrain them.

The Franciscans were poisoned by duplicity. He knew the challenge was a bluff to embarrass him and already the Franciscan was wavering after Domenico accepted. It was not gentle Domenico they wanted. They wanted him and he would not be coerced to play into their hands. In a letter to the Signoria and a pamphlet distributed on the streets, he had argued against the Ordeal, using reason and evidence to expose the true designs of his enemies, hoping to silence his critics in the Palazzo while reassuring his followers. But the officials rejected his appeal and his enemies persisted in spreading their lies. So Domenico pleaded to be allowed to silence them through a miracle and cause the blaspheming Franciscan to burn in Hell.

Domenico believed and more and more men, women, children had come to the convent to offer themselves as champions and demonstrate their belief. Perhaps such faith was the Lord's way and should not be denied. They needed a sign, something easily understood, something to gird their faith. Like a flood, the momentum could not be stopped.

"My brothers, it is with a great unwillingness that I give my blessing to this affair. You well know the time and place of miracles is not by the design of men, but only by the hand of God. As it is written: *Thou shalt not tempt the Lord thy God…*"

His brethren murmured and Fra Girolamo read their minds: Would their champion refuse to redeem them and punish their enemies?

"But Silvestro had the dream, Prior," one of the young friars implored.

He nodded. "Yes. Brother Silvestro had a vision and his visions have always proved true. God revealed to him the two guardian angels of myself and Domenico who came down and spoke with him, assuring him Domenico will pass through the flames untouched."

The brothers cheered: "And the Minorites will suffer for their blasphemies!"

Fra Girolamo hushed them again. "I've written to the Holy Father and the College of Cardinals, explaining how more than three hundred from among you and other citizens have offered to accompany Domenico through the flames. I asked if our challengers dare to do the same."

More cheers rose from the ranks. But Fra Girolamo had hoped his letter would alarm the Holy See and alert his allies in the College to the wicked designs of the Borgia and their Franciscan puppets—for canon law established by the Fourth Lateran Council of 1215 under Innocent III expressly forbids ordeals as a method of proof in civil trials.

In the ensuing pause, Fra Malatesta spoke. "Prior, it's said Fra Francesco has already withdrawn his challenge— that he will propose another in his place. Some say it's all a ruse to turn the people against us."

"Yes, Brother, I believe this. Our enemies do not wish to challenge our articles of faith or the propositions for reform expressed in my writings. They wish only to cause a commotion, to subjugate the city and return to the old order of things. But we shall call their bluff and they will resign and be exposed."

Fra Silvestro strutted forward. "And if not, we shall prevail! And let them be consigned to burn in Hell!"

Enthusiasm overflowed the room and Fra Girolamo was forced to hold his hands up again. "Brothers, in recent days I too have had a dream and a vision. In it I saw our blessed founders, St. Dominic and St. Francis, together at the edge of the Inferno. As one, they took hold of the evildoers and the condemned souls and hurled them into the flames while those souls who were saved clasped hands in a circle and danced and sang together. May this be our inspiration."

He motioned with his arms to gather them closer together. "Let us too pray and sing together for our salvation."

He nodded at Fra Bonifazio, who sang the first strains of *ecce quam bonum*.

Later that night Fra Girolamo wandered through the cloister in darkness. His thoughts pulled him in opposite directions as his eyes absorbed the frescoed images of Fra Angelico painted around the perimeter. He stopped for a moment before the large crucifixion scene that dominated this area of the cloister. The image was almost twice life-size and the subtle light and shadow with which Beato Angelico modeled the body of Christ imparted a living quality to the suffering Savior. St. Dominic knelt at the base of the cross with his arms wrapped around it in a tormented gesture of empathy.

The vision helped him focus his thoughts on the sacrifice of Our Lord, achieving its purpose here in the cloister. The image was repeated throughout the convent, with more than a half dozen renderings in the second floor dormitories alone. Outside the communal area where the brothers sought inspiration for nocturnal meditation and prayer there was a smaller replica of this same fresco. More recently, the convent had commissioned and received a moving wooden sculpture of the crucifixion carved by a local artisan. He had placed this precious icon in the choir of the church, to inspire the brothers as well as the worshippers who came to San Marco. At these moments, late at night, it called to him.

He went into the church and knelt before this sublime

representation, with its softly molded features and fine details. When he saw the red blood pouring from gaping wounds and the thin parched lips of death beckoning for mercy with lifelike pathos, the prior was moved to tears. He closed his eyes to check his tears and embraced the base of the cross in his arms.

Lord, you have given me this sign...

He dropped to his knees to pray but his mind traveled back to his last vision of his mother and her pity at his youthful pain. And to a father who could never understand; to a dark night when he left them without a word to embark on his journey to God. What did they do when they had returned and found him gone? They wept, but it was only for themselves—his father in shock, his mother in sorrow. He remembered how happy he was when he had arrived at Bologna, a new home to redeem the old. But he could not help feeling he had always been alone, cut off from communion, with each place a waystation before the next dark road. He prostrated himself before the crucifix.

Lord, is my journey at an end? Will You abandon me at the last moment? Will You test me as You tested Your own flesh and blood, Your son? Lord, show me a sign, preserve Domenico...

CHAPTER 40

THE SIGNORIA DEBATES THE ORDEAL

NICCOLÒ AND PIERO SODERINI CROSSED over the Old Bridge on their way to the Palazzo. Today a Pratica was called to discuss the Ordeal by Fire and decide whether to permit or prohibit the spectacle. Niccolò listened intently to the gossip and incessant quarrelling of the citizens they passed. Some argued both friars would burn, freeing the city from the cursed plague of priests. Others were convinced Brother Domenico would prevail, settling once and for all the question of God's favor; then their evil opponents would be silenced for good.

Piero confided in a low voice: "This morning Tommaso told me the *Arrabbiati* are eager to press the Ordeal, with Spini and his *Compagnacci* fanning these fires on the streets. The Signoria and the Gonfaloniere are sympathetic and we could lose control of the situation if the rabble have their way."

"Yes, but I'm almost sure the *Arrabbiati* are in league with Rome or Milan. This perception will brace the public against them, even if the people do turn against the friar."

"I'm most curious to see Fra Girolamo pull another miracle out of the fire. That would be an interesting development." Piero chuckled at his pun. He was amused, but no longer surprised by the fortunes of the friar. "Paolo's half-convinced."

"It's not an outcome I would wager on, Signor Piero. This 'unarmed prophet' has placed himself in a precarious position. He's more likely to go up in smoke with his ardent brethren. We must distance ourselves."

"Nevertheless, it's a situation we must exploit, or Vespucci and the *ottimati* will gain."

Niccolò's thinking was more acute. "The Frateschi may suffer the same fate as their friar, but it will be primarily by the hand of Vespucci and Spini and their foreign conspirators."

He spread his hands apart. "So, it opens a wide space in the middle for a true champion of the republic."

Piero smiled as he looked at Niccolò. "For the good of Florence?"

Niccolò's smile hid behind his eyes. "*Sì*, naturally, for *popolo e libertà*."

Piero suddenly looked grave. "One more thing—I didn't tell you before. Paolo said an anonymous accuser has denounced you to the Office of the Night."

"*Sodomiti!?*" Niccolò exclaimed. Then his astonishment turned to outrage spewing forth in a stream of curses.

"Shhhh, *basta*, don't be insulted," said Piero, smiling to calm him, "they said it was with a woman."

Niccolò almost burst out laughing, then reflected on the gravity of the charge, despite its absurdity. At least they got his preferences right; but sodomy was sodomy, it didn't matter whether the act was committed with a man, a woman, or a chicken. He was guilty, yes—who wasn't?—but the cowardly accusation aroused a burning anger toward his faceless enemy. Obviously, it was politically motivated: someone wanted to be sure he was not nominated for office. Could it be the *Compagnacci?* He knew there was no love lost between him and the Spini gang. Or maybe one of the pious *Frateschi*—perhaps Braccesi? The Weeper Braccesi was becoming more insecure in his position and it was obvious he suspected Niccolò's close relationship with Piero Soderini and First Chancellor Adriani. And Braccesi had reprimanded him handily for his correspondence with Ambassador Becchi. It must be him—Braccesi knew where power and influence lay and was striking preemptively.

From Niccolò's perspective this changed everything.

***

"The issue, as I see it, is whether God the Father or Christ is the ultimate authority over questions of religious doctrine and, more importantly in this case, Church affairs."

This statement issued from Guidantonio Vespucci, always the lawyer, always the polemic. Seated next to him was a smug Doffo Spini. With all its members now trapped in the Hall of Two Hundred, the blustering of the Pratica had begun.

Niccolò leaned over to whisper to Soderini. "Is this a theological conclave or…?"

Piero's eyes smiled back as Vespucci continued: "It would seem the friar's arguments for God's ultimate authority is misplaced. His Holiness governs here on earth as the appointed Vicar of Christ and must be accorded the ultimate authority to oversee the Church and Church matters. He exercises power to that end."

Another lawyer seated near Vespucci and Spini, interjected. "Actually, the question of whether the friar represents the word of God Almighty or not is still unresolved. Thus, this argues in favor of the Ordeal as a way to determine the truth of the matter. The friar vows his political aims are divinely ordained, accusing the government of standing in the way of God's plans. But this is an absurd notion—it effectively makes government officials superfluous, like *castrati!*"

Many laughed roundly, but Niccolò saw the friar's outnumbered supporters were not amused. At the end of the hall, Enea della Stufa stood and raised his voice derisively: "Enough evidence has been presented over the last four years to confirm the divine guidance of Fra Girolamo. The pope's authority is limited to spiritual matters; do we need to discuss *his* history there in comparison? On this question then, for the ultimate good of the city we shouldn't tempt fate with these foolish spectacles."

But another opponent rose to counter this view. "As I've said before, whether one chooses to believe in the friar's prophecies or not should be a matter for individual conscience; the city should not deal with matters of faith. For that we should defer to the Roman Pontiff or his representatives."

At this an angry Francesco Valori jumped to his feet. "Would you place our fate in the hands of Rome?! The true intentions of those who promote this affair are transparent."

This raised another objection from a merchant: "For now, Excellencies, we *are* at the mercy of the pope. Roman prelates never lose an opportunity to take money from us. If he declares the interdict, we will be ruined."

Niccolò noted the Pratica had split into several camps, with the favored position determined by whether one believed the Ordeal would resolve the issue of the friar versus the pope once and for all. Frankly, Niccolò was convinced it would and the friar was destined to lose this battle—though many of his own Weepers were most anxious for the Ordeal to confirm his divine mission. As Vespucci pressed his point, Niccolò realized he and Spini were clever enough to drive this wedge between their enemies.

"My colleagues, this is why we must endorse the Ordeal—to determine whether the friar is true or not."

As Vespucci opened his arms to affirm the reasonableness of his logic, Valori shouted back: "This is absurd. Fra Francesco has already withdrawn and placed another hapless friar in his place to challenge the substitute for Fra Girolamo. Two substitutes—what will this prove? And Church law expressly forbids the use of Ordeals to determine the outcomes of civic matters. Can the pope condone such a violation?"

Vespucci was nonplussed. "Actually, this is not a civic matter at all but a religious one. As such it is not proscribed by canon law and can only be prohibited by a special decree from the pope. The Signoria has not yet received any objection from His Holiness, and we cannot influence the mendicants as to whom they choose to submit."

Valori lost his temper. "If it's not a civic matter, WHY are we discussing it HERE?!"

Niccolò heard the shuffling of feet and embarrassed coughs. The truth could not be spoken aloud, but the answer was clear: sentiment had turned against the friar and the *Frateschi*. The debate also confirmed what he suspected: Vespucci and his *Arrabbiati* party were in league with the pope and other enemies of Florence.

The pregnant silence was broken by another clever lawyer suggesting a safer 'trial by water': "Better to require the friars to walk across the Arno without getting wet, like St. Peter—this would be a more convincing display of miraculous powers."

His droll suggestion brought snickers, prompting one wealthy merchant to express his indignation: "If our forefathers could see how we've chosen to become the laughingstock of the whole world, they would turn red with shame and refuse to have anything to do with us. I implore your Excellencies to deliver us from all this wretchedness at any cost, either by fire, air, water, or any other means you choose!"

This statement elicited shouts and exhortations against the interference of religion into business and government affairs. Unless of course, Niccolò had wryly observed, one could wield it to one's own purpose. He caught Piero Soderini's eye. Now was the moment.

Piero rose to speak, addressing the Signoria in a serious tone.

"Excellencies, if this conflict is allowed to fester it may cause a great deal of chaos and harm to our city. I believe we've suffered more than our share of pandemonium in the last few years so I suggest we resolve it as expediently as possible. I say let the Ordeal be our judgment. Now, let us vote."

As quickly said, it was decided. The official declaration had already been drawn up and was now read out to the assembly. It explained the various propositions to be decided by the Ordeal and the various consequences of the outcome: if the Dominican prevailed, the propositions were proved and the Franciscans would be banished; if the Dominican or both were consumed, the friar would be required, like the Divine Poet, to quit Florentine territory at once and forever.

CHAPTER 41

THE ORDEAL BY FIRE

EARLY ON THE MORNING OF the appointed day Niccolò wandered through the Piazza, curious to observe the preparations for the Ordeal. He had a delicate role to play in the proceedings and wanted to familiarize himself with the situation.

The area just in front of the Palazzo was busy with workmen. A long, narrow platform had been constructed of earth, wooden beams and fired bricks, almost fifty *braccie* long, ten wide and four high. It projected out from the entranceway toward the Pisan canopy on the far side of the Piazza. On top of this platform the workers were stacking two long rows of wood, packed with gunpowder and pitch, leaving a narrow corridor in-between for the two candidates to walk. It was intended for the fire be lit at the far end and then, after the two friars entered the corridor, to close off escape by lighting the entranceway, after which the frightful entertainment would begin.

The workers were cheerful, executing their tasks with eager efficiency while egged on by groups of joking *giovane*. Around the Piazza there were a number of banners being raised and barricades being moved into place at the entrances. A frantic flight of pigeons momentarily distracted Niccolò, as the activity flushed them from their comfortable roosts. Turning to go back to his house in the Oltrarno, he noticed a familiar figure hailing him. It was Filippo Giunta. With him was the First Chancellor, Marcello Adriani.

"*Buon giorno*, Messer Niccolò. Getting an early preview? *Dio mio*, what a travesty we have conceived."

As they embraced Niccolò noticed Filippo's smile set off by the dark furrow of his brow. "Thank God they've forbidden women to attend this circus. Such a spectacle is barbaric, no matter what the purpose. Today I'm ashamed to call myself a Florentine."

"Yes," said Adriani, "but it will pass."

"And leave a black mark on us all. Look at those *giovane* there, they joke as if it's Carnevale. Will they enjoy the putrid smell of burning flesh? No offense Niccolò, but letting young wastrels into the Great Council has brought us to this. The Golden Age of Lorenzo doesn't look so bad now."

"I can't disagree," said Adriani. "But then, youth are our only link to the future, no? Better to test them early."

"I've had enough of them. And I'll be staying home as I imagine there's a good chance of violence."

"The magistrates have put the Piazza under heavy guard," Niccolò assured him. "Three hundred soldiers under Salviati to protect the Dominicans and more than five hundred of the Signoria's guards to maintain order—it should be more than enough."

"Is this then how we maintain order in our city? Incite riots and then bring out the pikes and swords? May God preserve us."

With a grunt Filippo pressed his cap down tighter on his head. "Yes, I'm old so I'm told, but must we behave like Huns? Perhaps a Mass or two with a sermon is not such a bad thing?"

Niccolò nodded in agreement. "Most assuredly, I would say, ...provided it's said in Church."

"Well, this is your world now, my young friend," said Filippo. "Make the best of it. *Piacere*."

Messer Filippo turned away as Adriani smiled at Niccolò with forbearance. Then he followed Messer Filippo in the direction of Filippo's bookshop.

Niccolò called after them: "The pleasure is mine, Signori. *Addio*."

He was thinking how men cling to the past all the while it is receding. But if things went as planned, there would be no burning of monks. He turned to hurry back to his house. It wouldn't be long before he must meet Piero Soderini.

***

The sun was high in the sky over the Palazzo when Luca Landucci pushed his way through the crowd to find shelter under the Pisan canopy. Messer Luca looked from face to face, searching for someone familiar. He pulled his fitted wool cap low on his head, gathered his lucco around him and leaned his back up against the wall to watch and wait.

A throng of men and boys swarmed the Piazza like wasps, filling the loggias, and peering out from every window and balcony. Youths scampered like monkeys scaling the lampposts, clinging to the rustic stonework, and hanging from iron torch-rings fixed to the walls of buildings. Even the rooftops were crowded with heads bobbing like pigeons from their high roosts. A tight cluster of bodies closed in on the platform piled high with dry logs and webbed with sticks. Luca wondered how the guards would control this clogged mass when the roaring flames drove them back.

It was close to the appointed time and it seemed the entire male population was crammed into the square, most laughing, jesting, and carrying on. An insistent drumming grew louder, gaining momentum and assaulting the ears, before trailing off again. Everyone had come to see the miracle, or better. Either way, they were guaranteed a *spettacolo*. Banners of the Gonfalons hung from the buildings while supporters waved flags and hawkers shouted out their wares of food and drink for sale. Messer Luca thought this must be what the Circus Maximus was in ancient Rome. He heard raucous laughter and just in front saw a large group of *Compagnacci*. They were spewing out a litany of insults and derisions to torment the quieter, isolated pockets of somber *Piagnoni*.

"*Andiamo, dai, dai*, let's roast a porker or two!"

Though unnoticed, the apothecary felt surrounded and regretted his choice of vantage point. Even the younger boys were dancing and singing, caught up in the pent-up emotion of their elders. He wondered if some of these were former Boys of Friar—how quickly they had melted away. Then he overheard several men who were reading the official declaration of the Ordeal posted around the city.

"So, the friar isn't even going to enter the flames himself?" asked one, holding the announcement.

"No, no, his substitute, Fra Domenico from Pescia accepted the challenge. But the Franciscan has withdrawn as well. He's convinced one of his dim-witted brothers to offer himself up for the sacrifice. Someone named Fra Rondinelli."

The first man shrugged and then struggled to read the rest of the declaration. "So, these propositions are true or false depending on who burns."

Another bystander broke in. "It's the same as the friar's original prophecy: the Church is reprobate, will be scourged and renovated and all will happen soon."

"I thought that all happened already."

"The Franciscans claim the prophecies are a hoax, but Fra Girolamo insists Florence will be more rich and glorious. Even the infidel Turk will be converted."

"Bravo to that. I'll root for the Dominican's miracle."

"If he walks through untouched, the friar's excommunication is void and all sins of the Weepers washed away."

The man gestured with a flourish but Luca caught his eye and warned him with a nod toward the *Compagnacci*. Luca turned the other way and struggled to see through the crowd across to the east entrance of the Palazzo and the Loggia dei Priori along the south side. The Loggia was still empty, awaiting the two large delegations of the Franciscans and Dominicans. The cavernous Loggia was separated by a constructed partition with a small altar erected on the far side, closer to the Palazzo. The whole area was cordoned off from the crowd by a ring of infantry. Behind the soldiers, Luca's eye caught a flash of bouncing light. It was the long, gleaming sword brandished by the striding figure of the military captain, Marcuccio Salviati, appointed as the steadfast protector of the friar.

Girding the Palazzo was a larger force of the Signoria's armed guards, protecting the ringhiera where the priors would sit and watch as the two candidates entered the tunnel of fire.

The crowd cheered and Luca looked over to see a procession of gray-frocked Franciscans entering the Piazza along the Via Vaccherecccia on the right. Their hoods were drawn up to hide their faces as they quietly passed through Salviati's infantry and filed into the near side of the Loggia.

Close behind, Luca heard a spirited chant announcing the approach of the Dominicans. Strains of a hymn floated across the Piazza.

"Let God arise, and let his enemies be scattered..."

Stirred, the friar's supporters in the crowd echoed the response.

"Hosannah! Hosannah!"

This only provoked another outburst from the *Compagnacci*: "Snivelers!" "Prayer-mumblers!" "Enough with the grace, let's get on with our roast!"

Messer Luca stood tall to catch a glimpse of the procession. Fra Domenico was in the lead—his head bare and a flame-red cape covering his ample girth. He carried a large wooden crucifix, raised high in front of him. Marching directly behind was Fra Girolamo, dressed in a white cassock and holding up the silver-figured monstrance containing the consecrated Host. He was flanked by two other friars and followed by the entire San Marco congregation. Both Fra Girolamo and Domenico were chanting confidently and appeared insensible to the commotion around them.

Suddenly, a strong hand grasped Luca's shoulder, startling him. He turned into the exasperated face of Cronaca.

"It wasn't easy finding you in the middle of this rabble."

Luca said softly, "We're surrounded by *Compagnacci*. There could be trouble."

"These jackasses only bray," said Cronaca, looking around and flexing his arms. "They want no trouble with a sturdy builder."

Luca nodded his head toward the Loggia. "They just arrived."

"Not a bad vantage point. From here we should be able to see Fra Domenico emerge right from the flames of the Inferno, God willing."

In the *Sala dei Signori*, Niccolò huddled next to Piero Soderini, notebook and quill in hand. They were seated at a bench with several other members of the Eighty while Gonfaloniere Popoleschi presided. All were listening calmly to the petitions and allegations of the Franciscans. Fra Rondinelli, their candidate for the Ordeal, sat listless next to them. He looked forlorn and chagrined, no doubt pondering his fate.

"We humbly request, Excellencies," Fra Francesco pleaded, "that the Dominican be ordered to remove the red cape in which he is draped."

Niccolò felt a sense of mirth rise in him as Fra Francesco argued how, with magical powers, Savonarola may have bewitched Fra Domenico's robes. The request was granted and agreed to, but after the robe had been shed the Franciscan then insisted the Dominican trade all his robes for the plain ones of a brother and then not be allowed to stand next to the friar, lest he cast another spell. The official secretary of the Signoria was deputed to race up and down to deliver these directives and convey the responses of the Dominicans below. Soon these various pretexts had consumed more than an hour and exhausted the poor secretary. The Franciscans sat nervously while the magistrates deliberated among themselves.

Niccolò wrote a note in his journal and passed it to Piero, who then requested permission from the Gonfaloniere to speak.

"Fra Francesco, apparently Fra Domenico has changed his vestment and is now anxious to commence the Ordeal. But he wishes to carry the Host into the fire with him."

Fra Francesco sparked to life. "No, no, no. We cannot accept that he carries the symbol of Our Lord, Our Savior, to protect him in the flames! Excellencies, do you see what diabolical tricks these Dominicans play?"

"And what of the sacrament?" asked Soderini.

"This is impossible!" cried Fra Francesco and threw up his hands.

This new point raised sufficient cause for further objections and the secretary was dispatched again.

Outside the sun passed its zenith, causing the crowd to become impatient. Men and boys had grown weary, precariously clinging to their hard-won perches.

"What are they waiting for? *Che cazzo fai!*"

A young boy, hanging from a balustrade announced: "The red one has gone in and out of the Palazzo and now has changed his frock. He's kneeling before the altar."

"Where is this Fra Rondinelli? Has he shown his face yet?" yelled

Cronaca.

"The Grays are still in the Palazzo," replied the lookout.

In the distance one could see arguments and gesticulations between the two delegations and the official representative of the Signoria but from afar one could only guess what transpired.

"Perhaps Fra Girolamo has decided to test the fire himself?"

"No," screamed an opponent, "the *frate* delays. He's afraid, he plays for time. Are we to be taken for fools?"

"No," another bold supporter yelled, "Fra Girolamo has performed miracles before and this time he'll silence all his enemies for all time!"

Messer Luca looked up to see clouds cover the sky, blotting out the sun as it passed behind them, casting a dark shroud over the Palazzo and the far end of the Piazza.

"Come on!" a voice screamed, "Light the fire! Do we have to wait here all day?!"

Several of the *Compagnacci* screamed: "*Porco frate!* Pig Friar! The *frate* is a false prophet, a son of the devil! He cheats us of the trial!"

"Shut up, you blasphemers! It's all a scheme of the Franciscans."

The two groups pushed and squabbled and the mass of *Compagnacci* surged toward the platform and the Loggia.

Under the Loggia Fra Domenico was distraught with the delays and Fra Girolamo sought to calm him. Poor Domenico had confidently accepted the ultimate test of his faith, but for reasons he could not understand he was being denied the chance to enter the fire. Seeing his eyes fill with tears of frustration, Fra Girolamo told him to kneel at the altar and pray before the Holy Sacrament of the Body of Christ.

Just then the secretary of the Signoria returned insisting the Dominican must now surrender the consecrated Host, so the sacrament would not be burned. But this was a specious argument, Fra Girolamo contended: all theologians knew the substance of the sacrament is not consumed with the Host. This was an obvious ruse by the Franciscans and their enemies in the Signoria. There was a game being played here and he feared the worst. After all this time, the magistrates had still not come down to take their places at the ringhiera. He insisted there should be no more delays and for the Franciscans to show themselves at once.

Suddenly the commotion of the surging crowd off to the side alerted Fra Girolamo and the other friars to the threat of violence. He looked out over the sea of bodies and saw a dark surge with the white flash of steel coming toward the Loggia like a wind-whipped wave. The *Compagnacci* were attacking. The Dominicans fell back behind their prior.

In front of the steps Capitano Salviati reacted quickly, drawing his sword and concentrating his troops in front of the Loggia. He commanded them to hold fast and then shouted over the crowd that any man to cross his line would "taste the steel of Marcuccio Salviati!" This gave pause to those in front of the mob, as they braced themselves against those surging forward.

Fra Girolamo noticed the Signoria's guards arrayed in front of the Palazzo standing ready. But they had not advanced to quell the riot. At his ear, Fra Malatesta, who had previously sworn to enter the fire with Domenico, clamored for him to do something as the crowds surely meant to kill them. Then, as emotions rose to a feverish pitch, a black thunderhead moved in over the city, blotting out the light.

In the Sala dei Signori, Niccolò watched the priors huddle in discussion, equivocating for more time. With immoveable indignation, the Dominicans had now refused to concede any more points to their opponents. The conflict was at an impasse and the light of day was quickly fleeing. So here we sit, mused Niccolò, in The Hall of Two Hundred Reasons Not to Make a Decision. But Niccolò had learned how this game was played and everything was going according to plan. Only a little more time before they would throw up their hands and declare a forfeit.

Niccolò excused himself and returned to his office to steal a glance at the scene below. It was growing dark and the Piazza was still packed with bodies. He was fascinated by the seething mass and wondered if and when this powder keg would explode. He glimpsed Doffo Spini in the middle of an angry gang of *Compagnacci* and wondered where Tommaso was. This was a dangerous game and he hoped he and Piero had not miscalculated. It must be brought to a conclusion soon.

He was startled by a sudden crack of thunder that quieted the confused crowd into submission. All eyes looked up with trepidation at the sky and Niccolò looked too, half-expecting to see a lightning bolt hurl down and ignite the Ordeal with a fireball. Instead the skies opened up and a torrential rain doused the hordes outside.

Niccolò shook his head in disbelief. Che bella Fortuna! By the grace of God Almighty, that should cool them for a while.

Outside the jam-packed crowd was trapped under the deluge and the drenching only worsened their distemper. It was apparent they would be denied the pleasure of their day's entertainment, but they refused to retreat.

"It's a sign! It's a sign!" a voice shouted, but the surly crowd was not appeased. The rain shower ceased but still none left. They pushed and jostled each other and waited. Tired, hungry and wet, they spied the friars huddled together, dry under the protection of the Loggia.

There was a trumpet blast and all eyes focused on the green-liveried representative of the Signoria standing on the ringhiera to make his announcement. They listened, but all knew the message before it was delivered—the late hour and the inclement weather made it impossible for the Ordeal to take place. The crowd was ordered to disperse until a new decision on the Ordeal could be issued.

The malcontents cried: "Decision?! Who can wait for a decision from the Signoria? We only have one lifetime!"

Then the crowd called out for the Gonfaloniere to appear on the second floor balcony and address them, but to no avail.

Under the Loggia, Fra Girolamo and his brothers prepared to march back to San Marco escorted by Captain Salviati and his troops. As Savonarola held the monstrance aloft and the friars fell in behind him, Salviati's men were forced to drive a wedge through the crowd, brandishing their pikes and halberds. Pushed back by the soldiers, the mob turned ugly and hurled insults upon the Dominicans.

"False prophet!" "Deceiver!" "Sons of Satan, may you all burn in Hell!"

The friar's supporters were overwhelmed and ran for cover as the insults turned to rocks and stones and other materials torn from the platform. The angry crowd followed behind the Dominicans and threatened them with bodily harm all the way back to San Marco. Trembling from fear and cold, the retreating friars found refuge at last behind the heavy doors of the Church of San Marco. They huddled in prayer together with the female worshippers who had remained there during the day.

CHAPTER 42

AFTER THE ORDEAL

PAOLO SODERINI PACED BACK AND forth before the crackling fire as Niccolò stared, mesmerized by the licking flames. He and the three brothers—Paolo, Piero and Giovanvettorio—were waiting impatiently for Tommaso to return after the failed Ordeal and near riot in the Piazza. As a precaution, Niccolò and Piero had slipped unnoticed from the Palazzo more than an hour after the cancellation of the Ordeal and on their way back they had warily noted the unrestrained fury and passion of the mobs roaming the streets. A judiciously imposed curfew had since chased the rabble home, but Tommaso was still unaccounted for.

"It was a fiasco. We should have prevented it," fumed Paolo, indirectly criticizing his brother.

Piero, feeling the sting, said forcefully, "There was no possibility of preventing it—the Signoria and the people were both clamoring for it, even the Dominicans! The best we could do was try to manage it and maintain order. Anyway, I view the day as a qualified success."

"A success? What about Tommaso? What about peace in the city? And what happens now? It's dangerous to invite such chaos. I've already lost two sons, will I lose another to this foolishness?!"

"I'm sure Tommaso's fine," said Piero. "But I'd like to know what Vespucci's little troublemakers are planning."

"*Figlio mio*, where is he?" demanded Paolo, his frustration marked by his pacing.

Niccolò noted the personal differences between the brothers. The elder, Paolo, adhered to Christian virtue and placed his faith in the divine guidance of the friar; but the friar was reckless and bold, whereas Paolo was conservative. Equally cautious, Piero was more skeptical of religious beliefs and relished the intrigue of civic affairs. But Niccolò knew Piero was less sure. The irony was the religious Paolo had less faith in men and more in God, which was why he thought firmness was required to keep them from doing evil, whereas Piero professed an unwarranted faith in the goodness of men, based solely upon an appeal to civic virtue. Despite his own differing views concerning the friar, Niccolò found himself closer to Paolo's position on the nature of men.

Piero said, "You know, it would've been helpful if your friar had demonstrated a miracle or two in the Piazza today."

"I'm in no mood for jokes. The man is a preacher and priest, not a miracle-worker. Let's hope we don't pay the price of our false pretenses."

Paolo was right. Niccolò had seen it often enough: an unruly mob turned its wrath in unpredictable directions and today they had gambled dangerously.

"Don't worry, the Signoria and the Angry Ones were leading the charge, while we were the model of fairness. Right, Nico?"

"We were most fortunate, Signor Piero," he said, hoping their luck held.

The four men heard a commotion outside in the courtyard and after a long moment Tommaso burst into the room. He was out of breath and his words spilled forth in spurts.

"I was with Spini... and the others... they chased the Dominicans to San Marco...Salviati and his men stood guard until the crowd dispersed."

"That must have been hours ago," said Piero.

"*Sì*, ...then we roamed the city, cursing the friar and chasing the Weepers into their homes. They're too afraid to fight back... they're filled with doubt..."

Paolo started to pace again, torn between relief to see his son safe and fury over the plots and lies of the *Compagnacci*. "Have you lost your senses—,"

"Father, it's his own fault. The people have turned against him."

Paolo just stared, too angry to reply.

Niccolò had a million of his own questions. He quickly asked, "What's Spini planning?"

"I'm not sure. There was a Milanese with him and they spoke of another man, a Spaniard from Valencia who's staying somewhere in the city. I imagine both are spies. What will the Signoria do?"

Piero scoffed, "The Signoria? Bah...nothing, they'll never make a first move. Each night they sleep in the Palazzo, hoping to wake up in a paradise of their own design, without effort." He looked toward Paolo. "I wonder what the friar will do."

"He's not stupid," replied Paolo. "He knows the games his enemies are playing. I imagine he'll wait safely in San Marco...and pray."

Tommaso was disdainful. "He's doomed. He had his chance and failed. Spini's desperate to kill him and the Signoria won't stop it."

Before Paolo could reply Niccolò broke in. "I agree. The friar only has the support of the people to save him from his many enemies. Now they've exposed him and the *popolo* will turn against him."

Tommaso nodded. "*Sì*, did you see the *fanciulli* throwing stones again?"

Niccolò restated his thesis with confidence: "Fra Girolamo fashions himself a prophet favored by God, like Moses. But as I said before, Moses had an army and he didn't hesitate to use it to destroy his enemies. Perhaps the friar does speak with God, but where is his army? The pope has an army."

Paolo was disturbed by his son's rashness. "You two speak with the recklessness of youth. You forget Christ prevailed over the Romans with nothing but his humility."

"Yes, and his own people crucified him for it," Niccolò muttered.

"Perhaps you're right, if you care only for the preservation of your body. But what of your soul? You're young, but I fear for my immortal soul."

Niccolò fell silent. How could he reply? He could not insult the older man by belittling his faith. Someday, he too would look into the abyss and perhaps then he would say the same. This life was filled with death. But the problem was here, now, on earth. The people of Italia did not rise up to vanquish evil, they submitted to it, waving their blasted crucifixes. They let the foreigners have their way, raping and stealing, turning them into slaves in their own land. They wait for God to do their bidding, just as the helpless Hebrews who submitted to Pharaoh before Moses led them out. But God, thought Niccolò, does not wish to do everything for us. When the time came to fight violence with greater violence, cold-blooded Moses had wielded a merciless sword. They must do the same.

Perhaps it is unfortunate the Roman Church contributed to this decay, without Dominic and Francis it might have fallen by sheer weight of its own avarice generations ago. At least the friar deserved praise for rebelling against these corrupt prelates. But he'll never succeed with his army of the despairing; they'll be slaughtered.

No, Niccolò revised himself, as typical Florentines they'll desert *en masse* in the face of danger.

Tommaso still adamantly defied his father. "I'm sure Spini plans some attack tomorrow. It's Palm Sunday—so there'll be a sermon in the Duomo."

"*Basta*," interrupted Piero, standing up. "I see we have the same divisions in our own house that plague our city. Vespucci will attack the friar from one side while Valori and the *Frateschi* will resist from the other. They'll go on gnawing on each other like two demons in the Inferno. And the doubting Thomases will drift between the two, ready to heed our quiet voice of reason. But the middle road is open and we best take it. This way we survive to lead the city when the dust settles."

Then Piero looked at Paolo and Tommaso. "I would suggest neither of you attract attention to yourselves until all this has passed."

For once, Piero surprised Niccolò with his decisiveness.

As the group broke Piero motioned for Niccolò to accompany him to his rooms on the pretext of discussing the next day's affairs in the Palazzo.

"Don't be discouraged, Nico. My brother's a practical man and he suffers much over his sons."

"I understand. I too appreciate the power of faith and God's grace. Perhaps the friar is even a true prophet of God. It doesn't matter. The people believe it. Or they did... Now he should fight fire with fire, but cannot. We must not follow him."

"You're right. The people are in a fever to spill blood. I say let it not be ours. The Signoria will do nothing to restrain Spini's ruffians. But Valori will do his utmost to defend the friar."

Niccolò forced a smile. "As the friar is no Moses, Valori is no Maid of France."

Piero nodded. "So we must tread carefully. Let the Signoria fall in behind Vespucci and the *Arrabbiati*. Let Valori and the *Frateschi* do their best in the name of the friar. And let us not be so rash and foolish."

Piero put his hand on Niccolò's shoulder. "Nico, you have become like a son to me."

Caught by surprise, Niccolò smiled and averted his eyes as he wondered at Piero's sincerity and what was meant.

Piero continued: "If the *Frateschi* lose this battle, Braccesi will be deposed. Your letters and analysis have attracted notice and I've heard favorable words regarding your potential candidacy. Adriani is in favor, but much depends on whether we can prevail over both the *Arrabbiati* and the *Frateschi*. If either gains the upper hand our cause will suffer."

As Niccolò made the short walk home in the dark he felt both empowered and exposed. Chancellor Braccesi was closely identified with the friar and Valori, and Niccolò was sure he was behind the anonymous accusations of sodomy. Thank God it had been buried under the cascade of disasters. If Braccesi was dismissed the only obstacle would be the *Arrabbiati* candidate, whoever he may be. Braccesi was now the enemy and Piero Soderini and Maestro Adriani would be important allies. He felt his chances were good, but he could not help feeling another crisis was imminent and his destiny was in the hands of capricious Fate.

Was politics ordained to be this way? Men forever ricocheting from one folly to the next? It was inevitable, he imagined, an unending cycle. Man is born with envy in his heart because he desires all that's denied him. Then envy leads to discontent and rival factions and factions lead to rebellion. And rebellion foments chaos and fear, giving free reign to hate and the sins of true evil. Until the tyrant imposes order again.

The vicious cycle could be broken only by civic *Virtù* served by religious faith. And these must be enforced by action, violent if necessary. To avoid ruin, the good ruler must learn to be able to *not* be good, as necessity demands. He must be a fox to avoid snares and a lion to frighten the wolves. And still it's not enough—to achieve success one must be lucky or blessed, favored by *Fortuna,* or granted the grace of God.

He was, he admitted, a confirmed cynic of this world with little hope for the next; and still just a month away from his twenty-ninth year.

CHAPTER 43

ATTACK ON SAN MARCO

IT WAS THE MORNING OF the feast of Palm Sunday and the streets were calm. But as the day wore on they gathered force like clouds advancing before a storm. It was said the friar had locked himself away after a short sermon to his supporters early that morning at the Church of San Marco. Later, during Vespers, the traditional Mass and sermon was to be delivered in the Duomo by another friar from San Marco. In anticipation of trouble, a large crowd gathered in the Piazza San Giovanni as the *Compagnacci* swore to disrupt the sermon where they had failed the previous year. Members of the friar's party were also present and some said they meant to make a preemptory strike against their enemies. Many in the crowd bore arms—some with swords, some with concealed daggers, others with clubs and stones. When a band of *Piagnoni* arrived from San Marco, the ruffians barring the Cathedral doors declared the sermon would not take place. The Weepers spit back at them to stand aside, as they meant to enter. One wave pushed up against the other like the clash of wind and tide in a narrow strait.

Doffo Spini stepped forward, drew his sword, and flailed at his nearest adversary. The blow glanced off the shoulder of one of the Weepers, igniting an explosion as Spini's henchmen charged headlong into the throng, scattering the Weepers like pigeons. Screams and shouts erupted and shook the Piazza, then radiated out to alert the entire populace to the disturbance. In the midst of the madness the *Compagnacci* began chanting a refrain:

"To San Marco! To San Marco! With fire in hand!"

Soon the square and the surrounding streets were a pandemonium of fleeing bodies. Small bands formed, coalesced with other bands to form larger clusters, which then ran together to create a seething mass. It moved spontaneously toward the center, finally swarming in the Piazza della Signoria. The commotion they raised reverberated inside the Palazzo.

In his office, Niccolò jumped up from his desk and raced to the window to view the commotion. He was unsure what prey this beast was intent on devouring and wondered if the guards had secured all the doors. He was about to rush out into the corridor to alert the Signoria and the Chancellor when he heard the rabble unite behind a single chant: "To San Marco! To San Marco!"

***

Fra Domenico knelt in prayer before the carved crucifix in the church choir. It was now past vespers and there was only a small group of worshippers, mostly women, remaining. Domenico had reverted to his simple frock with black mantle, a contrast to the regal red cape and white garments he had worn to the Ordeal. He still saw himself carrying the crucifix of the Savior before him like a crusader. But he had failed his ordained mission. With a heavy heart he looked up at the icon before him, into the eyes of the crucified Christ and whispered his apology.

Lord, forgive me.

He heard a small commotion in the Church but blocked it from his senses by focusing on the figure of the Savior. He begged for one more chance, but how could it happen now. It seemed they were defeated. Exhausted and distracted, the prior had sequestered himself in the small refectory for most of the day, praying while waiting for word from the Signoria.

A sudden clash of thunder startled Domenico. It struck the large doors of the Church with a boom that threatened to break them down, growing larger as it reverberated inside the empty nave. Fra Domenico rose up from his prayer, confused by the frantic parishioners running toward the altar. He saw a group of men at the far end barricading the doors and realized the thunder was an attack on the convent. He raced through the side door connecting the church with the cloister.

The normally peaceful courtyard was in a furious commotion. Domenico saw Messers Valori and Tosinghi leading an armed band of lay supporters and brothers running to and fro in a panic. He was shocked to see several brothers carrying muskets and swords—led by Fra Luca della Robbia, Fra Benedetto and the passionate young artist Baccio della Porta. Then the young German brother, Fra Enrico, rushed past him, crossbow in hand, leading a band of his fellow countrymen back into the church.

In the center of the courtyard Valori was barking out commands: "Lock and bar all the doors. And guard the walls. Send a lookout into the bell tower!"

Domenico saw his doves fluttering in their cage and immediately went to them. He opened the door to calm them in his hands but they flapped their wings in fear and flew out of the cage. He quickly realized it was their best chance and shooed them all through the open door to fly free. He watched them as they rose up, like holy spirits disappearing into the sky. Surely they would return when it was safe.

Fra Domenico heard a shout and saw Valori, who shouted again: "Father, where is the prior?"

Domenico, speechless with tears, motioned toward the small refectory behind the Chapter House. Following in confusion behind Valori and Tosinghi, he heard an inner voice say "Fly away. Be safe!"

Valori burst through the door and exclaimed: "Fra Girolamo, attenzione! The mob is to attacking the convent. We arrived just ahead of them."

Seated behind his desk, the prior appeared dazed, slow to comprehend.

"Prior," flustered Domenico, "a mob is throwing stones against the Church doors and the worshippers are taking refuge in the sacristy."

"They mean to burn down San Marco and kill you," Valori cried, trying to rouse him.

The prior shook his head. "No, it's not possible. The Signoria will send a guard. Where is Captain Salviati?"

Valori was adamant. "He's not here. We sent a messenger to the Palazzo, but the Signoria will not act soon enough. We must defend the convent."

Fra Girolamo stepped out into the corridor where he saw the pandemonium in the courtyard. A small group of friars huddled along the walls of the cloister, frozen in fear. Others were running this way and that, mixed in with laymen hauling weapons and shouting commands. He cried, "No, no, no. They must not stain their hands with blood! They must not disobey the teachings of the gospels..."

Fra Silvestro, seeing the prior and Domenico, darted from the Pilgrim's Hospice across the courtyard. Out of breath, his eyes danced in fear. "We just came from the Cathedral. The mob of Angry Ones has already murdered two innocents in the Via Cocomero. They just ran them through with their swords like beasts. They're going to burn the convent!"

Valori and Tonsinghi hurried away to command the defense as the prior stood and watched his panicked brethren. "Domenico," he cried, "we must stop it...stop them—,"

Just then a hail of rocks came hurtling over the roof and landed in the courtyard.

***

The fortress-like Palazzo was barricaded and secured by a deployment of guards. Inside, the Signoria, the Eight, and several members of a Pratica were huddled in conference in the Sala dei Signori. Niccolò caught Piero Soderini's eye and saw concern. The Signoria was antipathetic to the sudden attack on San Marco. Gonfaloniere Popoleschi was obviously hostile to the friar and Valori and was using delaying tactics to avoid sending a division of guards to quell the disturbance.

Niccolò wondered about Tommaso and Paolo, who remained sequestered in their home. No one can predict an uncontrolled mob, where it will turn or when it will spend itself. The madness struck fear into the hearts of those with something to protect and excited the passions of those with nothing to lose. But this time we invited it, thought Niccolò, and who knows where it will end. Who will be murdered to settle old scores under the convenient mask of chaos? Which innocents will die? Who will be chased from the city gates, thankful at least to have survived?

***

At San Marco the battle raged as the day wore into evening. The large convent bell, *La Piagnona*, rang out its alarm but no help arrived from the Signoria. Those trapped inside could only wonder about what was happening outside the convent walls as a barrage of rocks, arrows, and fireballs rained continuously into the cloister.

To defend the convent, some of the brethren and laymen organized themselves into a formidable force. Apparently, several weeks earlier Fra Silvestro and some of the other Florentines had secreted a cache of weapons and armor in a room below the cloister that was quickly deployed, despite Fra Domenico's excited protestations. Two of the Florentines, Fra Francesco Davanzati and Fra Baldo organized brigades of friars, ordering them about and stationing groups at the weakest points. All along the roof on the outer perimeter, Fra Benedetto stationed friars to throw stones and roof tiles down on the rabble outside.

Earlier a mob had breached the Church doors and Domenico had watched as Fra Enrico and his band, armored in breastplates and helmets, beat them back, firing muskets and brandishing their swords and halberds, leading with the battle cry of "*Vivo Cristo!*" Fra Enrico exhibited his skill with the crossbow, felling several attackers from the height of the pulpit while singing out "*Salvum fac populum tuum, Domine!*" Surprised to meet this armed resistance, the mob had been turned back.

Unfortunately these small victories came at great cost, as several friars and lay supporters were seriously wounded. The fallen were carried into the Church and lain on the steps of the altar, where they received last rites from their fellows. Fra Girolamo remained in the Chapter House before moving to the choir to pray with many of the brethren who heeded his call for nonviolence. Domenico stayed there with him and prayed before the crucifix while Valori and the others directed the defenses.

The battle ebbed and flowed until a contingent of macebearers from the Palazzo arrived soon after dark with orders from the Signoria. Admitted into the cloister, their leader announced an official edict ordering all those in the convent to lay down their arms. It declared Fra Girolamo was sentenced into exile and ordered to quit Florence within twelve hours or suffer arrest.

Fra Girolamo was shaken as he looked to the others. "I will surrender myself to the Signoria. Only that will stop this madness."

"No, it's a trick!" cried Silvestro. "The mob will tear you to pieces and we shall be left defenseless."

Valori, too, was opposed. "Father, this is no justice. Who began this attack? Are our enemies not to be disarmed?"

While Fra Girolamo insisted again he should surrender, Domenico and the others tried to dissuade him. Valori assured them all that the arrival and departure of the macebearers would calm the mob temporarily. He would take this opportunity to escape over the back wall to return to fortify his family house and also raise a larger force of *Frateschi* to fight in the streets. Faced by a rear guard action, he was convinced the mob would quickly disperse.

"You take a great risk, *signore*," said Fra Davanzati, the Florentine who had helped direct the defense forces.

"Yes, Francesco," said Tosinghi. "If you are caught alone they'll—,"

Valori waved them off. "The Signoria won't dare risk insulting a respected citizen. I am a former Gonfaloniere."

Promising to return with reinforcements, he went to the rear of the gardens and was hoisted over the wall.

***

After a brief recess Niccolò returned to the confusion in the Sala dei Signori. Except for the frequent runners sent out to gather reports that were often conflicted or confused, the magistrates were in the dark on what was transpiring on the streets. The macebearers had returned from San Marco, reporting the siege was still engaged and there had been no surrender of arms yet. They reported seeing Francesco Valori and several other supporters of the friars there, so several contingents of guards were immediately dispatched to the houses of the leading *Frateschi,* to bring them before the Signoria to explain their roles in this disturbance.

The temper of the Signoria and many of the citizens present was clear. They were out to eliminate the problem of the friar permanently, but they wished to do so while wearing the mask of republican justice and moral virtue—this was the reason for all these pained contortions. Piero Soderini and many of the others avoided eye contact, so Niccolò occupied himself by taking his quill and scribbling cartoons and chicken scratches in his journal. He wondered where Braccesi was hiding now.

After about an hour another runner came to report to the magistrates that one of the macebearers had delivered the summons to Valori, who had been found at his house, besieged by an angry mob. Signor Valori had immediately surrendered and agreed to report to the Palazzo. This news was greeted with nods of approval from the Gonfaloniere and the opposition magistrates.

But then the messenger continued his report: Unfortunately, the macebearer was unable to protect Valori from the mob. Outside his house several ruffians had set upon him with daggers and killed him on the spot.

The sudden reversal of Valori's fortune sent the room into a fit of contortions over the senseless violence—even though, Niccolò noted, it was violence of which they were the prime architects. The runner went on to report Valori's house had been ransacked and he believed the man's wife and other family members had also been murdered in the mayhem.

Piero Soderini, visibly disturbed, stood up to address the Signoria and the Eight: "Excellencies, please, we must do something to end this now—before we devour ourselves!"

Niccolò knew he was thinking of his own house and family across the Arno. The magistrates succumbed and it was quickly decided to dispatch a deputation of guards and macebearers to San Marco immediately, where they were to arrest Savonarola and his two confederates, Fra Domenico Buonvicini and Fra Silvestro Maruffi, and safely transport them to the Palazzo under armed guard. The rioters were to be dispersed and a curfew enforced. Contingents of guards were also ordered to various points in the city to protect the houses of private citizens. This brought a noticeable look of relief to Soderini.

As the arrest orders were given, the captain of the guards stood rigidly in place and then inquired with military precision, "On what charge, Excellencies?"

The question hung, suspended in stony silence.

"For disturbing the peace and order of the city," said Gonfaloniere Popoleschi in a perfunctory tone of authority.

Niccolò looked down at all the little 'x's he had scratched in his notebook and noticed how much they resembled so many little crosses of various sizes.

***

After a brief respite, the attack on San Marco resumed with greater ferocity as the night wore on. The *Piagnona* rang out the alarm again and again but still no reinforcements arrived. The Church doors were set ablaze and the dense smoke choked those in the choir and the sacristy. Fra Enrico and his band of holy warriors were still defending the church but a retreat deeper into the convent was necessary. Fra Girolamo removed the Host from the tabernacle and placed it into the monstrance. He raised it up and held the Body of Christ before him and commanded the group of friars praying with him to follow him into the inner sanctum of the library on the second floor. He called for Domenico and Silvestro to accompany him.

At the top of the stairs of the dormitory, as they turned to enter the library, they confronted a determined Fra Benedetto racing down from the roof with a wild look in his eye and halberd in his grasp.

Fra Girolamo stopped him and commanded him to throw down his weapon and take up the cross, saying, "Benedetto, I never intended my brethren to shed blood."

Red-faced and ashamed, Fra Benedetto dropped his weapon and followed the prior and his fellow brethren into the library. Inside they lit torches, then closed and fastened the heavy doors behind them while Fra Girolamo deposited the monstrance with the Host just inside the entranceway. He stood and turned to behold the large hall as he gathered his disciples around him. They looked to him but his eyes looked past them.

This library was the garden of knowledge the architect Michelozzo had designed for Cosimo de' Medici with such subtlety. It was designed to open the mind and raise it to new heights, to provide refuge from the storm of man's pride and envy, and to succor the pursuit and discovery of hidden truths. The long straight hallway was framed by rigid columns and springing archways with a white ceiling, flat across the center and vaulted on the side corridors. Tonight the columns and ceiling were illuminated and shaded by the dancing light of the torches and resembled an arbor of trees under a knitted canopy.

Normally, the hallway shone with abundant natural light through the many softly arched windows along each outside wall. But tonight, shuttered and barred, it had become a walled garden protecting its precious fruit. Down the side corridors rows of upright lecterns held the heavy but fragile manuscripts. These were the repositories of the ancients, the Church fathers, the Holy Scriptures and even some of the moderns, like Petrarca—all these volumes were written in the secret Latin codes of the initiated, their pages filled with so many words only as valuable as the truths they embodied. In sum, this place revealed a perfect natural beauty, as if one were in a white, misted forest. This was his Gethsemane—the garden of knowledge that would betray his soul. As his brethren formed a ring around him, he sat down to lead them in prayer.

Before he began the door rattled and Fra Malatesta entered to announce the macebearers had arrived again from the Palazzo. The Signoria had issued and an edict for the three—Fra Girolamo, Fra Domenico and Fra Silvestro—to present themselves at the Palazzo without delay. "They said no harm would come to any of you."

"Where is the edict?" Fra Silvestro snapped.

"There was no written order." Malatesta replied.

"Then tell them they must get one," demanded Silvestro. Then Fra Girolamo spread his arms in an open embrace to comfort his disciples.

"My beloved children, in the presence of God, in the presence of the Holy Body of Christ, I confirm the truth of my doctrines. All I have said has come to me from God. He is my witness in Heaven."

Several friars quietly hummed *ecce quam bonum* to drown out the commotion outside as others fought to smother their sobs.

"I had not foreseen how all would turn so quickly against me. But may the Lord's will be done. My last exhortation to you is this: let prayer, faith and patience be your weapons. I leave you with anguish and grief, to surrender myself into my enemies' hands. I know not whether they will take my life, but if they do I am certain I will greet you in Heaven, where we shall fare far better than we have here on earth.

"The Lord said: 'unless a grain of wheat falls to the earth and dies, it remains but a single grain. Yet if it dies, it yields a rich harvest. Whoever loves his life will lose it. Whoever hates his life in this world will keep it for eternal life. Now my soul is troubled. Shall I say: 'Father, save me from this hour'? No, for this is the very reason I have come to this hour.'"[15]

Fra Girolamo grasped and held out the wooden crucifix around his neck. "Embrace the cross, take comfort in communion with the Lord and follow this path to eternal salvation."

He embraced those close to him and said, "Brothers, we must heed the words of Augustine: 'Resist and refuse to the point of martyrdom. The wars for Christ are won not by killing but by dying.'"

The brothers sobbed and quaked with fear. To comfort them, the prior knelt down and sang with them in an unwavering voice.

Soon after, Fra Malatesta returned with several others to join them huddled in the library. As the noise grew more immediate one of the laymen burst into the library, blood spurting from his head. It was a young artisan who had long desired to join the Dominican Order and had fought fiercely throughout the day to defend the convent. His wound was serious and, as he collapsed before the prior, he begged to be invested immediately, in case he should die. Fra Girolamo granted his request instantly, without hesitation.

The grateful brother stammered his gratitude from his prone position. "Father, the others can hold off the attack before the palace guards return. Take this chance now to slip away under cover of darkness."

"Yes, Prior, please," several of the brothers begged. "Once they take you in the Palazzo surely they'll kill you."

Fra Girolamo looked into the faces of his disciples—Domenico, Silvestro, Benedetto and the others. He had steeled himself to his fate, but perhaps he was mistaken. He had misgivings: perhaps this madness would blow past; perhaps this was not the right time; perhaps confrontation would not gain him the advantage. His work here was not done and his enemies were determined to defeat him. What would happen to his flock if he did not protect them from the wolves? Could he best shield them by fleeing or by confronting the Signoria? If he fled he could return when it was safe. But would he be denounced? Would his followers lose faith? If he stayed, could Valori and Soderini defeat their enemies? The next elections were still three weeks away but by then his supporters could regain the upper hand. Or he could flee north to France and return with Charles and his army to punish their enemies. The Christian kings required his guidance in calling for a Church Council to depose the Borgia wolf in Rome. God's work is not yet done. The moment is not right for this. *Lord, show me a sign...*

"What about Valori? Perhaps he's on his way with more troops," said Malatesta.

The wounded man disagreed. "Father, you mustn't wait, leave now. Give us your blessing."

Fra Girolamo was ready as he searched the faces of his disciples. But he saw fear and a shadow of anger and hesitated.

Then Fra Malatesta looked directly into his eyes and asked without emotion, "Prior, should not the shepherd lay down his life for his lambs?"

The ringing cry of the *Piagnona* fell silent and the silence swallowed him whole. It became clear: If he should flee, his disciples would fall away in shame and his name would be vilified for all eternity. The words of the Evangelist whispered in his ear: *I am the good shepherd. I lay down my life for my sheep. I know mine and mine know me. Just as the Father knows me and I know the Father.* Satan has made this challenge, now he must slay the beast in its own lair. He was in God's hands and may God's will be done.

"*Bastardo*," cried Silvestro at Malatesta, "you only wish to save your own neck!"

Fra Girolamo put his hand on Silvestro's arm to restrain him. "No, Brother Malatesta is right. What sort of shepherd would I be if I were to flee at first sight of the wolf? God is with us and God will determine our fate. Let them come, we are ready."

MICHAEL HARRINGTON

BOOK III

PARADISO

Only man's sins annuls man's liberty,
makes him unlike the Highest Good, so that,
in him, the brightness of It's light is dimmed;
And man cannot regain his dignity
unless, where sin left emptiness, man fills
that void with just amends for evil pleasure.
...

Either through nothing other than His mercy,
God had to pardon man, or of himself
man had to proffer payment for his folly.

- Dante Alighieri
[*Paradiso*: VII; 79-84;90-93]

O Highest Light, You, raised so far above
the minds of mortals, to my memory
give back something of Your epiphany,
And make my tongue so powerful that I
may leave to people of the future one
gleam of the glory that is Yours, for by
Returning somewhat to my memory
and echoing awhile within these lines,
Your victory will be more understood..

- Dante Alighieri
[*Paradiso*: XXXIII; 67-75]

CHAPTER 1

THE ARREST

THE MACEBEARERS RETURNED TO SAN MARCO within the hour, led by a company of armed guards. They pushed their way through the cursing throng in the Piazza San Marco, parting the pressing bodies with their pikes and halberds held crossways. They were admitted through the main door into the cloistered courtyard, still vigorously defended by a small band of friars and laymen.

The captain of the guard and the two macebearers ascended to the library where they found the friars still huddled in prayer behind closed doors. The captain read out the arrest warrant, specifying the names of Fras Girolamo, Domenico and Silvestro, and ordered them to accompany him downstairs. But Silvestro had slipped away and was nowhere to be found. As they descended to the cloister with Fra Girolamo and Fra Domenico in hand, the captain and his guards argued over what to do— to search for the third friar or return to the Palazzo with just the two. Fra Benedetto, impetuous and overcome with grief, stepped forward and demanded to be arrested as well, but Fra Girolamo reprimanded him again.

"*Basta*, Benedetto, I forbid it," he said. "You must remain here with the others and await my return."

The gesture angered the captain, believing Benedetto was making a mockery of his official duty. So he commanded his guards to bind the two friars, adding, "We'll come back for the other one later. He won't get far."

When his defenders objected, Fra Girolamo ordered them to put down their weapons. "Brothers, remember the words of Our Lord: 'Love your enemies, and pray for those who persecute you, so that you may be children of your Father in heaven, for He causes His sun to rise on the wicked as well as on the good, and He sends down His rain on the just and the unjust alike.'"

Then he extended his hands to be bound by the guards. One of the *Frateschi* tried to inject a note of hope: "Don't worry Father, we shall wait for Signor Valori to return and then petition the Signoria for your release in the morning."

The captain of the guard looked at them with dismay, then flatly announced: "Valori is dead, slain at the hands of the Ridolfi and Tornabuoni."

The *Frateschi* swallowed silent gasps—the bonds of community were now stretched by dread as each one now recalculated his individual chance of survival. The captain smelled their fear but was matter-of-fact: "I suggest you lay down your weapons immediately and return to your homes. A curfew is imposed by order of the Eight."

Then the captain and his company of guards pulled the two friars by the arms out into the pulsing fever of the Piazza San Marco.

An angry mass filled the square, brandishing sticks, poles and other makeshift weapons. Their torches licked the night sky and cast a menacing glow that danced among the shadows. As the guard and the two friars squeezed out the gate, a shout went up. "Here he comes, *il porco Frate*! The pig Friar!"

The crowd pushed forward until Fra Girolamo saw the whites of their eyes and felt the heat of their rage. The light of the torches blazed yellow-hot and glinted off drawn swords and protective armor. It was an inhuman wrath and even the guards drew back, holding their shields up and making a fence with their weapons to restrain the crowd. Fra Girolamo was sure the beast would devour them all at any moment.

"Hey, *Frate*, behold the true light," yelled one knave as he thrust his threatening torch close inside the protective ring of guards.

A hail of stones opened a small cut on the side of Fra Girolamo's head, causing a dark trickle of blood to flow. Domenico cried out with a plea of surrender as the captain raised his sword and screamed above the noise for the crowd to stand back and disperse, by order of the Signoria. But the grasping hands and fists of the crowd reached out to abuse the friars. One insistent fist shot out to strike Fra Girolamo from behind, its owner shouting: "Tell us now, prophet, who struck you."

The crowd laughed, spit, and cursed them as the escort made its way down the Via dei Servi behind the Cathedral. The taunts marked their slow progress:

"See now if God will save the false prophet!"

"May you burn in hell, heretic!"

"Anti-Christ!"

Fra Girolamo felt the fear he saw in Domenico's eyes and his confidence deserted him. His ears blocked out the noise around him but his eyes registered his horror. He was in shock. Valori was murdered and who knows whom else. So many of his brethren and supporters died for nothing in defending the convent this night. Would this ravenous beast now slaughter them all? What terrible thing had he done to incite this evil? *Lord, forgive me!*

As he looked around he was sure he saw the black eyes of Satan staring back at him from the darkness. So many contorted demons rising out of the dark, as if they were rising out of the black pitch of Hell. He saw those ghastly images of the Inferno, the sharp teeth and claws of demons reaching out to tear his flesh. But this was the Inferno as even Dante could not describe. Was this how the Savior felt, cursed by the Jews, whipped by the Romans, a crown of thorns cutting into his flesh, and the cross crushing him with its weight? *God, give me strength...* No, no, he rebuked himself; *I dare not compare myself to His Son.*

He gazed at the faces around him. There were no angels here, no women, no Magdalena here to offer him pity—only mad young men. He became confused. Where was his congregation? Where were the ones who came to every sermon in the Duomo, who worshipped in San Marco, who prayed with him? Who were these people who hated him so? Where have they come from? It was Satan's army rising up from the grave to steal the souls of the innocents and blacken the hearts of the pure. *Lord, ...give me strength...*

He looked again at Domenico but his brother's eyes were shut tight, letting his body be pushed forward by the persistent thrusts of the guards. He saw Domenico's lips move in prayer. Only two days before Domenico had walked tall, resplendent in his priestly robes, a champion eager to sacrifice himself for God's love. He was a true saint ready to ascend to his rightful place in Heaven. Now he was being dragged through Hell like an unrepentant sinner, an innocent betrayed. *Lord, You made Domenico pure of heart but have forsaken me, for I am plagued by doubts... Please forgive me my sins...*

He stumbled and fell when someone kicked him from the rear. He felt himself being hauled up under the arms and hurried along by the guards as a voice cut him like a knife: "There's the seat of his prophecies!"

He felt warm blood on his face and heard jeering and laughing. This unrepressed hatred tried to strangle him as another voice screamed out: "Let him trust in the Lord. Let God rescue him, then, see if He delights in him!"

Finally they arrived before the Palazzo and he looked up to see the dark shadow of the fortress, even blacker than the night. The tower rose up before him, against the sky like a centurion's sword standing guard. But protecting whom or what?

Then he realized this was the seat of man's earthly power. But it was a tomb, unlike the womb of the convent, the Cathedral or the Heavenly Church. He did not belong here; this was not his house. No, it was the yawing mouth of the ninth circle, which opened wide to swallow him whole.

He was pushed forward into the fortress where the noise of the mob died away in silent darkness. He and Domenico were tossed into a holding cell on the ground floor armory where they remained, bound and discarded like refuse for the remaining hours of the night.

CHAPTER 2

THE SIGNORIA DEBATES

"EXCELLENCIES," ANNOUNCED THE NOTARY OF the Signoria, "the charges against the prisoners are several. First, there is the matter of organized political *intelligenzie*—collusion between the accused and the *Frateschi*—that violates the laws of the Republic. Second is the question of violations of the sacrament of penance to reveal the private thoughts of individual citizens involved in civic affairs. Third is the religious heresy of false prophecies that violates the laws of the Holy Church. Finally, there is the charge of the failure of the Ordeal and the accused's refusal to quit the city, whereby he and his supporters provoked an armed resistance at the Convent of San Marco. Interrogations of the prisoners will determine the evidence and extract confessions on each of these charges."

As the notary read the report of the Eight of the Guard, Niccolò noticed the magistrates had barely flinched, though they were fully aware of what tortures lay behind the sterile wording. No criminal could be expected to confess truthfully unless the necessary inducement was applied, and no heretic would admit to the mark of Satan without a confession being torn from his or her breast. The accused would be deliberately 'put to the question' according to those subtle arts practiced by the Bargello 'interrogators.'

Evidenced by the smug expressions on the magistrates' faces, things had gone fairly, if unexpectedly, well. The Eight had arrested the three Dominicans: two on the night of the riot at San Marco, with the third betrayed by one of his brethren the following day. Savonarola was now imprisoned in the small prison cell high in the tower above, the one called the *Alberghetto* or "little inn," while his two colleagues were being held in the dungeons of the Bargello. Nineteen of the *Frateschi* were also arrested the day after and detained in the Bargello. The remaining friars at San Marco were severely reprimanded and the convent's bell tower silenced. A curfew was imposed and the city had returned to a more controlled temper in anticipation of the Signoria's final decision concerning the accused 'heretics.' Meanwhile the *Arrabbiati* were doing their part to intimidate many of the Weepers from showing their faces in public.

News from their foreign ambassadors had added to the Signoria's smugness. Two days ago word arrived from France that Charles VIII had died from, of all things, a bump on the head. It was an absurd end for an absurd little creature. In one of those mischievous tricks of the Fates, the deformed king's demise had occurred on the same day as the Ordeal and this fortuitous accident freed the Signoria from concern over possible armed intervention from the French.

From the pope the Signoria had received yesterday a dispatch full of congratulations over the imprisonment of His Holiness's arch-nemesis with a request the heretics be delivered up to the Holy See as soon as possible. But no decision had yet been made regarding the sacrifice of the lamb to the wolf. To weigh this question as well as the ultimate fate of the noisome friars and their seditious band of followers, today's Pratica of seventeen examiners had been appointed.

After the notary finished, a member of the Ten—a body still disposed toward the friar—voiced his objection: "Excellencies, is the religious matter one for us to decide? By what authority are we to put matters of faith to the question?"

Yes, Niccolò noted, the proceedings had conveniently glossed over the jurisdictional issue of canon law prohibiting secular authorities from torturing ecclesiastics. The pope had not yet granted such dispensation to the government.

The notary was matter-of-fact with his answer. "*Signore*, such authority is often vested in the secular authority by a written decree of His Holiness in Rome."

"Then let us wait until we receive it."

Then Bernardo Rucellai, appointed as one of the examiners, stood to address the assembly. "Excellencies, the pope's most recent letter raises the matter of whether the accused should be tried here or in Rome. Perhaps we might discuss this matter first. The city is in a state of disarray due to these events. If we forfeit to Rome our sworn duties to decide and administer justice, the open sores within our city will fester and we will continue to suffer."

Another examiner, a known *Arrabbiati*, disagreed, citing again the classical reference of Troy's destruction: "We should wash our hands of this matter and send our troubles on to Rome, lest we suffer the same fate."

"Yes," added another, "the pope still holds the threat of the interdict."

But Rucellai held firm. "The pope will not object if we remove this thorn from his side. Moreover, I suggest we propose to relieve the Holy Father of this burden in return for the *decima* tax upon Church properties to reduce our public debt."

This last point elicited encouraging nods of approval from around the room. Rucellai continued: "But most important is how we restore political order to our own city. We can best accomplish this by managing our own affairs. Let us put the blame on this friar and turn the city clean."

At this, Bartolo Zati, an examiner with an honest reputation and a long record of civil service turned red-faced as he exclaimed: "Messer Bernardo, you sound like Caiaphas. Like him, you reason fewer will die if we do our own killing. Are we then the Pharisee? Has this verdict already been decided?"

His accusation caused an outcry, during which Zati stepped down from the bench and renounced his appointment. Then he boldly condemned the proceedings saying, "I will take no part in this homicide!"

Bowing to the Signoria, he stalked out and the magistrates felt the heat as Gonfaloniere Popoleschi banged his gavel to return to order.

During this commotion Niccolò quickly discerned the purpose behind Rucellai's firm insistence on trying Savonarola in Florence, rather than Rome. Most Florentines were already convinced the Borgia wished to murder the friar. If the pope were allowed to execute the task with extreme prejudice, the people might rally behind the friar as a matter of civic pride. To break the back of the *Frateschi* party, who had so recently driven Rucellai and other Grays from political office, it would be better to submit the friar to republican justice.

Niccolò looked over at the bench of examiners and briefly caught the eye of Piero Soderini, who nodded knowingly.

Having restored order, Popoleschi loudly stated, "May we confine further discussion to the question of violations of Florentine law, a jurisdiction over which we should all agree. The organization of *intelligenzie* is a seditious act against the Republic."

The representative of the Eight interrupted: "Excellencies, this is a matter which may require wider 'interrogations' and examinations of written records to ascertain guilt."

Rucellai stood again. "Excellencies, I would argue again, to the same end, order will best be restored if we limit our interrogations to the accused. When Caesar defeated Pompey, in the interest of healing the rift in the empire, Caesar wisely refused to read his vanquished rival's correspondence to discover the true depths of the conspiracy."

"Perhaps if he had, he might not have been assassinated!" retorted one of the *Arrabbiati*.

Rucellai snapped back. "As recent tragedies show, our city can ill afford a new cycle of retribution and revenge."

All knew this objection was rooted in the *grandi's* fears of wider retribution, a transparent reference to the ignominious fate of Francesco Valori among others.

Feeling like an old hand in these matters, Niccolò watched the proceedings unfold in predictable patterns. It was finally decided the pope's request would be put off with a counter-proposal requesting permission for the *decima*. In the meantime the prisoners would be interrogated to elicit the evidence concerning the charges brought against them. The *Arrabbiati* successfully pushed to have the interrogators force the accused to reveal names in a wider conspiracy. In this way they hoped to eliminate more of their enemies. After the interrogations the Eight and the examiners would report the evidence and make their recommendations to the Signoria within ten days time.

As all this was transpiring, Niccolò observed his superior, Second Chancellor Braccesi had remained stoic throughout the proceedings. With satisfaction Niccolò imagined him as a fat pigeon cowering under the eaves while the hawks circled overhead.

CHAPTER 3

THE FIRST INTERROGATION

DAWN BROKE OVER THE SECOND night of Fra Girolamo's confinement in the Alberghetto. He had spent his time in this limbo praying and sleeping fitfully, frequently awakened by troubled visions. On occasion he heard a curious footfall outside the door and twice each day, in morning and late afternoon, the guard opened the door to deliver meager victuals and empty the chamber pot when needed. The man had been gruff and Fra Girolamo heard his mumbled accusations of 'false prophets' and 'devilish monks' each time he slammed and bolted the door.

The Good Men of San Martino, the charitable confraternity whose members tended to the sick and the imprisoned and provided comfort to the dying, had visited him on the first day. These were the ones that had benefited so generously from San Marco alms distributions and he knew they were embarrassed by this twist of fate placing him in their pity. But the news they brought confirmed his darkest fears. All his allies, friends and protectors had been vanquished: Charles of France had died suddenly on the same day as the tragic Ordeal; Valori had been murdered; and most of the other *Frateschi* had been arrested the day after the attack on San Marco. And the Weepers, the Good Men whispered, stayed hidden in their houses, locked away in mortal fear of the gangs of Angry Ones.

His brothers, Domenico and Silvestro, were locked away in separate cells in the Bargello and he knew their ordeals would soon begin in earnest. He tried to imagine them steadfast. Bodily torture was the only way to truth and even he had advocated it for criminals and heretics according to the doctrine of the Dominican Order and the severity of their Holy Inquisition. The power of Satan was strong and would control the spirit unless the body was broken. But each night he shuddered with fear of the ordeal to come and struggled to focus his mind by reciting from scripture: *If someone strikes you in the right cheek, turn the other to him as well.*

He grasped the small crucifix hanging round his neck and tried to imagine the surrender of his body to the Glory of Life Everlasting. But the thought made him shudder.

Lord God, my soul is in turmoil! See Fear has entered. She has not retreated from yesterday's battle but comes now with different weapons. What can I do? What shall I do, unarmed and weak?

He could not sleep and rebuked himself for his weakness. He felt the unshaved stubble on the crown of his head. He saw his frock worn foul with filth and his unclean body and wondered how long before he would be permitted to make his toilet and wash himself. Or if he would be left to squalor like a dog infected with the pestilence.

Then he heard the footsteps of the jailor on the stone stairway and heard them multiplied. The door rattled open and two macebearers entered with the guard. They recited their orders to escort him to the Bargello and then gruffly bound his wrists behind his back and placed a hood over his head. As the hood's blackness enveloped his head, his eyes widened like those of a rabbit paralyzed with fear. As they marched him through the darkness he could not suppress the sense of a small, terrified creature whose scream rose in his heart, choked on his tongue, then suffocated in his chest.

When they removed the hood he found himself in a large, Spartan hall on one of the upper floors of the Bargello. The room's emptiness made it seem larger. In addition to the macebearers there was an official of the Eight assisted by two others who wore hoods. The hooded ones took hold of him and sat him on a stool in the center of the room. He faced a bench behind a large raised table where he imagined the Inquisitors would be seated. And then, as he looked around, his eyes came face to face with their instruments of torture. He had imagined these instruments many times, made familiar by his reading of Dominican history. But he was unfamiliar with the fine mechanical details of each implement and up close he beheld their horror.

A large complicated framework covered with shackles rested on two large rollers with shafted wheels and ropes. This was the rack. He viewed the shackles that grasped the wrists and ankles, the ropes and rollers that tightened, imagining them stretching and twisting his limbs to the point of breaking by small, excruciating degrees.

In the far corner was a brazier filled with several iron implements like a smith's tools; presumably some hellish sort of flesh-burning firebrands. He shuddered inwardly and felt his flesh squirm as he imagined how they were applied. He released his breath when he realized the fire was still cold.

On the ceiling, he saw the pulley and rope—the merciless *strappado*. As it dangled before him he tried to close his mind to the image of himself hanging there. He had read of this fearsome apparatus and how it obliterated both body and mind. Despite his privations and scourging, he knew his flesh was weak and he could not endure pain. What did they want from him? What would save him from this pain?

The official announced the charges and read the decree charging the appointed examiners to interrogate the prisoner by all means necessary to extract the truth. Then he heard his name pronounced as "Fra Girolamo Savonarola of Ferrara."

So he was to be regarded as a *straniero*, a foreigner, the other, and not a privileged citizen in the City of Flowers.

After the statement the official and the macebearers abruptly left the room and the hooded ones laid their hands upon him. One turned him away and wound a chain around his wrists bound behind his back. Then he heard the deadly squeak of the pulley as the rope was pulled through. Knowing his fate, he shuddered in anticipation.

He felt the rope being wound through the chains and pulled tight, reversing his arms upward in an unnatural angle behind his head. His shoulders strained as he was slowly raised and he heard the pained pop of his joints as his feet left the floor. They hoisted his body higher toward the ceiling and he cried out at the tearing in his shoulders. But his screams only echoed back to him in the hollow room and his pain was overcome by the frantic thought of the floor racing back up at him before the rope snapped and wrenched his body apart. He reached the ceiling and the pulley fell silent.

In an instant he fell like a stone. It was a fall from the height of denial to the depths of despair. And just before he hit the floor he heard a thunderclap explode in his head.

Four times. The friar had no other sense of the passage of time except that they raised him four times and four times he fell. Four times dying and four times raised up. Or was it three? Or five? It ceased to matter. When they propped him back on the chair, his flesh had no feeling. His arms were something separate and apart from himself— broken, useless and discarded. There was a foul, pungent stench and he realized he had soiled himself. In shock, he closed his eyes to shut his mind and embraced the black void as his body slumped forward in the chair.

He was brought back from the abyss by the sound of voices. He had blacked out—for minutes, or perhaps hours, he didn't know. He felt hands on his shoulders as they propped him up in the chair and he screamed at the stab of pain. When he opened his eyes he saw several of the examiners seated at the bench before him and off to the side was another man turned away from him, seated at a notary's desk.

He focused on his inquisitors and recognized several of his enemies from the *Arrabbiati* party. They pricked him cautiously with questions, to which he answered yes, or no, but his clouded mind divined no purpose to their methods. Then certain words flocked together as they reached his ears: "hypocrisy, pride, vanity, worldly glory, false prophet."

Off to the side the notary was writing anxiously in his notebook, transcribing the words of the inquisitors. The friar recognized this man. It was Ser Francesco di Barone, the one they called Ceccone, a former Medicean supporter. Last year, when the mob's anger had turned against those who plotted with Piero, this Ser Ceccone had come seeking refuge at San Marco. He didn't remember much about the man except Fra Silvestro and some of the other brothers treated him with suspicion, though he was humbly offered refuge. Another who betrayed him.

The inquisitors' constant prodding slowly aroused the friar to a state of awareness and he began to resist. "No, no, no..." he said, "I have never professed to be a prophet...I am neither a prophet nor the son of a prophet. I received visions in my dreams and I have told of them truthfully..."

They persisted, trying to trap his tired mind with contradictions, but he held firm, saying, "Leave this matter be, for if my visions were from God you shall receive manifest proofs, but if not, they will fall to the ground. It is no concern of the State and no man has the right to judge or condemn..."

Disgruntled, his inquisitors left him again to his tormentors, who resumed their dutiful task of breaking their victim's will with relentless precision.

***

After another sleepless night, the friar was dragged again to the interrogation room, his muscles and joints aching. He was placed roughly on his back across the rack with his wrists and ankles tied to the rollers. Then his tormenters slowly cinched the wheels and the suffering in his joints became excruciating. His screams were wrung from his twisted body until they loosened the ropes once more. This time he remained affixed to the rack when the inquisitors returned to their bench to pose their questions. They asked again about his prophecies and then about the Ordeal and why God had failed him. They were mocking him. Finally they asked about the citizens who came to San Marco to confess or plot with him against the government. He denied all, he denied their accusations and insinuations, but then the ropes were tightened by degree until they received the answers they desired. Ser Ceccone scratched his notes with a furious purpose.

The interrogators continued with these methods each day without interruption and the friar lost count of the days and the hours. He slipped into a haze of unremitting pain, as the relentlessness of the rack alternated with the terror of the *strappado* until soon the mere sight of the roped pulley was enough to break his will. He slowly began to understand the methods they used on his body were solely for the purpose of breaking his mind. It was the mind's anticipation of the body's imminent agony that became unbearable long before the body registered pain. And so they broke him and he let his tongue speak freely toward the single goal of stopping the pain. "Yes, yes, yes," he replied to the answers they fed him. And they took special care to spare his writing hand so he could sign the depositions scribbled by Ser Ceccone after each session.

Each night he was returned to his cell in the tower, where he crouched like a wounded beast. He lost faith as he suffered through the long dark nights and then in the morning light he drew on the power of prayer to deny his bodily suffering and gird himself for the coming day's ordeal. He prayed for God's mercy and begged forgiveness for his weaknesses.

O God, like Peter I have denied You, I have denied You, I have denied You out of fear of torture!

He begged and pleaded for a chance at redemption. When his tormentors came again, he steeled himself with resolve and submitted to his fate without complaint, provoking them by retracting the confessions he had made the day before. But his resistance failed.

Back in his tower cell he noticed the changed demeanor of his jailor—the scowl had softened, replaced by a look of pity. One night the burly sentinel lingered in his duties and prodded the wounded priest with questions. The jailor was like a wary but curious fawn at the edge of a lush garden. The next day, like a miracle, the cell was cleaned and the nightly gruel and wine warmed.

Then one morning, as Fra Girolamo awaited his fate, the macebearers did not come. With the morning broth the jailor announced cautiously he had received no order for interrogations for the prisoner, but the Good Men of San Martino would visit later. When his visitors arrived, Fra Girolamo turned away from the shock and embarrassment on their faces, but before they left he begged them to leave a quill and some paper so he might compose his prayers and epistles.

CHAPTER 4

MACHIAVELLI AND PIERO SODERINI

NICCOLÒ KNOCKED ON THE DOOR to the Soderini house shortly before curfew and was quickly escorted to Piero's wing. He did not see Tommaso or Signor Paolo or any other members of the family on his way. A nervous Piero greeted him in his private chambers.

"Niccolò, things did not go well today, eh?"

No, things had not gone well. At today's Pratica the Eight had delivered the report on the interrogations and the proceedings, stirring up much controversy over the trial of the *frati*. Savonarola had been tortured continuously now for nine days and the proceedings had been transcribed by the notary, Ser Ceccone, and signed by the prisoner. But today, in the Sala dei Signori, when the transcriptions of the friar's confessions were read out, the inconsistencies raised accusations of fabrications and falsifications. The friar himself was too unwell to attend the hearing and testify to its accuracy, so the matter of a trial and verdict went unresolved with a widening split between factions for and against the friar's guilt. The magistrates of the Ten and Eight were still sympathetic while the Signoria and the Twelve Good Men were adamantly opposed. The sixteen gonfalons were sharply split by neighborhoods.

By now the news of this discord had spread all over the city, causing more unease and uncertainty among various factions for and against the *frati*. On his way from the Palazzo Niccolò had noticed those passing him moved with their heads down and their eyes averted. There was an uneasy wariness and the longer this matter went unsettled, the greater the risk of further unrest.

Piero shook his head in dismay. "The interrogations are an ugly affair; and that buffoon Ceccone is making a mess of the confessions. He's not clever enough to mold the friar's words into the proper shape. More of the magistrates worry we've unlawfully tortured priests without the pope's permission."

"Do you really think the Borgia will disprove of the way we've handled this affair?"

"Of course not, but that's not the point. The examiners are hesitating, which gives new hope to the *Piagnoni*. We must insure we don't have a massive religious uproar on our hands."

Niccolò crossed his arms. "Rucellai is right. We must break the friar's support here and now or suffer the constant threat of fanatical religious fervor. The results of today's hearings on the matter reveal the dangers of being overly cautious."

He wandered over to inspect an ornamental sword hanging on the wall and traced its edge with the tip of his finger.

He said, "Since the *Arrabbiati* only wish to accelerate the tortures, why not encourage them? Let Tommaso provoke his Bad Companions to increase their harassment of the Weepers and brag about their wish to eliminate the friar. This will paint them as fanatics in opposition. I'm sure the pope intends to send word of his permission to 'question' the priests and perhaps even allow us to tax Church properties in return. Such a *quid pro quo* will appeal to the calculating Borgia mind."

"Yes, but Paolo…" Soderini pondered.

Niccolò continued, "Don't forget, the Eight will be replaced next week on May Day and it will be mostly against the friar. I hear Doffo Spini has been nominated."

"If the *Arrabbiati* become too strong, we, and most certainly Paolo, will be in danger," said Piero. "It may wise for him to leave the city until things settle. Vespucci and Alberti are already demanding the Signoria remove Braccesi for his support of the friar."

Piero gave Niccolò a wan smile. "Incidentally, this may be your best chance for the Secretariat, but not if the *Arrabbiati* control the election."

Niccolò felt gratified, but he knew it was no coincidence. *Fortuna* has presented a golden opportunity not to be wasted. He knew he was not the ideal candidate because he was not a trained notary like most of those nominated to become the Secretary of the Ten. But he had proved himself well over the past few years and was more skilled than most in the subtle art of negotiation and diplomacy, especially more so than his immediate predecessor. "Vespucci, Spini and the other *Arrabbiati* can always be counted on to go too far. As always, Signor Piero, we remain safely in the center. It's there we must stay."

Soderini retreated into his customary caution. "Don't say anything to Tommaso or Paolo, I'll speak with them."

CHAPTER 5

THE PIAGNONI

OUTSIDE THE BARGELLO THE CROWD gathered like angry wasps. Fra Benedetto was there with several others from San Marco, including the young lay painter, Baccio della Porta. The hoods of the Dominicans were pulled up as they stood near a small group of nuns and penitents kneeling in prayer at the walls of the prison while armed militia warily guarded the main gate. The crowd was distressed by the intermittent screams and cries emitting from the torture chambers inside and echoing off the stone walls, floating out over the city streets. With each scream the nuns let out a heart-rending, empathetic cry.

Others with blacker hearts had also come to celebrate the sounds of vengeance meted out in the name of justice. These were angry *Compagnacci* and their younger allies enlisted from the ranks of the *fanciulli,* some formerly angelic Boys of the Friar. They had come to provoke the Weepers who dared show their unwavering support for the despised friar. These same Rabid Ones had paraded around the city with a wagon full of weapons confiscated from San Marco, shouting: "Behold the miracles of San Marco! Behold the miracles of the friar and the tokens of his love for the people of Florence!"

Fra Benedetto shut his eyes and prayed with determination to overcome his remorse. Each scream for mercy was a firebrand of grief burning into his chest. He should have done more to protect the convent. He should have forced the prior to flee. Instead, he had stood by and watched that Judas, Malatesta, betray them from within their own sanctuary. Today was the final day of shame, when the traitors led by Malatesta had revealed their black hearts by sending a letter to the pope. In it they begged forgiveness for their errors in following their prior, who had "seduced them with his cunning guile." The traitors were the same ones Fra Silvestro had suspected—the Tournabuoni, Salviati, and Vespucci—all sons of *Arrabbiati* families, so quick to abandon their false pretenses of priestly brotherhood. These were the tepid ones the prior had warned of, those who would sell their souls in a moment to save their own skins. Now these *tiepidi* had cowed the other friars into electing Fra Salviati as the new Prior of San Marco, whose first task would be to erase the memory of the errant 'Prophet.'

Benedetto could no longer live within the same walls as these Judases but didn't know yet what he should do or where he might go.

Everywhere the fever of the Inquisition had caught fire and the faithful were terrified of its capriciousness. Suddenly, cutting through the taunts behind him he heard a loud chorus fall like a lash on the backs of the *Piagnoni* and penitents. It was a verse from the *Inferno*:

> *Master, what shades are these who lie*
> *Buried in these chests and fill the air*
> *With such a painful and unending cry?*

He turned to see a group of young ruffians standing together on a wagon. In answer to their verse, one gaily-dressed man stepped forth to answer. Benedetto saw it was Francesco Cei, the mediocre poet and inveterate social nuisance, who sang out his reply in a clear, mocking tone:

> *These are the arch-heretics of all cults,*
> *With their followers… Far more*
> *Than you would think lie stuffed in these vaults.*
> *Like lies with like, in every heresy,*
> *And the monuments are fired, some more, some less;*
> *To each depravity its own degree.*[16]

Fra Benedetto felt the hot blood of his anger rise. He should have turned away but too late Cei caught his eye, calling out over the crowd. "Bettucio! Still weeping for your prophet? Surely you know his fate lies down in the sixth circle of Hell!"

Fra Benedetto fought to contain his fury but Baccio, unrestrained by the monk's habit, yelled back, "*Bastardo!* Cei, where's your pretty boy, Spini? *Sodomiti!*"

Cei only laughed at the malicious insult and called back. "Haven't you heard, friends? He's been nominated to the Eight. He's in the Palazzo now to decide the fate of your lying heretic. *Allora*, are you mute, Bettucio? Have you lost your wit?"

The poet played to his cohorts as he mocked Benedetto. "I think you must be filled with too many prayers: '*Lord save me, help me, have mercy!*' when you should be saying '*Dio mio, thank you, thank you, thank you!*'"

His crowd roared back in laughter as Benedetto clenched his teeth.

In a moment another blood-curdling scream echoed out the towers of the Bargello to be greeted by a cacophony of hoots, cackles and wails.

***

Inside the Bargello the friar's body was suspended from the

strappado. It was naked except for a cloth tied around the loins, looking more like a trussed chicken carcass hanging in the butcher's window than a man. The Bargello's hooded tormentors had been instructed to intensify their methods for these sessions, rendering the friar semi-conscious as he hung limply before his examiners. After being dropped several times from the ceiling, burning coals had been applied to the souls of his feet. Unbearable pain and the horrifying smell of seared flesh had caused the agonized screams that carried over the rooftops of the city. After each application the examiners waited for the friar to regain consciousness before renewing their interrogation. Looking down on his tormentors, he pleaded and begged for mercy as they plied him with endless questions. Finally, he affirmed the truth they desired as their relentless methods proved more than his weakened spirit could bear. Slowly he faded from consciousness. The examiners left, satisfied in achieving their purpose.

The hooded ones lowered the friar's body from the roped pulley and laid it on the rack but did not bind his hands and feet. Then they revived him with a wine-soaked cloth. There he rested with the bitter taste of the wine on his dried lips. He drifted in and out of consciousness as his mind struggling to escape from his tortured body. At some point his spirit drifted high up to gaze down upon the broken body, surveying the carnage:

Have mercy, O God, have mercy on me and free my soul from this decrepit body. I will leave behind all affections for the flesh... wash me of my iniquities and cleanse me from my sins... Let me hear You say the words "This day you will be with me in paradise," then I shall rejoice and be glad and these bones you have broken will rejoice.[17]

The friar's spirit drifted back between light and dark, sinking slowly into the dark depths of a black sea before bursting forth to gasp the light of air. Then he heard a dark voice speak softly in his ear: "Hear me now. Do you think the things Faith preaches are true? Do you want to see how they are only human fabrications? Tell me, where are the promises of your God? What good have your tears done you? What have your prayers brought you from heaven? Where is consolation? Where is deliverance? You called out and nobody answered you. You call upon your God, and He is silent."

He tried to shut his ears and prayed.

Lord, Fear besets me! ...she has returned and mouths these blasphemies in my ear... "Choose death," she says ...and I hear her army of devils roar, "Death is your only recourse!" Help me Lord! Why have you forsaken me?

He rolled and moaned on the wooden rack as his hooded tormentors watched in curiosity. Finally one of them took a handful of water from a bucket and splashed his face with it. "Padre, padre! Wake up. You're dreaming. The macebearers have come to take you back to the Palazzo."

He felt the pain in his bones and joints return as he was lifted like a child's doll by sturdy hands and half-carried, half-dragged back to his cell in the tower.

CHAPTER 6

THE JAILOR

FRA GIROLAMO PASSED THAT NIGHT and the next day huddled in prayer on the floor of his cell, tormented in spirit and oblivious to his bodily pain. Sleepless, he saw his life unfold in empty darkness. He tried to conjure up comforting visions of his grandfather, but felt only loneliness. Why was he alone? He saw his family gathered round him: his mother and father, his brothers and sisters. He tried to see into their eyes, but he was lost to them. He thought of his solitary youth, the melancholic songs so haunting they frightened his mother. Why was he so afflicted? Then he saw the young maiden Laodamia, laughing at him from her window. He wanted to drive this defects from his mind but could not. He could not save himself. He was a stranger in this world, alone. Forever alone. *Only with You by my side Lord, was I not alone. Only with Your words could I touch them.*

Turning his eyes upward, he struggled to envision his triumphs for his Lord. He saw the magnificent Hall of the Great Council and the processions of the angels and the faithful, all singing together. He saw the packed Cathedral and the rapture on the faces of the congregation lifted up to receive his words—*they were Your words, Lord.* He saw the flaming of the vanities and the miracle of the Impruneta. *God, you have given me these joys, these gifts...why have you taken them from me?*

He plunged into darkness again and twitched as he glimpsed devils escaping like vermin from their hiding places. He saw the gargantuan Antichrist, Pope Alexander, sitting high upon his throne, grinning like a wolf. *My enemies surround me, Lord...they have chained me and walled me in ...these creatures are the instruments of Your divine will... Your sword rends me asunder and cuts me down! ... Why?*

As the last rays of daylight came peeking through the small, high window he pleaded: *Tell me how I have failed You, Lord? Why do You desert me?* Then the sound of footsteps outside his door gripped him with fear. *No, Lord, please! ...Don't abandon me!*

But it was only the jailor carrying in the evening supper of stale bread and thin, but warm broth. He set down the bowl and bread near the friar, who was kneeling on the floor. Then he remained there, shuffling his feet as he cleared his throat. Fra Girolamo opened his eyes.

"Father," said the guard, "please, excuse me for disturbing you. I..." his voice trailed off, embarrassed.

"What troubles you, friend?"

"Me? ...Me? Oh nothing, Father, nothing!" The man was filled with consternation; he hesitated. "I was thinking to ask if perhaps there was something I could do for you, for your comfort?"

The friar saw the shame in the jailor's eyes. This was the power of faith and humility before God.

"Do you have a Bible I might read?"

"No, I'm sorry," he replied, looking at his feet. Then, anxious to please, he added, "But I could get one. Perhaps tomorrow."

Fra Girolamo smiled weakly as he tenderly rubbed his left shoulder, dislocated by the *strappado*. "It would greatly ease my pains."

The jailor searched for some words of solace. "Father, today I heard the examiners are finished with the interrogations for now. The Signoria will deliberate next week and you will be left in peace for a while. Today the Good Men of San Martino will visit you; perhaps they can bring some liniment to tend to your injuries?"

"Yes, yes. Perhaps you can bring some more paper and ink with the Bible? The interrogators were careful to spare my right arm, so to be able to write and sign the confessions. But I would like to write down my meditations. What I really need are my spectacles."

The jailor nodded vigorously. "*Sì*, of course. If you ask, perhaps the Good Men can bring the spectacles."

"*Grazie*, my friend. What's your name?"

The jailor colored slightly. "Salvatore, Padre."

For the next several days Fra Girolamo was left alone to recuperate in the tower. Except for frequent visits from Salvatore and occasional ones by the Good Men, he was left to himself. He prayed and wrote feverishly, jealous of his time, trying to stave off the moment when his interrogators would summon him again. He found comfort and peace of mind by glossing meditations on the verses of the Psalm, *Miserere mei Deus*. Salvatore became curious about his meditations, asking questions regarding the teachings of scripture. This caused him to recall his days in the convent as a lector. Rejuvenated, he recovered his meaning through the daily writing of his meditations.

One day, Salvatore made a small request.

"Father, I'm not a learned man. I attend Mass with my wife and make contributions to the collection plate when I can. We venerate the feast days of the saints, especially the Virgin Mary. I do my best to follow the teachings of the Church, Father. But, I'm ashamed when ...I go astray. Sometimes I'm not even aware of my errors. I beg you to provide some guide to aid me in achieving a state of grace and favor with our

Lord."

Fra Girolamo looked at the guileless expression on Salvatore's face. Suddenly the simplicity struck him with force and he saw clearly. *This* was the way of our Savior. Jesus was a humble teacher, who encouraged his followers through virtuous example. He answered their questions and girded their faith in small steps. This was in sharp contrast to the way of Moses, who had dictated God's laws to his people. Christ refused to wield a sword against His enemies and the enemies of God the Father. The New Testament broke with the Old when Christ laid down His own life for the sins and the salvation of man. *The Lord is my shepherd, I shall not want.*

Fra Girolamo felt an unburdening. "Salvatore, my friend, we are saved through grace alone. To live virtuously we must strive to attain grace through the Lord's favor."

The simple man was confused. "Yes, Father, but how?"

"By examining our sins and meditating on the vanity of earthly things. Through the Holy Sacraments we can open our hearts and receive God's saving grace. So perseverance in virtuous living, in good works, in confession, in prayer, in communion, in all that draws us nearer to grace is the only true and certain way."

"Would you write me a list of guidelines for virtuous living, Father?"

The friar grimaced as he rubbed his injured shoulder and arm. The left side of his body was rendered useless by the strappado, but this was but a small sacrifice compared with the crucified Savior. How could he dare complain? He nodded his assent.

CHAPTER 7

Niccolò and Chiara

Niccolò stood in the shadows of the Loggia dei Priori watching the investiture of the magistrates with feigned interest. The new Signoria as well as new company of the Eight were dominated by the *Arrabbiati,* ironically including even the archenemy of the friar, Doffo Spini, who would be one of those sitting in judgment. Niccolò looked over and saw Spini at the far end of the Loggia, a satisfied smile on his face. The friar's enemies were now in ascendance, but they were also enemies of the Republic. The *Arrabbiati* and their dupes were in league with both the Sforza in Milan and the Borgia in Rome and, given free rein, they would quickly reassert their privileges—just like the Medici they despised, they would place their cronies in office and subjugate the laws to their own narrow purposes. Yesterday they were emboldened by the pope's letter authorizing the trial and torture of the three priests while granting blanket amnesty for those seduced by the excommunicant. The pope also promised to send an official papal legate to question the heretics and confirm the findings of the examiners. Thus, it appeared the government would be forced to belabor several weeks more over the fate of Fra Girolamo.

Today was the first of May, normally the occasion for the communal festival of Calendimaggio to celebrate the arrival of spring, but Niccolò could not remember a time when the city had been more divided. The rowdy *Compagnacci* made every effort to intimidate the religious by forcing a celebratory mood—gambling, drinking, whoring and provoking the game of stones among the gangs of *fanciulli*. Meanwhile, the oppressed Weepers suffered in silence behind closed doors at home or in the refuge of the churches, in fear for their lives. Neither faction was sure of the fate of the *frati* and the final consequence to their own positions. But just yesterday, as a warning, those nineteen citizens who had been arrested with the friar after the riot at San Marco were sentenced to exile for periods ranging from several months to two or three years.

Niccolò looked on and regarded the overdressed, sweating magistrates as they acted out their grand ceremony, draped in their ermine-lined crimson cloaks, each preening on the public stage. He considered how every man of consequence in Florence hoped to receive this—his sixty days of glory—then wear it as a badge of honor in perpetuity to his family name. In spite of the obvious foolishness, this honor was the currency of Florentine society, just as valuable as any other. But Niccolò suspected such civic vanity was dangerously overvalued—in a fast changing world the past was cheap and the future became the prize. Fortuna favors the bold. And he was hoping the excess granted by Fortuna's favor would be quickly followed by the backlash of Nemesis's revenge. These *Arrabbiati* were drunk on their recent victories over the friar and perhaps with a little encouragement their arrogance would be enough to reverse their fortunes.

As the investiture wound to a close and the magistrates prepared for their procession, Niccolò noticed a group of white-habited nuns exiting the main door of the Palazzo. When they passed he was sure he recognized one of the nuns. He rushed down from the Loggia as they hurried down the street toward the river. He called to get her attention and she turned. It was Chiara.

"Oh, *buona sera*, Messer Machiavelli. Forgive me, I cannot stop as we are on our way to Santo Spirito and I must visit my family first."

"Then I'll escort you. I'm going to the Oltrarno myself. I need to stop by my home before I visit the house of your cousin later this evening."

He saw her weighing her reply. "*Prego?*" he entreated.

Chiara nodded her assent and called to her fellow sisters she would rejoin them at the convent of Santo Spirito.

Niccolò slowed his pace so their conversation would be private, but he was unsure how to begin. There seemed such a wide gulf between them. He noticed the Bible she carried under her arm.

"You were in the Palazzo?" he asked.

"Yes, we visited Fra Girolamo."

She shot Niccolò a sharp look. "I was shocked. They've treated him mercilessly. But his spirit is unrepressed, they cannot shake his faith."

"Well, I'm afraid his ordeal is far from over. The pope is sending his Inquisitors."

Niccolò saw a dark fury cross her face as she fought to maintain her composure. Then the floodgates broke and tears streamed down her face as she looked away. He put his hand on her arm and she wheeled around to face him. She pointed back to the Loggia where the magistrates were still gathered, as she sputtered in anger and confusion. "I cannot live in this world! Look at them! What kind of place do we live in, Nico? They preen and congratulate themselves on their cleverness, while they allow a man of God, a man of Christian faith be treated worse than a dog! Where is Justice and Virtue? Where is Christian Mercy and Forgiveness?"

Niccolò was struck speechless as Chiara continued to harangue him, waving her Bible in his face.

"I look into the hearts of men and I see only hate and envy, pride and ambition. I don't wish to live in this world."

She turned away in tears and quickened her pace toward the river as Niccolò hurried to catch up to her. "*Aspetta*, wait. Was it ever not this way? Like the sky, the sun, the river, the hills... men haven't changed, they are weak and vile. Man spoiled the garden God gave him. Expelled to nature we have the same passions, the same ambitions, the same inner nature and thus the same results. And from this comes both good *and* evil."

"So, why then do we choose to ignore the teachings of Christ? Did he not come to take on the sins of the world, to save us from our nature?"

Niccolò knew on this question he could never convince her of his views. There was a necessary difference between Heaven and earth. We may follow the stars in the heavens, but our feet are still firmly planted on earth. Only God can make the perfect—men cannot. But he couldn't explain. He only wished to comfort her—he needed to comfort her—so he replied, "Men are so created by nature to desire all things, but which they cannot acquire. So men are never satisfied: when they have a thing, they're not happy, but desire something else. I cannot see that religion has changed this."

"Yes, I'm sure you're right. And I choose not to be one of those *things* or to covet them myself. This is why I've taken my vows. To endlessly desire those things of the world only creates a poverty of the soul."

They reached the Ponte Vecchio and turned to cross over the river. The bridge was crowded with young people eagerly enjoying the spring weather and the feast day. The affairs in the Palazzo did not touch these innocents.

A slight smile brightened Chiara's face and she became wistful. "I remember when we used to come here in the evenings, to enjoy the *passegiata,* to laugh with my sisters, my cousins and friends... Tommaso, Fiammetta, Alessandro... and you, Nico, you were always the cleverest. It was a long time ago."

"Not so long ago."

Niccolò smiled again in a carefree manner but couldn't help noticing the stark difference between Chiara in her nun's habit and the crowd of fashionably dressed young girls and boys on the bridge.

She stopped and looked down the river toward the setting sun. "No, it is very long ago. Fiammetta and Alessandro are gone..."

Suddenly she looked at him directly. "Do you know what he said to us?"

"*Che?*" asked Niccolò, confused.

"Fra Girolamo. In all his torment, with us 'brides of Christ' lamenting, he said, 'Daughters of Jerusalem, weep not over me, but weep for yourselves and for your children.' *Weep for yourselves and for your children...*he meant for us to tell the *Piagnoni* there were worse things in store for all of us, for all of them."

She gestured toward the young revelers on the bridge. "As we lose our souls, we lose all."

She turned to him suddenly. "Nico, do you remember your wonderful *trionfo*, from Carnevale? The one with all the allegories?"

"Of course. It seems childish now."

"I remember it and I think of it often. It was a beautiful myth. I also remember the Triumph of Death and it makes me shudder. Satan has sown his devils in our midst. They infect the Palazzo and spread their poison through the streets. Sometimes I wonder if their pestilence has infected you as well."

She looked at him and recited a verse of the Divine Poet, spoken in the voice of Beatrice to Virgil:

> *O spirit of the courteous Mantuan,*
> > *whose fame is still present in the world*
> > *and shall endure as long as the world lasts,*
> *my friend, who has not been the friend of fortune,*
> > *is hindered in his path along that lonely*
> > *hillside; he has been turned aside by terror.*
> *From all that I have heard of him in Heaven,*
> > *he is, I fear, already astray*
> > *that I have come to help him much too late.*
> *Go now; with your persuasive word, with all*
> > *that is required to see that he escapes,*
> > *bring help to him, that I may be consoled...*[18]

Niccolò was dumbfounded. Under different circumstances he would have snickered at such female sentiment and harsh judgment of his character. 'Better to burn in Hell with the wise ancients than tag along with those snivelers who go to Paradise!' he often said. But now he could only force an embarrassed smile.

Chiara turned away to watch the carefree flirtations of the *giovani* on the bridge. "I used to love Carnevale—the pageantry, the pretending, hiding behind masks. But now I see our whole city is a Carnevale and there's no truth to it. It's a strange place and I don't recognize it."

"What is truth, anyway?" Niccolò scoffed, his voice tainted with cynicism. "Truth belongs to those who make it."

She regarded him again with a forlorn look. "No, Nico, not that. Prayer and faith have helped me find the truth within. You cannot understand him, Nico, because you use your reason, but there is no reason in faith. Faith is the absence of reason. We need this faith to survive the chaos of this world and prepare for the next."

Then she laid her hand with the Bible on her breast, over her heart. "It is here. Faith and the courage to be true. In the convent I discovered this and now I can pursue the only truth that matters—truth in God. I can never wear that Carnevale mask again."

Niccolò was almost amused by her overwrought religious sentiment but stifled his sarcasm. She was truly transformed by this experience, yet it baffled him. Perhaps she was right, who could ever know. He was embarrassed as he felt her pull the mask from his face and he turned to gaze down the river, running red like blood, and closed his eyes. He imagined himself adrift in a boat, looking toward the shore's edge where a Madonna stood gazing toward him. She was lifting her arms out and he tried to picture her face. She grew small and faint as he slipped farther out to sea with the tide, soon lost in a foggy mist.

That evening he sat alone in his study. Wasn't the friar's own fall from grace, his hypocrisy, his betrayal of the truth so obvious? How could Chiara forget her saintly friar had forsaken her fine cousin Lorenzo for political expediency? Even this priest had blood on his hands. How can she forgive him this? He would never understand the ways of women. This ambitious friar could not be the voice of God.

Niccolò looked at his books shelved along the wall. It was a small collection, bequeathed by his father, but one with a deliberate purpose. Knowledge was built upon itself and he craved the lessons of history. Cicero wrote that politics is made up of force and reason, both human and bestial. The man who wishes to rule must be the Centaur—half-man, half-beast—striding between Platonic dreams and brute realities. To achieve great things it's sometimes necessary to act against faith, against charity, against humanity, and against the Church. But our religion glorifies humble and contemplative men rather than active ones, so we adapt to suffering rather than act with purpose. Virgil's pagans esteemed honor and the glory of the state, while Christians esteem suffering and sacrifice. The ancients were great lovers of liberty, but modern men follow Christ. It will be the ruin of us all.

He also knew, as precisely as did all those princely churchmen, that this knowledge was power in itself. And *they* wielded it ruthlessly. He reached for his copy of Dante's *De Monarchia,* but then changed his mind and pulled down the *Vita Nuova.*

CHAPTER 8

ARTISTS DISCUSS TRIAL

FRANCESCO GRANACCI WANDERED THROUGH THE quarter of Santo Spirito on his way to the Church of Santa Maria del Carmine. His mood was as gray as the afternoon sky and at such times he felt the need for a painter's inspiration. Folded in his tunic was Michelangelo's last letter from Rome. News of the Ordeal and the torture of the friars had spread quickly throughout the 'infernal city,'—as his friend liked to call it—and rumors were the pope was anxious to dispense with the 'heretical' priests as swiftly as possible. It was said a representative of the Curia would be dispatched to seal the friar's fate, but surely, Michelangelo asked, the Signoria would not allow this? His letter begged for more news regarding tempers in Florence and he peppered Francesco with questions: what of the *Piagnoni* and the *Frateschi*—had they all abandoned him? Would the friar be exiled?

His friend was unaware that the *Frateschi* had already been driven out, while the Weepers were afraid to show their faces. With the constant uproar over the trial, many of Francesco's fellow artisans were also feeling the backlash due to their previous devotion to the friar.

Even more than Michelangelo, Francesco was perplexed by the trials and tribulations of men. He agreed these sad public affairs were beyond the realm of humble artisans, whose only recourse was to work and create. But he was a poor painter now, without paid commissions and without good prospects. In this climate one felt almost fortunate just to escape notice.

Michelangelo suggested again he come to Rome, where work was plentiful and one could do well to stay clear of politics. He was busy carving his *Bacchus* for the Galli banker and had begun planning the *Pietá* for the French cardinal. It was a nice thought but, except for Michelangelo, Francesco knew not a soul in Rome. And Michelangelo was a sculptor, whereas he was a painter. At least in Florence, he had some hope of receiving piecework through the Ghirlandaio workshop.

As Francesco entered the Brancacci Chapel he immediately felt a sense of liberation. Lit by candles, the walls came alive with the brilliant frescoes of Masaccio. The scenes were drawn from the life of St. Peter, framed by two panels depicting the Temptation of Eve and the Expulsion from the Garden of Eden. This was the school where all the painters and sculptors in Italia came to study the painter's art and learn how to execute figures properly. Before Masaccio, everything was flat and crude, whereas the young genius brought his subjects to life with perspective and lifelike modeling of human figures and their expressions. These were men and women, not heavenly ghosts. They seemed to breathe. He remembered how he and Michelangelo used to joke how before Masaccio all figures were painted as if standing on their toes, suspended like puppets in the air.

As he surveyed the room Granacci noticed another devotee standing in front of *The Tribute Money* and saw it was his fellow painter, Baccio della Porta. Baccio was regarding the depiction of Christ instructing Peter to pay tribute to Caesar.

Hearing him enter, Baccio turned. "*Ciao* Francesco, I see we have the same need for peace."

"*Sì*, it seems these days one can only take refuge and fine divine inspiration between these walls, eh. *Come va?*"

"Not well. I was in the convent when the mobs attacked. I, …I must admit I was not brave. Only the Lord knows my true shame."

"There is no shame in fear, Baccio."

"But one must stand for what one believes. If not, what hope is there?" Staring up at the fresco of Christ and the Apostles, he added, "We live in Caesar's world, Francesco, we must pay him tribute. But can we render unto God the things that are God's?"

"Your soul runs deeper than mine. I simply want to paint to enjoy this life and not suffer too much. But it seems we painters are forever caught between the heavenly and earthly worlds, between the spirit and the flesh, between the mind and the soul."

"And to survive we must have heart. This is where I've failed."

"You have heart, my friend. The beauty of your art is a testament."

"Perhaps. But during the riot I made a vow if the Lord spared me I would devote my life to him under the Order of the Preachers. I will paint no more. I'm here today merely to observe this sublime beauty one last time. I'm thinking of departing for Prato, where I might live free of persecution for my devotion to Fra Girolamo. My last painting was a portrait of him in profile. It's my best, but I'll have to take it to save it from destruction."

Granacci did not know what to say. Florence, the most superior of cities, was now cutting out her heart and soul by driving away her best artisans. He looked around at the frescoes, soaking them in with his eyes. "Filippino and Masolino are admirable, but it's a shame Masaccio did not live to complete the cycle himself."

"We cannot know our fate. All is in God's hands."

Granacci nodded vacantly as he eyed the fresco. Such mysteries were beyond the vanishing point for his eye. "I'm on my way to Sandro's *bottega* to meet some of the others. Come along?"

"Yes, I know. Simone told me," said Baccio. "Di Libri printed the friar's epistle on the *Miserere mei Deus* he wrote while in the Alberghetto. I've seen it and Simone wants to distribute it. But first I must stop by Piero's workshop." He made a sour face. "*Madonna*, I hope he threw out those rotting eggs!"

Francesco laughed in a carefree manner for the first time in days. Baccio had apprenticed under the eccentric and cantankerous Piero di Cosimo, the infamous designer of Carnevale *trionfi*, who lived on nothing but boiled eggs.

***

When Granacci arrived at Botticelli's workshop, Cronaca and Lorenzo di Credi were already there, along with Simone and Sandro. Sandro seemed tired and depressed but Simone was agitated, waving a printed pamphlet in his hand.

"Could the truth be more plain? By tomorrow Fra Girolamo's epistle will be read all over the city and then all over Christendom."

"It's in Latin," sighed Cronaca.

"No, some brothers have translated it into the vulgate, so there will be versions in both."

"And you think that will make a difference? It's said the Holy Father is ready to pronounce the sentence. And the *Arrabbiati* in the Palazzo have tasted blood," said Sandro wearily.

Simone sneered at the mention of the Anti-Christ pope. "Even in this golden age of bastards, the truth cannot be denied. The power of faith demonstrated by Fra Girolamo's words and the crime of his torture will once again incite his followers against his enemies."

Sandro stood up and walked over to his unfinished paintings of the Crucifixion and the Nativity. "I wish my faith was as unshaken as yours, brother."

"Don't forget Fra Girolamo still enjoys the favor of the new French king," responded Simone.

Lorenzo said, "Perhaps we can organize a petition for the *frati* to be exiled? Fra Girolamo is still revered in most towns in Italia."

Cronaca threw up his hands. "And who would dare sign it with the *Compagnacci* and *Arrabbiati* ready to attack and murder any supporter of the friar? We're all caught in this war between princes, popes and merchants. I thank God the Strozzi need me to finish their monstrosity."

"I see you're almost finished with the second floor façade. Any new work for painters?" Francesco inquired.

"Not yet, my friend. I still miss our good master stone-carver, Benedetto. Any word from Michelangelo?"

They were interrupted by the arrival of Baccio and Piero di Cosimo. Baccio greeted the others while Piero grunted and wandered over to look at Sandro's paintings. He seemed in a foul mood.

Francesco turned back to Cronaca. "I received a letter just yesterday. He says there's work in Rome, but he's carving marble and I only paint. I'm not much of a stone-carver. He also says the pope is sending an inquisitor."

Simone jumped up again. "An executioner, no doubt! The Black pope is a murderer, I saw many dark Spaniards lurking at the Ordeal—"

"Simone! *Calma*," Sandro cut in. "What good is it to see a devil behind every corner? Didn't the friar say Florence would be punished for its sins? I suspect our own ordeal has just begun. You yourself quote the chapters of John on the Apocalypse: that we shall suffer 'three and a half years of the reign of Satan before *il Papa Santo,* the Angelic Pope, comes; when evil priests will be removed and holy men sent into the Church. And the whole world will be converted to Christ.' It seems we have more tribulations to come."

Piero snorted from across the room. "From these sketchings one would almost think you believed it, Sandro. For all his good intentions, your *frate* is caught in a web of earthly ambition and the affairs of the Republic. It's only that—there's no divine significance to these events."

Simone protested heatedly. "The friar performed miracles, he foretold prophecies—the scourge by the French king... and he saved the city by his reforms. You know nothing because you spend all your time locked up in your *studiolo* eating eggs!"

"Did he?" Piero was cool in his reply, ignoring the insult. "So you say."

"Yes," snapped Simone, "and so do the *popolo*. Only now the tepid ones come forth and reverse themselves. Before they sang his praises when they wished to be associated with his holiness, but now these traitors call him the son of perdition!"

Cronaca intervened to restore peace. "Piero, no one can deny the friar performed good works and provided solace and charity to the poor of the city, as well as the impoverished in spirit. For this he deserves better than his fate at the hands of the *grandi*."

"*Sì, maestro*," added Baccio, "if you read this epistle you will find nothing written to condemn him and much to admire in his heart and soul. I was in the convent when it was attacked and most of us cowered in fear or fought back. I myself was like a frightened child. But Fra

Girolamo counseled surrender and forgiveness when seriously threatened with bodily harm. For faith and courage alone he's more saint than sinner."

Piero smiled condescendingly. "I've already conceded your preacher has good intentions. But he's a fool to expect men to change and the world to stay the same. How can one declare man's nature is evil? Or good? It is both, but your prophet denies that nature. Do you fail to see the impossibility of the situation?

"Shall we follow the written Word in all things? Even in dress? Unchanging for all time? If so, how to change? How does one explore *anything* new? No, my friends, there are many ways to heaven and many other ways to hell, but the friar demands one way and the choice of a single direction. In this he errs and thus he suffers."

"*Cave canem*," Francesco heard Simone mutter.

"So you believe God plays no role in these affairs?" asked Sandro.

Piero smiled devilishly. "Oh, I dare not blaspheme. I'm sure God watches over the folly of men. I'm sure He's most amused and we shall be subject to His terrible judgment. But we shouldn't attribute our idiocies to His design. As much as I seek to glorify the Almighty with sacred images, I assume I amuse Him by frightening His silly subjects senseless with my own devices. This is why I gain such pleasure from devising my Carnival *spettacoli*."

Cronaca shook his head. "Well, Piero, you're free to speak your opinions, but I can't say I agree."

The others nodded in affirmation.

"May God preserve us," added Simone darkly.

CHAPTER 9

THE SIGNORIA DEBATES

NICCOLÒ WAS BACK AT HIS desk, carefully transcribing his notes while waiting for Piero Soderini to arrive. As he wrote he wondered who would read these dispatches now that Braccesi had been dismissed. He suspected Chancellor Adriani would have to share some of these duties, but until a new Secretary was appointed defense policy would be adrift and all external affairs ground to a halt. This was his opportune moment, but everyone was distracted by this battle over the friars. Niccolò put his quill down with a sense of frustration and went to the window.

The city he surveyed should be at the height of its republican glory. The reign of the Medici was over and the French army had come and gone. The famine and the plague had taken their toll, but the city breathed new life again. Still, all teetered on the edge of turmoil. Down on the streets he watched the citizens busy themselves like insects scurrying about in their daily affairs. On his walk to the Palazzo this morning he had heard them chattering on the street corners, arguing for and against the merits of the friar's case and the pending judgment. Mostly they sounded wearied: his fellow Florentines were exhausted by their clash with the three Furies—famine, pestilence, and turmoil. Soon they would be begging for a respite.

He knew no matter what happened with the friar, the future remained precarious. The city's finances were bankrupted by the war with Pisa, its defenses a shambles, and its alliances untrustworthy. Very few of the problems plaguing the Republic had been resolved. It was rumored the pope might soon appoint his son Cesare as Papal General of the Vatican armies to conquer and extend papal territories in the Romagna. The Borgia presented serious problems for the Republic and Niccolò felt a pang of regret Savonarola had been unable to win his battle against this naked usurper of the Christian faith.

To the north, the shifty Duke of Milan still had only his own survival in mind, while Piero de' Medici and his brothers were pursuing every means of regaining their lost position and would exploit any alliance to achieve it.

Most serious were the imperialist ambitions of the French and Spanish monarchs, and the German Emperor. It would impossible for Florence or any Italian city-state to stand alone against these forces.

There was little appreciation in the Palazzo for these impending calamities. The government ministries had degenerated into embittered battles over Savonarola, with his supporters presently in retreat. But Niccolò believed the success of either faction would be detrimental to the Republic and especially to his own fortune. Though it appeared the friar was destined to be the sacrificial lamb, it was still unclear who would wield the axe. It would take some delicate maneuvering to make sure theirs was the last faction standing at the end of this affair. Just then a voice interrupted his thoughts.

"The Pratica begins in an hour?"

Niccolò turned to find Piero Soderini at his door.

"*Sì*, Signor Piero, please, come in."

Piero smiled easily. "Let us use the Udienza dei Dieci. It's empty now, no?"

Niccolò nodded and they crossed into the larger salon where the Secretary of the Ten would normally host his audiences. When Piero's smile faded, Niccolò asked, "Is there a problem?"

"No, not really. The street corners are filled with people discussing the epistle the friar wrote while in the Alberghetto. Have you read it? I don't know how he accomplished it, but printed copies are flying all over the city like pigeons. It's reviving the Weepers and inciting the Angry Ones. It makes everything more difficult."

"I didn't read it or take much notice—there's always the same inane chatter on the streets—but the magistrates grow more hesitant. I believe we must be decisive and stay our course."

Piero scratched his chin, a mannerism that typified his caution. "But if we find them guilty and treat them harshly we may invite the fury of the religious. The *popolo* turned against Savonarola with the failed Ordeal, but they're turning back—the harsh treatment of the prisoners, the rumors of fabricated confessions, and now this gloss of the *Miserere*... I don't wish my house to be the target of an angry mob... Many of the *grandi* are already wavering as their wives pressure them to show mercy."

Niccolò became exasperated. "Do you suggest a bunch of leaflets and some nattering women should determine our policy? And Paolo is safe in Lucca for now."

"You forget the French king and his army. You know our ambassador sent word the French court is sending an emissary."

Soderini's caution was exactly what Niccolò feared at this juncture. He replied too vehemently, "No, forgive me, Signor Piero, I do not forget the king, nor do I forget the pope. If either wins this battle we are lost—the city will fall as spoils to the victor and the Medici will be their puppets."

Piero's face betrayed his bewilderment.

Niccolò calmed his tone. "However, their mutual enmity provides us with the opportunity to secure our freedom. Think of it," he explained, "All of France is under the foot of the king; the same as in Spain and the German states with the Emperor. The reason we are not subjects of Rome is because we can play kings against pope, and pope against our Italian rivals. This is what Lorenzo knew well, and as long as none can dominate, we are safe."

Niccolò was convinced this keen political insight was the secret of Lorenzo's long success to the benefit of the Florentine Republic.

Piero scratched his chin some more. "So, what is the best strategy with the friar? Should he be exiled?"

Niccolò now became direct—the protégé now lectured his mentor: "No, this will never satisfy Rome and the pope is the immediate threat. If exiled, the friar will return with the next favorable Signoria, and we'll be back where we started. But," he paused deliberately, "we need not pronounce the verdict ourselves. Let the *Arrabbiati* continue to discredit themselves with their blatant hatred of the friar. They're truly mad dogs. Also, we'll hear testimony today from many of the friar's former supporters, including Maestro Marsilio and some of the Dominicans at San Marco. I think no further condemnation will be required on our part. And if by some chance another '*miracolo*' should occur, we can't be held directly accountable."

Signor Piero looked up to the ceiling, as if he wondered if this conversation was escaping the scrutiny of the All-Seeing and All-Hearing. "But this puts Vespucci and the *Arrabbiati* in a dominant position after the friar is gone."

Niccolò shook his impatiently. "This is why the pamphlets the friar writes and the Weepers distribute are not a bad thing. They help discredit the *Arrabbiati's* methods in the minds of the people, which may just promote a backlash."

"Of course, already there's a bad feeling against Ser Ceccone with his fabrications. You know Vespucci and the Popolani-Medici have nominated the knave for the Second Chancery?"

Niccolò hid his surprise as Soderini smiled like a cat. No, he had not heard, but he had already calculated this possibility and the wise man keeps his own counsel. Soderini was holding out his potential nomination as an added incentive but Niccolò was tiring of Signor Piero's little game. He shrugged to feign disinterest and continued his explanation.

"The pope is sending his examiners within the fortnight to interrogate the *frati*. Let *them* pronounce the verdict of heresy. This way the friar's followers will focus their vitriol on the Borgia together with the *Arrabbiati* while we stay safely between the two extremes."

Soderini's eyes finally lit up as he clapped Niccolò on the back. He exclaimed, "But of course!"

***

In the Hall of Two Hundred, the notary called the Pratica to order. With all the magistrates and ministries in attendance, the Hall was filled to capacity again. Niccolò could not help note the semblance to a large *cucina* filled with cooks, where everybody wished to have a hand in the preparation, but no one wanted to touch the hot pot.

Many leading members of the *Arrabbiati* were present, including Vespucci and Spini. With their party dominating the Signoria, they looked confident of their purpose. If left up to these judges, the cards were already stacked against the poor *frati*. But Niccolò would shed no tears for the friar; he had brought this calamity down upon himself.

Looking over to the other side he saw Piero Soderini seated next to Bernardo Rucellai. On the visitors' bench was the esteemed Marsilio Ficino, the poet Ugolino Verino, and several priests, friars and lay citizens. Ficino was the first called to give testimony.

Despite his advanced years, the philosopher appeared invigorated by the questioning. He viciously denounced the friar and his group of followers as a "demon" and a "whole swarm of devils who had seduced the gullible Florentines."

One of the priors asked him if he, a man acclaimed of wisdom, prudence, and learning, had not also been seduced by the friar. Ficino answered forthrightly:

"Yes, Excellencies. I admit I, too, was seduced by the friar's words in the first years. I remind you at this time the situation in the city was difficult and dangerous. When driven out, the Medici left the government in confusion and the French king threatened our lives with his huge army. Who would not have followed a man who delivered us from such ruin? You cannot fault citizens for this and the pope should forgive us this."

He continued: "But after the new government was installed the friar became seduced by power, and so his true nature was revealed to me. I quote to you the words of Cicero: 'everything in excess is usually changed into its opposite.'"

Ficino's testimony greatly satisfied the judges. Then they called the poet Ugolino. He had also been a fervent disciple, dedicating many of his poems to the friar. But now he described him as "an incarnation of the Antichrist," and "the son of perdition and corruption." He related how the hypocritical Friar had persuaded the whole city of his divine mission, how he had enlisted the poor innocents through an appeal to virtue and the simple life just to further his designs and unjustly impeach those who disagreed with his reforms. He did all this with "incredible slyness and cunning."

'Incredible' is right, Niccolò mused, confident things were going as planned.

Ugolino's testimony was followed by a Dominican from San Marco, Fra Roberto Ubaldini. This priest was obviously a member of an old, noble family with that sense of privilege that came with his name. Fra Roberto denounced his three fellow Dominicans as that "triumvirate of *gran maestri* who usurped all authority and settled everything among themselves and then expected the rest of the community to ratify their decisions." This mode of government was a tyranny, he said, and thus the prior had lost all credit and reputation in the convent. Then he stated he saw Fra Silvestro spending whole days in the cloisters surrounded by groups of citizens and gossiping about the city's affairs.

This spoke to the serious charge of *intelligenzie* and political intrigue and immediately Doffo Spini interrupted the testimony: "Do we need more evidence? The three *frati* were in constant communication and thus passing secrets concerning the government in violation of the law. Even his own followers have condemned him."

Another outburst forced the Gonfaloniere to silence the assembly with his gavel. "There is additional testimony to be heard."

Several citizens were deposed next, declaring they knew of no intrigues of a 'political nature' at the convent and stating they had frequented San Marco for religious purposes only. Nevertheless, several admitted Fra Silvestro was imprudent—a busybody who became the center of a good deal of political gossip—but this could not be faulted against the friar. Niccolò noted these several witnesses seemed more intent on deflecting any blame from their own persons than ascertaining the guilt or innocence of the accused.

The pendulum swung back and forth like this for most of the afternoon. Then Ser Ceccone read out the recent 'confessions' extracted in the Bargello from the prisoners. But these too failed to resolve differences, only provoking more controversy. Niccolò sensed the growing weariness of the assembly and impatience of those who wished to pass final judgment and be done with it.

One of the examiners suggested the evidence seemed sufficient to ban the friar and his colleagues from the city, but not strong enough to condemn them to death. One of the Eight then rose to complain: "If we banish the friar and do not deliver him to the pope, the interdict will fall upon us and we'll be ruined!"

"If freed, he may create a new sect of *fraticelli,* of which we have had previous experience."

Citing the friar's latest epistles written while imprisoned, one examiner stood in his defense: "Even a good man may err, and mistake his own imaginings for the spirit of prophecy."

"Such imaginings have ruined us! Shall we wait for the new French king to march down and occupy our city, or the pope's League to attack us directly? *Basta!* A sermon unheard will not be the cause of anyone missing heaven."

Doffo Spini rose to second this. "We've covered all this before. No new evidence refutes the guilt of these despicable priests. I agree with Signor Bernardo, let us be rid of this blight upon the city."

As pandemonium threatened to break out again, Piero Soderini rose to claim the floor. When order was restored he said: "Excellencies, we've received word the pope has dispatched his own examiners from the Roman Curia to question the *frati*, no? They will arrive within the week; surely they'll be able to pass judgment on the *frati*."

Niccolò watched the faces around the Hall. The *Arrabbiati* adamantly expressed their opposition—they wished to execute the friar immediately, before he slipped through their grasp—but most were nodding their approval. One could always count on the natural disposition of Florentine officials to put off to tomorrow what decisions need not be made today. It was a Tuscan golden rule that the prudent man may live to see tomorrow. Signor Piero's proposal was quickly agreed to.

CHAPTER 10

PRISON MEDITATIONS

IN THE DARKEST MOMENTS OF the night Fra Girolamo felt the shadow of death loom over him. The walls of the prison cell closed in as he huddled on the floor, frozen with his hands clasped in silent prayer like some stone angel on an altar frieze. Sleepless, he struggled with his thoughts during the worst moments in the last hour before dawn, when fear became a crushing weight on his chest. It was like a giant wave breaking over him again and again, drowning and suffocating him, pulling him under.

Lord, save me! What a wretched man I am!

But he was abandoned to his fate. He was alone; his followers had scattered and his enemies surrounded him. The Almighty would not reach down to end this torture, even though he pleaded feverishly:

Sadness besets me...she counsels me to despair...O Lord I confess, I confess! I have betrayed you in my fear...show me Your mercy, O God... give me a sign You have not abandoned me...I confess O Lord, that I have sinned against You alone and done evil before You. Take pity on me...

He shook catatonically as his muscles struggled to free his body from its paralysis, wondering: Was this the final grip of death? Pressing his fists into his closed eyes, he mouthed silent words into the darkness:

"O you wretched creature," he castigated himself. "Divine kindness bestowed on you the knowledge of the Scriptures and put God's Word in your mouth and set you up among the people as one of the great men. You taught others and neglected yourself. You cured others but could not save yourself. Your heart lifted you up in your beauty and so you have lost your wisdom. You have become nothing and you will be nothing forever. Don't you know how God resists the proud?"

He unclenched his fists and dropped his hands as he sensed the milky gray of dawn seeping through his eyelids. Somehow the light lessened his fear and he listened for the birds. He became conscious of his senses—the painful soreness of his limbs, the tenderness of his blistered feet, and the hollowness in his belly. Then he heard the morning song of the birds. He imagined them flying free, out over the city, before returning to their nesting places around the tower. These were God's innocent creatures and they reminded him of the beatitude of Francis. He imagined himself flying free, free of his tormented body, free of his tortured flesh.

Lord, did You not say: On any day a sinner moan, 'I shall not remember his iniquities'? See how I, a sinner, am moaning... my sores are festering because of my folly...my strength has deserted me...

Then his eyes opened slowly and the sudden shadows along the floor of his cell frightened him. He knew his fate was a chasm of emptiness and despair. Was this the abyss? Then he saw a vision in the form of a woman and she came close to whisper in his ear, beckoning him: "Death is your only recourse. Death is your only salvation."

No! No! His mind fought back. It was an illusion, *nothing but an illusion.*

Were they all illusions? Everything he saw in his dreams? Was his burning need to believe the true source of his visions and his gift of prophecy?

Lord, You leave me in the desert of the unknown.

As the light of day slowly grew stronger, it reached down through the high window and bathed the walls in white. His eyes adjusted as the dark corners retreated from its path. "Who will come to my aid? Where can I go? How can I flee?" he asked.

The small birds chattered more insistently somewhere outside his window and he reached out to pick up the Bible, clasping it to his breast. He felt his heart beat against it as it rested there. Again he felt the breath of life pulse through his veins and he thought: "Lord, You are my hope. It is Your divine grace and my profound faith in You that gives me strength. Please."

Suddenly he found his voice, insistent and alive, and it cried out, "*In Te, Domine, speravi.* In You, Lord, I have hoped!"

The sound echoed off the stone walls and startled him. Like a physical slap it roused him and slowly he straightened to unwind his cramped and broken limbs. Then he forced his hand to pick up the quill again and scratch out the words.

***

Salvatore turned the key and opened the door. He saw the friar huddled on the floor writing with his quill amid a nest of small scraps of paper.

"*Scusi*, Padre. I have your soup."

The friar ceased his work and invited Salvatore to sit as he shuffled through his papers. The scraps were covered with what appeared to be tiny chicken scratches of writing.

"I have something I promised you," the friar said, handing him an intricately transcribed page. He struggled to mouth the words as he read it.

The friar explained it for him: "It is a listing of *The Rules for Virtuous Christian Living.* There is the title. Can you read it?"

"*Sì, sì*, Padre. You write with a very small hand."

Salvatore was flustered with gratitude. This was a special gift from the celebrated friar and he held it tightly—his family and neighbors would be greatly impressed. "*Grazie, grazie*, Fra Girolamo. I will strive each day to follow its guidance."

Salvatore looked at the pages strewn around the floor of the cell. "What are you writing now, eh? Everyone in the city has read your epistle on the *Misereremei*. There are not enough copies for everyone who wants one, it is greatly esteemed by all."

Actually the pamphlet had aroused as much vitriol as praise, but he did not think this small omission a sin.

"I've been writing on the psalm *In Te, Domine, speravi.* As the prophet says, 'Lord, you are my hope.' I therefore call upon Hope. She will come and bring joy in this, my hour of despair."

The jailor nodded and wrinkled his brow, so the friar continued: "In the long dark night, Salvatore, a deep sadness weighs upon me. Fear creeps into my heart and I cannot shake its grip. Sadness besets me with the darkness of the void and I fear the coming interrogations and bodily pain. And I fear the end to come if I am alone, forsaken by my God. But, in the morning Hope comes and keeps me company. She chases Sadness, scatters her army, and gives me strength. Hope has taught me to fight and she says, 'Cry out and cease not!'"

"She?"

"*Sì.* Last night I had a vision. I saw Sadness descend upon me like a she-wolf. She set upon me with her army of jackals and saddled me with fear. She barked like Cerberus at the gates of the Inferno and I feared for my soul. But Hope came down with the light of Heaven, like the Virgin Mother, and she spoke to me and consoled me."

"What did she say?" he asked, trying to imagine the visage of the Virgin.

"She said, 'See, O wretched man, open your eyes and witness God's lofty refuge. He alone is God; He alone is an infinite ocean of substance. It is He alone who knows how to deliver you; He alone who can console you, He alone who can save you.' Then Sadness returned again to chastise me and belittle my faith in God. She told me God had abandoned me and that everything is ruled by chance, nothing exists but the things of this world and our spirits pass away like smoke. She filled me again with despair."

The jailor was transfixed. This was a strange dream, but perhaps one that came from God. "What happened then?"

"Hope returned, sparkling with divine splendor. She smiled and said, 'Don't fear! Evil is not going to take you captive. See, I am with you to deliver you. Sadness made these statements like some foolish woman.' Then she asked, 'Did you begin to doubt the faith in your heart? Faith is a great gift from God. Arise and fear not. You must descend, so then you may ascend. Understand this: the Lord will not desert you.' And so Hope has given me strength."

"What a beautiful dream, *fantastico!*" exclaimed Salvatore. He was amazed as a child at Carnevale, but then reddened, feeling embarrassed.

"No, not fantastic, Salvatore. Perhaps the vision of two women is merely a device God uses to help us to understand His meaning. But I wrote the same idea of Hope there in your Rules. Faith fills the void of darkness with Hope, just as day follows night. And Faith together with Hope leads to the perfect knowledge of God and participation in all His glory."

"*Sì*, Padre, your followers need these words of Hope. Their enemies have attacked them and spread lies about you. And the sick and poor have nowhere to turn. The plague officers have expelled all those afflicted with the pestilence and banished them, under threat of torture and death. They have even constructed a crude *strappado* outside the Armourer's Guild to torture those who try to return."

The friar closed his eyes with a pained look and Salvatore immediately felt remorse for mentioning the *strappado*. "I'm sorry, Padre. I shouldn't have—"

"No, Salvatore, it's not that." He opened his eyes. "I only weep for the suffering of the innocent. You, too, have helped rescue me in my faith. I'm sure God has sent you to me for my own redemption."

Salvatore shook his head in denial, but beamed with pride mixed with a natural shyness. This friar was a strange one, beyond comprehension. But all the lies he heard had convinced Salvatore that Satan himself was opposed to the friar, and so God must favor him, like St. Francis. When he exited the cell he carried his *Rules for Virtuous Christian Living* with exaggerated reverence.

*** *

Alone again, Fra Girolamo looked down again at his pages of notes. These were his only salvation and slowly he put them in order as he silently recited a prayer of apology.

Peccavi, Lord, I have sinned. I adopted the ways of my enemies, thinking I could subject them with power. I was wrong and they have trapped me with their own devices.

Your Son Jesus shows us the way but I, your servant, was blinded by my pride. But who is it that is more renown: Caesar or the crucified Savior? Herod the tyrant or the Christ child? Who remembers Caesar now? Who remembers Herod? But all worship the sacrifice of the Savior on the cross. He shows the way that leads all Christians to salvation.

Then he wrapped the fingers of his left hand tightly around the small crucifix hanging from his neck and once more commenced to write.

CHAPTER 11

THE PAPAL COMMISSIONERS

TOMMASO SAT WAITING ON HIS horse outside the Porto Romano, the city gate leading south to Rome. He was with Doffo Spini together with a contingent of guards of the Eight. Spini, reveling in his new political role had invited him to ride out this morning to meet the two papal commissioners from Rome. Cardinal Francesco Romolino was Bishop of Ilerda and Auditor to the Governor of Rome, both powerful and lucrative benefices granted him by Pope Alexander. Bishop Giovacchino Torriani was Master General of the Order of Dominican Friars, charged by the Roman Curia to oversee the convents of the Order and thus directly responsible for the problems related to the fractious Prior of San Marco.

As the two clerics approached from the distance, Spini said, "Here they come. I'd like to see that sniveling bastard preacher escape his fate now."

After Cardinal Romolino offered greetings from His Holiness the group turned to escort the visitors to the Palazzo. Tommaso rode next to Spini, who rode close to the cardinal with the bishop on the far side. Romolino was a tall, dark Spaniard and his mood was jovial. He appeared energetic and eager in contrast to the Italian bishop, who seemed wearied by his journey and discomfited by the long ride. As they rode through the streets toward the Ponte Vecchio many of the wizened old crones poked their heads out their high windows to watch the procession ride by. Meanwhile, young *fanciulli* scampered alongside the horses, shouting and cheering the clerics.

"Death to the friar! Death to the friar!" they yelled, laughing at their own cleverness.

Romolino smiled as he turned toward Spini. "Don't worry, he'll die, ...even if he's another Baptist," he said with a soft chuckle. Then he added, "By the way, Cardinal Borgia sends his greetings and his congratulations."

Spini acknowledged the compliment with formality. "Your Eminence, we are pleased if the Holy Father is pleased. Our city has suffered greatly under the spell of this devilish monk. But you shall see for yourself soon enough—how he conjures up his seductive lies."

As they approached the Ponte Vecchio the accompanying crowd had grown so large the guards were forced to drive a path by extending their pikes and halberds. When they arrived in the Piazza dell Signoria, the crowd cheered and the cardinal responded with a wave.

"How is it this Friar is still alive? It would appear the entire city is against him. Is this the place where they burned the vanities?"

"Yes, Eminence," said Spini. "We put an end to such nonsense, but this monk is a snake in the art of escape. Many of his supporters, Snivelers and Weepers, still hide behind closed doors. We mean to kill the beast by cutting it off at the head."

Tommaso for once was in agreement with Spini. He leaned over to address the cardinal. "Eminence, we hope His Holiness will grant his pardon to our city after we have resolved this matter to his satisfaction. I, myself, have witnessed the execution of one my family and the banishment of several others due to the injustices of this friar and his supporters."

Romolino shook his head with disdain. "I can't imagine how your government can fall prey to such a creature," he said. Patting his breast, he added, "Well, it matters little, for we shall make a fine bonfire of our own. I bear the sentence with me, already prepared."

CHAPTER 12

ROMOLINO'S INQUISITION

THE NEXT DAY CARDINAL ROMOLINO took his place at the inquisitors' bench in the Bargello. He and Bishop Torriani were flanked by the government's representatives—a couple of merchants, a magistrate from the Ten, one from the Eight, and one from the Twelve Worthies. Noticing the complacent looks on the Florentines' faces, Romolino remembered Cesare Borgia's damning assessment: "A republic of preening fools," he called them and Romolino was inclined to agree. After this, only God will be able to save them from the Borgia's rapacious clutches.

The subject of all this trouble was bound and seated on the prisoner's stool facing them: this poor Dominican friar looked like man of little consequence. Apparently he had already been tortured and broken and his body showed the ravages. This morning he had been racked and his limbs stretched to the tenderizing point just to remind him of the pain to come absent a forthright confession. He did not look like he would be able to endure much more.

Cardinal Romolino had already reviewed the accused's signed confession, submitted by this fawning notary who sat scribbling off to the side. Next to him Bishop Torriani looked ill. Obviously he was not up to this unpleasant task, but the Church could not survive heretical fanatics; they must be rooted out. It was the cardinal's appointed task and he intended to get on with it. He began by repeating those questions that had already been put to the prisoner as noted in the deposition:

As regards these matters, have you had any dealings with other ecclesiastical persons besides those named in your confession?

Have you had any dealings with princes? And which of them did you trust, and why?

What cardinals were your friends, and what dealings have you had with them?

Did this Fra Domenico Buonvicini or Fra Silvestro Maruffi reveal to you matters heard in confession?

The prisoner struggled to answer but did not depart from his previous confession: stating only several of his San Marco brethren shared his confidence; he had no dealings with princes, but had hoped to appeal to them as good Christians; he had considered Cardinal Caraffa of Naples to be favorably disposed toward him; and no confessions were revealed to him.

Romolino pressed on. "Do you claim to receive visions from God?"

"I had dreams and I interpreted these visions as messages from God. And I interpreted these messages as prophecies that then bore fruit. But I have made no claim to be a prophet. The Lord only wished me to know and to speak out."

"So you believe yourself to be a divine visionary," stated the cardinal.

"Eminence, as seeing is believing, so is believing seeing."

Romolino scoffed, looking to his fellow examiners. "Why, this is just Scholastic nonsense. It may be a clever way to deceive the ignorant, but we are another matter."

He shook his head in warning and redirected his inquiry to more concrete issues. "And what about your defiance of the excommunication?"

The Dominican hung his head. "Your Eminence, on this I have sinned and I pray for mercy from His Holiness."

The cardinal sensed an opening and moved to corner his prey. "Did you say the pope was not a Christian, had not been baptized, and was no true pope?"

The friar seemed dazed and hesitated before he replied. "I can't remember, I believe…no, I never said so, but I think I wrote a letter in which this was said, but I never published it."

Romolino pounced. "How then," he cried, "would it have reached my ears?"

He stood up to let his anger show. "Have we not commanded you to tell the whole truth and nothing but?"

In a show of annoyance, he commanded the blackhoods to strip the prisoner for the *strappado*. When they laid their hands on him, the friar threw himself down before his inquisitors. He looked up toward the ceiling and cried, "Now, please hear me! O God, you have caught me! I confess I have denied Christ, I have told lies."

Then he lowered his gaze to the magistrates. "O Lords of Florence, bear me witness I have denied Him for fear of torture. If I must suffer, let it be for the truth. All I have said I have had from God! O God, grant that I may repent of having denied Thee for fear of the torture."

Romolino waved his arm and the blackhoods grabbed the friar roughly and tied his wrists to the roped pulley. As he was hauled toward the ceiling with his arms up over his head and the pain shooting through him, he cried out, "Jesus, save me!"

Romolino signaled for the friar to be held at the top, suspended in his terror. He suspected the anticipation of pain was likely more effective than the actual experience of it. He stood up and walked around the table to stand under the dangling prisoner.

"Why have you made these claims? Why do you cry out to God, when you know He only demands the truth to be saved?"

The friar was overcome, replying in a whimper. "That I might be thought a man of faith, a good man of faith. Please, don't torment me, for I will tell you the truth now, for sure."

Romolino signaled for the friar to be lowered, then asked, "Why did you just deny what you have confessed?"

The man looked deranged as he stammered: "Because I am a fool. I thought perhaps you would be afraid to lay hands upon me. When I see the tortures, I lose my self-control, but when I am in a room with a few men who deal peaceably with me I express myself better."

Romolino was dismayed; truly this heresy must be exorcised. He continued wearily. "So, the process which has been drawn up, is it true?"

"All I have written in the confessions is true."

Romolino noted the cleverness of the friar's reply, which could be interpreted as denying all he had *not* written, alluding to the embellishments of the notary. But the cardinal let it go. He had most of what he needed and as long as the prisoner put his signature to the confession, his guilt was assured. Romolino would review the depositions tonight and continue the interrogation tomorrow if necessary. There were still several matters he wished to pursue concerning the conspiracy for a Church Council and he was now sure the friar could not bear up under even the mildest of tortures. Furthermore, the Florentine officials wanted to question the friar about political interference and collusion among officials who had been in the government and what part the friar had played in the execution of the five citizens last August.

That evening, at the house of their host, Cardinal Romolino rested in his room and carefully reviewed Ceccone's transcriptions of the depositions of all three accused. Romolino was determined the case be resolved quickly, and to the satisfaction of His Holiness. He remembered well the pope's cold and resolute tone when he had been appointed to this commission. The Borgia's words clearly stated he wanted the "heretics silenced, without delay." Romolino was too aware of the costs to himself if his mission failed in any way.

While reading the confessions his felt his disgust rise at the notary's crude attempts to distort Savonarola's answers. This would need to be rectified, especially when contrasted against the testimony given by the other two prisoners. Both had been separately informed their prior had confessed to false prophecies so to make further denial futile. After, the Florentine named Silvestro broke immediately under torture, confessing readily to all charges. He begged for mercy, attributing his guilt to an illness that caused confusion in the mind. He was a somnambulant possessed by strange dreams and visions. Ask anyone, he said. He had been misled by the prior to believe these dreams were signs from God. He also confessed to the desire to be held in greater esteem and so had embellished and gossiped about information he had obtained while administering the sacrament of confession. This was all damning enough.

However, the one called Domenico had borne up well under the torture and refused to recant. Subjected to the *strappado* and the rack, he repeatedly denied all the charges, even after the painful torture of the boot. This was the foolhardy one who had embraced the challenge to the Ordeal by Fire.

Later, when the cardinal and bishop were entertained by their host—a merchant who seemed eager to denounce the whole affair as a travesty to Florentine trade and good will—the point of Fra Domenico was raised again. Yes, Fra Domenico had the power of faith, Romolino conceded, but it was a misplaced faith. Anyway, it was of no consequence because, from the point of view of the court, Domenico could not separate his guilt from the other two. The important point, he explained for the benefit of his host and to make the grievous nature of the charges perfectly clear to Bishop Torriani, was that Savonarola had openly procured the deposition of the pope by means of a General Council. This was a direct contravention of the Bull *Execrabilis* issued in 1459 by Pius II explicitly condemning an appeal to a General Council to override decrees of the His Holiness. Essentially, Savonarola had deliberately defied the excommunication and then sought to depose the pope. By these actions he openly demonstrated his contempt for the Holy See and was justly condemned.

"As for the other two, well," said Romolino as he smiled at his host, "Perhaps we should spare the brave one as a sign of the pope's benevolence."

It was at this point Bishop Torriani excused himself to retire for the evening.

CHAPTER 13

MACHIAVELLI VISITS FILIPPO GIUNTA

NICCOLÒ STEPPED OUT OF THE Palazzo into the harsh sun during the midday *pausa*. He desperately needed a respite from the mounting tensions among the various ministries. Just this morning he had procured from one of the priors of the Signoria an undisclosed copy of the friar's confessions 'undoctored' by Ser Ceccone. The discrepancies and inconsistencies with the 'official' version were glaring. This was just what he needed to sink the ambitions of that puppet Ceccone, though he would need to be cautious because public knowledge could threaten an expedient outcome to the trial.

Niccolò thirsted for some company of an apolitical nature. He thought of Del Corno's, but no, even the taverns these days offered little respite from the hellpit and he had no energy for an afternoon tryst. Thinking of other avenues of escape, he reflected with irony on those words of Tuscan wisdom: "If you have someone to whom you wish evil, send him to Florence as a city official." How true.

Wandering aimlessly, he suddenly realized he was only steps from Messer Filippo's bookshop and made his way there directly with the hope of catching him. When he arrived Filippo was just locking his door to return home for the midday meal.

"*Saluti*, Messer Niccolò, where are you off to?"

"I've come here directly to catch you before you go home."

"Well, you arrived just in time. Will you stay and join me?" he asked. When Niccolò nodded he unlocked his door again and ushered him in. Then he leaned out to shout at one of the neighborhood boys to go tell Signora Giunta he must stay at the shop and to bring back the food she had prepared, with enough for two. Then he invited Niccolò to sit down and pulled out a flask of wine.

"It's been awhile, my young friend. Official business leaves you no time for books?"

"I know why they say 'be careful what you wish for.' But I have great hopes after the current troubles pass." He held up his goblet in a toast and drank.

Filippo drew from his own goblet but looked grave. "And how exactly will they pass? Do you know?"

Niccolò sighed; there was no escaping this controversy. "Who knows? But the papal commissioners appear to have their orders from the pope. The *frati* have come up against a most serious adversary."

Filippo took another draught of wine. "It seems doubtful anyone will step forward to pull these poor *frati* from the fire. It's a travesty of justice nonetheless, no matter what you think of Fra Girolamo's prophecies. I suspect the Franciscan challenge to the Ordeal was nothing but a sham to trap the friar into promising a miracle and then insuring he would fail. Then they could denounce him as a false prophet."

Niccolò hesitated for a moment, wondering what Filippo would say if he knew about the unspoken conspiracy among those in the Palazzo to eliminate the friar as an inconvenience.

Filippo continued. "Though my own tastes in worship have differed, my wife has attended almost every sermon delivered by the friar over the past four or five years. And she swears to me she never *once* heard him depart from the teachings of Scripture, even in exhorting sinners to change their ways. True, his style of preaching is prone to exaggeration and occasional outlandish metaphor, but how can one twist this into heresy? Do the *grandi* take us for idiots?"

Niccolò was willing to concede the obvious. "Actually, you're correct in many respects, especially where justice takes second seat to the desire for peace and order. A copy of the friar's confessions obtained under torture was given to me in secret by Berlinghieri in the Signoria. The confessions reveal little that would violate law, either civil or canonical."

"So how can they convict him? How can they allow the pope to commit this injustice?"

Niccolò emptied his goblet. "I suppose the depositions will be altered to obtain the desired results."

Messer Filippo appeared dismayed. "And so, what will become of a society of Christians that violates its most fundamental principles of justice? How far down into the abyss will we slip?"

"It's a necessary evil in this case," Niccolò declared defensively. "I can't find it possible to excuse the man who got himself into this mess. He made the mistake of denouncing the simplest pleasures of life as unholy vanities. The people could not tolerate it. And he was unyielding in all other matters: even Christ found it in his heart to forgive the Magdalena."

Before Filippo could respond, he continued: "And in the matter of the Grays, he foolishly allowed himself to be persuaded by Valori to allow the death sentence to stand. But the crime was less treason than a struggle between factions for control—Del Nero's offense was egregious, but banishment would have been the appropriate sentence for the others. So Valori incited the hateful revenge of the condemned men's families, a mistake for which he paid with his life. It's the same penalty these families now wish to impose on the friar."

Filippo was surprised. "This is a strange argument coming from you. You would then excuse those who seek to overthrow the Republic? I had the impression you believed in liberty above all else. Is Brutus still a hero?"

"I do not excuse traitors, but if Caesar had killed Brutus, would we still admire him? Or call him a fool? And hasn't Valori suffered the same fate as Cassius? In the past few years, I've seen little virtue in a weak republic. Men die unjustly and the whole community is seen to suffer from constant unrest. Thus liberty is best supported by ruthlessly eliminating the weaknesses of a republic and replacing them with strengths. The friar and his lot have become a weakness. He committed the most serious sin by threatening the peace and stability of the community. Inciting fear in the people is the one thing they can never forgive. Even Maestro Adriani concedes this."

Filippo replied, "Learned men are sometimes blinded by their intellect to the neglect of their souls. I see the cold efficiency of your logic, but hasn't justice then become just another weapon for those with the mightier sword."

"Has it ever been any other way?"

Niccolò could never understand his fellow Florentines' persistence in confusing heaven and earth.

Messer Filippo fell silent. How was one to derail such simple rationalizations—they were like moving pieces on a chessboard toward a single objective. He wondered if religious virtue and civic virtue had become so divided. Is nature just a reality for one to accept or reject? He got up and walked over to a wall case filled with bound volumes. He gently caressed the bindings. He knew these better than back of his own hand. His eyes sought out a copy of the Hebrew Bible. He quoted softly: "Behold, I will send prophets to you, and wise men. Some you will kill and some you will crucify; some you will persecute from city to city. And upon you will fall all the righteous blood shed upon the earth until this day." Then he added, "May God save us from ourselves."

The door opened and the boy came in to deliver the meal from Signora Giunta. Filippo smelled his wife's fragrant aromas of spices and cooked tomatoes as he put away the empty flask of wine and flipped the boy a coin.

"I hope you're hungry, Messer Niccolò. Unfortunately, I think I've lost my appetite."

CHAPTER 14

THE SIGNORIA'S VERDICT

NICCOLÒ AGAIN SAT AMIDST THE magistrates, ministers, and examiners in the Hall of Two Hundred Reasons Not to Make a Decision as they entered their third day of deliberations. Actually, the verdict was a foregone conclusion and the differences were now merely over the appropriate punishment. Yesterday there was a closed Pratica with the examiners and the ministries and some of the friar's supporters had made a spirited effort to spare the prisoners. One said the prophet was "one man in a hundred years," and had made an impassioned case that, with the friar's richly endowed learning and sincere piety, he would soon succeed in restoring Christian faith to the world. While not excusing the friar's mistakes in involving himself in political affairs, the man importuned the Signoria to imprison the friar and grant him use of writing materials so "the world may not lose the fruits of his learning."

But the *Arrabbiati,* in the voice of Vespucci and Alberti, smelled the rottenness of that fruit and made a strong counter-argument that given the rapid changes of Florentine government, the life of such a prisoner would be a constant menace to the peace of the city. They wisely feared the unceasing threat of a constant flow of the friar's epistles, as were now peppering the populace.

Today the magistrates would hear the final report of the papal Commissioners after their two days of interrogating the prisoners. Both the Spaniard Romolino and the Dominican Torriani sat comfortably at a place reserved for visitors at the end of the Signoria's table as Ser Ceccone read the report to the assembly. It was no mystery what the recommendations of the pope's representatives would be, nevertheless all ears and eyes riveted on Ceccone as he stood up to deliver the report.

Niccolò saw the looks of satisfaction on the faces of the *Arrabbiati* as Ser Ceccone referred to the friar as a "nefarious monster," stating that all his appearances of goodness were but a "pretense and a cloak for ambition, a base desire to attain worldly glory." Niccolò took up his quill to make notes in his journal. He thought it useful to record the language used by his principal rival for the Chancery, who so obviously served as a mouthpiece for the Commissioners and thus ultimately the pope. This *beffato* was not aware of the trap he was setting for himself.

Ceccone elaborated with ever-greater invective and far-fetched hearsay, so the accusations soon became as transparent as the lies and fairytales they were. He reported the friar had often turned to the crucifix and said, "If I lie, You lie," thereby committing a most heinous blasphemy. Then he accused the friar of never having made a confession for fourteen years and abusing the sacraments.

Niccolò wrote all this down as he reflected on the reaction of Messer Filippo yesterday. While he firmly believed the older scholar naïve and idealistic when it came to matters of state, and that Niccolò's own fortunes were enhanced by the demise of the *Frateschi* and the friar, he also realized Filippo's intuitive reaction to the whole affair was more representative of the majority of the population. This affair was all a game played by the *grandi* and the people knew it. Changes in the world were being thrust upon all and when the *popolo* realized the friar had represented their best hope for change for the better, there would likely be a backlash against those who perpetrated his downfall. Ceccone's obvious complicity would be his downfall.

Niccolò looked up when the notary paused and saw Doffo Spini whispering to another member of the Eight at their bench. Spini was enjoying the warmth of *Fortuna's* embrace just now, another pawn in this game but oblivious in his own ignorance. He, his *Compagnacci*, and their *Arrabbiati* patrons were the symbols of anti-religious invective in the minds of the Florentines, especially among the *poverini* and the *popolo*. They were also suspected of conspiring with the Sforza and Borgia agents against the friar, thereby putting their own interests above those of the commune. Niccolò expected their arrogant nature would eventually invite Nemesis to wreak her mischief.

Ser Ceccone finished by announcing the papal Commissioners' determination that the three accused were all confessed heretics and schismatics and they be remanded and turned over to the secular arm for sentencing and punishment. For Fra Girolamo and Fra Silvestro they recommended the sentence of death, but only imprisonment and banishment for Fra Domenico.

There was a brief commotion among the magistrates' benches as Ser Ceccone read out these sentences. The member of the Eight who had been whispering with Spini immediately rose to object, saying to allow Fra Domenico to live would mean all of the friar's pernicious doctrines would be kept alive as well.

Bishop Torriani responded with a look of consternation: "We have advised to spare Fra Domenico to placate your citizens and heal the divisiveness in your city. He never confessed directly to many of the charges, even under the most …rigorous questioning."

Torriani had struggled to find an acceptable word, and Niccolò sensed his shame as he averted his eyes. Romolino suffered no such compunctions of guilt. With a dismissive gesture he said, "One vile friar, more or less, matters little. Do with him what you will."

After the papal Commissioners departed, a final vote by the Eight and the Signoria was tallied. Niccolò briefly caught the eye of Piero Soderini who for the past two days had sat quietly observing events unfold. There was no emotion betrayed in his eyes. As the votes were announced, Niccolò opened his journal to record them: of the Eight, seven for death and one against; for the Signoria it was unanimous, eight plus the Gonfaloniere all for death. So now it was settled: Death by hanging and burning at midmorning the following day.

As the vote was confirmed, Niccolò looked up at the high angle of the sun coming through the windows of the Hall. It was only late morning and soon they would break for the midday *pausa*. By early afternoon the sentence would be spread across the entire city. He was sure Piero had encouraged Tommaso to spread the gleeful reaction of the *Compagnacci*. And the performance of Ser Ceccone would be richly mined for street theater. For his part, he would merely relate the events to his good friend, Nello the barber. As for the prior of San Marco, if he escaped his terrible fate now, Niccolò would don the frock himself and become a Weeper.

CHAPTER 15

The Gibbet

It was early evening when Luca Landucci, preparing to close his shop for the day, swept the dust back out the front door into the street. As he stepped outside he looked across at the ever-present construction of the Palazzo Strozzi across the way. Just this week they had finished installing the second row of arched windows. This monstrous beast had struggled to be born for now more than nine years. Through war and chaos, fire and flood, famine and plague, the beast would outlast them all, emerging slowly from the backs of dying men. Already many who had begun the project had died and Luca wondered if even Cronaca would survive it. But then, the master builder was still a relatively young man.

The small piazza was subdued, though this had turned into a momentous day. Following the recommendations of the papal Commissioners, the Signoria had finally pronounced a sentence of death on the three condemned friars. The execution would take place tomorrow morning in the center of the Piazza della Signoria, at the center of the city. Everyone knew the inevitable result, yet still it was a shock. Death was final and the prior of San Marco would be silenced and walk no more among them. Luca himself had felt the weight of the friar's presence and he wondered what he would feel tomorrow. He looked up from the dust to see Cronaca coming across the piazza.

"*Buona sera,* Messer Luca. You've heard?"

Luca nodded.

"It's a tragic moment for our city, and for us," Cronaca lamented.

"In voluntate Domine omnia sunt posita…"

Cronaca looked at him closely. "Yes, all by God's will, but do you think He meant us to be so fatalistic?"

Luca made no reply and then realized with shame his comment was more of a personal absolution. He had not attended a single sermon since the excommunication, avoiding all public contact with the friar's ardent supporters after the Ordeal. He told himself it was because he could not go against Holy Mother Church, but when he searched deeply within himself he found the true reason: he was afraid. He had confessed as much in his diary. He professed faith in his heart, but he knew he was one of the *tiepidi* who hid when evil slithered into the room. When he had attended the reading of Fra Girolamo's confession in the Great Council and heard the words written in the friar's own hand—about how he was no prophet and had not received from God the things he preached—he had felt a sad sense of vindication. It was a tragic sense that the veil of false piety had slipped to the ground and left them all naked. Then the shame returned because he knew it was not true. The contrivances of the government, the pope's agents, and the conniving notary Ser Ceccone were too transparent to be believed. But there was nothing to be done—it was like an unstoppable flood of the Arno when one could only hope to escape with one's life from the cascade of sludge and debris.

Cronaca asked, "Are you heading home? Let's go together, we can pass through the Piazza."

Luca hesitated. A morbid sense of curiosity pulled him toward the public spectacle, but he was ashamed. Yet, if he stayed away would it mean he sought to deny his own guilt and complicity in this evil, pretending it did not exist? He assented and locked the door of his apothecary to accompany Cronaca.

When they arrived it was almost twilight and the preparations were almost complete. A scaffold of wood covered the entire ringhiera, wrapping the corner of the Palazzo with a platform and walkway extending out into the middle of the square. The walkway terminated in a large circular platform head-high with space below for combustibles. Out of the center of this platform was erected a solid piece of timber more than twenty *braccie* high. Attached to this was a crosspiece placed horizontally, and one could not fail to notice the resemblance to the Cross. This was the gibbet, from which the condemned would be hanged and then consumed in the flames from the bonfire below. The carpenters were still working feverishly to complete the walkway and reinforce the platform around the ringhiera as the crowds milled about and harangued them.

Cronaca and Luca shied away and moved toward the shelter of the Pisan canopy. There they came upon Sandro Botticelli standing alone, staring out at the cross.

"A grim affair, eh?" Cronaca said solemnly.

Botticelli nodded without interrupting his stare. "It's the calamity I've been trying to envision in my painting. A crucifixion."

A small group nearby overheard the artist and nodded in agreement, saying, "*Sì, sì.* Look, it's a cross."

Their voices carried out over the crowd and a celebrating group of *Compagnacci.* One turned and snarled with contempt, "He's a thief and a traitor." Another added, "He's not Christ, you whiners, he's Barrabas. But this time the thief and murderer is not going free!"

Botticelli turned away from the argument toward his companions and said, "Simone received some secret copies of Fra Girolamo's confessions under the torture."

"How?" asked Cronaca.

"He received them from Fra Benedetto, who procured them from Ser Ceccone's wife."

Cronaca whistled. "Ser Ceccone's wife? I wonder if the fool knows he's being cuckolded this way."

"He'll receive his reward in the next life. Simone has read these 'confessions' and has shown me how they are obvious fabrications of a not-too-clever imagination."

"And the Signoria knows this?"

"They must. The Eight is packed with *Arrabbiati* and so is the Signoria. In the eyes of both Christian and Roman law, this is murder."

Cronaca shook his head in disbelief. "Will you come tomorrow?"

"Yes, I intend to burn this scene into my mind's eye."

CHAPTER 16

THE LAST NIGHT

FRA GIROLAMO WATCHED THE LIGHT shining on the wall slowly fade as the sun disappeared, unseen, somewhere over the horizon. Earlier a messenger had brought official word of their sentence. It was no surprise; declared heretics and schismatics, they were to be cleansed of their sins by the holy fire. He heard the echoes of hammering rising up from the Piazza. Soon his ordeal would be over.

Please, O Lord, take me quickly from this place.

After, he had requested Salvatore to send for one of the *Compagnia dei Neri*, the lay confraternity whose black-hooded members comforted condemned prisoners in their final hours. He also wished to make his last confession. Much to Salvatore's grief, he had refused his last supper—with Death coming so soon, he wished to prepare his soul and not be occupied with bodily needs.

He looked down at the strewn pages of his psalm of Hope. It would go unfinished. Now he only had time left to prepare, so he knelt once more in prayer. When Salvatore announced the Nero, Savonarola opened his eyes to see the forbidding figure, his face hidden behind a black cowl, enter the cell. He was the angel of mercy and the angel of death for now they were one and the same.

The two spoke for some time and the friar listened to the hidden voice of the blackhood as he spoke of faith and repentance, redemption and salvation. The Nero quoted from the book of Matthew with the same words he himself had used that terrible night weeks ago at San Marco and they recited the verse together:

You have heard how it was said: "You will love your neighbor and hate your enemy. But I say this to you: Love your enemies, and pray for those who persecute you, so that you may be children of your Father in heaven, for he causes His sun to rise on the wicked as well as on the good, and He sends down His rain on the just and the unjust alike.

As the Nero urged him to accept God's will, he slowly surrendered and felt a wave of peace wash over him. His eyes grew heavy and he professed a desire to sleep. When the Nero asked if he had any other request, he begged to be granted a last interview with his two companions. After the Nero left to take his request to the Signoria for approval, he closed his eyes and slept.

He awoke when the Nero and Salvatore returned and, as he

accompanied them down from the tower to meet with Domenico and Silvestro, he realized he had not dreamt at all. Slowly he descended the stairs, fighting the pain in his knees and ankles, and feeling lost. Upon meeting his companions and seeing Domenico's unquestioning eyes and Silvestro's apprehension, he was reassured: his followers still needed him, they still revered him. They knelt to receive his blessing.

Domenico was effusive, saying he had written a letter to his brethren at the Convent of Fiesole to collect all the writings of his master, to bind and keep them in the library with a copy made available to all who should desire to read them.

Fra Girolamo looked deep into his eyes and then admonished him, saying, "Brother, I am told you wish to be burned alive. But it's not for us to choose the manner of our death. You must joyfully accept what is prepared for you by God."

As Domenico bowed in humility Fra Girolamo looked to Silvestro, who had lost control of his wandering eye. "And I know you, Brother, wish to loudly protest our innocence before dying. But remember not even Christ professed his innocence from upon the cross. We must do likewise, for every act of Christ is an example to us and we must be a testament to the true faith according to the will of God our Father."

"But I fear for my soul," he whined, tears clouding his eyes. "I can't bear the sounds of shouting and the noise of hammering from outside where they are…"

"*Sì*," said Domenico in support, "The cardinal told us we would burn in Hell."

Fra Girolamo again assumed the role of teacher and confessor. "Brothers, know I too have felt the same grip of fear in my heart. But in the last few days God opened my eyes to an infinitely greater force. What then, is the antidote to Fear? What will save us from despair?"

He paused and then continued: "Of course it is Hope. Fear is the Devil's handmaiden, pay her no mind. She causes us to despair and wrongly follow Satan's path. But the light, the light of Hope and salvation—by the grace of God alone—will overpower the darkness of Fear. And we shall rise up, like angels, into the light."

He looked into Silvestro's unfocused eyes and said, "Do you remember your dream, where angels came and bound us together with a chain of gold? How they sang: *ecce quam bonum et quam iocundum habitare fraters in unum*? How they told us we should remain united together, and to make one heart and one spirit of our three? And God wanted it thus? God gave you that vision as a prophecy and now it is being fulfilled."

Silvestro smiled through his tears, pleading, "Please, let us sing it now, Father."

Fra Girolamo knew singing the psalm would calm them so he grasped his brothers' hands in his own and said, "Remember, if Jesus had not been crucified, He could not have been resurrected. We must rejoice because we three will ascend together into His Kingdom in Heaven."

They softly sang three refrains and then, reassured in their mutual salvation, they knelt and prayed together. Fra Girolamo led them slowly and deliberately, reciting the words of John the Evangelist:

> *I am the good shepherd.*
> *I lay down my life for my sheep.*
> *I know mine and mine know me,*
> *Just as the Father knows me*
> *And I know the Father.*
> *The Father loves me*
> *Because I lay down my life*
> *In order to take it up again.*
> *No one is taking it from me.*
> *I lay it down of my own accord.*

Reciting the prayer three times over, Fra Girolamo looked at his brothers. His final words were: "Remember what the Lord said to His disciples, '...I am going to prepare a place for you in my Father's house...'"

CHAPTER 17

THE EXECUTION

FIRST LIGHT CREPT INTO THE small window of the Alberghetto, slowly waking Fra Girolamo from a short but restful nap. His head was cradled in the black lap of the Nero, who had faithfully stayed awake through the short night. As his mind cleared, he realized again he had not dreamt while asleep.

The Nero spoke. "The Signoria has granted permission for a last Mass and Communion in the chapel. You may receive the Body of Christ one last time."

Fra Girolamo smiled dryly. "I wonder how it is they can allow a heretic to receive or administer the Sacrament?"

Seeing the Nero's consternation, he quickly added, "Don't worry, I won't press my wonder upon them."

The three *frati* assembled in the Palazzo chapel for the Mass and Fra Girolamo raised the Host one last time. Holding it before his fellows, he recited his last prayer to God:

Lord, I know the You are the true God, Creator of the world and of mankind... You are the everlasting Word that came down to earth in the womb of the Virgin Mother, and was crucified to shed Your blood for us miserable sinners...

I pray to You, my Lord, that Your sacrifice shall not have been in vain, but in remission of all my sins, ...for which I ask Your forgiveness. I confess my sinfulness to You, O Lord... and I ask Your forgiveness for anything in which I may have offended this city and this people, in spiritual and in temporal matters, and for everything in which I may have erred without knowing...

I humbly beg forgiveness of all these people and ask that they may pray to God for me, that He may give me strength at my final end and the Enemy may have no power over me...

After the Mass they comforted each other while awaiting their final summons from the Eight.

***

In the grand piazza the stage was set. It was mid-morning and the sun ducked behind a thin veil of clouds. The public space was filled to capacity; its windows, balconies, and roofs overflowing with spectators eager for a view. For this was a *spettacolo* not to be missed, greater than all those in recent memory. Either the Black friars would make a splendid bonfire or the Almighty would enact a great miracle for the benefit of his faithful servants.

The crowd grew restless with anticipation. Many *Compagnacci* were gloating as their leader, Doffo Spini, sat on the ringhiera with the Eight. But there were also quiet pockets of Weepers and silent sympathizers, who stood alone or in small groups to avoid attention. Many of these clung to the desperate hope that God would grant one last sign to affirm the words of their prophet. At the very least they were compelled to witness the final earthly moment of their gentle master on this day of infamy.

Sandro Botticelli stood near the constructed walkway with Simone, who wore a dark woolen cowl over his head despite the warm weather. Among a group of young artisans nearby were Granacci and Cronaca. Fra Benedetto, Baccio, and several of the younger friars from San Marco, now censored, huddled together at the far northeast corner of the Piazza, while Luca Landucci observed alone from a shadowed area near the exit to the Street of the Hosemakers.

With his painter's eye, Sandro seared the scene into his memory. Situated where he was he had a full view from left to right of the entire scene in front of the Palazzo. The platform along the ringhiera was festooned with officials, both ecclesiastical and secular. Arranged in three tribunals were the civic officials including the Gonfaloniere, the Signoria, and the magistrates of the Eight, the papal ambassadors, and the leading clerics of the city.

On the far right side in the Loggia dei Priori stood members of the Chanceries and ministries. They were surrounded by hundreds of citizens from the Great Council and the Eighty who had come to watch the triumph of order and right reason while taking reassurance from the guards stationed like centurions all around the Piazza.

Sandro had heard the Eight had released numerous prisoners from the *Stinche* to amplify the anti-religious fury and noticed a filthy rabble gathered around the gibbet. Apparently they were intended to contribute their own vitriolic fuel to the straw, twigs, and wood piled underneath. He also noticed the crossbeam of the gibbet had been cut short to lessen its resemblance to the cross.

Suddenly a single trumpet blast hushed the crowd and all eyes turned to the entrance of the Palazzo as the prisoners, bound in chains, were led out. The three were halted in front of the first tribunal to be defrocked and slowly stripped piece by piece of their clerical robes. Simone flinched as Fra Girolamo cried out when the frock was lifted from his shoulders. Then the friar murmured an apology to his worn frock as it was taken from him, as if parting from a dear and faithful friend.

The reigning cleric, Bishop Pagagnotti, was now required to pronounce the ritual separation of the friars from the Church but appeared distracted by the friar's mumbling. Finally he raised his scepter and loudly proclaimed, "I now separate Thee from the Church Militant and Triumphant."

"Non é giusto," cried Simone and Fra Girolamo suddenly raised his head to speak: "Excellency, from the Church Militant, yes, but not Triumphant. That is not in your power."

There was a moment of embarrassed silence followed by a buzz of confusion as many heads nodded in agreement—the Church fathers could not separate the soul of a Christian from God in Heaven, only God could do so on the Day of Judgment. Flustered, the bishop quickly repeated for all to hear, "I separate Thee from the Church Militant."

At the next tribunal they stood half-naked in their worn tunics before the Papal Examiners who had condemned them. The stark contrast with their accusers' sumptuous ecclesiastical robes was not lost on the friar's silent supporters. Cardinal Romolino proceeded to read out the charges with an officious air as the bishop avoided eye contact with the prisoners. As the cardinal read the friar's signed confession, the audience murmured with snickers, but he ignored them. Finally he read out the official judgment pronouncing the three degraded clerics "heretics" and "schismatics" and remanding them for punishment to the secular arm. This verdict elicited cheers from some in the audience, but Romolino silenced them with a raised hand and a stern look.

Softening his hard features into a more benign smile, he directed his gaze at the defrocked clerics before him and spoke with an exaggerated tone of compassion: "I've received word from His Holiness Pope Alexander VI this very day granting you a plenary indulgence in the moment of death with release from all canonical censures and excommunications. His Holiness sets you back into your original state of sinlessness. You will not undergo the punishment of Purgatory for your sins. Do you accept?"

The friars cowed without speaking, so Cardinal Romolino took their bowed heads as an assent and blessed them as they were escorted to the civil tribunal.

The condemned men were then brought up before the Eight (of which, Sandro noticed, only seven were present—the missing one obviously had no stomach or too much dignity for this sort of thing). Sandro and Simone saw Spini smirk as the official vote on the sentence was repeated for the public record. It passed unanimously (except, of course, for the single abstentia).

"*Bastardo*," growled Simone, who passed his eyes from the face of the friar to Spini, but Sandro reached out to put a hand on his brother's arm. The spokesman for the Eight announced the sentence loud enough for the entire Piazza to hear:

"The Eight, having considered the depositions of the three friars, and the atrocious crimes committed by them, and having considered the sentence pronounced by the Commissioners of the pope, who have now handed them over to the secular arm to be punished, hereby decree each of the three shall be hung from the gibbet, and then burnt, so their souls shall be entirely parted from their bodies."

A voice close by whispered, "*Sì*, they've sold him for thirty pieces of silver."

Sandro turned to give this informant a puzzled look. "*Sì*," the man repeated, nodding his head. "The Signoria received permission from Rome to apply the *decima* tax against Church properties three times over. And three times ten makes thirty."

As the prisoners were escorted down the long walkway through the jeering crowd toward the gibbet, Sandro heard them softly reciting the *Te Deum* in unison, accompanied by the black-hooded Battuti: *Te Deum laudamus: te Dominum confitemur. Te aeternum Patrem omnis terra veneratur...*

As they passed close by he thought he heard whispers rise up and flutter like a stiff breeze through fallen leaves. It was a faint chorus of unseen voices reciting with the condemned: *Sanctus, Sanctus, Sanctus, Dominus Deus Sabaoth...*

Suddenly the three friars stumbled and cried out. Under the walkway Sandro saw a gang of mischievous *fanciulli* poking through the wooden planks at the friars' bare feet with sharp-pointed sticks.

"*Bastardi!*" Simone lunged toward the youths, who easily scampered out of reach.

"Simone!" hissed Sandro, trying to distract and calm his brother. He reached out to pull him back.

When they finally reached the gibbet Fra Girolamo closed his eyes and ears to recite a last prayer: The Lord is my shepherd, I shall not want. He maketh me lie down in green pastures, He leadeth me beside still waters. He restoreth my soul, He leadeth me in the paths of righteousness For His name's sake.

Silvestro was brought forward first and a sea of anger erupted around the platform. "*Porco frate!*" "*Occhi del Diavolo!*"

Poor Silvestro's lips moved feverishly in silent prayer as he was pulled up the ladder and the noose tightened, his eyes closed tight. Unceremoniously, the executioner pushed his body off the ladder as

Brother Silvestro's last words, "*Gesú, Gesú,*" slowly strangled in his throat.

Fra Girolamo felt a sharp pain followed by a wave of numbness, as if a limb had been torn from his body. He steeled himself for the next blow as Domenico was raised up. At the last moment, sweet Domenico exclaimed loudly over the crowd: "The Church will be purified! The Holy Spirit will send His heavenly fire!"

Then he jumped willingly into the abyss with the words of "*Gesú, Gesú,*" expiring with his last breath. The crowd cheered again and Fra Girolamo, numb to all pain, was left alone with his Savior.

Yea, Lord, though I walk through the valley of the shadow of death, I will fear no evil. For thou art with me, Thou preparest a table before me in the presence of mine enemies, Thou anointest my head with oil, my cup runneth over. Surely goodness and mercy shall follow me, And I will dwell in the house of the LORD forever. For thou art with me, thou art with me…

Reaching the top of the gibbet Fra Girolamo looked through the noose into the heavens beyond. He heard nothing and saw only the Gates of Paradise through which he would soon travel. The roiling sea of faces below were angry waves licking at him as the life-ring was placed over his head and pulled taut. He heard the written word of the Hebrews in his ears as he stared into the sky:

Then I saw a new heaven and a new earth. The old heaven and the old earth had passed away, and the ocean no longer existed. I saw the holy city, a New Jerusalem, coming down out of heaven from God, arrayed as a bride adorned for her husband.

With clear eyes he saw the heavenly bride of Christ, resplendent in her white robes, beckoning him forward.

Then a voice shattered the interminable silence. Cutting like a razor's edge through the still, heavy air, it ricocheted hard off the cold stone walls of the Palazzo:

"O Prophet, NOW, …NOW is the time for a miracle!"

But it was not a single voice, it came from nowhere and everywhere and its echo filled the square. It was primal and it was communal. All these Florentines, with their eyes glued to the top of the gibbet, moved their lips as they silently mouthed the same words resounding in each heart and belly. Some jeered, some begged. This was the dreaded moment they would never forget. Filled with sin, they had exhausted themselves and now needed a sacrifice to purge their guilt. They could not stop. It was an instinct, a force of nature, a mortal finitude pulling them forward to the point of no return. Somewhere inside it pulled taut against their resistance, and they sensed the sinews holding their flesh intact would snap and they would be torn in two and flung in opposite directions. It proved unbearable to some and their taut bows snapped, releasing their arrows of taunts and curses to annihilate their tormentor.

"At last I can burn the friar... who would have liked to burn me! A just reward!"

"He saved others, but he can't save himself!"

"Come back, Friar, and tell us if the Inferno suits you!"

But Fra Girolamo only stared at the opening in the clouds and moved his lips in prayer: *In manus tuas, Domine, commendo animam meam...*

The executioner pushed him off the platform and with a sudden gasp the noose tightened, the rope pulled taut, and the body jerked.

The Florentines held their breath and looked up as one in fear. This was a clash of the gods and they searched for a sign—a murderous thunder of anger or lightning bolt of wrath; perhaps the raining tears of the saints or the warm, sympathetic light of the Madonna. But oddly, there was nothing, no pigeons flying, as the sun ducked behind a darker cloud and a chill breeze blew down off the mountains.

In the shadow of the imposing palazzo the three forsaken corpses swung from their nooses and halters. A torch was set to the sticks and faggots and the flames rose up, licking the swinging feet of the lifeless bodies.

The breeze blew the flames to one side, provoking exclamations of "*Che miracolo!* Look, the bodies don't burn!"

But the breeze passed and the flames rose again. The sickening smell of burning flesh soon permeated the air, shaking the crowd from its numbness as it exhaled in a crashing wave of wails and jeers. The *fanciulli* began shouting curses and throwing stones at the bodies. When the rope ties burned through, the friar's right arm broke free and rose up in benediction, provoking more cries of miracles.

Soon the assault on the senses overcame Simone. He threw back his hood and exhaled a final rasping cry: "O Jerusalem, Jerusalem, you have killed the prophets and stoned those who were sent unto you!"[19]

***

As the conflagration consumed the bodies, the stench overpowered the officials crowded near the Loggia, sending them scurrying back into the refuge of the palazzo with their silk robes over their noses. After Piero and Tommaso bid him farewell to return to their house for the remainder of the day, Niccolò retreated to his office.

It was over, he said to himself. The meddlesome friar had taken his last breath and existed no more, his soul dispatched to the next life, may God preserve him. The Signoria ordered the bodies completely consumed, the ashes collected and then thrown into the Arno so there was no possibility of scavenging a piece of clothing, a burnt piece of flesh or a charred bone for a relic.

Niccolò couldn't help but admire the pope's final touch. These churchmen were in a class all their own, promising 'all will be forgiven, just burn for a while in the purifying fire and your soul will find everlasting salvation in the next world.' A mere moment's discomfort for an eternity of happiness: How could one refuse? And how could one fault Holy Mother Church after displaying such magnanimity?

As he climbed the stairs he became preoccupied with more immediate concerns. In the next few weeks the offices occupied by the friar's supporters would need to be refilled. It was important that he and Soderini plan their next moves. The *Arrabbiati* were celebrating the successful conclusion of their campaign against the friar and the office of the Second Chancellor would be hotly contested. But the prospect of reporting to Ser Ceccone was almost laughable. Meanwhile the Pisan conflict was deteriorating and the Borgia would try to press their advantage.

Reaching the Sala dei Dieci, Niccolò crossed into the Udienza to look back down on the Piazza. It was still roiling with packs of *fanciulli* running this way and that, throwing stones and creating havoc amid clusters of black-cloaked old women mourning around the smoldering embers. At the same time the guards frantically tried to chase away both from the accumulated ash. It was a vision almost comic if it didn't also give him a troubling sense of tragedy: He knew the black smoke floating up had poisoned the air and blanketed the city with a stench that would not so easily dissipate.

His gaze took in the now empty Loggia and then fell upon the blue-enameled medallions decorating its façade. These representations of the cardinal virtues of Prudence, Justice, Temperance, Strength; and the Christian virtues of Faith, Hope, and Charity provided an ironic contrast to the vices and passions that had consumed the city on this day.

Epilogue

Faith disappeared, or was transformed; men became at once skeptical and intolerant. It is not at all the modern, serenely cold, and imperturbable skepticism; it is a violent movement of the whole nature which feels itself impelled to burn what it adores; but the man is uncertain in his doubt, and his burst of laughter stuns him; he has passed as it were, through an orgy, and when the white light of the morning comes he will have an attack of despair, profound anguish with tears and perhaps a vow of pilgrimage and a conspicuous conversion.

    – J.J. Jusserand, *English Wayfaring Life in the Middle Ages*

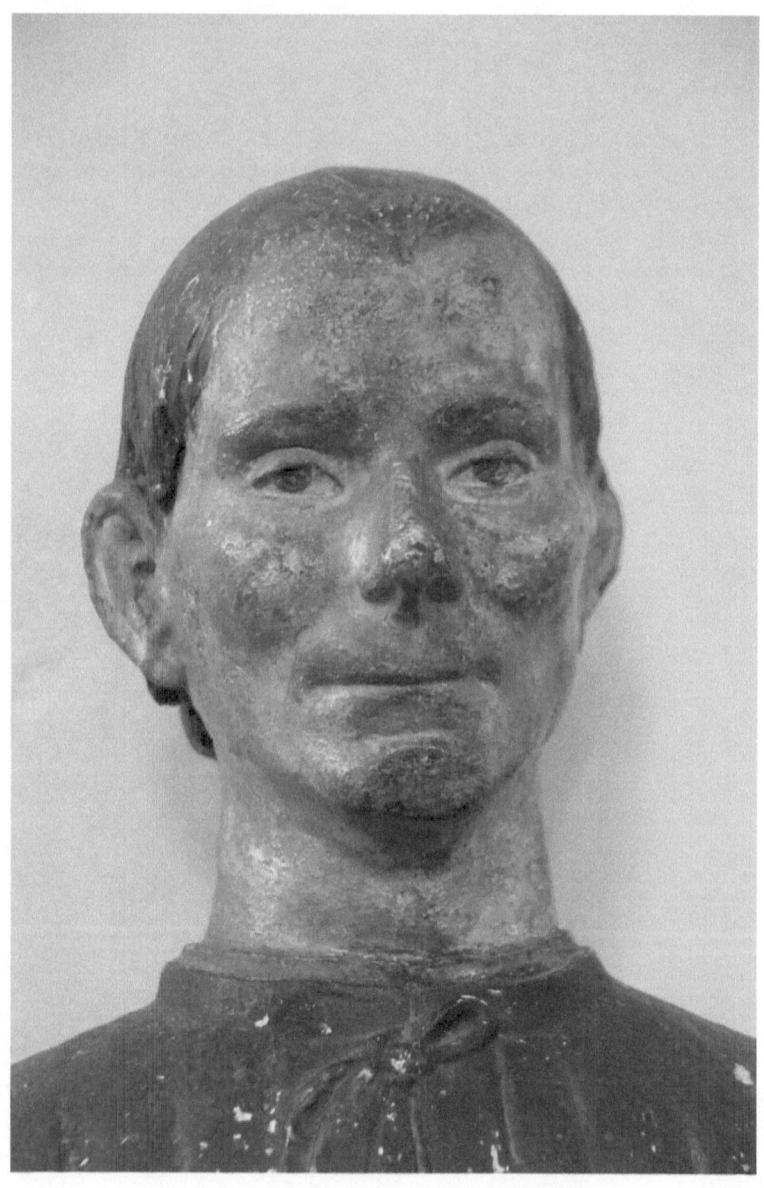

NICCOLÒ MACHIAVELLI 1475-1527

MUSEO PALAZZO VECCHIO

JUNE 24, 1498

FESTA DI SAN GIOVANNI

THE CROWD ROLLED WITH LAUGHTER as Pantalone [*wiki*]paced back and forth barking orders at his frantic servant, Pulcinella [*wiki*], badgering him to collect contributions from the audience. The archetypical *padrone*, Pantalone wore a black-faced mask with a long, hooked nose, over which his bushy eyebrows twitched like a squirrel's tail. A red woolen skullcap covered his head and his tight red breeches and vest contrasted richly against his full-length black cloak. He waved his arms as he strutted back and forth with his gait impeded by an enormous codpiece. The codpiece doubled as a fat money pouch into which he secreted the coins Pulcinella collected and each time he changed direction, he thrust his crotch out to display his proud endowment overflowing with coins spilling out to the ground. At each turn a colorfully dressed trickster snuck out and stole the coins, sneaking them back to Pulcinella, who then humbly returned them as new treasure to his master. The farce continued as Pantalone proudly displayed his ever-accumulating wealth while demanding more and more.

His abused servant Pulcinella was a little chicken with a long-beaked mask, dressed in a baggy blouse with saggy trousers topped by a sugar-loaf hat. He was poor and bent, oppressed by his master ordering him about with disdain. When he lingered his *padrone* swung a paddle—called a slapstick—that made a large clapping sound when it made contact with Pulcinella's buttocks. Each clap of thunder sent him jumping into the air as the audience exploded with laughter.

Pulcinella's accomplice, the colorful trickster, was the clever Arlechino [*wiki*] or Dante's little devil. He obscured his identity with a black silk stocking wound round his head and his costume was festooned with a colorful, diamond-patterned patchwork. With acrobatic agility he hopped and skipped in crisp staccato movements, moving his head first to change the direction of his gaze and then snapping his body around in the same direction. As he snatched the fallen coins, he ducked up and over, around and under the stage to avoid the glance of the rich *padrone* Pantalone.

Standing in the audience, Niccolò interrupted his stroll near Orsanmichele in the Piazza del Grano to watch the antics of this troupe of actors—one of many that criss-crossed Italia performing the Commedia dell'Arte during festivals. On this feast day of San Giovanni the mood of the Florentines was returning to one of abandon. The revelers in the streets again wore the comic Carnival masks of jesters and fools, clowns and kings. Though Niccolò knew many were still traumatized by the dramatic burning of the friar, it was perhaps because of these tribulations that they yearned to enjoy these simple pleasures.

Niccolò himself had dressed extravagantly in a fine silk blouse and hose under a brocade doublet. Later in the day he was required to participate in the civic procession from the Piazza della Signoria to the Baptistery to pay annual tribute to the patron saint. This was the most important ritual marking the Florentine civic calendar; when the merchant-rich city honored its benevolent deity.

Suddenly, the roving Arlechino confronted Niccolò in front of the audience. The colorful scamp mimicked a wide grin on his masked face by drawing it out with his gloved hands. Then extended one hand in a common gesture of friendship. As Niccolò grasped the hand, he was momentarily shocked. It had fallen off as he gripped it in his own.

The one-handed Ellechino hopped around like a madman, feigning horror at his lost appendage while the crowd roared in laughter. Niccolò quickly recovered with a self-deprecating smile and returned the hand to its chagrined owner together with a generous contribution to the troupe's coffer. The actors bounded off to plot their next victim and he backed away through the crowd, feeling a momentary chill as he sought to regain his anonymity. How much easier, he suddenly realized, to be the unseen observer rather than the unsuspecting victim. Shaking off his embarrassment, he headed back toward the Palazzo to prepare for the procession.

***

"Salute, Messer Secretario!"

Niccolò looked up to see Tommaso in his doorway with a hand entwined around a wine flask. The words sounded strange to the ear, but it was true: Messer Niccolò Machiavelli, Florentine citizen, nominated as Secretary of the Ten of War only days after the burning of the *frati* and then confirmed Second Chancellor of the Florentine Republic just four days ago. He was now the highest-ranking minister after First Chancellor Adriani. For once everything had gone according to plan—the guilt of the Florentines was heaped upon the Arrabbiati and Ser Ceccone was vilified by the Council. For Niccolò it proved that when man makes his fortune, Fortuna finally smiles.

Tommaso was unrestrained: *"Basta! Andiamo!* Let's enjoy the festivities. It's a holiday, no time to be in a stuffy old office! Care to test your luck with a game of *tarocchi?"*

"No, *grazie*," Niccolò said soberly. "I'm just collecting my official robe and cap before the procession. Where have you been?"

Tommaso spread his arms wide as if to take in the whole world. "Everywhere! Here, share some of my precious treasure."

Niccolò took the flask as Tommaso continued babbling. "I was just enjoying the carefree life we once knew: drinking, eating, gambling, ...whoring—well, not yet, but later. It takes a lot of effort to get my fellow Florentines to forget their stupidity and get on with life, but they're trying."

Niccolò felt compassion for Tommaso. He was still desperately trying to overcome the accumulated losses of the past year by drowning his bitterness in wine. It seemed as Niccolò's fortunes had risen, his friend's had fallen.

"It seems you've succeeded," he replied.

Tommaso winked back at him. "Machia, *senti*. I was just in Piazza San Giovanni. It's a madhouse. There was a large *girandola* with exploding rockets and spinning wheels of fire. On the vehicle platform some clever fellows arranged several figures of pigs and dogs and a large, dead giant. As they pulled the wagon the big giant kept falling down and the *fanciulli* were yelling '*Quel porco del Frate*! That pig of a friar!' Then someone said the dead giant symbolized Valori. It was strange and hilarious at the same time."

Niccolò rose from his desk. "I'm not surprised, but it would be better if they all forgot the friar and his folly."

"Fat chance," said Tommaso. "Early every morning the old women Prayer-mumblers sneak out to kneel and pray at the very spot where they torched him. They think he's a saint, a martyr! Holy relics popping up all over the place...the usual pieces of cloth, charred bones and flesh. Even 'Fra Girolamo's caterpillars!'"

Everyone had heard this fable from the gossipmongers. Two weeks ago the *fanciulli* had found a strange species of caterpillar in the fields outside the city that devoured everything in its path. The creatures were described as having a human-like face with a crown on their head, a halo, and a small cross on their backs. After four days they turned a golden color. They had never been seen before and then they disappeared after turning into butterflies. The Weepers swore it was all a miracle, signifying the golden life of the friar who had attempted to root out the ill weeds of the city, but then was resurrected like a winged angel.

"I'm well-acquainted with the fertile imaginations of our townsfolk," he said dryly. "It's why the Signoria found it necessary to confiscate the bell from San Marco. How do you know so much about all this?"

"Chiara—," Tommaso stopped abruptly, but Niccolò waved in an off-hand manner to reassure him it was nothing. Tommaso continued: "She still talks with my father, though she has yet to forgive me. Eventually she'll understand."

Perhaps family blood could over come such differences but Niccolò was not so sure Chiara would ever forgive him. He knew she partly blamed him, and not unjustly, for playing the game of politics too well. He was not sure he would ever get the chance to explain. He wasn't sure he could.

Tommaso continued, filling the awkward silence. "Yes, she's decided to devote the remainder of her life to good works and veneration to the memory of our famed prophet." He added, "She means well."

Then he changed the subject. "Anyway, a bit of good news: the *Arrabbiati* have fallen out of favor. When Ceccone botched his candidacy even Spini ceased his strutting. You know, Doffo told me he bore no ill feeling for the friar; it was Berlinghieri who had it out for Savonarola. He even said had he known Fra Girolamo sooner he would have been his fervent disciple!"

They both laughed at the irony.

"*Incrediblile,*" muttered Niccolò. "I suppose now he'll be attending Mass regularly?"

"No doubt," Tommaso said, "to save his wretched soul. But I've renounced my former *Compagnacci* anyway."

Niccolò crossed the room to look out over the city. Down below he watched the ritual procession of the massive *ceri*—enormous wooden candles with statues of saints on top, each carried upright on litters by eight struggling men. In between the *ceri* marched the various religious orders and parish clergy representing the various religious communities paying homage to their parish patron saints. The Piazza was overflowing with workers and country peasants.

"Do you believe in God?" Niccolò asked Tommaso softy.

"Naturally. I guess. Don't you?"

"Personally I've never been convinced it matters." Nodding down at the crowds, he added, "for them it surely does."

"Who?"

Niccolò turned to face Tommaso. "Who rules the great cities, Tommaso? Who holds power?"

"The *grandi* of course… and the Roman Curia?"

"I thought so myself. But then, how did this insignificant, poor, frail, little friar rule our city for these past four years? You saw him, a wisp of skin and bones. How did he control us? I've asked myself many times, what *was* the source of his power?"

"He was full of lies and deception," Tommaso said sharply. "A clever one, like Satan."

Niccolò heard the hate in Tommaso's voice and challenged him: "Was he? Are we such fools then? The pope too? And your father, have you asked him?" He had been contemplating these questions for the past few days and was not sure he had the right answers.

Tommaso frowned. "He believed yes, but he'll come around. We saw through it soon enough, no? The common people are fools, so we used the friar to rally them to our purpose. My father and uncles foiled the assassination plots of the *Arrabbiati* and the *Compagnacci* after I informed them. We're the ones who saved him."

Niccolò shot him a look of surprise and then smiled knowingly. But of course, who else? He was only surprised he had been kept in the dark. He might be an ally but he would never be a Soderini. His eyes silently begged the next question: Who?

Tommaso shrugged. "Mostly the Tosinghi and their men. We didn't think it wise to speak about it."

Niccolò turned away. Tommaso was not as guileless as he appeared, but even when perfectly clear-headed he could not grasp the obscure patterns of history and twisted paths of fate. His friend, unlike himself, had no appreciation for the lessons gleaned from the histories of man's follies. Niccolò remembered reading in Plutarch and Livy about the story of Numa Pompilius, the second king of Rome, who wished to civilize and pacify his people. This king claimed to consult a nymph with the power of prophecy and with the religion he established under her guidance made the Romans obedient citizens and disciplined soldiers. Then Niccolò thought of the more recent case, when the king of France, Charles VII, had made war against the English under the counsel of a girl sent by God. Called everywhere the Maid of France, they said she was the cause of his victory. Was it true or *Fortuna* with a helping hand?

There was some latent power in the hearts and souls of men that defied the simple logic of nature. He did not, perhaps could not, understand it. Perhaps Chiara could have better explained, since it burned in her breast. He decried the Christian faith, how it glorified humble and contemplative men above those who were strong and decisive. It was a faith that worshipped suffering and sacrifice, to the detriment of honor and noble virtue. And he decried it even more for the brazenness of its leaders, the prelates and popes who exploited this faith with their own deceptions. Yes, perhaps the corrupted papacy was strong enough to keep Italia divided, but it was not strong enough to unite its warring dominions and to resist the invasions of monarchs and sultans. At the core he knew it had made them weak.

And yet, the true faith displays surprising resilience.

He found his eyes looking down again on the procession in the piazza. The priors and other magistrates were beginning to gather under the Loggia and he knew it was time to join them. He watched the brigades of the guilds approaching. The *arti maggiore* came first, merchants with their sumptuous displays of fine silks and woven wool textiles, dyed to every shade of the rainbow; followed by bankers, lawyers and notaries, then doctors, apothecaries and furriers. After this followed the *arti minori*: artisans, shopkeepers and innkeepers; builders, masons, butchers, and bakers. Then he saw the choreographed march of standard bearers and flag-throwers with each troupe of the sixteen gonfalons displaying its colorful banners to the accompaniment of drummers, pipers and trumpeters. The Red Lion, the Green Dragon, the Golden Lion, the Viper, the Unicorn, St. John's Dragon, and others. Sixteen in all, brandishing flags and coats-of-arms, those same coats-of-arms reflected in the medallions around the façade of the Palazzo. It was a magnificent display of order, hierarchy, and power.

The citizens cheered lustily, waving the small pendants of their local gonfalons as all paid tribute to the glory of San Giovanni for the continued prosperity of the city. They marched in lock step, brimming with civic pride as they passed under the government fortress with the echoes of their passions filling the Piazza. The reverberations multiplied off the stone façades, reaching him with a sound larger than life.

"The friar has departed this world, Tommaso, but the power he wielded remains. It makes me wonder how clever he was and just who was using whom."

"You talk nonsense, Machia. Look at you, our new Secretary of the Ten. Would you care to trade places now with the good Fra Girolamo?"

Niccolò smiled his enigmatic smile. "I guess it depends on where he is." Then he motioned at the spectacle below. "*Vieni*, Tommaso, come here. Look at the *poverini*. Look."

He gestured toward the crowds in the Piazza. "*They* believe. *They* were persuaded he talked with God. I don't know whether it's true or not, but I want to argue it doesn't matter. Our religion is a treasure for the poor and hungry. Driven perhaps by fear and death, they have Heaven and Hell to guide them through the void. We grow fat but they grow more powerful. You don't believe it but tell me: What silly creed allows a man to kill his enemy, but not in church?"

Tommaso had no reply. After a pregnant pause, Niccolò continued, "That's the power of Christ and the crucifixion. We've created another martyr from a mere mortal and long after we're dead, *he* will live on in their hearts and souls."

Then, without knowing why, Niccolò said a strange thing,

completely out of character: "I'm persuaded God has not yet castigated us in the way that he wishes; that He is reserving for us a greater scourge."

Tommaso scoffed. "Don't be ridiculous! You've heard a silly rumor that the *Frate* made a last prophesy of a terrible scourge that would befall us during the time of a pope called Clement? I remember you used to joke about such things. Surely you're joking now."

Niccolò remained silent.

"Come now," Tommaso cajoled. "The world is a great crime, someone must be made to pay for it. And, Messer Secretary, you're going to be late for your first official procession."

Niccolò didn't move. It was the same argument they had made for Christ and the crucifixion. Finally he said, "It's strange, no?"

"*Madonna*, what now?" Tommaso was exasperated

"Who did the Messiah come to redeem?"

"The Jews."

"Yes, and who vilified and crucified him?"

"The Jews. And we've branded them Christ-killers ever since."

It took a moment for Tommaso to follow the analogy to its conclusion. Suddenly his devilish face lit up as he exclaimed: "Hah! As the Jews crucified Christ, with this Friar we have our own 'bad nails,' those *mal clavellus*, that fixed him to the cross." Tommaso pointed accusingly at his friend and laughed. "That, Machia, is *your* legacy."

His back turned, Niccolò winced at the damning reference to the Latin origin of his family name. He gazed out over the glorious city as the sun dipped and the sounds of pageantry filled his ears. He heard the trumpets and the hurrahs; saw the standards weave and wave; the guilds and gonfalons marching in lockstep—the harmony of sound and color. He was guilty as charged, but he did not drive the nails.

He couldn't regret the way things turned—it was the way it must be; the bargain was set, the friar's fate sealed. Let God administer His Justice on Judgment Day. Down below in the piazza passed the earthly glory that descended through the ages. This was his inheritance: the real, the tangible, the ordered world. There could be no doubt for him. Faith had its place but this—this must be the world as the Almighty intended. Like Pico had stated in his oration: this world was given to Man, and from here they would pass into either the light above or the darkness below. This was the world he, Niccolò Machiavelli, would take up his sword and defend. *Virtù, Libertà, Patria:* for these he would trade his immortal soul. And perhaps he too would burn. So be it.

He took one last long look down on the Piazza before descending to take his place there among the city magistrates under the shade of the

Loggia dei Priori.

THE END

Dear Reader,

If you have come this far and enjoyed this book, or found it wanting, please offer a review on Amazon or Goodreads for the benefit of other readers and as feedback for the author. Crowd-sourcing through social media networks provides the new forum for book promotion and reviews. Digital publishing has expanded the number of books available to more than several million new books each year and informative reader reviews are the best means to help us all find the particular books we desire to read. If you wish to contact me directly, my contact information is on the copyright page at the frontispiece of this book. Thank you kindly for reading.

Michael Harrington
February 2014

HISTORICAL AFTERWORD

FOUR DAYS AFTER THE EXECUTION of Savonarola and his companions, Niccolò Machiavelli was nominated as Secretary of the Ten of Liberty and Peace, referred to as the Second Chancery. On June 19, 1498, the Great Council confirmed his nomination. He served continuously in this capacity until 1512.

In 1502 the Great Council appointed Piero Soderini as Gonfaloniere for Life. Machiavelli served under Soderini for the next ten years as the principal architect of Florence's defense policy and diplomacy. One of Machiavelli's many proposals was to conscript a citizen army for Florence's defense and in 1512 he led these Florentine forces into battle against the invading Spanish and Neapolitan infantry. They were crushed and the Medici, with the help of Pope Julius II (Giuliano delle Rovere) and the armies of the Holy League, returned to power. Piero Soderini fled and Machiavelli was turned out of office. He never again served the Republic in an official capacity and was forced into retirement. He spent the last fifteen years of his life writing extensively on politics and history, as well as composing plays and poetry. His most famous study, *The Prince*, was based on the political strategies of Cesare Borgia. After Piero Soderini's death in exile in 1522, Machiavelli ridiculed the political skills of his former superior with this short epigram:

> *The night that Piero Soderini died,*
> *He left for Hell via the common stair.*
> *But "Not for your sort!" was what Pluto cried;*
> *"We have a Hell for little boys. Go there!"*

The Republic of Florence was briefly restored in 1527, but Machiavelli was shunned. He died that same year. This revived Republic was rife with the same divisions between the *Arrabbiati, Piagnoni, Palleschi*, and a new group of young Republicans called the *Libertini*. Besieged by the Imperial army of the Spanish Holy Roman Emperor Charles V allied with Pope Clement VII, the Republic fell for the last time three years later. The Medici were restored as the Grand Dukes of Florence and Tuscany with the Pierfrancesco 'Popolani' line, which survived the line of Cosimo the Elder and Lorenzo the Magnificent. They ruled over the Duchy until the line died out in 1732.

Paolantonio Soderini was killed in 1499 in the ongoing war against Pisa. Tommaso Soderini remained widowed and childless until he married Francesca di Jacopo Pandolfini in 1515.

In August 1498, Cesare Borgia was relieved of his Cardinalate and appointed General of the Papal Forces by his father, Pope Alexander VI. He led the Papal armies on a campaign of conquest to expand the Papal States and conquered many of the smaller independent cities of the Romagna and Umbria before his father died under mysterious circumstances in 1503. It was said Pope Alexander's corpse became bloated and turned black, suggesting poison or disease. Soon after, the Borgia's enemy, Giuliano delle Rovere, was elected Pope Julius II. Cesare's power and influence waned after the death of his father and, after fleeing Italy, he was killed in battle in Spain in 1507.

Piero de' Medici never ceased trying to regain his family seat of power in Florence but failed repeatedly. He drowned in 1503 while serving in the French army. His son Lorenzino became Duke of Urbino and briefly governed Florence from 1516-1519. Lorenzino's daughter, Lorenzo the Magnificent's great granddaughter, Catherine de Medicis, later became Queen of France.

Piero's brother, Cardinal Giovanni de' Medici was elected Pope Leo X in 1513. During his reign as pope, he excommunicated Martin Luther as a schismatic for his defiance of the Roman Church. Pope Leo died in 1521. His younger brother Giuliano, given the title of Duke of Nemours, died in 1516.

In 1523, Cardinal Giulio de' Medici, the bastard son of Lorenzo the Magnificent's brother Giuliano, was elected Pope Clement VII. During his reign the French and English armies overran Florence and the armies of the German Emperor sacked Rome. Pope Clement also provoked a schism between the Anglican and Roman Church by excommunicating the English king, Henry VIII, for divorcing his wife in 1533. Clement VII died in 1534.

Michelangelo went on to carve the *Pieta*, the tomb of Pope Julius II and paint the Sistine Chapel in Rome. In Florence, he carved the *David* and competed with Leonardo da Vinci to fresco the Great Hall in Florence. Unfortunately, these wall murals were never completed. In 1536-41, in his sixties, Michelangelo frescoed the *Last Judgment* in the Sistine Chapel. His powerful interpretation attests to the importance of faith and the power of divine will and is strongly suggestive of Savonarola's profound influence on the artist.

Sandro Botticelli labored to finish his Mystic Nativity and Mystic Crucifixion, but ceased to produce any significant paintings after Savonarola's execution. His most renowned paintings are the pagan allegories that he painted for the Medici, including Springtime and the Birth of Venus.

The apothecary and diarist Luca Landucci kept his detailed journal until 1516.

To this day, in Florence every May 23, devotees of Savonarola lay wreaths of flowers around the brass plaque inlaid in the Piazza della Signoria that commemorates the exact spot where he was hung and burned in 1498.

FLOWERS PLACED ON MAY 23, 1998

500TH ANNIVERSARY OF THE EXECUTION OF
GIROLAMO SAVONAROLA AND HIS TWO COMPANIONS,
DOMENICO BUONVICINI AND SILVESTRO MARUFFI.

APPENDICES

THE SODERINI FAMILY TREE

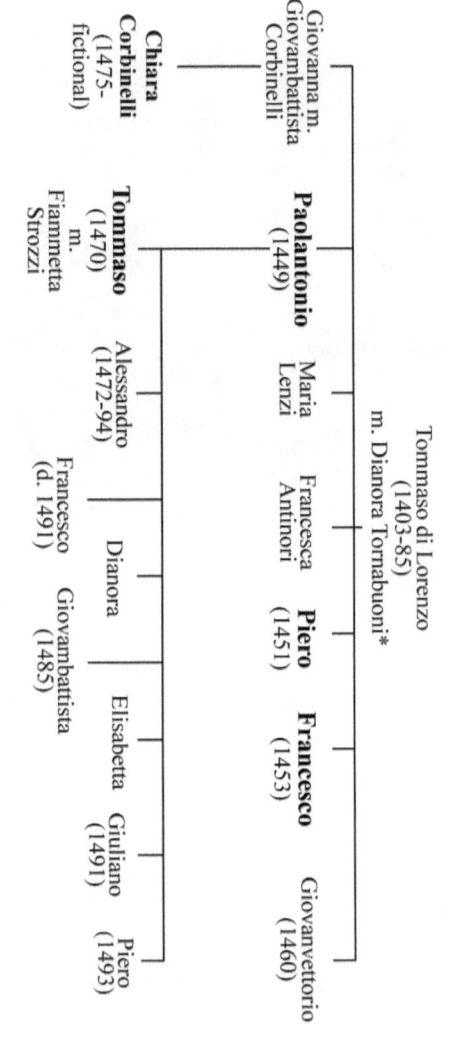

The Soderini

Tommaso di Lorenzo
(1403-85)
m. Dianora Tornabuoni*

Giovanna m. Giovambattista Corbinelli

Paolantonio (1449)

Maria Lenzi

Francesca Antinori

Piero (1451)

Francesco (1453)

Giovanvettorio (1460)

Chiara **Corbinelli** (1475-fictional)

Tommaso (1470) m. Fiammetta Strozzi

Alessandro (1472-94)

Francesco (d. 1491)

Dianora

Giovambattista (1485)

Elisabetta

Giuliano (1491)

Piero (1493)

*Lucrezia and Dianora Tornabuoni were sisters.
(See Medici family tree.)

THE MEDICI FAMILY TREE

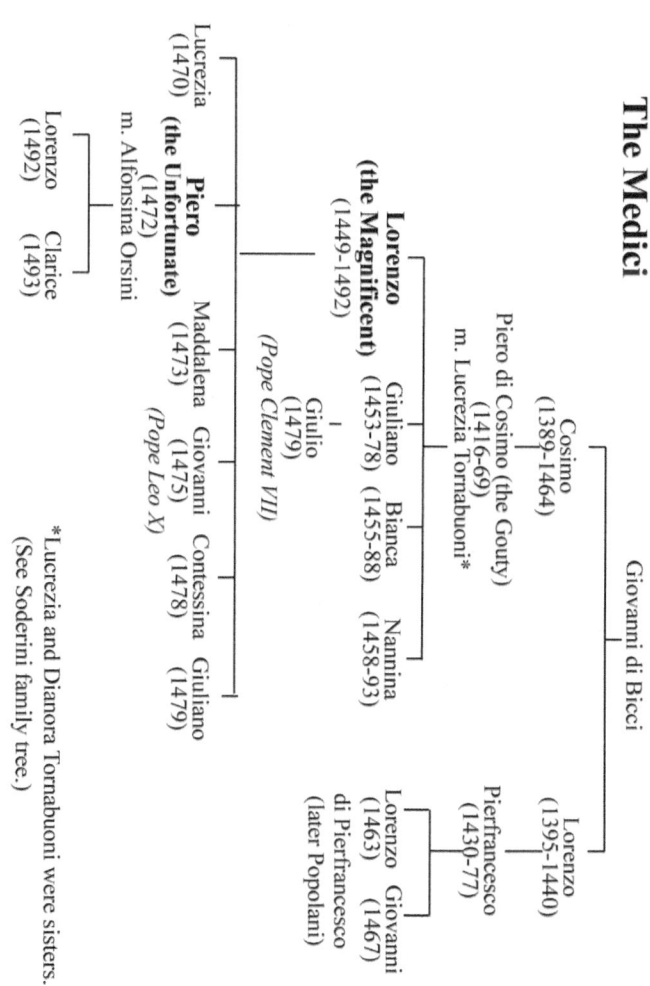

The Medici

Giovanni di Bicci

Cosimo (1389-1464)

Lorenzo (1395-1440)

Piero di Cosimo (the Gouty) (1416-69) m. Lucrezia Tornabuoni*

Pierfrancesco (1430-77)

Lorenzo (the Magnificent) (1449-1492)

Giuliano (1453-78)

Bianca (1455-88)

Nannina (1458-93)

Lorenzo (1463)

Giovanni (1467) di Pierfrancesco (later Popolani)

Lucrezia (1470)

Piero (the Unfortunate) (1472) m. Alfonsina Orsini

Maddalena (1473)

Giovanni (1475) *(Pope Leo X)*

Contessina (1478)

Giuliano (1479)

Giulio (1479) *(Pope Clement VII)*

Lorenzo (1492)

Clarice (1493)

*Lucrezia and Dianora Tornabuoni were sisters. (See Soderini family tree.)

505

MICHAEL HARRINGTON

CAST OF CHARACTERS

Fra Girolamo Savonarola – Dominican Friar and Preacher, Prior of Convent of San Marco in Florence.

Niccolò Machiavelli – young Florentine, neighbor of Soderini; becomes secretary to the Second Chancellor, then eventually Second Chancellor himself.

Medici family (see family tree):

Lorenzo the Magnificent – grandson of Cosimo, son of Piero the Gouty and brother of Giuliano (all deceased).

Piero de' Medici, the Unfortunate – first son of Lorenzo; married to Alfonsina Orsini of Rome.

Giovanni de' Medici – second son of Lorenzo, becomes Cardinal and then Pope Leo X

Giuliano de' Medici – third son of Lorenzo

Giulio de' Medici – bastard son of Lorenzo's slain brother Giuliano, becomes Pope Clement VII

Lorenzo's Circle:

Marsilio Ficino – philosopher, head of Plato's Academy

Giovanni Pico della Mirandola – philosopher and Count of Mirandola (portrait)

Angelo Poliziano – poet,

Domenico Benivieni – poet

Braccio Martelli – aristocrat, friend and business partner of Lorenzo

Bernardo Rucellai – aristocrat, brother-in-law to Lorenzo; leader of the Grays (*Bigi*)

Soderini family (see family tree):

Brothers Paolantonio (Paolo), Piero, Francesco (bishop), Giovanvettorio

Tommaso – son of Paolantonio, nephew of Piero, marries Fiammetta Strozzi

Chiara Corbinelli (*fictional*) – daughter of Giovanna Soderini and Giovambattista Corbinelli, niece of the four Soderini brothers and first cousin of Tommaso

Borgia family:

Rodrigo – Spanish Cardinal who becomes Pope Alexander VI, four

bastard children by his former mistress, Vanozza Catanei
Juan – first son of Rodrigo, Duke of Gandia, murdered
Cesare – second son of Rodrigo, appointed Cardinal, (portrait)
Lucrezia – daughter of Rodrigo; married to Giovanni Sforza
Jofre - youngest son; married to Sancia of Aragon, daughter of Alfonso I
Giulia Farnese, "La Bella" – pope's current mistress, younger than Lucrezia

Sforza family:
Lodovico (Il Moro): Duke of Milan, regent to nephew Giangaleazzo
Cardinal Ascanio: brother of Lodovico, cardinal in Rome
Giangaleazzo – young heir to Duchy of Milan; married to Isabella of Aragon, granddaughter of King Ferrante of Naples

By Political Factions:

Frateschi: **(Friar's Party)**
Francesco Valori – former Medicean, leader of *Frateschi*
Domenico Bonsi – former Medicean
Paolantonio Soderini
TommasoTosinghi
Alessandro Braccesi – Second Chancellor

Grays (Bigi)
Bernardo del Nero: former Medicean leader of *Bigi*
Bernardo Rucellai

Whites (*Bianchi*)
Piero Capponi: former Medicean, leader of *Bianchi*
Piero Soderini (Whites)
Niccolò Machiavelli (Whites)

Angry Ones (*Arrabbiatti*) and Bad Companions (*Compagnacci*)
Guidantonio Vespucci – lawyer, aristocrat and leader of *Arrabbiati*
Doffo Spini – young aristocrat, leader of *Compagnacci* (Bad Companions)
Francesco Cei: poet
Ser Ceccone – notary

ARTISTS & WORKS:

Michelangelo Buonarotti – sculptor
  Battle of the Centaurs
  Madonna of the Stairs
Francesco Granacci – painter
Sandro Botticelli – painter
  Adoration of the Magi
  Primavera
  The Birth of Venus
  Mystic Crucifixion
  Mystic Nativity
Cronaca (Simone Pollaiuolo) – architect and builder
Lorenzo di Credi – painter
Piero di Cosimo – painter
Filippino Lippi – painter
Benedetto da Maiano – sculptor
Baccio della Porta (becomes Fra Bartolomeo) – painter
  Portrait of Girolamo Savonarola

OTHER REFERENCED ART WORKS

Fra Angelico
  Annunciation – San Marco
  Crucifixion with Fra Domenico– San Marco
Benozzo Gozzoli
  Adoration of the Magi – Ricciardi-Medici Chapel
Massacio
  Holy Trinity – Santa Maria Novella
  Adam & Eve – Brancacci Chapel
  Tribute Money – Brancacci Chapel
Donatello
  St. George – Orsanmichele
  Judith and Holofernes
Ghiberti
  Gates of Paradise – Baptistery Doors

RELIGIOUS:

Fra Domenico Buonvicini da Pescia – friar at San Marco (SM)
Fra Silvestro Maruffi – friar SM

Fra Benedetto (Bettucio) – friar SM
Fra Malatesta – friar SM
Fra Roberto Ubaldini – friar SM
Fra Mariano da Genazzano – Augustinian opponent of Savonarola, Medicean partisan
Fra Menico da Ponzo – Franciscan opponent of Savonarola
Fra Francesco di Puglia – Franciscan opponent of Savonarola
Cardinal Giuliano delle Rovere – most powerful rival to Pope Alexander VI, elected Pope Julius II
Cardinal Caraffa – Cardinal of Naples
Cardinal Francesco Romolino – Papal Inquisitor
Giovacchino Torriani – Master General of the Dominican Order

OTHERS:

Charles VIII – King of France
King Ferrante, Alfonso I, Alfonso II – successive kings of Naples
Lorenzo Tornabuoni – cousin of Piero de' Medici, also cousin of Soderini
Bartolomeo Scala – First Chancellor
Marcello Adriani – humanist scholar, replaces Scala as First Chancellor
Alessandro Braccesi – Second Chancellor, succeeded by Machiavelli
Ricciardo Becchi – Florentine ambassador to Rome (Vatican)
Fiammetta Strozzi – first daughter of Filippo Strozzi (deceased), richest family in Florence
Chiara Corbinelli (*fictional*) – first cousin to Tommaso Soderini; second cousin to Piero de' Medici
Filippo Giunta – printer, bookseller, and humanist scholar
Simone di Filipepi – Dominican lay brother, brother of Sandro Botticelli
Luca Landucci – apothecary and diarist
Don Michele (Michelotto) – Spanish captain (assassin) serving the Borgia
Salvatore degli Angelini – jailor (name *fictional*)
Jacopo – Neri confessor
Nello – barber

GLOSSARY

SOCIAL CLASSES:

grandi
> Wealthy aristocratic class; originally referred to the *magnati* nobility but with the rise of the merchant class and the decline of the landed aristocracy the term came to refer to the wealthy families in general (*magnati* and *ottimati*).

magnati (magnates)
> Ancient, land-owning aristocracy, often allied with the *ottimati* through marriage; in the 14th century excluded from direct participation in Florentine politics; many subsequently lost their preeminent status to merchant banking families and over the 15th century intermarried with the *ottimati* or became commoners with little more than illustrious names

ottimati (optimates)
> Upper class of nouveau rich merchants and bankers with the highest social status and greatest political influence; new aristocrats; some allied with the *magnati,* some allied with the *popolani*

popolani
> The middle-class traders, bourgeoisie, craftsmen, merchants, professionals comprising the minor guilds and artisan classes; source of the 'new men.' The Medici were *ottimati* who appealed to the *popolani* for support

popolo minuto
> The "little people," the working poor, often refers to some of the minor guilds

contadini – peasants

stranieri – foreigners

fraticelli
> Radical religious sects of the mendicant Orders, demanded reform of Catholic Church. The offshoot of the Franciscans were called Spirituals and the offshoot of the Dominicans were called Observants. *Fraticelli* is a generic term applied to those friars accused of heresies against the Church.

POLITICAL FACTIONS:

Arrabbiati
> The **Angry Ones**, the Rabid Ones (anti-Savonarola, anti-Medici); led by Guidantonio Vespucci

Bigi
> The **Grays** (pro-Medici, anti-Savonarola); led by Bernardo Rucellai

Bianchi
> The **Whites** (pro-Republic, anti-Medici, neutral on Savonarola); led by Piero Capponi and Piero Soderini

Compagnacci
> The **Bad Companions** (anti-Savonarola, anti-Medici); led by Doffo Spini

Piagnoni
> The **Big Weepers**, religious followers of Savonarola

Frateschi
> The followers of the friar, Girolamo Savonarola's political supporters; led by Francesco Valori and Paolantonio Soderini

Palleschi
> The followers of the Medici, from the *palle* on their coat-of-arms

Popular Party
> Amorphous party label assumed by anyone claiming to represent republicanism and 'the people.' Mostly comprised of the Whites and the Frateschi.

accoppiatori
> Special advisory committee to select candidates eligible for office; after the expulsion of Piero de' Medici, an accoppiatori of twenty was appointed to recommend a new constitution and electoral system

parlamento
> A plebiscite of the whole body of citizens, which possessed full legislative powers in that it represented the will of the people; it was often called during a crisis suspending the constitution

Signoria
> Main governing body comprised of eight Priors of Liberty (magistrates) and the Gonfaloniere of Justice; members referred to as *Priori* or *Signori*

ITALIAN WORDS AND EXPRESSIONS:

a posto – in place
accoppiatori – special advisory committee to select candidates eligible for office (see Political factions)
addio – good-bye
allora – interjection = well, now
amico(i) – friend(s)
andiamo – let's go
animo – spirit, courage
aspetta – wait
avanti – come in
barlacci – bigot, lit. rotten eggs
basta – enough
bastardo, -ino – bastard, little bastard
beffato, buffone – dupe, buffoon
beffatore – con artist
bella, -issima – beautiful, most beautiful
bene – good
beneficiati – those designated eligible as members of the Great Council under the post-1994 republic
borsa – small leather pouch
bottega – workshop
braccia – an arm's length, a unit of measure about two feet
buon giorno; buona sera – good morning; good evening
canzoni – songs
capito – understand?, understood
car'amici – dear friends
casino – a brothel, a metaphor for chaos
castrati – castrated eunuchs
catasto – city head tax, instituted under Cosimo de' Medici and assessed somewhat arbitrarily
cazzo – prick
c'era una volta – Once upon a time...
certo – surely, of course
che – how, what
chiachiarone – chatterbox
cittadini – citizens
collegi – the various ministries that make up the government of Florence
condottiere – hired military captain
contadine – peasant girls

cucina – kitchen

culo – ass (posterior)

d'accordo – okay

davero – really

decima – wealth tax of 10% instituted by Savonarolan Republican government

diavolo – devil

Dio mio – my God

discorsi – discourses, title of Machiavelli's major study of politics

divertimenti – diversions

Doge – elected leader of Venetian Republic, Duke

domani – tomorrow

donna – woman, lady

dottore – doctor

fagioli – beans

fanciulli – street urchins, aged 5-15, many orphaned or abandoned

ferro roto - a broken tool

festa – festival

fica – lit. fig; vulgar euphemism for woman

figlio –a,-i, – son, daughter, children

figlio di putana – son of a whore

fondacci – factory

Fra, fratello – brother

frate – friar

fraticelli – *see Classes*

galli – roosters, slang term for French, or Gauls.

giovane(i) – young men (and women), aged mid-teens through mid-twenties

gonfalone – neighborhood administrative district (16 in all; four per quarter); the gonfalon originally was the basic military organization of the citizenry for defense

Gonfaloniere – Standard Bearer of Justice

governo stretto/largo – narrow/wide government

grandi – see Classes above

grazie – thank you

guarda – look

insieme – together

intelligenzie – political conspiracies

Lasciate ogne speranza, voi ch'intrate – "Abandon all hope, you who enter here." From Dante's Inferno.

la dolce vita – the sweet life

Le temps revient – (French) times past return; Lorenzo de' Medici's motto *loggia* – a covered portico or outdoor porch area, usually on the ground floor

Madonna – My Lady

maestro –master, teacher

magnati – magnates, see Classes above

marranos – Spanish Jews exiled during the Inquisition

medico – doctor

merda – shit

mio – my

miracolo – miracle

miserere mei Deus (Latin) – Have mercy on me, O Lord

misericordia – Latin prayer, the miserere

momento – (wait) a moment

Monte Comune – public debt fund

Monte di Doti – public dowry fund

non rompere i miei palle/coglioni – don't break my balls

ottimati – see Classes above

palazzo – palace

palle – balls, reference to the balls on the Medici coat-of-arms, also slang for testicles

pane – bread

parlamento – a plebiscite of the whole body of citizens, (see Political factions)

passegiata – promenade

patria (Latin) – patriotism

pazzo – crazy

popolo – the people; term used to refer to commoners as opposed to the aristocratic families or *ottimati*

popolo e libertà – power to 'the people and freedom'

popolani – see Classes above

porco cane, Dio, Madonna – expletive, lit. pig dog; pig God; pig Madonna

Pratica – government advisory board, appointed

prego – please, lit. "I pray"

Priori – Priors in the Signoria; a prior(ess) is also the head of a convent of mendicants

putana, -e – prostitute, whores

vieni – come

ragazzo, –a, -i, – boy, girl, guys

ringhiera – a seating area that ringed the outside of the Palazzo della Signoria for the magistrates to sit during public ceremonies.

saluti – greetings

scrutino – scrutiny, determination of eligibility for political office *scusi* – excuse me

senti – listen

sfortunato – unfortunate

Signore – Lord

Signoria – main governing body comprised of eight Priors of Liberty (magistrates) and the Gonfaloniere of Justice; members referred to as *Priori* or *Signori*

sodomiti – sodomizers

spettacolo – spectacle, extravaganza

stranieri – strangers, foreigners

strappado – torture instrument comprised of a pulley that hauled a prisoner to the ceiling and then dropped him toward the floor, snapping taut and dislocating one's arms and shoulders

tarocchi – tarot, a game played with tarot cards

terza rima – *ababcbcdc, etc...*– rhyming pattern, used by Dante

tiepidi – tepid ones, luke-warm ones

tramontana – seasonal north wind blowing down from the Appenine mountains

trebbiano – regional red wine

triche-tach – early version of backgammon

trionfo – parade vehicle, *lit.* Triumph

Trionfo di Morto – Triumph of Death

tutti – all

va bene? – okay?

va bene cosí – okay, just so

vaffanculo – Up yours!

LATIN TRANSLATIONS:

Anathema sit – excommunicate

Cave canem – beware the dog

Duce virtute comite Fortuna – Under the guidance of virtue, accompanied by good fortune.

Ego veni ut vitam habent et abundantius habeant – I came that they may live, and that they may live more abundantly.

Genus irritabile vatum – the irritable race of poets, sages and seers who make divine utterances.

Homo homini lupus - man is wolf to man.

Missus a Deo – Sent by God.

Mal clavellus – lit., bad nails

Virtú vince Fortuna – Virtue conquers fortune.

Voluntas Dei – By God's Will

PRINCIPAL TEXTS AND SELECT BIBLIOGRAPHY

The principal texts that form the backbone of this Florentine trilogy are
  The Bible, both New and Old Testament;
  St. Augustine's *City of God*;
  Dante's *Divine Comedy*;
  Machiavelli's *The Prince, The Discourses*

The following are the most useful selected texts used in researching this book. They are arranged and ordered by principle subject.

SAVONAROLA:
Selected Writings of Girolamo Savonarola: Religion and Politics, 1490-1498
Prison Meditations on Psalms 51 and 31.
The Life and Times of Girolamo Savonarola by Pasquale Villari
The Life of Girolamo Savonarola by Robert Ridolfi
Fra Girolamo Savonarola : a biographical study based on contemporary documents by Herbert Lucas
Savonarola: A Study in Conscience by Ralph Roeder
The Elect Nation: The Savonarolan Movement in Florence 1494-1545 by Lorenzo Polizzotto
Savonarola and Florence: Prophecy and Patriotism in the Renaissance by Donald Weinstein
The World of Savonarola. Edited by Stella Fletcher, and Christine Shaw

MACHIAVELLI
The Prince
The History of Florence
The Discourses
The Life and Times of Niccolò Machiavelli by Pasquale Villari
The Life of Niccolò Machiavelli by Robert Ridolfi
Machiavelli in Hell by Sebastian de Grazia
Machiavelli: A Dissection by Sydney Anglo

THE ITALIAN RENAISSANCE
Dante Alighieri: The Divine Comedy
History of Italy and History of Florence by Francesco Guicciardini
A Florentine Diary from 1450 to 1516 by Luca Landucci
Florence the Magnificent: A History by Piero Bargellini.
The Renaissance by Walter Pater

MICHAEL HARRINGTON

The House of the Medici: Its Rise and Fall by Christopher Hibbert
Daily Life in Florence in the Time of the Medici by J. Lucas-Dubreton
The Social World of the Florentine Humanists 1390-1460 by Lauro Martines
The Borgia Pope, Alexander VI. by Orestes Ferrara

AUTHOR NOTE

GIROLAMO SAVONAROLA CAN HARDLY BE considered an obscure figure in European history. Many people are readily familiar with his infamous Bonfire of the Vanities and have a vague understanding of his relation to the art and politics of his day. I have always been astounded, however, by the way in which this friar's tale, set within its particular historical circumstances, so closely approximates the great myths and legends that transcend both time and place. To borrow the words of one scholar, the life of Savonarola in Florence approximates "the battle between good and evil, played out against a background of order and chaos, fought for the redemption of fallen and painfully self-conscious man."[20] In this sense we may appreciate its universalism and relevance. My interpretation is presented along three important dimensions of historical literature: context, character, and theme.

CONTEXT: MOST OF US HAVE a basic knowledge of the Italian Renaissance, primarily within the context of art history and the genius of such figures as Leonardo da Vinci, Michelangelo, and Raphael. Standard reference texts characterize this remarkable cultural period as one in which new conceptions of the individual in relation to the universe contributed to a great flourishing of scholarly, literary, philosophical, scientific, and artistic achievement. This novel arose from my desire to comprehend the richness of the Renaissance and the causality of historical events. How did such a great flowering of human achievement come about? Was it a historical accident? An unfathomable mystery? Cultural or religious destiny? Plain dumb luck?

The most helpful view in understanding the conceptual framework for this novel is the classic one that characterizes the Renaissance as a *transition,* a bridge between the Middle Ages and the early modern world. It was a rapid period of change between the Age of Faith and the Enlightenment, brought forth by an upheaval of social, economic, and political institutions. Such periods of transition and change are not unique in history. We may look to the Age of Pericles in Athens, the Age of Rome under Julius Caesar, the nineteenth century's Industrial Revolution, and our own technological information age for parallels ancient and modern.

History, of course, is littered with winners and losers and every remarkable period of human advancement has been accompanied by rather less appealing characteristics and events. The great flowering of ideas and creativity during the Renaissance occurred on a continent beset with low life expectancy and high death rates due to famine, plague, and frequent wars. Medical and sanitary conditions were abysmal and the Black Death still haunted the urban landscape. Great disparities in wealth, combined with the tyranny of ruthless despots and oligarchs, resulted in constant economic and political instability. The imperialist nations of France, Spain and the Ottoman Turks were in their initial phases of expansionary conquest. The Roman Catholic Church engaged in corrupt practices, such as selling indulgences, and the Popes themselves were hardly paragons of virtue with their large retinues of mistresses and bastard children. The entire European countryside was largely mired in poverty, brutalized by war and famine, and ruled by despots and superstitions.

The two sides of the Renaissance—its glory and brutality—bring many important issues into sharp relief. Periods of social and cultural upheaval have motivated mankind to ponder deeper philosophical and religious questions concerning the purpose and meaning of existence. As the Renaissance bridged two periods classified as the Ages of Faith and Reason, such questions were particularly momentous because of the immediate conflict between the worldviews that defined these two eras. Prior to the Renaissance, the West was gradually becoming aware of new ways of relating to the universe. In fathoming the mysteries of the unknown, the intellect, employing reason and scientific inquiry, seemed to hold more promise than the traditional touchstones of spiritual faith and superstition. God and the universe became centered in Man, and the experience of man became paramount for understanding the world. As coincidence would have it, self-serving church leaders ensured that Faith was being corrupted just as Science and Reason were emerging as powerful cornerstones of a new philosophical humanism. Existing structures of power were challenged by the new usurpers to that power and the ensuing clash was violent.

The highest ethical objective of the new philosophical humanism became the salvation of the soul through the earthly good of humanity and the perfectibility of man. Such a philosophy justified the mass accumulation of wealth and power—ostensibly for the ultimate glory of God—and represented a significant shift away from the church's moral teachings of poverty, humility, and penance. The result was an explosion of new expression through art, poetry, architecture and philosophy that overwhelmed the piety and reverent morality of Christian doctrine. Savonarola was acutely aware of the conflict in which he was engaged as his program of reform was symbolically represented by the transformation of the sinful, earthly city of Man (Babylon or Rome) into the heavenly city of God (the "New Jerusalem").

These issues remain sharply delineated in our own societal distinctions between Church and State. Whereas we, in the modern West, presume a separation between religious and secular institutions, the concept of a unified religious state has been widely pursued in both western and non-western societies. The most obvious recent example is the rise of the Islamic fundamentalist state, but one must also consider the Victorian Age of morality, Puritanism, and modern Christian fundamentalism. From the perspective of the dramatist, these philosophical positions are often manifested in the attitudes and characters of real persons. Girolamo Savonarola can be viewed as the last vestige of the medieval age of faith while Niccolò Machiavelli can be celebrated (or vilified) as the harbinger of a new, enlightened age of science and reason. In my interpretation of the Renaissance I explore these two archetypal historical characters in depth.

CHARACTER: THE CHARACTER OF SAVONAROLA is particularly intriguing within the aforementioned historical context. Here was an obscure, ascetic monk who rose to the height of power and influence in the richest and most sophisticated city of his day. Under Savonarola's guidance, Florence developed new institutions of government, economic justice, and religious charity. Evidence suggests that many of Florence's cultural icons—Michelangelo, Botticelli, Pico della Mirandola, to name only a few—were quite taken with the charismatic preacher's message and became his devout followers. Ultimately, however, Savonarola became a victim to his own overreaching ambitions and emotional weaknesses. His story is a classic, earthly Greek tragedy. In posterity, Savonarola has been immortalized by history and his message has inspired religious reformers from Martin Luther to our present day.

Most modern characterizations of Savonarola appear to reflect a contemporary bias that finds horrifying any assault on the primacy of reason and scientific inquiry. Many studies portray him as a fanatic and a reactionary, a religious fundamentalist who resisted science and reason by burning books and art and condemning the enlightened views of his day. But if he were a madman, how are we to judge Michelangelo, Botticelli, Lorenzo de'Medici and thousands of other Florentines who were deeply impressed by him? Were they all mad as well?

Niccolò Machiavelli is another figure who holds a significant place in our cultural imagination and, like Savonarola, is in some need of reevaluation. Like Marx and 'Marxist', Machiavelli and 'Machiavellian' suffer a strained, uneasy relationship warped by time. Machiavelli was blessed with an analytical mind and is often cited as the first political scientist. He studied the human drive for power and sought to devise a strategy to harness that drive to the greater good. His reputation, however, has been hijacked throughout history in the service of those who pursue power as the means to any ends. In this he is certainly misunderstood—perhaps not wrongly, but surely not fully.

We have no writings and little knowledge of Machiavelli that predate a letter he wrote near the end of the Savonarolan episode. We can conjecture that many of Machiavelli's early ideas derived from his experiences in Florence in the 1490s at which time he was a young man in his twenties. I have tried to employ his eyes to view the Savonarolan phenomenon from a modern perspective. I use Machiavelli's *The Prince, The Discourses,* and *History of Florence* from which to extrapolate back to those youthful experiences when he must have struggled to make sense of a rapidly changing world. In my interpretation Machiavelli seeks to impose order and restrain chaos by the most efficient means he can imagine. In this respect he is no different from Savonarola, who seeks the same through faith in God.

THEME: THE AGE OF REASON that commenced more than five hundred years ago is the age in which we still reside. In this age, the immense and vast capability of man and his intellect is expected to solve all puzzles and answer all questions that plague existence. From such a perspective, Savonarola is inevitably dismissed as a reactionary who resisted a new world that he could not understand. But perhaps he understood it all too well. At the turn of the twenty-first century we have discovered that science overpromises, at least in the sense of immediate gratification, and that we need to recognize the limits imposed on reason. For Savonarola, the salvation of the soul was paramount, but certainly not to the exclusion of the development of the mind. The preacher was a man of considerable intellectual talents and was an avid proponent of Augustine and Thomas Aquinas (and, by implication, Aristotle) on the reconciliation of philosophy and Christian theology. The conflicts and tensions within the heart and mind of this one individual cannot be dismissed by caricaturing him as a zealot.

The story of Savonarola and Machiavelli is, above all, a story of the conflicts within the human spirit—what we might refer to as the soul of mankind. As the human soul is a prisoner of the body, the struggle of mankind, like that of Savonarola, is *the struggle to free the soul from the body,* or the flesh. The material world imposes itself on our sense of the spiritual world of the soul and, indeed, to reconcile the demands of the material with the needs of the spiritual has been the struggle of Buddhists, Hindus, Christians, Muslims, and Jews alike. This struggle has profound dimensions, such as the search for a higher being or the experience of love, and also mundane ones, such as how to function within the world of industrial employment in order to secure a living. A long literary tradition addresses this struggle and includes works by such renowned and celebrated authors as Dostoyevsky, Hesse, Hugo, Kafka, Kazantzakis, Mann, Conrad, Camus, and Kundera.

I believe this eternal struggle of the soul is why the life of Girolamo Savonarola is so compelling. Today, more than five hundred years after his death, his story seems as relevant as ever to the universals of human experience. More Ancient Greek than modern Western hero, Savonarola is a man of shining virtues and tragic flaws, and in this he is all too human.

Through the struggle of the friar and the observations of Machiavelli, this novel also examines the question of mankind's capacity for both extreme good and evil. The Florentines glorified Savonarola, and ultimately crucified him when he became an inconvenience. The guilt of this contradiction lives on today as humble citizens honor him with the memorial marking the site of his hanging and burning on May 23, 1498 in the Piazza della Signoria in Florence. (Every May 23 flowers appear in the morning to cover the brass plaque in the Piazza.) The trials of history reveal that the barbarism of men extends well into our own time. Our collective experience defies our faith in both God and reason to fathom the depths of the human heart and soul. And this is, perhaps, how it should be. We are, and will remain, a mystery.

In addressing "The Modern Spiritual Problem," Carl Jung captures the dilemma from the perspective of the psychoanalyst:

> The modern man has lost all the metaphysical certainties of his medieval brother, and set up in their place the ideals of material security, general welfare and humaneness. But it takes more than an ordinary dose of optimism to make it appear that these ideals are still unshaken. Material security, even, has gone by the board, for the modern man begins to see that every step in material progress adds just so much force to the threat of a more stupendous catastrophe. The very picture terrorizes the imagination. What are we to imagine when cities today perfect measures of defense against poison-gas attacks, and practice them in "dress rehearsals"? We cannot but suppose that such attacks have

been planned and provided for—again on the principle 'in time of peace prepare for war.' Let man accumulate his materials of destruction and the devil within him will soon be unable to resist putting them to their fated use.

> ...if [modern man] turns away from the terrifying prospect of a blind world in which building and destroying successively tip the scale, and if he then turns his gaze inward upon the recesses of his own mind, he will discover a chaos and darkness there which he would gladly ignore. Science has destroyed even the refuge of the inner life. What was once a sheltering haven has become a place of terror.[21]

Jung, writing in the 1930s before the conflagration of the Second World War, was eerily prescient of future experiences with terrorism and genocide. The evidence continues to accumulate that mankind is both good and evil, light and dark. One particular hypothesis explored in this book is that change, which we often label progress, can have corrupting influences on society, well apart from its positive effects. When it is the harbinger of chaos and crisis, change incites fear and lays bare the most base and cruel of human instincts. Only by understanding this dimension of ourselves, either consciously or intuitively, can we hope to resist the temptation to evil. Faith, whether it is in God or science, fellow man or self, is the only antidote to fear. Faith props up efforts to reestablish order and maintain control of human destiny. Savonarola put his faith in God and the Bible while Machiavelli put his in Cicero, the Republic and Realpolitik.

BACKGROUND TEXTS: TO TEASE OUT the thematic elements of the story, I have drawn heavily upon three principal texts: the Bible, Augustine's *City of God*, and Dante's *The Divine Comedy*. The Bible, especially the Old Testament, was the primary reference from which Savonarola drew his sermons and developed his prophesies. His particular gift was to draw parallels between the Old Testament and events of his day and in so doing, reiterate the teachings of the Gospels. His intellectual sources for the ideal organization of earthly society, along religious guidelines, were Augustine and Aquinas. Savonarola liberally used the Old Testament and Augustine's *City of God* to delineate a clear moral distinction between the earthly and heavenly cities. He employed Aquinas' writings on politics for practical implementation. His mission was to transform the earthly city of Florence into the heavenly City of God.

Dante's *The Divine Comedy* can be viewed as a mythical, Christian text delivered from a more secular, historical perspective. Dante's pilgrim takes us on a journey that first plunges into the depths of sin in Hell, finds redemption in Purgatory, and ultimately ascends to salvation in Heaven. On this journey Dante takes us through the Florence and Italy of his day, exposing the factionalism, conflict, and corruption that impedes the good and the just. In so doing he, much like Savonarola, provided a framework for common Florentine citizens to comprehend their everyday world. Dante is Florence's most famous son and all Florentines were intimately familiar with his verse. Furthermore, his three-stage pilgrimage through condemnation, redemption, and salvation presages Savonarola's own brief journey across Florence's stage.

This interpretation of the events of Savonarola's life is uniquely my own and is intended to adhere closely to the historical record of Renaissance Florence, and to the words attributed to Savonarola, Machiavelli, Lorenzo de' Medici, Pope Alexander VI and others. The only purely fictional character is Chiara Corbinelli and those created by her circumstances, such as the Prioress at the Convent in Fiesole. The relationships between Tommaso Soderini and Machiavelli, as well as those between Tommaso and the *Compagnacci* are inferred from historical evidence, but there is no indication that Tommaso and Niccolò were close friends. I have assumed they were because they were neighbors, close in age, and because a close mentor relationship did exist between Niccolò and Piero Soderini, Tommaso's uncle. Certain plot elements have been created to tie the characters together but do not, to the best of my historical research, contradict any historical evidence. The historical background is gleaned from the professional research of respected scholars and historians. Artistic license, though kept to a minimum, and mistakes, hopefully minimized as well, are the sole responsibility of the author.

The Renaissance city of Florence was a moment of promise—a promise of the mind, body, and spirit of man; a sensual awakening, the puberty of modern civilization; the birth of *l'uomo universale*; the blossoming of intellectual discipline and humanistic interpretation. We have embraced its ideals and continue to uphold the myth. But we should always question how well it serves us and never forget that every man is modern to his times.

I welcome the opportunity to correspond with readers with comments, critiques, corrections and suggestions. I can be reached

through the following websites/email accounts:
   casinocap.wordpress.com
   author@michaelharrington.info
   mharring54@gmail.com

Michael Harrington
Santa Monica, 2003

ABOUT THE AUTHOR

MICHAEL HARRINGTON IS A POLITICAL ECONOMIST, public policy analyst, and author. He holds advanced degrees in political science, finance, and economics and his scholarship has garnered several national awards, including the American Political Science Association's Harold D. Lasswell Prize for best research in policy studies. His research interests include trade policy; capital markets; the politics of finance; risk, uncertainty and social insurance; voting patterns in American politics; agent-based modeling techniques; and the economics of inequality. He has worked in the securities and venture capital industries as an investment portfolio manager and financial analyst. In more recent years he has taught political science as a lecturer at the University of California and worked as a research fellow and public policy analyst. He currently writes on economic policy and politics on the blog, Casino Capitalism and Crapshoot Politics.

Harrington has harbored a life-long fascination with the art, culture, and politics of the Italian Renaissance, and has lived and studied in Italy, near Florence. His enduring interest in the social movements and artistic creativity of this period led him to study the life stories of Girolamo Savonarola, Niccolò Machiavelli, Michelangelo, and Leonardo da Vinci. As a visiting scholar to the Bridwell Library at Southern Methodist University in Dallas, he conducted research with primary Renaissance materials for his dramatized history-fiction trilogy on Savonarola and Machiavelli. This work, titled The City of Man: Inferno, Purgatorio, Paradiso, has been an Amazon Kindle bestseller for more than four years running.

An early convert to digital technology, Harrington is a pioneer in the development of digital book formats, or eBooks. His eBooks are programmed to take full advantage of the search and link capabilities of digital text, as well as incorporating the enhancements of images, illustrations, tables, and indexes. These features give the reader the freedom to pursue their own path through the story with direct access to historical information on the Internet.

He recently published two more works. Saving Mona Lisa is a novel about the world's most famous painting told through the eyes of Leonardo da Vinci's young assistant and eventual archivist, Francesco

Melzi. The story is inspired by two real mysteries: Why did Leonardo insist the painting was never finished, refusing to surrender it to its rightful owner? And, who painted the copies, several of which depict Mona Lisa bare-breasted? The story delves into the conflicts inherent to artistic creativity and love by examining one of the most creative and complex personalities in history.

Political Economy Simplified: A Citizen's Survival Guide is a condensed public policy primer that integrates analyses of economics, financial markets, and American politics into a broad overview of national policy for citizen-voters. This primer derives from and supplements the author's weblog, Casino Capitalism and Crapshoot Politics.

His latest book, published November 1, 2013 is a political novel that modernizes the Renaissance conflict between religion and politics to the current era of religious fundamentalism and secular politics. This work, titled In God We Trust, develops a Machiavellian plot that dramatizes Washington politics during the period from the Millennial through 9/11 and the build-up to the Iraq War.

NOTES

---

[1] Hesiod's *Theogony*.

[2] Trans: Behold how good and pleasant it is for brethren to dwell together in unity.

[3] Augustine, *City of God*, [2:20]

[4] From Giovanni Pico, "On the Dignity of Man."

[5] Dante Alighieri, *Inferno*, VI: 49-75.

[6] From Luca Landucci, *A Florentine Diary*.

[7] Dante Alighieri, *Inferno*, XXVII: 74-78.

[8] Ezekiel, 28th Sermon, in Will Durant, *The Renaissance*.

[9] Translation: I came that they may live, and that they may live more abundantly.

[10] From Pitti, *Storia Fiorentina*, recounted in Villari, p. 561.

[11] Abridged, translation from Atkinson and Sices, *Machiavelli and His Friends: Their Personal Correspondence*.

[12] "Going to Canossa" refers to the ploy of the German king, Henry IV, to travel to Canossa in 1077, to ask forgiveness and seek absolution from excommunication imposed by Pope Gregory VII. It is said that he knelt in the snow to kiss the pope's feet as a sign of subjugation to the authority of the Church.

[13] Michael of Cesena and William of Occam were prominent Franciscans who were excommunicated by John XXII for criticizing the material wealth of the Church and supporting the Spirituals, a heretical offshoot of which were known as the *fraticelli*.

[14] *amor nummi* = love of money; *amor patriae* = love of country.

[15] John 12:20-32.

[16] *Inferno*; IX: 121-129.

[17] Dream dialogue adapted from *Prison Meditations: Psalms 51 and 31*.

[18] *The Inferno*, II, 58-69.

[19] Matthew 23:37.

[20] Jordan B. Peterson, *Maps of Meaning: the Architecture of Belief*.

[21] Carl G. Jung, from "The Modern Spiritual Problem," in *Modern Man in Search of a Soul* [p. 204].

www.ingramcontent.com/pod-product-compliance
Lightning Source LLC
Chambersburg PA
CBHW021834010726

47493CB00005B/1397